DEADLY TREASURES

Second Chances

DEADLY TREASURES

Second Chances

RACHELLE JONES

ARPress
45 Dan Road Suite 5
Canton MA 02021

Hotline: 1(800) 220-7660
Fax: 1(855) 752-6001

Ordering Information:
Quantity sales. Special discounts are available on quantity purchases by corporations, associations, and others. For details, contact the publisher at the address above.

Printed in the United States of America.

ISBN-13:	Softcover	979-8-89330-404-6
	eBook	979-8-89330-405-3
	Hardcover	979-8-89330-406-0

Library of Congress Control Number: 2024900499

Works by Rachelle Jones

<u>**Deadly Treasures Series**</u>

Deadly Treasures
Deadly Treasures: Second Chances

<u>Coming Soon</u>

Deadly Treasures: What are the Chances
Deadly Treasures: Last Chance
Deadly Treasures: Out of Luck

DEDICATION

The Deadly Treasures series is dedicated to the men and women who have served and who are serving in our armed forces. Thank you, for your time, dedication, and devotion to serving our country, protecting our way of life, and preserving our freedom.

NAVY SEAL CREED

"I will never quit. I persevere and thrive on adversity. My Nation expects me to be physically harder and mentally stronger than my enemies. If knocked down, I will get back up, every time. I will draw on every remaining ounce of strength to protect my teammates and to accomplish our mission. I am never out of the fight."[1]

Except from "The SEAL Code"

Military Time

0100 = 1:00am	1300 = 1:00pm
0200 = 2:00am	1400 = 2:00pm
0300 = 3:00am	1500 = 3:00pm
0400 = 4:00am	1600 = 4:00pm
0500 = 5:00am	1700 = 5:00pm
0600 = 6:00am	1800 = 6:00pm
0700 = 7:00am	1900 = 7:00pm
0800 = 8:00am	2000 = 8:00pm
0900 = 9:00am	2100 = 9:00pm
1000 = 10:00am	2200 = 10:00pm
1100 = 11:00am	2300 = 11:00pm
1200 = 12:00pm	2400 = 12:00am

Military Alphabet

A = Alpha	N = November
B = Bravo	O = Oscar
C = Charlie	P = Papa
D = Delta	Q = Quebec
E = Echo	R = Romeo
F = Foxtrot	S = Sierra
G = Golf	T = Tango
H = Hotel	U = Uniform
I = India	V = Victor
J = Juliet	W = Whiskey
K = Kilo	X = X-Ray
L = Lima	Y = Yankee
M = Mike	Z = Zulu

---

[1] https://navyseals.com/nsw/seal-code-warrior-creed/ (2023) (This direct quote from the Navy SEAL Code appears in multiple locations in this book. Please refer back to this notation for reference to the original source.)

PROLOGUE

November 30
6 years ago
The ice tundra of Siberia

Navy SEAL team Echo waited in the back of a cargo plane preparing for a HALO jump over Siberia. Their mission was to raze a chemical weapons research facility to the ground.

Just past dusk, Echo dropped fifteen miles south of the installation. According to satellite intel, the facility was heavily guarded, but the hike through the treacherous glacial snow and ice would be the first challenge.

Once Echo was safely on the ground, Master Chief Kyle Masters signaled the team to move out. Halfway there, the ground dropped out beneath Kyle. He plummeted into the darkness of an ice crevasse. He was stopped short by the rope linked to the rest of the team. His helmet slammed into the hard, ice surface, and he felt the impact reverberate inside his skull. Before he could process what happened, John Rusk was pulled down into the crevasse right behind him. Kyle felt his body swing back over the open air, and his right arm slammed into the ice. Above them, the rest of Echo was digging in with ice cleats and pick axes. Kyle heard Lydell Fry in his earpiece.

"Echo 1, Echo 3, what's your status?" Fry asked.

"Echo 1, minor head and arm injury," Kyle replied.

There was only silence from John.

"Echo 3, what's your status?" Fry repeated.

Silence answered back.

"Echo 1, give status for Echo 3."

"I have no visibility on Echo 3." Kyle grimaced in pain.

"Hang tight. We are working to get you out," Fry said.

Once Echo pulled them out of the crevasse, Cord Murphy, the team medic, checked them over. Kyle had a minor concussion, and his right arm was sprained. John didn't fare as well. He was unconscious with a severe concussion.

"We can't take him with us. He'd be a liability. We'll have to leave him here and come back for him," Fry said.

"No!" Kyle said. "If our exit south is cut off, that leaves Echo 3 alone and unprotected. We stay together!"

"You're the boss," Fry said unhappily.

"Echo 2 take the lead. I'll fall back and carry Echo 3. Keep your eyes open. Move out!" Kyle commanded.

Kyle tied himself and John in to the rear positions, and they made it to the coordinates without further incident. Soon, Echo moved into flanking positions. Kyle knew his men were questioning his judgement. He didn't care. He would never leave an injured man behind again.

After taking out the external guards, Echo entered the facility, and went about taking out targets and placing C-4 in strategic locations. On the second floor, they encountered a door with state-of-the-art security protocols. Kyle gave Axel the go-ahead to blow the door. They spilled into the room with guns drawn ready to open fire, but they encountered the unexpected.

The room was filled with two hundred, heavily sedated male human test subjects in hospital beds. They were hooked up to monitors and drip bags. Each test subject's face was covered with a strange breathing apparatus.

Kyle scanned the large room. There were ten rows with twenty beds each. He walked over to the nearest hospital bed, and his eyes were drawn to the drip bag. A luminescent green liquid was being pumped into each test subject. He'd never seen anything like it in all his years of service.

This was not the intel they'd been briefed on. They were supposed to blow up a research facility experimenting with chemical warfare not whatever this was. It was obvious that testing in violation of the Geneva Convention was taking place here. Echo was on radio blackout until extraction. It was Kyle's call.

"Echo abort mission. I repeat. Echo abort mission," Kyle said into his coms. Then he turned to Dorian Axel. "Video document all of this. We are pulling out in five!"

Axel and the rest of the men proceeded to video as much of the experiment as they could while Kyle hacked into a computer terminal and downloaded the data to a flash drive. Then he ordered Echo to the extraction point.

On the chopper ride back to base, Kyle sat staring at John, who lay unconscious strapped down to a spine board on the floor of the chopper. His own head was pounding from the blow he'd taken, and his arm was throbbing, but he pushed all that down. He wasn't concerned for himself. All he could think about was John. The entire flight back to base, Kyle prayed that John's injuries wouldn't be serious, that he wasn't paralyzed, and that he hadn't suffered a traumatic brain injury.

When they reached base, John was immediately taken to medical, but Kyle couldn't go with him. He had a duty to perform. He had to report what they'd witnessed to his C.O., Commander Rowen. He turned over the flash drive and the video footage to Rowen and was dismissed.

The following morning, Kyle reported to Rowen's office as ordered.

"Masters, you didn't complete the mission," Rowen said.

"No, Sir," Kyle answered. "There were civilians present that could not be transported to safety."

"I read your report and the data you recovered. That was a super soldier project. If you had blown up the facility as ordered, you would have destroyed the evidence. You made the right call regardless of your reasons," Rowen said.

"Sir!" Kyle saluted his C.O.

"Dismissed, Soldier!" Rowen said.

Kyle turned sharply on his heel and left Rowen's tent. He walked to the infirmary to check on John's condition.

"How are you feeling?" Kyle asked.

"Like something crushed my skull," John said.

Kyle nodded. "Good thing you have a hard head."

John chuckled. Then he abruptly stopped. "Don't make me laught. It hurts to laugh."

Kyle's face remained stoic and serious. "You missed the fun. That installation was no chemical weapons facility."

"What was it?"

Kyle glanced around to ensure they were alone. "It was a super soldier project. They were testing live human subjects. Rowen has scheduled a debrief with Echo this afternoon. The doctor said you have a severe concussion, but otherwise you are undamaged. Get some rest. I'll come collect you before the meeting so you'll be up to speed with the rest of the team."

Kyle headed toward the door.

"Hey, Kyle!" John called after him. Kyle turned and walked back. "Nick said Fry wanted to leave me behind, and you refused. Why didn't you leave me and come back for me after Echo completed the mission?"

Kyle shook his head. "I'll never make a mistake like that again."

John gave him a questioning look.

Kyle dragged his hand over his black burr. "I told you before that I lost my whole team. It started with me leaving an injured man behind and taking the team ahead to complete the mission. Due to the circumstances of the mission, it seemed more logical to send the rest of my team ahead to the rendezvous point while I circled back to pick up the medic and the injured man on my own. It was a bad call. It cost thirteen men their lives. It's something I'll never be able to make right. I have to live with that every day. If I had left you behind and something had happened to you, or our way back to you was cut off, I'd have to face the consequences of another bad choice. I know the mission always comes first. I know what my duty is. The problem is, I just can't do it. I can't leave a man behind. I can't do that to you or any of the men on Echo. I'll find another way to accomplish the mission, but I won't leave anyone behind, ever again."

"I think I'm starting to understand you a lot better, Kyle."

Kyle nodded. Then he left.

CHAPTER 1

Present Day
May 28
North Carolina

As the wedding guests were seated and the reception dinner was being served, John Rusk, Nick Novack, and Sonny Eldridge stood near the dance floor watching Owen and Anna Wiley. A Waltz began, and the newlyweds glided elegantly across the floor caught in each other's eyes in a perfect moment. Her beautiful bridal gown swished as Owen led her through the steps of the dance.

Grinning, Kyle Masters walked over to John, Nick, and Sonny. "I don't see you dancing."

"We don't know the Waltz." John watched the happy couple on the dance floor.

"You all better learn how to dance soon," Kyle said.

"Why is that?" Sonny tugged at the bow tie around his neck as if it were choking him.

"Megan's going to have you all married off soon." Kyle winked at them.

"Like hell she is! I ain't gettin' caught in no Megan net. I'm a Mustang. I roam free," Sonny drawled, his Texas accent thick and exaggerated.

They all laughed.

"Laugh it up," Megan said from behind Sonny. "Soon you'll all be caught in the Megan net."

The laughter died suddenly, and John, Nick, and Sonny turned to face her. She was grinning from ear to ear.

"Hey, Megan," Sonny said nervously.

"Hey, Sonny." Megan wore a mischievous grin.

"You been there long?" Sonny tugged at his collar again.

Megan laughed. "Nervous?"

"Why should I be nervous?"

"Because I have someone I want you to meet." She gave him a wink.

"I'm not the marrying kind." Sonny protested as Megan grabbed him by the hand and tugged him after her.

Kyle shook his head. "He's a goner, Boys. He's already caught, and he doesn't even know it yet."

All three men laughed again.

Kyle grinned slyly. "Don't laugh too hard. You two are next."

"Why do we keep coming stateside again? Why don't we stay in Afghanistan where it's nice and safe?" Nick joked.

"It's all Kyle's fault." John grinned.

"Don't blame me." Kyle laughed. "Blame Megan."

"Yeah, blame Megan," they all said in unison.

"Blame me for what?" Megan asked.

"Uh—nothing, Babe." Kyle took her hand.

She grinned at him, and he grinned back.

"I love you," he said.

"I love you more," she said.

"Not possible," they both said in unison.

Megan turned to Nick. "You're next." She dragged him off by the hand.

Kyle looked at John. "I really appreciate you guys coming back to be groomsmen in Owen's wedding. Anna wanted all her sisters to be bridesmaids, and they needed three more guys."

"Anything for you, Kyle. I'm just confused. Why didn't he have some of his own friends stand up for him?"

"Owen doesn't have any friends. Megan and I are his only friends."

John frowned. "He doesn't have any?"

Kyle shook his head. "He had a rough childhood."

"You told me his dad was an abusive alcoholic, but—"

"The kids at school didn't treat him much better. After I started working with Owen, he told me how some of his classmates beat him up, ridiculed him, and did their best to make him feel worthless. They were really cruel."

"What about after school? He's twenty-eight-years-old. He hasn't made any friends since school?"

"No. He thought he was friends with the guys on Buck's old crew, but after Buck fired him, he quickly discovered they weren't really his friends. He spent very little time with his own crew, so he was never close to any of those guys. It's really just me and Megan."

"I'm actually surprised you are friends with him after all the bad blood between you two."

Kyle shrugged. "It's ancient history. I got the girl I wanted. Owen got the perfect girl for him. It's all good. We are all happy. Owen and I buried the hatchet a long time ago."

John nodded. "That's good. Hey, if you're cool with him, so am I."

"Thanks for the favor, John. I owe you."

"You don't owe me anything, Kyle. If you hadn't saved my life, I wouldn't be standing here right now. I'm the one who owes you."

Kyle grinned. "That's just what friends do for each other."

Megan walked up behind John with a pretty blonde in tow and tapped him on the shoulder.

"John, this is Felicia."

A smirky grin spread over Kyle's mouth. John's jaw tightened, and he gave Kyle an accusing look. Then he turned to meet the woman Megan was trying to set him up with.

"Hey." He gave Felicia a smile.

Felicia's eyes roamed slowly up John taking in his six-foot-tall, slim, muscular build, short, dark brown burr, angular jaw, perfect kissable lips, and finally met his brown eyes.

Wow! Megan was right. He is totally hot!

"Hi, John. Megan's been telling me all sorts of good things about you." Felicia winked at him.

John cleared his throat. "I'm sure she exaggerated."

"Not in the least. You are everything she promised and more."

John glanced briefly at Kyle, but he could see he wasn't going to get any help. He had been thrown into Megan's matchmaking trap. There was no way to escape without being rude. So, reluctantly, he went along with it—despite his better judgement.

Felicia took his hand and dragged John out onto the dance floor where Sonny and Nick were already dancing with their respective Megan traps. John felt his heart racing faster as his eyes took in Felicia's slim, curvy figure. He forced his eyes back up to her beautiful face and vibrant blue eyes.

She's beautiful and way out of my league. This is going to go badly. I can already tell.

"How do you know Megan?"

Felicia slid her hands up the front of his tuxedo jacket and gently locked her fingers behind his neck. "We are in the same Martial Arts class."

He bit his lip and glanced away from her too intense eyes. She had that look—the appraising look—the judging look—the look that always spelled disaster.

"Megan didn't tell me you were shy."

He forced himself to make eye contact again.

Her eyebrow rose. "Am I making you nervous?"

"No."

Wow! She is so pretty. I'll just stay calm, and I won't talk any more than I have to. Maybe I won't screw up this time.

He felt his heart racing out of control. This was worse than going on a mission—far worse! On a mission he knew what to do. The objectives were clear. However, women were unpredictable. They were full of expectations, and he had a proven track record of disaster where women were concerned. He let out a heavy sigh and raked a hand over his burr as his gut twisted into a hard knot. He glanced down at his shoes and cleared his throat nervously.

Felicia couldn't help but notice his awkward behavior. She found it endearing, and she couldn't stop the grin that sprang to her lips.

"You can put your hands on my waist. I don't bite."

As his hands slid over her slender hips, his heart rate sped up its already frantic beat. He did his best to keep pace with the slow dance, but John was not a dancer. After a few minutes, he accidentally stepped on her foot, and she lost her balance. He grabbed her and pulled her up against him to keep her from falling. As soon as she had her balance, he quickly let go of her and took a step back.

"Sorry. I'm not good at this. I don't really dance."

"I can tell." She grinned up at him. "Let's take a walk outside and talk instead."

Bad idea! Talking is what always gets me in trouble.

John felt like he'd just been thrown into the ocean with a thousand-pound weight strapped to him. He was about to drown, and he knew it; he could see it coming like an inevitable storm on the crest of the next wave. She took him by the hand and led him to a side door. They were soon strolling through the beautiful grounds of the country church.

"How long have you been in the military?"

"Since I graduated high school."

"So, how old does that make you?"

"Twenty-eight."

"What do you do in the military?"

"Mostly, I kill people."

Felicia frowned. "That's morbid."

"It's less morbid than allowing the scum of the Earth to perpetrate evil on the innocent."

"I suppose that's true. How much longer are you planning to serve?"

"I don't know. I guess as long as I'm needed."

"So, you have no plans to get out any time soon?"

"No."

Her frown deepened as they walked toward a large shade tree on the far edge of the property.

"Would you categorize yourself as a violent person?"

"Only if I'm faced with an enemy."

They stopped under the tree. She leaned her back against the trunk and gave John an inviting smile.

"How do you feel about marriage? Do you want to have kids?"

He bit his lip and dropped his gaze to the grass. "I don't think about that kind of stuff."

"Why not?"

"My parents had a toxic marriage, and I had a horrible childhood. I don't plan on repeating it."

Her arms crossed over her chest. "What is that supposed to mean?"

Aw! Crap! I think I just pushed a button. She looks perturbed.

"Nothing. It doesn't mean anything. My parents hated each other. They weren't too fond of me. It was a bad situation."

"So, your parents had an unhealthy relationship, and now you think every woman is bad news?" Her tone was clipped, annoyed.

"That's not what I said."

"That's what you implied. Are you automatically assuming I'm the kind of woman who would do you wrong?"

He shook his head. "No. I don't even know you. We just met. I haven't formed an opinion of you yet."

"It sounds like you have a very negative view of marriage."

"That's fair."

"Do you have a negative view of women as well?"

"I haven't had any good experiences with them."

"What does that mean?"

"I'm not good at it—I don't really know what I'm doing. I always—" He shrugged faltering for the right thing to say.

Is he referring to sex? I've never had a man admit he's not good at it. That's a new one.

"I always end up saying the wrong thing."

Oh good! I'm glad he wasn't referring to sex.

"No one is perfect. I'm not looking for the impossible. I'm just looking for a good man who wants a future with me."

I'm just looking for one conversation that doesn't end in the girl hating my guts.

"What are you looking for, John?"

"I'm not really looking for anything."

Her lips formed a hard line, and she glared at him. "If that's the case, why are we wasting time talking?"

His jaw tightened. He could see the conversation was headed in the wrong direction. "Can we start over?"

"Why would you bother? It doesn't sound like you are looking for a serious relationship."

He dragged a hand over his burr. "I'm sorry. I'm coming across the wrong way. I'm not good at this."

"Not good at what?"

"Talking. I didn't mean to offend you. I apologize."

She took a deep breath and tried to calm her nerves.

Maybe he didn't mean it the way it sounded. He does seem nervous. Megan said he's really sweet. She said he's a good guy. I'm going to give him another chance.

"I just need to know one thing."

"Okay."

"Be honest. Do you ever see yourself getting married and having children?"

He stared at the grass for a moment. "Honestly, no. I'm pretty sure I'm not any girls' type."

She stared at him with a confused expression.

Not any girls' type! He's every girl's type. He's so hot! Why is he acting so insecure?

"Why do you think that?"

He shook his head and let out a frustrated sigh. "I don't know what women want. You are all too difficult to figure out. Trying to think of the right thing to say to a woman is more stressful than facing down an enemy on the battlefield. Nothing I ever say or do seems to be right. You take anything I say and twist it into something you find offensive. To be honest the thought of going out on a date with someone like you is nauseating."

Her lips turned down. "You find dating me nauseating?"

I haven't twisted anything! I asked him a simple question, and he turned it into an opportunity to complain about women. What is wrong with him?

"Yeah. You're beautiful, confident, focused. You walked into this encounter already knowing what you wanted to get out of it."

Where is he going with this?

"Is there something wrong with that?"
"No."
"I don't understand what the problem is, John."
He raked a hand over his burr and sighed. "I guess I'm the problem. You got me instead of Mr. Right. Between my parents and what years as a soldier has done to my head, I'm pretty screwed up."

Is this just him being insecure, or is he trying to admit to some serious flaw?

"Exactly how screwed up?"

She's looking at me like that again. She's judging me. I've already stuck my foot in my mouth. This isn't going to get any better. There's no point in even trying to fix this. She's already made up her mind. I can see it in her eyes.

He smirked. "Screwed up enough to know that you wouldn't be happy with me. I wouldn't fit into your little mold of the perfect husband. You're looking for a man who will fall in line and do whatever you want him to. I'm not the nine-to-five career kind of guy. Taking kids to after school practice and living in the suburbs isn't my thing. I'm a soldier. I'm not the guy who will jump through your little hoops."
"My little hoops!" she huffed annoyed.

He has a lot of nerve! I don't like his condescending attitude or his prejudice against women.

"Yeah. Don't pretend you don't have hoops. You met me twenty minutes ago, and you're already trying to pin me down on marriage and children."

"Pin you down? Wow! For your information, I don't have hoops!"

This guy is not ready for a serious relationship. His negative view of marriage and women borders on hostile.

John stared down at her. "What exactly do you expect from me? Be honest."

She took a deep breath. "I thought you would be sweet and charming. Obviously, I was way off. You are neither."

"Yeah, way off. Charming isn't my thing."

"No, apparently, rude is your thing."

"No, honesty is my thing. I'm not going to waste time trying to feed you whatever pretty lies you want to hear. I've tried that before. Women don't like lies any more than they like the truth."

She's already formed an opinion of me. Nothing I say is going to change that.

Her eyebrow rose, and her mouth fell open.

Women don't like the truth? Where did he get that from? I don't want to be lied to! I want the truth! He is so full of it!

"Honesty! That's your thing? Then be honest! When you first laid eyes on me, what did you think?"

"I thought, you were pretty."

That's a safe answer! A safe, rehearsed answer! Is that all Mr. Honesty can come up with?

"What else were you thinking? I'm sure that wasn't the only thought in your head! If honesty is your thing, be honest! There's something else! Tell me the whole truth, John!" she sneered.

His lip curled in irritation. He didn't like her tone or her accusing eyes. "Fine! You want the whole truth? I tried to picture you naked."

A hard slap stung his cheek.

Yeah. I deserved that. That's not the honesty she was looking for. She wanted me to lie. She wanted me to say I thought she was pretty, and sweet, and the kind of girl I could spend the rest of my life with. These girls expect too much from a first date. Hell! This isn't even a date. It's just an introduction. I am so tired of trying to please women. It's impossible! Who the hell knows what they really want? I bet they aren't even sure what they really want! All I know is they never want me!

John watched her storm back toward the church and disappear inside. He figured it would be safer if he hung outside for a while. She looked furious.

By the time he came back in, the cake had been cut and toasts had been made. Everyone was milling around conversing and eating cake. He noticed Felicia glaring at him from across the room. He did his best to ignore her. Soon enough, the bird seed was thrown, and the happy couple got into the just married limo that was decorated with flowers. They waved to the small crowd and disappeared on a month-long honeymoon to Hawaii.

Sonny, Nick, and John helped Megan and Kyle round up Owen and Anna's kids who were having too much fun with Anna's family. The little Wiley clan didn't want to go home, but they were soon buckled in their car seats.

The following morning, Kyle and Sonny gave the kids rides on Sassy, Owen's miniature Shetland pony. Nick helped Megan change the seemingly endless number of diapers produced by the three infants. He also helped her feed them, burp, them, and generally gave her a hand with anything she needed. After the pony rides, John entertained the kids with stories and piggy-back rides. Then he and the kids played on the living room floor with toy cars, dolls, and a small mountain of stuffed animals.

Megan sat on the couch holding Kyle's hand and watching Sonny asleep on the other couch with their three-month-old daughter, Mandy, napping on his chest. Nick sat in the rocking chair with Owen's three-month-old twins, Grayson and Bryson, in his arms. Her eyes went to John playing with the rest of Owen's kids, five-year-old twins, Mason and Carter, four-year-old, Julia, three-year-old, Cassie, and Becca, who was almost two-years-old. He was currently giving them rides on his back as he crawled around on the floor.

"John is so good with the kids," she whispered in Kyle's ear. "He needs to settle down and have a bunch of his own."

Kyle grinned as he watched his best friend tickling the kids and playfully growling as he chased them around the room on his hands and knees.

"When I introduced him to Felicia, she was more than interested. I don't understand why she didn't want to go out with him after the wedding."

Kyle cleared his throat and glanced at his wife. He lowered his voice so John wouldn't hear him. "John repels women, Babe."

"Why? He's handsome, sweet, and—"

"He just does. He told he me he's never gotten a girl to agree to a second date with him."

"I don't get it"

"He has a gift for sticking his foot in his mouth and pushing a woman's buttons."

"According to Felicia, he's hot as sin, but a complete jerk. She said she's dated men like him before, and the handsome face and hot body were not worth the emotional rollercoaster they put her through. She never wants to see John again."

"I believe it. He's perfectly nice to everyone on the SEAL team, but when it comes to women, John is a bumbling idiot with a knack for making them hate his guts."

"Why do you think he sticks his foot in his mouth? Is it self-sabotage?"

Kyle shrugged. "Not according to John. He wants to find a girl, but every time he gets one to agree to a date it all goes to hell. I don't think he means to anger their inner beast; he just stumbles onto the very thing they can't tolerate. He told me one girl he took to a steak house only to discover she was vegan when she began lecturing him on the evils of eating meat; he said the wrong thing, and it was all over in a moment. She got up and left. Another girl got angry that he held doors open for her and paid for her meal. Apparently, she was the independent type and felt he was treating her like a 1950's wife."

"Well, they both sound like unreasonable women. It didn't have to end badly. They could have communicated their point of view to John and worked through it."

Kyle shook his head. "Not according to John. I guess when women go off on him, he makes snide comments back, and it escalates. After the independent girl accused him of being a chauvinist pig from the 1950's, he grabbed her, slung her over his shoulder like a sack of potatoes, and carried her across the street to her car When he set her down, he snidely told her a 1950's chauvinist doesn't allow the little woman to walk across the street in traffic. She screeched at him and swatted him with her purse."

"He did that!" Megan gasped in shock.

"Apparently, she pushed some of his buttons too. It didn't end well for either of them. He's told me about a dozen dates that went horribly awry. I don't think he means to act like a jerk. He just responds to them the wrong way."

"Well, I'm not giving up. I have a date set up for him this evening with Linda."

"The new woman in your yoga class?"

"Yeah. She's very pretty, and she seems really sweet. I think it could be the perfect match."

"That's what you said about Felicia."

"Well, apparently, John ruined that. I'm going to coach him before she picks him up at 7:00."

Kyle rolled his eyes. "I'm guessing you haven't told John yet."

"No, I'll tell him later. He's having too much fun with the kids. I don't want to interrupt."

Kyle let out a long breath. "I'm staying out of this. If you want to play matchmaker, have fun."

She chuckled. "He just needs to find the right woman."

"I agree, but John is a walking disaster. Why not set Linda up with Nick? The girl you introduced him to at the wedding decided not to pursue him. He's more charming than John."

"Because Nick is going out with Charlette tonight, and Sonny is going out with Rita."

Kyle groaned softly. "Do Nick or Sonny know this yet?"

She shook her head and winked at her husband. "Not yet."

"You are a trouble maker."

"No, I'm just trying to help your friends find happiness like you and I found."

CHAPTER 2

May 29
1900
North Carolina

Linda Westing pulled up in front of Kyle and Megan's house. She was excited about the blind date despite the last-minute call from Megan the night before. She had visited the salon earlier that day for a manicure, and she was wearing the new outfit she'd purchased that morning. When she parked and got out, her nerves hit her full force. She hadn't been out on a date in a long time.

Her stiletto heels clicked on the concrete sidewalk as she hurried to the front door. A doorbell ring later and she was walking through the front door where she came face to face with John.

He is hot!

Her eyes roamed over him taking in his long legs, slim waist, and sculpted chest hugged by a thin, tight t-shirt. When she reached his face, her breath caught. He was so handsome. The only thing she wasn't crazy about was his short burr. She preferred longer hair. Military buzz-cuts weren't really her thing. Still, in her opinion, even his short buzz-cut did not deter his appeal.

Megan grinned at Linda's reaction. "Linda, this is John Rusk." She glanced at John who had a slightly stressed look on his face. "John, this is Linda Westing."

John's eyes briefly took in Linda. She was tall; he guessed five foot nine, taller than Megan. Her bright, curly, red hair was pulled back in ornate combs. She had engaging green eyes, demure lips, and cute freckles across her nose and cheeks. He only allowed himself a quick look at her slender, curvy form before jerking his eyes back to her face.

"It's nice to meet you, Linda." His deep voice held a slight rasp to it that sent a shiver down her spine.

"It's nice to meet you too. Are you ready to go?"

John gave her a smile that nearly melted her insides. "Yeah, sure."

He followed her out to her truck and slid into the passenger's side. On the drive into town, he was extremely nervous. Megan had only told him about this date an hour ago. He'd barely had time to shower and listen to her sweet, albeit unhelpful advice on how to impress a woman. He'd already tried everything she suggested on previous dates with no luck.

Linda chatted about her job and random things—none of which he was paying attention to. He was too focused on the short mini-skirt that was so far up her long, beautiful legs that he was sure if he really tried, he could see her panties. His eyes wavered between staring at her legs and staring at her cleavage that was practically spilling out of her halter top. She had a few random freckles on her abdomen that was exposed by the short top, and occasionally, he caught a glimpse of her belly-button ring. She was a vision of temptation.

It wasn't his fault he wasn't listening to anything she said. When a woman dressed the way she did, it put a man's mental faculties at a disadvantage. His brain had gone far beyond picturing her naked. He was in full-on dirty fantasy territory.

Halfway to town, Linda asked him what branch of the military he was in. When he didn't answer, she glanced over at him and saw the way he was staring at her.

I think he likes me. The way he's looking at me is so feral.

"Is it top secret or something?" She grinned as she looked back at the road.

"What?" John came out of the daze he'd fallen into.

"Your job."

"What about my job?"

She chuckled. "Were you even listening to me?"

John cleared his throat and stared out the front windshield for the first time. "Sorry. I must have zoned out."

She stole a quick glance at him. He was intently staring straight ahead.

"Was I boring you? I tend to ramble when I'm nervous."

"No, I just—um—I'm not really good at this."

"Not good at what?"

"This. Small talk. I'm sorry."

A sly grin spread over her lips as she ogled him for a moment before returning her attention to the road. "So, what are you good at?"

"Killing the bad guys."

"What?"

"That's what I do for a living. I'm a Navy SEAL. I get sent in to eliminate threats and end conflicts."

"By killing people?"

"Well, most of the scumbags we encounter aren't interested in surrendering, so yeah."

A shiver went up her spine, and her pulse raced. "So, are you a total badass?"

John shrugged. He kept his eyes on the road where it was safe.

When he didn't answer, she looked back at him.

He looks so serious. I wonder what he's thinking right now?

"You're awfully quiet. What are you thinking about?"

I should keep my mouth shut. So far, it seems like I haven't offended her.

She looked back at him, and her eyes scanned him and caught on the bulge beneath his zipper.

Oh! Wow! He's definitely turned on. He must like me.

"What kind of food do you like?"

He didn't look back at her. "We can go wherever you want. Anything is better than an MRE."

"What's an MRE?"

He chuckled. "Meal Ready to Eat. They taste like cardboard. That's mostly what I end up eating. We are gone on missions most of the time. Getting a real meal is a luxury I don't get to indulge in very often."

"Really. What other luxuries are you deprived of?" Her voice took on a suggestive tone.

Is she trying to flirt with me?

He looked over and caught her sly grin.

Yep. She's definitely flirting. This is going better than ninety percent of my previous dating attempts. Usually by now, I've already said something to tick the girl off.

"Pretty much any luxury. Sleeping on a bed or just sleeping at all. Most of the time I only get to sleep if we are in a safe zone. So, I guess sleeping would probably top my list of deprivations."

"What other deprivations are on your list?"

"I don't know. I don't really think of them as deprivations. It's just my normal routine."

"What about women?"

"What about them?" he asked warily.

"Are women on your list of deprivations?" Her voice took on a slightly husky, flirty tone.

"Uh—yeah. Definitely."

"Exactly how deprived are you?"

"Completely."

She glanced at him again. "How long has it been since you were with a woman?"

He cleared his throat and stared out the passenger's window. "I—um—never."

Awkward silence filled the truck.

Finally, Linda broke it with a smirk. "No, seriously."

John bit his lip as he stared at the green blur of trees passing by. He did not want to look back at Linda. He did not want to see whatever look was on her face.

She glanced his way several times as she drove the last few miles into town. He didn't make eye contact or speak again. She pulled into a Mexican restaurant near the center of Main Street.

"Is Mexican okay?" she asked breaking the long silence.

"Yeah."

John got out of the truck and walked to the entrance ahead of her. He held the door open and avoided eye contact. When she didn't complain about him holding the door open, he mentally checked one concern off his list.

The hostess seated them in a tall corner booth at the back of the crowded restaurant, and John focused on reading the menu. He wasn't ready to look Linda in the eyes. After the waitress took their orders, he forced himself to look up at her.

"So, what do you like to do for fun?" she asked with a warm smile.

Fun? What kind of question is that? Fun! I just focus on trying to survive every mission so I don't come home in a body bag. How am I supposed to answer that?

He shrugged. "I don't know."

"You don't know what you like to do for fun?"

He shook his head. "Not really. Fun is a luxury."

She smirked and chuckled. "That's an odd statement."

"We are on duty most of the year. We don't get that much leave time. When I'm on duty, I focus on training and on the mission. If I don't stay focused, I put the team in danger. That's not an option. Fun is for civilians."

Linda frowned. "So, you never have any fun?"

"Well, I wouldn't say never. I had fun this morning."

"What did you do?"

"I played with Owen's kids."

She grinned at him. "You like kids?"

John grinned back. "Yeah, kids are great! They are so literal and honest. You never have to wonder if they have an ulterior motive."

She bit her lip. "But you wonder if adults have ulterior motives?"

"I don't wonder. Adults always have an ulterior motive."

Her eyebrow rose. "Do you think I have an ulterior motive?"

He swallowed hard. He knew he'd just wandered into dangerous territory. He bit his lip studying her. Then he gave her a crooked grin. "Don't you?"

She chuckled. "I'm not really sure how to take that, John."

Lucky for him, the waitress arrived with their food. The conversation died as they both dug into their steaming plates.

John was halfway through his meal when he felt her foot sliding up the inside of his left calf. His brain immediately snapped to attention, and his jaw muscle tightened. He looked across the table at her. She grinned at him. He swallowed hard as her bare toes slid up past his knee.

What the hell should I do? No girl has ever come on to me like this.

Her grin turned sly.

His eyebrow rose as he felt her toes slide up his inner thigh to the rock-hard bulge under the zipper of his jeans.

"Lisa—" He gently grabbed her ankle and slid her foot onto the wooden seat next to his leg.

"It's Linda."

"Right, Linda. Uh—" His tanned cheeks were turning pink.

"Megan didn't tell me you were shy."

He cleared his throat. "I'm not shy."

"Are you sure?"

He looked down at his plate and let out another long breath.

"Earlier in the car, you said you'd never—you were joking—right?"

He bit his lip and forced his eyes back to hers. "No."

She smirked. "You know, you're not the first guy to use that line to try to get in my panties."

His jaw tightened. "I just met you. I don't even know you! Why would I be trying to get in your panties?"

"You're a man."

"I'm not that kind of man."

"There is only one kind of man. That's all men think about. Don't play innocent; you're hard as a rock. It's obvious what you want."

"Obvious! You don't know what I want, but it's clear what you want. I'm guessing you sleep with all the men you date. Does the line stretch around the block?"

Her eyebrow rose, and her lips formed an angry line. "I don't sleep around!"

They both stared at each other for an awkward moment.

"Yeah, right!" he muttered.

"I was only trying to flirt with you! A normal man would have liked that."

"A normal girl wouldn't come on to me like a whore thirty minutes into the first date."

"You're an ass!"

"I've been called worse."

John glared at her for a moment. Then he stood up and walked out of the restaurant. He headed down the road in the direction of Kyle and Megan's house. He needed a long walk to cool off. He felt like punching something.

I don't care if she is Megan's friend; I don't have to put up with that! It's not my fault this time! She's the one who started it! I'm not going to sleep with a skank like her!

Ten minutes later, John felt his phone vibrate in his pocket. He pulled it out and grimaced. Megan's contact photo displayed on the screen. He took a deep breath and answered.

"Hey, Megan."

"John, what happened? Linda just called. She said you insulted her, walked out halfway through the meal, and left her with the check. She was very upset."

John bit his lip. "Is that all she said?"

Megan cleared her throat. "She said you called her a whore."

"I did."

"Why?"

"Didn't she tell you?"

"No. She said everything seemed to be going great, and then you got angry with her, called her a whore, and stormed out of the restaurant."

He smirked. "That's the abbreviated version."

"What's the long version?"

"She's your friend. I don't want to say anything to ruin a friendship."

"You're my friend. I've only known Linda for a month. Tell me what happened."

"I wouldn't say the date was going great. I suck at small talk, so the drive in was awkward. When we got our food, she slid her foot up my leg and started rubbing my—equipment."

"She did what!"

"Yeah—well—I pulled her foot off my crotch, and she took offense to the fact that I wasn't comfortable with it. She said most men would like it. That's when I called her a whore. Maybe I went a little overboard with my accusation, but she seemed like a dirty slut to me. She acted like she was ready to jump me right there in the booth. She's not my kind of girl, Megan. I don't like fast women. That's when she called me an ass. I figured the date wasn't going to get any better from that point, so I left. I should have left money for the meal. I wasn't thinking clearly. All I could think about was getting away from her as quickly as possible. I'll give you some money. You can reimburse her for dinner."

Megan gasped. "She did that?"

"Yeah."

"You don't need to pay for the meal, John. I'm sorry I set you up with her. I had no idea she would act like that. She seemed so nice."

"No, I'll pay for it. I shouldn't have left her to pay the whole thing. Lousy date or not, it wasn't right. I'm not that kind of guy."

"I know you're not. I apologize for setting you up with her. Where are you?"

"I'm walking home. I needed some fresh air."

"Where are you? I'm already on my way in town to pick you up."

John gave her his location, and a few minutes later, Megan pulled up next to him. He got in, and she turned the SUV around and headed home.

"I'm so sorry. Next time I set you up, I'm going to make sure she is nothing like Linda."

"Forget it. I have lousy luck with women. Maybe I'm not meant to be with anyone."

"Don't say that. You are a great guy. We just have to find you a great girl."

"I don't need a girl, Megan."

"You definitely need a girl, and I'm determined to find the perfect girl for you."

John let out a heavy sigh and stared out the window.

When they reached the house, John wasn't in the mood to rehash the date with Kyle or anyone else. He took a walk down to the beach to think. He sat on the pristine sand and stared at the vast ocean ahead of him.

An hour later, Nick walked up and sat down next to him. "I heard your date was a bust too."

"Yeah."

"My date said she wasn't into the military vibe."

John chuckled. "Then why did she agree to go out with you?"

Nick chuckled too. "Good question. She asked me how soon I was getting out. I told her I'll probably retire from the Navy. She didn't like that. That pretty much ended the date. She didn't want to waste any more time on me. I heard her on the phone; I think she was going to hit the club scene after she dropped me off."

"She'll probably run into my date there. I think that's more her vibe."

"Megan told me what she did. I'm glad she didn't set me up with her."

"She told you?"

"If you didn't want everyone to know, you should have kept it to yourself."

John buried his head against his knees and groaned.

"If it makes you feel any better, Sonny's date ditched him too. Kyle is on his way in town to pick him up now. Apparently, she didn't appreciate his aggressive flirting."

John smirked. "He should have gone out with Linda. Sonny is more her speed."

Nick nodded. "Ironically, he seems to have the luck of the gods with all women. His date must be one of the few exceptions if she's immune to his charms."

A short while later, Sonny joined them on the beach.

"I heard you two had a speck of bad luck." Sonny chuckled as he sat down next to John.

Nick smirked. "I heard you didn't fare so well either."

"Says who?"

"Megan."

Sonny chuckled. "She only heard the filly's side of it. That girl was purring sweet until—"

"Until you tried to get too handsy," Nick said.

"Too handsy! There's no such thing. Women like a take charge man. It turns them on when you get handsy. That's free advice, Boys. The friskier you get, the more they like it."

"If that's true, why are you sitting here with us?" Nick asked.

Sonny chuckled. "That filly just wasn't ready for my brand of romance. She's young and inexperienced."

"When has that ever stopped you before?" John muttered.

"True, but she had too much church in her. She was one of them sweet, innocent, savin' it for marriage types. It can be hard to overcome the religion hurdle. Believe it or not, Ol Sonny doesn't always bed the girl. There's been a few times I got turned down, but only a few."

Nick smirked. "Not to hear you tell it."

Sonny grinned slyly. "I have a reputation to uphold, Boys. That information goes no further than this beach."

"What about the girl yesterday?" Nick asked.

Sonny winked. "Why do you think they invented coat closets? It ain't fer the coats."

"You had sex with that girl at the wedding?"

"I gave it to her good—five times in that closet."

"Then why did Megan set you up with a new girl?" Nick asked.

Sonny winked. "A girl can only handle so much Sonny. Didn't you notice she was walkin' funny when we came back to the wedding? That's signature Sonny. When you give it to them good, they don't need it again for a week."

"You're a piece of work!" John muttered. He stood up and walked away.

"Don't be jealous, John. The right girl will come along for you eventually. They won't all turn you down." Sonny called after him.

John walked down the beach in the dark muttering under his breath.

"The girl tonight didn't turn him down. He turned her down," Nick said quietly. "Apparently, she got a little too handsy for John's liking."

"Yeah, I know. Kyle told me on the drive back."

Nick gave Sonny a questioning look.

Sonny winked. "John don't want some easy chic that's been around. He's holding out for someone special—a nice girl with good morals. What he wants is another Megan."

"I wouldn't mind finding a Megan of my own," Nick said. "Girls like her are hard to find."

"Yeah, you virgins are all looking for the same thing. You're all lookin' fer yer Megan."

"What are you looking for, Sonny?"

"A good time, no attachment, and a hot piece of ass."

"That's it? Don't you ever plan to settle down and raise a family?"

"Nah. That's fer guys like you and John. I'm a wild stallion. I got to roam free."

"You don't ever plan to find Mrs. Right?"

Sonny shrugged. "I don't think there is a Mrs. Right fer me, Nick. Besides, you know the mortality rate for SEAL operators. I'm lucky I've lived this long. The chances of me coming home fer good are in a bag, not to the arms of a pretty girl. So, I enjoy the pretty fillies while I'm alive. You never know when yer clocks goin' to strike midnight."

"That's morbid."

"Don't tell me you don't consider your own demise. Hell, every operator has to face that possibility on every mission we get sent on. It's just a fact of life."

Nick grimaced. "I think about it, but I try not to dwell on it."

Sonny nodded. "I don't dwell on it either, but it's always floatin' in the back of my head. So, I take what I can when I'm able to. Besides, there ain't a Megan out there for me. No nice girl would have me. I'm tainted goods. Nice girls see me coming a mile off and run the other way."

"So, she saw through your cowboy charm and realized you're just a man-whore."

"Yeah. It didn't take her long either. She was a real sweet, little thing, but after the first kiss, she bolted like a scared little bunny. She couldn't get away from me fast enough."

"You came on too strong."

"Nah. I barely came onto her at all. I slid my hand up the inside of her leg, and that was it for her. She was as skittish as an unbroke horse in a corral. Too bad I didn't get to break her in."

The next day, the SEALs' short leave was up. Sonny, Nick, and John said goodbye; the kids hugged Sonny and Nick, but none of them wanted to let go of Uncle John. It was a tearful detachment when Kyle and Megan had to pull their tiny hands free of John's legs.

"I'll be back to see you all before you know it," John promised. "Maybe you can draw me some pictures, and Aunt Meg and Uncle Kyle can mail them to me at work. I would love that."

John gave them all one last hug and kiss before he left. It was hard to say goodbye to their precious little faces. It made his heart hurt, but he didn't have a choice. Duty called. He had a job to do. He had a country to defend. He had bad guys to kill.

CHAPTER 3

May 30
0730
Guantanamo Bay, Cuba

Corporal Sophia Maria Louisa Armanda Gonzalez packed her duffle bag and prepared to officially end her four-year stint in the Marine Corp at Guantanamo Bay. She reported to her C.O. Sergeant Steadly and stood at attention in front of his desk.

"Gonzalez, your exit paperwork indicates you are joining the Navy to pursue SEAL training."

"Sir, yes, Sir," Sophia said respectfully.

"You know eighty percent of all candidates who enter the BUD/S training program drop out."

"Sir, yes, Sir."

"You realize no woman has made it through BUD/S."

She stood at attention. "Sir, I am aware of that. I intend to be the first."

"Is your ego propelling you to pursue this?"

"Sir, no, Sir. Permission to speak freely?"

"Permission granted."

"I wish to pursue a career with the Navy SEALs because they are the best of the best. They are the most elite fighting force our nation puts forward. I wasn't trained to settle for less than the best. I know the statistics, but I'm determined to put forth my best for myself and my country.

He sighed heavily. "The odds are stacked against you, Gonzalez."

"I'm a Marine. I've been trained to overcome the odds and press forward, Sir."

Sergeant Steadly nodded. "Good luck Gonzalez! Dismissed!"

CHAPTER 4

May 31
0600
Afghanistan base

Echo reported as ordered to Commander Rowen's briefing. Rowen's gaze fell on the team. They were sitting around the table anxiously waiting to hear what the new mission would be. To Rowen's right sat Echo's leader, Chief Lydell Fry. Rowen's gaze traveled around the table to the medic, Cord Murphy, and then to the remainder of the team, John Rusk, Ben Obasi, Nick Novak, Camron James, Sonny Eldridge, Zachary Hurst, Rob Dover, Grant Donnell, Dorian Axel, Cliff Ellwood, Ian Irwin, Ezra Lombard, Porter Prescott, and Eric Coll.

Every man on Echo was highly trained in a variety of diversified skills. Every man was lethal in the extreme sense of the word. They had all seen some of the worst combat situations, and they were ready for more.

Rowen took a deep breath and started the briefing for Echo's next mission.

"There's been an uprising in Congo. General Tacari Negassi of the Chacha army of the new Chimelu Republic has declared war on the current government. He's set his site on dominating the region through force. His guerrilla army operates from secret bases in the Mitumba mountain range. For the past two years, they have been attacking small villages and forcing the men and young boys into servitude to the Chacha army. They become slave labor, mining for diamonds and precious metals to support the rebel cause. They live under the threat of the annihilation of their home villages if they don't cooperate.

Until now, the Democratic Republic of the Congo has attempted to subvert Negassi's efforts and subdue his army with their own forces. This has proven difficult due to the defensive mountain terrain where the Chacha army operates from. The current Congolese government has recently requested assistance from the United Nations.

Echo and Delta will be sent in to take out these militants in a joint effort with the U.N. England, France, and Spain will be offering assistance with supplies and coordinating strike locations, but you gentlemen will be the tip of the spear. Delta should be arriving on base within the hour. We will have a joint meeting with Delta in two hours to coordinate efforts from our side. Are there any questions?"

Sonny cleared his throat. "Yeah, how long will this deployment be?"

"As long as it takes to eradicate, capture, or kill the Chacha army and its leaders. Rough estimation is a few months to a year. We are fully committed to this endeavor. We have the support of the world court behind us. The Congo region has been unstable for decades, and the U.N. wants to see that come to an end as much as the people of Congo do. We are there for as long as it takes," Rowen said.

Sonny nodded. "Good, cause I hate doin' a half-ass job. I say we kill all the cockroaches even if we have to burn the whole damn house down!"

Rowen smirked. "Let's not burn down the house. There are innocent victims who don't deserve to deal with the aftermath of an all-out war. That's why we are sending in the best of the best. Echo and Delta will be there strictly to kill the cockroaches. We don't want collateral damage."

"I wasn't talkin' bout collateral damage. I meant burn Negassi's house down. Don't give that rat bastard anywhere to hide and scurry. I'm talkin' bout annihilation of him and all his pathetic little army minions," Sonny clarified.

Rowen nodded. "Glad we are all on the same page, Sonny."

Nick raised his hand. "You said we are there. Are you coming with us on this mission? You normally just coordinate the SEAL teams from here."

"This is a critical mission that has the potential to affect global politics. The United Nations wants this region stabilized. It has been plagued with disease and civil war for too long. They want Congo to return to a stable economic entity. Success will be a positive not only for the people of Congo but also for global trade. I am being temporarily assigned to this task until we are done in Congo. Commander Taggett will replace me here for the duration of this mission."

Dorian whistled. "This is serious."

"Yes, it is serious," Rowen said sternly. He looked around the table for more questions, but everyone seemed content with his answer. "If that's all the questions, you men are dismissed. Go pack up the appropriate gear. Our flight leaves at 1600. Meet back here in two hours for a briefing with Delta. Then we ship out."

Echo headed back to the supply building to pack up and assemble all the necessary gear.

Two hours later, Echo and Delta were jointly briefed, came up with a strategy, and made their flight at 1600. Several hours later, they landed in Kinshasa, the capital of Congo. U.N. troops were already busy securing a base of operations in Kananga, but until the red tape was sorted out, SEAL teams Echo and Delta were forced to play the waiting game.

CHAPTER 5

June 1
0600
Coronado, California

BUD/S Day 1

Petty Officer Third Class, Sophia Gonzalez reported to NSWO (Naval Special Warfare Orientation) for BUD/S (Basic Underwater Demolition/SEAL) training. The moment she stepped off the bus, her ears were greeted by the sound of orders being shouted at the group of SEAL candidates. They were soon assembled in rows on the grinder for uniform inspection. Anyone who failed inspection was sent on the crawl of shame.

All around her, men were being sent to the remediation group for infractions like unpolished boots, loose threads on their uniform, crooked collars, and dusty helmets. The slightest imperfection in uniform presentation was awarded with a stern speech. Men who failed the inspection were told if they can't be trusted with a uniform, helmet, and boots than they won't be trusted with a rifle, pistol, gear, or communications equipment. Those who failed inspection were forced to crawl on their hands and feet to the remediation group.

When the officer inspecting her row stepped up in front of Sophia, he wore a smirk. He checked and rechecked her uniform, but he found no infractions. His smirk turned to a frown. He passed her through to the next group. She took her place in the evenly spaced rows of men who all wore pristine uniforms like hers. When the last uniform was inspected and the SEAL candidates were split into those who passed and those who

30

would face remediation, Sophia's group was addressed by Senior Chief Petty Officer Reynolds.

Reynolds walked down the rows staring a hole into each soldier assembled before him. A long, jagged scar snaked down his right cheek. He was weathered—perfectly seasoned—totally relentless—he was all SEAL. He took up a post in front of the group and barked his intimidating rhetoric.

"Here at BUD/S, you will face fear and inner demons you didn't know you had. You will suffer. You will know pain, humiliation, failure. If you discover that SEAL life is too hard, you can end your personal hell by ringing the bell three times. If you DOR (Drop On Request), you will be sent back to your Naval unit where you will serve out what remains on your contract. Those who stay will come to know the O-Course (Obstacle Course), swimming, running, and PT (Physical Training) with an intimacy you have never experienced before. Teamwork will become like breathing. You will demonstrate integrity and humility. Your physical, mental, and emotional limits will be pushed until you push through or until you break. Those who are weak in mind or body will be driven to your breaking point. You will quit! It is my duty to push you until you break. I would not be doing the SEAL program justice if I passed through sub-par candidates who will fail under the rigors of the job. To be a SEAL is to be the best of the best! Only the toughest, most dedicated soldiers can endure what is required out in the field. Our SEALs not only handle the pressure, they thrive under the most extreme conditions. If you are not worthy to wear the SEAL Trident, we will discover it here at BUD/S. There is nowhere to hide inadequacies inside this compound. You will be stripped down to your naked core and exposed to everyone here. Eighty percent of you will ring the bell. There are no exceptions! By the end of today, at least three of you will ring it!"

Sophia stood at attention with the rest of the men and listened to every word. She knew she wouldn't be ringing that bell. She was here on a mission. Nothing was going to deter her from making it to a team.

Reynolds' speech was followed by PT. They were directed through a series of push-ups, sit-ups, and pull-ups. It was followed by a one-and-a-half-mile run. Chow time was brief and was followed by surf torture in the Ocean at a cozy fifty-two degrees.

Sophia sat on the sand with her arms linked with the man to either side of her. With every wave that rolled in, the water reached her neck. Her teeth chattered, and her body grew numb just like every man on that line. After surf torture, they were told to roll in the sand until they were covered from head to toe.

Men who failed to fully coat themselves with sand were reprimanded and given more surf torture before being told to get sandy again.

Sophia stood at attention with the rest of the men who passed the sand test. Her body shivered, and her teeth chattered. She was coated in sand from the top of her short, black burr, to the bottom of her combat boots.

Surf torture and getting sandy was followed by more PT. As Day 1 dragged on, every SEAL candidate began to feel the effects of a full day of physical exercise and near hypothermia.

At the end of the day, Sophia cleaned up in the communal showers with the rest of the 206 SEAL candidates. She ignored the gawking stares of some of the men. After a shower, she went to bed. At midnight, they were all awakened by the sound of a loud bull-horn. SEAL training officers called them out of the barracks to the grinder where they were marched on a midnight two-mile run.

BUD/S Day 2

Sophia woke before dawn with the rest of the candidates. They were put through PT, surf torture, the O-Course, and chow. After chow they were told to do laps in the pool.

Reynolds was there front and center to shout directions to the candidates. "You will race to the end of the pool! The first man to touch the side of the pool will be excused from the rest of this exercise! You will swim back! The winner of that lap will be excused from the rest of this exercise! You will continue to race laps until each man has been excused in like manner! If you decide this exercise is too much for you, get out and ring the bell! I expect at least four of you to ring the bell before this exercise is over. Jump in and swim for your life!"

All the candidates dove in the pool and swam as fast as they could. Every man was hoping to be first to avoid further physical exertion.

Sophia knew better than to sprint the first lap. She knew she wasn't the fastest swimmer. She also knew that if she wore herself out during the first sprint, she'd never be able to finish what promised to be a long, grueling exercise. She paced herself, and soon she was near the back of the pack. She could hear the instructors yelling, but she tuned it out and stayed focused on the mission at hand—swim to the edge of the pool.

She had a minute to rest when she reached the edge of the pool. There were still ten men behind her that were struggling to make the swim.

After five laps, she was no longer coming in at the back of the pack. She was finishing near the middle of the pack and had a little longer to rest. As promised, one man was pulled out of the exercise after each lap, but that still left 194 candidates to compete with. Six men had already rung the bell since yesterday morning. The class of 206 was currently 200.

When Sophia's turn came to be pulled from the exercise, she finished 142 out of 200. Her legs were shaking, and she could feel a muscle cramp coming on, but she ignored it. She'd made it through one more test.

The afternoon of swimming was followed by PT. By the time she showered with the rest of the 197 candidates and went to bed, she was utterly exhausted. At midnight, they woke to the bull-horn and another two-mile run.

BUD/S Day 3

An early morning run was followed by PT, surf torture, getting sandy, and the O-Course. Chow was a welcome break from the physical exertion, but it was short-lived. They were soon back outside enduring the extreme conditions of BUD/S training. By the end of the day, there were 186 candidates left.

BUD/S Day 4

The morning was a repeat of the previous mornings, and after chow, there was another long, grueling swim. This time, Sophia finished 127 out of 180. The class of SEAL candidates was dwindling slowly but surely, just as Reynolds had predicted.

BUD/S Day 5

While the SEAL candidates were going through their usual morning physical torture of PT, a run, surf torture, and getting sandy to finish it off, some of the SEAL training officers were doing room inspection. Half the candidates failed room inspection. Sophia was among those who failed. She'd forgotten to tuck in one corner of her bedding tightly enough. When the candidates were assembled on the grinder, she was called out along with the rest of the men who failed inspection. They were given a speech about responsibility, dedication, and attention to detail. Then they were dismissed to rectify their respective mistakes.

At lunch Sophia sat across from men who were still strangers, but who she felt a simpatico connection with nonetheless. The man sitting across from her was Cafferty. She recognized him vaguely, as much as she recognized the 175 who were left.

"I thought about ringing the bell this morning," Cafferty muttered. "Then I saw you show up on the grinder, and I decided to tough it out. If you can take this, I can take it."

Sophia didn't respond. She merely shoveled food in as fast as she could before chow was over.

After chow, they were assembled on the beach for surf passage. Sophia was assigned to a boat crew of six men. When the race started, her team pulled their ten-foot rubber raft into the water and paddled out against the rough surf coming into the San Diego shore. The water was cold, but she was getting used to being perpetually cold. She dug into the water with her paddle and pulled through the surf with her team. Beside them, a team hit the surf at the wrong angle, and the rubber raft flipped spilling all six men into the violent surf. Sophia didn't have time to ponder whether the men would be able to flip their raft and continue the exercise. She had to remain focused so her own team didn't suffer the same fate.

BUD/S Day 8

The morning began with the usual run followed by PT, and the O-Course. After chow, she was assigned to a team of six men to carry a toothpick. A toothpick is a 400 to 500-pound telephone pole. Cafferty was one of the men assigned to her team.

Sophia ignored his muttering and complaining. She focused on carrying her portion of the 400-pound log. They were required to carry it on their shoulders, up the hill in the loose sand, and back down to the water. Once they reached the surf, they were ordered to carry it in knee deep water down the beach.

Halfway to the finish line, Cafferty collapsed in the surf in front of her. The sudden shift in weight distribution coupled with the added challenge of stumbling over him was too much for Sophia. She went down too as she stumbled and fell on top of Cafferty. The weight of the toothpick shifted, and the end came down on her back.

She found herself unable to move, unable to get off of Cafferty, and unable to breathe with her face buried in the surf.

While Sophia and Cafferty were both dragged from the surf, her team was ordered to finish the mission with two men down. Sophia and Cafferty were both immobilized and immediately sent for medical evaluation and treatment.

After x-rays at the hospital, Sophia was given the bad news; she had three cracked vertebrae. She was told if her recovery went well that she would be permitted to reenter the BUD/S program provided she could pass the PST (Physical Screening Test). It was hard news to hear, but she took it in stride with a renewed determination. Sophia was not about to quit.

CHAPTER 6

June 9
2400
Kinshasa, Congo, United Nations Embassy

John lay on his assigned bunk staring at the peeling ceiling. Echo and Delta had been waiting impatiently at the embassy for days, and it was starting to wear on him. Rowen had explained that negotiations between the cooperating nations were holding everything up. A chain of command had to be established and responsibilities assigned to each group.

Like most SEALs, John was a war machine. He kept a clear head. He stayed focused. Losing focus could cost you your life; he was all too familiar with what one moment of distraction could bring. If not for Kyle, John's one serious mistake would have cost him his life. After stepping on that land mine, John had never allowed himself to lose focus again. He was fully committed to the SEAL way of life. He wasn't interested in the politics of the situations they were dropped into. Politics wasn't his mission. He left that to the politicians. All he wanted to know was the target package so he'd know where to point his rifle. That's all he cared about. The red tape that surrounded every little decision annoyed him more than anything else.

He didn't understand what the holdup was. They'd already been told that Negassi was the target, that he was a murderer, kidnapper, and that he used innocent children to promote his own agenda. What more needed to be debated? It was obvious to John that Negassi needed a bullet to his head. He was itching to get in the field and put that bullet where it belonged. His philosophy was the more scum he eliminated the better the planet became. Every bullet that met its mark was one less scumbag wasting oxygen. That's how John viewed the world. It was simple, clean, and left no room for second guessing. Kill the bad guy; move on to the next bad guy.

At 0500, the Embassy breakfast hall hummed with conversation. Echo stood quietly in line waiting for food. There was nothing to say. A meeting was schedule with Rowen at 1300. Rowen was currently engaged in more negotiations with military leaders from the U.N. John got a plate of food and headed to the far end of the dining hall where most of Echo were already sitting. He took a seat next to Sonny at a small table in the far corner.

"So, John, you were talkin' in yer sleep last night." Sonny grinned mischievously.

John grimaced. He wasn't sure he even wanted to know what Sonny had overheard. He didn't look up from his plate of bacon, scrambled eggs, and toast.

"Good thing I was the only one awake to hear it."

John let out a weary sigh. "You don't plan to repeat it at the breakfast table, do you?"

Sonny chuckled. "Why? Worried I might have heard something embarrassing?"

"Did you?"

"Yep."

John groaned, leaned back in his chair, and raked both hands over his burr.

Sonny lowered his voice and leaned in closer. "You just need to find yourself a woman."

"It's not that easy to find the right girl. You think I don't try? I've tried and tried. I'm tired of the whole scene. Dating is too complicated. I can't figure women out. They don't like me. I think there's something really wrong with me."

"There ain't nothin' wrong with you, John. Granted, I ain't a woman, but I've got eyes. You're an attractive guy. I see the way women look at you. It's just that dang-fool tongue of yours. Next time we go on leave, you can go to the bars with me, and I can be your wingman. I can help you keep from saying something stupid and talk you up to the fillies. You really need to get laid. If you just get that monkey off yer back, women won't seem like such a challenge."

John shook his head. "Thanks for the offer, but I don't think so. That's not the kind of man I am. I don't want to be that guy. I'd rather get rejected than be like you."

"What's that supposed to mean?"

John picked up his fork and absently pushed his scrambled eggs around on the plate. "I'm not a player like you. I won't use a woman just to fulfill my needs. I'm not looking for a one-night-stand, Sonny. I want a real relationship with the right woman or nothing at all."

"See, that there is why you're still a virgin. You're so stubborn!"

John smirked. "You make it sound like I have a disease."

Sonny chuckled. "Nah. Yer just so—"

"What?"

"Yer just so—good. I swear if I knew any good-girls, I'd hook you up with one, but all I run into are bar-skanks. They're only interested in a one-night-stand."

"Yeah, I'm not interested in one of those."

"What exactly are you looking for in a woman?"

John shrugged. "You mean besides a woman who can tolerate me and my idiotic mouth?"

"Yeah."

"I don't know. Someone with good morals."

"That's all?"

John grinned. "Well, I wouldn't mind if she were pretty."

Sonny laughed. "What kind of pretty are you looking for? Brunette, blonde, red-head—"

"I don't have a type. I'm attracted to all kinds of women. They just aren't interested in me."

"I think part of your problem is you have zero self-confidence."

John shrugged. "It's hard to have self-confidence when I get shot down harshly every time."

"You expect them to reject you, and you orchestrate it so they will."

John took a bite of his eggs and glared at Sonny. "I don't do it on purpose."

Nick slid into one of the empty chairs. "Don't do what on purpose?"

"Nothing," John mumbled as he shoved a piece of bacon into his mouth.

"Me and John were just discussing the reason why he gets turned down by women. I was trying to share some wisdom with the boy."

Nick smirked. "Sonny, why can't you leave him alone? Just because you're God's gift to the female species doesn't mean the rest of us have to follow in your promiscuous footsteps."

Sonny chuckled. "Now, Nick, don't get your feelings hurt. I'll let you join the class too."

Nick shot Sonny an accusing glare. "No thanks. I'm not interested in being schooled by you."

Sonny grinned. "Don't get so snippy, Nick. All I'm sayin' is that I know a few things about women. A little advice could go a long way toward helping you find the woman yer lookin' for."

"What advice?" Nick's lip curled up in sarcastic derision. "One-liners? What kind of alcohol gets them drunk enough to agree to anything? How to lie to them? How to use them and lose them? What, Sonny? What can you teach us?"

"Damn! You sure are crabby this mornin'." Sonny stood up and left the table.

As soon as Lydell finished his breakfast, he went to the main lobby where the cell phone reception was better. The large room was dark, deserted, and eerily quiet. It would be dawn in a few minutes, but the sun hadn't quite peaked the horizon. He put in a call to the states. He'd been trying to reach his grandparents since coming to Africa.

"Hello," Benedetta Fry answered.

"Grammy?" Lydell's voice betrayed his relief.

"Lydell? It's the middle of the night. What's wrong? Are you alright?" Her voice was shaky.

"I'm fine, Grammy. I'm sorry to wake you. I've been trying to get ahold of you for days. I've left several voice-mails and texted you. I was getting worried." He dragged a hand over his burr as he paced back and forth in the lobby.

"Oh, I'm sorry. You know I can't figure out this new phone you bought me. I can barely figure out how to answer a phone call on it. All this new technology is so complicated."

"I texted Ellery and Ridley too. I haven't heard back from them either."

Benedetta sighed. "Well, Ridley went on what he calls a walkabout. He said he's going to see the world before he starts college in the fall. He packed a backpack full of his things the day after graduation and left. I think all that money your friend gave you is a bit of a curse. Ridley emptied his bank account before he took off. He's too young to have that kind of money. You shouldn't have given him so much."

Lydell sighed. "I didn't give him that much. I only put a thousand dollars in his account. I paid his college tuition directly from my account."

"A thousand dollars to a boy who is barely eighteen is like a million dollars to you or me. The boy has no concept of the value of money. He's probably on a spending spree wasting it all. I doubt it will last him all summer; though he thinks he can see the whole world on it. I do appreciate you paying off the mortgage on the farm with some of your money. It has taken a heavy burden off your Gramps and me, but you didn't have to do that. It's your money. Your friend gave it to you. You shouldn't be using it to bail us out of a bind."

"Kyle gave me plenty of money, way more than I need. When he found that treasure, he gave all the guys on Echo money so we could take care of ourselves and our families. Which is exactly what I'm doing. I don't want you and Gramps worrying about how to pay off loans. I want to make sure Ellery and Ridley both get a good education. I'm just taking care of my family."

Benedetta smiled. "You are such a good boy, Lydell. Your parents would have been so proud of the man you've become. The way you've stepped up to take care of your brother, sister, me, and Lonan shows character."

"How is Ellery? She didn't take off too, did she?"

"Your little sister is fine. She spends too much time in town with her friends mooning over boys, but other than that she is keeping her head on her shoulders."

"Mooning over boys! She's only fifteen! She shouldn't be thinking about boys. She's too young for that. Besides, teenage boys only have one thing on their minds. Keep her away from boys. Ground her. Tie her up if you have to—"

Benedetta chuckled. "She's not serious about any particular boy yet. She's just starting to show more interest in boys than she used to. Don't worry; I've got my eye on her. Speaking of romance, is there anyone special you have your eye on? You'll be thirty-three-years-old in July. It's high time you settled down, young man."

"Grammy, I'm a SEAL. We don't have time for relationships. We are never in one place long enough to get to know anyone anyway. The life of a SEAL doesn't leave room for—"

"What about Freya?"

"What about her?"

"She's been asking about you."

"Why? She's married."

"Actually, she's recently divorced."

He grimaced. "I'm not interested."

"She's still in love with you. She wishes she'd married you instead. She knows she made a huge mistake, and she's looking for a second chance."

Lydell scoffed. "She didn't love me enough to marry me when I asked her. She said she couldn't see herself tied down to a man who wouldn't be around and who might never come home from war. She made her choice. I made mine. I don't love her anymore. I'm completely over Freya. You can tell her that next time you see her."

Benedetta frowned. "I hope you're not closing your heart off to ever finding love."

"I don't have time right now to pursue love. I have a duty to my country. That comes first."

"Don't wait too long. You're not getting any younger, Lydell."

He halted his nervous pacing, and the muscle in his jaw tightened. He rolled his eyes and a half-annoyed smirk parted his lips. "I gotta go, Grammy. Duty calls. If you hear from Ridley, have Ellery text me."

"I will. She's the only one left in this old house who can figure out these new phones."

"I love you, Grammy. Tell Gramps I love him too."

"I love you, Sweetheart. Take care of yourself."

Lydell hung up and slid his phone back into his pocket. There was more he wanted to discuss with Grammy, but his love life or lack thereof was not one of them. He knew better than to think he could steer the conversation in a new direction. Once Grammy got started on that particular subject, there was no stopping her. He glanced toward the window where the morning sun now illuminated the empty lobby. Then he sank down onto one of the lobby chairs, buried his head in his hands, and sighed in frustration. He knew Grammy was right. He wasn't getting any younger, but being a SEAL was a very demanding responsibility. There simply wasn't time or opportunity to meet a woman much less pursue one.

"It can't be that bad." A woman's clipped, British accent echoed through the empty lobby.

Lydell looked up, and his eyes took in the petite beauty walking toward him. She was barely five-foot-tall with blue eyes and long, blonde hair pulled back in a clip to reveal her delicate jaw and her beautiful face. She wore a khaki colored uniform with the Union Jack insignia. His grim expression did not change as he stared at her.

She gave him a warm smile and held out her hand to him. "I'm Bretta."

He looked at her hand as if it were a poisonous viper. Then he looked back up into her eyes with wary curiosity.

Bretta dropped her hand after a moment. "A man as handsome as you should smile. A smile would complement your face more than the scowl you are wearing now."

His upper lip curled up on one side in irritation. "Do you need something?"

Bretta gave him another smile. "I was just trying to cheer you up a bit."

"Mission accomplished." His tone was sardonic as he gave her a mocking salute.

Her lips pursed together as she studied him. Aside from the hateful scowl on his face, he was extremely handsome. Her eyes slowly traveled down from his bright, copper-orange burr, to his piercing green eyes, to the freckles on his nose and cheeks that were barely perceptible under his tan. Her eyes paused on the pink scar that snaked down the right side of his neck; it started at his ear and disappeared inside his tan, camo t-shirt. She continued her appraisal noting his sculpted chest, accentuated by the tight t-shirt. Her eyes dropped to his tan, camo fatigues. He had long, muscular legs. He suddenly stood up, towering over her.

"Get a good look?" Lydell snarled as he took a step toward her.

Bretta stared up into his accusing eyes and smirked. "Not quite. I could go for a bit more."

"Sorry to disappoint you!" he growled.

He stepped around her to leave and felt her slender fingers close around his wrist.

"Where are you off to?"

"None of your business!" He jerked his arm free of her grip, glared at her for a moment, and then turned and headed toward the stairs.

Bretta hurried to cut him off. She stood on the step blocking his path.

"What do you want?" he growled.

He didn't mean to, but his gaze dropped from her beautiful face to the swell of her breasts beneath the British uniform. His eyes traveled down to her narrow waist and continued down her khaki pants to her black combat boots. He slowly dragged his ogling eyes back up to her flirty grin, and his gut tightened. He mentally berated himself for trying to picture her naked. Then he side-stepped and hurried past her up the stairs. Bretta stared after him with a sly grin.

Chief Lydell Fry is even more handsome in person. His service record photo doesn't do him justice. I'm looking forward to finding out if he's as intriguing in person as his file was to read. He's had quite a career in the SEALs. This assignment promises to be—fun.

CHAPTER 7

June 11
0900
Kinshasa, Congo, United Nations Embassy

Rowen sat in a meeting listening intently and taking notes. As always, when multiple countries were coordinating in one massive effort, there was red tape to wade through and negotiations to be made. The U.N. wanted to ensure the mission was a success. They were hopeful that the region could be stabilized politically. If they could build good relations with the current government structure, it would be one step closer to bringing another third world country into healthy relations with the rest of the civilized world. Congo was once a thriving contributor to world trade. The entire region was rich in vast deposits of precious stones, minerals, and metals. If the region could be stabilized, in time, Congo could once again be a thriving nation.

The U.N. agenda seemed clear to Rowen. It was motivated by the promise of trade; which equated to profit. The fact that everything in government always seemed to center around turning a profit disgusted Rowen. He truly wished people would do the right thing for the sake of doing the right thing. He knew it would never happen that way, but it didn't stop him from wishing. Still, in this case it seemed clear that Negassi was pond scum. To use children to mine and fill his militia was unforgivable. If Negassi was all that stood between Congo achieving peace and eventual prosperity, then he hoped Echo and Delta could end Negassi's tyranny soon.

In the end, a chain of command between the cooperating countries was established. That afternoon, Echo and Delta sat in the conference room on the third floor waiting for Rowen to give them an update.

"Things are amping up. We should be shipping out soon. The chain of command has been established, and we will be reporting directly to General Loredo, of Spain, who will be in turn reporting to his own chain of command within the United Nations military ranks," Rowen said. "I know this isn't what you are accustomed to, but we are cooperating in a massive joint effort with the U.N. here. It will require us to do things a little out of the norm. Our own chain of command has made it clear that we are to cooperate with the U.N. to resolve this conflict."

After a short briefing to go over strategies and procedures, Rowen dismissed the SEAL teams. They went to the mess hall to eat dinner. As usual, the line was long, the conversations around them were in foreign languages, and the food was mediocre.

After chow, Lydell stood leaning against the south wall of the lobby with his phone to his ear. A frown marred his handsome face as he listened to his Grandmother recount his sister's activities from earlier that day. After a brief discussion, Benedetta handed the phone to Ellery.

Ellery rolled her eyes as she took the phone. "Hello."

"Ellery, your behavior is not acceptable," Lydell said sternly.

"I didn't do anything wrong," she retorted, as she glared at her grandmother.

"Kissing a boy is crossing the line. You're not old enough to kiss a boy!"

"You are all being ridiculous!"

"It's not ridiculous!" Lydell grated as he dragged his hand over his burr. "Boys are not trustworthy, Ellery—especially a seventeen-year-old boy, who kisses a little fifteen-year-old girl! He is only after one thing! You're too young for boys. Stay away from them!"

"Yes, Master!" Ellery sneered sarcastically.

"I mean it!"

"I'm not going to get pregnant. All I did was kiss him. That's all I was going to do. You are all making this into something much bigger than it is."

He sighed and started pacing around. "You may only mean to kiss him, but he has a lot more than kissing on his dirty, little mind. Just steer clear of boys until you are much older, Ellery. I don't want you to get hurt. Me, Grammy, and Gramps are just trying to protect you."

Ellery sighed. "I know, but you are all smothering me. I can take care of myself."

"Don't grow up too fast. Enjoy being a kid. Promise you won't kiss anymore boys.

Ellery rolled her eyes and let out a frustrated sigh. "Fine! I promise! Are you happy now?"

Lydell hung up and shoved his phone back into his pocket.

"Why do you always seem like you are carrying the weight of the world on your shoulders?" Bretta asked.

Lydell jerked his head up at the familiar sound of her British accent. His frown deepened.

"There it is again."

"There what is?" he asked gruffly.

"That look. You look at me like I'm up to skulduggery."

"Are you?"

"No, I'm here serving just like you."

He gave her a curt nod and walked off toward the stairs. Bretta followed him and fell in step beside him.

"I'm busy!" he said, as he lengthened his stride.

She matched him and started up the stairs right next to him.

"Busy doing what? You Yanks don't ship out to Kananga until tomorrow at 1100. What's your hurry? You have a few minutes to talk."

Lydell stopped on the landing, grabbed her wrist, and pulled her off to the side of the crowd traversing up and down the stairs.

"Where did you get your information from? We haven't been informed of that!" he growled.

Bretta breathed in his male scent and smiled. "You smell good."

"Answer the question!"

"You Yanks are at the bottom of the food chain. This is a U.N. operation. Navy SEALs are just the grunt labor. Your orders won't be made official until tomorrow morning."

"Then how do you know about it?"

"It's my job to know, Chief Fry."

He pulled back and looked into her beautiful blue eyes. "Who are you?"

"Bretta Brairton."

"What's your rank?"

Bretta leaned in closer, slid her hand behind his neck, and pulled him down to whisper in his ear. "That's classified, and you don't have clearance, Lydell."

He felt a warm shiver race down his spine. Her floral scent assailed his senses. He closed his eyes and breathed in her scent. The sensual, searing heat of her hand on his neck was far too pleasant. Just as he pulled back from her, a throng of people descending the stairs jostled against his back and shoved him up against her. She was pinned against the wall, and she could feel the firm planes of his sculpted chest pressing against her.

"Sorry," he mumbled in her ear as he was pressed even more firmly against her by the crowd hurrying down the stairs.

"Don't apologize. I like being close to you."

"Don't waste your time."

"You're not a waste of my time. Actually, you're starting to grow on me, Yank."

"Don't get your hopes up, Brenda," he smirked against her ear. "I don't like fast women."

"It's Bretta."

"I know." A sly grin spread over his mouth as he stared down at her near white-blonde hair and her perfect, delicate ear. He could feel her soft breasts pressed firmly against his chest.

"What makes you think I'm fast?" Her hands came up to rest on his waist.

He could feel her fingertips caressing over the thin fabric of his t-shirt. He did his best to ignore the tingling sensation spreading out from her gentle touch. Just then the crowd behind him bumped into him pushing him even closer against her. He brought his forearms up and pressed them against the wall above her head to brace himself against the jostling crowd behind him.

"I've met your kind before," he said in her ear. "I'm immune to your particular bag of tricks."

"Are you?" Her voice purred in his ear like a challenge.

Bretta reached up and softly caressed the scar that snaked down the right side of his neck. "How did you get this scar?"

"It's classified, and you don't have clearance," he smirked.

"You got it in the Swiss Alps when you fought with a mercenary who had taken hostages at a ski resort. According to your file, you're quite the bad-ass, Chief Fry."

His jaw tightened, and he pulled back a little to look her in the eyes. "If you knew, why ask?"

Bretta grinned. "I just wanted to see if you would volunteer it."

"I don't volunteer anything."

Her hand slid up to frame his face. She could feel his tensed jaw muscles beneath her palm as he glared at her.

"I don't know you. Keep your hands to yourself!" he growled.

"Don't try to play that game. You like being touched. I can feel exactly how much you like it."

He stared down into her eyes. "Don't read into things."

"Reading into things is what I do for a living."

"Don't read into me. I'm not interested."

Just then the last of the throng passed them heading down the stairs. Lydell took a step back from her with the now familiar scowl on his face. Her eyes dropped to the bulge beneath his camo zipper, and a sly grin spread over her plump lips.

"What else do you know about our team's assignment?" His lip curled in irritation.

Bretta's eyes slowly traveled up to his face. "Have dinner with me, and I'll fill you in."

"I already ate."

"If you're not willing to spare a few minutes to talk in private, you can wait and get your orders through normal channels."

He gritted his teeth, glared at her, and stalked away. Her lip curled as she stared at his ass until he disappeared around the corner at the top of the stairs.

As soon as he was out of sight, Bretta left the Embassy and headed through the busy streets to a dingy, crowded watering hole. The bar tender nodded at her and glanced to the far corner table. She showed no outward sign of recognition, but she walked over to the dark corner table at the back of the dimly lit room. She slid into the empty chair across from a man with jet black hair, a full beard, and dark wary eyes. He was dressed in a traditional, Arabic, white thawb with a ghutrah covering his head. He blended in perfectly with the majority of the men in the bar. It was Bretta who looked out of place, but it was impossible to blend into a bar full of men when her beauty could not be subverted regardless.

"Were you successful?" Jakeem Sayad asked quietly.

Bretta's eyebrow rose. "Have you ever known me to fail?"

Jakeem's lips formed a hard line. "No."

"Fry will be useful."

"He is a bad choice."

"No, according to the data he's the perfect choice."

Jakeem's jaw tightened. "I don't like this. Navy SEALs are trained not to trust anyone. He will not be easy to handle. There are other options."

"Trust me. I know exactly what I'm doing."

"Yes, that is what worries me."

Her lips formed a sly grin as she stared into Jakeem's dark, almost black eyes.

"I'll be in contact." Bretta stood up and left.

She took an indirect route back to the Embassy down dark, back alleys. In her small, private room, she pulled up surveillance cameras on her laptop. Then she pulled off the long, blonde wig and her British uniform. She took a quick shower, towel dried her short, cropped brunette hair, and slept for a few hours. Her job depended on her ability to operate with a clear head, and the operation was about to begin.

CHAPTER 8

June 12
0800
Kinshasa, Congo, United Nations Embassy

Rowen walked into the briefing room and addressed Echo and Delta.

"We've received marching orders from General Loredo."

Lydell frowned. "Let me guess. We are shipping out to Kananga at 1100."

The room fell silent as Rowen stared at Fry. "I just received that order. We are shipping out to Kananga at 1100 to set up our base of operations. Where exactly did you get your information?"

"From Bretta Brairton. She's a British officer here at the Embassy," Lydell said dryly.

"What's her rank?"

"She refused to tell me. She said it's classified and above my pay grade. She insinuated we are at the bottom of the totem pole when it comes to the flow of information."

Rowen's mouth turned down in a frown. "I'll find out who she is. In the meantime, pack up all of our gear. Our transport helo leaves at 1100."

Rowen left the SEALs to follow his orders while he went to inquire with his British contact as to exactly who Bretta Brairton was.

At 1000, Echo and Delta were on transport vehicles headed to the airport. Fry made sure he was on the same transport as Rowen.

"Did you find out who she is?" Lydell asked.

Rowen shook his head. "I'm either being stone-walled, or she gave you a false name. According to the British general overseeing things here, there is no record of any Bretta Brairton stationed here. He contacted London; there is no such person listed in the British data banks."

Lydell frowned. "I don't like this. She was wearing a Brit uniform with the Union Jack on it. She had a British accent. What do you think is going on here?"

Rowen shrugged. "I'm not sure, but if you encounter her again, keep your guard up."

"Trust me it was up from the moment I first met her. I've run into her twice now, and I'm not so sure the first time was a coincidence. I don't trust her. She could be trying to earn my trust to develop me as an asset. We've done similar things in the field to gain tactical information."

A few hours later, Delta and Echo were setting up their equipment at the temporary U.N. base camp in Kananga. It consisted of several abandoned warehouse buildings near the air strip on the outskirts of the city. The U.N. troops were already busy setting up perimeter fencing and generators to compensate for the unreliable electrical service throughout most of Congo.

Delta's Master Chief, Wes Chilven, noticed that the number of U.N. troops far outnumbered the thirty-two SEALs and their commander. One warehouse had been converted to house all the troops. The SEAL's bunks took up one small corner of one floor. There were five floors to house the troops. He estimated that there were over 3,000 U.N. military personnel on base in Kananga. He wondered why the U.N. even bothered to include the Americans in the endeavor. Thirty-three Americans was a drop in the bucket, compared to the number of U.N. troops present. That only included the U.N. troops stationed in Kananga. There were even more U.N. personnel present at the capital in Kinshasa. This seemed to be a massive undertaking in Congo.

June 14
1300
Kananga base, briefing room

Rowen pulled up a satellite image on his laptop and projected it on the wall for the SEAL teams to observe.

"Gentlemen, we have been given the green light. Our first mission will be deep in the Mitumba Mountain range on the western border of Congo."

He pointed to an area of densely forested land on the image. Then he clicked to the next image, an aerial view of a small populated area with a dirt road and a handful of houses.

"The closest settlement is Ugoma, twenty klicks north of our strike zone. The U.N. is sending us in to ensure there are no civilian casualties. The politics surrounding this mission don't leave room for mistakes. The Congolese government requested U.N. intervention to prevent a civil war. They do not want innocent civilians to come to harm. We have been invited here to ensure that doesn't happen. Our orders are clear. We are to take down military targets only. There is to be zero collateral damage. That's why they requested SEALs be the tip of this particular spear. The U.N. troops are here to back us up, but we will be handling all target packages."

"What time do we leave, Sir?" Dorian Axel's serious expression matched the rest of Echo's.

"At 2100, you will be dropped in by chopper twenty klicks south of the target. Make your way north through the mountain forest to the encampment and eliminate or capture any militants you find there."

"I don't see a camp," Ezra Lombard said.

Rowen pointed to the dense forest marked by a red X. "It is located here according to our sources. The dense trees in this region block the satellite view. We believe this is one reason why Negassi has chosen the mountains as a base of operations. It is hard to access and is shielded from spy satellites. We can't track his movements from the air. U.N. recon teams on the ground in these mountains are tracking movements and identifying military targets for us to take down."

For the next two hours, Rowen went over all the intel he had, and Echo and Delta came up with a strike plan for the mission. Everyone was itching to get into the action.

At 2107, Echo and Delta repelled from their respective U.N. helo transports and took up position on the forest floor. The choppers left, and the SEALs made their way through the forest toward the strike zone. Without a clear line of sight, the SEALs lost communication with the drone in the night sky flying high above them. Their plan was to send Delta's communications officer up into the forest canopy to reacquire communications once the mission was complete.

The SEALs took up positions on the perimeter of the camp. It was just before dawn, but the militants in the camp were already preparing to leave. Sonny watched Lydell's hand signals with his night vision goggles. The order was given, and Sonny focused his scope on the target in front of him and pulled the trigger. He took out three of the enemy before the militants in camp realized they were under attack.

The battle that ensued was easier than the SEALs had expected. The Chacha soldiers were committed but inexperienced against the superior, highly trained SEALs. The Chacha army chose not to surrender; they fought until the last man went down in a blaze of bullets. It confirmed what the SEALs had been told; General Negassi's men were radicalized, committed, and a force to be reckoned with.

After a few weeks, the missions became more difficult. Word spread through the Chacha ranks that they were being hunted. Negassi's forces fortified their mountain strongholds with more men, more weapons, and a greater determination. Hunting them down became increasingly difficult as time went on. The SEAL teams were forced to use every means at their disposal to track the scattering groups of guerilla platoons.

The problem wasn't taking out the small militant groups. The problem was that for every soldier they killed, three more seemed to spring up in their place. The Chacha army was multiplying faster than the SEAL teams could take them out. The solution seemed simple; cut off the head. Taking out Negassi was the obvious solution, but he was illusive and impossible to track. He was much smarter than anyone had expected, and he seemed to have the luck of the gods on his side. Orders came down from above to find Negassi at any cost and eliminate him before the rebellious uprising grew out of control.

CHAPTER 9

September 30
1600
Navy Medical Center, San Diego

Sophia walked down the corridor of the rehabilitation wing in the Med Center. She was on her way to consult with her assigned physician about her prognosis. She entered his office, and Dr. Sharang gestured for her to take a chair opposite his desk.

"How are you feeling today, Sophia?"

"Like I can move a mountain."

Dr. Sharang frowned. "Your rehabilitation is going well, but I don't see moving mountains in your future."

"What do you see, Sir?"

"I see you leaving our facility at the end of this week and returning to your assigned duty."

"Respectfully, Sir, when can I return to BUD/S?"

Dr. Sharang frowned. "You're so determined. Why is it so important for you to pursue Navy SEAL training? There are far less dangerous and less demanding jobs in the Navy. You could have a long, successful career. I see in your file that you are a language and communications expert. That is a far less demanding career path than the life of a SEAL."

"I intend to become a SEAL, Sir."

Dr. Sharang closed his eyes and squeezed the bridge of his nose between his thumb and forefinger. "Must we have this conversation again?"

"Apparently so, Sir."

"Your spine is on the mend, but if you suffer any further damage to those vertebrae, you could end up paralyzed. I advise you against returning to SEAL training."

"Respectfully, Sir, that's a risk I'm willing to take. I know the hazards of the job. There are no guarantees in life, Sir. I request to be returned to SEAL training as soon as possible."

Dr. Sharang took a deep breath and let it out slowly. "I'm granting your request, but I think you are making a huge mistake, Sophia."

"Thank you, Sir!"

"You're dismissed."

Sophia stood and respectfully saluted the doctor. He saluted her back, and she turned and left his office. When she exited the Med Center, she pulled her phone out and called her father.

"Hola, Pequeña," (Hello, Little One) Juan Gonzalez greeted her.

"Hola, Papa." (Hello, Dad.) She grinned. "In English, Papa."

"My English is not so good," he grumbled.

"The more you practice the better you'll get," she playfully scolded.

"I am trying, but English is not so easy. I'm not so smart like you." He sank into his armchair and opened a bottle of Mexican lime soda. "Why you want me to speak English?"

"Papa, we've had this discussion before. Speaking English will open up so many opportunities for you. During my long months of recovery, I learned Russian. Now, I speak English, Spanish, Farsi, and Russian."

"Why you need to learn Russian and Farsi?"

"As a Navy SEAL, I could get sent anywhere in the world, but I'm hoping for an assignment in Afghanistan or Iraq. I just want to be prepared."

"So, they let you back in the program?"

"Yes, the doctor is going to clear me to re-enter BUD/S."

"A tu madre no le va gustar esto." (Your mother is not going to like this.)

Sophia frowned. "In English, Dad. You promised me you would practice."

Juan sighed and humored his daughter. "Your mother no like this."

"Your mother isn't going to like this," she corrected.

"You know what I'm saying!" Juan was frustrated with his only daughter. "Your brothers don't like it too!"

Sophia sighed in frustration. Her and her family had butted heads over her joining the Marines. She had ten brothers; five were older, and five were younger. They had all tried to talk her out of joining the military.

"They are sending me back to BUD/S at the end of November. I hope you and Mama will support me in my decision, but if you choose not to, I'm still joining the SEALs."

"*¡Ay dios mío!*" (*Oh my god!*)

"Papa!" Sophia scolded. "Please don't start with me!"

"Fine! Have it your way *mi pequeña!* I just hope you no get killed! You are our only daughter! *¿Por qué debes romper el corazón de tu madre?*" (*Why must you break your mother's heart?*)

"I'm not breaking anyone's heart, and I'm not going to get killed. You raised me to be tough, Papa. I can handle whatever comes my way."

"I know. You are tough. I just worry. I love you, Sophia."

"I know, Papa. I love you too. Tell Mama I love her too, and all my brothers."

"You come visit soon."

"I will visit as soon as I get leave."

"Your mama wants to speak." Juan handed the phone to his wife.

"Sophia." Amparo greeted her daughter in a curt manner.

"Hi, Mama."

"I'm assuming from your father's reaction that they said yes!"

"Yes, I'm going back to BUD/S at the end of November."

Amparo shook her head and started pacing. "Sophia! Why? You should have taken the way out! How do expect to find a husband when you are traipsing around the world with a gun in your hand and a shaved head! No man in his right mind is going to see you as a proper wife!"

Sophia smirked and rolled her eyes. "You're English is getting better every day. Those classes you've been taking are paying off."

"Don't try to change the subject, Young Lady!" Amparo huffed. She was wearing a path between the kitchen and the television. "You are not getting any younger! You are twenty-two-years-old! By the time your contract is up you'll be twenty-six! Do you have any idea how hard it will be to find you a husband at that age especially if you are all scarred up from war?"

Sophia took a deep breath and steeled herself. "Mama, I'm not looking for a husband. You have ten sons to give you grandchildren. You don't need me for that."

"Don't you start with me, Sophia! This isn't about how many grandchildren I have. It's about you finding a proper husband to settle down with!"

"I don't want a husband! I don't need a husband! I have dedicated my life to serving and protecting our country. You and Papa came to the United States to start a new life. You wanted your children to benefit from all our country has to offer. I am just trying to preserve that way of life for you and my brothers. Why can't you understand how I feel about this?"

"Because it's not natural for a woman to go off to war! That's man's work!" Amparo huffed.

"No, Mama. It's whoever chooses to take up the call and serve. Our military is open for all races, genders, and religious beliefs to serve. They don't discriminate. Why do you insist on discriminating? I choose to serve. This is the life I'm choosing! Please learn to accept it."

Tears streaked down Amparo's cheeks, and she swiped them away. "I don't know how to accept it, Sophia. When you were born, I dreamed of all the wonderful things you would experience as a woman. Why do you insist on taking on the role of a man? This isn't who I raised you to be!"

"You raised me to do the right thing. This is right. I know you don't understand, but maybe someday you will. I have to go now. My bus is here."

Sophia stepped on the bus and turned her phone off. She sank down on the bench seat and sighed. It was no use arguing with her mother. It was like hitting her head against a granite mountain. There was no moving it no matter how hard she tried. She sat staring out the window as the bus pulled away. She knew she was a huge disappointment to her mother, and there was nothing she could do about it. They were at such opposite ends on the issue. Her parents couldn't understand why she wanted to serve, and no amount of explaining had made it any easier on anyone. They wanted her to be something she wasn't.

CHAPTER 10

October 1
0700
U.N. base, Kananga

Echo waited in the briefing room for Rowen. He entered with a grim expression.

"Somethin' wrong, Boss?" Sonny asked.

"Just the usual political runaround."

Rowen plugged in his laptop and pulled up their next mission package.

"Intel has confirmed via satellite that five trucks are making regular visits to Kalemie."

He pulled up the satellite images and displayed them on the wall.

"According to the U.N. scouts, these trucks do not belong to any of our troops. The mountains are too dense for trucks to be useful. All recon in this area is being done on foot, by satellite, or by chopper."

"Do they believe these trucks are Negassi's?" Fry asked.

Rowen nodded. "U.N. scouts have surveilled the trucks on the road to Kalemie four times in the last month. They have been unable to ascertain what the trucks are carrying, but the frequent stops in Kalemie are highly suspicious. They could be using them to transport weapons, troops, or something worse. Echo is being sent to Kalemie to investigate and gather intel."

"When do we leave?" Fry asked.

"Your helo transport leaves at 1300. You'll be dropped south of Kalemie after dark. Don't interact with the locals. There is obviously someone in Kalemie who is collaborating with Negassi. We don't want to tip them off.

Your mission is to track the trucks back to Negassi's base of operations. We want to know where his headquarters are located."

October 4
0947
Kalemie, Congo, Mitumba Mountain Range

Half of Echo waited on the southern edge of Kalemie just outside the town's perimeter. They were lying in wait hoping to tail the militant force back to their hidden base. The guerilla forces under Negassi had taken to hiding in small villages and in the mountain wilderness as an evasive maneuver. Delta was on their own mission tracking a group in the north.

Chief Fry spoke quietly into his short range comlink. "Echo 1 to Echo 2 do you copy?"

John Rusk responded back. "Echo 2, copy. Go for Echo 1."

"All is quiet near the southern perimeter. What does it look like from your position?" Fry's eyes were watchful, observing everything for as far as he could see.

John surveyed the tree line for the thousandth time in the last three hours. Nothing moved. All was quiet in the forest, save the occasional sound of nature. "All is quiet on the western front."

Fry stretched his fingers that had grown numb over the long wait. Then he repositioned his trigger finger and scanned the edge of the town with his rifle scope. There was a small group of children playing with a ball on the outskirts of the town and a mangy-looking canine skulking around near an overturned garbage can. Nothing looked out of the ordinary from his vantage point. He chewed at his lip. Something felt off. He was getting a gut check.

"Echo 1 to Echo 7 do you copy?"

Zachary Hurst whispered into his comlink. "Echo 7 to Echo 1, I just saw movement in the forest on the northwest border."

"Copy that," Fry responded. "Can you confirm an ID?"

"Negative," Zach whispered. "It could be gorillas, the ape kind."

Fry smirked. "You can't tell the difference between a hairy gorilla and a militant guerilla with a gun?"

"I just see movement in the underbrush. It could be anything," Zach whispered.

"How close are you?" Fry yawned and refocused his attention. Echo had been in position for nearly three days watching Kalemie for sign of guerilla movement.

"Almost close enough to smell them." Zach edged a little closer on his belly as he kept his scope trained on the movement in the undergrowth. "It's the ape kind. False alarm."

All was quiet for the next half hour until Sonny broke the com-silence. "Echo 8 to Echo 1."

"Echo 1 copy. Go for Echo 8," Fry answered.

"We got company on the northern perimeter, and it ain't the ape kind. There's a five-truck caravan headed for the port in Kalemie."

"Copy that. Take up positions and wait for my command," Fry ordered.

The small caravan of trucks stopped at a warehouse near the docks. Guerilla soldiers hopped down from the back of the covered trucks. Sonny watched through his scope as they made their way up the rutted dirt street in a loose formation.

"Echo 1 to Echo 14," Fry said quietly into his coms.

"Echo 14, Go for Echo 1," Ezra Lombard whispered.

"Are you in position?" Fry asked.

"I'm under the first truck," Ezra whispered. "I just finished securing the tracker. Moving to the second truck now."

Ezra did a slow belly-crawl to the front of the truck and waited. As soon as it was clear he crawled under the second truck and secured the magnetic tracker to the undercarriage.

"Second tracker secured. Moving to the third truck," Ezra whispered.

"Copy that," Fry said quietly.

"Echo 14, I advise you hold up," Sonny said from his overwatch position on the roof of a nearby building. "There's movement at the fourth truck. It looks like they are loading supplies."

"Copy that," Ezra whispered. "I'm under the third truck planting the tracker. I'll hold position until you advise it's clear."

Sonny trained his scope on the small group of guerilla soldiers, who were loading wooden crates into the back of the truck. He bit his lower lip as his eye caught on a large, red cross painted on the side of all the crates.

He watched the soldiers and counted. Once he was sure they had all left the area he let out a long breath.

"Echo 8 to Echo 14, all clear to proceed," Sonny said quietly. He scanned the street and the surrounding buildings for any sign of movement. The only thing he saw were two stray cats fighting over garbage scraps.

Ezra crawled to the fourth truck, planted the tracker, and proceeded to the last truck in the line. He was on his back securing the last tracker when he heard Sonny in his ear again.

"Echo 14, I advise you to move your ass. They are coming back with more crates. Get the hell out of there before you get caught!" Sonny said tersely.

"Copy that," Ezra whispered as he belly-crawled out from under the truck and took cover behind a cluster of garbage cans in a nearby alley.

Sonny smirked. "Echo 14, you do realize this is the twenty-fourth time you've taken cover behind garbage cans since I've known you."

Ezra grinned as he kept his gaze trained on the soldiers a mere ten feet from his position. They were loading wooden crates labeled grain and beans.

"Don't be a wise-ass, Echo 8," Ezra whispered.

Sonny lay on his stomach on the sun-heated, tar roof. He could feel the hot surface burning through the thick fabric of his camo fatigues. The only part of his body that wasn't on fire was his torso; the flak jacket provided him some protection from the searing heat. It was mid-day and he'd been lying on the roof for three days waiting for the guerillas to arrive. He kept his finger on the trigger and his scope trained on the group of soldiers loading crates.

"How 'bout I call you Double-D from now on," Sonny said with a mischievous grin.

"I know I lift a lot of weights, but my pecs aren't that big," Ezra whispered with a grin.

"Double-D stands fer Dumpster-Diver, Dumbass!" Sonny smirked.

Ezra bit his lip to keep from laughing out loud. After a minute he whispered into his comlink. "Go ahead and call me Double-D. I'll just start calling you S-man."

"S for Super?" Sonny grinned. "I can't fly, and I'm not susceptible to kryptonite, but you can call me Super—"

"S for Sterile," Ezra whispered. "I figure, as much time as you spend lying on your belly on hot roofs, hot sand, and hot rocks, you have to be shooting blanks by now. You do know that extreme heat kills your little swimmers, don't you?"

Sonny shifted his arm a quarter of an inch to reposition his scope on a second group of guerillas heading to the trucks with wooden crates.

"Echo 14, be advised we have more incoming. Hold your position," Sonny said.

"Copy that," Ezra whispered.

Sonny smirked. "Not that it's any of yer business, but my swimmers work just fine."

"How would you know? Do you have a kid out there you haven't told us about?"

"Nope, but unlike yer uneducated ass, I've studied biology." Sonny aimed his rifle on a guerilla soldier headed in Ezra's direction. "Little swimmers are renewed in cycles. Even if these guys are burned to a crisp before this day is done, I'll get more on the next go around. I don't shoot blanks, Double-D."

"Cut out the trash talk, and keep your focus!" Lydell Fry's voice interrupted Ezra and Sonny. "Zip it, and keep your eyes peeled! If you two blow this mission, you'll have me to answer to!"

"Copy that," Sonny said. His rifle followed the soldier as he drew near Ezra's position. "Echo 14, be advised; the bogey is right on top of your ass."

Ezra sat still behind the group of garbage cans. He could see the glint of the rifle slung over the young soldier's shoulder. He stopped at the entrance to the alley and looked in Ezra's direction. Ezra took aim through the scope of his rifle and positioned his finger on the trigger. He didn't want to pull the trigger and blow the entire surveillance op, but if the guy came down the alley, he wouldn't have a choice. He watched the soldier readjust his rifle on his shoulder and dig in his pocket. The soldier—Ezra guessed to be in his late teens—produced a cigarette and walked a few feet into the alley. Ezra watched him light up and take a long drag. Then the boy leaned against the wall of the alley a mere five feet from Ezra and thoroughly enjoyed the entire cigarette before returning to the street to rejoin his comrades. Ezra and Sonny both breathed a sigh of relief. The guerillas finished loading supplies and pulled out after an hour. Fry verified that the trackers were working before giving the order for Echo to regroup.

Once the convoy of trucks left Kalemie, they split into two groups. Fry figured they were heading to two separate camps to replenish supplies. On foot there was nothing he could do to follow the trucks. He reported back to Rowen, and a chopper was sent to pick them up.

Fry watched the signals on the screen. The trucks seemed to be staying in two groups. One group was headed north; the other was headed south.

Once Echo was on the chopper, he contacted Rowen again to update him.

"Delta finished their mission yesterday. I'm sending a chopper to pick them up. They are already north, so I'll have them track the northern group. You stay with the southern group and see if they lead us to Negassi. The U.N. scouts have been unable to locate Negassi's headquarters. Let's hope these trucks lead us straight to him."

"We'll track them and find out where they are going. I'll report back to you at 0500," Fry said.

The chopper dropped Echo at the southern end of the Mitumba mountain range. Lake Tanganyika lay to the east, and nothing but trees and an occasional break of small farming plots surrounded them. There were no visible settlements in the area, but the trackers showed two of the trucks north of their position traversing the mountain terrain. The trucks were headed their way. There were no visible roads from the air. Echo headed into the forest on foot. According to the tracker, the trucks were moving slowly away from each other in the dense forest.

"Do you think they are headed to their base?" Cameron James asked doubtfully. "If they are, why would they split up?"

Fry shrugged. "This area is awfully remote to set up a base of operations. It would be difficult to load in supplies to any location in these mountains. It's amazing they've been able to traverse the forest in those trucks."

"So, what's your call, Chief?" Ian Irwin asked.

"Reconnaissance," Fry said. "Half of Echo will shadow the first truck, half the second."

Fry split the platoon. The first group under him was comprised of the medic, Cord Murphy, Ben Obasi, Cameron James, Zachary Hurst, Rob Dover, Cliff Elwood, and Ian Irwin. The second group under John Rusk was comprised of Nick Novak, Sonny Eldridge, Grant Donnell, Dorian Axel, Ezra Lombard, and the two newest members of the team, Porter Prescott, and Eric Coll.

Fry's group took the truck to the northeast of their position and started off through the dense forest to cut across the truck's current path. John's group took the truck to the northwest.

After half a day of double-time marching through the dense forest, Fry signaled his team to hold up. His tracker showed the truck had stopped three klicks to the east of their position. The team took up flanking positions around the perimeter of a primitive, hut village deep in the forest.

John's team took up similar flanking positions around a small, primitive village about thirty klicks to the west of Fry's position. They were out of com range with Fry's team, and John ordered them to stay out of sight and record anything of interest.

Sonny quietly climbed a tree on the western edge of the small village and started recording everything he could. Echo spread out around the village in the forest to do reconnaissance.

Sonny zoomed in on the guerilla soldiers. Their camo uniforms were dirty and tattered. They were unloading a crate of beans, grain, and medical supplies. Then he recorded several parents carrying small children out of the huts. The children all appeared to be sick and lethargic.

He filmed the soldiers administering antibiotic shots, first to the sick children and then to the remaining members of the village. They distributed bags of grain and beans to the villagers and then made a brief speech to the people there. In essence they asked if anyone was interested in coming with them to fight the conditions of poverty and lack of medical care to the people of Congo. One boy who looked to be about fifteen spoke briefly to the chief of the village and then got in the truck with the guerillas.

After the truck pulled away, Echo regrouped in the forest outside the small village and resumed a path through the forest to cut off the truck at its next stop.

Sonny jogged up to the front of the line and fell in step next to John. "My Lingala is rusty, but I did pick up a few phrases back there. It didn't look like they were forcing anyone into servitude. It looked like they were mainly offering aid."

John nodded. "That's what it looked like from my vantage point too. This is not what I expected based on the other militants we've encountered so far. Something is off. Once the data is translated, hopefully, we'll have a better understanding of what's really going on out here."

Fry's team witnessed the same scenario in another small village. He ordered his men to shadow the truck to their next stop. It was nightfall when the truck stopped at another small, primitive village deep in the southernmost mountains bordering Lake Tanganyika.

The villagers had been ravaged by Trypanosomiasis, more commonly known as Sleeping Sickness. There were fresh graves just outside the circle of primitive huts, and many of the villagers showed signs of varying stages of the disease.

Fry ordered his team to record everything that transpired. What they witnessed was the soldiers offering more food and medical aid to those suffering from the disease. The guerillas camped just outside the village for the night. Fry and his team took up a watch rotation so they could get some sleep too. When it was Lydell's turn to keep watch, he stood guard over the other seven men, and his mind wandered.

He intended to contact Rowen in the morning to let him know about this village. He was certain if the villagers didn't get real medical assistance soon every one of them would die. Trypanosomiasis was fatal only a few months after infection. From the look of the villagers, most of them had been infected quite some time ago. He'd noticed several with the tell-tale skin rash. Others were having trouble walking. Two he witnessed seemed disoriented, and the remainder of the villagers were lying around in a lethargic state. He was certain everyone in that village had been bitten by an infected tsetse fly. The meager antibiotics the guerillas were administering were no match for the level of infections displayed by the victims. They needed real medical assistance from real doctors. Fry intended to relay the coordinates of the village and have Rowen report the epidemic to the CDC (Centers for Disease Control and Prevention). From Rowen's briefings, he knew the WHO (World Health Organization), and UNICEF (United Nations Children's Emergency Fund), were both in Congo working to bring the current health crisis under control. He only hoped these organizations could assist the villagers in fighting the disease.

When Fry's watch ended, Rob Dover took over until dawn. Lydell lay down next to Cameron and tried to go to sleep, but the faces of the suffering villagers haunted him, and sleep eluded him. He thought about his younger brother and sister back in the states. His brother had just started college after wandering on his walkabout all summer, and his sister was a sophomore in high school now. He hadn't seen them since May. He hadn't been able to call them for over a month. Cell service was as unreliable as the electricity in this country. Despite the massive hydro-electric dam on the west coast near the capital, the dilapidated state of the electric lines did not guarantee reliable power to many parts of Congo.

He tried to push thoughts of home down deep. It was best not to think of home while on a mission. It was too easy to lose concentration. He closed his eyes and tried to empty his mind. He finally drifted into a restless sleep. An hour later, he was jolted awake after a horrible nightmare. He'd seen his baby sister and his grandparents in a twisted, mangled, car wreck. His heart was racing, and his breath came in short gasps. He sat up in the darkness and buried his head between his knees.

It was just a dream. They're fine. I only dreamed that because Mom and Dad were killed in a car accident. It was just my imagination. I have to stay focused. We have a mission to complete.

CHAPTER 11

November 26
0700
U.N. base, Kananga

After nearly two months of intensive surveillance by Delta and Echo, both SEAL teams were choppered back to base camp in Kananga for debriefing.

Commander Rowen stood before his SEAL teams in the briefing room. His eyes roamed over the tired, weary SEALs seated at the tables in front of him.

"The surveillance footage you've brought back is being translated and analyzed. Until I hear word back on what you've found, consider yourself on a short break. Rest up and enjoy the down time while it lasts."

Lydell raised his hand. "Is there any word on the villagers we reported ill?"

Rowen grimaced. "The CDC intervened on all the coordinates you men gave us, but most of the villagers were too ravaged by disease to be saved. Those who were still alive were transported to hospitals in the cities, but according to the last report we received, most of them were not responding well to treatment. There are ten thousand people for every one doctor in this country. It's an uphill battle to administer care to so many. There just aren't enough qualified doctors in Congo to care for all the sick and suffering. They are doing the best they can. The WHO and UNICEF are trying to help, but the numbers in need are overwhelming."

Lydell dragged both his hands over his thick, copper-colored curls. His jaw tightened in frustration as he stared at the chipped corner of the table in front of him.

"I'm sorry I don't have better news," Rowen said solemnly. "I know it must be hard for all of you to see so many people suffering in need and feel helpless to do anything about it. Believe it or not, we are seeing things here in Kananga that make us feel the same way. For too long, civil war, poverty, and disease have made survival a daily struggle for the people of Congo. Less than thirty percent of their population is over the age of thirty. This country is in a state of crisis on multiple levels."

Lydell's hand fisted against his thigh, and his jaw tightened tighter. "How many of those villagers does the CDC expect to pull through?"

"They can't say for sure, but their rough estimate is five to ten percent," Rowen said.

Lydell let out a long breath and looked up to meet Rowen's eyes. What he found there was sympathy, but no projection of Rowen's usual confidence. He could see this deployment was taking a toll on Rowen as much as it was on the members of Delta and Echo. Lydell nodded and forced down the emotional pain that was roiling in his gut. There was nothing he could do; he felt utterly helpless.

"Are the phone lines up?" Ben asked.

Rowen nodded. "They are up as of an hour ago. There is no guarantee how long that will last. I suggest you men make any necessary calls as soon as I dismiss this briefing before the lines go down again."

"How is the electric situation?" Wes Chilven, Master Chief over Delta asked.

"It's the same as before. We are using generators to ensure our most vital equipment has power," Rowen said.

After an hour of exchanging information between the two teams, Rowen dismissed them. Echo and Delta headed to the mess hall to get the first real meal they'd had in a month. Surviving on MRE's was just that, surviving. They were all looking forward to sitting down at a real table with a hot plate of food in front of them.

Lydell took his place in line and pulled out his cell phone. He tapped his grandmother's number and listened to it ring; as usual, it went to voice-mail.

"Hi, Grammy. It's Lydell. I'm just calling to check on everyone and make sure you're all okay. I'm still on deployment. I've been out of cell phone range for a while, but I'm back in a real city for a few days. Call me when you get this message."

Echo and Delta found a table in the crowded dining area. They were surrounded by United Nations people from Spain, France, and Great Britain. There was a hum of conversation all around them in various tongues. Nick sat across from John and Sonny. They were discussing yet another Thanksgiving feast they were missing back home.

"This ain't as good as my mom's but it sure beats the hell out of an MRE," Sonny drawled.

"Yeah, but it's been so long since I've tasted my mom's Thanksgiving dinner that I can't really remember what it tastes like anymore," Nick said.

John smirked. "This is much better than the Thanksgiving dinners I grew up with. My mom's idea of cooking was to throw some TV dinners in the microwave and yell at me and my dad to come get them. Then everyone would take their plate off to other parts of the house and avoid each other as much as was humanly possible."

"Ya know, John," Sonny said, putting his fork down for a moment to look John in the eyes. "I do believe this is the first time since I've met you that you've ever mentioned your family. Hell! For all I knowed you was an orphan or somethin'."

John bit his bottom lip and dropped his eyes to the table for a moment. Then he looked back at Sonny. "I don't talk about them. I don't know why I brought it up. I guess it just slipped out."

Sonny nodded. "They still alive?"

John shrugged. "I don't actually know. We don't speak to each other. My teenage years were—difficult. When I graduated high school, I joined the Navy, and we parted ways for good."

"What happened between you to drive such a wedge?" Nick asked.

John shrugged. "My mom was not the nurturing type. My dad was a work-a-holic. Those two never really got along. They mostly tolerated each other. You'd think they would have just gotten a divorce, but they didn't. Instead, they ignored each other, lived separate lives in the same house, and hated the fact that they had a kid together. Growing up I think my presence in the house annoyed them more than anything else. They tolerated me about like they tolerated each other. I don't have any happy childhood memories. In high school, I was rebellious. I got into trouble at school—spent a lot of time in detention. That only made things worse between us."

Nick frowned and Sonny grimaced.

"You have no happy childhood memories—not even Christmas?" Sonny asked.

John shook his head. "We never celebrated holidays. My mom wasn't into that, and my dad was always working. There was no Christmas tree, no presents, nothing at all. Christmas at the Rusk house was like any other day of the year. I do my best to forget the first eighteen years of my life. There's nothing there worth remembering. It was just loneliness and depression—best forgotten and buried in the past where it belongs."

Nick frowned. "I'm sorry, John."

John shrugged. "It's just the way things were. I wouldn't have known it was supposed to be different except for what I saw on television. The older I got, the more I realized just how messed up my family really was. They weren't physically abusive. They provided me with food, shelter, and clothing. They were just absent in everything else that mattered."

Sonny studied John. He was surprised by the lack of emotion John had when he talked about his family—his past. It was as if he were rotely telling a story that had nothing whatsoever to do with him. There was no personal connection to it.

Those rat bastards really screwed John up good. He has zero attachment to them. It's a wonder he turned out to be such a nice guy. You'd think he'd be totally screwed up in the head growing up in an environment like that.

Sonny picked up his fork and finished the last few bites of his meal. "I don' know 'bout ya'll, but I'm gettin' me another plate." He stood up and left to get in line.

John chuckled and looked at Nick. "Sonny has the right idea. I think I'll follow his example."

Nick grinned at John. "Me too."

As John and Nick stood up the rest of Echo and Delta all seemed to have the same idea. Nick and John were stuck waiting behind the rest of the SEALs as they filed down the narrow aisles toward the food. Lydell was the only SEAL still sitting at the table. He wasn't eating; he was staring absently at the contents of his plate. His mind was preoccupied with the troubles only a C.O. has to worry about. The food smelled delicious, but he didn't feel hungry anymore.

"Why do you have to look so damn sexy when you scowl? It really isn't fair."

Bretta's lips brushed against his ear as her hands came to rest on his shoulders. He could feel her fingers kneading his sore muscles; it felt good. For a moment, he allowed himself to give into the pleasure of it. He closed his eyes and moaned softly.

"You're so tense," she murmured in his ear. "You should let me give you a full body massage."

He smirked. "You'd like that, wouldn't you?"

Her hands slid over his shoulders, down over his sculpted pecs, and her fingers lightly, repeatedly grazed his nipples over the thin fabric of his t-shirt.

A soft groan escaped his lips. "Do you have to do that?"

"Why? Is it turning you on?" She grinned mischievously as she pressed a soft kiss to his neck just below his ear.

"No."

She took the seat next to him and pulled his hand down onto her thigh with his palm facing up. He gave her a questioning look as her fingertip traced softly over the lines of his palm and up his forearm with a featherlight touch. It sent a warm shiver up his spine. He watched her fingers for a moment; then his eyes slowly traveled up until they met hers.

She grinned. "You are quite handsome for a Yank."

He continued to stare at her with a wary expression.

"You have a girlfriend?"

He cleared his throat. "I don't have time for a girlfriend. I stay busy."

"I stay busy too, but I won't be busy tonight at 2200. Meet me at the front gate."

"Why would I do that?"

She leaned in and stared into his eyes. "Because you're curious."

"I'm not curious."

He stared back into her blue eyes with a defiant, wary gaze until he felt her hand slid up the inside of his camo covered thigh and reach its destination before he could stop her. A sly grin spread over her lips as she leaned in closer.

"It feels like you're very curious."

He pulled her hand away as his gaze traveled down to her cute, upturned nose, and then to her full, ruby red lips. Then traitorously his gaze dropped to the enticing swell of her breasts beneath her uniform. His pants suddenly grew too tight, and he jerked his eyes back up to meet hers.

A low growl erupted from his throat. "I'm not curious. Don't touch me."

Bretta leaned in and pressed her lips to his. Lydell froze. His heart beat faster, and his pants grew tighter as his lips parted to her coaxing kiss. His tongue met hers; she tasted sweet, and he wanted more. He leaned into the kiss sucking her lip between his. Suddenly, she pulled back grinning at him.

"See you at 2200 at the front gate, Love." She winked at him and left.

He watched her walk away. His eyes lingered on her swaying hips. Then he forced himself to look away.

I'm definitely not meeting her tonight. She is trouble! I shouldn't have kissed her back. That was stupid! Why did I do that? So, she's beautiful—so what! Nothing good can possibly come of letting her inside my circle. She's an unknown. Rowen can't find out who she really is. She's dangerous. She could be working for the enemy for all I know. I need to avoid her from now on.

Cliff Elwood slid onto the seat across from Lydell and smirked. "Who's your girlfriend?"

Lydell glared at Cliff. "She's not my girlfriend!"

"I saw her kiss you." Cliff chuckled. "In fact, you're wearing her lipstick."

Lydell grimaced and grabbed a napkin. He attempted to wipe the ruby red lipstick off his lips, but Cliff shook his head to let him know he wasn't successful. He stood up, grabbed his plate, and deposited it in the trash on his way out the door. In the bathroom down the hall, he scrubbed his lips and neck with a wet paper towel until all the evidence was gone. Then he exited the building and took a long walk around the base. He needed to clear his head.

November 26
2200
Front gate of the U.N. base, Kananga

Bretta stood in the shadows waiting for Lydell to show up. After twenty minutes, she looked at her watch and frowned. She walked away with a grim expression on her beautiful face.

He's not going to show. Apparently, I wasn't persuasive enough. He's much more stubborn than I gave him credit for. I'll just have to take things to the next level.

Lydell lay on the cot he'd been assigned to, stared up at the tall ceiling, and tried to empty his mind. It was dark on the floor, and everything was eerily quiet. He wasn't used to quiet. He'd been living outdoors for months. His ears missed the sound of nature. After half an hour, he got up and walked down the hall to the bathroom. He stood at the sink staring at his reflection in the mirror. His copper hair had grown out during his time in the field. It was time to shave it again. Short hair equaled low maintenance. He decided he'd shave it off first thing in the morning. He started down the hall toward the bunk room, but turned down the stairs instead of going back to bed. It was pointless to lie down. He knew he wouldn't be able to sleep. Instead, he went outside.

From the shadows, Bretta watched Lydell walk the perimeter of the makeshift, military compound. They were surrounded by U.N. guards intermittently, but otherwise they were alone in the dark. The electric in the city had gone out an hour ago. Only the inner buildings of the compound were being powered by generators. The stars were out in force, but they didn't illuminate enough. It was a new moon. It was very, very dark. She preferred it that way; it was easier to stay concealed in the pitch-black darkness. She followed him at a discreet distance before ducking into an alley and cutting him off at the end of a row of buildings where there were no U.N. guards posted. Lydell stopped in his tracks when he saw her emerge from the shadow of the building.

"What do you want?" he asked warily.

"What do you think I want?" she asked, with a sly grin. She walked over to him, and he backed away. "Are you scared of me?"

"No."

"Then why are you retreating?"

He stopped and glared at her. He could barely make her out as she sauntered toward him.

"Did I cross the line with you earlier, Yank?" She stopped right in front of him.

"Yeah." His heart rate kicked up as he stared down at her.

Bretta slid her hand up his chest and hooked it behind his neck. Lydell's whole body grew tense, and his breath grew shallow. He could feel her fingers gently caressing his neck for a moment before she slid her fingers up into his hair. His whole body shivered in response.

"You're not used to being touched, are you?" she asked softly.

His jaw tightened, and he took a step back disconnecting contact. She grinned up at him and took a step toward him. He backed up again, and their dance continued until his back met the wall of the metal building.

"What do you want?"

"Isn't it obvious?"

He glared at her. "Why don't you spell it out."

"I like you."

"You don't even know me." His voice was a soft growl.

Her hands came up to rest on his abs, and he grabbed her wrists in a gentle, vice-like grip and pulled her hands away from his torso.

"I didn't say you could touch me." His fierce, green eyes studied her in the darkness.

"I didn't ask your permission." She winked at him and gave him her most winning smile.

"I don't like fast women."

"I don't like fast men."

"Why are you following me?"

"I think you're hot, and I'd like to get to know you better." She leaned in close until her breasts pressed against his chest.

He let go of her wrists and gently pushed her back by her shoulders. "I don't know what game you're playing, but you can stop now. I'm not falling for it."

"Falling for what?" Her tone was laced with affected innocence.

"I don't go out with sluts. Don't waste your time."

Bretta smirked. "Is that how I came across? I think you have the wrong impression of me. I don't sleep around, and I really do want to get to know you better. You're so mysterious and aloof. You've piqued my curiosity."

"I'm not buying any of that, and I'm not interested."

He felt her hand caress over the rock-hard bulge in his camo dungarees.

Bretta grinned up at him. "Not interested, huh? You're not a very good liar."

Lydell shoved her back a step and started walking away.

"Where are you going?" she called after him.

"There are thousands of men stationed at this site. Why are you bothering me?" he growled over his shoulder. "I don't sleep around. Go get what you need from some other smuck."

Bretta hurried to cut him off. He stopped and glared down at her as she curled her fingers into the front of his shirt and looked up into his fierce, green eyes.

"You're even cuter when you get angry."

"Don't call me cute! I'm not a damn puppy!"

He stepped around her and had barely taken two steps when he felt her kick the back of his left knee. He stumbled, and before he could regain his balance, she was on his back with her legs wrapped around his torso and her arm wrapped around his neck in a tight choke-hold. He struggled to free himself, but she had him at a disadvantage. He knew the only way to get her off his back was to get rough with her.

He spun and took a stumbling step back as pain shot through his left knee. He slammed her back against the side of the building. He didn't slam her as hard as he could. He wasn't trying to hurt her. He was just trying to get free. To his dismay, she didn't let go. He could feel the oxygen supply to his lungs being cut off as she tightened her arm over his throat. He took a step forward and slammed her against the wall again with more force this time.

"Is that all you've got? That's a piss-ant move for a badass Navy SEAL."

He reached up and grabbed her arm, but he couldn't get free of her grip. Then he went for her ankles locked over his stomach. He didn't have the leverage to get free of her. Unless he was willing to really hurt her, he didn't see an escape.

"Better hurry, Fry. You're running out of oxygen."

Who is she? Why is she really here?

He limped down the wall slamming her repeatedly until he got to the corner of the building. Then he shoved her spine up against the corner and pressed as hard as he could, but his combat boots were sinking into the muddy soil next to the building.

"Better, Love, but not good enough." She squeezed his throat harder.

I can knock her out or try to find out what she really wants. She didn't come here for a tryst.

Lydell took a step forward and put his hands up in the air. "I surrender," he gasped in a garbled whisper; it was all he could manage.

Bretta grinned as she loosened her grip around his neck a little. He sucked in a deep breath.

"I didn't think SEAL's were trained to ever surrender."

"You're hilarious!" Lydell growled. "What do you want?"

She caressed her free hand up into the copper curls on the back of his head. "If you promise not to run, I'll let you go."

Lydell smirked. "I could have killed you. You're not letting me go. I'm choosing not to use lethal force on you."

She smirked. "If that's what you need to believe to keep your ego intact, I can concede to it."

He slid his hand up between her arm and his throat and yanked, pulling free of her grip. Then he threw his weight forward bending at the waist and catching her off balance. She was thrown over his head onto the muddy ground in front of him. Bretta gasped—the wind knocked out of her—but she was not deterred. As he leaned forward to further subdue her, she kicked him in the jaw knocking him off balance. She popped up to her feet, and hand-to-hand combat ensued, but neither could gain the upper hand. They were equally skilled in martial arts. After several minutes, she backed out of his range.

He focused on taming the chaos swarming in his brain. There were so many variables to this encounter. He wasn't sure what was going on, but he was sure he'd been set up. She'd caught him alone, she was obviously trained in combat, and she was a lot tougher than she looked.

She shook her head. "Fighting is getting us nowhere. You're wasting valuable time."

He grinned at her. "I wouldn't say that. I needed a good workout. Thanks."

She grinned back. "You're even sexier when you smile."

"Don't waste your breath. You're not my type."

"What is your type? Let me guess. You want a sweet, small-town, country girl from back home. She should be a protestant like you, with no sexual experience whatsoever—you'd prefer to break her in yourself. She should have a high school education, but you'd prefer no college. You don't really want her to have too broad a mind or too much ambition. You want a girl you can keep in line easily. You want someone who won't ask you too many difficult questions. You basically want her to; how do you American's say it? You want her barefoot and pregnant in your kitchen, taking care of your little ones."

"You think you have me pegged?"

"Tell me I'm wrong."

He smirked. "You forgot. She should be brunette, not a blonde like you. I don't like blondes."

"Don't be a smart-ass. The girl you dated in high school was blonde—Freya, wasn't it?"

His jaw tightened, and his eyes narrowed. "Whatever you want from me you're not getting it!"

"You really are stubborn, Fry."

He felt a sting in his left thigh. He looked down and saw a small injection dart sticking out of his leg. Suddenly, everything looked a little blurry, and he didn't feel right. He took a few stumbling steps in the mud while she watched him from a safe distance. It only took a few seconds before he sank to his knees. She walked toward him with a smirky grin and slid the tranq-gun into the holster on her hip.

"What did you hit me with?" He couldn't feel his arms or legs.

"Tranquilizer." She gently trailed her fingertips down his smooth-shaven jaw.

"Bitch!"

His tongue felt numb. Everything felt numb. His peripheral vision was gone. All he could see was her face right in front of him. Anger boiled up inside him, but he couldn't do anything to act on it. He was fading quickly.

"Don't worry, Lydell. I'm not going to hurt you. I'll take good care of you. I promise; I'll be gentle with you."

His heart sped up as Bretta leaned down and captured his lips with hers. Her hands slid up into his copper curls, and he could feel her mouth on his—caressing, licking, sucking. He could do nothing to stop her. He was paralyzed. All he could do was stare into her mischievous eyes as she took what she wanted. She pulled back from his lips, and dragged him over to the fence.

Damn! She is a lot stronger than she looks. I'm in a lot of trouble! She set me up—and I fell for it. What the hell does she want with me?

He watched her cut the fence with expert precision. Then she dragged him through the opening to the dark, deserted street on the other side. He felt panic rise inside him. Then everything went black.

CHAPTER 12

November 27
0100
Kananga

Lydell woke to find himself handcuffed to a bed. His feet were tied with rope to the metal footboard. It took his groggy brain a few moments to assess his situation. He was naked except for his black boxer-briefs. The room was dirty, derelict, and sparsely furnished. There was a rusted twin bed, a small wooden table, and one metal chair. On the table set a heart rate monitor. That was all his eyes could see.

What did I get myself into? This is bad!

After a few minutes, Bretta entered the room. "Good, the tranq wore off. We don't have any time to waste." She pulled out a hypodermic needle and injected him.

"What was that?" he demanded angrily.

"Truth serum." She dropped the needle in the trashcan.

"Who are you?"

"Bretta Brairton."

"That's not your real name."

She winked at him and blew him a kiss.

"MI6 or just a lousy merc?"

She grinned slyly at him. "Are you going to cooperate? I want us to be civil to each other."

"Sorry to disappoint you, Bretta!" he sneered.

She walked back to the bed and sat down beside him. Her eyes traveled up his ripped abs to his sculpted pecs. She traced her fingertips over his freckled shoulders, and her gaze moved up lingering on his perfect lips before traveling up to his freckled nose and cheeks for a moment. Then she met his angry, green eyes.

"Before that serum takes effect, I have a question for you."

"I'm not going to answer any of your questions."

"I think you will." She gently trailed her fingertips down the firm ridges of his abs.

He flinched involuntarily under her touch.

"I was right. You're not used to being touched by a woman."

"Don't," he whispered, as her fingertips reached his naval.

"Don't what?" She grinned at him.

"Don't touch me like that."

Bretta licked her lips seductively. "You're really not in any position to tell me what to do."

Her fingers traced featherlight circles all over his abs. Lydell closed his eyes and tried to focus on something else. He tried adding complex numbers in his head, but he couldn't ignore how nice her touch felt. His body responded to her gentle caress against his will.

"Stop," he groaned softly.

"You don't really mean that. I can see just how much you like it."

He glared at her. "Why am I here? What do you want?"

She didn't answer him. Instead, she crawled on top of him straddling his hips. His eyes traveled over her. She'd changed clothes; the British uniform was gone. Now, she was braless and wore a tight, white tank shirt that showcased her generous, perky breasts. His eyes traveled down to where their bodies met. She wore a silky, black G-string. She was a feast for his eyes, and despite his best effort, he felt himself grow even harder against her.

"Damnit!"

She grinned down at him. "I knew you liked me."

"Get off me!"

She leaned down and licked the ridges of his rock-hard abs, and his whole body tensed in response. He pulled futilely against the cuffs on his wrists. Every muscle in his arms bulged with his efforts. His breath grew shorter, and his heart raced faster. She could see the desperate plea on his handsome face.

"You want more?"

"No," he groaned, gritting his teeth. "Get off me!"

She sat up grinning. Her fingertips caressed over his chest as he pulled against his restraints.

"Please, get off me."

Bretta scooted up to straddle his stomach and leaned down to claim his lips. He didn't kiss her back. She pulled back and stared into his defiant, green eyes.

"Kiss me, and I promise I'll be gentle with you," she whispered against his lips.

"Let me go now, and I promise not to kill you."

"You are so adorably cute when you're hostile." She slid her hand up into his curls.

When she leaned down for another kiss, he turned his face away from her and buried it against his bulging bicep.

"What's the truth serum for? What is it you think I know?"

He felt her tongue drag up the scar on his neck and suck his earlobe. He shivered and turned back to her with begging eyes.

"Please stop. Don't do this to me."

"You know you want me. Just give in to it."

"I don't sleep with strange women. I don't know you."

"But you want to know me, don't you? You like me."

"I—"

He was interrupted by her mouth on his. He could feel her tongue. He could taste her. She tasted good. He wanted more, but logic propelled him to resist. He turned his face away and broke the kiss. She crawled off of him and walked to the door.

"If you're not in the mood for fun, then I'll be back when the truth serum has taken affect."

Lydell watched her leave the room. It wasn't long before he began to feel light-headed.

Bretta sat at the small kitchen table watching the clock. She didn't have long to accomplish her mission. She had to have Lydell Fry back before dawn. No one could know he'd been missing all night. This was a zero-footprint mission. When her watch beeped, she returned to the bedroom.

"Hey, Sexy." Lydell grinned at her from the bed.

Bretta grinned back. She crossed the room and sat down on the bed next to him.

"How are you feeling?" she asked.

"So good."

The dopey grin on his handsome face let her know the serum was in full effect. His defenses were down. The serum made subjects compliant— susceptible to suggestion. It destroyed all pretense of inhibitions. His inner thoughts and desires were hers for the taking. She gently took his jaw in her hands and brought her lips down to his. This time he kissed her back with fervor. When she finally pulled back from his frantic kiss, he groaned in protest. She stared into his eyes and gently traced her thumb over his lips. Then she leaned down and pressed her forehead against his.

"You're my assignment, but I wasn't supposed to get personally involved or emotionally attached to you," she whispered.

"Are you going to seduce me?" Lydell gave her another dopey grin.

"No."

"Then why did you strip me down naked?"

"That's need to know, and you don't need to know."

"But you kissed me."

"Sorry, Love. I can't help myself. You're so damn sexy. I just want to eat you up."

He groaned softly. "You're straight out of my dirtiest fantasy. I want you so bad."

"I want you too, but I can't cross that line. I'm not supposed to have sex with you. I'm only supposed to interrogate you and verify information."

Lydell turned his head and captured her lips in another feral kiss. When she finally pulled back breathing hard, he stared up into her beautiful blue eyes.

"Cross the line," he groaned softly. "Take me right now. You're torturing me."

"I have to take you back before dawn. No one can know you went missing."

"I need you, Bretta. You're torturing me. Uncuff me. It won't take long. I'll be quick."

She shook her head. "That's not how I want our first time to be. I don't want you to rush."

"Then uncuff me, and I promise I'll pleasure you until the dawn."

"Bloody Hell, Yank! If you only knew how much I wish we could do just that. Why did it have to be you? Of all the SEALs assigned here, they had to ask me to interrogate you! It's just not fair. You're my Achilles heel, Lydell. I've wanted to make love to you since the first moment I bloody laid eyes on your sexy ass—sitting in the lobby with that scowl on your face."

"No one will know. I'm yours for the taking—so take, Bretta."

He leaned his head in closer and pressed his lips to hers again. She gave into the moment and kissed him back. He could feel her hands caressing over his bare chest.

It was hard for Bretta to break the kiss this time, but she had a duty to perform regardless of her personal feelings. She walked over to the small table.

"Lose the panties and come here. You can ask me questions while you screw my brains out."

She smirked at him. He grinned at her and winked.

"Just so you know, you won't remember any of this later," she said. "That's another reason not to screw your brains out. You'll never remember our first time. I want you to remember."

"What did you give me?" His speech was becoming a little slurred.

"That's classified."

"It will make me forget? How much will I forget?"

"You'll forget everything that's transpired in the last twenty-four hours."

"Well, damn! I don't want to forget this. I don't want to forget you— how you make me feel."

"Sorry, Love. I wish it could be different."

"I'm not going to tell you what you want to know. You'll get nothing out of me."

"I know you believe that, but that injection was only the first. The next one will force you to talk whether you want to or not. No one can resist it."

Bretta walked over to a small case, set it on the table, and opened it. She removed a syringe with a red liquid inside and injected Lydell with it.

He felt it burning through his veins, and he screamed in pain. A tear streaked down Bretta's cheek as she watched him writhing in pain against the restraints.

"I'm sorry, Love," she whispered.

After half an hour, he stopped writhing, stopped screaming, and lay docile on the bed. She walked over and caressed her hand down his jaw. She leaned down and gently kissed his lips. He didn't kiss her back. He merely stared blankly up at her.

It was time to begin the interrogation. She got out electrode pads, and stuck them to his chest. Then she connected the pads to the EKG monitor on the table.

After three hours, Bretta knew everything there was to know. It was time to return her baby bird back to his cage before his owners discovered he was missing. She retrieved his now clean uniform and redressed him. Then she led him by the hand down the dark streets of the abandoned industrial park and back to the U.N. compound. She breached the fence line at the same place she'd extracted him from and led him through the dark compound avoiding the U.N. guard details. When she reached the building where the soldiers bunked, she pulled him in close and hooked her hand behind his neck.

She pulled him down for a kiss, but he didn't kiss her back. He didn't resist, but there was nothing behind his blank stare. She knew he wouldn't remember any of it. Still, she knew she would never forget him. He was burned into her like a brand. The heat of his earlier impassioned kiss burned inside her chest like a fire that couldn't be quenched. She led him around the corner to the door and told him to go inside and go to bed. He rotely turned from her and walked inside the building.

November 28
0600
Bunk room, U.N. base, Kananga

The next morning, Lydell woke with the worst headache he'd ever had in his life. He felt sick. He felt dizzy. He felt disoriented, but he forced himself to get up and trudge through the day. At lunch Cameron sat down across from him.

"Are you okay?" Cameron asked.

Lydell stared down at his plate in silence.

"Lydell!" Cameron waved his hand in front of Lydell's face.

He jerked and looked up at Cameron.

"Is something wrong?" Cameron asked.

Lydell shook his head and with a blank stare began shoveling his food in. Cameron left him alone and dug into his own plate. Once he finished eating, Lydell stood up and left the cafeteria without a word to anyone. He went outside and walked the perimeter of the compound.

Bretta followed him at a distance. The serum combination affected people in different ways. It was her job to ensure that nothing out of the ordinary happened to draw suspicion.

Lydell stopped at the fence perimeter where they'd scuffled the night before. He shook his head as if he were confused. Bretta watched him from the corner of the building just out of sight.

Something seemed familiar to Lydell, but he couldn't put his finger on why this particular spot on the compound was drawing him. He walked over to the fence where she'd breached the perimeter with him. He stood staring at the alley on the other side of the chain link.

Surely, he can't remember. That serum's been tested and proven.

"Are you authorized to be here?" Bretta asked from behind him.

Lydell jerked at the sound of her voice and turned to face her. The blank stare on his face put her a little at ease but not completely. He'd come straight to this exact spot without hesitation.

"I—uh—Bretta! What are you doing here?"

She frowned. "What are you doing here?"

He winced in pain and grabbed his head. "I don't know."

"Are you okay?" she asked concerned.

He sank down on his knees holding his head with both hands. "My head hurts."

She knelt down, cupped his chin in her hand, tilted his head up, and stared into his eyes. There were small red lines marring the whites of his eyes. She grimaced. He was having a reaction to the serum. He needed an antidote immediately. She reached into her pocket and produced a small sealed patch that was an inch in diameter. She peeled off the protective backing and pressed the medicated side of the patch against his neck just below his squared jaw.

"That tastes horrid," he mumbled.

"I know, but it will make you feel better."

He stayed still and allowed her to hold the patch against his neck, but his thoughts were a jumbled mess. She caressed her fingers down his jaw. He lowered his hands and looked up at her. His head pounded like it was being beaten with a sledgehammer.

"What did you give me?"

"My grandmother's remedy for a hangover."

"I don't have a hangover."

"Are you sure?"

"I don't drink. It dulls the senses."

Her thumb caressed over his lower lip. "Maybe you should; it might loosen you up a little."

His head hurt so bad it took him a moment to realize her thumb was still on his lip. He reached up, pulled her wrist up, and inhaled the sweet scent of her perfume.

She always smells so good. Why do I want to kiss her? I don't know her. Damn! To hell with getting to know her. I really want to kiss her.

"You smell so good," he murmured, as his lips pressed against the inside of her wrist.

Bretta had been trained to be immune to a man's advances, but she wasn't immune to Lydell. She felt her insides melting under his tender caress as his lips worked their way up her wrist.

Suddenly, the pain increased, and the pounding inside his skull became unbearable. It was the worst pain he'd ever endured. He grimaced and let go of her wrist. His breath grew short as he tried to breathe through the pain. He felt her gentle hands on his neck, but it was overridden by the intense pain inside his skull. He groaned, closed his eyes, and passed out.

Bretta caught him as his body went limp against her. She laid him back on the ground and continued to press the patch against his neck. It would take five minutes for the patch to take full effect, but she didn't expect him to wake up after that. The patch would do nothing for the pain. It was only designed to counteract the effects of the serum on the brain.

After five minutes, she disposed of the patch and dragged Lydell into the building behind them. It was the warehouse where the supplies were kept. She found a crate labeled blankets and opened it. Then she wrapped him up in one and sat on the floor with his head on her lap.

It took him an hour to wake up. He sat up feeling groggy and confused.

"Does your head still hurt?"

"Yeah. This is the worst headache I've ever had."

"It will go away eventually."

"Maybe I should go see the U.N. doctor on base."

"No, you should just lie down and rest."

He looked at her confused.

She reached up and slid her fingers into his copper curls. He leaned into her gentle caress.

"I love your hair. It suits your face. You are so handsome."

"Who are you?"

"Bretta Brairton."

He shook his head and winced in pain. "We both know that's not your real name."

"What does it matter?"

"Why are you—"

Bretta put a finger to his lips to silence him. "Talk is overrated."

Their eyes locked, and neither took a breath. Bretta leaned in a little closer and waited for him to make the move. Lydell stared into her beautiful blue eyes for a long, heated moment. His eyes dropped to her perfect lips, and his heart beat faster. The urge to kiss her was almost unbearable, but he resisted it. He reminded himself that he didn't know this woman, and no matter how beautiful—she was off limits. She was an unknown entity. She could be the enemy for all he knew. He pulled back, and her lips turned down in a frown.

She wants me to kiss her.

Bretta rose up on her knees, slid her leg over his, and sat straddling his lap. His eyes roamed over her curves and back up to her plump, kissable lips.

"What are you doing?" he whispered, as her lips drew close to his.

"Whatever you want me to do."

She pressed her lips to his, and he kissed her back. After a long, heated kiss, he pulled back. A dull ache throbbed in his head, but he couldn't ignore the feral urges she was waking inside him.

I don't know her. Why do I feel such overwhelming attraction to her? I don't trust her. I don't know who she works for. She's lied about her name. What else will she lie about?

He stopped her from reclaiming his lips and gently pushed her back.

"I need to know who you are. You don't exist as far as the British general is concerned. He checked the data banks. No one named Bretta Brairton works for the British military. Who do you work for?"

Bretta smiled at him. "That's classified."

Lydell smirked. "Why are you targeting me? I don't know anything of value. Like you said, I'm just the grunt work around here. I don't have access to any top-level information. Hell! You knew about my orders before I did. You don't need me. What's your game?"

"I like you."

"That's a lie!"

"Would I kiss you if I didn't?"

He glared at her and then winced in pain. "Girls kiss guys for a lot of reasons. It doesn't always equate to love. Women use men the same as men use women. What are you really after?"

"Freya really did a number on you, didn't she?"

He studied her with suspicion. "How do you know about Freya?"

"She's in your file."

"What file? I never told anyone in the military about her. She's not in any damn file!"

"I never said it was a Navy SEAL file."

Freya completely destroyed his trust in women. During his interrogation, he told me what she did. The only good thing she did was refuse to marry him. She would have made him miserable.

"What do you want from me?"

Bretta grinned slyly. "A lot."

Lydell growled at her. "You'll get nothing!"

Suddenly, a jolt of pain shot through his head again. He cried out and grabbed his head. Bretta reached up and took his pulse.

"Your blood pressure is spiking."

She reached in her pocket and produced a small syringe. She injected him with it, and within seconds he slumped unconscious against the wooden crates. Just then she heard his cell phone buzz in his pocket. There was a text from Sonny.

S: Hey, where are you? It's nearly chow time.

She quickly texted back.

L: Not feeling well. I'm going to see the doctor on base. Eat without me.

Bretta checked her watch. It would be dark in an hour. She looked back at Lydell and frowned. She needed to figure out why he was having such a severe reaction to the serum.

November 29
2415
The derelict apartment, Kananga

Bretta sat next to the small bed in the dingy apartment watching Lydell sleep. She was waiting for her contact, Jakeem Sayad. When she heard him knock on the apartment door, she let him in.

"Did you bring your equipment?" she asked eyeing the case he carried in his hand.

He glared at her. "You broke protocol! Meeting here is too risky. Why did you miss our predetermined rendezvous?" he demanded in a terse tone.

The sound of his agitated voice woke Lydell. He saw his left wrist was handcuffed to the metal frame of the bed. Then he heard Bretta's voice, and he closed his eyes and pretended to sleep.

"That was not an option. Our subject is having an adverse reaction to the serum."

Jakeem's dark jaw tensed as he stared at Bretta. "Where is he?"

She pointed to the small bedroom and followed Jakeem. He set the case he carried on the table and extracted a med kit. He took Lydell's blood, and ran a series of tests on it. An hour later he looked up from the microscope and frowned at her.

"He's type J."

"What does that mean?"

"It means he falls into the one percent of the population who are not fully susceptible to the serum. Type J's have genetic factors that interact with the serum. The memory wipe cannot be guaranteed in type J's. Unfortunately, the test won't indicate a type J until after they've been exposed to the serum. That is a flaw we are working to correct in the next serum."

"He doesn't remember anything."

He glared at her. "That doesn't mean he won't remember in the future. Type J's are completely unpredictable. We can't take that kind of risk. He must be eliminated immediately."

"I'll take care of it."

"No. I have an assignment for you."

Bretta nodded. "What's the assignment?"

He reached into his case and handed her a small manilla envelope. "It's all in there. It must be done immediately. Destroy the evidence after you're done. You must leave now. Your window of opportunity will close quickly. There is no time to waste. I'll kill him once you've gone and dispose of his body."

Lydell watched through slitted lids mentally preparing to defend himself and kill Jakeem as soon as he walked close enough to the bed. He would strangle the man with his legs and hope Bretta was already gone by then. Then he would figure out how to get out of the handcuff before she got back. His body tensed waiting for the perfect moment to strike.

Bretta watched her contact pull out his 9MM Beretta from its holster and walk toward the bed. When his back was to her, she yanked her gun out and shot Jakeem in the back of the head. Then she opened the envelope and sat down at the small table to read over her new assignment.

Lydell continued to watch her through slitted lids.

She just saved my life and killed her partner in cold blood. She has no remorse. Who the hell is this woman?

Bretta glanced back to the bed and let out a sigh.

I'll have to leave him here unsupervised for a while. I'll dispose of Jakeem on the way out.

She dragged Jakeem's corpse to the doorway.

"Are you just going to leave me here helpless, handcuffed to the bed?"

Her eyes jerked back to Lydell. He was watching her intently.

She grinned slyly. "You are hardly helpless, Lydell. Don't worry. I'll be back soon. Get some rest while I'm gone. You're safe. No one else knows about this place."

She walked back to the bed, leaned down, and pressed a soft kiss to his lips. He slid his free hand behind her neck and kissed her back until she finally pulled away. He watched her drag Jakeem's body out of the room. He still felt a little disoriented, but the throbbing in his head had subsided to a dull ache. After she left, he felt grogginess overtaking him, and he fell asleep.

Bretta dragged Jakeem down the hall, shoved his body into an empty apartment, and shut the door. The entire apartment building was abandoned. It had been empty and derelict for quite some time. The only inhabitants brave enough to live in the condemned building were the rats.

Bretta walked down eight flights of stairs and walked back to the U.N. base camp six blocks away. There she proceeded to carry out her orders to the letter before returning to the apartment to check on Lydell. By the time she made it back it was 0330. It would be dawn soon, and she didn't have much time to finish her task. Lydell was now in stable condition, but she had to maintain the cover story. He had to wake up in the infirmary on base.

She changed into a U.N. medical staff uniform and woke Lydell. The serum still lingered in his system; he was still mostly compliant. Dizzy and disoriented, he followed her downstairs and back to the base. She snuck him into an infirmary bed, wrote up the necessary medical chart, and slipped away unnoticed by the U.N. nurse on duty, who was sleeping at the front desk.

She returned to the derelict apartment building and set incendiary devices on each floor. It was just before dawn when she finished. As she walked away, she glanced at the burning building. It was completely engulfed in flames, and she was the only witness. The area was completely deserted.

CHAPTER 13

November 29
0700
U.N. base infirmary, Kananga

Lydell woke to the sight of Rowen, John, Nick, Sonny, and Cameron around his bed.

"What happened?" Lydell mumbled.

"You tell us," John said.

Rowen cleared his throat. "You texted Sonny yesterday, told him you were sick, and you were going to see the base doctor."

"I did?"

Rowen nodded. "Trouble is, I came to the infirmary to check on you only to find they knew nothing about you. You've been MIA for hours. When the medical staff changed shifts at 0600 this morning, I got a call saying you were here. Can you explain what happened?"

Lydell shook his head and winced in pain. "I don't remember any of that. All I know is my skull feels like someone cracked it open with a wrecking ball."

Rowen nodded. "According to your chart, you suffered a severe concussion. It says you were suffering from hallucinations."

"It does? I don't know, Sir. I can't remember any of that."

"What do you remember?" John asked.

Lydell struggled to focus for a few moments. "I remember being on the chopper."

"That was three days ago," Nick said. "Do you remember anything after that?"

"I don't think so."

"You must'av knocked yer skull pretty hard to forget the last three days," Sonny drawled.

"The rest of the guys are waiting to see you. They won't let more than five visitors back here at a time. We were all worried about you," John said.

"I'll be fine. I have a thick skull." Lydell forced a grin.

Soon the rest of Delta and Echo had paid a short visit to Lydell. Once they were gone, Rowen came back in.

"The nursing staff said you should be able to get out of here in a few hours. They are just going to monitor you for a while. Get some rest. I'll be back to check on you after my meeting with General Loredo."

Once Rowen was gone, Lydell looked around. He was in a small area partitioned off by hospital curtains. He could hear patients around him coughing. He could hear the monitors beeping. He could hear everything, and it was all too loud. It was making his head hurt worse. He'd had plenty of concussions. This felt nothing like a concussion. It was far worse.

He closed his eyes and tried to go to sleep.

When he finally fell asleep, hazy images filled his mind. He tried to make sense of them, but they were disjointed and illogical. He saw Bretta straddling his lap, kissing him. Then he saw his arms and legs secured to a bed with handcuffs and rope. His last image was of Bretta dressed in scrubs leaning over him with a wistful smile. She leaned down and kissed his forehead. Then she softly kissed his lips. He wanted to tell her not to go, but he couldn't speak. He wanted to kiss her back, but he couldn't make his lips work. It was like being completely paralyzed watching things happen to you. When he woke, he could only recall very hazy images of Bretta kissing him.

November 29
1600
Mess hall, U.N. base, Kananga

Bretta followed Lydell keeping a discreet watch over him. He no longer seemed to be in pain, and his behavior had returned to normal. He sat at the dinner table with the rest of Echo wearing his usual grim expression. She didn't know why, but his stern scowl turned her on. She sat three tables over, but he hadn't noticed her. Even if he had looked up from his plate, he wouldn't have noticed her. Her own mother wouldn't recognize her today. She was well disguised.

Lydell finished his meal and left Echo and Delta to their banter and jokes. Bretta disposed of her meal on the way out the door and followed him. He walked the perimeter and stopped at the exact spot he'd tangled with Bretta two days ago. She halted around the corner of the building and flipped open the face of her watch. She watched the red dot on the tiny screen.

Why did he come back here? Is he remembering?

She ran a digital diagnostic on the tracker she'd injected him with during his interrogation. It was functioning perfectly, but Lydell hadn't moved. She peeked around the corner. He was staring at the fence and the street beyond. She held her position and waited too. After a few minutes, he walked back to the infirmary. Bretta eavesdropped on his conversation with the nurse on duty. He was asking about his injury and when he was admitted. The nurse on duty did not speak English. Bretta took the opportunity to quickly change into scrubs and emerge from behind a curtain. She spoke to Lydell in French with a perfect French accent.

She asked him what his inquiries were. He spoke back to her in French and repeated all his former questions. She checked the computer and relayed the nature of the false injuries she had put on his chart. Then she informed him that he had checked himself into the infirmary at 0350. Lydell seemed satisfied with her answers, though he was no more enlightened. He left the infirmary, and Bretta changed back into her generic, black, U.N. uniform and followed him with the tracker. He left the base and wandered the streets. When he turned down the street where the burned-out apartment building lay in crumbled ruins, her heart skipped a beat.

Is he starting to remember?

She breathed a sigh of relief when he walked past the still smoldering remains without so much as a pause. It did not appear that he recognized anything. Still, the fact that he was aimlessly wandering the streets in search of something was cause for concern.

Bretta stopped by her new apartment during Lydell's aimless wandering. After removing the makeup and false nose, she changed back into the British uniform and donned the long, blonde wig. Then she took up her surveillance again.

It was well after dark when he returned to base. Lydell rounded the corner of the bunkhouse on his way to the door and stopped short. Bretta was leaning against the wall by the door.

"What are you doing here?"

"Looking for you."

"Why? What do you want?" he asked suspiciously.

Bretta grinned at him. "I have a gift for you."

"What is it?"

His eyes roamed over her petite figure without his permission, and images if her straddling him and licking his abs slammed into his brain. His heart beat faster as he slowly dragged his eyes back up to meet hers.

"You'll be briefed on this in the morning, but the SEALs are being shipped back to the field."

"When?"

"Tomorrow at 1200."

He rested his forearm on the wall beside her and leaned in closer. He could smell her enticing perfume as he grinned down at her. Suddenly, she was in his head again, caressing his jaw, kissing his forehead, and looking at him tenderly. He leaned down and claimed her lips. She parted her mouth, and their tongues met. At first their kiss was a gentle exploration, but the longer they kissed the more passionate it turned. Soon he was devouring her mouth and pressing her up against the wall with his body. He knew he shouldn't give in to his urges, but it was impossible to quell them. Something about her pulled him in. She was the forbidden fruit, and he was tempted as hell. He felt her leg snake around his thigh, and he grinned against her seeking mouth as he slid his hands down her luscious curves and pulled her legs up around his waist. Bretta moaned in approval as he staked his claim on her lips. After a long, flirtatious bout of kissing, he pulled back and stared into her eyes.

"I had a dream about you. You were wearing a black G-string."

"What else was I wearing?"

Lydell grinned slyly. "Who says you were wearing anything else?"

Is he remembering, or is this just a fantasy of his? I was wearing more than a black G-string.

"What happened?"

"You were on top of me, and we were making love."

"Really."

He leaned in to whisper in her ear, as his arms encircled her, holding her tightly against him.

Her eyes grew wide as she listened. Then she grinned. "Really? I did all that in your dream?"

He pulled back with a mischievous grin, and his right eyebrow rose playfully. "That's only part of what we did. I can show you the rest."

"You said you don't like fast women."

"I don't." He went in for another passionate kiss.

When he came up for air, she grinned. "You're coming on awfully strong, Fry."

He grinned back. "Can't handle it?"

"I didn't say that."

He stared at her for a moment. "How many guys have you been with?"

"What makes you think I've been with any?"

"The way you carry yourself. You don't have a shy bone in your body."

"So, that makes me a slut in your book?"

He chewed on his bottom lip. "I can't read you. I honestly don't know what to think."

"Do you still think I'm the enemy?"

Do I trust her? She did save my life. Wait! Did she? She had a gun. She killed a man and dragged his body away—I think. I'm not sure. Did she? Where did that come from? Did I imagine that? I want to trust her, but that would be foolish. She's lied to me. I don't know who she really is. I should walk away, but I don't want to. I want to rip her clothes off and make love to her all night.

He tilted his head a little and studied her. "I don't know. A voice in my head is telling me not to trust you, but some other part of me thinks you're not entirely evil."

She chuckled. "Thanks for the vote of confidence."

He put her down, took a step back, and raked his hand over his short burr. "I probably shouldn't have kissed you. I don't know what got into me. I should go."

He turned his back to her and was halfway through the doorway.

"I liked your hair better before you shaved it all off."

He halted in his tracks, and a grin spread over his mouth. He looked back over his shoulder at her, and his gut twisted into a knot.

She's beautiful, sexy, and a great kisser. She's also dangerous, deceitful, and probably up to no good. The right call is to walk away. So, what am I still doing here?

He turned to face her. "You're dangerous."

"Does that scare you?"

He shook his head. "You're also a liar. I think you're up to something."

Bretta walked to him. "What am I up to, Lydell?"

He rubbed his wrist as the sensation of metal against his skin slammed into his conscious.

"I haven't figured that out yet."

She smiled up at him. He smiled back.

"Damn! Why do you have to be so sexy?" he murmured as he slid his arms around her. "Your whole body is a weapon, and I'm defenseless."

"I guess you better surrender."

"Bretta—or whatever your name is—"

She chuckled. "It's Bretta."

"Okay, Bretta. One day you'll have to tell me the whole truth, including your real name."

Don't hold your breath on that, Frogman. I'm not allowed to tell you the whole truth.

"How do I find you again in the masses here on base?" he asked.

"I'll find you, Love. I've got my eye on you."

He leaned down and teased her lips with his before pulling back just out of her reach. Then he gave into his urges, backed her up against the wall, and went in for a long, passionate, feral kiss.

An hour later, Lydell showered, dressed for bed, and flopped down on his cot. Sonny walked over and sat on the empty cot next to his. His mouth turned up in a sly grin.

"Who's the sexy, little filly? I practically had to squeeze past you two to get in the building. You were all over her. You didn't even notice me."

Lydell sat up grinning. "She's the Brit. Her name is Bretta, or so she says."

Sonny's eyebrow rose. "How long has this been going on?"

He shrugged. "I ran into her after dinner."

Sonny smirked. "Hope you used protection."

"I didn't sleep with her!" Lydell bit his lip and looked away. "I shouldn't have kissed her. I don't know what got into me. She's probably the worst kind of trouble."

"See—You can't let your urges control you, no matter how hot the girl is."

"You're one to talk, Sonny. It doesn't sound like you ever reign it in."

"Yeah, but that's me. I know how to handle trouble; I like trouble; trouble can be a lot of fun. You ain't like me, Lydell. You can't act on a crazy impulse. What if next time you go farther than a kiss? What if you get her pregnant? What would you do then?"

Lydell let out a long breath. "I don't know. I guess I'd marry her."

Sonny shook his head. "What if she is the enemy? She could be a spy or something worse. You told us you don't trust her."

"I don't—exactly trust her."

"But you thought it was a good idea to practically screw her by the bunk house door?"

"No. I knew better. I just couldn't seem to help myself. She makes me so—"

"Trust me. I know that type. They get you so hard you can't think straight. Then you do the stupidest thing possible. You screw them. Screwing a woman like that only makes the situation worse. Them's the kind you should run away from as fast as yer little feet can carry you."

"You're probably right." A mischievous grin spread over Lydell's lips. "Still, I bet she would make a good wife."

Sonny studied him for a moment. "If you was to get hitched—what country would you live in? She's a Brit. What if she don't want to move to the U.S.? Would you be willing to move across the ocean and join the Red Coats?"

Lydell chuckled. "That wasn't really a topic of conversation. We didn't do a lot of talking."

"Uh-huh! So, yer tellin' me you was just a hare in heat a racin' fer the finish line?"

Lydell dropped his eyes to the floor and fell silent for a moment.

"So, when do you plan to see her again?"

He shrugged. "She told me we are being sent back out to the field tomorrow at 1200."

"What did she want in return for that information?"

"Nothing."

"Suspicious."

"Yeah, I know."

"Yet you practically sucked her lips off anyway." Sonny shot him a disapproving frown.

Sonny got up and went back to his own cot. Lydell lay awake for a long time. He was restless, pent up, and worried about what Sonny said. He finally drifted off to sleep only to have more of the weird, disjointed dreams about Bretta. Something in his subconscious was trying to break free. He felt fear roiling inside him like a hurricane, and there was no subduing it. A short while later, he was in the bathroom hurling his guts up. He sat on the cold tile floor for a while waiting for his stomach to calm down. His thoughts turned back to Sonny's comment.

What if Sonny is right? What if she is a spy or something worse? She's too secretive. I don't trust her, and yet all I can think about is how much I want her. Damnit!

This is crazy! I was never this desperate over Freya. What's so special about a mystery girl with a fake name? She's definitely trouble! I should stay away from her.

November 30
0800
Briefing room, U.N. base, Kananga

Lydell sat at the table with the rest of Echo and Delta waiting to find out why Rowen had scheduled a last-minute briefing. Rowen walked into the room with a grim expression.

"I have some bad news," Rowen said with a heavy sigh. "All the footage you men brought in for translation and analyzation was stolen."

"Why would someone steal that?" Wes Chilven asked incredulously.

Rowen shrugged. "That is the question of the day. The translators had the first couple of weeks translated. They made written transcripts of their work, but that was stolen too."

Sonny raised his hand. Rowen nodded to him.

"I smell a conspiracy," Sonny drawled. "I may not have understood everything we heard out there, but it was pretty clear what we was seein'."

Rowen gestured for him to continue.

"We was told that Negassi's guerilla's were kidnappin' little kids and forcin' them to join their army or forcin' them to work in the mines to fund his regime. That ain't what we saw out there. We saw them guerilla's acting like amateur doctors, and handin' out food. They wasn't kidnappin' nobody. There was some recruitin' goin' on, but they wasn't forcin' none of them boys to join their army. Them kids was voluteerin' all on their own."

"That's what Fry and Chilven reported when you guys first came back. The intel we are getting from our U.N. counterparts is not lining up with what you guys are witnessing in the field," Rowen said.

Wes added. "Delta saw the same thing with our group of trucks, but these soldiers were different from the one's we have been fighting since we arrived in Congo."

"Different how?" Rowen asked.

"Their weapons were old and not well maintained. Their uniforms were barely better than tattered rags. We saw no hostility from this last group toward anyone. Our previous engagements with the guerillas seemed better organized. They had better weapons, better uniforms, and they were definitely hostile. It was like looking at two completely different armies."

"I agree with Wes." John sighed in frustration. "None of this makes sense. I'm not sure we are on the right side in all of this. I don't think we have been fully informed of all parameters."

Rowen nodded. "I'm not arguing with you, John. It's apparent there are hidden agendas going on here. Unfortunately, our hands are tied by U.N. regulations. The Congolese government didn't invite the U.S. to resolve this conflict—they invited the U.N. To compound these issues, I was given orders this morning for Echo and Delta to ship out at 1200. There have been reports of guerilla movement in the south. The Katanga province is where the majority of the mining operations are located. Your orders are to locate and take out any guerilla strongholds."

Nick frowned and raised his hand to speak. "I thought the whole point of us surveilling Negassi's men was so we could determine what is really going on in the guerilla army. I thought we were trying to locate his headquarters. Now the video footage has been stolen, and we are suddenly being ordered to go in and wipe out more of Negassi's army rather than track him down and take him out. It's damn fishy!"

Rowen nodded. "That's why I'm sending you in with orders to take out the army if you find them doing anything nefarious. If you witness more of the same humanitarian aid—use your best judgement in the field. I think something is off too. Be careful out there, and watch your backs."

At 1200, Delta boarded a helicopter enroute to Kolwezi. Echo boarded a helicopter destined for Kabalo. From those cities they would travel into the countryside in search of Negassi's militants. Echo would travel by truck from Kabalo to Bukama before heading south to investigate the mining operations to confirm if the allegations against Negassi's militants were accurate.

For the moment, Echo was enjoying the landscape rushing by below the chopper. The raw beauty of nature was inspiring. John stared out at the beautiful, African land zipping past below them. When the chopper passed over the grasslands of the southern plateau in the Katanga province, he watched a pride of lions chasing down an antelope. It was a thing of beauty to witness the dance between predator and prey.

CHAPTER 14

December 1
0600
Coronado, California

BUD/S Day 1

Petty Officer Second Class, Sophia Gonzalez reported to NSWO for her second attempt at BUD/S. The moment she stepped off the bus, her ears were greeted by the sound of orders being shouted at the group of SEAL candidates. Like before, they were assembled in rows on the grinder for uniform inspection, and anyone who failed inspection was sent on the crawl of shame to the remediation group. Sophia passed and took her place in the appropriate group. When the last uniform was inspected, Sophia's group was addressed by Senior Chief Petty Officer Reynolds.

Reynolds' eyebrow rose when he spotted Sophia. "Back for more punishment, Gonzalez?"

"Sir, yes, Sir!" Sophia answered respectfully. "If you can dish it, I can take it!"

Reynolds' lip turned up ever so slightly in the corner. Sophia noted his amusement and kept her expression stoic. Reynolds continued with his opening speech to the candidates, and things proceeded in much the same way as she'd experienced the first time, six months ago.

Reynolds wound down his speech. "There are 217 BUD/S candidates in this class. Those who don't deserve to be here will ring the bell! By the end of today, at least 6 of you will ring it!"

After Reynolds' speech came PT, chow time, surf torture, and getting sandy from head to toe. Once again, Sophia stood at attention with her body shivering, her teeth chattering, and her determination to succeed undeterred. At the end of the day, she hit the communal showers with the 209 men who hadn't rung the bell that day.

She stood under the cold water and washed off all the sand and grit. She ignored the gawking eyes of the men around her. She wasn't here for them. She was here for a higher purpose. Their lascivious staring was nothing new to her. She'd endured it for four years at Gitmo. She'd learned to tune it out and press on with her duties. She didn't see the men she served with as men, or as potential romantic candidates. She viewed them as fellow soldiers and nothing more. She couldn't afford to allow emotions to enter any equation, or she'd end up on the wrong end of a court martial. The UCMJ (Uniform Code of Military Justice) was strict, unyielding, and punishable by time served in Leavenworth.

Week one progressed in the same manner as before. There was PT, runs, surf torture, lap races in the pool, and Surf Passage. There was one other familiar entity, Cafferty. He didn't approach her. He didn't speak to her. He didn't even acknowledge that he recognized her. Sophia treated him in the same aloof manner. She focused on what was important, hanging in through the worst of the physical strain. She deliberately didn't allow herself to dwell on the fact that Cafferty was the reason she hadn't passed the first round. It was his refusal to ring the bell that had caused the accident that cost her months of recovery and physical therapy.

BUD/S Week 2

It was once again time to tackle the toothpick. Reynolds split the remaining 187 candidates into teams to carry their respective logs. Sophia did not delude herself into thinking it was coincidence that she and Cafferty were assigned to the same team.

Cafferty gave her a wary glance as they assembled together as a team.

"I want the front of the line," Sophia said without hesitation.

"You're the shortest one on the team. You should bring up the rear," Wescott said.

"I want the front," Sophia insisted. Her eyes narrowed on Cafferty.

He swallowed hard and gave her a nod. "Give her the front," Sam Cafferty said sternly.

Wescott bit his bottom lip pondering for a moment.

"She's earned it. Give her the front," Sam growled. He turned his gaze on Sophia, and the corner of his lip turned up as he winked at her.

She merely nodded in response. Their team retrieved a cable and began the arduous task of carrying the 430-pound log. It was a struggle, but Sophia made sure she wasn't the weak link in the chain. She noticed that Cafferty took up the rear position. She couldn't help but wonder if he would collapse again. She'd tried to keep an eye on his progress over the last week, but it was impossible to watchdog him and stay focused. All she could do was pray that he was in better physical condition to handle it this time around.

Carrying the cable put them all through their paces, and when the exercise was over, they were beyond exhausted. At the end of the day, Cafferty took the showerhead next to Sophia's. She did her best to ignore him.

"You did good today, Gonzalez."

"So did you." She kept her eyes averted from his perfect body as she scrubbed herself clean.

"I'm sorry about what happened last time. They told me about the accident when I was recovering in the infirmary."

"It wasn't your fault. It was an accident."

"I shouldn't have attempted to carry it last time. I was sick and depleted. I should have gone to medical that morning, but my pride got in the way. I was determined that if you could handle it so could I. I made a bad call, and you paid the price for it. I'm officially apologizing."

She nodded without looking at him. "Noted, Soldier."

Sam smirked. Then he glanced over at her for a moment and quickly averted his eyes. Her naked body was far too enticing. He hadn't broken silence to get tangled up with her. He only wanted to apologize.

"You can call me Sam." He stared at the tile wall in front of him.

"It's better if we keep things professional. You're just another soldier here, Cafferty"

He grinned. "So, you do remember my name."

She rolled her eyes and tried to hurry through the rest of her shower.

Sam ducked his head under the cold water and rinsed the soap out of his short, blonde burr. Then he turned under the water so his back was to the wall. He turned his head in her direction.

"I think we are way beyond professional, don't you? I nearly cost you your career. I'd rather we move on as friends."

A smirky smile tugged at the corner of her mouth. He noticed.

"Friends?" she mused. "I've never had one of those since I joined the Marine's four and a half years ago. I'm used to being the lone wolf. It was the only way to survive at GITMO."

Sam chewed at his lip as the water cascaded down his ripped body washing away the soap.

"You were stationed at GITMO?"

"Yeah."

"You're tougher than I thought. I've heard GITMO is no joke."

"You heard right."

"So, friends then?"

Sophia glanced up at him, and he winked at her again. She felt her heart skip a beat.

Is he trying to flirt with me?

"Friends," she agreed.

She made sure to keep her eyes focused on his eyes and nowhere else. She wanted to ensure she didn't give him the wrong idea.

That night she lay on her bed pondering the exchange with Cafferty. She'd had plenty of men come on to her during her service in Cuba. Cafferty didn't seem like he was trying to get in her panties. He seemed genuine and sincere. She decided to give him the benefit of the doubt and take his offer of friendship at face value. Though she doubted anything would come of it. The likelihood of him washing out was high in her opinion. She figured she wouldn't see much more of him. This was week two. It would only get more difficult from here.

CHAPTER 15

December 13

0400

Deep in the heart of the Katanga province

Sonny lay still on the eastern ridge of a massive strip mine. He surveyed the area with his night-vision binoculars. Dawn would break the horizon soon, and he would have to move, but for the moment, he was taking advantage of the cover darkness provided to get a clearer picture of what this place was about.

John and Nick skirted the perimeter to the southern ridge where a large tent community lay sleeping. The primitive tents offered the only housing for the large group of miners. Five guards lay sleeping with their rifles in hand. John provided cover while Nick crept down to take a closer look at the inhabitants and their living conditions.

Nick made his way along the eastern perimeter of the tents. His night-vision goggles painted a bleak picture for him. Every tent was full of small children ranging from six-years-old to fourteen-years-old. They all lay on the dirt floor of the tents dressed in what amounted to rags. When Nick circled around to the back of the tent encampment, a boy about twelve-years-old woke and saw him. The boy spoke to him in Swahili.

"Are you going to hurt us?" the boy asked.

Nick shook his head and answered in Swahili. "I'm here to help you."

"What can you do?"

"Do the men with the rifles hurt you?"

The boy shook his head. "They protect us from the lions and hyenas."

"How did you end up working the mine?"

"My village was sick with the sleeping sickness. When my parents died, I left to find work."

"They pay you to do this?"

The boy nodded.

"What about the others?" Nick gestured to the other children sleeping in the tents.

"Some lost their families like me. Others came because they were starving in their villages."

"Were any of you forced to work here against your will?"

The boy shook his head. "No, we are all grateful to have a job and food to eat."

Nick nodded and thanked the boy. Then he crept back to John's position.

"I don't think this is the mining operation we are looking for," Nick said into his comlink.

"I heard the boy," Fry said. "Still, since we are here, let's observe the operation for ourselves.

At dawn three trucks rolled in loaded down with adult workers. Breakfast rations were distributed to the child labor, and the day began. The adults ran the heavy machinery while the children had the tedious job of sifting through piles of freshly dug earth for precious minerals and gems.

Echo watched the operation all day. They saw nothing to warrant action on their part. The children were fed three meals, and they were treated with kindness from the adult workers. It was obvious to Fry and the rest of the team that this mining operation was not abusing anyone.

At a distant mining operation farther north, Wes Chilven and the rest of Delta witnessed a similar scenario. There was nothing to be done but to move on to the next mine and investigate.

CHAPTER 16

December 15
0500
Coronado, California

BUD/S Day 15

Sophia reported to the grinder with the other 142 candidates. Senior Chief Petty Officer Reynolds stood in front of the group.

"This class started with 217 candidates. There are 143 of you left. I expected a lot more of you to ring the bell by now. You surprised me, but it won't matter. After this week, those of you unfit to become a SEAL will ring that bell. I expect at least 100 of you to ring that bell! Welcome to Hell Week, Gentlemen," Reynolds said with a smirk.

The candidates all stood at attention waiting for further instructions. Reynolds scanned the group assembled before him. His eyes landed on Sophia, and his mouth turned down in a frown.

Reynolds began his speech. "This is Hell Week! You will all be pushed to your breaking points. Those who don't ring the bell will endure hell!"

Sam Cafferty stood at attention. He listened intently to every word Reynolds yelled at them. He did his best to stay focused, but he was distracted. Sophia stood at attention directly in front of him. His eyes kept drifting down to her perfect, camo-covered ass. Lascivious thoughts invaded his brain, and he had to continually refocus his attention on Reynolds.

At the end of his speech, Reynolds kept his promise. Hell Week officially began.

Hell Week Day 1

Sophia did her best to keep up with the rest of the men during the morning sprint. It was twice as long as usual, and the BUD/S instructors were yelling at them the entire run. Despite her best effort, she finished in last place.

"Is that all you've got, Gonzalez?" Reynolds yelled in her face as she stood at attention.

"Sir, no, Sir!" she yelled respectfully.

"You think last place will get you there? If this was a battle situation, you'd be dead! Last place isn't good enough! SEALs strive to be number one! I haven't seen you finish first in anything yet! Why are you still here?"

"I'm here to serve my country, Sir!" she yelled respectfully.

"How will you serve your team, much less your country, if you're the last one to make it to cover? When the bullets start flying in the field, your ass will be on the line, Gonzalez! Tell me how you expect to survive? How will you serve your team when you're dead? How will you pull your weight when you can't even run four miles without lagging behind the team?"

"I will strive to do better, Sir!"

"You will all strive to do better!" Reynolds yelled at the entire group. "This exercise doesn't end until everyone, including Gonzalez, makes this run in under thirty minutes! You are all part of the same team!"

Everyone stood at attention trying to catch their breath. When Reynolds gave the word, they all started the four-mile sprint again. This time Sophia wasn't the only one who didn't make the cut. Seven of the 143 candidates finished over the thirty-minute mark. They endured another lecture from Reynolds about the importance of teamwork and giving everything you have for the sake of the team.

Reynolds wrapped up his speech. "SEALs are not individuals. A SEAL is part of a team. If there is a weak link in the team, the whole team fails. Fifteen men can do exactly what they are required to do to complete a successful mission, but if the sixteenth man fails to do his part, the mission fails! The team fails. There is no place in the SEALs for weak links. This team now has twenty-nine minutes to run this sprint. If even one of you fails to make it back in that time, the entire team fails."

The third attempt thirty-seven didn't make the time. Reynolds decreased the time to twenty-eight minutes and told them to run it again. By the sixth attempt, the required time was twenty-six minutes. They had sprinted a total of twenty-four miles that morning. Ninety men didn't make the time. Fourteen rang the bell. That left 129 candidates. Day 1 of Hell Week was half over.

They were given a short break for lunch and told to report to the pool. Sophia was dragging herself through the paces. At the pool, they were split into teams of three. They were tethered by the waist to their teammates and told each team had to do their laps in less than twenty minutes or they would repeat the exercise as a team until they met the required time.

Sophia did her best, but she wasn't used to swimming with someone tethered to her. She was used to pacing herself somewhere in the middle and finishing when she finished. This was a whole new ball game. Sam Cafferty was tethered in the middle and Sophia and Bob Laggerson were tethered to either side of him. When it was their turn, they dove in the pool together and began their laps. At first, they were keeping a decent pace with each other, but after three laps, Sam and Sophia were falling behind and they could all feel the pull of the rope on their abdomens. Bob attempted to tug them along, but it soon became apparent that the only way to accomplish their mission was to swim together at the same pace. Bob had to slow his pace to accommodate Sophia and Sam. They finished their laps in thirty-seven minutes.

Needless to say, Bob cussed them both out when they pulled themselves out of the pool. No one was happy to have to repeat all those laps. They were all exhausted.

"Your time was pathetic! If this were a real-life situation all three of you would be dead! Learn how to work as a team and live, or keep doing what you're doing and die!" Bruchard yelled at them as he recorded their lap time. "You now have nineteen minutes to complete your laps. Back in the pool! Go!"

They dove in together and swam as fast as they could, but it wasn't good enough. They managed to shave two minutes off their previous time. Bruchard yelled at them again, just as he yelled at the other teams for being too slow. He decreased their time to eighteen minutes and ordered them to swim it again. By the time Sophia's team pulled themselves from the pool after five attempts, their completion time had increased to fifty-seven minutes.

Not one of the three-man-teams met their time mark. Seventeen men rang the bell that afternoon. That left 112 candidates to meet in the mess hall for dinner. After dinner, they assembled on the grinder to do two hours of PT. Then they were told to shower and prepare for room inspection.

Cafferty stepped up to the showerhead next to Sophia with a weary sigh. "They said it would only get harder and harder after you stepped off the bus. They weren't exaggerating. I think I had about five heart attacks today."

Sophia's lip turned up in the corner. "BUD/S is definitely no joke. They don't give you any mercy here. GITMO was a vacation paradise compared to BUD/S."

"Well, this is Hell Week. This is where most of the candidates fall short and quit. You have any plans to ring the bell, Soph?"

Sophia glanced up at him, and he winked at her.

"I'm not quitting. I'm here to become a SEAL. It's make it or die for me. They'll have to kill me and drag my body away."

"Damn, Girl! That's some attitude." Sam chuckled as he lathered soap on his ripped abs.

"Are you planning to ring the bell?" Sophia smirked as she lathered up.

"No, they'll have to drag my dead body away too."

Room inspection was brutal. Men were brought low by the tiniest infractions. Any infraction from anyone in the room and the entire room was sent to the surf. It wasn't long before 97 candidates were sitting in the frigid ocean with their arms linked together. The remaining 15 men were sent to stand on the beach and watch the rest endure surf torture. Once surf torture was over, they were dismissed to their bunk house.

Of the 97 only 84 returned to the shower to clean up. The others all hit their bunks no longer caring about being clean. Exhaustion was already taking a toll.

Two hours after they were dismissed to their bunks, Jaxson called reveille at 0230. The candidates were assembled on the grinder for a midnight run. The two-mile run was followed by PT, which was followed by timed practice on the O-course. At dawn twelve men rang the bell.

That brought the count down to 100 candidates at the start of day 2 of Hell Week.

Hell Week Day 2

Breakfast was at 0600. Immediately following breakfast was more sprinting on the beach. Like the previous day, when the entire team didn't make the four-mile run in thirty minutes, the entire team had to run it again and again and again. Each time they had one less minute to accomplish their mission. Like day 1, Sophia was at the back of the pack every time. She tried as hard as she could, but she never could make the time. The other men in the group did their fair share of cussing her out during and after each failed attempt. It didn't matter. She was pushing herself as hard as she could. Her disadvantage was her stride length. The last three sprints, Cafferty fell back and paced himself with her. He did his best to motivate her to run faster, but even he could tell she was giving it her best shot.

When the entire team failed to ever complete the run in the allotted times, they were lined up on the beach, yelled at, and surf torture followed.

At lunch Cafferty got in line behind Sophia and took a seat across from her.

"You okay?" he asked.

She nodded as she shoveled in a big bite of food.

"You thinking about ringing the bell?"

She shook her head and shoveled in another bite.

"Good. I don't want you to quit. You can do it."

"Why don't you want me to quit? I'm the slowest runner in the group."

"But you're not the slowest swimmer."

She smirked at him, and he winked at her.

"Besides, you're pretty good at the O-course. A lot of the men can't do some of those obstacles as well as you. There's a lot more to being a good soldier than being the fastest runner. You probably have mental skills that these other guys don't. What's your poison?"

Sophia shrugged.

Sam shoveled in a bite. "Computer guru?"

Sophia shook her head.

"Communications?"

"Language."

"What language?"

"Spanish, Farsi, and Russian," she said around a mouthful of food.

"Damn! Three languages?"

She grinned as she watched Sam shovel in several more bites. Lunch time was nearly over, and then it would be back to the pool for more physical exertion.

Bruchard was ready to yell at them the minute they stepped into the massive pool room.

"Today you will be tied in groups of five. Work as a team, and do your laps in twenty minutes or less. You all know the drill. In the pool! Go!"

Teams of three had seemed hard the day before. Teams of five was much worse. Cafferty wasn't on her team this time. She was tethered to four new men. Jeff Collier, who everyone called Collie, she had worked with on the toothpick one time, but the others she didn't know at all. Not one team made the required time. Like the day before they were directed to swim it again and their time was reduced by two minutes every time they failed. Not one team passed that day. Eight rang the bell after the pool exercise. That left 92 candidates on the grinder for PT.

After dinner there was another room inspection. Only 25 men passed inspection. The entire group was then assembled back on the grinder at 2217. Burkins addressed the group.

"Why is it important for your sheets to be tucked tightly? Why is it important that your fatigues be folded according to regulation?" Burkins glared at them as their silence hung in the air. "It's a pattern of behavior! If you don't keep your quarters in ship shape, why would we expect you to keep your weapons in proper functioning order? Would you like to be in a firefight with a man who never cleans his rifle?"

"Sir, no, Sir!" the group answered in unison.

"If your focus is on the team and not on yourself, you will be ready and able to protect your teammates. You don't matter. The team is all that matters. The mission is all that matters. Is that clear?"

"Sir, yes, Sir!"

"Is this sinking into your thick skulls yet?"

"Sir, yes, Sir!"

"You're all lying! If you were acting as a team, there wouldn't be 67 candidates failing room inspection!"

The air fell silent as Burkins glared at the 92 soldiers lined up in neat rows in front of him.

"Until you learn to act as a team you will never be a team. If one of you fails, you all fail! Sprint to the surf, now! Get in, and stay in until I say it's over!"

The group left the grinder at a dead run, but only 90 made it to the surf. As they plunged into the freezing water with their arms linked, they heard the bell. It rang three times. There was a short pause, and it rang three more times.

"We lost two more," Sam said to Sophia, whose arm was linked through his.

"Only 47 more until we hit the eighty percent mark," Sophia said.

The cold ocean waves crashed against their backs as the 90 remaining candidates huddled close together and endured surf torture. When it was over, they were ordered to get sandy for the twentieth time that day. Being cold, wet, dirty, and miserable was slowly becoming second nature to Sophia.

Reynolds addressed the sandy group on the beach. "Have you men had enough yet?"

"Sir, no, Sir!" they answered in unison.

"You will! Back to the grinder! You're all doing PT!"

PT was followed by the O-course, which was followed by more surf torture and getting sandy. That was followed by a lecture at top volume from Reynolds. The group was dismissed for the night. They went to the showers and hit their beds immediately. Two hours later, Burkins called them out for reveille at 0200.

Burkins addressed the group. "How many of you men are tired?"

"Sir, no, Sir!"

"How many of you want to quit?"

"Sir, no, Sir!"

"Good! We have a mission for you. Assemble on the beach!" Once they were all on the beach Burkins addressed them again. "You will swim out to the buoy and back! Then you will repeat that swim tethered to your new swim buddy!"

When each man returned from the beach, he was tethered to a man who did not match his swim speed or time. Then they were ordered to swim it again and again. By the time every man struggled against the ocean surf to make the swim five times they had nothing left. That's when Reynolds ordered them to the O-course for more drills.

At dawn, 9 men rang the bell. That took the group down to 81 candidates.

Hell Week Day 3

Sam sat across from Sophia shoveling in his food as fast as he could. When his plate was clean, he laid his head down on the table and fell directly to sleep. Sophia felt bad for him as well as the other candidates. In the last forty-eight hours, they had only been allowed a total of four hours sleep. She knew it was about to get worse. She'd heard stories about Hell Week. Sleep deprivation was part of the training. When she saw Burkins heading down the aisle toward Sam, she knew he was in trouble. She reached over and slapped Sam hard across the cheek.

Sam bolted up and stared at her in shock. She darted her eyes in Burkins direction. Sam swallowed hard. He saw the angry look on Burkins' face. He knew he'd just screwed up. Burkins stopped behind Sam with his arms crossed. He focused on Sophia and shook his head.

"Gonzalez!"

"Sir, yes, Sir!"

"You think it's okay to let your boyfriend sleep on a critical life and death mission?"

"Sir, no, Sir!"

"Yet you did just that! You only woke up Loverboy when you saw me heading his way!"

"I apologize, Sir! It will never happen again!"

"You're damn right it won't! You don't understand what it means to be a team player yet, but you will! Report to the beach immediately. I mean all of you. Throw your plates away on your way out! Breakfast is over! You can all thank Gonzalez for cutting your meal time short!"

At the beach, Burkins ordered Sophia to stand in front of the other candidates while he yelled at her.

"You think you can save the world all by yourself?" Burkins yelled.

"Sir, no, Sir!"

"You think you are the only one affected by your actions?"

"Sir, no, Sir!"

"You think the rules don't apply to you and your boytoy, Cafferty?"

"Sir, no, Sir!"

"Pick up that toothpick and carry it down the beach! If you fail, the rest of these candidates fail with you! You think you can do it alone! So, do it alone! The rest of the class will stand here and watch you. If you fail to get that toothpick across the line, every candidate will be punished!"

Sophia swallowed hard.

"Turn around, and walk this line. Look every man in the eyes as you pass him. He is you. You are him. If you fail, he fails, and you will all skip lunch, and there will be absolutely no mercy on the O-course. You are responsible for their fate! Now move your ass, Gonzalez! You have a toothpick to get across the line!"

Sophia walked the line and looked every man in the eyes. She could see sympathy in some and anger in others. When she passed Cafferty, she saw a fresh tear roll down his cheek.

"I'm so sorry, Soph," he whispered.

She bit her lip and finished the line. Then she sprinted over to the toothpick and struggled against the weight of the 400-pound log. She managed to lift it a few inches off the sand, but it was too much for her. She dropped it, panting hard from her efforts. Her eyes scanned the 80 candidates assembled on the beach watching her. She bent over and tried again. The second time she raised it an extra two inches before dropping it.

"If you fail, they fail!" Burkins yelled at her back.

He turned and ordered all 80 men into the surf for torture. They sat arm in arm in the freezing water, watching her. Burkins walked back to Sophia and stood watching her with his arms crossed over his broad, muscled chest.

"They don't come out of that surf until you cross the line with that toothpick or until you ring the bell and quit, you worthless, loner!"

Sophia stood at attention, saluted Burkins with an angry glare and then walked to the far end of the toothpick. She got down on her knees and began digging in the sand, until the end of the log was completely exposed.

Then she crawled down into the shallow hole and wedged her body against the log. It took every ounce of her strength to move the end of the log two feet in a circular direction. It was now slightly angled from the goal.

Burkins smirked. "Is that all you got, Gonzalez? Your team is dying of hypothermia while you play with your big stick! Ring the bell, weakling!"

"I won't ring that bell, Sir!"

She looked back at the men in the surf, and her chest hurt. Then she looked back at her enemy, a 400-pound log, and anger rose up inside her. She dug out more sand and managed to move the log two more feet. After struggling in the sand, she managed to move the log a total of thirty feet. The goal was still 90 yards away. She looked back at the men in the surf and went right back to work.

"By the time you move this toothpick across the line your entire team will be dead from hypothermia. Is that what you want? Do you want to murder your whole team because of stubborn pride? Ring the damn bell!"

"I will never that ring the bell, Sir!"

"Is this what you call teamwork, Gonzalez? You're willing to sacrifice your entire team to complete the mission?" Burkins barked at her.

Sophia continued to dig as she began shouting her favorite part of the SEAL Creed. "I will never quit. I persevere and thrive on adversity. My Nation expects me to be physically harder and mentally stronger than my enemies. If knocked down, I will get back up, every time. I will draw on every remaining ounce of strength to protect my teammates and to accomplish our mission. I am never out of the fight."

Sam grinned when he heard her voice drifting over the sound of the surf. He let go of the men on either side of him and stood up. He started wading toward the shore.

Burkins turned to face Sam. "Cafferty if you step one foot on this beach you are washed out of BUD/S. There will be no second chance. Return to the surf, or go ring the bell!"

Sophia stopped digging, stood up, and yelled, "Sam, go back! It's not worth losing your chance. I got this! I'll get it across the line!"

"The human body can only take so much at this temperature. Soon these men are going to reach the critical phase. After that, they'll all be dead from hypothermia. That's all the time you have, Gonzalez! Are you going to sacrifice their lives to prove you're a badass? Get this toothpick across the line, or Cafferty will ring that bell, and so will you."

Sophia glared at Burkins. Then she ran over to the rope they had used to tether them together for the swim in the ocean. She cut a long length from the spool and ran back to the toothpick. Working quickly, she secured the rope to the giant log and tethered the other end around her waist. Then she started pulling as hard as she could. She managed to drag it a few feet before she had to stop and take a short breather. Then she pulled again. By the time she dragged it a third of the way, she was beginning to feel light-headed.

Burkins stood watch over the men in the surf, who were all glaring at him. Then an evil smirk crossed his lips.

"If she fails, you all fail. Your lives are in her hands. The mission is to get that toothpick across the line. Is this the soldier you want fighting next to you? Someone who puts her own ambition above your welfare? She refuses to ring the bell knowing that every minute she forces you to be in that water is another minute of hypothermia you have to endure for the sake of her pride! She's not a team player! She's a worthless woman, on a mission to prove that she's tougher than every one of you men. She doesn't care about you. She only cares about winning. She only cares about proving me wrong. She only cares about getting that log across the line."

Butch Simonis stood up in the surf and started walking toward the shore.

"Simonis! You step one foot on that shore and you, Cafferty, and Gonzalez wash out!"

Sophia turned and met Butch's gaze. "Don't do it, Simonis!"

Butch halted two feet from the beach and stood glaring at Burkins.

Sophia redoubled her efforts. It wasn't in her to quit. She would never give up, no matter what it cost her personally. She would finish the mission.

She started shouting the SEAL Creed again.

Then she heard 80 male voices rise in unison from the surf, all altering the SEAL Creed to acknowledge her. "She will never quit. She perseveres and thrives on adversity. Her Nation expects her to be physically harder and mentally stronger than her enemies. If knocked down, she will get back up, every time. She will draw on every remaining ounce of strength to protect her teammates and to accomplish our mission. She is never out of the fight."

Burkins glared at the candidates sitting in the water, arm in arm, enduring surf torture. He knew they had to be hypothermic, but not one of them were giving in to the pain. He looked back at Sophia who was struggling with everything she had to pull a log four times her weight down the beach to an arbitrary line in the sand.

After several more minutes of struggle, Sophia fell to her knees breathing hard. Burkins walked over to her with his hands on his hips and laughed.

"You fail, Gonzalez! You're still thirty yards from your goal! Give up now! Go ring the bell! You've blown the mission, and your entire team is dead! You're a loser! You're a murderer! You just killed every man on your team!"

All 80 men in the surf stood to their feet, arm in arm, and began shouting the SEAL creed.

Burkins glared at the men. Then he heard Sophia struggle to her feet and grunt as she began pulling against the log.

"You've already lost, Gonzalez. Your team is hypothermic. There's no saving them. They'll be dead before you complete this mission. Give up. Go ring the bell!"

"I will never ring that bell!" she shouted.

She began reciting the SEAL creed over and over until the entirety of the toothpick lay on the opposite side of the line.

Whooping and shouting came from the surf as 80 men sprinted to Sophia.

She received 80 of the coldest, wettest hugs of her entire life, and more than a few men planted a wet kiss on her lips.

"That was the most bad-ass thing I've ever seen in my entire life! Will you marry me?" Butch Simonis said in her ear, as he gave her a firm, wet, hug.

"I did not tell you men to get out of that surf!" Burkins yelled.

All 80 men turned and glared at Burkins. Then they obediently returned to the surf. Sophia went with them and sat down in the surf with her arms linked with Sam on one side and Butch on the other. Burkins crossed his arms over his chest and stood on the beach watching them.

Butch leaned in close to her. "I meant what I said. Just say yes."

Sophia grinned.

"Yes, to what?" Sam asked.

"To marrying me." Butch grinned.

"Get in line!" Sam glared at Butch. "If she marries anyone, it will be me!"

Sophia grimaced in pain as the cold surf pounded her back.

"You okay, Soph?" Sam asked concerned.

"They'll have to drag my cold, dead body out of here," she grunted.

Sam frowned. "You're hurt, aren't you?"

Butch frowned as he stared at her grimace of pain. "Yeah, she's hurt."

"I'm fine." She gritted her teeth and closed her eyes.

"Is it your back?" Sam asked.

"No, it's my whole body."

"What are you going to do?" Butch asked.

"I'm going to suck it up and push on. That's the SEAL way."

"I'm sorry. This is all my fault. If I hadn't fallen asleep—"

She shook her head. "No, Burkins is right. We are a team. I shouldn't have let you fall asleep."

"Burkins is an ass! He's just looking for an excuse to punish you for being the only woman to make it this far in BUD/S," Butch growled.

"Burkins is right. If we had been on a mission, letting a teammate fall asleep could mean death for the whole team. I shouldn't have felt sorry for him. I should have slapped his ass the moment he laid his head down on that table."

Sam grinned mischievously. "Damn! Slap my ass, huh? You're kinkier than I thought."

"Don't push me, Cafferty! I'm not in the mood right now!"

Sam leaned in and kissed her cheek. "Sorry, Honey. I'll try to be more sensitive."

Butch glared at Sam. "Don't kiss my future wife, Cafferty!"

"In your dreams, Simonis. She wouldn't marry you if—"

"Can you both shut the hell up!" Sophia snapped. "I'm in too much pain to listen to you two get into a bitch fight like two little girls!"

Butch and Sam both leaned in and kissed her on the cheek at the same time.

"Stop kissing me!"

Burkins watched the exchange from the edge of the beach. The waves lapped at his combat boots as he surveyed the 81 candidates in the water.

"Out of the water! Report to the mess hall immediately. Gonzalez bought you back your chow, but she lost hers.

Everyone stood up and walked to the beach arm in arm.

"Sir, respectfully! If Gonzalez doesn't eat, none of us eat!" Collie shouted.

A smile played at Burkins' mouth, but he squelched it. "So be it! Report to the O-course!"

They sprinted to the O-course where Reynolds was waiting to put them through the paces. They were all grateful for the physical exertion. All their extremities were numb; they were all hypothermic. Their biggest challenge was holding on to anything with numb fingers.

Dinner that night was eaten in silence. They all shoveled in their food as fast as they could. They all watched each other to make sure no one dozed off. No one wanted to risk any further punishment. By the time they were dismissed for the night they all felt weak and depleted.

Half an hour later Chapman sounded reveille, and they were assembled on the grinder for a midnight run. The rest of the night was spent doing a series of PT and O-course exercises.

At dawn five men rang the bell. The class was now 76 strong.

CHAPTER 17

December 18
0630
Coronado, California

Hell Week Day 4

The day started with carrying the toothpick. The five other men on Sophia's team insisted she be in the middle so they could carry most of the weight. They all felt bad that she'd had to move a toothpick by herself. Sophia didn't argue. Every muscle in her body felt like it was on fire, and she was a little light-headed from being dehydrated.

After carrying logs all morning, they ate lunch and reported to the pool. Bruchard was waiting to give them the good news. Today they would be practicing the Deadman Drag. They would alternate the role of the dead man and the rescuer. As if swimming laps weren't enough, they would now have to tug a man across the pool. Bruchard made sure to alternate partners after every lap so no one could anticipate what their partner would do.

Sophia was happy to be in the water. It took all the pressure off her spine, which was causing her some trouble. She found after pulling the log, it had become painful to put any weight down on her left leg. The pain would shoot up her leg and into her lower back with every step.

When it was Cafferty's turn to partner with Sophia, he walked over to her with a grin on his face. His grin soon turned to a frown when he saw her wince in pain as she stepped toward him. They waited for their turn in the water.

"You're really not okay."

"I'll survive."

"Is it your back?"

"My left leg and my low back."

"Need a massage?"

Sophia smirked. "Nice try, Cafferty."

"That wasn't a line. I was being sincere."

"I'm honestly not sure a massage would help. I think I pinched a nerve or severely strained a muscle. I can't tell. All I know is it hurts every time I put any weight on it."

Cafferty went down on his knees behind her and started working his hands up her left leg kneading the muscle. Bruchard gave him an accusing look.

"Leg cramp," Sam said.

Bruchard gave him a curt nod and refocused his attention on the men in the water. Sam worked his hands up to her lower back and continued all the way up to her neck.

"Any better?" he asked.

She took a step forward and grimaced. "It still hurts, but not quite as bad. Thank you, Sam."

"Anytime."

Then it was time for them to take a turn in the water. Sam played the rescuer with his hand firmly holding her chin above the water as he swam the length of the pool with powerful smooth strokes. They traded places and Sophia tugged him back. Then they switched partners. Several partners later Butch Simonis stepped up to her.

"I don't like seeing Cafferty's hands all over you like that," he murmured in her ear.

"Don't read into it. He was just trying to help."

"Yeah, I could tell," he said derisively.

"My back and leg have been hurting since the toothpick yesterday. I think I pulled something."

Before Sophia could protest, Butch's hands were on her neck and shoulders slowly working their way down her spine until he reached her ankle.

"Thanks, Simonis."

He stood up and put his hands on her bare shoulders. Then he leaned down to her ear. "You might as well start calling me Butch. It won't do for my wife to go around calling me Simonis."

Sophia pressed her lips together to suppress the chuckle. Then it was their turn in the pool. She had to admit that the massages did help some. Her pain had diminished a little.

After a full round of the Deadman Drag, Bruchard had them do multiple underwater exercises to test their lung capacity and ferret out any fear of the water that might have slipped by so far. He could see that all the men were severely fatigued, but it went with the territory. He'd been in plenty of situations himself where functioning under extreme sleep deprivation had been a necessary part of the mission. It was important to see who could handle the stress of it and who would wash out.

After dinner 10 men rang the bell taking the remaining candidates down to 66. The ringing of the bell was immediately followed by PT and a long, grueling surf torture. They were ordered to get sandy and line up on the beach.

Reynolds and Burkins took turns interrogating candidates as they stood shivering on the beach. The questions were extremely difficult and complicated for the state of hypothermia the candidates were in.

"What's your full name soldier?"

Sam stood shivering violently. "My-my n-name is S-Samuel N-Nolan C-Cafferty."

"What's your rank soldier?"

"S-Senior Chief P-Petty Officer, Sir!"

"Where were you born?"

"Th-The USA."

"Wake up soldier! What town were you born in?"

Sam didn't answer for a moment. He seemed confused by the question.

"What town soldier?"

"T-T-Topeka, Kansas, Sir!"

"How old are you?"

"26—no—27, Sir!"

"Which is it? Are you 26 or 27?"

"27, Sir! My birthday was yesterday."

The inane questions continued. By the time they came to Sophia she was struggling to endure not only the pain of her injury, but also the pain of hypothermia, and extreme sleep deprivation.

"When did you cross the border?"

The question threw her. Then her tired brain caught up to his rude, prejudiced jibe.

"I was born in Los Angeles, Sir!"

"What year did your parents illegally cross the border?"

Sophia's mouth turned down in a frown, but she wasn't going to let him goad her. She'd had to endure this sort of prejudice her entire life. It was nothing new to her.

"Sir, my parents came to the United States twenty-nine years ago. After which, they became legal citizens."

"I didn't ask you if they were legal! I asked what year! Stick to the questions you're asked!"

"Sir, yes, Sir!" she shouted respectfully.

"How many times have you been to Mexico?"

"Sir, I have never been outside the United States, except for my tour with the Marine Corp in GITMO, Sir! The only country I've served in was Cuba, Sir!"

Burkins smirked as he stared at Sophia.

"What makes you think you can be a SEAL? Doing a tour in Cuba doesn't prepare you for the life of a SEAL!"

Sophia's jaw tightened. "Sir, respectfully, I am committed to becoming a SEAL. I will do whatever is necessary to serve my country and my team. I'm here to train. I'm here to learn!"

Reynolds studied Sophia from a short distance. He hadn't asked her any questions yet. He wanted to observe how she handled Burkins intentional racial slurs and provocations. He wanted to see if she would lose her cool, her concentration, or her temper under pressure.

Burkins continued his interrogation. "What are you going to do when you are living all alone in a camp full of men and they come sniffing around you like a dog in heat?"

"I will perform my duty and remain professional, Sir!"

"I see you've got two on your little fishing line already. Cafferty and Simonis are already distracted by your hot little ass! How will you handle men like them when you're in the field?"

Sam and Butch both glared at Burkins.

"I have not thrown out a fishing line, Sir! My duty is to the Navy and the SEAL team I'm assigned to. I had no personal life during my time in the Marine Corp. I do not intend to have one in the Navy, Sir! I'm here to serve my country! I'm not here to find a husband!"

Burkins smirked. "Who said anything about a husband? What if one of these men just want a tryst with you in the supply building, or out in the field where they won't be caught?"

A low growl escaped Sophia. "I am not here to have relations with any man for any reason at any time. I'm here to serve my country! That is all I'm focused on, Sir!"

"You'll be in the field alone with a whole team of men. What if one of them rape you?"

"The Uniform Code of Military Justice would have to prevail if that happened, Sir! I expect the men I serve with to give me the same respect I give them. If they infract the rules of conduct, then they will be the one's paying the price for their actions, Sir! I leave justice in the hands of the legal system. I'm not here to be judge and jury. I'm here to be a SEAL. I'm here to protect and serve my country to my dying breath, Sir!"

Burkins opened his mouth to ask her another question, but Reynolds shook his head. Burkins nodded respectfully to Reynolds and took a step back. Reynolds stepped in front of her.

"What's your favorite color, Gonzalez?"

A slight smile turned her lips up. "Red, white, and blue, Sir!"

"Who's your favorite actor?"

"I don't have a favorite. I don't have time for television. I'm too busy doing push-ups, Sir!"

Reynolds' lip turned up. "What's your favorite song?"

"I have two favorites, Sir! The Star Spangled Banner and America the Beautiful."

"Those sound like rehearsed answers."

"Sir, no, Sir!"

"Who is your favorite, Sam Cafferty or Butch Simonis?"

Sophia looked Reynolds directly in the eyes and shouted respectfully, "I don't have a favorite, Sir! All SEALs are equal in my eyes. I respect each man here with equal measure."

"These men aren't SEALs yet. Don't bestow titles on them that haven't been earned."

"Sir, yes, Sir!"

Reynolds continued questioning her. Then he moved on. When he came to Butch, he smirked.

"I hear you asked Gonzalez to marry you!"

"Sir, yes, Sir!" Butch shouted as his body trembled from the cold.

"Are you in love with Gonzalez?"

"Sir, yes, Sir!"

"What would you do if ordered to send Gonzalez into a firefight that could get her killed?"

Butch stood shivering as he contemplated the question.

"Answer me, Soldier!"

"I would do my duty, Sir!"

"Would you? You took a long time thinking about that answer!"

"We are all here to serve, Sir! If Gonzalez ordered me into a life-threatening situation, I would not hesitate. That's what we signed up for, Sir! If I had to order her into the same, I would expect her to act without hesitation as well."

"That's a very diplomatic answer, Simonis. What would you do if you witnessed Gonzalez being sexually harassed by other men in the field?"

"I would put a stop to it and report them to the appropriate chain of command, Sir!"

"Has Gonzalez accepted your proposal of marriage?"

"Not yet, Sir!"

Reynolds smirked. "Do you think she will?"

"I don't know, Sir!"

"What if she doesn't and you see her flirting with or displaying affection toward another man? How will that affect your mindset in the field?"

"If she says no, I'll accept her answer, and it won't affect my performance of my duties, Sir!"

"Gonzalez announced earlier that she does not intend to pursue any personal relationships. She said her first love is the Navy. How did that make you feel?"

Simonis grinned. "Like we have a lot in common. The Navy is my first love too."

"What is your rank, Soldier?"

"Petty Officer First Class."

Burkins stepped in with more questions until all 66 candidates had been questioned.

They were ordered back into the surf for more torture. Then they ran the O-course until dawn.

Hell Week Day 5

At dawn they were ordered back to the beach for surf torture. Then they were ordered to get sandy and line up on the beach.

Reynolds walked the line studying each man. Then he stood in front and addressed the group.

"How many of you men have thought about ringing the bell?"

The only sound on the beach was the breeze.

"How many are afraid to ring the bell because you don't want to get shown up by a woman?"

Again, silence reigned on the beach.

"I have news for all of you. She's already shown you up. If you want to be as bad-ass as Gonzalez, tie yourself to a toothpick, and drag it across the line! That's your next mission! If you can't handle the toothpick, then take your ass to the bell, and ring the sucker! You can get a shower, breakfast, and go back to regular Navy. The rest of you have a log to pull. Get started!"

Grumbling could be heard from some of the men in the line, but no one stepped out of line to go ring the bell. Six men at a time were tethered to a toothpick and sent on the 100-yard drag.

Reynolds stepped up to Sophia who had gotten in line with the rest of the men.

"Gonzalez! You already completed that mission. Your mission today is to sit in the surf for as long as it takes every one of these men to drag their toothpick to the finish line."

"Sir, yes, Sir!" She saluted Reynolds and sprinted to the ocean.

She sat in the frigid water shivering. She knew she would get a taste of what she'd put the other men through, but she was grateful not to be dragging a toothpick today.

The first six men managed to get their toothpicks across the line with extreme effort. Six more men were tethered to those toothpicks and required to drag them back. Reynolds was yelling at the men the entire time.

"How does it feel to be a loner? You like getting all the glory? You like carrying the full burden alone? You don't need your team! You can do it all by yourself! You're a bad-ass!"

Every time one of the men stumbled and fell from the weight of the toothpick, Reynolds was there in his face taunting. Every man managed to get his toothpick across the line, but Reynolds wasn't done with them yet.

"That's great! You've all proven what bad-ass loners you are. Unfortunately, Gonzalez's mission isn't over yet. She's required to sit in that surf today for the same amount of time you did and watch you struggle alone like she did. This time twelve of you line up, and each of you pull a log. You will take turns dragging them across the line until I tell you to stop! Are we clear?"

"Sir, yes, Sir!"

The candidates were all exhausted, but they were made to endure extreme physical exertion to prove the point and drive it home. Sophia sat in the surf shivering violently. She watched as the men stumbled and fell while pulling their enemy, the log, through the loose sand of the beach.

"You men having fun yet?" Burkins barked.

"Sir, yes, Sir!"

"Do you think once you pass today it's going to get easier than this?"

"Sir, no, Sir!"

"You're damn right it's not! The few of you who survive today will know what real torture and hardship are in the next phase of your training. If you don't like today, you'll hate tomorrow and every day that comes after it. I know some of you are thinking, if I can just make it through today,

Hell Week will be behind me, and it will all be easier after this. You're wrong. It doesn't get easier! It gets harder. If your only goal is to make it through today than you might as well quit now and go ring the bell. A nice cold shower and a hot meal are waiting for anyone who wants to quit now. What's waiting, for those of you who make it through the toothpick this morning, is no food and no rest. You'll go straight to the next mission of the day. Hell Week isn't over. Hell Week is never over. If you are a SEAL, Hell Week is every day!"

One of the men pulling a log stopped in his tracks and sank to his knees.

"You quitting, Son? You're not as much of a bad-ass as you thought!" Burkins taunted.

He stood up, and grunting he strained against the rope. He managed to pull the log another ten feet before he sank to his knees again.

"I bet you wish you had a team behind you to help with this burden!" Burkins yelled.

"Sir, yes, Sir!" he yelled as his hands planted in the hot sand.

"Who thinks Sallisaw should get some help?" Burkins yelled.

"Sir, yes, Sir!" several of the men shouted.

"Too bad! You men don't know the meaning of the word teamwork! You all think you're so tough! If you can't pull your log, go ring the damn bell, and get out of the way!"

Sallisaw gritted his teeth and struggled back to his feet. He strained against the weight of the log and managed to move it another three feet before sinking back to his knees.

"Give it up, Sallisaw!" Burkins taunted. "You're a pathetic weakling! Gonzalez is a better soldier than you!"

Sallisaw struggled back to his feet and looked a Burkins with a glare in his dark brown eyes. "She only had to drag it once! I know what you're doing! I won't ring that bell!"

"We are not passing 66 candidates into the SEAL program!" Reynolds shouted. "This is not a psychological game. This is the real deal! If you don't like punishment and torture than you are not SEAL material. Burkins was telling the truth. Hell Week is not the worst you'll endure in SEAL training. It's a vacation compared to the next phase! If you pass the next phase, it only gets worse from there. You'll be tested mentally, physically, emotionally, and made to endure the worst moments of your life. If you get assigned to a team, it will get worse. You'll be treated with the respect you deserve which is zero. You'll be puke on the bottom of your SEAL team's boots. You'll have to earn your way slowly up the ladder to earn any measure of respect from your team. Get used to being mistreated and abused. It's the life of a SEAL."

Sallisaw grunted as he pulled against the rope. The other eleven men pulled their logs across the line ahead of him, and he still had thirty yards to go when a new set of eleven men started pulling logs in the opposite direction. As Simonis reached Sallisaw with his log he looked over and stopped. He grabbed Sallisaw's wrist and met his eyes.

"Keep going, Jim. You can do it," Butch said. "Don't give in. The team is depending on you. Gonzalez is depending on you. Don't let her down. She didn't let us down yesterday."

Jim nodded and kept pulling.

Butch got his log across and looked back. Jim was ten feet from the finish line, but he was on his hands and knees panting hard. Butch walked back to Jim, pulled his arm over his shoulders, and helped him to his feet. Then he unhooked Jim from the log and fastened it to his own waist. Jim grimaced. Butch grinned at him. Then pulling the log with Jim's arm around his shoulders, they both crossed the line and handed the log off to the next man.

Reynolds walked over to Jim and Butch. "Did I say you could help him?"

Butch shook his head. "No, Sir!"

"Then why did you pull his log for him? Why not let him wash out and ring the bell?"

"Sallisaw is part of the team sir! If he fails, I fail, we all fail!"

Reynolds suppressed the grin and nodded curtly at Butch.

When the other men heard the exchange, they all grinned at each other. From then on, they formed teams of six men per log to pull it across the line. They did their work chanting, "If he fails, we all fail."

Reynolds and Burkins watched with suppressed grins.

"Took them long enough to figure that out, this group seems to be a little slow to catch on," Burkins said quietly.

"Let's see if it translates past the toothpicks," Reynolds said.

By the time Reynolds ordered them to stop pulling toothpicks not one man was standing. The last men who crossed the line did so on their hands and knees.

"Get up! It's time for more hell!" Burkins yelled.

All the men struggled to their feet.

"Line up on the beach!"

They all lined up.

"Gonzalez! Out of the water and line up!" Burkins yelled.

Sophia struggled to her feet and forced her legs to take one step and then another. She was shivering violently. She'd barely heard the order to get out of the water. Her mind was beginning to shut down. When she reached the line, Burkins ordered her to stand directly in front of him. Her teeth were chattering, and her whole body was shaking from extreme hypothermia.

"You ready to ring the bell?" Burkins yelled in her face.

"S-S-Sir, n-n-no, S-S-Sir," she mumbled softly.

"I can't hear you!"

"S-S-Sir, n-n-no, S-S-Sir!"

"What's your name, Soldier?"

Sophia stared at him blankly in a hypothermic daze.

"I said, what's your name, Soldier?"

"I-I-I—" She trailed off staring at the sand.

"Answer the question or ring the bell!"

The men behind her watched her shivering violently. They knew exactly what she was going through. They'd endured the same hypothermic torture. Several of the men closest to her stepped up and pressed their hot, sand-coated bodies against her.

"You can do it, Sophia," Collie said encouragingly, as he wrapped his arms around her shivering body.

Burkins smirked. "What's your name?"

"S-S-Sophia M-M-Maria L-L-Louisa Ar-Ar-Armanda G-G-Gonzalez"

"What time is it?"

"I—d-don't kn-know."

"Tell me the time, Soldier, or ring the bell!"

Sophia stared blankly at Burkins.

"Look at your watch, Soph," Sam said, as he reached down and pulled her arm up.

Sophia looked down at her watch and tried to focus on it. Sam held her arm still, but her head was still jerking, making it hard to see the watch.

"1300, Sir!" she managed to chatter out.

"Do you men think Gonzalez is a bad-ass now? She can't even tell me the time without help. Take her up to the bell so she can ring it!"

"Sir, no, Sir!" the men shouted. "Gonzalez is part of the team. If she fails, we fail!"

Burkins asked her a series of inane questions that she had a very difficult time answering. She was doing her best to focus, but her mind just wouldn't engage. Everything seemed unfocused and far away. She honestly felt like she was going to pass out.

Then she did.

Butch caught her as she slid down inside the circle of sand-coated men.

"Take her to medical! She just washed out!" Burkins yelled.

"Sir, she's just hypothermic. We can get her back," Collie said.

"She could die. Do you honestly want her death on your hands?" Reynolds asked.

"Sir, Gonzalez said she'd rather have her dead carcass dragged out of BUD/S than ring that bell!" Sam said. "We'll get her back!"

Butch began stripping her out of her wet uniform. Once she was stripped down to her bra and panties several of the men knelt around her gently rubbing her limbs to restore circulation.

Sophia woke to the sight of Collie staring down into her eyes. It took her a moment to realize that he was shirtless. He was lying on top of her on the hot, sandy beach.

"Welcome back. You ready for more hell?" Collie asked.

"Wh-What happened?" she mumbled.

"You passed out from hypothermic shock," Butch said, as he gently ran his hand over her short, black burr. "You okay?"

"Yeah," she mumbled.

Collie winked at her. "We've been taking turns warming you up."

Collie got up off her, and offered her a hand up. That's when she realized she was stripped completely down to her undergarments. She quickly redressed with 65 candidates and all the BUD/S instructors watching her.

"You ready to ring the bell now?" Burkins asked.

"Sir, I will never ring that bell!" Sophia said.

"Any of the rest of you men ready to ring the bell?" Burkins barked.

"We will never ring that bell!" all the candidates said in unison.

"Report to the O-course! Your Hell Week has only begun!" Reynolds shouted.

December 20
0600
Coronado, California

At dawn, the candidates stood on the beach in front of Reynolds and the rest of the BUD/S instructors.

Reynolds addressed the group. "Look around at the other candidates standing here. Three weeks ago, 217 men were issued identical uniforms, identical boots, identical helmets, and identical equipment. 170 men rang the bell. You 47 are all that's left standing.

Monday you start your next phase of training, and it will be a bitch! If you thought Hell Week was bad, you'll wish you were back in Hell Week. It only gets harder from here. Physical skills are not enough; they only equal ten percent of the equation. Your mind and your will control ninety percent of your reality. Your BUD/S instructors are preparing you for what you will face in the field physically, mentally, and emotionally. To know exactly what you are capable of, you must stretch to your breaking point. Only then will you know the true limits of your potential. You can overcome any obstacle if your determination is strong enough. How far are you willing to stretch yourself before you tap out and ring the bell? If you have what it takes to make it through all the phases of SEAL training, you will be welcomed into the brotherhood and receive your trident. Wear it with pride knowing you have earned it."

Reynolds walked the line and shook every SEAL candidate's hand. Then he addressed the group.

"Gentlemen! Hell Week is secured!"

Everyone yelled in unison, "Hoo-Yah!"

A short celebration of whooping commenced. Then every candidate made sure they shook every BUD/S instructor's hand and thanked him for putting them through the paces to become a SEAL.

CHAPTER 18

December 21
0630
Strip mine in Katanga province

Sonny lay still on the western ridge of another massive strip mine. He surveyed the area with his binoculars. Dawn had broken the horizon, but there was no immediate need for him to change positions. From what he was witnessing, the men in charge of this strip mine had more urgent business than scanning for possible spies.

They were too busy whipping the child labor to notice a team of SEALs infiltrating their space. With every lash of the whip, Sonny's eye twitched. He wanted to aim his sniper rifle and pop the brute in the back of the skull, but he'd been ordered to observe. Observing children being abused did not sit well with Sonny. In truth, watching children working like dogs at the previous three mines hadn't set well with Sonny.

Damnit! A child should be allowed to be a child. They should be playing, going to school, and learning, not working til they drop and being beaten for not being able to carry the workload of an adult! I really hate this assignment! I just want to—fix this! I wish I could fix everything that's wrong here. Their economy is busted. Their electric lines are mostly inoperable. There's rampant disease and practically no medical care. They are starving and working for pennies. Watching this and not being able to do anything about it is giving me an ulcer! Even if we capture or kill Negassi, it won't solve the real problems here in Congo. These people need so much. I wish I could—I swear if I had a magic lamp—my first wish would be to make things better for all the poor and suffering people on the Earth. There are so many, everywhere.

Below, in the strip mine, Nick and John had crept up to the massive earth movers before dawn. Nick was recording the children being beaten and whipped. John was standing watch.

"Echo 1 to Echo 2," Fry said.

"Echo 2, go for Echo 1," John whispered.

"Get whatever video you can and fall back to the ridge when it's clear."

"Roger that."

"Echo 1 to Echo 15"

"Echo 15, go for Echo 1," Porter Prescott said quietly.

Porter and Ezra Lombard were positioned behind the small wooden shack near the entrance of the mine.

"Have you infiltrated the shack?" Fry asked.

Porter grimaced. "Negative. There is too much traffic. We are holding position until the trucks move out. This mine is not like the others. It is well guarded, and the guards are well armed."

"Yes, and they patrol around the clock. Maybe the chaos of the workday will mask our presence here," Fry said.

"Overwatch here," Sonny interrupted. "That's a negative on masking our presence. Echo 15, you have two bogeys headed your way. Suggest you find better cover ASAP."

Sonny positioned his sniper riffle to follow the two guards. They were armed with AK47 rifles, hand guns, and grenades. Whoever owned this mine wanted their investment protected. Sonny had spotted a stack of wooden crates near one of the trucks just before dawn. Rob Dover had confirmed that the crates were loaded with surface-to-air Stinger missiles; he counted a total of thirty-eight. This operation was full of surprises. Stinger missiles meant no air strike.

So far, the SEAL presence had gone unnoticed, but that was about to change.

"Echo 15 to Echo 1, advise on action regarding bogeys coming our way," Porter said, as he and Ezra crawled under the shack and secured the plywood skirt around the foundation of the small wooden building.

"Echo 1 to Echo 15, you are out of sight. Hold position for now," Fry said.

The two bogeys made their watch rounds and headed back down into the mine.

"Echo 1 to Echo 15, you are clear to investigate the shack," Fry said.

"Going in from below," Porter confirmed.

He and Ezra carefully removed one section of planks in the middle and Porter hoisted himself up onto the wood floor. It was dark in the small square space. The only light filtered in through the cracks in the planks of the outer walls. Porter flipped his night-vision goggles down and surveyed the small space.

"Echo 15 to Echo 1, the shack does not house ammo or valuables. The only thing in here is dried blood on the floor and manacles anchored to the wall. I don't like the looks of this, Sir." Porter said.

"Copy that," Fry said. "Record it all and get out of there before you're discovered."

"Roger that."

Porter scanned the small room with his camera and crawled back under the shack. Ezra secured the planks back in place. Then he muted his comlink and looked at Porter.

"You know what this shack is," Ezra said quietly.

Porter muted his coms and nodded. "What are we going to do about it?"

"Whatever we have to. I won't stand by and allow these sick bastards to hurt one more child. I'll burn this whole place to the ground before any of them have a chance to blink," Ezra growled angrily.

"Shouldn't we coordinate with Echo 1?"

Ezra didn't answer. He lay on the dirt thinking. "How far away are those crates of Stingers?"

Porter's eyebrow rose. "Two klicks west. Why?"

Ezra grinned. "I haven't blown anything up in a while. My trigger finger is feeling itchy."

Porter nodded. "What are you planning to blow up?"

"Every damn thing here. How many trucks and earth movers did you count?"

"Ten trucks and five earth movers."

Ezra unmuted his com and contacted Fry with his plan. Fry wasn't opposed to the plan, but he ordered Ezra to stand down until they could coordinate a strike after dark. He'd seen enough already to know that every man working at that camp deserved death. He'd witnessed nothing but abuse to the children from the moment he'd arrived.

When darkness fell, the SEALs quietly took out the guards one by one. Then they freed the children from the work camp. Once the children were clear of the strip mine, the SEALs used the Stingers to blow up every piece of equipment there. Fry was going to call for an extraction for the children, but the SEALs soon discovered that the children were long gone.

"They probably headed back to their home villages," Dorian Axel said.

The SEALs tried to scan the area with night-vision, but there was no sign of any child. They had all disappeared without a trace.

"What now, Chief?" Ben Obasi asked.

"We move on to the next mine. Negassi wasn't here, but maybe we'll get his attention when he realizes his mining operation is blown to hell," Fry said.

CHAPTER 19

December 22
0600
Coronado, California

At dawn the SEAL candidates ate breakfast and assembled for further instructions. Reynolds addressed them.

"You have just completed the first three weeks of BUD/S. This is a six-month training course that will put you through hell. We will train you in six stages.

Stage 1 will test your mental capacity. You will spend time in the classroom learning about what your body can handle. You will learn the Core Values of the Navy. You will learn ORM (Operational Risk Management). You will learn what it means to become a Navy SEAL.

Stage 2 is NSWO (Naval Special Warfare Orientation). If you don't know what that means, you will soon enough.

Stage 3 is Basic Conditioning. Physical training, water competency, mental tenacity, and teamwork are the fundamentals of this stage. You will learn the value and necessity of teamwork.

Stage 4 will bring you up to proficiency in Combat Diving. You will learn the difference between Open Diving and Closed-circuit Diving. You will become experts in both!

Stage 5 you will be trained in Land Warfare. You will become proficient in basic weapons, demolitions, land navigation, patrolling, rappelling, marksmanship, and small unit tactics. If you prove yourself worthy, you will go to the Island to complete your training in a real-world environment.

The safety net will be off, boys! It gets serious from here on.

Stage 6 is learning core tactical knowledge necessary to join a SEAL platoon. If you do not pass every phase of your training, you will not be joining a platoon. Only the best of the best get sent to the field.

To pass this final phase you must prove yourself in SQT (SEAL Qualification Training). That's weapons, small unit tactics, land navigation, demolitions, cold weather survival, medical proficiency, and maritime operations.

You must also prove yourself in SERE (Survival, Evasion, Resistance, and Escape).

Last but not least, you must prove yourself in Static-line parachuting and Freefall parachuting ops. In Freefall you must successfully perform HALO (High Altitude Low Opening) and HAHO (High Altitude High Opening) jumps.

If you fail even one of these tests, you will not become a SEAL. You will not receive your trident. You will wash out and go back to regular Navy to finish out your contracts.

Are there any questions?"

Butch raised his hand. "Sir, what are we waiting for? When do we start?"

At lunch Butch sat next to Sophia. "Have you thought about my proposal?"

A shy grin parted her lips, and her cheeks turned pink. He leaned in and closed his eyes. Images of her in the shower with water shimmering over her naked body flooded his mind. His fingers dug firmly into the camo fabric covering his thigh as he fought urges that threatened to overwhelm him. He'd never felt so desperate about a woman before. It took him more than a moment to get control.

From across the cafeteria, Sam could see Butch leaning in far too close to Sophia. His gut twisted into a knot. He sat down across from Sophia and glared at Butch. Then he noticed the blush in her cheeks. The knot in his gut twisted tighter.

"What did I miss?"

Reluctantly, Butch pulled back from Sophia and glared at Sam. "It's private."Sophia dropped her eyes to her plate and started shoveling in food. She did not wish to get in the middle of an argument between Sam and Butch.

CHAPTER 20

January 4
0800
Katanga province

Echo rendezvoused with a U.N. chopper on the savannah to pick up more supplies. To their surprise, Rowen was onboard. He hopped down and met them twenty yards from the chopper.

"Things have gotten dicey back at base," Rowen said.

"What's going on?" Fry asked.

"The upper echelons of power are pushing for Negassi's assassination. They want him taken out of the picture immediately."

"That's great, except no one knows where he is," John chimed in.

Rowen produced a file from his jacket. "The latest satellite footage shows his base camp here."

John and Fry studied the satellite image for a few minutes.

"This camp looks like it's been there for a while," Fry said. "Look at the deep-rutted tire tracks leading up to the camp. That dirt road looks well-traveled.

"Why are we only now seeing these satellite images? Why wasn't this camp investigated by a U.N. team months ago?" John asked.

Rowen frowned. "I'm not so sure it wasn't. The entire time we've been in Congo our chain of command has had us running around wiping out random groups of guerillas claiming they were part of Negassi's army. They've repeatedly stated that taking out Negassi would leave these guerillas with no funding and no leadership. They've been adamant about us finding and eliminating Negassi, but he mysteriously managed to evade satellite detection and spies on the ground searching the forest. Now suddenly, this image shows up, and the recon team claims it is Negassi's base camp."

Sonny crossed his arms over his muscular chest. "That's just damn fishy."

"Agreed," Rowen muttered. "Per our chain of command, this ISR (Intelligence, Surveillance, and Reconnaissance) indicates that we should strike this camp in two days to wipe out Negassi and his entire army."

Fry chewed on his lip. "Is that your order, Sir?"

Rowen let out a frustrated breath. "I'll be honest. I don't know what the real agenda here is, and I don't know who is trustworthy anymore. It seems like everyone in Congo is playing multiple sides with multiple agendas."

Fry nodded. "The footage we got at the last mine is pretty incriminating, and it fits with what we've been told about Negassi, but there's no hard evidence those men were actually working for Negassi."

Rowen dragged his hand over his dark brown burr. "Per Loredo, your current order is to assassinate Negassi and end the revolution, but it feels like our SEAL teams are being manipulated and used as a tool for some unidentified purpose."

Fry grimaced. "What does our U.S. command say?"

"On the unsecured, unreliable communications available in Kananga, our U.S. command says to cooperate with our U.N. chain of command to end the revolution," Rowen said.

"What about Delta? Will they be joining us on this mission?" Fry asked.

Rowen shook his head. "Loredo still has them investigating mines down here."

Fry nodded. "I see. In other words, if this goes south, Echo will be the scapegoat."

Rowen nodded. "The U.N. sees us as expendable, boys. Let's prove to them why we are not."

"So, exactly what are our orders, Sir?" Fry asked.

"Your official order from General Loredo is to assassinate Negassi and his militants at this camp immediately. Just watch your backs. Don't let this go sideways on you."

"Are you here to give us a ride to the strike point?" Sonny asked.

Rowen looked over his shoulder at the U.N. soldiers unloading supplies for the SEALs. "This U.N. chopper has other assignments. I just hitched a ride, so we could talk in private."

Rowen walked back to the chopper, got on, and it disappeared into the thunderhead rolling in.

"Let's secure the supplies and head out," Fry ordered.

"What are we going to do?" John asked.

Fry sighed. "We are going to do the right thing."

Echo packed up the spare ammo and MREs and headed north.

Sonny jogged up to Fry, who had taken the lead. "Don't you think it's a little odd that the U.N. has enough ammo on one of those choppers to take out Negassi's entire camp?"

"What's your point?" Fry asked.

"So, why don't they just fly in there and wipe out his whole army? Why are they sending us on foot to a camp that's been there for at least a year? Do we even have enough ammo to take out his entire army?"

Fry let out a frustrated sigh. "Are you second guessing our orders?"

"Hell, yeah, I'm second guessing!"

"Join the club."

Sonny frowned. "So, what's the real plan, Chief?"

"I'm still working on it, Sonny."

January 6
0130
Mitumba Mountain Range

Echo reached the camp specified on the satellite image. Three of the trucks were there. The tracking devices were still active. Fry found it highly suspicious that the trackers were not what the U.N. used to find the camp. A convenient satellite photo was the evidence they'd presented. He didn't like the way this mission was being laid out before them. It smelled rotten to its core.

After doing recon of the area, it was obvious this camp had been around for quite some time. There was even a grave yard on the east end of the camp. The small huts built from the surrounding forest had not been erected overnight; they all showed signs of weathering. Before the SEALs finished recon, the other two trucks pulled into camp, and young boys in tattered uniforms piled out of the back looking weary.

With the stealth of a cat, Sonny took up a post in one of the trees to do surveillance. He'd been studying up on Swahili and Lingala in his spare time. He was getting fairly proficient at both languages, and the only orders he heard Negassi giving his men involved humanitarian aid to the mountain villages. After tracking the trucks from Kalemie, it had become obvious to the SEALs that Negassi and the Red Cross were working hand in hand to subvert the spread of disease in the mountain villages. From the look of the rag-tag army in this camp they were not well funded, and Sonny noted several among them who were showing signs of the same sleeping sickness that plagued the mountain villages.

He wondered who was backing this army with weapons, fuel, and food. Their weapons were meager. They ate the same rice and beans that they handed out to the villages. They had enough fuel stored in the trucks to get them to Kalemie, but not enough to launch any sort of attacks on mountain villages. Their uniforms had all seen better days. This group was not like the other guerillas the SEALs had taken out in previous months. This was not a force to be reckoned with. These soldiers, if they qualified as such, seemed more like a desperate group of half-starved boys. Nothing about them seemed threatening or dangerous.

When the small army took an afternoon rest inside the shade of the small, primitive huts, Sonny climbed down from the tree and crept over to where John lay in the woods watching the camp for any signs of aggression.

"We're bein' set up," Sonny said quietly.

John nodded.

"This ain't no army, and it sure as hell ain't no revolution. Half them rifles are so dirty I doubt they'd even fire. These kids don't know how to handle or take care of a weapon. Negassi don't strike me as the all-powerful, dictating ruler type. He ain't runnin' no revolution here. These boys are halfway down the road to starvation. How much you want to bet that graveyard on the east end of camp is full of victims of sleeping sickness from them damn flies. Hell, these boys probably contracted it while trying to stop it from killin' all them villagers," Sonny drawled.

"Yeah, I see it," John agreed.

"All that video we took of these boys administering aid conveniently disappeared. Then boom! We get orders to take them all out. I don't think that mine belonged to Negassi. If he was skimming that kind of profit from a mine, that man would have money to feed this army and weaponize them better. Shoot! Negassi is walkin' around in rags like the rest of these boys."

John nodded. "This definitely smacks of a coverup, and we are the scapegoats. There's no doubt about that."

"Who do you think owns that strip mine we blew to hell?" Sonny whispered.

John shrugged. "We only blew up the equipment. Whoever owns it will have new equipment and new men with better training and better weapons by the end of the month. We only delayed their operation."

They fell silent for a few minutes.

John let out a long breath. "What's bothering me is how quickly the order to assassinate Negassi came after we blew up that mining operation. Maybe, whoever owns the mine wants us out of the country. Our reason for being here was to locate and eliminate Negassi's threat. We've been here for a long time with no direction as to where Negassi was hiding. Now, his location is suddenly dropped in our lap out of nowhere. I don't think Negassi is a revolutionist like they claim. I think something else is going on here. Negassi would make a pretty good scapegoat to blame things on if you were trying to cover up something big. I don't like the way this picture is being painted. Something is very wrong here, and we are being kept in the dark."

Sonny nodded. "What we need is intel. We need to find out the truth."

"Agreed," Fry said over the coms. "You two maintain surveillance. I'm going to take the rest of Echo and come up with a plan. Rendezvous with the rest of Echo at the rally point at sundown."

"Roger that," John said into his coms.

At dusk, Sonny and John rendezvoused with the rest of Echo east of Negassi's camp.

"What's the plan?" Sonny asked.

Fry quickly filled them in on his plan as darkness fell in the woods.

January 6
2300
Negassi's camp

Lydell Fry and Nick Novak crept into Negassi's camp. The trucks were lined up at the edge of camp ready to depart the following morning on their next mission of mercy. The soldiers were all sleeping in the primitive huts. Sonny had Overwatch, but there wasn't much to watch. The rest of Echo had surrounded the small camp awaiting further orders from Fry.

Nick entered Negassi's small hut just after Fry. They surprised Negassi in his sleep.

"Don't alert your army!" Fry warned.

"My army?" Negassi sat up on his woven mat on the dirt floor and stared blankly at Lydell.

"Your men." Fry stared back.

"My volunteers. We are no army. We are here to administer medical aid to those in need."

"All your volunteers are carrying rifles."

"For protection," Negassi sighed wearily. "We have been attacked before. Our medical supplies and food were stolen. My boys only carry weapons to defend themselves."

"How many other camps are you running?"

"None. This is our only camp," Negassi insisted.

Fry nodded and holstered his handgun. "We need to talk."

Negassi frowned first at Fry and then at Nick. "We have nothing here of value. If you are here to rob us, there is nothing to steal."

Fry shook his head. "We are not here to steal anything."

"I do not understand."

"Who funds your operation?"

"Techno Corp funds our humanitarian aid."

Fry nodded. "What about the Red Cross? Do you work directly with them?"

Negassi shook his head. "Techno Corp set up a weekly drop in Kalemie. We pick up the supplies and fuel and distribute it to as many villages as we can."

"Who is your contact with Techno Corp?"

"John Smith."

Fry frowned. "How do you contact him?"

"I don't. I only met with him once. That was almost two years ago. He gave me the instructions on when and where to pick up supplies. I have not had any contact with him since."

"Are you aware that the Congolese government has labeled you a radical revolutionist?"

Negassi laughed. "Me a revolutionist? No."

"Our SEAL unit was brought in by the United Nations in a joint effort to subvert your attempts to overthrow the government. We're authorized to use lethal force to stop you from kidnapping and forcing small children to join your army and work in your mine to fund your rebel regime."

Negassi's expression grew grim, and panic showed plainly on his face. "I am only here to prevent the spread of disease. My boys are not an army. They only wish to help their countrymen in need. I force no one to join us, and I know nothing about a mining operation."

"The U.N. and the Congolese government have ordered us to assassinate you. They perceive you as a threat. They want you taken out."

Negassi buried his head against his knees. "I am nobody. Why would they want me dead?"

"How did you first make contact with John Smith at Techno Corp?"

"I used to live in Kinshasa. I worked in the hospital there. I saw so much suffering and death. I just wanted to do something about it. First, I tried to talk to anyone in the government, but no one seemed to care about the problem. So, I set up a website to accept donations. A few months later, John Smith contacted me. Techno Corp gave me five trucks, and they provide food, medical supplies, fuel, and the occasional crate of uniforms or ammo for the rifles. Their support has been steady; they are never late with a shipment."

"Why would your government paint you as a revolutionary and have you assassinated?"

Negassi shook his head. "I have done nothing to provoke such a response. There is much unrest in Congo. We have been through civil war, and our economy has suffered greatly. Most people eke out a simple existence here. I have never sought political power. I simply want to stop the spread of disease. I have no other agenda."

Fry nodded. "I hate to say this, but I believe you are being targeted as a scapegoat for something much bigger. This all smacks of a coverup. From what we've witnessed, we don't believe the reports that you are a revolutionary. If you trust us, we will try to save your life."

Negassi nodded his head with a weary sigh. "What is to become of my boys?"

"Can they return to their villages?"

Negassi shook his head. "Most of these boys have lost their entire family to disease. Some are very sick. I cannot abandon them."

Fry nodded. "If this camp remains occupied, the U.N. will destroy it. Our orders are to destroy it. If we fail in that mission, they will send someone else to do it. You can't stay here. You have to leave. Everyone here must leave. We have a plan. You have to trust us and do exactly as we tell you."

January 6
0530
Negassi's camp

Just before dawn broke the horizon, Negassi instructed his ragtag group of volunteers to load up the boys who had fallen ill onto the first truck. Then the remaining boys crowded into the second truck. Negassi climbed in the cab of the first truck, and within minutes the entire camp was abandoned.

Fry ordered his team to detonate the explosives once the trucks were a safe distance away. Then Echo rendezvoused with the trucks a klick north of the decimated camp. Echo climbed in the back with the boys, and they headed northeast.

It took two days to reach Lake Tanganyika by truck. Under the cover of night, Echo procured a boat and transported Negassi and his boys across the lake to Bujumbura, the capital and main port of Congo's neighboring country, Burundi.

Fry and Nick took the sick boys to the hospital to be treated immediately. John and the rest of Echo took Negassi and the remaining boys to secure an apartment. Negassi was given a new identity, curtesy of Echo's wide array of skills.

"How can I thank you?" Negassi asked, as he sank down on the couch in the apartment.

Fry slid a folded piece of paper to Negassi. "I had some money wired to you in this account. It should help you get settled with the boys and be able to take care of them."

"I thank you. You are a kind man," Negassi said gratefully.

"Unfortunately, you will probably never be able to return to Congo. You are being hunted for reasons we have yet to decipher."

Negassi nodded. "If everything you say is true, I would not be alive much longer to enjoy living in Congo. Sometimes a man must adapt to survive."

That night, Echo snuck back to Kalemie where a sting operation was put into motion. Fry checked the warehouse, and the supplies had not been delivered yet. The SEALs were positioned in strategic positions to catch whoever made the next delivery.

The SEALs were surprised when the supplies came in not by truck but by boat. It took the three young men on the boat over two hours to load in the supplies. By the time the men were finished, they were exhausted and put up no fight when the SEALs confronted them.

"Where did these supplies come from?" Fry asked.

The men looked dumbfounded. Then they began speaking in their native tongue.

"I think they are speaking Bemba," Dorian Axel said. "I picked up a few familiar words."

"Can you translate?" Fry asked.

Axel shook his head. "I'm not fluent, but I can try to ask them about the supplies."

Axel spent a few minutes conversing with the men in Bemba. Then he looked at Lydell, and shook his head.

"This looks like a dead end. These men are from Zambia. They were contracted by a man in their town to ferry supplies to Kalemie once a week. They get paid in cash, and they don't know the man's name. They said, he has the supplies at the dock. They load them on the boat and get paid once they return. They don't seem to know much more," Axel said with a heavy sigh.

Fry nodded. "It looks like we are going to Zambia, boys. We'll hitch a ride back with them."

Four hours later, Echo stepped foot on the dock in Zambia. They were introduced to the man who had employed the ferry service. He knew little more than his employees. He told them he was contacted by a man named John Smith and asked to make deliveries. The money was wired to his account once a week. The supplies were delivered via air freight. He had to pick them up from the airport and transport the crates to the dock. Like Negassi, he had no way to contact John Smith. He said he'd never had a need to. Smith was never late with his payments. The mystery seemed no closer to being unraveled.

The next day, Echo paid one of the ferrymen to take them back to Kalemie. They had hit a frustrating dead end for the time being.

Fry made contact with Rowen, and a chopper picked up the SEAL team the following morning just outside of Kalemie. The ride back was fraught with tension. No one was sure what to expect when they reported back to Rowen.

Sonny gave Fry a questioning look as the chopper landed at the airport. "Plan A or plan B?"

Fry let out a long breath. "I'm honestly not sure. I need to see what Rowen has to say first."

CHAPTER 21

January 17
1400
U.N. base, Kananga

When Echo arrived at the U.N. base in Kananga, Rowen was in a meeting with General Loredo. The team cleaned up and met in the mess hall for chow. Fry got in the back of the line, and a moment later he felt a hand slide into his. He looked back to see Bretta.

"Hey." He grinned down at her.

"We need to talk. Now!" she whispered.

His brows knitted, but he turned and followed her outside. She led him to a secluded spot where the guards were not present, and there was no camera surveillance.

"You can not tell Rowen the truth!"

"What?"

"Don't play dumb. I know what Echo did. Not only could you spend time in Leavenworth, but it could get you killed. You were ordered to assassinate Negassi. I know that's not what you did."

"I don't know what you're talking about or where you're getting your information from—"

"Don't bother denying it." Bretta pulled a satellite photo from inside her jacket.

Lydell studied the photo. It clearly showed the SEAL team loading Negassi and the boys onto a boat. His jaw tightened as he crumpled up the photo and jammed it into his pocket.

"I didn't feel it was necessary to bring the photo of you sneaking them into Burundi to prove my point. I don't know what you were thinking, but you could get in a lot of trouble for this! If this information falls into the wrong hands, you and the rest of the SEALs won't leave Congo alive. Convenient accidents tend to happen when powerful people feel threatened."

His lips turned down in a frown. "I take it you don't intend to expose our operation."

"I'm on your side, but what you did was stupid."

"What we did was the right thing to do. Negassi was being used as a scapegoat. He's no revolutionary. I found out who's been funding his humanitarian aid—"

"John Smith from Techno Corp," Bretta interrupted.

His eyebrow rose in surprise.

"John Smith is an alias, and Techno Corp is a front company for a lot of nefarious business."

"If you knew that, why not do something to stop it?" he asked annoyed.

"Because, Negassi is a drop in the ocean. You don't know the bigger picture. You have no idea what the SEALs were dropped into here. This is a hotbed of deceit, corruption, and international powerplays. Negassi's mission of mercy, while commendable, was ill-advised and foolish. You can't stop the spread of massive disease with a few antibiotics and meager food portions. He was a dreamer with no common sense."

"He is a dreamer with a kind heart. He doesn't deserve to be assassinated to serve some agenda!" he growled.

"You don't have the authority to make that call. Your job is to follow orders."

"My job doesn't include blowing an innocent man's head off along with innocent children who are only trying to help those in need. That's not the job I signed up for, and I'd rather take a bullet to my own head than murder a bunch of innocent people."

"Regardless, Negassi will be tracked down, and his army will be taken out with him."

"They are not an army! They are not revolutionaries! They are just kids!"

"It doesn't matter. Powers bigger than you want Negassi to take the fall for an attempted coup. There are bigger things in play here than you know. This is about more than one man's life."

"You knew all of this months ago! You knew he was being set up as a scapegoat!"

"I suspected. My suspicions have been confirmed."

"And you're just going to stand by and watch while an innocent man's life is destroyed!"

"Should I wire him money from my own personal bank account to his new alias, Tobias Rigg? That was foolish Lydell. You didn't even bother to launder the money through a Cayman account first. You're an amateur!"

Lydell dragged his hand over his copper curls and groaned. "How easy is it going to be for someone to discover all of this?"

"No one will discover Echo's part in Negassi's escape. I've already altered the satellite footage and digitally reversed and erased your banking trail. Report to Rowen that you hit the camp, but Negassi wasn't there. He'll be tracked down by U.N. forces and used for his intended purpose."

"How long does he have?"

"Not long. A few days."

"I have to warn him."

"How do you plan to do that? Your cell phone is being monitored. All the lines here on base are compromised. The SEALs are being watched like hawks. If I were you, I'd be worried about my own ass, not an expendable nobody like Negassi."

"He's not expendable!"

"He's walking dead. There's nothing you can do to save him. Stop wasting valuable time on a lost cause. It was decided long before you came to Congo that Negassi would take the fall to provide a catalyst for the change that is coming."

"What do I have to do to convince you to save Negassi and his boys? If you have access to all this information, surely there's something you can do to stop this tragedy from happening."

Bretta bit her lip as she studied Lydell. "You're not going to let this go, are you?"

He shook his head.

"Using the dead bodies from the graves to make it look like you wiped out his army was clever. However, if I do what you're asking, it would cost me much more than you can possibly imagine. I'm here to do a job. That job is not to protect a nobody like Negassi. There are much bigger things in play, Lydell."

"Do it."

"If I do this for you, you're going to owe me, Lydell."

"I know."

"Are you prepared to pay up when the time comes?"

He let out a sigh and looked down into her beautiful blue eyes. "Yeah, I'll pay up."

"Then consider it done."

"Are you sure you can pull it off?"

Bretta grinned. Her fingers curled into his t-shirt as she tugged him in closer. "Trust me."

Lydell planted his hands against the wall behind her and leaned down until his lips barely brushed over hers. He pulled back and looked into her eyes.

"The only people I trust are the men on Echo."

"You don't trust Grammy, Gramps, Ridley, or Ellery?"

His eyes narrowed on her. "Exactly how much do you know about me?"

"Everything."

He grinned. "Everything, huh?"

She grinned back.

"If you know everything, what am I thinking right now?"

She slid her hands slowly down his camo shirt, curled her fingers into the waistband of his camo dungarees, and tugged him closer. He leaned in and claimed her lips with a possessive kiss. He felt her hands exploring as they kissed. She pulled his shirt free, and her fingers caressed over the firm ridges of his abs. Soon he was completely lost in the kiss.

Her lips left his, and she worked them up his neck to his ear. "Is this what you had in mind?"

"Not exactly."

His fingers freed the buttons on her shirt as he claimed her lips again. Bretta moaned against his mouth as his fingers caressed her, sending tingling pleasure throughout her entire body.

"You make me so crazy. I want all of you, Bretta. I want you right now."

"You can have all of me, but now is not the time. You'll have to wait a little longer."

Lydell pressed his forehead to hers and groaned. "You shouldn't have started something you knew we couldn't finish. You're killing me, Bretta."

She pulled his mouth down to hers, and his body molded against her as he ravished her lips with his. It was hard to pull back from his impassioned plea, but she knew this was neither the time nor the place for any sort of romantic interlude. His needs and her own would have to wait.

He groaned softly. "I've dreamt about you every night. You have no idea how badly I need you."

"Oh, I have a pretty good idea, Love. I don't think you can get any harder, but it will have to wait. Meet me tonight at 0100. I promise you can take anything you want then. In the meantime, you have a meeting with Rowen. Don't tell him the truth or Negassi is a dead man."

"Are you saying Rowen is dirty?"

Bretta bit her lip. "I don't know. I only know some of the players in the coup that is coming. I'm still working on understanding all the variables here."

"Rowen is not dirty. He doesn't like this any more than we do."

Bretta nodded. "That may be true, but Rowen did give you the order to take Negassi and his army out. Even if he isn't pulling any strings, he's following orders, unlike you."

"Fine. Where do I meet you tonight?"

"Just take a walk, and sneak outside the fence line. I'll find you."

"This isn't exactly a small place. How are you going to find me?"

"I'm always watching you. I always know where you are."

Lydell smirked. "Always watching me? Careful. You sound like a stalker."

"Maybe I am."

He grinned and pressed a soft kiss to her lips. "You can stalk me anytime."

"You should eat before your meeting. You don't eat right, Lydell. You worry me."

His lips turned down in a frown. "Damn! How much do you watch me?"

"Every spare minute I have."

"If I didn't know better—I'd say—you were in love with me."

Bretta stared up into his eyes, and silence fell between them.

Lydell stared back, and an ache bloomed in his gut that hadn't been there before.

"Damn! You do—don't you?" he asked softly.

He swallowed hard, and his voice caught in his throat in a strangled rasp. "Bretta, you barely know me. You can't possibly be—"

She shut him up with a kiss.

Lydell spent as much time as he could making out with Bretta before she shoved him away and disappeared around the corner before he could stop her. He trudged back to the mess hall and got a plate of food. He sat down and stared at the plate for a while. Too many ideas were crowding his brain and killing his appetite.

Is Bretta really in love with me? Can she save Negassi? What should I do about Rowen?

He picked at his food for a while before he finally ate half the plate. Then he tossed the rest and left to find Echo. Most were crashed out on their cots sleeping. The few who were awake, he pulled outside for a walk. John Rusk, Sonny Eldridge, Nick Novak, Zachary Hurst, and Dorian Axel followed Lydell. He circumvented the U.N. guards and led them out through the hole in the fence behind the supply building.

Once they were a few blocks away from the base, John asked, "Where are we going?"

"Somewhere private. I don't want anyone listening in on our conversation," Fry said.

He led them past a burned down apartment building and stopped short. He turned and stared at the blackened rubble. Confusion warred in his brain. Something seemed familiar, yet, he was sure he'd never been here before.

"Something wrong, Chief?" Zach asked.

Lydell shook his head. "What used to be here?"

Dorian shrugged. "Beats me. We've never been down this street before."

"I think I have. There was an apartment building here before. Eight stories tall—I think."

"Looks like a recent fire," John said, studying the rubble. "When were you here?"

Lydell bit his lip, closed his eyes, and tried to focus the jumbled images that had suddenly invaded his brain. "I don't know. I remember—a dirty, derelict apartment, handcuffs, and Bretta. She was wearing a black G-string."

Sonny chuckled. "Sounds like a dirty fantasy to me. Was she any good?"

Lydell glared at him. "It wasn't a fantasy. It feels real, but I don't actually remember. It's just bits and pieces of images in my head."

"Dirty dreams are like that," Sonny drawled. "That's the hell of it. You want to remember, but all them really juicy parts are just out of yer reach when you wake up."

"No. It wasn't a dream. It—I can't piece it together."

"Is this why you brought us here?" Nick asked.

"No. This is not where I intended to go. We need to talk inside somewhere." Fry said.

They continued to walk until they found an abandoned building.

"So, what's this about? Does it have to do with Negassi?" John asked.

"Yes. We weren't as stealthy as we should have been. All our actions were caught on satellite footage. Bretta showed me a satellite photo of us sneaking Negassi onto the boat. She claims she has one of us sneaking them across the border too. She knows I wired money to Negassi under his new alias. She seems to know everything we did."

"Well, hell!" Sonny grumbled. "So, what are we going to do?"

"Nothing. She's already destroyed all the incriminating evidence, and she's agreed to keep our secret."

"Why would she do that? What's in it for her?" Dorian asked.

Lydell let out a frustrated sigh. "I had to agree to owe her one."

"What the hell does that mean?" Zach asked.

"She didn't specify what sort of favor," Fry said.

"It will most likely be unethical and illegal," Dorian said grimly.

Lydell nodded. "She had no intention of saving Negassi. She would have been fine with letting him die. Whatever she has planned for me is going to be painful. I'm sure I'm not going to like it, but I can't watch an innocent man and all those kids be slaughtered and take the fall for what's coming. She said someone wants Negassi to be blamed for an attempted coup."

"Damn!" Sonny exclaimed. "If there's a coup coming, shouldn't we warn somebody?"

Fry shook his head. "According to her, the SEALs don't have a clear picture of the bigger situation. Someone in our chain of command is dirty. We can't tell Rowen the truth. If he reports it up the chain of command, whoever ordered Negassi's assassination will be tipped off. Whether it came from General Loredo or higher up is impossible to know. Bretta also told me that the communications are all being monitored. That includes our personal cell phones. In essence, we are cut off from the outside world here. She said some very powerful people want things here to go their way. If things don't go their way, accidents tend to happen to eliminate the problem."

"In other words, we are the problem, and if we open our big mouths, we might encounter one of these so-called accidents," John sighed.

Fry nodded. "She also knew about John Smith and Techno Corp. She said Smith is an alias and Techno Corp is a front for a lot of dirty, underhanded business world-wide. We are treading in dangerous water here. We don't know who our enemy even is. I think until we leave Congo, we should keep Negassi a secret from everyone."

"Even from Rowen?" John asked.

"I trust Rowen, but should we put him in the position of having to lie to his C.O.?" Fry asked.

"If we don't tell him, we could be putting him in danger. If someone finds out what we did, they'll assume that Rowen ordered us to do it. He'd be walking in blind," John said.

Lydell dragged his hand through his copper curls and groaned.

"It's up to you, Chief. We'll follow your lead," Zach said.

The rest of the men agreed.

"Okay, when we meet with him today, we'll tell him the official story. Negassi is dead. I'll tell him the truth in private away from prying eyes," Lydell said.

"Good. I don't like lying to my C.O.," Dorian said. "I think that's exactly what we should do. Rowen is a good man. He flew out on that chopper to give us a warning. He knows things here are not what they appear to be."

"Who does Bretta think is behind all of this?" Nick asked.

Lydell shrugged. "Obviously Techno Corp is dirty, but she didn't say who else is involved. She's still trying to uncover the whole truth."

Echo returned to base and snuck back inside the perimeter through the hole in the fence.

"Did you cut this hole?" Nick asked. "You can't even tell it's been cut unless you look close."

Fry shook his head. "I've been through this fence before at night, but I can't quite—it's hazy."

"Who cut the fence?" John asked.

Fry shook his head. "I think Bretta did."

"When were you here with her?" Nick asked.

"I—can't remember," Fry mumbled.

They fixed the fence back in place and followed Fry back to the bunk house. Fry informed the rest of Echo that they were going with plan B. Then Echo reported to their temporary HQ for a briefing with Rowen at 1600.

Before Rowen had a chance to speak, Fry handed him a piece of paper that was folded up. Rowen unfolded it, and his eyebrows knitted together as he read Fry's scrawl.

> Don't say anything out loud. Everything we say and do
> is being watched. Everything we are about to tell you is a
> necessary lie. I'll explain it all later. You'll have to trust us.
> Someone up the chain of command is dirty.

Rowen looked up at Fry and nodded. Then he listened to their account of the incursion on Negassi and his army. He recorded their false accounts of the battle and the slaughter.

"I'll make my report to General Loredo. Take it easy, Men. Enjoy your down time until further notice," Rowen said.

January 17
1800
U.N. Base, Kananga

Commander Rowen sat in a meeting with his C.O. General Loredo as well as several other high-ranking officers from various countries under the United Nations umbrella. Bretta Brairton sat in the small apartment she'd procured off base. Her laptop was recording multiple views of the meeting, and she was watching them intently.

It was no surprise to her that General Tacari Negassi of the Chacha army of the new Chimelu Republic, as he had been labeled by the corrupt powers in play, was the center of the discussion. Commander Rowen reported the facts of Negassi's demise just as Fry had laid them out in the meeting two hours earlier. There was much discussion about Negassi's residual armed forces that could retaliate once they learned of his assassination.

Bretta smirked as she listened to the pile of lies being shoveled in the meeting. There was an agenda in play, and finally, the players were making their move and showing their hand to her. She made note of who told what lie. One U.N. officer went so far as to suggest that Negassi might have escaped the hit on his camp and could be assembling his armies as they spoke. He recommended immediate action to protect the current government.

"Bingo! That was what I was waiting to hear," Bretta mumbled to herself, as she typed up an encrypted message to send to her boss.

> Coup is in play. Attaching a list of the major players.
> Advise course of action. Awaiting your response.

She hit send and refocused her attention on the meeting. Ten minutes later she received a response.

> Couse of action recommended is as follows. Allow coup
> to proceed. Document all players in the game. Collect
> data for future analysis. Do not allow the SEAL teams to
> interfere with the overthrow of the government. Extract
> them from Congo at the first opportunity.

Bretta bit her lip as she read the response. Then she immediately pulled up her contact list on her computer, encrypted a message, and sent it to Admiral Svenson.

> Admiral Svenson,
> Dispatch the American SEAL teams. They have completed their mission. The United Nations military force is to handle the coup.

Admiral Svenson read the message and slid his SAT phone back into his jacket pocket.

"Gentlemen," Svenson addressed the men at the table. "Seeing how this has escalated to a serious offensive on the part of General Negassi's army, the United Nations forces will be handling the protection of the government here in Congo. The United States SEAL forces are no longer required here. They should be dispatched from Congo immediately.

There was a quick assent to Svenson's statement. Commander Rowen was summarily dismissed from the remainder of the meeting and ordered to get his men on the first transport out of Congo the following morning.

Rowen walked out of the meeting feeling like he'd been shoved out of their private club. He didn't like what was going on, but there wasn't much he could do about it. The United Nations had the final say, and they had spoken.

A U.N. chopper was dispatched to locate SEAL team Delta and return them to base. Once they arrived, Rowen met with the SEALs to apprise them of the sudden change.

"I don't like this. We are being kicked out so they can do whatever the hell they please!" Fry growled angrily.

Rowen nodded. "Unfortunately, we are not in control here. We've been politely invited to leave. We aren't being given a choice. Pack up the gear. We fly out at 0600."

At 0100, Lydell left the bunk house. He had no idea where he was supposed to meet Bretta. He started walking, making sure to avoid any encounters with the U.N. guards posted around the compound. He snuck out of the hole in the fence and wandered aimlessly.

"Funny you should choose this burned down rubble as a meeting place," Bretta said.

Fry grinned as he turned to face her. "You really do watch my every move, don't you?"

"This is an odd place for a romantic date."

"Is that what we are doing?"

She sauntered over to him and curled her fingers into his shirt. "Isn't that what you want?"

"That's before I knew we were being kicked out of Congo on the first flight in the morning."

She frowned. "Yes, I only found out about that myself a few hours ago. We don't have much time. We should make the most of it."

"Am I ever going to see you again?"

"Do you want to?"

Lydell groaned softly as he pulled her firmly against him. "Desperately."

"Then we will."

"How? I'm leaving at 0600. We're not even from the same country. I don't even know your real name."

Bretta chuckled. "I told you, it's Bretta Brairton."

"We both know that's a lie."

"Do you trust me?"

He grinned. "Not even a little bit."

"Negassi and the boys are safe. I took care of it. No one, not even you will ever be able to track them down. I've squirreled them far away from prying eyes."

He cleared his throat. "They're not in Burundi?"

"No. They are currently on their way to a new location that only I am privy to. They will never be found. Stop worrying about them. I kept my promise. Your tracks are covered."

"Who are you really, Bretta?"

"I'm just a soldier following orders, like you."

He shook his head. "I don't believe you. You are nothing like me. I'm guessing MI6."

She grinned at him and winked. "Let's not spoil the mood with any more shop talk."

"I don't want to start something that can't be finished, Bretta."

"Neither do I."

"I'm about to leave. You're staying here. Am I missing something?"

"You're missing everything."

"Draw me a picture."

She pulled his mouth down to hers and ravished his lips. It wasn't long before they were in her bed making passionate love to each other. He'd stopped caring about the consequences. His only focus was making her his all night long.

At 0600, SEAL teams Echo and Delta boarded a transport and lifted off on time. Lydell sat staring at his combat boots while his mind replayed his night of passion with Bretta. The only other woman he'd ever been with was Freya. That hadn't ended well. She'd dumped him right after he signed up for the Navy. She didn't care that he'd been willing to commit his life to her. She only cared that he was leaving. She wouldn't wait for him. It had been an ugly breakup.

His parting with Bretta had been the opposite of his experience with Freya. Bretta had promised she would find him again. His gut reaction was to distrust her, but his heart wasn't listening. Something about her drew him in a way he'd never been drawn to any woman before.

Once they were back on base in Afghanistan, the familiar surroundings of the base took his mind off of Bretta's absence but only a little. He missed her already, but he had a big fish to fry. He had to report to Rowen and tell him the truth about Negassi.

CHAPTER 22

February 14
0600
BUD/S

It had been eight weeks since Hell Week. As promised, things at BUD/S had not gotten easier. The training was brutal every day. The sheer amount of information they had to absorb and retain on a daily basis was daunting. Yet, the physical training kept pace with the psychological and technical training. Every part of her brain and body was being tested.

Sophia woke early, dressed, and went to chow with the 44 candidates who were still in the program. Three more had washed out after Hell Week. They hadn't been able to keep up with the brain bending, and their scores were too low to pass.

She sat shoveling in her breakfast as she studied her notes from the day before. Sam Cafferty sat down on the bench next to her. He was too close for her liking. She could feel the heat of his thigh against hers. It was distracting. She refocused on her notes without even glancing his way. After a moment, she felt his warm breath feather against her ear.

"Happy Valentine's Day, Sweetheart."

She didn't respond. Instead, she shoved in another large bite of food and kept reading. That's when a single red rose obscured her vision of her notebook.

"This reminds me of you, Soph—delicate, beautiful, and full of sharp, dangerous thorns."

She mentally grimaced.

Why does he have to be such an idiot! Does he not realize what kind of trouble he can get me in by openly flirting like this! BUD/S instructors are always watching!

She set the rose off to the side of her book and shoved in another bite.

"Have you considered my proposal?" he asked.

"I'm focused on passing my quals at the moment."

He grinned. Then he leaned in and pressed a soft kiss to her cheek. "I'll let you study, just make sure you say yes to me and no to Butch."

Sophia resisted the urge to roll her eyes. The two men hadn't given her a moments peace in over a month. Usually, they were fairly sly about it, but everyone at BUD/S had noticed. The instructors had given her hell over it, but they hadn't been any easier on Butch or Sam.

Giving her a rose in the mess hall was really pushing it. She was sure there would be consequences for this. The BUD/S instructors were all business.

"Are you trying to earn me extra PT, Sam?" she asked around a mouth full of food.

"No, I just couldn't let the chance to tell you how beautiful you are pass me by."

"Sam! I'm just trying to pass BUD/S right now. You have to stop this. I really need to focus!"

"So, you find me distracting. That's good to know."

"Yes! You're distracting! Please, scoot over, and eat your breakfast! I need to concentrate!"

Sam grinned. Then he glanced down to where his thigh was firmly pressed against hers. He leaned back down to her ear.

"If just touching my leg turns you on, imagine how great it's going to be when we are both naked, making love to each other. You make my heart race, Soph. I can't wait to marry you."

She cleared her throat nervously and tried not to imagine Sam naked. She failed miserably. She'd seen him naked too many times in the shower. His blonde burr, warm brown eyes, perfect lips, and ripped body slammed into her brain. Everything about Sam was perfect.

"Sam, please! You are going to make me fail the test this morning if you don't let me study."

His hand slid up the inside of her thigh, and her body tensed in response. She reached down and pulled his hand away.

"Sam, stop now! Take that rose and go sit somewhere else!"

"I'll let you study." He winked at her and moved to another table.

Right after Sam left, Butch Simonis sat down on the other side of her. His thigh pressed firmly against hers, and she felt her heartrate kick up when he caressed his fingertips up her arm.

"Good morning, Sweetie," he murmured in her ear. "Happy Valentine's Day." He laid a card on top of her notebook. It was red with flowers, hearts, and sentimentalism.

Sophia groaned inwardly as her eyes scanned the romantic, sweet words on the paper.

I never knew how much I despised Valentine's Day until this moment! Why do men feel the need to make a grand gesture on today of all days? Of course, these two have been bubbling over with charm and romantic gestures every stinking day! Can't they just leave me alone and let me focus on BUD/S. I didn't come here for this. This is not what I want! I need to focus. I need to block them both out. I need to pass my test this morning, or I'll be the next one ringing the bell!

"Good morning, Butch. I'm studying for my test."

She willed herself not to think about Butch's naked body either. He was equally as beautiful as Sam. Her mind rebelled. She pictured Butch standing under the shower with water cascading over his ripped body. His ebony burr and the dark, sexy stubble on his chin were far too appealing. It was hard to pound the image of him naked out of her mind.

Okay! They are both beautiful. They are both sweet. They are both madly in love with me, but this can't happen. I can't allow either of them to distract me from becoming a SEAL. One mistake in the field could be fatal. I have to focus! I have to block them both out!

Her test that morning was far from easy, but she managed to pass. Her afternoon was spent in the pool doing drown-proofing exercises. She had no time to think about Butch or Sam until dinner that night. Then the Valentine's Day charm rained down on her once more. She did not appreciate that both men were drawing so much attention to their pursuit of her.

Damnit! I really hate Valentine's Day! Could there be a worse holiday? The one thing I need them both to back off of is the very thing this day encourages in men!

That night during room inspection, Reynolds pulled Sophia outside for a private discussion.

"I can't help but notice that your presence here is causing a lot of distraction. Men aren't used to having a female in their midst like this. There are two candidates in particular that are walking the fine line. I want to know if you are encouraging this behavior in them?" Reynolds demanded.

"No, Sir! I have done my best to ignore it and discourage it, Sir!"

He nodded. "If it is unwanted, then I have to ask if you plan to file charges of sexual misconduct or harassment on their part?"

"Sir, no, Sir! I did not come here to cause trouble. I came here to train to become a SEAL, Sir! Becoming a SEAL is my only goal and my only concern. I have no interest in derailing any man's career based on a momentary lapse in his judgement, Sir!"

"This is what you are up against in BUD/S; it will be worse out in the field. How you handle it here is a direct correlation to how you will handle it there. I'm watching you, Gonzalez!"

"Sir, yes, Sir!"

She went to bed with a heavy weight on her mind. She'd done her best to ignore Butch and Sam. She knew that would have to change. She couldn't handle this situation the same way she'd handled the Marine's at GITMO. She was going to have to address this problem head on.

The next morning at breakfast, Sophia told Sam and Butch that she needed them to back off. She did her best to make it clear that she was here to become a SEAL not a wife. They both agreed to back off during SEAL training, but neither man intended to let her slip through his fingers. She felt a hard knot form in her chest. It was clear the problem wasn't going away. All she'd managed to do was postpone the inevitable.

CHAPTER 23

March 1
1100
Afghanistan U.S. military base

It had been over a month since the SEALs had been kicked out of Congo. Between missions, Echo checked the news to see what was going on in Africa. Nothing newsworthy had transpired since their absence until now. They were all crowded around Fry's laptop watching the breaking news. A WGNL reporter was on the air. She was covering the morning skirmish in Kinshasa that had led to an all-out conflict in the capital.

Shelly Mayheart held a microphone and stared sternly into the camera. "U.N. troops have blocked off many of the streets here in Kinshasa in an attempt to subvert the attempted coup by the Chacha army of the new Chimelu Republic. Formerly led by General Tacari Negassi until his recent death in a skirmish, this army is a force to be reckoned with. For the last two years, General Negassi built up an army. His frequent proclamations about the necessity for change and the inadequacy of the existing government to lead its people have been well documented. It seems now that General Negassi's guerilla forces have taken matters into their own hands. In retaliation for his death, they intend to replace the existing government with one of their own making. The sudden, unexpected attacks this morning have left many civilians dead and wounded. Among the reported fallen are many of Congo's leading government officials. The bomb that destroyed a significant portion of the capital building this morning came at the worst possible time. The leading heads of state were in a meeting to discuss the growing epidemics here in Congo. Disease has ravaged this struggling country for too long, and plans were underway to bring in much needed medical help to contain the spread of disease. Now, that will have to wait until peace can be restored and a government can be repaired. Fighting in the streets continues behind me as the U.N. forces attempt to subdue the radicalized Chacha army and restore peace to this troubled city. I'm Shelly Mayheart reporting for WGNL."

Sonny dragged his hand over his blonde burr as he let out a groan of protest. "What the hell! Negassi never had an army. What army is the U.N. even fighting there. I knew something dirty was going down!"

John chewed at his lip for a moment. "My guess is whoever attacked the capital this morning belongs to the same militant forces that we encountered when we first deployed in Congo. Obviously, Negassi had no army, nor was he any of the things they are accusing him of. His reputation is being smeared to serve someone else's agenda. The question is whose agenda is in play now?"

Fry let out a frustrated breath. "No, the real question is, if they knew a coup was coming back in January, why did they let it come to fruition? Who would gain the most if Congo fell into upheaval?"

"The mining operations?" Zach offered.

Fry nodded. "I agree. A lot of countries have their fingers in the pot of Congo's mining industry. If the new government were to pass new legislation that increased their profits—"

"It always boils down to money, doesn't it!" Nick growled. "We were just being used. The question is, who was doing the using?"

"Everyone with something to gain by this," Fry said. "My guess is there were a lot of fingers in this particular pot. Bretta told me that setting up Negassi to take the fall had to be in the works from the beginning. They used him for two years while they plotted how to get what they wanted. It looks like they are succeeding!"

"If Bretta knew all of this was coming, why didn't she try to stop it?" Ezra asked.

"Maybe she did try, but how much can one person do against a conspiracy as big as this was? Maybe saving Negassi and his boys was the only thing she had any power over in this situation. I didn't get the feeling she went through official channels to save him. I think it was her own private covert op, just like ours," Fry said.

"Do you think you'll ever see her again?" Cameron asked.

Fry shook his head. "No, she's a ghost. She has to be MI6. None of us will ever lay eyes on her again."

"How do you feel about that?" Sonny asked.

Fry sighed. "I feel glad that our paths crossed. She helped us save a lot of lives that would have been needlessly killed to promote this propaganda on the news right now. Without her, things could have gone south on us all."

"Yeah, but how do you feel about never seeing her again?" Sonny asked.

Fry looked down at his combat boots and back up at Sonny. "I don't. SEALs can't allow personal issues to cloud their judgement in the field. She's in the past. That's where she'll stay. Right now, I'm focusing on what lies ahead. I'm keeping my head on a swivel just like all of you should be doing."

Sonny nodded. "Right, Chief."

CHAPTER 24

March 15
0630
BUD/S

The candidates were assembled at the pool. Reynolds stood before them with a stern look on his rugged, scarred face.

"Today we will continue Combat Dive training. Each day we will continue to build on what you learned the previous day. It only gets harder from here. Anyone want to ring the bell?"

"Sir, no, Sir!" they all answered in unison.

"When I blow the whistle Group A will dive into the pool holding all your equipment in your arms. You will put on all your equipment at the bottom of the pool, swim the length of the pool, and exit the water. Then Group B, C, and D will repeat the same exercise."

Sophia was in Group C so she had an opportunity to watch the other groups before attempting it herself. Some struggled with the exercise more than others, but all of Group A and B successfully navigated it. The whistle blew, and she went into the pool with the rest of her group. Since December she'd spent a lot of time in this pool. It was familiar, it was comfortable, but she'd never had to put on all her scuba gear after diving in before.

It turned out to be much harder than she'd imagined. Getting her mask on and clearing the water out was the first challenge. Once she'd done that, the rest was easier. Still, the feeling of panic that washed through her when she couldn't see, was nothing to laugh at.

The rest of the day went well. They learned some underwater combat moves and practiced them with the instructors all afternoon.

The following morning, the candidates were split up into four groups again. However, unlike the previous day, they were scheduled a block of time in the pool for their specific group. Sophia was in Group A today. They entered the pool area, and Reynolds was waiting for them.

"This morning you will enter the water as a group. You will put on your equipment at the bottom of the pool. The instructor assigned to you will perform a series of underwater attacks. You must fight off your opponent and accomplish your mission. Your mission is to untie the ten-pound weight at the bottom of the pool and successfully transport it to the far end of the pool. You will exit the water with it. If you fail to complete this mission, you fail today's lesson. If your head comes above the surface of the water before you complete this mission, you fail! If you fail, you will be given an opportunity tomorrow to repeat this exercise. If you fail twice, you will be given one final chance to complete this exercise. If you fail thrice, you wash out of BUD/S, and you will ring the bell. Are we clear?"

"Sir, yes, Sir!" Group A said in unison.

"It only gets harder from here. I expect you to give me 150 percent. I expect you to succeed. Anything less than perfection is a fail!" Reynolds shouted to the group.

Everyone grabbed their scuba gear and lined up at the deep end of the pool. Reynolds blew his whistle, and everyone on the line made the plunge into the water.

When Sophia reached the bottom, she began the task of putting on her scuba gear. No sooner had she completed that task than she felt her instructor grab her from behind, pull her air hose loose, and yank her mask off her face. Panic shot through her, but she willed herself not to give in to it. She worked through the combat moves she'd learned the day before. The problem was, she had no air, and she was fighting blind.

Every time she attempted to restore the air hose, her instructor blocked her. The struggle ensued until Sophia was out of air. She shoved off from the bottom of the pool ditching her scuba gear as she frantically kicked her way to the surface. She broke the surface gasping for air.

"Gonzalez! You fail!" Reynolds barked from the side of the pool.

Sophia dove back to the bottom of the pool, retrieved her scuba gear, and exited the pool. She stood at attention at the edge of the pool and watched as the other men still in the pool worked to untie the knots while fighting off their instructor. She noticed that the attacks did not stop.

Every moment they were in the pool working to keep their equipment intact and free their ten-pound weight, their instructor was trying to cut off their air supply and their vision. Only half of the men in Group A were successful at getting their weight to the far end of the pool without surfacing.

Reynolds assembled all those who failed into a line and paced back and forth in front of them as he began reciting the SEAL creed.

"SEALs never quit. Your nation expects you to be physically harder and mentally stronger than your enemies. If knocked down, you will get back up. Every time. You will draw on every remaining ounce of strength to protect your teammates and to accomplish your mission. You are never out of the fight!" Reynolds stopped pacing and stood facing them with a stern frown on his face. "You did not complete your mission! Thousands of innocent people are going to die now, because you couldn't fight off the enemy and accomplish your goal. You are not SEAL material! If that's your best, if that's your 150 percent effort, then you might as well ring the bell now and go home!"

"Sir, no, Sir!" they all said in unison.

"Report to Bruchard on the O-Course! You have a long way to go before you can call yourself a SEAL!" he shouted at the group.

The O-Course was brutal that afternoon. They were put through the paces as they climbed walls, climbed rope, balanced on beams, and ran as fast as they could through the obstacles over and over. By the time Sophia hit the showers that night, she was beyond exhausted. She fell asleep as soon as her head hit the pillow.

The following morning began her second attempt in the combat training exercise. She stood on the edge of the pool with her scuba gear in her arms waiting for the whistle. This morning she was determined to succeed. No matter what, she had no intention of surfacing. The whistle blew, and she plunged into the water. This time she knew the attack would come immediately. She was a little better prepared for it, but not by much. It was difficult to reattach her air hose while fighting off an attacker. Still, this time she managed to get the knots untied. She had to reattach her air hose three times while fending off her assigned instructor, but she freed the weight and started for the shallow end of the pool.

It was not easy. He was on her the entire way, pulling off her mask, detaching her hose, and struggling to pull the weight away from her. She only made it halfway down the length of the pool before he was able to yank the weight away and take off swimming with it. He made it to the end of the pool before she did and exited with her prize. Sophia pulled herself up on the edge of the pool.

"Gonzalez! You fail!" Reynolds shouted.

After the exercise was over, Reynolds lined up the ten candidates who failed that morning in a row. He yelled at them and gave them a more severe version of the speech from the previous day. Then he sent them to the O-Course.

At lunch Sophia sat at the end of a table shoveling in her food. Her mind was racing with the horrible possibility of failure. She only had one more chance to prove herself in the pool tomorrow. After all the hard work she had put in to get here, she felt sick at the thought that it could all end tomorrow.

Sam sat down next to her. "Hey, I heard you didn't pass today."

She let out a sigh. "I came closer. I made it halfway, but he got the weight away from me."

Sam nodded. "Don't give up. You still have one more test tomorrow. You can do it. You're the biggest bad-ass I've seen. Just remember, you don't need air. You don't need to see. You just need to hang on to that weight and get it to the end of the pool. Just don't let go of it."

A sardonic smile curved her lips. "Piece of cake. I'll just hang on to the weight this time."

"That's my girl."

The next morning began her final attempt at the combat dive training exercise. This was it. Her last chance to make it to the next phase of SEAL training was upon her. She stood on the edge of the pool. She emptied her mind of everything. Then one thought filled her. Don't let go of the weight! The whistle blew. She plunged in. The battle began.

CHAPTER 25

April 1
0700
The Island

Excitement did not begin to describe how Sophia felt. She'd passed everything necessary, and she was on her way to The Island. Finishing Hell Week had been the first goal. Getting to The Island had been the second. Every candidate was filled with the same anticipation. The instructors had all preached about how hard The Island would be, but none of the candidates cared. They just wanted to get there. It was a benchmark in their training. It was an achievement worthy of bragging rights. No one wanted to be denied The Island.

When they arrived on the beach, they set foot on hallowed ground. Every SEAL who'd made the cut before them had walked this beach. It felt like standing on the shoulders of giants. Sophia's heart was beating hard inside her chest. The adventure was about to begin.

Two weeks later, dawn broke the horizon to find Sophia staring at the ocean waves rolling in from the Pacific. Going to The Island had been nothing like what she expected. She thought she'd prepared for it physically and mentally. She was wrong.

All the practice in the pool seemed like child's play now. Swimming in the ocean with its unforgiving currents, tides, and frigid temperatures was the real deal. They swam in the ocean every day. They practiced underwater missions. They ran the beach. They practiced overland combat training. They practiced concealment and sneaking up on an enemy. They worked hard every day, all day. They were sleep deprived, hungry, and the instructors never let up on them for one second. They were tested and tried. They were pushed past their breaking points. They were remolded into relentless fighting machines.

There was no sleep schedule on the island. They were woken from sleep often to gear up and go on a practice mission. They were put through live ammo training, in combat situations. They were taught to move and think as one cohesive unit.

It did not take long for Sophia to adapt to the new way of life. She no longer thought of protecting her own six. Instead, she constantly scanned and evaluated her surroundings to determine how best to defend her unit and to stealthily sneak up on an enemy and take him out.

Her scores went up dramatically from her first day on The Island, but she was still in the bottom quarter of the pack. She made her new goal to become so good at what she did that she would rise to the top score on the board.

She ran harder. She got faster. She worked and worked, but rising on the score board was difficult. The other candidates were working just as hard as she was to improve their own scores. It was a constantly fluctuating current of improvement, and she was struggling to swim against that current.

By the time training ended on The Island, Sophia had risen to the midpoint of the pack. She felt it was quite an accomplishment to make any headway among such fierce competitors. It came as no surprise to her that Butch finished at the top of the score board. Sam finished in the third spot.

They all left The Island to embark on the next phase of training, the parachute course. This would be a new experience for Sophia. She had never jumped out of a plane in her entire life. The only time she'd even flown in a plane was on her way to GITMO and back. She was ready—at least she hoped she was ready for it. The instructors kept telling them—it only gets harder from here. So far, they hadn't lied about that. The Island had been the hardest thing she'd ever done in her life; she couldn't imagine how parachuting could possibly be harder.

She was about to find out.

CHAPTER 26

April 17
1400
North Carolina

Kyle Masters stood at the baggage claim area at the airport waiting for the plane to arrive. His phone buzzed with a text from Megan.

M: Are you on your way home yet?
K: No. John's plane hasn't arrived. It was delayed half an hour.
M: Ok. Can you stop and get milk on your way home?
K: No problem. I love you.
M: I love you more.
K: Not possible.

He slid his phone into his pocket and leaned back against the column to wait. When he spotted John headed toward the baggage carousel, he walked over and intercepted him.

"Kyle!" John grinned as he hugged him.

Kyle pulled back after a minute. "It's good to see you. How are you doing?"

"I'm good. Everything is good. How are you? How are Megan and Mandy?"

"Everyone is doing great. Mandy is walking now and getting into everything. I have some news; Megan is pregnant with our second baby."

"Congratulations! Trying to catch up with Owen and Anna?"

Kyle chuckled. "That mission is impossible. "They pop them out two at a time. Anna is pregnant with another set of twins."

John grinned. "Boys or girls?" he asked.

"Girls this time, but Megan is pregnant with a boy, so it evens out."

John laughed. "Aw man! The triangles just keep on coming."

Kyle joined his laughter. "We'll have to think of a plan to separate them from trouble."

"Good luck with that. You live across the driveway from Owen. There's no separating these kids. You should have thought twice before you agreed to build a house on his property."

"I don't regret building a house there. Once I got over my initial hatred of Owen, I realized he's a great guy. He was meant to find Anna, just like I was meant to find Megan. Everything worked out like it was supposed to. Owen and I are good friends now."

"And business partners—How's the classic car restoration business going?"

"We stay busy, but we make sure to make plenty of time to spend with our families."

John nodded as he grabbed his bag from the carousel. They headed toward the parking lot.

"So, what's new in your world, John?"

"Nothing. It's the usual. It's nice to get stateside for a little while. I really miss you."

Kyle nodded. "I miss you too."

They climbed into Buck's old Chevy truck, and Kyle pulled out on the highway.

"Owen really did a great job restoring this old truck," John mused. "I should have you guys restore something for me."

"What do you have in mind?"

John shrugged. "I don't know. I don't really need a vehicle right now, but it would be nice to have something cool like this to drive when I do get stateside. A road trip would be great."

"You'll be here for two weeks. We can take a road trip. What do you want to go see?"

John shrugged again. "I don't know. Something awesome. Got any ideas?"

"Tons! We can check my maps at the house and come up with a plan."

April 17
1600
West Virginia

When Lydell's plane landed, he was greeted by Grammy, Gramps, and Ellery. They had made a hand-painted banner to welcome him home. He gave them all hugs, and they headed to the car. On the long drive from the airport, Grammy made her play.

"Lydell, it's been too long since you were home."

"I know. They've kept us busy, but I'll be here for two weeks. We can make up for lost time."

"Speaking of lost time, Freya has been asking about you. She'd like to see you."

Lydell rolled his eyes. "I don't understand why she keeps at this!"

"She's in love with you."

"No, she's in love with the idea of me. She burned our bridge to the ground before I left for the Navy. I have no desire to resurrect it from the ashes. She should move on with her life!"

"You're alone too much," Grammy sighed. "It's high time you settled down with a wife and started a family. All this traipsing around the world has gone on for too long. How many years do you plan to serve, Lydell?"

He groaned softly. "Grammy, don't start with me. We've had this conversation before."

"And I didn't like your answer."

He let out a long, frustrated breath. "Can we just have a nice family visit? I don't want to be set up with anyone. I'm not interested in settling down right now. Okay?"

"Fine! Break your poor, old Grammy's heart."

Gramps drove the Jeep in silence. He knew better than to get in the middle of one of his wife's lectures. Ellery slapped Lydell on the arm and gave him a scolding look.

Lydell dragged his hand over his copper burr and sighed. "Okay, look. I know you think eventually I'll cave in and take Freya back, but that's not going to happen."

"Why not?" Grammy huffed, "She's a perfectly sweet girl."

"Because—I—"

Awkward silence fell in the car.

"I'm listening."

"Because—I'm in love with someone else, okay!"

A grin spread over Grammy's wrinkled lips. "What's her name?

Lydell stared out the window watching the beautiful forest zip past in a green blur.

"Who is she, Lydell?" Grammy asked impatiently.

He cleared his throat. "Her name is Bretta."

"Is she a good, God-fearing girl?"

I don't know! Probably—I hope. What difference does it make? I'll never see her again anyway! She's long gone! So, why tell Grammy about her?

"She's a good girl."

He glanced over at his sister. Ellery had a big grin on her face as she watched him intently. Heat began to creep into his cheeks, and he looked away.

"Where does she live?" Ellery asked.

"She—uh—she's British, but she's stationed in Africa right now."

"Is that where you met?" Grammy asked.

"Yeah."

"When do we get to meet her?" Ellery asked.

"I don't know. Our schedules aren't exactly cohesive at the moment."

Ellery grinned. "Have you asked her to marry you yet?"

"No."

"Why not?" Ellery grinned as she tickled his ribcage.

Lydell jerked away as he laughed. Then he grabbed her hand and gave her a warning look.

"Why haven't you asked her?" she repeated.

He cleared his throat again. "It's complicated."

"Love is not complicated," Grammy piped in.

"Love may not be complicated, but the military is. We are not even stationed in the same country now, and even if we were—"

"Yes?" Grammy encouraged him to continue.

Lydell smirked. "As Sonny said, she's a Brit. It's not like I'm going to quit the SEALs and join the Red Coats."

Ellery chuckled. "Sonny is funny. Why didn't you bring him with you so we could meet him?"

Lydell's lips turned down in a frown. "You are never going to meet Sonny."

"Why not?" Ellery asked.

"He's not—little sister friendly."

"What does that mean?" Ellery huffed.

"It means, Sonny is a player. He sees women as a thing to conquest. He is never going to meet you. It's my job to protect you from the evils of this world and from guys like Sonny."

Ellery rolled her eyes. "You can't protect me from a guy. You're never here."

Lydell thought about her comment. "You're right. I'm not here, but if a guy so much as looks at you funny, and I hear about it, they'll never find his body!"

She rolled her eyes again.

For the rest of the drive, Grammy and Ellery peppered him with questions about Bretta. He gave them very little information and side-stepped the more dangerous questions. By the time they arrived at the farmhouse, his brain was tired from the onslaught. He got out of the Jeep and headed up the porch steps. Then he spotted something he didn't like. A teenage boy sat in the porch swing. The boy's eyes were glued to Ellery as she walked across the yard to the porch.

"Who are you?" Lydell growled.

"Donovan Jerzy." The young boy stood up and extended his hand to Lydell. "You must be Lydell. It's nice to meet you."

Lydell shook the boy's hand with a wary curiosity. "What are you doing here?"

"I work here, and I'm here to study with Ellery. We have a big Spanish exam tomorrow."

"You work here? Since when?" Lydell asked, dropping the boy's hand.

"Since Ridley went away to college. Your grandparents needed someone to help out around here. I live just down the road. I come over after school and on weekends to help your grandpa."

Lydell's eyes narrowed on Donovan. "You live down the road? I've never seen you before."

"We just moved here about a year ago."

Lydell crossed his arms over his chest and stared at Donovan.

Ellery walked past Lydell on the porch. "Hi, Donovan."

"Hey, Ell. Are you ready to study?"

"Yeah, I'm just going to change clothes first. I'll be back down in a few minutes."

Lydell heard the screen door tap loudly against the doorjamb as she went inside, but he was still watching Donovan who was intently watching Ellery disappear into the house. Lydell didn't like the look on the boy's face.

Lydell helped his Grammy up the porch steps. Then he retrieved his bag from the Jeep. By the time he showered and changed into clean clothes, Ellery and Donovan were already absorbed in studying for their exam. Lydell leaned in the doorway of the dining room and watched them. He didn't like what he saw. Donovan could barely take his eyes off of Ellery. It was infuriating! He walked down the hall to the kitchen where Grammy was chopping vegetables for dinner.

"Who is this kid?" Lydell asked.

"He's such a sweet boy. He's been a lot of help to your Gramps since Ridley left last May. We offered to pay him, but he refuses to take any money. He said he just wants to help out."

His jaw tightened. "Is that so? How much time does he spend with Ellery?"

"They usually study together after he helps with the chores. He came over right after school today to do the chores while we went in town to pick you up."

"You know what he's doing, don't you?"

Grammy looked at him with a confused expression.

"He's just hanging around to get close to Ellery! Have you seen the way he looks at her?"

Grammy chuckled. "Calm down, boy. He's a perfectly sweet kid. I'm not blind. I know he likes Ellery, but you can relax. She has no interest in him. They study together. That's all."

"Yeah, right now! Wait a few months or a year, and I bet she sees him differently! What if he tries to kiss her? I guarantee that will change the way she sees him!"

"Lydell, you need to relax. Your Gramps and I raised your dad and Ridley. I think we can handle Ellery too. I might be old, but I'm not senile. I still know what's what."

He bit his lip and sat down at the kitchen table. "I'm just worried about her, and you, and Gramps. I worry about you guys all the time."

"I know. You need to stop that before you give yourself an ulcer, Boy. We are fine. Now, about this Bretta girl, when are you going to ask her to marry you?"

"I'm not."

"But you said you're in love with her."

"I am, but I honestly don't know that our paths will ever cross again."

"So, make them cross."

"It's not that easy."

"The path to true love is rarely easy, Boy."

He sighed and shook his head. "I never said it was true love."

"You never said it wasn't."

"Do you really believe in soulmates?"

"Yes. Your Gramps and I are soulmates. He's my other half. I'd be lost without him."

Lydell grinned at her. "How did you know he was the right one for you?"

She grinned back. "I felt it deep down in my bones. When I was with him, I was so happy and when we had to part it felt like a piece of me was missing. That's how I knew."

"What does that feel like?"

"You tell me? How do you feel about Bretta?"

"Ever since I left Africa, I haven't been able to eat, and I can't sleep. My guts feel twisted inside. I can't stop thinking about her, even though I know I'll probably never see her again."

"Yep, you're definitely in love. There's no doubt about it. The question is, what are you going to do about it? Are you going to let her slip through your fingers, or are you going to do whatever it takes to hold onto her?"

Hold on to her? I don't even know if she's still in Africa. I'm pretty sure her real name isn't Bretta Brairton. I have no way to find her. Like she said, she'll have to be the one to find me. That's assuming she wants to find me.

That's assuming she wasn't just using me as an asset to further her own agenda. I know practically nothing about who she really is. All I really know is I miss her, and it hurts.

"I need to go for a walk. I need to think." Lydell headed for the back door.

"Dinner will be ready in an hour."

"I'll be back before then."

April 17
1600
Nebraska

Nick Novak met his family at the airport. All five of his younger sisters, his parents, as well as several aunts, uncles, and cousins were there to extatically greet him with hugs and kisses. It was an hours drive out to the farm, but dinner was waiting when they arrived. Three of his aunts had been busy in the kitchen all afternoon. A feast was set before them, and Nick gratefully dug into the delicious home cooking. It took him all evening to make his rounds and talk to all his relatives that had traveled to see him.

By the time he dropped off to sleep in his bedroom that night, there were aunts, uncles, and cousins scattered throughout the sprawling farm house in sleeping bags. Most of them would be leaving after breakfast the next morning, but a few would be staying for a couple of days to visit.

Breakfast came at the crack of dawn. Nick was used to getting very little sleep. He was used to being jet-lagged. He was used to running on empty. So, a full night's sleep in a soft bed was like a vacation to him. He was up before dawn helping his mother in the kitchen. His father was already working in the fields.

"How are things?" Trish Novak asked, as she peeled potatoes.

He stood at the stove cooking sausage. "Things are good. Is the corn crop doing well?"

"Yes, it is doing very well this year."

"How about the girls?"

"They are all doing fine. Tara will be graduating with a masters next month. Violet is halfway through college. Time sure flies by fast," she sighed.

"I can't believe Tara is married with kids. It seems like yesterday she was in middle school."

"She was in middle school when you joined the Navy."

Nick nodded.

"Violet might be getting married soon. He hasn't asked her yet, but we all know he's going to. Those two were meant for each other."

Nick sighed. "I feel like I've missed out on most of their lives."

"Being gone for months at a time will do that. Are you planning to stay in or get out?"

"I'm going to reup. I'm not really suited to hold down a regular job. All I've ever done was be a soldier. I don't think I'd fit in too well around here."

"That's not true. You were a farmer long before you were a soldier."

"Yeah, but I just can't see myself working a farm."

"Not enough action for you?" Brook his 17-year-old sister asked, as she walked in.

"Honestly, no. I think I would be bored out of my skull waiting around for the corn to grow."

"So, what are you planning to do after Navy life?" Brook asked.

"I have no idea."

Sasha his 15-year-old sister peeked around the doorjamb and chuckled. "You could always become an assassin. Isn't that what you do for the SEALs anyway?"

Nick chuckled. "Not exactly. We do a lot of different jobs in the SEALs, but I can't tell you about any of it, or I'd have to kill you," he teased.

Olivia, the youngest sister at 14-years-old soon joined the group, and they spent the next half hour joking, laughing, and making a large breakfast to feed all the visiting relatives.

April 18
0700
A cheap motel in Texas

Sonny forced his eyes open despite the pounding headache that begged him to sleep it off. It wasn't his style to stick around and entertain a one-night-stand. He carefully pulled his arm out from under the beautiful girl sleeping next to him. Then he quietly pulled on his clothes and left.

His trusty, old pick-up truck was parked outside the door. He got in and pulled away from the motel parking lot. As he drove down the dusty, dirt road, he passed the bar that was responsible for the atrocious hang-over he was suffering through. He'd lost count of how many shots of whiskey he had chased down with a beer the previous night. He could barely remember dancing with the beautiful blonde he'd just snuck out on.

Hell! I don't even remember her name. I think it started with a B or was it a D? What difference does it make? I'll never see her again anyway. Though she was quite the spirited little filly last night. I haven't had sex that good in a long time.

Sonny drove until he was two hours away from the motel. Then he pulled into a diner for breakfast. He sat at a booth trying to focus on the menu, but his brain didn't want to cooperate.

"Looks like you had a rough night," the waitress said.

"Can I get coffee, black."

"Sure thing, Hon."

She returned with a steaming cup of coffee a minute later. Sonny sat sipping the bitter liquid as he tried again to read the menu. When she came back, he ordered. He wasn't hungry, but he knew he needed to put something in his stomach. That much alcohol on an empty stomach had done a number on him. He'd known better, but at the time it had seemed like a good idea.

After he left the diner, he found another cheap motel and slept off his hangover for the rest of the day. He decided to be smarter the second time. He stopped for dinner before hitting the bars. By the time he made it back to his motel room with a gorgeous red-head in his arms, it was just after two in the morning. She was as drunk as he was and equally as willing.

Sonny didn't hesitate to undress them as quickly as possible before pulling her down on the bed under him. Once he'd satisfied them both, he collapsed on the bed and fell asleep.

The next morning, he repeated his usual routine. He snuck out while she was asleep, drove several towns away, and started the cycle again. After a week of getting drunk and getting laid by random strangers, he finally cleaned himself up and drove to his parent's ranch.

His mother wasn't expecting him though that was nothing new. He never called ahead to tell her he was coming for a visit. He would just show up, stay for a few days, and hit the road. He saw no reason to change his routine. He came in the sprawling ranch house and hugged his mom.

"Sonny!" she exclaimed in surprise. "It's good to see you. How are you?"

"I'm good."

"You look tired."

Sonny nodded. "It's been a rough week."

His mother frowned. "Don't pretend like you just came in from Afghanistan. I know you've been out drinking. I can smell the liquor on your breath. You're not fooling anyone."

"I never said I didn't stop on the way to have a drink."

She shook her head with a scolding expression on her face. "A drink and a woman no doubt. How long have you been stateside?"

Sonny grinned at her. "About a week."

"How many women have you had in that week?"

He shrugged. "I lost count. I think eight."

"Eight!"

He grinned mischievously. "Well, one night there were these two women who were both—"

"I don't want to hear details, Sonny! You need to stop whoring around and get your act together! You'll be thirty-two years old this year. Don't you think it's time you grew up and quit acting like a man with no future! You need to lay off the booze and the cheap women. You need to find yourself one good woman, marry her, and start a family."

"A family! Oh, hell no! First, I ain't the marrying kind. Second, I'd make a terrible dad. What kind of example would I be to a kid? No, I have no plans to ever get married or have kids."

"I should have spanked your little ass more when you were young. Maybe you wouldn't have turned out to be such a mess!"

He grinned at her. "I turned out fine."

"Fine! You're a sniper! You call killing for a living an honorable profession?"

"I only kill the bad guys, Mom. You worry about me too much."

"Of course, I worry! You give me plenty of reasons to worry and fret. I know you have a good heart down deep, but I'll be danged if any of it shows on the outside of you. You drink like a fish. You swear like a sailor, and you whore around like a heathen sinner on his way to the eternal lake that burns with fire!"

"Settle down, Mom. First of all, I am a Navy SEAL. So, technically that makes me a sailor. Therefore, I'm entitled to swear like one. Second, I only drink like a fish when I'm on leave. The rest of the time, I don't touch the stuff. I have to keep a clear head in the field. It wouldn't do to be hung over in a firefight. And third, I probably will burn in hell for my sins. The likelihood that I'll repent before I take a fatal bullet is pretty low. I don't get to church except when I come home to visit you. So, I've accepted my fate. I figure as long as I'm going to hell anyway, I might as well have as much fun and as many women as possible before I get sent there."

"Sonny! Don't be ridiculous! God is everywhere. Church is not the only place you can repent, and you know it. So, don't try using that as a crutch to excuse your choice to sin. You need to stop all this wicked partying. You need to get your life straightened out!"

He chuckled. "But sin is so much fun, and being good all the time is so boring."

"I swear, if you weren't taller and bigger than me, I'd pull your pants down right now and tan your rebellious little hide. How you got to be so disrespectful toward God and women I will never know. This is not how I raised you to act, Young Man!"

"I'm not disrespectful toward women. I make sure I satisfy them thoroughly before I leave."

She sighed in frustration. She had no idea how to get through to her thick-headed son.

"How many of the eight women you were with did you get their name?"

Sonny grinned and chuckled. "None. I don't need names. They was all bar sluts just looking for a good time. That kind of girl don't expect you to stick around and remember her name."

"Which is exactly why that kind of girl is the wrong kind of girl. You need to find a good woman before it's too late to find one. At some point, no woman will have you and your checkered past. You can only survive on your good looks for so long, Sonny."

"What? You mean I won't be able to survive on my charm?" he smirked.

"Don't you sass me, Young Man! I'm trying to have a serious conversation with you."

"I don't really like serious conversations, Mom. I don't see the point in them. It won't change anything. I'm already damaged goods. No good woman in her right mind would have me anyway. What's the point in looking for one?"

Gina studied her son for a moment in silence. "So, that's what this is about? You think you've already ruined your chance at a good woman and real happiness because of your past? So, what's the point in trying to turn your life around? Am I getting warm?"

Sonny looked away from her accusing eyes and chewed on his lip. "Something like that."

"Well, I hope to God you are wrong about that. The moment you give up trying to be a better man is the moment you doom yourself to failure. I still believe the right woman is out there for you, but if you don't stop all this foolishness, she will slip through your fingers. If that happens, you'll end up alone and miserable for the rest of your life. Grow up before it's too late!"

"I'll think about it."

"Stop thinking and start doing! I want to see you do a one-eighty, Sonny!"

Sonny closed his eyes and groaned loudly.

"Why don't you go get cleaned up. You smell like a brewery. I'll put on a pot of coffee."

"Thanks, Mom," he said to her retreating back.

Sonny took a long, hot shower. It didn't help much with his hangover. Ever since his dad passed away, his mother wouldn't allow alcohol on the ranch. She'd dealt with his father's alcoholism for too many years. After he died, she put her foot down and fired any ranch hand who didn't comply. Sonny knew better than to bring any on the property. So, he knew over the next few days he'd sober up. He also knew that the minute he'd had enough of his mother's lectures, he'd be hitting the road again. He loved his mother, but he didn't like being told what to do. That was the only source of conflict between them. She didn't approve of his lifestyle, and he had no intention of changing the way he did things.

When he came back downstairs, his mother had made him breakfast.

"I'm not really that hungry."

"Sit down and eat. You know an empty stomach and alcohol are not good friends."

He sat down and started on the plate of food.

She folded her hands together on the table. "Now, back to our previous discussion."

He groaned.

"If you could just give sober life a chance, there is a really sweet girl I want you to meet."

"I'm not interested. If I have to be nice and remember her name, there's no point in it."

Gina rolled her eyes and sighed. "Well, too bad, Young man! I already spoke to her on the phone and told her you will pick her up this evening at seven."

"You set me up on a blind date?" Sonny scoffed.

"Yes."

"I don't do blind dates."

"You did eight blind dates in the last seven days. I'm not giving you a choice. It's time you learned how to act like a gentleman instead of a drunken man-whore. I want you to behave yourself. She's a very sweet girl. Treat her with respect. She's not a bar slut."

"No-no-no! I told you; I'm not the marrying kind."

"I didn't say you have to marry her, but you are going to take her out to dinner at a restaurant. Do not take her to a bar. She doesn't drink. Treat her with respect. Then take her home at a decent time. It will be good practice for you. Maybe one day you'll actually learn how to be a decent man who someone will want to marry."

"Practice! What the f—!"

"No swearing in this house, Sonny!"

He slunk down in his chair. "First it's no booze. Now, it's no swearing. What's next?"

"I'll let you know when I decide."

"You know I could just leave now. Then what? Your little blind date will be a no go."

"You could do that, but you'll be the one missing out. She's very pretty. She's about to graduate college. She wants to teach kindergarten. I think you'll like her."

"What? A kindergarten teacher! Oh, no. I can't do it. If there's no booze, and I actually have to talk to her, it's going to be a nightmare. We won't have anything to talk about. It will be awkward. Cancel it. Tell her your son is a no-good piece of—tell her you made a mistake."

Gina smirked. "Why, Sonny. I do believe you are scared of this little girl. A tough Navy SEAL shouldn't be afraid to have dinner with a pretty girl. You can't seriously be thinking about tucking your tail between your legs and cowering away like a scared dog."

"That's low, Mom. Using the coward card is not fair."

"Are you scared?"

Sonny glared at his mother.

"Oh! You really are scared. Afraid you might actually like her? Afraid she might make you consider changing your wicked ways?"

His jaw tightened as he continued to glare at her. "Fine! You want me to go out with this stupid girl? I will! But I'm only going out with her to prove you wrong. You think I can't behave myself? Watch! I'm going to take her out to dinner. I'll be so charming she'll be begging me for it, but I'm not going to screw her! I can control myself when I want to. I'll have her groveling at my feet by the end of the night, but she'll get nothing from me. And—this is a one-time deal! I won't go out with her twice, so don't try anything funny! I'm only doing this to prove a point!"

"Good. I'm glad you're beginning to come to your senses."

"Didn't you listen to anything I just said?"

"I heard every word."

He rolled his eyes and shoved in another bite.

Gina pulled a folded piece of paper from her apron and slid it across the table to Sonny.

"What's this?"

"Her name, address, phone number, and the restaurant where I made reservations for you."

He snatched the paper off the table and jammed it into his back pocket.

"Sonny, the restaurant is fancy, so no ratty jeans or camo. You have to wear a suit and tie."

"What the— You're doing this on purpose!"

She grinned slyly. "Of course, I am. Have fun, but not your usual kind of fun."

He smirked at her as she got up to wash the dishes.

CHAPTER 27

April 25
1900
Texas

Sonny pulled up in front of a small but well-kept bungalow in a sea of sprawling suburbia. He'd gone the extra mile that afternoon and washed his truck—his mother had insisted. Then he spent the time to properly groom himself; he was sporting a fresh shave and cologne.

Mom tricked me into this! She caught me when I was hung-over and not thinking straight! It's too late to back out. There's nothing to do now but meet the girl.

He got out of the truck, walked up to the door with flowers in hand, and knocked.

Myla Heart quickly pulled rollers out of her hair and hurried to answer the door. When she laid eyes on Sonny, her heart skipped a beat. He was even more handsome than the picture his mother had texted her. He was five foot, ten inches tall with gorgeous brown eyes and a smile that made her heart race wildly.

"Come in. I'm sorry. My class ran late, and then I got stuck in traffic," she rambled nervously.

Sonny stepped through the door, and his grin grew wider. He reached up and tapped the tip of his finger to a roller still attached to her dark brown hair.

"You missed one."

Myla's cheeks grew red. "Oh, my gosh! I'm so embarrassed. Excuse me."

She turned and hurried down the short hall to the bathroom. Sonny chuckled. Then he walked into her kitchen to find a vase for the flowers. He was filling it with water when she walked in.

"Thank you for the flowers."

"Pretty flowers for a pretty girl." He turned and looked at her. "You changed clothes!"

"Your mom said this restaurant is coat and tie fancy. You look very dashing in your suit. If I had known about this date sooner, I would have went shopping for a suitable dress, but I literally had no time today. I don't want to embarrass you, but this is the fanciest dress I have."

"Okay, let me stop you right there. You are not going to embarrass me. I'm not the fancy restaurant kind of guy. My mom made that reservation, not me. She also made me wear this suit. The last time I wore this suit was to my father's funeral. This isn't the real me. I'm a blue jean, t-shirt kind of guy."

Myla chuckled. "Were the flowers your mother's idea too?"

"No, just the suit. Everything else is me."

"So—is this dress okay?" she asked nervously.

He let his eyes roam over the slinky, strapless, black dress that hugged her curves perfectly. "That dress is so hot it's about to melt off of you."

Myla blushed. "It was my prom dress."

"Too bad I wasn't your prom date." He gave her a flirty wink.

She cleared her throat nervously. "I didn't actually have a date to prom. I went alone."

"You might have started alone, but I'm guessing you didn't end up alone. Car or motel?"

"What?"

"Where did you lose your virginity? The back of his car or a motel?"

"Oh! At prom?"

"Kinky. Where at prom? Was it a public place?"

Oh! No! I didn't mean it that way. I didn't even get asked to dance. I'm still a virgin, Sonny."

"What? Were the guys at your school blind or just idiots. If I'd been there—I would have snatched you up and rocked your world."

Myla's cheeks turned bright red. "I—uh—thank you for the compliment—I think."

Sonny walked over to her and feasted his eyes on her a second time. She was beautiful.

Myla swallowed nervously when she saw the predatory look in his eyes.

Sonny took her by her bare shoulders and pulled her close. Then he leaned down and whispered in her ear, "You look beautiful."

Myla felt her cheeks grow even hotter. She breathed in the enticing scent of his cologne as his lips grazed lightly down her delicate jaw. Caught up in the moment, she leaned in.

"If we don't leave right now, we are not going to make our reservation."

She pulled back. "Is it that late already?"

"I wasn't referring to the time." He winked.

"Oh—I—uh—you mean?" She sucked in a sharp breath as she stared up into his wanton eyes.

A sly grin parted his lips. "Are you really a virgin?"

"Y-Yes."

She looked away shyly and bit her lower lip.

If I hadn't promised my mom, I wouldn't sleep with her, I'd strip her out of that dress right now and break her in. This is going to be a long night. I don't know if I can do it. Damn my mom! She set me up with the one temptation I can't resist! Shy, sweet, naïve virgins are my favorite.

Sonny stared at her for a little too long. Then he took her hand and walked out to his truck with her. He helped her into the cab, and a short while later, they were enjoying delicious—albeit overpriced—food. As promised, Sonny abstained from alcohol that evening. When they left the restaurant, he planned to take her home, but he ended up driving to the middle of nowhere.

Myla finally asked, "Are you taking me somewhere special?"

That's when Sonny snapped out of the daze he'd fallen into. "No, I'm just enjoying your company. I like listening to you talk. You're so imaginative and expressive. I wasn't even paying attention to where I was headed."

"Sonny, I want to be honest. When your mom told me you were a soldier, I wasn't sure about going out with you. I almost backed out of the date. Soldiers are so violent; they kill people."

Sonny cleared his throat. "Not all soldiers kill people. There are all kinds of jobs in the military. Saying all soldiers are violent is quite a stereotype."

"I'm sorry. You're right. I didn't mean to judge. I try not to be prejudice about anyone, but isn't the whole point of the military to wage war?"

"Actually, some could argue that the point of a strong military is to prevent war. I like to think we are more like peacekeepers. We are the big dog who walks around with the big stick to keep the little dogs in the yard from getting out of hand."

"I guess I've never considered it from that perspective before."

Silence fell for a moment.

"So, what is it you do in the Navy?"

"I'm a Navy SEAL sniper."

Myla swallowed hard. "So, you kill people."

"Yes. It's my job to take out threats before they can carry out their evil plans."

"So, you kill them before they can do something bad?"

"Yeah."

"How do you know they are actually going to do something bad? What if they grow a conscience and decide not to go through with whatever they are planning?"

"The people they sick me on don't have a conscience. They've spilled the blood of the innocent long before I spill theirs. The people I kill are very bad. They don't deserve mercy."

"Are you sure about that?"

"I'm pretty damn sure. I've seen a lot of evil things in this world. It's my job to protect you and the rest of the world from that evil. I wish I could squash every evil thing so everyone could live in peace, but that's never going to happen. Everyone has a demon inside them just itching to get out; some are just worse than others. Some people turn into murderers, others abuse those around them, and some just abuse themselves. We are inherently destructive as a species."

"Which demon is itching to get out of you, Sonny?"

He grinned. "At the moment it's a lust demon. That dress you're wearing woke him up. He's been torturing me all evening. He's just itching to get out and—well you know what he wants."

She chuckled. "I've never met anyone as blunt as you. It's nice to know what you're really thinking and not wonder if I'm being lied to."

"Myla, you're too sweet and innocent for your own good."

He glanced over at her. The innocent, curious look on her face was far too enticing. He jerked his eyes back to the road and tried to talk himself down.

Why does she have to be so perfect? I really want to corrupt her, but I promised I wouldn't. Damnit! Damnit! Damnit! I'm going to take her home. Then I'm going to leave. Damn my mom!

Myla watched him, and a grin spread over her lips. She could hardly believe she was on a date with a man as beautiful, charming, and sweet as Sonny.

"So, what is your plan tonight? Where are you taking me?"

Where am I taking her? Hell! I don't even know where we are. On this dark, deserted road it could be morning before another car passed by. Perfect for—

Sonny groaned loudly and slammed on the brakes. He threw the truck in park, got out, and paced back and forth beside the truck on the deserted, two-lane road.

Don't even think about it! She's a good girl. She's sweet, innocent, and perfect. Don't take that away from her. She deserves better than a one-night-stand with a man-whore like me! I should take her home right now, walk away, and never look back.

Myla walked around the back of the truck and stood in front of him blocking his path.

"Did I do something wrong? Are you mad at me?"

He groaned softly. "You didn't do anything wrong. Hell—you've done everything right. That's the problem."

"I don't understand."

Sonny raked a hand over his short, blonde burr. "I'm trying to be the nice guy. The problem is—I don't know how to be a nice guy."

Myla's expression showed her confusion. "I think you are nice. You've been very sweet. You brought me flowers, took me out to a nice dinner. You even wore a suit when you obviously aren't a suit kind of guy. I think you've been a perfect gentleman, Sonny."

He groaned and looked down at the broken line of yellow paint at his feet. "I'm no gentleman, Myla. Hell! I'm the opposite of that."

She walked toward him and stopped in front of him. "I think you are very sweet."

He forced his eyes up to meet hers. Her eyes were full of trust, happiness, and something else. His gaze dropped to her too enticing lips. He leaned down until his lips were almost touching hers. He argued with himself and lost.

His lips pressed down against hers in a soft caress. As soon as her lips parted to his, he delved his tongue and found hers. He continued the kiss into a soft, sucking exploration as his hands came up to frame her jaw. When she leaned into him, he slid his arms around her and slowly backed her across the lane until she was pressed firmly between the bed of his truck and his body.

His kiss grew passionate—possessive—feral. Myla put up no resistance; that only weakened what little resolve he had. His hands caressed up her sides and covered her breasts over the satin of her dress. A heat bloomed inside her; she knew he was crossing the line, but she didn't want him to stop. No man had ever kissed her—touched her. It felt good to be wanted. She slid her hands up to caress his burr and let herself get lost in the moment.

Sonny slid his hands down, reached up under the short skirt of her dress, and found her lacy panties. He hooked his thumbs securing the fabric before a quick yank rent the lace. It fell to the ground, and Myla gasped.

A sly grin spread over his lips as he enjoyed the shock in her eyes. Then his jaw clenched tight, and he took a step back from her.

"I'm sorry, Myla. I shouldn't have done that."

"It's okay."

"No, it's not. I promised my mom that I would treat you with respect, and instead I—"

She chuckled. "You promised your mom?"

Sonny grimaced. "Yeah. If I sleep with you, she'll know. I can't lie to her. She sees right through all my bull hockey."

She cleared her throat nervously. "You want to sleep with me?" she asked hesitantly.

Sonny groaned, turned his back to her, stared at the dark field across the road, and let out a frustrated breath.

"Of course, I do. What man in his right mind wouldn't want you? You're beautiful—sweet—innocent. Hell! You're perfect!"

"You would be the first to think so."

He turned to face her. "I'm sure that's not true. I don't know what kind of men you've dated before, but they must all be fools."

"You're my first date—ever."

He swallowed hard. "Ever?"

She nodded.

His eyes dropped to the lace panties lying on the road. He picked them up and shoved them into his pocket.

"I'm sorry. I shouldn't have done that. My brakes don't work."

"Your brakes don't work?" She walked to him, took his hands in hers, and grinned up at him. "But—you did stop."

"Not really. My brain hasn't stopped. It's just getting started."

"What's your brain thinking right now?" she asked softly.

He took a step back from her and shook his head. "I won't do that to you. You deserve better. The right man will come along. You'll be glad you didn't waste your first time on a loser like me. I'm doing you a favor."

"I don't think you are a loser. Any girl would be lucky if you fell in love with her. You would be a good husband. You're honorable, honest, and sweet."

"I should take you home before I lose my resolve. You deserve a good man; I don't qualify."

"You don't think you are a good man?"

"Not where sex is concerned. I'm about as bad as they come. I don't date good girls like you. I bang easy sluts who are eager and willing. It's a one-night only thing. I never see them again. No strings attached is easier—there are no complications. When I'm on deployment, I have to have a clear head. My job is very dangerous. I can't afford distractions."

"Distractions—like a girl back home."

"Yeah. Like that."

"When was the last time you were with one of these easy sluts?"

"Last night."

She swallowed hard; a grimace marred her pretty face, and her voice trembled. "So, you're just looking for a one-night-stand with me. No strings—no complications. That's why you took me out."

"That's not why I took you out. My mom made me promise not to sleep with you after she reverse-psychologied me into this date. She accused me of being a coward. She said I was afraid to go out with a good girl because I was afraid, I might actually fall for one."

"Were you afraid of that?"

"Maybe."

"Did you fall for me?"

Sonny fell silent and looked away at the grassy field across the road. A cow mooed in the dark and broke the silence.

"Did you?"

"I don't know. I mean—I like you. I think you're sweet. You're a good girl. I don't know what to do with a good girl. Usually, I just corrupt them, but you—"

"Yeah?"

"I'm trying to be good for once."

"So—do you like me?"

He cleared his throat. "I'm no good for you."

"I think you're good for me."

He shook his head. "I'm not. Right now, I want to rip that sexy dress off you and take you up against the side of my truck. The problem is—I don't deserve you."

Silence fell again. Myla stared at him in the darkness. Sonny stared at the pavement.

"If I could pick the perfect guy for you, I would. In fact, I know a couple of guys who would be perfect for you if you're not opposed to marrying a soldier. Nick and John don't believe in sex before marriage. They are both two of the best men I've ever known."

"I think you did fall for me. This is our first date, and you're already thinking about what's best for me and what kind of man I ought to marry. I think you already care about me."

"Well, of course I care." He looked back up at her. "What kind of heartless ass would I be if I didn't care about what's best—"

He was interrupted by her lips pressing against his. He kissed her back with a tender, seductive, playful, flirty kiss. Sonny got lost in the kiss, and—like before—his kiss turned feral. He backed her up against his truck again as his hands caressed firmly, possessively over her. It took every bit of his will power to pull back from her lips. He touched his forehead to hers and stood pressing her body against the truck with his.

"Myla, I'm sorry. I'm having a hard time controlling myself. I'm not used to holding back. I'm trying to be good. I'm failing, but I am trying. I should never have kissed you, but you're so damn adorable. I couldn't help myself."

Her hands slid up his dress shirt, over the hard ridges of sculpted muscle, to his smooth jaw. "I like the way you kiss. Maybe, I'm crazy, but I think I'm falling in love with you."

Sonny jerked his head back and took a step back from her. "No, not that. You don't want to do that. I'm not worthy of love, Myla. You can't fall for me. You deserve better."

"But I'm already falling, Sonny."

He shook his head and took another step back. "No—no—no! Fall in love with a good man, not a scumbag like me."

"You're not a scumbag. I believe you are a good man. I can see that you have a good heart. So, maybe, you've made mistakes in your past. That doesn't mean you have to keep making those same mistakes. You can change. You can be the good guy that's just itching to get out. I can see him. He wants to be good. He wants to do the right thing. He wants to protect me even from himself. I like that guy. Be that guy, Sonny. Let the past go."

Damn! She sounds like my mother. Is it possible to let the past go? Is it possible for me to change my ways? Do I even want to change? I didn't want to change this morning. Do I want to change now—for her? Am I falling for her?

He stood staring at her for a few minutes. Then he walked back and opened the driver's door. "Get in. I'm taking you home before I completely lose control."

He helped her into the truck and headed back toward town. Neither of them said anything the entire way back. The silence was awkward, but not as awkward as the thoughts racing through Sonny's mind. It was more than difficult for him to walk her to her door and let her go inside without him. He waited until he heard her locks click in place before he returned to his truck. He slid in and sat behind the wheel staring at her door.

Don't do it! Be the good guy for once. Walk away and leave her alone.

He turned the key, and the truck roared to life for a moment. Then it sputtered and died. Sonny cursed as he looked at the gas gauge on the dash. It read empty. He sat in the truck for a while arguing with himself. Then he got out and walked up to Myla's door.

She was just about to crawl in bed when she heard the doorbell. She grabbed a robe and tied it around her as she walked to the front door. As soon as she realized it was Sonny, she breathed a sigh of relief and opened the door. Then she saw the grimace on his handsome face.

"What's wrong?"

"My truck is out of gas. We must have coasted here on fumes."

"Is it really out of gas, or is that just a line you use to get in girls' panties?" she teased.

He grinned at her. "It's really out of gas, but that's actually not a bad line."

"It's late, and I'm already dressed for bed. Why don't you just sleep on my couch tonight, and I'll take you to get gas in the morning."

"That sounds like a dangerous proposition. Maybe, I should just sleep in my truck."

"Then why did you ring my doorbell?"

He placed both hands on her doorjamb and stared at her for a long—silent—awkward moment. Then he leaned in closer until his nose almost touched hers. The only sound was their breathing as they stared into each other's eyes.

"Because I'm weak," he whispered. "You should tell me to leave. I'm nothing but trouble."

Her heart sped up, and her breath caught. Her thoughts became muddled. She wanted him to come in, but she knew he was right. Everything he'd told her about himself was a warning, but she was finding it hard to believe he was as bad as he claimed. He seemed so sincere, so sweet, so good.

She grabbed the lapels of his suit jacket and tugged him inside.

Sonny groaned softly. "You're making a mistake, Myla. You're inviting a hungry lion into your meadow."

"I know."

She hooked her hand behind his neck and pulled him down for a kiss. While his lips sucked and pulled her lips, his hands slid the robe off her shoulders. He pulled back to feast his eyes on her lingerie, and his eyebrow quirked up in surprise. She was wearing a snug pajama t-shirt with a kitten painted across the chest. His eyes traveled down to the matching pajama pants that featured small kittens playing with balls of brightly colored yarn.

He grinned. "Sexy."

She grinned and rolled her eyes. "Sorry. I don't own anything sexy."

He caressed his fingers over the snug shirt where her taunt nipples pressed against the thin fabric.

"So, damn sexy." His voice was low, husky, and filled with unabashed desire.

His fingers trailed down her shirt to the elastic waistband of her pajama pants. He hooked his fingers down inside her panties and tugged. Then he stared down inside her pants for a moment before letting the elastic snap back in place.

"Damn! I want you so bad."

His lips found hers again, and he backed her slowly toward the hall. When they reached her room, she slid his suit jacket off his shoulders, loosened his tie, and went to work on the buttons on his shirt. Sonny watched her—arguing with himself the entire time. When she finished, he shed his shirt on the floor and Myla gasped.

Her fingers came up to trace the crescent shaped scar over his right collarbone. Then they gently trailed down his ripped abs to a small circular scar just above his right hip bone.

"How did you get these?"

"Bullet, knife."

She swallowed hard. "Are these your only scars?"

He shook his head and unzipped his slacks. They fell to the floor.

"The one on my left knee was a parachuting accident with a tree. I had to have knee surgery."

Her eyes dropped to his knee and quickly came back up to stare at the hard bulge in his black, boxer briefs.

He grinned. "First time you've ever seen one?"

She cleared her throat and jerked her eyes back up to his.

She's going to be fun to break in. She's so innocent—so sweet—so naïve.

When dawn shattered the dream playing in Sonny's head, he woke with a start. He started to slide his arm out from under Myla to sneak out when the weight of what he'd done came crashing down on his groggy brain. He froze staring at her.

Sorry mom—I couldn't help myself. You shouldn't have thrown her across my path. I tried to be good, but she's so perfect. I had to taste her forbidden fruit. I'm a sinner. That's what I do.

She stirred in her sleep and rolled facing him. Her arm found its way around his bare torso as she snuggled against him.

He knew he could get out of bed without waking her. He'd done it a hundred times before. Every instinct in him was telling him to sneak out and run like he always did, but his heart wasn't listening. He lay watching her sleep until she woke up.

"Good morning." She smiled at him and caressed her hand down the light brown stubble that covered his jaw.

"Morning." He smiled back.

"Want me to make you some breakfast?"

He slid his hand over her hip and pulled her snugly against him. "I could go for some breakfast. I worked up quite an appetite last night."

While she was making pancakes, he got in the shower and scrubbed up with her girly-smelling soap and shampoo. It was only after he got out that he remembered his only clothes were his suit and dress shirt. He opted to come to breakfast wearing a towel instead. Myla's eyes roamed over him appreciatively.

"Do you have plans today?" she asked when she sat down a tall stack of pancakes on the table in front of him.

He smirked. "Five hours wasn't enough for you last night?"

She grinned at him as she sat a much smaller stack of pancakes in front of her and took a seat across from him.

"I don't have any classes today. If you're not busy, we could go do something."

"Go do something? Like what?"

"It's your vacation. What do you like to do on leave? We can do anything you like."

Sonny shoved a big bite of pancakes into his mouth to give himself time to think of a diplomatic answer that did not involve admitting the only thing he ever did on leave was screw sluts and hang out on the ranch with his mother.

After a minute of chewing and contemplation, he drew a blank. He said the first non-sexual thing that popped into his head.

"We could go horseback riding."

Myla beamed. "I've never been horseback riding, but I've always wanted to try it. It looks like so much fun."

I should have thought that through before I blurted it out. Horseback riding means going to the ranch. Going to the ranch means facing my mother. I've been gone all night. If I show up with Myla, she's going to know I screwed her. This is bad.

"Will your mom be at the ranch? I haven't seen her in forever. It will be nice to visit with her."

Yep! I'm screwed!

Sonny dodged a bullet when they arrived at the ranch. His mother's truck was gone. He hurried up to his room and changed into jeans, boots, a t-shirt, and his black Stetson. When he came back down, Myla was in the kitchen. He could hear her talking—then he heard his mother's voice, and he froze in the hall just out of their sight.

"I hope Sonny behaved himself," Gina said.

"Oh, he was a perfect gentleman. We had a lovely dinner. Then we took a drive and talked."

Yeah, and then I screwed her brains out.

"That's good. I'm glad you had a good time. So, you two are going horseback riding?"

"Yes. I mentioned to Sonny that I've never been on a horse before, and he insisted that I come out today and go for a ride."

My mom will never believe those lies. She knows me too well.

Sonny stepped into the kitchen. "You ready to break in our new stallion?" he joked.

Myla laughed. "I think you better saddle me up an old nag that likes to go slow."

Gina grinned. "You two have fun."

Myla walked into the hall, and Gina caught Sonny by the arm. She gave him a stern look and lowered her voice.

"I know you didn't come home last night. I'm not buying that you were a gentleman. You're not capable of it, but you better not hurt this girl. She's a real sweetheart. Be good to her!"

"Don't worry, Mom. She's safe with me. I'm not going to hurt her."

Gina glared at him. "You better not!"

Sonny spent the afternoon teaching Myla how to mount a horse, reign it, and find the rhythm of riding. She was clumsy at first, but after an hour she got the hang of it. Then they took a ride on the ranch property. He couldn't remember the last time he'd had so much fun. They ate dinner on the ranch with his mom, and then he drove her home.

The voice in his head told him not to spend the night, but he didn't listen. When he woke up the next morning with her sleeping peacefully on his arm, he had no desire to bolt. The only desire he had was to spend another day with her and make love to her as often as humanly possible.

Is this what it feels like to stick around? This is nice. I could get used to this.

CHAPTER 28

April 28
1100
North Carolina

Kyle and John pulled into the driveway after a week-long road trip. The minute they walked in the front door, Mandy ran up to Kyle.

"Dada!" She threw her tiny arms around Kyle's calf.

He bent over, scooped her up, tossed her in the air, and caught her. She squealed in delight.

Megan waddled into the foyer. "Hi, Honey. How was the trip?"

"We had a blast, but I missed you."

"I missed you too." She wrapped her arms around him.

John grinned at her. "Hey, Megan, thanks for letting Kyle off the ball and chain for a few days to hang out with me."

She smirked at him. "Speaking of ball and chain, when are you going to settle down?"

"I—uh—"

Megan grinned at John. "I know quite a few eligible young women. You'll be here for three more days. I could set you up with someone."

"Thanks, but no thanks. All the blind dates you set me up on were a fiasco. I suck at dating. I always say the wrong thing or do the wrong thing. When it comes to trying to impress a girl, I'm a bumbling idiot."

"Maybe, you should try being yourself instead of worrying about impressing them."

He shook his head. "I've done that. Girls don't like the real me either. Going on a date for me is like opening a book and not knowing how to read. Everything I do is wrong. I can't interpret any of their signals. If I think she wants a kiss, what she really wants is for me to get lost. If I think she would like me to be a gentleman and hold the door open, she'll be a feminist who doesn't want a man controlling her or telling her what to do, and she'll take it the wrong way. If I think it's okay to hold her hand, I'll be wrong every time. It's impossible."

Kyle chuckled. "Megan, you know he doesn't want to be set up. Why do you keep pushing him?"

She sighed and looked up at John. "I'm only trying to help you. You're a great guy. I just want to see you happy. I want you to find the right girl."

"I appreciate it, Megan, but I don't think she's out there. I'm a hopeless case. Stop worrying about me. Besides, I stay busy with the SEALs. I don't have time for a woman. She'd be here alone most of the time, and I'd be overseas. It wouldn't work. Long distance relationships are too hard."

"Kyle and I made it work."

"Yeah, but you guys are the exception to the rule. I can't even get a girl to like me for one date. I'd never be able to keep her happy if we were half a world apart."

"Don't sell yourself short, John. You have a lot to offer," she said encouragingly.

"Not to interrupt your sales pitch, but John and I are starving," Kyle said. "Do you want to go grab some lunch?"

Megan pulled him down for a kiss. Then she grinned up at him. "Owen is already making lunch. They invited us all over."

"Good, I'm famished. What's he making?"

"Lasagna."

"Oh yeah! He makes the best lasagna," Kyle said enthusiastically.

A short while later, they walked over to Owen and Anna's. They were greeted at the door by the little Wiley clan.

"Uncle John!" they all cried in unison.

He was immediately accosted by the kids and was easily convinced to give them all piggy-back rides around the house. After giving several rides to each kid, he sat down on the fireplace hearth, and all the kids crowded around him.

"Okay, now it's been a while since I saw you. How old are you again?" John asked.

Mason took over the narrative. "I'm Mason. Me and Carter are six. Julia is five. Cassie is four. Becca is almost three, and Grayson and Bryson just turned one, but they're just babies. They don't talk good yet. Mandy is one, but she's not our sister. She's just our friend, even though we call Uncle Kyle and Aunt Meg our uncle and aunt. They're not really related to us. It's just an honorary title, because they are friends with mom and dad."

John nodded and managed to quell the grin. "You're very smart, Mason."

"I'm smart too," Carter piped in. "Mom and Dad said we are all equally smart. Nobody is smarter than nobody else."

"That's very true. You are all very sweet too. Who taught you to be such good kids?"

"My mom and dad," Carter said proudly.

"And Uncle Kyle and Aunt Meg teached us too," Julia added.

"Well they are all doing a great job," John said grinning.

"Did you know we is going to have new babies soon?" Cassie asked. "Mommy and Aunty Meg have babies in their tummies, but they aren't finished yet. They is still growing."

"I know. That's going to be exciting," John said.

"Yeah, but babies poop in their diapers, and it stinks," Carter said wrinkling his nose.

John chuckled. "That is true, but they don't wear diapers forever."

"Yeah, they has to get potty trained," Becca said. "I'm potty trained. I go on the big chair like a big girl."

"That's very good, Becca."

Becca threw her tiny arms around John's neck and kissed him on the cheek. "I love you, Unka John."

"I love you too, Becca. I love all you kids." He was soon given a hug and a kiss by each child.

Megan watched from her seat on the couch, and a tear rolled down her cheek.

John is so sweet. I don't understand why he has such a hard time with women. Any woman would be lucky to have him. I have to find him a wife. He really needs a good woman in his life. He deserves to be happy too.

A few minutes later, Anna announced that lunch was ready. They all sat around the dining room table and dug into Owen's lasagna.

"Oh, Kyle, I forgot to tell you that Eli called while you and John were gone," Megan said.

"What's my little brother up to?" Kyle asked with a grin.

"He wanted to know if he could visit us on his next leave. I told him that he doesn't need to ask. He's always welcome."

Kyle nodded. "I don't think we've seen him since—"

"Your birthday right after we got married," Megan finished.

"Well, he is a SEAL. They keep us busy," John said.

"Have you ever worked with Eli on a mission?" Anna asked.

John shook his head. "No, my team is based out of Afghanistan. I think Eli is based out of Brazil."

Kyle nodded. "Yeah, Eli works on the other side of the world from Echo."

"Your mom called too," Megan said.

"How is she doing?"

"She wants you to call her. They are planning a trip down here in June."

Kyle nodded. "I'll call her when we get home."

John grinned. "Not to change the subject, but do you ladies know what you're going to name the new babies?"

"Buck Allen Masters, after my dad," Megan said.

"Gabrielle and Bianca," Anna said. "I haven't settled on middle names yet."

The rest of their lunch was filled with good conversation and lots of laughter. The kids piped in with their own cute observations which usually brought more laughter. Everyone enjoyed themselves, and after the dishes were done, Kyle, Megan, Mandy, and John returned home.

When Mandy went down for a nap with Megan, Kyle and John went for a walk down to the beach.

"You were right," John said. "Owen really is a nice guy. I like him too. I see now how you two became such good friends even after the whole Megan triangle fiasco."

"Told you, but your still my first best friend."

"Yeah, Me, Nick, Sonny, and Owen. Too bad Nick and Sonny didn't come with me. We should plan a trip with the five of us some time. If Nick and Sonny get a chance to hang out with Owen, they'll like him too."

"I'd like that. We'll have to make it happen soon. I really miss all the guys. I love my new life, but some part of me misses the old life too."

John nodded. "Yeah, all the guys miss you too. It's not the same without you. Fry is a good leader, but he's not you. He does things a lot differently. It took some getting used to."

Kyle grinned. "Fry is his own man. Every leader has to find their own way of doing things. That's just the way it is, but he's a good man."

"I agree. We had some serious trouble in Congo. I wasn't sure what Fry was going to do, but he made the right decision."

"I've been in that hot seat before. Hard decisions are just that—hard."

John cleared his throat. "Have you ever had to lie—to your C.O.?"

Kyle's eyebrow rose. "I've never lied to my C.O."

John grimaced. "I didn't like it. It felt wrong, but it was necessary to protect innocent people. Things are really screwed up in Congo right now. Some very bad people are running the show. I'm still waiting for it to come back and bite us all in the ass."

Kyle frowned. "Did you do something illegal?"

"We disobeyed a direct order."

"Does Rowen know you disobeyed his order?"

"Yes, Fry told him the truth later, but it wasn't exactly Rowen's order. We had to report to a U.N. representative. The order came down from him and his superiors. The order was wrong. It was unethical and reprehensible. Fry said Rowen agreed with our decision to disobey the order, but he can't officially commend us for it either. We all lied. We deceived the U.N. If it ever comes out that we didn't follow that order, there will be a severe backlash. It could damage relations between the U.S. and the U.N."

Kyle let out a deep breath. "I've disobeyed a direct order before. I was ordered to destroy that facility in Siberia. I didn't do it, because it would have meant killing a lot of innocent victims in that super soldier experiment."

John nodded. "I remember—well not technically. I was unconscious on that mission, but I remember what you told me about it later. If I was in your shoes, I wouldn't have blown up the place either. Killing the innocent would be far worse than facing the punishment for disobeying an order. That's what we faced in Congo. None of us wanted to kill the man we were ordered to assassinate. It would have been wrong."

"Like I said, hard decisions are hard. There's no easy road when you reach that particular fork."

"Not to change the subject, but can you ask Megan to stop playing matchmaker?"

Kyle smirked. "You think I haven't already? She's got a mind of her own. She's just trying to help. She wants you to be happy. In her mind, that means finding you a wife."

"I know, but I don't want to face that road anymore. I'm tired of the rejection. It's easier to be alone than to be made to feel like you're worthless."

"You're not worthless, John."

He nodded, but a frown pulled at his lips. "It just makes me feel worthless when the bad ending comes. It feels like there's something seriously wrong with me. You know the only woman who's ever really been nice to me is your wife. You might want to get her radar checked. I think she's wearing rose-colored glasses or something."

Kyle chuckled. "She is overly positive most of the time. That's one of the things I love about her. She's been through the fire, but she came through it without being seriously damaged like me. Hell—she's even managed to change me. I'm not the same guy I was before I met her. She pulled my ass back from the brink and made me look at life from a new perspective. Maybe she can help you find a new perspective too. If you let her, she might just find a happily-ever-after-ending for you too."

John shook his head and stared off at the ocean. "Nah. I don't believe in happily-ever-after. I've seen too much reality to be swayed by some fairytale in a book or movie. It doesn't exist."

"So, you don't think me and Megan are living happily-ever-after?"

John chuckled. "You two might be the exception, but I don't see it happening for me. Definitely not for Sonny."

Kyle laughed. "Well, Sonny is bringing that down on himself. You can't use women the way he does and expect a happy ending. His world is bound to crash down on him sooner or later. I don't think he cares about finding true love. He just wants to know where his next piece of ass is coming from."

"He doesn't care where it comes from as long as he gets some. He's really not that picky. He'll do any piece of hot ass that crosses his path."

"True."

"He's disgusting."

Kyle nodded. "I can't disagree with you."

"If he wasn't such a good friend, I wouldn't have anything to do with him. He's great when it comes to having your back, pulling your ass out of the fire, or just being there when you need a friend, but I can't stand to listen to him talk about women. He makes me want to puke. The things he's done—"

"We all make choices in life. Sonny's just made some really bad ones when it comes to women. If you take women out of the equation, he's really a great guy."

"Yeah, I guess none of us are perfect. I'm certainly not."

"What's bugging you, John?"

He shrugged. "I don't know. A lot of things. Nothing. Everything."

"It's something specific."

John let out a long breath, bent over, picked up a handful of sand, and watched it sift through his fingers.

"Time. That's what's bothering me. I'm not getting any younger. I'm starting to feel it creep up on me. If I—if I do come home in a bag—"

"That's not going to happen, John. Don't start thinking like that."

John swiped a tear away and looked back at the ocean. "If I come home in a bag, don't bury me. I want my ashes spread on the ocean. I don't want anyone visiting my dried-up bones and crying over them. I'd rather people just forget me and go on with their lives."

Kyle grimaced. "Where are these morbid thoughts coming from, John. You're worrying me."

"I've just been thinking about the end. I know it will come eventually. The longer I stay in the program the closer it gets. My body doesn't work like it did when I was twenty. It's starting to wear out. One day, I'll slip up, and that will be that. It only takes one tiny mistake to end you out there."

"The mine?"

John nodded. "I've been having nightmares about that day lately. Maybe you should have let me blow up that day. It might have put me out of my misery early on and saved me all this—"

"All what?"

"Disappointment. Getting my hopes up and planning for a future that's never going to happen is almost worse than a quick merciful death."

"You can't think like that. If it wasn't for you, I'd be dead. You saved me in Afghanistan. If you hadn't read my letter and forced me out of my self-destructive state of mind, I might have put a bullet in my head. I thought about it more than once."

"That's not what you told Megan."

"I know. Some things she is better off not knowing."

"You don't still think about it, do you?"

Kyle shook his head. "Not since I married her, but before—yeah. It crossed my mind more than a few times. When I worked for Buck, there were a few bad days when I thought it would be easier to just end it all and be out of my pain and misery."

"What kept you from doing it?"

"You and Megan."

"Me?"

Kyle nodded. "You're my best friend, John. I know I say that Sonny, Nick, and Owen are my best friends too, but you're my one, true, best friend. You know me better than anyone else on this Earth. You know all—well most—of my dark secrets." He grinned slyly. "The point is, without you in my life there would be a huge, dark, sucking hole in my soul. I love you. I don't want to think about life without you in it. You are more important to me than you know. We are like brothers—no—closer than brothers. I don't want anything to happen to you, and I truly want you to be happy. It makes my heart hurt to hear you talk about being in pain and misery. I want to help you, John. What can I do?"

"I don't know. I'll try to do better—think better thoughts. Sometimes, just seeing the ugly side of the world on a regular basis gets to me. It was easier when you were there. I had someone I could talk to about it, but now—I guess I just miss you. You're my rock. If I didn't have you to anchor to, I'd be lost at sea in a storm of misery and chaos."

Kyle nodded. "You and Megan are my rocks. You make a good place to anchor to. I'm glad that mine didn't kill you. I need you in my life."

Tears streaked down John's cheeks as he pulled Kyle into a tight hug. "Thanks, Kyle. I just needed—"

"I know. Anytime. I love you, John."

CHAPTER 29

April 28
1400
North Carolina

The minute Kyle and John walked through the front door Mandy ran to Kyle.

"Dada home!"

Kyle grinned, picked her up, spun her around, and enjoyed her delighted squealing.

"Hi, Honey. Hi, John," Megan called from the kitchen.

"Hi, Babe. Did you have a good nap?"

She walked out of the kitchen with her cell phone to her ear. She gave Kyle a thumbs up as she listened intently to the phone.

"Yeah, six o'clock will be fine. Are you sure you'll be able to get here by then? No, we are not on any kind of time crunch. Drive safe, and just get here when you can. No, don't be silly. It's going to be great. John's a sweetheart. He's not going to care about any of that. I'm serious. He's not that kind of man. No, really. Stop worrying. See you soon."

Megan hung up, eased herself down on the nearest couch, and rubbed her very pregnant belly.

"Please tell me you weren't just setting John up on another blind date," Kyle groaned as he gently set Mandy down to run and play.

"Actually, it's more like a double date."

John let out an exasperated breath.

Kyle's eyebrow rose, and he gave his wife a stern look.

"Megan. I told you, he doesn't want to be set up anymore."

"I know, but sometimes you men just don't know what's good for you."

Kyle let out a frustrated breath.

"It's okay, Kyle," John said quietly. "What's one more embarrassing evening in a long string of disasters?"

"It won't be a disaster, John. The four of us are going to have a nice quiet evening here at the house. Owen volunteered to make enchiladas and all the fixings for us. He and Anna are going to watch Mandy for a few hours. So, it will just be me, Kyle, you, and my good friend, Ursula."

Kyle raked a hand through his ebony hair and groaned again.

"Don't act like it's the end of the world, Honey. It's going to be fun. We will be here to help steer John and Ursula through the pitfalls of a blind date. I was thinking after last time, maybe a chaperone to keep John on the right track might be better than throwing him in the deep end to drown on his own."

John grimaced. "I appreciate the effort you are putting into this, but I don't want you to get your hopes up, Megan. For me, dating is like walking through a mine field. Something is bound to blow up in my face."

"Don't go into it with that attitude. You have to be positive. For all you know, Ursula could be the one."

He frowned. "I highly doubt it, but I'll humor you—again."

"Thanks, John." Megan smiled brightly at him.

At half past six, the doorbell rang. Kyle answered the door and let Ursula in. Megan was relaxing on the couch per Kyle's insistence. Her back had started to hurt, and he thought she'd exerted herself too much that day. She thought he was being over-protective. He'd argued that she was trying to do too much for the stage of pregnancy she was in. She'd reluctantly agreed to follow his advice and veg-out on the couch.

"Hi, Ursula. This is John," Megan called from the couch.

John stood up and politely offered Ursula his hand.

She grinned up at him. "Nice to meet you."

He smiled back as his eyes roamed briefly over her. She was blonde, petite, and pretty. He couldn't help but notice that she gave him the once over too.

"Megan forgot to mention that you are handsome as sin."

He stared at her unsure how to respond—afraid to respond. He was sure anything he said would be the wrong thing—so he said nothing.

Ursula gave John a playful wink. "Nice surprise."

Kyle helped Megan up from the couch, and they went to the dining room to feast on Owen's delicious dishes. The conversation moved along—thanks to Megan. John avoided talking any more than he absolutely had to. He noticed that Ursula was a talker. She had no problem talking—and talking—and talking—mostly about herself, her accomplishments, and her Quarter horses. She seemed particularly proud of her Quarter horses; she went on and on about all the races they had won. The more she talked the less interested John became in anything she said. He tuned her out and let his mind wander as he finished his plate.

She's completely self-absorbed, snobby, a typical—spoiled, rich girl. Not only is she out of my league, but she has nothing in common with me. I don't see this going anywhere. In fact, I don't want it to go anywhere. I'm actually a little disgusted with her. For the first time, I'm the one who's not interested. Okay, wait—this is the second time. How could I possibly forget Linda? I wish I could forget her.

After dinner, Megan suggested that Ursula and John go for a walk on the beach. John inwardly cringed. The last thing he wanted to do was spend more time with Ursula, especially alone. He didn't put up an objection because he didn't want to disappoint Megan. She seemed so excited about the date.

The walk to the beach was quiet and awkward.

Wow! Amazing! She can actually shut her mouth and stop talking about herself for more than a minute at a time. I didn't think she had it in her.

"You were awfully quiet during dinner. I barely know anything about you—except what Megan has told me."

Nope! I was wrong. She can't stop talking. Five minutes must be a record for her.

"There's not much to tell."

"I'm sure that's not true. You're a Navy SEAL. I'm sure you have stories from your missions."

"My missions are classified. If I told you—I would definitely have to kill you."

With your mouth—you'd blab every secret to the world in about thirty seconds.

The sound of her laughing snapped him out of his musing.
"You are so funny! Why weren't you this funny at dinner? Were you just saving all your good jokes for me?"
He glanced her way as they walked. She was smiling at him.

She's really beautiful. Most guys would probably like her. I'm just not one of them. She's vain, self-absorbed, and a snob. It's obvious—all she thinks about is herself. I just don't like her. I'm tired of listening to her prattle on. I've heard more about training and racing Quarter horses than I care to know. I wish she'd just shut up already!

Ursula studied John's stern expression as they walked down the dark path toward the private beach. Then her eyes slowly roamed over the rest of him.

He is so handsome. He would make such beautiful babies. Megan is right. He is very polite. Plus, he's got that sexy, brooding vibe that I just can't resist. I wonder if my parents would approve of him if I brought him back to Connecticut with me?

"I'm sorry, John. I've been monopolizing the conversation all evening. Tell me about yourself. I really want to get to know you. Are you really as perfect as you seem?"
John smirked. "Perfect? No. I'm far from perfect."
"Me too. I tend to talk too much. I ramble on and on when I get nervous. Awkward silences make me uncomfortable so I tend to fill them. That's just one of my flaws."

It's a big one. A really big, annoying one.

Ursula bumped his arm with her shoulder and grinned up at him. "So, tell me about yourself."

"What do you want to know?"

"Where are you from originally?"

"Iowa."

"Did you grow up on a farm?"

"No. It was a regular house in the suburbs."

"What do your parents do for a living?"

"My dad was—is—a lawyer."

"Did your mom stay home with you then?"

"She stayed home."

"Do you have any siblings?"

"No, one was more than enough for them."

Ursula chuckled. "Were you a handful?"

John shrugged.

"Were you always this quiet?"

"Yeah."

"What made you decide to join the Navy?"

"I wanted to get the hell away from my parents and do something worthwhile with my life."

She frowned. "You didn't get along with them?"

"I wouldn't say we had much of a relationship at all. There was no reason to stick around."

"How about now? Has getting some distance improved your relationship with them?"

He smirked. "Only if you count that I don't have to see them anymore."

"When was the last time you saw them?"

"When I left to join the Navy. I was eighteen."

"Oh."

Silence enveloped the woods. The only sound was the crunch of the fine, gravel path beneath their feet in the dark. When they reached the beach, John sat down on the sand near the water. Ursula sat next to him. She was a little too close for his liking. He was doing his best not to encourage her. He had no interest in her whatsoever. He stared at the ocean and avoided making eye contact with her.

To his dismay, she broke the long, awkward silence.

"Do you plan to get married and start a family soon?"

They always steer the conversation to this—family—kids—when are you getting out—I don't want to date a man who's never around—why would you put the military above a relationship with me? Blah—blah—blah. I'm tired of answering this question. I'm just tired of answering questions—period! I'm tired of dating. It's such a waste of time.

"No."

"How much longer do you plan to serve?"

"Until I come home in a body bag." His voice was terse.

Her eyebrow rose, and her mouth dropped open. "That's—um—"

He stared ahead at the ocean. "Too morbid for you?"

"That's horrible! Why would you say that?"

"Statistically, that's where I'm headed. Tier One Operators don't have good odds. Our job is very dangerous. The likelihood that we will die in the line of duty is pretty high."

"Why do it then? Why not get out before it's too late?"

Typical! Of course, that's what she'd think! Her rich, spoiled ass knows nothing about sacrifice or doing what's right because it's the right thing to do. She's so selfish! She disgusts me!

His jaw tightened, and his voice came out in a harsh, bitter growl. "Because if men like me don't stand on the front line and defend our country from the predators of the world, people like you won't be free to race your precious Quarter horses and become rich, spoiled, and self-absorbed. I do it to protect your right to live free—whether you deserve it or not."

She gasped, and the shock on her face was clear. She stood up and stormed off the beach toward the path back to the house.

Good riddance! At least now, I don't have to listen to her prattle on about her stupid horses anymore!

He lay back on the sand, stared up at the stars, and lost track of time.

"Really!" Kyle's annoyed tone rang clear over the sound of lapping waves.

John groaned.

"Apparently, you can't be left unsupervised for more than two seconds. Why in the hell would you call her rich, spoiled, and self-absorbed?"

He sat up and stared at the waves lapping the sandy beach. "Just called it like I saw it."

Kyle stepped in front of him and stood glaring at John. "Ursula is the opposite of that! She is too humble to say so, but she and her family do a lot of charity work to give back to underprivileged communities. Half the profits they make off of racing horses is donated to the needy. She is anything but spoiled or self-absorbed. Where did you even get that from?"

John let out a long breath. "I don't know. She kept droning on and on at dinner about her horses and all her many accomplishments."

Kyle shook his head. "Did you not notice that she was mostly answering Megan's questions about all of that? Megan was just trying to get a conversation started between you two, but you were like a tight-lipped clam all through dinner. You barely said five words the entire meal. Ursula, Megan, and I carried the entire conversation."

John shrugged and stared at the sand instead of looking up into Kyle's accusing eyes.

"Why in hell did you tear into her like that? You really hurt her feelings."

"Yeah—newsflash. I'm a jerk! Big surprise." John muttered.

"I think you should go up to the house and apologize to Ursula. She was bawling her eyes out when I left. Megan is trying to console her, but she's under the impression that she comes across as a selfish, spoiled bitch to all men, and that's why no man wants to date her. She's had a bad string of dating experiences—just like you. You've both had a similar experience when it comes to the opposite sex. That's why Megan thought you two would get along. Ursula is one of the sweetest people I've ever met. Of all Megan's friends—Ursula is my favorite. She's a caring, kind, moral, giving person. I can't believe you said that to her, John!"

"Damnit! I am a jerk. I'll go apologize right now. I'm sorry, Kyle. I really don't know what's wrong with me."

John sprinted up the gravel path and caught Ursula just as she was coming out of the house.

"I want to apologize."

He could see she'd been crying; her eyes were red, and there were mascara smudges under her eyes and fresh tears on her cheeks.

"Why? You only said what you were thinking. You're probably not the first man to think it. Apparently, I come across as a horrible person."

Her shoulders shook with a fresh sob as she passed him on the sidewalk. He gently grabbed her arm and spun her around.

"I'm really sorry, Ursula. I never should have said those things. I don't know you. I had no right to judge you based on a few comments over dinner. I'm the jerk. Please, don't leave."

"Please—just let me go." She pulled free of his grasp and headed to her car. "You've already shattered my dignity. I don't think I'll be going out on another date ever again. I'm just not meant to be with anyone. Everyone sees me as a self-absorbed jerk. It's hopeless."

John felt her words like a kick in the gut. He'd done this to her. He had to make it right.

"Look—just—don't go like this. You're upset. You shouldn't be driving when you're this upset. You could get into an accident."

He stepped up beside her and put his hand on the door to prevent her from opening it.

She turned facing him with trembling lips. "Why would you care? Why would anyone care?"

"I'm sure your parents would care."

"They are the only ones."

"Megan and Kyle would care."

"Fine! My only two friends in the world!"

"I would care."

She scoffed. "No—that I don't believe at all. You're just—"

John leaned in to kiss her, and she jerked back in surprise.

"Do you really think kissing me will fix this? It won't. You opened my eyes to the way the world sees me—truly sees me. They can't be closed now. I'll never forget what you said to me."

"I'm sorry, Ursula. I didn't mean it."

"Yes, you did." A tear streaked down her cheek.

He felt horrible for making her cry.

"You're right. I meant it in that moment, but that's not who you really are. I see that now."

"Why? Because Kyle came and set you straight? The moment he heard what you said, he stormed out of the house in a blaze of fury. I actually thought he might beat the crap out of you for what you said. Then I half hoped he would. You would have deserved it."

"I would have. I'm truly sorry, Ursula."

"You only voiced what you believed to be true. Still, in the future, maybe you should keep your opinions to yourself. Words can hurt more than a punch in the face. A bruise will heal over time. A broken heart never heals."

"I'm sorry I acted like an ass. I'm a walking disaster. You deserve better than the likes of me."

"That's just the way the dice always seem to roll for me. Please move so I can get in my car."

"Ursula, please don't leave like this. I'm worried about you. At least let me drive you home."

"Why? So, you can insult me some more? I don't think so. I've had enough for one night."

John leaned down and gently pressed his forehead against hers.

"I'm really sorry."

"I can tell."

"If I promise to be good and keep my mouth shut, will you give me a second chance?"

"No."

"Why not?"

"Because it hurts too much. I could have fallen for you, John—I was starting to like you, but you took a sledge hammer to my heart and maliciously pounded it into the ground. I don't trust you anymore. Megan told me you weren't like those other men I dated. She was right. You are a thousand times worse. The worst thing they did was not return my voice-mails, e-mails, or text messages. They simply ignored me and never told me why they were not interested in a second date. Now, thanks to you, I know what they were probably thinking about me."

He swallowed hard as he stared into her eyes. "I feel awful. What can I do to fix this?"

"Nothing. You can't fix it. There are some things that can't be taken back. You just have to live with the consequences."

"I'm sorry."

"Yes, you are sorry. You'll have to live with that too."

"Are you okay, Ursula?" Kyle called out as he walked up from the gravel path.

She looked over at Kyle and nodded as she wiped away her tears.

"I'll be okay. I was just leaving. I have an early day tomorrow. This morning my father picked up two new horses that have to be broken. I still have a long drive ahead of me. I'll call Megan in a few days. I'm going to be busy for a while training them."

Kyle nodded. "Call when you get back to Connecticut. Let us know you got there safely."

"It's a long drive. It will be the middle of the night. I don't want to wake you."

"I'll be awake. It doesn't matter how late it is. Just call. Megan and I will worry otherwise."

"Connecticut! You definitely shouldn't be driving that far tonight. If you insist on getting there by morning, than at least let me drive you It's the least I can do. I owe you—for being a jerk."

"You don't owe me, and I'd prefer to be alone right now. I have some unpleasant truths to face. I'd rather you not be there to make any more of your truthful observations. I don't think I can handle a second one."

"Please don't leave like this."

Ursula looked at Kyle for help.

"John!"

John looked at Kyle. "She's too upset to drive. She could get into an accident."

"I'm not going to wreck the car. I'm perfectly capable of driving myself! Please take your hand off the door and let me leave. We are never going to see each other again. I'll make sure of it. Go about your life and forget about me. It should be easy. I'm not worth remembering."

"That's not true. I'll never forget you or what I did. I was wrong."

"It's too late to take it back so step back and let me go."

He shook his head. "What if I change? Would you give me another chance?"

"No second chances for you, John. I don't ever want to see you again."

I don't ever want to see you again. Familiar words. I've heard them too many times. I don't ever want to hear them again. I wonder how many other women I falsely accused or wrongly hurt the way I did Ursula? Was it all of them? Well—not all—Linda deserved it.

Ursula is the last girl I'll ever hurt with my malicious mouth. From now on I'm steering clear of women—all women. Apparently, the only way to protect them is to keep my distance.

He took a step back, and she got in her car and drove away. John watched her tail lights disappear down the winding road through the woods.

He groaned loudly. "Damn! What is wrong with me? Why did I have to open my stupid mouth? I'm such an idiot!"

Kyle shook his head. "Megan is not happy with you. Ursula is a really close friend."

John grimaced. "I really screwed up this time. I deserve whatever punishment Megan dishes out."

To their surprise, Megan didn't come down on John. She finally understood the truth of Kyle's warnings. She didn't know what to say to John. There were no words.

John does have a knack for saying the exact wrong thing to a woman. He truly is a magnet for trouble. I should have listened to Kyle this time and not meddled. I feel so bad for Ursula. She's so sweet, and she really deserves a good man. John is sweet too. I don't understand why he would he say that to her? Why would he even think it? That's not who Ursula is at all.

CHAPTER 30

April 29
0800
Nebraska

Nick sat on the porch swing after breakfast staring out across the yard at the corn field.

"Penny for your thoughts," his mother said as she sat next to him.

Nick shrugged. "I was just thinking about what I would do when I retire from the Navy."

"What do you want to do?" Trish asked.

He rubbed his hand over his ebony burr and frowned. "I don't know. I mean, technically I don't really have to work. Kyle gave us all enough money to retire for the rest of our lives. So, it's not about earning a paycheck. I guess I'm just so used to the military life that I don't know what else I would want to do."

"You have a little time to think about it. You're not retired yet.

"It doesn't really matter anyway. I don't plan that far ahead. I just focus on what's right in front of me most of the time. It's the best way to live to fight another day. No distractions."

"Is that why there's still no woman in your life? You don't want any distractions?"

"Something like that. Honestly, I don't have time to pursue a woman."

"Do you ever intend to pursue one?"

"Sure, when I get out."

"It sounds like your friend, Kyle, is happily married. You could be too. There are quite a few eligible girls around here who—"

"Not interested."

"Not even to go on a date?"

"Where would that lead? I'm leaving for Afghanistan in two days."

"I just worry about you. The last time you went on a date you were in high school."

Nick cleared his throat. "Actually, Kyle's wife set me up on a couple of blind dates when we came stateside for Owen's wedding."

"You never told me that."

He shrugged. "It didn't go anywhere. I only went out on one date with each girl. It just didn't work out. There was nothing to report."

Trish rolled her eyes and sighed. "Nick, even if there is nothing to report, I'd still like to know what's going on in your life. I'm your mother. I love you."

"I know, Mom. I'm fine. I knew when I joined the SEALs that it wouldn't be easy. This is the life I've chosen. I am happy. I don't need a woman in my life right now, especially the wrong woman."

Trish sighed and hugged her son.

April 29
0900
West Virginia

Lydell was mucking out the horse stalls when his phone buzzed in his pocket.

"Hi, Ridley."

"Grammy said I needed to call you so I'm calling."

"But you didn't want to call me."

"I've got a lot going on right now. She said you've been worried about me."

"I guess I have been. How are your classes?"

"Tougher than I thought they would be. College is nothing like high school. I feel like I've been thrown in the deep end with a weight tied to my feet."

"Been there, literally done that," Lydell chuckled. "Hang in there, Brother. You can do it."

"I decided to major in structural engineering."

"Good for you."

"I gotta run. I have a class in ten minutes."

"Okay. Love you."

"I love you too."

Lydell slid his phone back into his pocket and went back to mucking. This was his least favorite chore on the small family farm. His grandparents had always grown enough crops to sustain the farm for the year and sell the other half at the local farmer's market. It was a meager living, but they had always gotten by. Now that he'd paid off all the loans against the farm, his Gramps had scaled back. He'd only planted what the family would need. He was getting too old to keep up with farming for a profit.

Lydell had kept a wary eye on Donovan, but he'd seen no sign that the boy acted inappropriately. In truth, Donovan seemed shy, but friendly. His Grammy had assured him that she was keeping close tabs on Donovan, and she wasn't worried in the least. According to her, Ellery showed interest in older boys but showed none in Donovan. That news didn't ease his mind in the least. He planned to have a serious talk about boys with Ellery this afternoon. The last thing he needed was his baby sister getting into boy trouble while he was on deployment.

April 29
1900
Texas

Sonny moved the food on his plate around with his fork, but he wasn't eating.

"Are you not hungry?" Myla asked.

"Huh?"

"Are you that distracted?"

He bit his lip and dropped his gaze to his plate. "Actually, I am."

"What's wrong?"

"Everything. I have to go back to Afghanistan tomorrow."

"I know. I'm dreading it. Maybe it won't seem like so long if we call or text every day."

He shook his head. "Can't do that. When I'm on a mission, which is most of the time, I don't have my phone on me. It's a safety protocol. If we are captured by the enemy, we can't have any personal items on us that could identify us or be used against us."

"Oh."

"I—"

"We could write letters, or I could text you and just wait for you to get back on base to return my texts."

He shook his head. "That's a bad idea."

"Why?"

"Look—I've been trying to think of the right way to say this, but there ain't no right way."

Myla swallowed hard.

"I can't go back on deployment like this."

"Like what?"

"I told you before that I can't have distractions when I'm in the field."

"Me being the distraction."

He nodded.

"Okay. We won't write, text, or call. You can just let me know next time you're going to be stateside, and we can—"

"Nope. That's just a different kind of distraction. See, if I know yer back here waiting around for me to come home, I'll be thinking about that, and I'll lose focus. I might not make it back home at all. The tiniest bit of distraction in a battle situation can cost a man his life. It's not just my life I have to protect. There are fifteen other men on the team counting on me to have their back. If I'm distracted thinking about you, I ain't watching their six the way I should. I got to be one hundred percent focused one hundred percent of the time out there."

"I understand. You can't think about me at all."

"I'm sorry, but it is true."

"So, don't think about me. I'll be here waiting when you get back, whenever that is. We can pick up where we left off."

He shook his head. "You just ain't understanding, Myla. I don't want you to sit around waiting for me. I want you to find happiness with the right guy. I'm not the right guy. We've had a good time this week. Actually, this is the best time I've ever had, but it's over now. There ain't no future for you with a guy like me. Find yourself a good one, get married, and have a passle of young'uns. That's what I want you to do. If I think of you, that's how I want to imagine you. I want you to be happy with some handsome feller with about six kiddos runnin' around."

"What if I want that handsome fellow to be you and those six kids to be your kids?" She grinned at him.

Sonny groaned.

She ain't gonna let this go.

"Look, Myla. You knew what kind of man I was from the beginin' I was honest with you. I sleep around. That's what I do. True, I usually do one-night-stands. I made an exception for you because—well—because I was really havin' fun with you. Trouble is, with one-night-stands there ain't no call to have a break-up conversation like this."

"So, don't have it. Don't break-up. Just leave the status quo. If you decide on your next leave to come back to me, I'll be here. If you decide you're through with me, then move on to the next girl. Leave the door open until you're really ready to decide what you want. I can wait for you to decide."

He buried his face in his hands. "This ain't how I wanted this to go. I don't like this. You think I want to break-up? I don't. I like you—a lot. That's the problem. I like you too much. If we don't break-up now, I'll definitely be distracted. I can't let myself have any attachments, Myla. It's the life I've chosen. Being a SEAL comes first. Everything else has to take a backseat—that includes my own personal happiness. There's no room for falling in love in that equation."

He is in love with me. I hoped he was; now, I'm sure he is. He's just too scared to admit it.

"I'm not asking you to fall in love with me. I'm just asking you not to break-up. Forget about me for the next six months or however long your deployment is. When you get your next leave, you can remember me then. We can have more fun like we had this time. Then you can forget about me again until your next leave. We'll just take it one leave at a time."

"No, that won't work. You was real fun for a week. The week is over. I'm done with you now. My next leave, I'll probably go back to bar sluts and one-night-stands. It's easier. I don't like breaking-up. This is too much of a hassle. When I get on that plane tomorrow morning, I'm going to forget all about you and this week. You might make it into a story to the guys about how I did this hot, virgin chic, but that's as far as this is gonna go. We are done now. There ain't gonna be no next leave. We ain't gonna get together ever again. You'll have to move on like I said."

"How long do you have before your plane leaves?"

"0700. Why?"

"Then we have until 0600 to have some more fun that you'll forget as soon as you board the plane."

Sonny closed his eyes and shook his head. "That's only going to make it harder."

"For who? You or me?"

"Probably both."

"I thought you said I'm just another conquest story for the guys? So, conquest me one more night, Sonny."

"Damn, Girl! You done figured out all my buttons."

She grinned at him. "I thought you only had one button."

He grinned back. "Well, maybe I do only have one. You sure been pushin' it all week."

"Have I worn it out yet?"

"That button don't never wear out. It's always ready to go."

"Good. Let's take this food to go. There's no sense in wasting time here when we could be enjoying each other in my bed."

"Oh, hell yeah! You said it, Woman! Let's get out of here."

April 30
0700
Military transport plane

All of Echo reunited for the flight back to Afghanistan. Most of them were sleeping off hangovers during the long flight across the Atlantic.

Nick sat down next to Sonny. "You look bright and chipper. You're usually sleeping one off."

Sonny shrugged. "I haven't had a drop in a week. I'm completely sober."

"There's a story there."

Sonny chuckled. "Nah, nothing worth mentioning."

"I don't buy that. In all the years I've known you, you've always come back from leave smelling like a brewery." Nick studied his friend.

"I kinda made a deal with my mom."

"What sort of deal?"

"A sobriety thing. I figured I'd give it a try and see how things go."

"Good for you."

"Eh! It's not all it's cracked up to be. I miss beer—and whiskey—and tequila shooters."

"So, why did you agree to it?"

"I figured I'd humor her for a week."

Nick smirked and shook his head. "So, back to your usual then?"

"You know me. I'll never change."

Nick got up to go sit next to John. As soon as he was gone, Sonny pulled his phone out and stared at the selfie he'd taken of he and Myla. Then he scrolled through the many pictures he'd taken of Myla. He would never admit it to anyone on Echo or his mother, but spending the week with Myla had been the best week of his life.

It had been hard to say goodbye to her, but he'd managed to break it off. He'd told her a lot of lies, but they were all necessary. They were all for her own good. They were all to protect her from him.

He sat staring at her beautiful face for a long time. Then he put his phone away and drifted off to sleep. He hadn't gotten any sleep the previous night. He'd been too busy making love to Myla.

His dreams on the plane were filled with his perfect week with the perfect girl. He only wished he could live in those dreams, but he had to face the reality he'd created. Now he had to live in it regardless of the consequences. Myla had been devastated when she realized he was breaking-up for good, but he'd made up his mind. He refused to ruin her life by being in it. He knew she'd be better off without him.

One important thing had changed for him. He'd gotten a taste of what the good life could be like. He'd sworn off any future pursuit of bar sluts. As his mother would say, he'd made a one-eighty. He just couldn't go back to the way he had been before Myla. She had changed him whether he wanted it or not.

CHAPTER 31

May 1
0300
HALO parachuting

Sophia sat on the transport plane waiting her turn. The parachute course had been tough. It wasn't just strapping on a chute, jumping out of the plane, pulling a cord, and floating down to the ground. They'd had to learn everything that went into making a successful jump. There were mathematical calculations to be made. You had to know what your altitude was and how fast you were plummeting to Earth to know when to pull the cord. If you were jumping with a load of supplies strapped to your chest, you had to compensate for the extra bulk. There was wind drag to calculate and a dozen other variables. If you thought about it too much, it would give you a migraine.

High over the Pacific Ocean Sophia was about to perform a HALO jump with approximately five hundred pounds of supplies strapped to her chest. If she had miscalculated how many buoyancy floats to add to the pack, the weight of the load would drag her under the ocean surface to her death. Every detail mattered.

When it was her turn, she walked up to her supply pack, hooked in, and made the jump.

The darkness enveloped her. It was a moonless night. The cold air whipped at her as she plummeted into the dark abyss toward what could be her death. This wasn't her first HALO jump, but it was the first with a pack strapped to her.

She tried to remain calm, but she could feel that old panic trying to creep up her spine. She willed it to stop. Then she focused on her altimeter.

It was almost time to pull the cord and find out if she was going to live—or become another training accident statistic.

When the pack hit the water, panic surged through her again, but once she realized it was going to float and not drag her under, she relaxed. She'd done it! She'd performed her first HALO with a pack.

They were right. Everything only gets harder and harder. The more you train, the more you realize how much more you need to train. This is so much harder than I ever expected it to be. I'm starting to understand why everyone says SEALs are the biggest badasses on the planet. You have to be the biggest badass, or you'll never live through the training program.

As she made the long swim to shore with her 500-pound supply pack, she thought about her parents. It was the first time in a while that she had allowed herself to think about home.

She wondered how her parents, her brothers, and their families were doing. She wondered if her papa had learned any more English. It had been five months since she had last scolded him for not using proper English. She doubted he'd learned too much more. He just wasn't motivated. Her mother was quite the opposite. Her parents had both come to the United States to give their children a better chance at financial success. Her papa often spoke of the small village he had come from in Mexico. There was not much opportunity to earn much money there. It had been a hard life for him growing up. His dream to come to the U.S. and make a better life had happened, but he still clung to his roots with a passion. He did not want to change. He only wanted his circumstances to change.

Sophia knew that if her papa did not adapt, he would be left behind in the constantly changing climate of culture and progress that the U.S. had become known for. Even in her lifetime, she had to grow and expand to keep up with changing technology. Her father barely knew how to use the text function on his phone. Navigating the computer programs on a laptop were beyond his abilities. He just didn't want to learn anything new. His stubbornness frustrated Sophia. She didn't want him to miss out on opportunities because of a language barrier or because of a lack of understanding of new technology. She only wanted the best for her family. She wished she had the ability to make everything turn out right, but there was nothing she could do about it. Her papa was stubborn and stuck in his ways.

Sophia shivered in the frigid water and kept a wary eye out for any sign of sharks. There were a thousand ways to die in the ocean. Sharks were just one of those ways. It took her nearly two hours to make the arduous swim, but when she dragged her pack up onto the beach, she felt like she'd really accomplished something.

Soon she would be moving on to the next phase of training. Helicopter rope suspension training couldn't be harder than a HALO jump with a pack—could it? She grinned as her instructor's words echoed in her head.

It only gets harder from here.

CHAPTER 32

May 25
0500
NSWC, BUD/S

Sophia had survived The Island, the parachute course, helicopter rope suspension training, and all her written and oral exams. She hadn't passed at the top of her class, but she had passed in the middle of the pack. She'd gone through the graduation ceremony and received her trident. The only thing left was to be chosen for a team. She was anxious to find out which team she would be serving with. She was ready to deploy and see real action.

She rose early and went to breakfast. Then she tackled the O-course to work off the stress of waiting to hear what team had chosen her. The lists hadn't been posted yet, but all the 38 surviving candidates were anxiously awaiting the same news.

When the lists were finally posted, she scanned every list twice, but her name wasn't on any of them. She hadn't been chosen for a team. It was a letdown, but she wasn't going to let it get her down. She immediately went to speak to Reynolds about her next course of action.

After a thorough discussion, Sophia understood what she had to do. She wasn't the only candidate who wasn't chosen for a team. Still, it hadn't escaped her attention that quite a few men who scored below her were chosen for teams. It seemed obvious to her that a gender discrimination was in play, but it wouldn't do her any good to complain. That wasn't who she was. She didn't want to skate by anything because of her gender. She wanted to be chosen on her merits, not on a government quota system. She decided to keep her mouth shut and buckle down.

Per Reynolds advice, she would continue to train while getting certified in additional skill sets. It wasn't the end; it was merely a setback she hadn't planned for. She was sure she would get placed on a team the next time around. She made up her mind to press on and make herself so invaluable that a team would have to choose her.

In the interim, she would learn more languages, go to sniper school, and get noticed for excellence as opposed to mediocrity. Her academic scores were at or near the top. It was her physical scores that needed work. She intended to condition her body to work like a well-oiled machine. She would become the biggest badass there was. She would make sure that the next time someone needed to fill a spot on their team she would be their first choice.

Calling her parents to tell them the news was the hard part. She wasn't looking forward to it.

"*Hola, Pequeña,*" Juan Gonzalez answered.

Sophia grinned. "*Hola, Papa.*"

"*¿Cómo estás?*" (How are you?)

"In English, Papa," she scolded with a smile.

"*¡Ay dios mío!*"

"Papa! Please don't start with me!"

"Your brothers no make me use English!"

"That is why you are not getting better at it. You are not practicing enough."

"I no have to use it for my job. Why I have to use it to speak to my *hija!*" (daughter)

"Because your daughter wants you to!" Sophia sighed in frustration. "Papa, if I can learn Farsi and Russian, you can learn English. Did you know I have to learn a few more languages for the SEALs? I've already started learning Mandarin. After that, I'm going to learn Oirat and Buryat."

"Why you need to learn all that?" Juan sighed.

"I plan to join a SEAL team stationed in that part of the world. I've officially graduated. I'm a SEAL, but I haven't been assigned to a team yet. I'm going to enter sniper school first."

"My only *hija* is in the army and running around with a gun! *¡Ay dios mío!*"

"Papa, I'm not in the army. I'm a Navy SEAL now. It's not the same branch of the military."

"Your Mama wants to speak."

"Sophia," Amparo said curtly.

"Hi, Mama."

"Why is your father carrying on about guns?"

"I told him I'm going to sniper school."

Amparo grabbed her chest and sank down into a chair. "Sophia! It's bad enough you insist on joining the military, but now you're going to be a trained sniper? I don't like this!"

"My scores were not high enough after BUD/S for me to be chosen for a team. I spoke to my C.O. He said the more skill sets I can offer a team, the more likely I am to be chosen by one. I'm going to learn three more languages over the summer while I'm attending sniper school. Hopefully, I will be able to score high enough to get noticed and picked up in the next round."

"Can't you just get out? If they don't want you, maybe that's a sign that you don't belong there. Come home, grow your hair, and find yourself a husband, Sophia!"

"No! No! And no!" Sophia huffed. "Why can't you just accept that I'm a soldier? You have ten sons who are not in the military. You have spares in case I get killed. I'm not quitting!"

"Spares! How dare you say that to me! I love all my children equally. I don't want to see any of you hurt, much less dead! It hurts me when you say things like that."

"It hurts me when you insist that I quit and settle down with a man to call the shots."

"A man to call the shots! Young Lady, you listen to me! That is not what a marriage equates to! Marriage is a partnership. Is that how you see your Papa and me?"

Sophia sighed and closed her eyes. "I'm sorry, Mama. That came out wrong. I just get so frustrated when you refuse to see things from my perspective. There's more to life than getting married and having kids. That's fine for my brothers, but I just don't see myself ever getting married. To be honest, two of the men in the SEAL program have asked me to marry them, but I just can't get tied down like that. Not now. I have so much I want to accomplish in this world before I tie myself down to cooking and cleaning and changing diapers and—"

"Tied down? You make marriage and motherhood sound like a weight around your neck. The best thing I ever did in this world was to marry your father and have you kids. My family is what makes living worthwhile. I just hope you fall in love before it's too late for you. I hope you don't wake up an old woman and regret living a life alone with no one in it that matters."

After a long silence, Amparo asked, "Are you coming home for a visit?"

"I have a few days before I start sniper school. I will be coming to visit tomorrow."

"Good. I will plan a big dinner with all your brothers. I may not approve of what you are doing, but I understand you have worked hard to get to where you are. You deserve a celebration for all your hard work. I worry about you. I only want to protect my child."

"I love you too, Mama. I only want to protect you too. That's one of the reasons why I serve."

The next morning, Sophia exited the bus and walked the rest of the way to her parent's house. She had a great time enjoying her mother's home cooking and visiting with her family. It wasn't until later that afternoon that the pressure to conform returned.

Her sister-in-law, Conseja, pulled her outside for a chat.

"So, Amparo tells me that you have two marriage proposals," Conseja said with a big grin.

Sophia rolled her eyes. "She told you about that?"

"Of course. So, what's the scoop? Which one are you going to marry?"

Sophia dragged her hand over her ebony burr. "I didn't say I was going to marry either."

"Which one do you like more?"

"I—uh—" Sophia's brain scrambled for an answer.

I try not to think about either of them. It's too distracting. I don't know which one I like more. What difference does it make? I'm not getting married right now to anyone.

"I don't know."

"Love triangles are so scandalous. Which one is cuter?"

Sophia shrugged. "They are both very attractive."

"But which one gets you hot?"

"I—"

Damnit! They both do if I allow myself to think about them that way. Which is exactly why I do my best to block them out.

She cleared her throat and looked down at her combat boots.

"You're blushing, Sophia."

"I haven't said yes to either one."

"But you haven't said no."

"We won't even be stationed in the same part of the world. Butch is on a team deployed in Guatemala, and Sam's team is deployed in Tanzania."

"Where are you being deployed?"

"I'm not on a team yet. I'll be starting sniper school in a few days. After that, I'm hoping to get on a team in the middle east. Either Iraq or Afghanistan. I want to be where the action is."

"If you got married, you could still see each other on leave, couldn't you?"

"Yes, but a long-distance relationship would be hard."

"But if you're in love, isn't it worth the hard work?"

Am I in love with Butch or Sam?

"I suppose you are right about that, but I'm not going to marry anyone right now."

"You should make a pros and cons list to compare them and decide who is the best choice."

"Is that what you did before you married my brother? Did you make a list?"

Conseja burst out laughing. Then she caught her breath. "No, definitely not. From the first moment I laid eyes on Julio I knew. It was love at first sight. He is my soulmate."

"Then why would you suggest that I make a list to decide?" Sophia asked annoyed.

"I'm not sure love at first sight is your thing. You seem a little too pragmatic to believe in it. Besides, according to Amparo, you're dragging your feet. Are Butch and Sam good men?"

"They are both loyal, dedicated, and good to their cores."

"Sounds like a good match to me. They obviously love you, or they wouldn't have asked you to marry them. Do you love either of them?"

"I'm not sure what it feels like to be in love. I don't allow myself to ponder love too much. It's dangerous to get distracted with emotions when you're in the field."

Conseja nodded. "I can imagine. Still, they are the one's deployed, not you. You're not in the field now. It's safe to explore your emotions and figure out how you truly feel."

Sophia bit her lip as she pondered her sister-in-law's words. "You're right. I'm not in the field. Maybe I should figure out how I feel before I end up on a battle ground. Thanks for the advice."

"What are sisters for?" Conseja hugged her. "Just don't elope. I want to be at your wedding."

Sophia laughed. "I doubt it would be anything to get too excited about."

Conseja smiled. "You will make a beautiful bride. I can see you now in a long, white dress with a big bouquet of flowers. You'll walk down the aisle at the church with your nieces dropping flowers in front of you. It will be beautiful."

"No, we would be wearing camo fatigues in front of a justice of the peace at the courthouse."

Conseja shook her head. "No, no, no. You have to do it right, Chica. Don't let Amparo hear you talking like that. You'll give your poor mother a heart attack. She's been planning a beautiful wedding for you since the day you were born. She has a savings account set aside just for your wedding. Don't break her heart, Sophia. Let her give you the wedding she's been dreaming of."

Sophia swallowed hard. "She saved money for my wedding?"

Conseja nodded.

A tear streaked down Sophia's cheek, and she quickly swiped it away. "Why would she do that? She and Papa struggle with money as it is. Why would she set money aside for me?"

"Because, she has high hopes for you, Sophia. She's very proud of you. She just wants you to have the best life possible. To her, that means a fine husband and loving children. I can't imagine my life without Julio and our children. We want the same happiness for you, Sophia."

Conseja hugged Sophia and then went inside. Sophia sat on the small patio and swiped at traitorous tears that would not stop. She couldn't understand why she was getting so emotional. She usually had much better control over herself. She almost never cried.

Once she tamped down her emotions, she went inside for a piece of her mother's *pastel de tres leches. (three milk cake)* She cut a big slice of the moist, delicious cake and sat down at the table to feast on it.

Juan sat down next to her.

"Your mama say you getting married soon. I no seen her so happy in a long time."

"Papa! I never told her I was getting married. I only told her two men proposed."

Juan chuckled. "I think she already plan the whole wedding."

Sophia shoved in a big bite of cake to avoid commenting.

"So, who you going to marry? What his name?"

Sophia swallowed the bite. "I never said I was going to marry either of them."

"What their names?"

"Butch Simonis and Sam Cafferty."

"They names no sound Hispanic."

"They are not Hispanic, Papa."

"Hmm, I no like that. You marry a nice Hispanic boy, eh?"

"So, now not only do I have to marry, but he has to be Hispanic or you won't approve?"

"Hispanic boy is same as you. You have more in common. You have same beliefs, same—"

Sophia put her hand up to stop him. "Look, Papa. I don't even know if I'm going to marry either man, but if I decide to marry, I will marry whoever I choose to. I'm not going to rule a man out just because he's from a different race than me. We are all human beings. We are all the same in God's eyes. I'm not going to discriminate. If he has a good heart, it doesn't matter what color his skin is. Don't try to paint me into that corner. I'll kick your paint bucket over!"

"Oh! She's feisty, Papa. You can't control this one," her older brother, Jorge chuckled.

Amparo walked in from the living room with her arms crossed over her chest. She gave her husband the look, and he snapped his mouth shut before he said what he was thinking.

"Our daughter finally has a man propose to her, two good men at that. Two honorable men who defend our country. If Sophia says they are good men, I believe her. It doesn't matter what background or race they come from. We moved to the United States. This country is the melting pot. That means there are no racial lines here. If our daughter wants to marry a good man from another race, you will not speak against him or her for it, Juan! You will accept him into our family with open arms! Do I make myself clear?"

Juan nodded and gave Sophia an apologetic smile. "If you say he good, than he good.

The following afternoon, Amparo had a long discussion with Sophia about the benefits of a happy marriage. She made Sophia tell her all about Butch and Sam.

CHAPTER 33

September 7
0100
SEAL sniper school

Sniper school was extremely difficult to master. There were so many variables to consider before taking a kill shot. Fortunately, Sophia was excellent at quick calculations in her head. Her instructors were very impressed with her focus and accuracy.

During her training, she had learned Mandarin and two Mongolian dialects, Oirat and Buryat. She was sure once she finished sniper school a SEAL team would pick her up in November.

At 0102, camouflaged, she lay on the dirt. Her sniper rifle was trained on her target. She checked wind velocity, barometric pressure, her watch, and then she zeroed in on the moving target. It was time to make the shot. She gently squeezed the trigger. The bullet exited the barrel of her rifle, and the cantaloupe on the moving stick burst into a mushy mess on the ground. Without hesitation she zeroed in on the second target, squeezed the trigger, and the watermelon behind the moving car door burst open a split second after the glass shattered. She immediately focused on the third target, the fourth, and then the fifth. All targets were moving. All targets had challenges that had to be overcome. It didn't matter how steep the hill; Sophia was there to conquer it. She was there to smash all previous course records to dust; she had to, but her biggest obstacle was getting others to see her as a soldier and not as a female soldier. She'd been butting her head up against that wall since the moment she first joined the Marine Corp.

Still, she wasn't a quitter. She would never give up. She would push as hard as she could until she dropped dead trying. She was utterly determined, and nothing was going to stand in her way.

CHAPTER 34

September 16
0600
Afghanistan

John was walking to the mess hall for chow when his phone buzzed. He retrieved it and grinned when he saw Kyle's picture on the screen.

"Hey, Kyle, what's up?"

"Megan just had our baby. Buck is six pounds, seven ounces. Anna is in labor with her twins. I think our babies are going to share a birthday." Kyle was grinning from ear to ear.

"Congratulations from me and all the guys. Tell Owen and Anna congratulations too!" John entered the mess hall and got in line.

"I will. I just wanted to share the good news. How are you doing?"

John took a deep breath. "I'm good."

"You don't sound good. What's wrong?"

"No, I'm good. I'm just tired. We've been busy, and I haven't gotten much sleep lately. The usual grind is starting to wear on me. I think I'm getting sick."

"Well, take care of yourself, and keep your head on a swivel."

"Always do. You take care of those babies and their mommies."

John talked to Kyle for a few more minutes. Then he slid the phone back into his pocket, got a plate of food, and sat down with the rest of Echo at the table. He shared Kyle's good news. Then he dug into the mediocre food.

"Are you okay, John," Nick asked.

John looked up at Nick who was sitting across from him. "Yeah."

"You look a little pale."

"I'm just fighting off something. It's probably a virus."

"You should get checked out by medical."

"I'll be fine. It's just a bug."

Nick grinned. "You're not afraid of doctors, are you?"

John rolled his eyes and ignored Nick. He also ignored the pounding headache that was relentlessly cracking his skull like an egg. When he finished his plate, he stood up to leave. He only made it a few steps before he face-planted on the floor.

Nick bolted over the table to examine John while Sonny called Rowen to apprise him of the situation.

"He's burning up!" Nick said.

A few minutes later, John was carried out on a stretcher.

It took John a week to kick the virus. He missed a mission that the rest of Echo insisted was a cakewalk. Still, he felt bad for not being there to do his part.

November 15

0323

Seven klicks northwest of Huma, China

Echo crossed the Russian border into China. Russian troops pursued and cornered them in a mountain ravine. They were taking heavy fire. Cord Murphy, the medic took several rounds while they headed for cover behind a group of boulders.

"Echo 2! See to his wounds!" Fry ordered as the rest of Echo took up defensive firing positions.

They were deep in enemy territory. Russia lay to the north, east, and west. China lay to the south. There were no friendlies in the area. There was no way to call for backup without alerting the Chinese military that they'd crossed into their realm. Even if Fry called for backup, no one would arrive in time. The Chinese military would intercept the transmission and get there first. The Russian force who had followed them over the border were determined to wipe them out. Echo was outnumbered. They were outgunned. The only things they had going for them were a few boulders and the cover of darkness for a few more hours.

John quickly opened the med pack to treat Cord, but Cord grabbed his arm.

"Don't waste supplies on me, John. I'm bleeding out. You can't save me."

John's jaw tightened as he cut Cord out of his body armor. There were three bullet holes in his chest and two in his legs.

"Don't give up; you're going to make it," John said, as he pressed dressing against Cord's chest wounds. He quickly tied tourniquets on his legs and went back to the chest wounds.

"John, you can't save me. It's too late."

"Don't say that!"

Cord's eyes fluttered shut as he exhaled his last breath. John immediately started CPR, but it was too late. Cord was gone.

The battle raged on, but John was too preoccupied to join it. The injuries kept coming. Ben Obassi took a bullet to his leg. No sooner had John tended to Ben's wound, than Ezra pulled Ian back to John with two bullet wounds to the chest. John felt panic rising inside him. It took effort to tamp it down and deal with Ian's injuries.

Unfortunately, the Russian force was relentless. The bullets kept coming their way, and the injuries kept piling up on John. He couldn't treat the wounds fast enough, and the men he worked on died while he was trying to save them. John could hear Fry in his earpiece giving orders; the situation was grim, and the sight of watching so many brothers die in front of him was gut wrenching.

At 0450, Nick pulled Fry back to John, and he immediately went to work on Fry. He could hear Nick take over command and start giving orders to the few SEALs who were left in the fight. Technically, John was the second in command after Fry, but since Cord, their only medic, was dead, John was the only other team member with medical training. The situation had gone from bad to worse, to worse, to worse.

The Russians were using armor piercing ammo. There were too many chest wounds and not enough time or supplies. John felt more than overwhelmed; he felt hopeless. The bullets never took a pause, and though both Fry and Nick had instructed Echo to conserve their ammo, John knew they had to be almost out. It would all be over in a matter of minutes for every one of them despite his best efforts to save everyone.

He examined Fry. He'd taken a bullet near his spine and two to his right thigh. The damage was bad, but John did his best to stop the bleeding and keep Fry alive for as long as they all had left. In his ear piece he could hear Echo reporting in to Nick as each man ran out of ammo.

This is it. This is how I'm coming home—in a bag. I knew it was going to end badly for me. I just hope when they kill me, they put a bullet right through my skull—quick and merciful.

A transport chopper flew south toward the battle in the ravine. It was dark, but the thermal vision windshield was lit up with warm bodies engaged in the firefight on the ground. The chopper circled the battle scene with barely a whisper of blades and came down behind the Russian military force. The pilot opened fire and made quick work of taking out every Russian soldier. The chopper landed, and the pilot jumped down and raced toward the SEAL team.

Nick spotted the chopper pilot waving them in. He relayed the information to John.

"Echo, move out immediately!" Nick ordered in his coms. Ezra carried Ben on his back. Sonny helped John carry Fry to the chopper, and John went back to work on Fry as soon as they were inside. What was left of Echo loaded their dead onto the chopper, and it took off.

The pilot navigated back toward the Russian border. The Chinese military had noticed the helo's incursion on their radar. China had ordered their own forces to intercept. There was no choice but to reenter Russian airspace to evade the Chinese, but Russian airspace was no safer. Their only hope of success was to fly low using the mountain terrain as cover.

John was busy in the back of the chopper trying to save Fry. No one on Echo cared who the mysterious, lone, chopper pilot was. They only cared that they had been saved from a complete massacre. The chopper had no insignia. They didn't even know what country had come to their rescue. All they knew was that they were still alive and hopefully headed to safety.

Once the chopper reached open airspace over the Sea of Japan, the pilot flew them directly to the nearest military medical facility in Japan. Fry and Ben were immediately taken in for evaluation and treatment.

While John hurried in with the medical team to give conditions on Fry and Obassi, the rest of Echo turned back to the chopper to tend to their fallen teammates. The pilot stepped down from the cockpit just as Sonny walked up.

"Thank you for the rescue," Sonny said, extending his hand.

"You're welcome, Sonny. If you'll excuse me, I need to check on Lydell's condition."

She removed her helmet and set it in the pilot seat. Then she turned and raced toward the door.

Sonny stared at her until she disappeared inside the door. He was perplexed.

Bretta! That's Bretta! What in the hell is she doing here?

The next day, Lydell woke to the sound of beeping and a bright, white light. He tried to sit up, but his arms and legs were dead weights. He couldn't make them work. He tried to speak, but his mouth was dry and parched. Then suddenly, Bretta was there staring down at him with a smile.

"Hey, Babe," she said softly.

"Hi—" His voice came out as a strangled rasp.

She gave him some water.

"What are you doing here?"

"Saving your ass as usual."

He grinned at her. "Where am I?"

"Japan."

"My men—"

"Don't worry about anything right now. Just heal up."

"I can't move."

"The doctor gave you tranquilizers to keep you immobile. They had to operate on you. You barely made it."

"How many of my men made it?"

"Sonny, Nick, Ben, Dorian, Ezra, Zach, and John."

Tears streaked down Lydell's cheeks as the men he lost flashed through his mind.

"I'm sorry I didn't get there sooner. As soon as I saw you were in trouble, I stole a chopper and headed your way. I just couldn't get there fast enough."

"How did you even know—"

"Remember, I watch you. I watch you all the time."

Lydell closed his eyes and swallowed hard. "You put a tracker in me, didn't you?" He opened his eyes and met hers.

"Yes, but only so I could protect you. I love you, Lydell. I just want to keep you safe."

"Who are you really, Bretta?"

"Your guardian angel, Love."

"You're not going to disappear on me again, are you?"

She leaned down and pressed a soft kiss to his forehead. "I won't disappear. I promise."

November 18
2100
Afghanistan base

John sat down on a supply crate, pulled out his phone, and called Kyle.

"Hey, John."

"Hey, Kyle." His voice was hoarse and raspy.

"You've been crying. What's wrong?"

"We lost half the team."

"Who's left?" Kyle sank down onto a chair feeling sick.

"Sonny, Nick, Ben, Dorian, Ezra, Zach, and Lydell."

"I'm so sorry, John."

"Ben took a bullet to the leg; he'll be okay, but Lydell is in bad shape. The bullets shattered his right femur. They'll have to replace it with a steel rod if he ever wants to walk again."

Kyle winced. "That's bad."

"Rowen wants me to take the number one spot on the team, but I don't know if I can do it."

"Why?"

"Because, now I know how you feel. We got pinned down in a nasty firefight. Cord was the first man down. I had to take his spot. By the time back-up arrived it was too late. I had to watch them all bleed out, Kyle. Damnit! I don't know how anyone can be a medic. How can you watch a man dying right in front of you and tell him it's going to be okay—that he's going to make it—when you know damn well, he's not!"

John broke down sobbing.

"I'm not a leader. I'm just a bad ass killing machine. How can I be responsible for fifteen lives? How do I rebuild a team with a bunch of innocent greens and tell them to follow me into battle? I don't know how you did it, Kyle! I don't think I have it in me."

"John, you don't have to take the number one spot. No one is going to lose any respect for you if you don't think you're up to the challenge."

"I can't step down. No one else has enough experience or training to take the number one spot. There's nothing but to suck it up and push through the pain. I don't have a choice. I have to take command. I can't let the team down."

Kyle sighed. "Are you going to be okay?"

"Yeah, I'm good. I guess I just needed to get that whiny-baby crap off my chest."

"Sometimes it's good to get it off your chest; otherwise, it will eat you up inside."

The next morning at 0800, John stood at attention in front of Rowen's desk.

"Now that you are in charge of Echo, you'll need to rebuild the team. I'm sending you stateside to choose nine men to replace the one's you lost. Your flight leaves in two hours."

"Yes, Sir," John said respectfully.

"I know you're being thrown into this position suddenly, but you are the best man for the job."

Rowen dismissed him, and John went to pack a bag. Two hours later he sat on a transport plane with the weight of the world on his shoulders. The mantel he was picking up was a heavy one, and despite Rowen's confidence, John wasn't entirely sure he was the best man for the job. All he knew was that he would give it 150 percent as always.

CHAPTER 35

November 20
0600
BUD/S

John reported to Reynolds at BUD/S.

"Rowen tells me you're in need of nine new SEALs. That's a tough loss. Sorry to hear it."

John nodded.

"We have quite a few great candidates about to graduate and a few who have been doing extra training after not being selected for a team in June. I'll let you take a look at all the files, and you can observe the candidates in action. Selection will begin in seven days. There are other teams looking for candidates too. They will be arriving soon."

John nodded. "I'll look the files over carefully. Thank you, Sir."

For the next two days, John sat in an empty conference room with the files spread out on long tables. He read them all carefully, made lists, and compared skill sets on paper. Then he gave the files back to Reynolds and spent a lot of time observing the candidates. He watched them on the course. He watched them in the mess hall. He even watched them during what little down time they had. He kept a running tab of everything he observed.

He wasn't sure yet how he was going to choose a new team. Trying to pick from so many candidates was overwhelming. There were too many variables. He had to take into consideration their skill sets, their previous experience, where they had served before coming to BUD/S, and last but not least the personal, social dynamics. A SEAL team is a close-knit unit.

If you have someone on the team who can't get along with the rest of the team, it will cause trouble. John was looking for the right fit, but not just one right fit. He had to find nine newbies who would mesh well with each other—and with the existing Echo members.

There were a lot of good candidates, but it wasn't just about picking your top nine. There would be other SEAL teams looking for a new member or two. They would all have to pick from the same group. John had to have his first choices, plus backup choices in case another team selected someone he had his eye on. After two days of observing, he started to get a headache. Then the returning BUD/S graduates who hadn't been picked yet came back from their respective training courses. John had to observe and evaluate the new arrivals as well. The night before selection was to begin, he went to bed with a stress headache.

November 27
0800
BUD/S conference training room

John sat at a table with twenty-three other SEALs who had come to make selections for their teams. There was a total of fifty-two candidates and only forty-one open spots on the teams. The SEAL team leaders discussed the merits of the green candidates, and then started selections.

"Echo, you get first pick," Mizerman from SEAL team Charlie said. "Who do you want?"

"Hogan Zeleno."

"Really? He didn't get top scores on anything."

Wentley from team Bravo smirked. "I thought Echo was supposed to be a top elite team. How are you supposed to stay the top team when you pick sub-par candidates?"

"Just because you make the top score in a training environment doesn't mean you'll be a good fit for the team," John said. "I have my reasons. I've made my choice."

The first round of picks was chosen, and it came back to John. He picked Chris Canby, and on the third round he picked Matt Pragun.

At that point, the remaining leaders filled their spots on their respective teams and left to turn in their choices to Reynolds. John was left alone in the room with the remaining candidate's folders. He still had six spots to fill. He sat staring at the board evaluating who was left. Then he began to second guess himself. He still had to pick six to fill his team. That meant eleven highly qualified, highly motivated SEALs were not going to make it to a team this round.

After an hour, Reynolds entered the room and saw John sitting and staring at the pictures.

"Having trouble deciding?" Reynolds asked.

John dragged his hand over his dark brown burr. "This is the first time I've had to make this kind of decision, and I have to pick nine. I'm just trying not to make a mistake."

"Would you like a recommendation? I know all these candidates as well as anyone."

"Sure, more information can only help. Who would you pick?"

Reynolds took a quick look at the twenty candidates left. Then he pulled out nine of them and arranged their folders according to how he would rank them on the team.

"I would pick Adam Amari, Kallen Gibor, Darek Orth, Marsh Largo, Grant Farley, Clay DeVoss, Brad Bogart, Lars Maro, and Jeff Minos," Reynolds said. "They didn't have the top scores of the group. It looks like the top scores have been selected by other teams, but these nine scored the best of the candidates left. Did you not make any choices during the meeting earlier?"

John sighed. "Actually, they let me choose first in every round. I've already picked three."

"Who did you choose?" Reynolds asked surprised.

"Hogan Zeleno, Chris Canby, and Matt Pragun."

Reynolds frowned. "Hogan Zeleno has the slowest response times across the board of any candidate. Why choose him over much stronger candidates?"

"I've been watching all the candidates for the last week. Hogan seems like the best fit for Echo. He never quits even when the odds are against him, and there's no hope of success. He's persistent. He gets along with everyone around him. He listens and pays attention to everything. He's very aware of his surroundings. Some of the top scoring candidates seemed to be going through the motions. They already knew what was expected and were ready to do it. In the field, you rarely know what you're really going to encounter. Surprises come up on every mission. If you can't deal with the unexpected, you will fail. If you are not hyper aware of your surroundings, you probably won't make it back alive. Also, Zeleno has seen real battle when he served with the Army in Iraq. He's no stranger to danger."

Reynolds smiled. "You know, John, you might be new at leading a team, but you already seem to grasp what it takes. A team isn't just made up of a bunch alphas and testosterone. If you can't work together in the field, you won't succeed. Who else are you thinking about and why?"

John grinned. Then he went over the rest of his choices and explained his reasons to Reynolds.

Reynolds pinned John's choices up on the board and stood studying them for a moment. "You know, of the 52 candidates we started with, I would never have pictured these nine ending up on the same team together, but after hearing your explanations, it all makes perfect sense. I think you have the makings of an excellent team. I'll post your choices with the others this afternoon."

"Could you hold off on that?" John asked.

Reynolds gave him a questioning look.

"These greens all think it's an honor and a privilege to be chosen for a SEAL team. They don't yet understand that it's really a sacrifice. You are required to sacrifice every part of yourself to the team and the mission to accomplish the objective. I want the recruits to be made aware of the strenuous conditions they will be subjected to before they are officially posted to my team. I only want the most dedicated on Echo. Our missions are too critical for it to be otherwise."

"This is highly irregular, Chief Rusk."

John nodded. "I want them to be given a choice. If they don't want to be on an elite team like Echo, it's better they stay here and train for a future team that won't be as extreme. Echo has to answer the call no matter where in the world it happens. We have to be extremely versatile and flexible. There is no routine in the field on our team. We continually have to adapt to meet the situation we are faced with. I don't want anyone on Echo who doesn't want to be there. If any of them decline their spot, I'll choose a replacement."

"Duly noted. I'm assuming you wish to be present during these private briefings?"

"No. I don't want to put pressure on these greens to accept. I want it to be their decision."

Reynolds nodded. "I'll take care of it."

John nodded. "Spot sixteen has a special circumstance. I need a medic. We lost ours."

"I'll make sure it's clear. Train to be a medic or wait for another team."

John saluted Reynolds. "Thank you, Sir!"

At 1300, the BUD/S posting hallway was crowded with candidates anxious to see if they were placed on a team. Sophia waited impatiently for her turn to check the posting list in the hall outside of Reynolds office. She'd just come from the mess hall, but she'd barely eaten a thing. The stress of wondering if she would get placed on a team this round was beginning to wear on her. When she got to the list, she read over it and then read it two more times.

My name is not on the list. I didn't get chosen for a team again! How many languages do I have to speak, and how many skills do I have to develop in order for a team to choose me!

She walked away feeling dejected. Just as she passed Reynolds office, the door opened.

"Gonzalez!" Reynolds barked at her back.

She stopped, turned, and saluted him.

"I need to see you in my office immediately!"

She followed him inside and shut the door. She stood at attention in front of his desk.

"Sir."

"At ease, Soldier."

She took the position and waited for him to speak. He sat down behind his desk and pulled out a folder.

"Have you checked the postings?"

She nodded. "Sir, I noticed I was not chosen for a team this round. What do I need to do to improve my chances of being chosen in the next round?"

"How do you feel about training to be a medic?"

She gave him a questioning look. "I don't have any feeling about it, Sir. It's not in my wheelhouse. All the skills I've developed are to take a life, not save one, Sir. I speak seven languages now. I would make an excellent translator. I received top marks in sniper school. I would make an excellent overwatch. I'm skilled in martial arts and hand-to-hand combat. I could kill a man with my pinky finger. I've trained to be a warrior, Sir. I have no medical training whatsoever. That's not really my calling, Sir," she said respectfully.

Reynolds stared at her in silence.

After a long period of silence, she asked. "Is there a special reason why you are inquiring?"

"How serious are you about joining a SEAL team?"

"Very serious, Sir. It's the reason I joined the Navy."

"Are you serious enough to learn a skill set that is not really your calling?" he asked snidely.

"Sir, yes, Sir!" she said.

"Are you willing to be deployed to any location on the planet? Are you willing to be put in extreme danger to accomplish your mission? Are you willing to sacrifice your life to your team and the mission? Are you willing to give up being Sophia Gonzalez, and embrace being number sixteen and the medic on a team?" he asked.

Sophia swallowed hard.

What is he asking? I didn't get chosen. I don't understand where he's going with this.

Without hesitation she said, "Sir, I'm willing to do whatever it takes to complete a mission. I'm willing to be a medic. I'm willing to eat dirt and drag myself across broken glass if it means our mission is successful. I'm willing to lay down my life for my country, my team, and the mission if that's what it takes to succeed. I will do anything it takes, Sir. There is no line I won't cross to defend this country and fulfill my duty. If you ask, I will perform it 150 percent, Sir!"

A slight smile turned up the corner of his mouth. "I'm not asking you to train to become the number sixteen spot and the team's medic. Your new team leader is asking you to. Echo lost nine members of their team including their medic. Chief Rusk sees something in you that none of the other SEAL team leaders saw. They all passed you over in this second round, but Chief Rusk thinks you'll make a good fit on his team as their medic. He doesn't want you to accept the position if you don't truly want it. He's giving you the option of declining and continuing your training in hopes of making it to a team next round. However, if you decide to accept—"

"I accept!" she said without hesitation. "If Chief Rusk needs a medic, then I will become the best medic in the entire SEAL division."

Reynolds nodded. "I thought you might say that. You'll make a good SEAL, Gonzalez. You display the kind of dedication and devotion that our outfit needs. You'll start med training next week. After you pass the course, you'll be deployed to Afghanistan to join the rest of Echo. Congratulations, Gonzalez. You just made one of the most elite teams in the SEAL community."

"Thank you, Sir."

As soon as Sophia left his office, Reynolds called in the rest of John's picks one by one. All eight men accepted the offer to join Echo.

The next morning at 0600, Sophia assembled in line next to Hogan Zeleno, Chris Canby, Matt Pragun, Marcus Macmahon, Joe Karsa, Jerome Holt, Falco DeShawn, and Andrew Angel. John stood in front of them. His eyes appraised, studied, and noticed everything. He walked down the line of the new greens on Echo. Then he returned to his original spot facing them.

"I see all of you have sewn your tridents to your uniform. Tear them off right now! You haven't earned those tridents! You might have passed BUD/S. You might think you've earned those patches, but you haven't. Until you prove yourself in the field, you haven't earned anything. Your trident will be returned to you when or if you've proven you deserve to wear it! Until such time as you show yourself worthy, you are the dirt on the bottom of a real SEAL's boot. I'm a fair leader, but I won't listen to any whiny baby crap from any of you. This is an elite team. You will be expected to act like an elite SEAL. If you can't measure up, leave now! I don't want anyone on this team who isn't going to give me 200 percent. That's what it takes to complete an Echo mission. We aren't given the easy load. Our country asks the impossible of us, and we deliver every time. To fail would mean lives lost. Echo is not in the business to fail! Failure is not in the Echo vocabulary! Does anyone here wish to leave now before you enter the gates of hell? If so, there's the door. If you like fire and you like to get burned, then put your trident in my hand right now!"

Nine trident patches were placed in his hand.

"Gonzalez will be the only one not joining me on the plane in two hours. She will be training in the med program and will join us in six months. The rest of you, pack your gear. We are going home to Afghanistan."

Eight greens filed out of the room to go pack. Sophia stood at attention in front of John.

"Is there something you need, Gonzalez?"

"I just wanted to thank you for giving me the opportunity to prove myself. I will do everything in my power to be an asset to your team, Sir."

John scoffed. "Don't thank me, Gonzalez. You have no idea what you're getting yourself into. I read your file. You scored top marks in linguistics, communications, and sharp shooting. Your P.T. scores were not impressive. While you're training to save lives, I suggest you work on your endurance and strength training as well. When you hit the field with the team, you'll have to keep up. If you can't keep up, it won't matter how good of an aim you have or how many languages you speak. A bullet will kill a smart woman as fast as it will kill anyone else."

"Sir, yes, Sir."

"Don't expect special treatment just because you are female. You'll have to carry your weight and then some. That's the life you choose when you choose Echo. In this unit, you are not a woman. You are a soldier. That is all you are."

Her lip turned up in the corner. "Thank you, Sir. I've worked for years to be seen as a soldier and not a woman. You are the first to make that distinction. I don't want special treatment. Treat me the same as you would treat any other male in your unit."

John's eyes narrowed on her. He stepped closer and stared down into her dark brown eyes. "Dismissed, Soldier!"

"Yes, Sir!"

She saluted him and then left to pack her own bag. Reynolds had granted her one day leave to visit her family before being shipped off to med training.

When she left BUD/S, she called her mother's cell phone.

"Mama, I got selected for a team!"

Amparo sighed dejectedly. "Congratulations. How soon are you being deployed?"

"I'm not being deployed yet. My new C.O. is sending me to train as a medic. I'll be in the states until I finish that course. I won't ship out until closer to June."

"Where will you be deployed after med training?"

"Afghanistan."

"Well, you got your wish. I'm not happy about it, but I'm happy that you're happy."

"Thank you."

"Have you decided which man you want to marry yet?"

Sophia rolled her eyes. "No, Mama. I have a lot on my plate right now. There is no time for a wedding or marriage. I promise you'll be the first person I tell when I decide."

"Okay, just don't wait too long, Sophia. You're not getting any younger. You'll be twenty-four soon. Your body can only bear children for so long."

"My biological clock is not ticking that fast. I have plenty of time!"

Amparo sighed.

"I'm on my way to come see you today. I have to report back in the morning."

"I love you. I'll see you soon." Amparo smiled as she hung up the phone.

At 0830, John sat on a cargo plane watching his green recruits. Some of them were reading technical manuals. Some were sleeping. Two were playing cards. He decided to get some sleep himself. It was going to be a long flight. The job of training the greens would be grueling. He still remembered the training sessions with Kyle when he first joined Echo.

He wasn't particularly looking forward to all the sleepless nights pushing greens to exceed their best.

His mind wandered to the men he'd lost in the firefight. His dreams were plagued by their haunting death stares after their last breath was expelled. He couldn't get it out of his head. He'd witnessed plenty of men die during his time in the SEALs, but it had never been men he knew. He'd never had to look into a teammate's dead-eyes—until now. This was very different.

At 1100, Sophia sat on the bus. It would be another hour before she reached L.A. There were only a few people on the bus. Most had gotten off at the last stop. The ride had turned quiet and peaceful. She stared out the window, and the meeting replayed in her head.

Chief Rusk seems fair and open-minded. I'm going to like working under him. This is going to be great! I'm finally going to be a real SEAL!

Over the long drive, she had too much time to think. Her thoughts drifted to Butch and Sam. She didn't know what to do. She wasn't ready to make a life-long decision like that. Besides, even if she was ready, how could she choose between two really great guys? There was nothing inherently wrong with either man. She couldn't make a pros and cons list like Conseja had suggested. There didn't seem to be any cons and the pros were basically an even match. The choice seemed impossible, and eventually, she pushed it back down. She didn't have the energy to deal with such a crucial decision. She had bigger things to think about. She would soon be on a SEAL team in Afghanistan. It was a dream come true. She decided to enjoy the time off with her parents and then refocus on her new task—med training.

I honestly never considered any sort of career in the medical field. It never even crossed my mind that I should save lives. Why is that? I've been so focused on learning how to efficiently take a life that I never considered the other side. This is going to be new, different, challenging. I'm actually getting excited about this. I wonder what made Chief Rusk decide to send me for medical training over one of the other candidates? Maybe one day I'll ask him.

She grinned at the thought of asking the stern, all-business Chief Rusk anything. He seemed more the type to bark orders than to answer inane questions. It didn't make sense to her given her sniper training and her background, but she wasn't about to question his wisdom in the matter. He'd chosen her. She was going to be on a team. That's all that really mattered—that and becoming the best medic she could for her team. She could hardly wait to get to Afghanistan.

The other eight men chosen were strangers to her. They'd come through this last round of SEAL candidates while she was in sniper school. Everyone on Echo would be complete strangers to her, but none of that mattered. She was sure she could make anything work as long as she got to serve and do what she'd been training for. It was finally happening, and it was great!

Soon enough the bus made it to her stop. She got off and walked to her parent's house. She paused on the front porch for a moment and took a deep breath. She already knew the questions, arguments, and lectures she was in for. It never changed. She opened the door and faced it head on—like always.

CHAPTER 36

November 30
0830
Afghanistan base

The new members of Echo stood at attention assembled in a line. John stood in front of them, and the rest of old Echo stood to the side with the exception of Ben Obassi who was in recovery.

"Welcome to hell, Gentlemen," John said sternly. "This is what you signed up for. Echo lost most of our team during a recent incursion. Those of us who survived are here to train you how we operate on Echo. You will do as you are told. You will not question orders from myself or any of the senior members of Echo. Some of our methods may be unconventional, but they are necessary for the success of our missions and for the survival of our members."

None of the newbies spoke. Silence fell over the empty mess hall for a few moments.

"I'll introduce you all to the team," John said. "Echo 2 is Nick Novak. His special skills are too many to name. You'll get to know them over time. Echo 3 is Sonny Eldridge. His special skills are also many, but his primary position on the team is Overwatch. Echo 4 is Ben Obassi. You'll meet him later. He is still in the infirmary healing from a bullet to the leg. Echo 5 is Zachary Hurst. Everyone calls him Zach. He is our primary reconnaissance man. Echo 6 is Dorian Axel. He is our explosives expert. Echo 7 is Ezra Lombard. He is our communications specialist."

The greens all shook hands with each member as they walked down the line.

John addressed the greens again. "I am placing each of you in the following position on Echo. Echo 8 is Hogan Zeleno. Echo 9 is Chris Canby. Echo 10 is Matt Pragun. Echo 11 is Marcus Macmahon. Marcus prefers to go by Mac. Echo 12 is Joe Karsa. Echo 13 is Jerome Holt. Echo 14 is Falco DeShawn. Echo 15 is Andrew Angel. Our sixteenth spot will be filled by Sophia Gonzalez as soon as she completes med training."

John paused as he stared at the group. "I shouldn't have to tell you this, but I'm going to cover every base. Gonzalez is the first female to pass the SEAL program. She is highly trained and highly motivated. However, the fact that she is a female brings its own set of challenges for her and for the rest of us. She has made it clear that she does not want special treatment. She wants to be treated the same as any other man on the team. That is exactly how you will all treat her. If I see anything to the contrary going on, there will be consequences! I know you are all well versed in the Uniform Code of Military Justice. If I see even the slightest infraction, I will nail your ass to the wall. Are we clear?"

"Crystal, Sir!" all of Echo said in unison.

"Commander Rowen is giving me a month to train you before he sends us on our first mission. A month is not much time. The learning curve is steep. I will assign you greens to a senior member of Echo to shadow. You will do everything he tells you to do. You will give 200 percent in everything you do!"

"Sir, yes, Sir!" the greens said in unison.

John divided them up and each group went to train. Hogan and Matt were assigned to shadow John. Chris and Mac shadowed Nick. The rest were paired up, Joe with Sonny, Jerome with Zach, Falco with Dorian, and Andrew with Ezra.

January 2
2400
Air transport over Afghanistan

The greens of Echo prepared for their final training mission before Rowen would approve them for a live mission. It would be a HALO jump thirty-five klicks north of base. John had given the greens instructions to drop on coordinates north of base. They were to make their way south to basecamp collecting target objects along the way. They had five target objects to obtain before their mission would be complete, and they could return to base. If they failed to collect every object and return to base before sunrise, they would fail the mission.

John wanted to see how the greens would perform as a team without senior Echo's leadership.

Echo 8, Hogan Zelano, was leading the charge. The eight greens made the jump and pulled their cords at the appropriate altitude. They quickly reassembled on the ground, and Hogan gave the command to move out. They collected the first target without any opposition. Half way to their second target package, Joe Karsa felt a sharp sting in his leg followed immediately by sharp stings to his arms. He looked down at the glowing green paint coating his flak jacket.

"Damnit! I'm hit!"

Joe sat on the ground, and Falco looked back to see Joe peppered in paint.

"Echo 12 is down," Falco said into his coms.

The rest of the greens dropped down and took cover. There was nothing more Joe could do. As per the rules of the training op, if he was hit, he could no longer participate in the exercise. He was officially deceased.

Hogan scanned the area with his night vision binoculars, but he saw nothing out of the ordinary. He knew the enemy, the senior members of Echo, were hunting them, but whoever made the kill shot on Karsa was well concealed.

"Move out men. Keep your head on a swivel. We are being hunted," Hogan said into his coms.

They collected the second target and headed out for the third.

Nick watched them pass within five feet of him. None of them noticed his presence. As soon as they were out of earshot, he contacted John.

"Echo 2 to Echo 1."

"Echo 1 go for Echo 2."

"I let the greens obtain target one and two as per your instructions. They are headed to target three now. I took out Echo 12. I could have easily taken them all out. These guys need more training. They are easy targets."

"Copy that. Rendezvous as per our plan."

"Roger that."

Nick moved with the stealth of a cat as he crept past the greens two klicks south of the second target. None of them noticed his passing.

As the greens approached the third target package, Hogan signaled them to hold up. He knew better than to think the object was unguarded. It sat in the middle of a valley. There was nothing there but a few scrub bushes and sand. It didn't feel right to Hogan. He ordered Falco and Jerome to scout the area and search for signs of a sniper's perch. After half an hour, Hogan requested an update. Silence answered back.

Damn! They've been taken out too!

That only left Hogan, Chris, Matt, Mac, and Andrew to collect the last three targets.

"Does it feel like we are sitting ducks to you?" Mac asked quietly.

"It's like shooting fish in a barrel. The trouble is, we are the fish," Matt muttered. "I say we do something unexpected. They know we are coming. Let's throw them off."

"How do you propose we do that?" Hogan asked. "We have to collect three more targets and return to base before sunrise, or we fail the mission. We've already lost three men."

They sat quietly for a few minutes pondering the problem.

Finally, Mac spoke up. "The object is for us to collect the targets. Echo seniors are expecting us to go straight for the targets in order. What if we don't do it."

"If we don't collect them, we fail the mission," Hogan sighed.

"No, I mean, why don't we collect them out of order and throw them off. We can skip this one and come back." Mac grinned mischievously. "I say we send in one of us as a decoy to draw out a shooter. Then the rest of us take out that shooter."

"Who will we sacrifice? There are only five of us. There are not enough decoys to accomplish a mission like that. Even if we sacrifice three men to obtain the targets, that only leaves two men to carry all five targets back to base with Echo seniors on our tail the whole way. Besides, the object of the mission is not to lose all our men. The object is to get the targets and return to base with the team intact," Chris said. "That plan is no good."

"I didn't say we sacrifice any of us," Mac said. "We use a uniform as a decoy, like a puppet."

Andrew laughed. "That's so stupid it just might work. They definitely won't be expecting it."

Hogan grinned. "I like it. Let's go for target four and see if it will work."

Target four was halfway up a mountain. There were clear shots in multiple directions. Andrew stripped down, and they stuffed his uniform with blankets from their packs. Then they rigged up their puppet, and Hogan, Chris, Matt, and Mac took up strategic positions to watch. Andrew slid his puppet over the ridge and began mimicking a belly crawl down the hill toward the target.

It did not take long before the puppet was riddled with glowing green paint. Hogan took out one sniper, and Mac took out the other with their own glowing orange paint. Zach and Dorian were both down. Andrew retrieved the target, and they headed back to target three.

"Echo 6 to Echo 1," Dorian said quietly into his coms.

"Echo 1 go for Echo 6."

"Per your instructions, we made sure we weren't well concealed and allowed the greens to take us both out. Be advised. They are using a puppet to draw fire."

"Copy that." John shook his head and muttered, "Amateurs."

After brushing off the dried green paint, the greens rigged the puppet with branches from a scrub brush. Andrew belly crawled with the puppet mounted to his back to mimic the puppet walking into the valley. He made sure to stay in an area that was riddled with scrub brush to mask his presence. All anyone at a distance could see was the upper quarter of the puppet.

As soon as the puppet took a hit, Mac and Chris trained their scopes in the direction the shots came from and took out two targets. Ezra and Ben were now out of the fight.

Andrew moved in, captured target three, and they rendezvoused at the top of the ridge.

Hogan grinned. "That's four down. That only leaves John, Nick, and Sonny between us and success. Let's go get target five and go home."

"Echo 4 to Echo 1," Ben whispered as he watched the greens walk away.

"Echo 1 go for Echo 4."

"We allowed the greens to take us out as per your instructions. You're right; success strokes their egos. They are getting too careless; we could have easily taken them all out. They aren't grasping the real purpose of this mission. They think the whole point of this exercise is to obtain the targets. They don't understand the point is to evade us, kill us, get the targets, and get home by the deadline. They are only accomplishing half the agenda and only because we are allowing it. They need a lot more training. They are still not moving in proper formation, and they aren't aware of their surroundings. Also, be advised, they are still using that idiotic puppet."

"Copy that." John shook his head and let out a heavy sigh. He had a lot of work to do.

As the greens approached target five, Hogan hand-signaled them to hold up. "I don't like this. The target is at the top of the ridge. No matter what approach we take, we will be exposed. We have to assume they have three directions covered. It's a suicide mission. We have to pinpoint their locations before we try to take the target."

"How do you propose we do that?" Andrew asked. "We are up against the best of the best. Echo 1, 2, and 3 are out there waiting to take us down."

Hogan nodded. "We have another problem. Four of us are carrying targets. If one of us gets killed in this exercise, that person's target will fall back into enemy hands. We have to secure our packages before we try to take target five."

Chris nodded. "I agree. These targets are all heavy. I say we stash them somewhere safe near home base and come back for five. If we don't all make it, at least whoever is left will be able to transport the last target back to base and collect the other four."

Hogan thought about it for a moment. "I like that idea. It's outside the box, but what if Echo 1 has anticipated that scenario? We could be walking into a trap. Besides, we are still seventeen klicks from base. We only have three hours until dawn. If we don't finish the mission by sunrise, we fail anyway. I say we go with part of your plan. We stash the targets here with one person to guard them. The rest of us find Echo seniors and take them out. Then we capture the last target."

"Who gets guard duty?" Chris asked.

"You do," Hogan said. "I'll stake out the scene from a distance and take Overwatch position. Echo 10, 11, and 15, advance slowly on the target from multiple directions. I'll cover your six."

Matt, Mac, and Andrew nodded in agreement.

At 0330, Matt, Mac, and Andrew advanced on the target. Mac was the first one to take a hit with the green paint. Hogan saw it and made the kill shot. Nick was down. Before Hogan could blink, he felt the sting and looked down to seen glowing, green paint on his flak jacket.

From their positions on either side of the ridge to the north and south of target five, Sonny and John scanned for any sign of movement. John took out Matt. Sonny took out Andrew.

John contacted Sonny. "That just leaves Echo 9. Where is he?"

"If he's out there, he ain't movin a hair on that dern head of his."

"He's not out there. This is some sort of ruse. We have to find him."

"He'll come to us. He has to have all five targets, or the mission is a failure."

John's jaw clenched. He scanned the south side of the mountain through his scope.

"You're right. He has to come to us. We wait him out."

When the greens didn't return at the scheduled time, Chris had a decision to make. He knew he was on his own now. He tied the four target packs together and dragged them sixteen klicks over the mountainous terrain. He stashed them in some heavy brush and headed back to target five as fast as he could move. When he reached the ridge, he crouched low and watched. The south side looked clear. He crept over the ridge and scanned with his night vision again. There was no movement, but he played a hunch and peppered the area all around the target with paint pellets.

I know that kid didn't see me. I'm completely camouflaged, and I wasn't movin' a lick!

Sonny was down. Chris saw no sign of movement anywhere. He walked up to Sonny who was smirking at him and collected the target. He strapped it on his back and headed down the south side of the ridge. If he sprinted most of the way, he would make base just before dawn.

Chris encountered no opposition. He wasn't sure where Echo 1 was, but he had no time to ponder it. He collected the remaining four targets, tied them on, and dragged them the last klick to base. The sun was almost up, but he crouched low watching for John. There was only 100 yards between his position and the gate. If he could make the last 100 yards, he would complete the mission, score the touchdown, and stuff it in John's face that he outsmarted him.

He saw no movement anywhere outside the compound. There was nothing suspicious to raise his guard. Still, he had half an hour until dawn broke the horizon. It would not pay to rush into anything and lose when he was so close to the goal line. He crept cautiously toward the open gate. He could see the sentries posted on the wall. He could see the convoy vehicles inside the gate in the courtyard area. What he didn't see was John. He didn't like it. It looked too easy.

Chris crept a little closer. He was thirty feet from the gate, and there was no sign of John. He decided to make a run for it. Ten feet from the gate he felt the sting. He looked down to see glowing green paint splattered on his flak jacket. He stopped in his tracks and growled in frustration. Then he frantically searched for John. He wanted to know how John had beaten him. He saw nothing. All he could hear was the smirking laughter of the sentry guards on the wall.

"He got you good!" one of the guards yelled.

"Where the hell is he?" Chris yelled back.

The guards said nothing. They just continued to laugh.

Chris growled loudly. "Where are you, Sir?"

Just then he felt the sting of another pellet hit his leg. He looked all around him and saw no sign of John. He searched frantically for an answer. Then the sand five feet in front of him began to move, and John sat up with his paintball rifle trained on Chris' chest.

"You're dead, Echo 9. Your entire team is down. You failed your mission." John stood up and dusted off most of the sand coating his uniform.

"Holy hell!" Chris exclaimed. "How long have you been buried there? All night?"

John shook his head. "I followed you from target five after you took out Echo 3. I watched you drag all five packs. I could have taken you out at any point from target five until now."

"So, why didn't you?"

"I wanted to prove a point to you. It's when you think you're home free that you have to be the most cautious. You never know what surprise the enemy has in store for you."

Chris nodded. "I see what you mean. I did think I was home free. I never suspected that you would be buried in the sand right beneath my feet. I never saw you coming."

"That's why we train, Chris. You are all very green. You don't know everything yet. The cockier you get, the more likely you are to end up in a body bag. If this had been real tonight, I would be writing eight letters home to your families to tell them you were killed in action. I don't want to write letters like that, Chris. I want the whole team to make it back— every time! I want us to accomplish our missions without losing any team members. When Nick, Sonny, Ben, Zach, Dorian, Ezra, and I tell you something, it's important. You need to pay attention. We went over concealment tactics a week ago. Yet, tonight the only time any of you could locate one of us was when we fired on you first. By then, you had already lost a team member. Sending out sacrificial lambs to draw fire is not how Echo operates. We use our head to outsmart the enemy. You have to start using your head, Chris, or you will end up in a body bag."

"I'm sorry, Chief. I won't make this kind of mistake again."

"I know you won't. We'll run this drill again tomorrow night. Rowan won't approve any missions until I tell him you guys are up to speed. Tonight proved that none of you are up to speed. You all have a long way to go."

CHAPTER 37

April 12
0557
Medical training facility

Dawn broke through the night to find Sophia on the running track just finishing her laps. She'd done what John requested. She was sprinting fifteen miles every morning before classes started. During her lunch break, she was weight training. After her last class of the day, she was sprinting an additional fifteen miles. She was keeping up with her medical studies and had top marks in all her classes. She had thrown herself wholeheartedly into this endeavor. In her spare time, she was practicing the various foreign languages she'd learned. She was getting by on very little sleep. She attributed her unnatural energy to adrenaline. She could hardly wait to finish the med course so she could be deployed and join Echo in Afghanistan.

Just as she crossed the imaginary finish line, she heard a male voice from behind a tree ahead.

"You've gotten fast, Soph."

She grinned as she slowed her pace and jogged up to the tree. "Hey, Sam."

"Hey—all I get is a hey? It's been almost a year since I laid eyes on my gorgeous fiancé. Can I get a kiss?" Sam grinned as he stepped out from behind the tree with a bouquet of red roses.

Sophia's heart skipped a beat. Sam looked so handsome.

"Are you stalking me, Sam?" she joked.

He grinned as he walked up to her and held out the roses. "You told me you run before class every morning. I figured this would be the most likely place to intercept you."

She took the roses and inhaled their sweet aroma. "Do you mind walking a lap with me?"

He fell in step beside her. "Soph, I was thinking since I'm stateside for a couple of weeks, we could get married before you deploy."

Sophia felt a pain inside her chest. "Sam—I—"

"I know I'm springing this on you, but this would be the perfect time for us to tie the knot. It will be easier now while we are both stateside. If we wait until we are on deployment it will be a lot more complicated."

"Let me think about it. How do you like being on a team?"

"It's awesome! My team is really great."

Sam pulled her into his arms and grinned as he stared down into her eyes.

"Sam, I really need to get ready for class, and you are a huge distraction right now."

"Am I a good distraction?"

Before Sophia could react, his lips were pressing against hers. At first, she froze. She'd never been kissed, and she wasn't sure what he expected from her. Then she felt his tongue slide along her lips as he coaxed her mouth open. His arms wrapped around her, and he pulled her up against the hard planes of his chest. Her heart beat faster as his tongue slid seductively against hers. She felt a heady rush, and she gave into it momentarily. It felt good to be held in his arms. He was strong, but he held her gently as if she were a fragile flower. It made her feel like something she hadn't felt like in a long time—a woman. His devotion to her was a hard thing to dismiss. It took her a minute to come to her senses. She reluctantly pulled back from his kiss.

"Sam, I'm truly sorry, but I have to go shower now, or I'll be late for class."

He took her hand in his and walked briskly beside her as they headed to the row of small apartments provided by the military.

"We could shower together. I've missed seeing you naked. We could make love and—"

"No, Sam. Get that out of your head. I'm catholic. I don't believe in sex before marriage."

He grinned slyly. "You can't blame me for trying. How about I pick you up for dinner?"

"Sure, dinner sounds great. I'll text you later. I have to hurry, or I'll be late for class."

She started to put her key in the door when he turned her, trapped her against the door with his body, and went in for a feral kiss. His aggressiveness turned her on in a way she'd never felt before. Everything about Sam was sexy—sweet—irresistible. It took her a while to come to her senses and pull away.

"Sam! I have to get ready. I'll see you tonight at dinner."

Sophia hurried through her shower berating herself for being so weak.

Sam is very sweet, but I got way too distracted from his kiss. Why did I allow myself to get so caught up in the moment with him? I didn't want that kiss to ever end. The only thing that pulled me back to reality was my duty to Echo. Chief Rusk is depending on me to complete my medical training. Echo doesn't have a medic right now. What if one of our men gets injured in the field, and I'm not there to take care of him? I have to stay focused. I'm here to learn. One day, one of my teammate's lives could be in my hands. I have to be the best medic I can be. I can't let my team down. Chief Rusk is trusting me with a crucial job. He is the only man who's ever believed in me. My Marine C.O. merely tolerated my presence. The BUD/S instructors did everything in their power to get me to wash out and ring the bell. The other SEALs passed me over—twice! Chief Rusk is different. He actually sees me as a soldier—not as a woman. I can't let him down.

Sophia quickly finished her shower and hurried across the campus to begin her busy day. She found it hard to stay focused in class. She had to concentrate to keep Sam out of her thoughts. His proposal that they get married while he's on leave kept surfacing at the worst possible moments—as did his feral kiss. Forcing thoughts of Sam out became quite a challenge.

She decided to skip her afternoon run figuring it was better to get dinner with Sam over with early. She had a lot of studying to do. She texted Sam, and he picked her up a short while later. He drove her to a nice restaurant. He was charming and sweet. He held doors open for her. He helped her into her chair. Then he sat across from her smiling and gazing into her eyes like she was the only thing in the world worth looking at.

Sophia's heart was doing flip-flops inside her chest. She found it difficult to read the menu and decide what to order. While waiting on their appetizers to arrive, Sam reached across the table, threaded his fingers through hers, and gently caressed her hand with his thumb. Sophia was so distracted she couldn't think straight. His gentle caress was sending tingles up her arm straight to her pounding heart.

I'm going to say yes. Sam is so sweet. He's such a good man. I know he'll make a good husband. We can make it work. If we love each other, we can navigate through a long-distance relationship. I'm actually glad he showed up. A weight has been lifted. I've been wavering between who to choose—Sam or Butch. Sam is so devoted; he makes me feel truly loved.

Their food arrived, and for a while, they were busy eating and making small talk. It was turning into the perfect date, not that Sophia had any experience dating. This was actually her first date ever, but it felt perfect. When they returned to her apartment, her heart was racing. She knew she shouldn't let him in, but when he started kissing her, she forgot why he should stay out.

It wasn't long before Sam had her under him on the couch. He wasn't pressuring her for sex, but Sophia had never felt so turned on in her entire life. She was sliding down the slippery slope of passion straight into the abyss of wanton pleasure.

It wasn't Sam who made the first move. She pulled his shirt free of his pants and slid her hands over the hard ridges of his abs. He groaned against her lips, and his kiss grew more possessive. She unbuttoned his shirt and caressed her fingertips over his sculpted chest until he pulled back from her lips. He touched his forehead to hers and groaned softly.

"Soph, I'm not trying to pressure you, but if you keep touching me like this—"

She grinned up at him. "Are you about to lose control?"

"Yeah. I'm trying to be good. I know you want to wait until we get married, but—"

"Maybe I changed my mind."

He stared into her eyes for a long, heated moment. "Have you?"

Her tongue flicked out to moisten her lips, and she swallowed hard. "I know we should wait until we get married, but I'm having a hard time resisting you, Sam."

"Is that a yes?"

"Yes."

He gently caressed her jaw with his fingers before claiming her lips in a tender kiss. He scooped her up and carried her to the bedroom.

"I've been dreaming about this for so long," he whispered, as he crawled up on the bed with her.

"Wait! Do you have protection?" she gasped.

He grinned down at her. "We don't need any. We are getting married this week. We belong to each other now."

"But I could get pregnant!"

"I hope you do."

Sophia's eyes grew wide. "What? Why? I can't get pregnant now. I'm about to deploy to Afghanistan!"

"Maybe if you're pregnant, they'll change your orders, and you can serve stateside where it's safe. I can come home on leave, and we can make more babies."

He leaned down to claim her lips, and she pulled away from him.

"Sam! Stop!"

"Are you afraid if we get pregnant before we are married that your parents won't approve?"

Sophia frowned. "My parents wouldn't approve, but that's a whole other issue. Are you seriously saying you don't want me to be deployed overseas at all?"

Sam sat back on his knees and stared down at her. "How honest do you want me to be?"

"One hundred percent honest."

He cleared his throat. "Okay. I love that you're such a badass. The fact that you're so tough turns me on, but the truth is, I would rather know you were stateside where it's safe. I'd rather you serve here and raise our kids than have you overseas in the line of fire. I love you. I don't want anything to happen to you. I just want to protect you."

"So, you think if I get pregnant that I can get out of serving overseas?"

"I've actually done some checking on that already. There are precedents where women who became pregnant were given special dispensations and allowed to serve out the rest of their contracts stateside. If you don't want to get pregnant tonight, we can get married tomorrow. I can get you pregnant over the next couple of weeks before I have to go back to Tanzania."

"You've really thought this whole thing through, but what if I don't get pregnant?"

Sam grinned. "I know this sounds extreme, but we could go to one of those places where they do artificial insemination. Even if I don't technically get you pregnant while I'm here, you can still get pregnant with our baby after I'm gone and get the dispensation. There's actually a clinic a few miles from here that performs those services."

"Wow! You've really done your research on this."

Sam grinned. "So, are we getting pregnant tonight or waiting until we are officially married?"

"I need to think about this, Sam. You are throwing me a pitch out of left field."

"So, not tonight?"

She shook her head. "Definitely, not tonight."

He let out a heavy sigh. "Okay. I'll see you tomorrow then. I love you."

"I love you too."

He leaned down and kissed her. Then he left.

Sophia went to the small table by the kitchenette. She got out her notes and sat down to study. It was impossible to concentrate. There were too many thoughts crowding her mind. It was pointless to study. She decided to go for a run to clear her head.

It was dark on the track. She was alone. This was exactly how she liked it. She felt like the night enveloped her in its cloak and hid her from the rest of the world. It was liberating. Running the track in the dark made her feel like she was invincible. That thought brought her right back to the source of her trouble.

Sam doesn't want me to serve overseas. He loves me. He wants to raise a family with me. Is that what I want? Do I want to marry him and start a family right now? No! That's the opposite of what I want. I want to go to Afghanistan. I want to be Echo's medic. I want to make use of all these skills I've been developing for so many years. I want to be the translator, the overwatch, and the lifesaver. I want to do it all. I'm finally on the cusp of getting everything I want, and Sam wants me to throw it all away. He wants me to stay home and be a mom. I'm not ready for that.

The next morning, dawn broke the eastern sky to find Sophia on the running track again. She had made a decision the night before. Now all she had to do was talk to Sam.

At dinner that night the atmosphere was full of tension. After dinner, they took a walk.

"Sam, you were honest with me last night. It's my turn to be honest with you. I want to go to Afghanistan. I want to serve with Echo. I want to live up to my full potential."

He frowned. "I know you want to, but is serving in such a dangerous environment really the best idea? You fractured your back in three places. I feel horrible that I played a part in that. Sweetheart, you can't dismiss a serious injury like that. I don't want to see you get injured again, or worse—killed. I couldn't bear it, Soph. I love you too much. It would break my heart."

"So, you're very serious about me not going overseas. You absolutely don't want me to go. You've gone out of your way to find a solution to what you perceive as the problem. If you get me pregnant, I don't have to go. I'll be safe and sound here at home. I can have your babies, and you can go off to Tanzania and save the world on your SEAL team."

He dragged his hand over his blonde burr. "Something like that."

"What if I don't want you to go overseas either? What if I think it's too dangerous for you? If we get married, and I stay here, are you willing to quit the SEALs when your contract expires?"

Sam's eyes widened, and his mouth fell open a little. Silence reigned for several moments until he broke it.

"I—uh—if that's what you want me to do, I'll do it."

"So, you're perfectly fine with giving up the SEALs if I ask you to?"

"I wouldn't use the word fine. I want to serve, but I can understand why you wouldn't want me to be in the line of fire. You would be worried about me. It's the same way I feel about you. If you want me to give it up at the end of my contract, I will. I'll do it for you, Soph."

She turned her back to him and stared out at the moonlight glistening on the water. There was a long awkward silence.

"You truly love me, Sam. You're willing to give up everything just to be with me."

Sam slid his arms around her and leaned down to kiss her neck. "I love you more than anything. There's nothing I wouldn't do to make you happy. There's nothing I wouldn't sacrifice to make sure you are safe. I love you more than life, Soph."

Sophia reached up and wiped away the tears that had escaped down her cheeks.

"I've never seen you cry before," he said softly.

"I'm not a crier."

He hugged her against his chest and kissed the top of her ebony burr. "I'm sorry, Sam."

"You don't have to apologize for crying. You don't always have to be a badass. You can be whoever you need to be with me."

She pulled away from him and turned back to stare at the water. "I'm not apologizing for crying. I'm apologizing because I've wasted your time. I'm not what you need me to be. I'm not ready to be a wife or a mother. I do love you, but I think you are more in love with me than I am with you. You are willing to sacrifice everything to make me happy. I'm not willing to do the same for you. I want to serve overseas. I've been preparing for the SEALs since before I finished my contract with the Marine Corp. This has been a long time coming, and I'm on the verge of getting everything I want. Last night, I realized that you are not on that list. I'm not willing to give up my career for you. I'm not willing to sacrifice my goals to stay at home and be a wife and mother. I'm not ready to settle down. I feel like the world is right at my fingertips. I'm about to walk through the threshold of a great adventure. I get excited when I think about going overseas and being put in dangerous situations. Last night, I forced myself to consider what life would be like sitting at home with kids waiting for you to come back. It made me feel claustrophobic. It felt like a heavy weight on my chest. It was like drowning. I just can't do it, Sam."

She turned back to look at him, and there were tears glistening on his cheeks.

"I didn't mean to make you feel trapped, Soph. If you're not ready, we can wait to get married. You can go serve overseas. I'll figure out how to deal with the worry. I don't want to be your dream crusher. I want you to be happy. We can get married after you've served out your contract or longer if you decide to reup. I just don't want to lose you. I've never felt this way about anyone before. I will do whatever it takes to make you happy."

She bit her lip and dropped her eyes to the ground. "I can see that. You are all in. The trouble is—I'm not. I don't want to make you wait indefinitely for me. What if I'm never ready to get married and settle down? I don't want you to waste any more time on me. I'm not worth postponing your life and happiness over. There are so many women out there who would make you a much better wife. You deserve to be happy. You deserve to find a woman who loves you as much as you love her. I wish you all the happiness in the world, Sam. I really do."

He swiped at the tears. "You're breaking up with me?"

"For your own good, I'm breaking up with you. I'm so sorry, Sam. I never meant to hurt you."

"Please, Soph. I don't want another woman. I only want you. Don't do this. I'll wait for you. I'll wait for as long as it takes."

She shook her head. "I won't do that to you. It wouldn't be fair to ask you to wait. I don't think I'll ever be the woman you need."

As she walked away, she could hear him sobbing behind her. She looked over her shoulder and saw him sink down on his knees on the path. She felt horrible. She didn't want to hurt him like that, but she had no choice. She wasn't in love with him. If she'd truly been in love, he would have been the only thing that mattered. She refused to string him along anymore. As she walked away, she cringed realizing there was one more man whose heart she would have to break. She would not string Butch along either. She would set him free, but not tonight. She would call him tomorrow. She didn't think she could take any more emotional heartache today. It hurt too much.

The next evening, she stood on the running track by the water's edge and called Butch.

"Hey, how's my beautiful, bride-to-be?"

A tear escaped down her cheek. "Hi, Butch. I need to talk to you."

He chewed at his lip for a moment.

She swallowed hard. "I need to break up with you."

"Whoa! Slow down! What are you talking about? Did I do something to make you mad?"

"No, you haven't done anything wrong. I'm the one in the wrong. I shouldn't have strung you along all this time. I'm not in love with you. I love you, but more like a friend."

"Sophia, look, I know going to med training is putting a lot of pressure on you. I know—"

"Sam came to see me."

"So, you're dumping me for him?"

"No, I broke up with him too. I thought it was just a matter of deciding which man I loved more. I was wrong. I'm not willing to put either of you ahead of my own goals, dreams, desires. I'm not in love. I want you both to be free to find happiness with the right woman."

"Maybe, we haven't spent enough time together for you to fall in love with me yet. It will come. Love grows over time. I don't believe that love hits you out of nowhere. I don't believe in love at first sight. I believe that real love is built on a solid foundation. It forms over time into something that is strong enough to withstand any hardship, challenge, or tragedy. Love is a journey that entwines two hearts. I want to entwine my heart with yours, Soph."

"Wow! That is really beautiful, Butch. You are going to make a great husband. The problem is, you want to build that solid foundation with me, but I don't want that. We truly are good friends, but that is all we are going to be. I don't want to give you false hope. I'm cutting ties now before I deploy. I need to be laser focused when I join my team. I can't have any distractions. My first and only love has to be Echo."

CHAPTER 38

May 8
0515
Afghanistan

John left Rowen's tent and headed to the mess hall. They had just returned from a mission two hours earlier. It had been messy and dangerous, but the greens had handled it. When he sat down at the table with a plate of food, he heard something he didn't like.

"Only a few weeks before that hot, little medic joins the team," Andrew said with a sly grin.

Joe grinned back. "Yeah, I can hardly wait to get injured so she can attend to me personally."

The two men laughed.

"Hey! Cut out the trash talk. You will treat Gonzalez with respect when she gets here, or you'll be off this team! I've already gone over the rules of the UCMJ with all of you!" John growled.

"Sorry, Sir!" Andrew and Joe said respectfully.

This is going to be a problem. She's not even here, and their minds are already in the gutter.

After breakfast, Master Chief Litton from SEAL team Sierra caught up to John.

"I heard some base gossip—is it true? Did you really choose a woman for your team?"

"Yeah."

Litton chuckled. "You do like trouble, don't you, Rusk?"

"What is that supposed to mean?"

Litton smirked. "Look around. You're on a base filled with sex-starved men. Most of these guys are single. They spend their time on missions. Throwing a woman in the mix is trouble."

"There better not be any trouble! Gonzalez earned her spot on the team the same as any other man. She deserves the same respect as everyone else!"

"She won't get it—not on this base. You've worked with these guys. You know how they think. To them she'll just be a welcomed opportunity for quick, easy, accessible sex."

John growled. "They better keep it in their pants if they know what's good for them. I won't tolerate anyone sexually harassing her. You can spread the word around here that any man who acts inappropriately with her will have me to answer to. I won't hesitate to file charges against him. She's here to work the same as the rest of us."

"Good luck with that, Rusk. Bucking the entire military is a lot of work."

Litton walked away laughing. John's jaw tightened as he looked around and surveyed the base in a completely new light. Suddenly, he saw dangers for Gonzalez everywhere he looked.

Litton is right. What if one of these guys gets it into his head to take advantage of her? It would be too easy—there are too many areas on base that are suitable for a tryst—or God forbid a rape! This is very bad. I'm going to have to make some changes before she gets here.

The first thing John did was order the men to change their sleeping arrangements.

"Why are you reassigning bunks?" Mac asked, as he started emptying his locker.

"Gonzalez will be here in a few weeks. We have to make some changes around here."

"Good call, John. Having her sleep next to the tent door wouldn't be wise. Anyone could snatch her out in the middle of the night without any of us knowing about it," Nick said.

"What other changes are you planning to make, Boss?" Sonny asked as he moved his things to the bunk across from John's new bunk.

"I'm still thinking about it. I'll let you know," John said.

Sonny grinned. "If you're worried about her virtue, she can share my bunk. She can sleep curled up right next to me. I'll hold her nice and tight all night. I'll cover her like a glove. I'll be her up close and personal body guard. Nobody will get near her, except me."

John smirked. "This isn't the time for jokes, Sonny."

"Who's joking? I heard from Joe that she's a hot, little senorita with the most luscious ass—"

"That's enough, Sonny!" John growled.

Sonny chuckled. "Don't get your gator in a snit. I was just joking."

"Don't joke! It's not funny!"

"I hear ya, Boss."

Nick moved his belongings to the far back bunk next to Sonny's and across from the empty bunk that would be Sophia's. John would bunk next to Sophia to ensure no one else got near her. After everyone settled into their new spots, John tagged all the lockers between the bunks with everyone's name.

"One more thing—" John addressed the whole team in the tent. "There will be no undressing in front of her. There will be no showering with her. We are going to treat her with the respect she deserves. I don't want to hear any comments from any of you that can be construed as demeaning or harassing in nature. If you don't comply, there will be serious consequences!"

CHAPTER 39

June 1
0600
Afghanistan

Sophia watched her first Afghani sunrise from the transport chopper. When the chopper sat down on base, she stepped down, and her foot touched Afghani soil for the first time. Her heart pounded as she slung her duffle bag over her shoulder and surveyed her new home.

It was sandy, and everything in sight was tan. The chopper was painted in tan shades of camo. The trucks sported the same pattern. The tents were tan. The tall stacks of wooden crates in the distance were tan. The buildings constructed of plywood were painted tan. The base virtually blended in with the surrounding mountains. Everything was tan save the occasional scrub brush.

She smiled. This was the start of her new life. She stepped away from the chopper, and it took off on its next assignment. She looked around, but she didn't see Chief Rusk or any of Echo in sight. She suddenly realized she had no idea what she was supposed to do next.

Don't be an idiot! Find someone, and ask them where Echo is. I have to report to Chief Rusk.

She started off in the direction of the nearest building. When she peeked inside, she realized it was the mess hall. It was deserted at the moment. She turned looking for anything that looked like an office. There was another structure on the opposite side of the compound. She headed toward it.

"You look lost, Little Lady," a man said from behind her.

She turned to find he was appraising her with lustful eyes—nothing new—typical behavior.

"I'm looking for Echo or Chief Rusk."

"Echo's been gone for a week. Talk to our C.O. Commander Rowen can get you squared away."

"Where is Commander Rowen?"

"Follow me."

He headed toward the north end of the compound. Sophia followed him. He stopped in front of a tent, gestured her to enter, and left. She expected Rowen to have a proper office not a tent.

"Commander Rowen?" she called out.

Rowen stepped out of the tent and nodded. "Gonzalez, follow me. I'll show you where Echo bunks. They are on a mission right now. I expect them back tomorrow assuming all goes well."

She followed keeping up with Rowen's brisk pace. He entered a large tent near the northern edge of the compound. It had a raised wooden floor and sixteen bunks. There were eight beds on each side of the tent with tall locker pairs between the beds. Rowen walked all the way to the back of the tent and gestured to the last bed on the row to her right.

"Chief Rusk assigned you to this bunk. There's your locker. You can stow your things. Chow is from 0500 to 0600, 1100 to 1200, and 1600 to 1700. If you miss it, that's on you."

"Thank you, Sir."

"The mess hall is the building on the west end. Medical and Ops building are behind it. The building on the east is ammo storage. The tents along the northern wall are troop quarters. Showers are behind the tents. Bathrooms are to the west of the showers. Welcome to Afghanistan, Gonzalez. We are glad to have you here."

"I'm glad to be here, Sir."

Rowen nodded. "I have critical work to get back to. I trust you can handle yourself."

"Sir, yes, Sir." She saluted him.

Once he was gone, she put her personal items in her locker and stowed her uniforms in the foot locker at the end of her bed. It was hot inside the tent, so she exited to explore her surroundings. She found the showers to the north of the tents. They were wooden stalls in squared groups of four. There were two sets of showers, making a total of eight stalls. There was no privacy. The showers had a swinging door on one end, but the top was open to the sky. Anyone taller than four foot could easily look over the shower wall into the adjacent stalls.

This is more primitive than I expected, but no less public. It won't be a problem. I'm used to showering with strange men. It won't bother me. I'll ignore them the same as all the others.

She found the bathroom. It was a small building that housed ten toilets with two long, trough style sinks outside. There wasn't much to familiarize herself with. The compound was fairly straightforward. The living quarters were all on the north end. There was an area on the northeast corner that was dedicated to P.T. There were weights and a basketball goal, though no cement court. Hard-packed sand served as the court floor. Food, Medical, and Ops were to the west. Ammo was to the east. Everything in the center seemed to be for transportation of one kind or another. It was simple and efficient.

By 0900, she was bored beyond measure and hoping Echo would be back early in the morning. She didn't like sitting around with nothing to do. Another day like this would make her crazy.

It didn't take her long to realize that the sand made everything worse. With every gust of wind, sand was getting in her burr, in her mouth, and creeping inside her clothes to places it did not belong. It was itchy, rough, and generally unpleasant.

She decided to buzz off what little burr she had to give the sand one less place to cling. That killed all of ten minutes. Then she was bored again. The minutes ticked by slowly until 1100. She was the first in line at chow time. She wasn't particularly hungry, but she was looking forward to the company of the other soldiers. She chatted with several men at her table while they ate. At 1200 on the dot, the mess hall emptied out. The only men left were the kitchen staff cleaning up.

With nothing to do, she decided to get in a good run around the inside of the base perimeter and begin acclimatizing herself to the environment. After a long run, standing under the cold water from the shower felt good.

The saving grace of the primitive shower was that it had a concrete floor with a drain in the center.

After her shower, she returned to Echo's tent. It was the heat of the day, and the temperature inside the tent was twenty degrees hotter than the outside. Still, there seemed to be nowhere else for her to go. She flopped down on her bunk and closed her eyes. She woke when her watch beeped notifying her it was chow time. In the mess hall, she found the group of soldiers she'd eaten lunch with and sat down.

"Back for more punishment?" one of the men joked as he gestured to her plate of food.

"This is fine cuisine," she joked back.

"Maybe for a wild dog," another man muttered. "I miss my wife's cooking. I only get to eat it a couple of weeks out of the year, but I live on those memories. She's a really great cook."

"Do you have any kids?" she asked.

"Three. I miss them like crazy. They are growing up so fast."

"How old are they?"

"Three, five, and seven."

She nodded and smiled at him. She tried to imagine what it would be like to leave kids behind and go off to serve. It seemed too painful to imagine, so she pushed it out of her head.

The following afternoon, Sophia sat on her bed playing solitaire. Choppers had come and gone all day, but Echo hadn't been on any of them. She'd stopped running out to greet them by 1030.

"Well, now! What have we here? Solitaire? No, no. That won't do. I'll have to teach you a better game. Have you ever played strip poker?" Sonny drawled from the doorway of the tent.

Sophia jerked at the sound of his voice and looked up.

"Sonny! That's enough!" John barked from behind him.

"Sorry, Boss. I just couldn't resist messin' with her a little."

She stood up, scooped up the deck of cards, and put them in her locker. Then she extended her hand to Sonny as he closed the distance between them. "I'm Sophia."

"*Enchante.*" (Nice to meet you.) Sonny took her hand, pulled her in close, and winked at her. "I'm Sonny. Don't believe the rumors you may have heard about me. I'm not as bad as the legends suggest."

She chuckled. "Legends? I guess I haven't heard them."

"Ow! Boys, she cuts me to the quick!"

Laughter erupted from several of the men heading to their bunks.

"Sonny! Let go of her! She's not one of your bar sluts!" John snapped.

Sophia's attention was drawn to John who was hobbling down the aisle toward them. She let go of Sonny's hand and rushed over to John.

"You're injured!"

John winced as he took another step. She quickly slid under his left arm and circled her arm around his torso. She couldn't help but notice that his dark brown burr was still damp from a shower, and he smelled clean—like soap—he smelled nice.

"Put your weight on me, Sir. You shouldn't be walking on it."

"I'm fine. I've had worse."

He grunted as he pulled away from her and finished the last few steps to his locker—next to hers. He opened the door, grabbed a bottle of pain pills, and swallowed two of them. Then he carefully sat down on his bunk with a groan. Sophia walked to his locker and examined the pills he'd taken. Then she turned to look at him.

"Do you take these very often?"

"Only when I need them."

"How often do you need them?"

"Only when I get hurt." John laid back on his bed and closed his eyes.

She shut his locker and stood staring at him. "Those are very strong pain pills, Sir. I think I should take a look at your leg. What happened?"

"I don't need you to baby me," he muttered.

"I'm not babying you. I'm doing my job, Sir. You want me to be the team's medic. My job is to tend to the sick and injured."

"I'm barely injured. I'll live. I just need to rest it."

"Where does it hurt?"

"Can you just leave me the hell alone, Gonzalez!"

Nick motioned her across the aisle to his bunk. She walked over.

Nick lowered his voice. "He twisted his knee saving Falco. He was dangling from a cliff, and John was the only one close enough to get to him. There wasn't time to secure a rope. John had to wedge his left foot in a crevice and twist his body around a boulder on the cliff face to reach Falco. That's how it happened."

Sophia nodded. Then she walked over to John's bunk and started untying his boots.

"What are you doing?" John muttered with his eyes still closed.

"I'm going to take a look at your knee. Pills will only mask pain. They won't treat the injury."

"I know that!" he growled. He watched her gently tug his boots off.

"Do you need help taking your pants off?"

"I'm not taking my pants off!"

"I need to look at your knee, Sir. I can't do that with your pants on."

John shook his head. "Leave it alone, Gonzalez! It's not your concern. I don't need your help."

"Sir, I insist."

Their eyes locked. He glared at her, but it was clear she wasn't going to relent.

Finally, he let out a frustrated sigh, sat up, and swung his legs over the side of the bed.

"Fine! Turn around!"

She gave him a confused look.

He cleared his throat. "I don't wear skivvies," he muttered.

A smirk twisted her lips. "You don't have anything I haven't seen before. I assure you; the only interest I have in you is purely medical, Sir."

John's jaw tightened as he glared at her. "If you insist on looking at my knee then turn around! Otherwise, shut the hell up and leave me alone!"

She turned her back to him with a grin. She heard him grunting with the effort to stand up.

"You can turn around now!" He groaned loudly in pain.

She turned to see him sitting on the edge of the bed with his blanket covering his lap. Her eyes grew wide at the sight of his left knee. It was badly swollen with dark purple bruises.

"How long ago did this happen?" she asked as she knelt down to examine his knee.

"Two days."

"Have you been walking on it for two days?"

"Didn't have a choice."

She gently pressed her fingers against his knee. He winced in pain.

"We need to ex-ray this. You might have torn something."

"It's not torn. I know what a tear feels like. It's just a bad sprain. I'll be fine if I rest it."

"Are you always this stubborn?"

Nick smirked. "Yeah. He is. Can you fix him, or do we need to drag him off to medical?"

Sophia gently lifted his ankle. He didn't react with pain.

"It doesn't hurt to move it this way?"

John shook his head.

"Why don't we put some ice on it and see how it feels in a couple of hours?"

"I'll go get some ice," Matt volunteered.

"Look at Falco's arm while you're at it," Nick said. "He's been favoring it ever since the fall."

She turned to see Falco sitting on his bunk rubbing his right arm. While she was examining Falco, John tugged his pants back on. He sank back down on his bunk and closed his eyes.

When she finished wrapping Falco's arm up in a sling to immobilize it, the last few stragglers from the showers made their way into the tent. Nick introduced her to everyone.

When Matt returned with an ice pack, she walked over to John's bunk to put ice on his knee. He was sound asleep. He didn't even stir when the cold pack was applied.

"Does he always sleep so soundly?" she asked.

Nick shook his head. "No, he's usually a light sleeper. We all are, but we haven't had any sleep in four days. We were behind enemy lines. Sleep was a luxury none of us could afford.

She nodded. Then she noticed that most of the men were already on their bunks snoring.

"Was anyone else injured?" she asked.

Nick shook his head. "Not seriously. Nothing requiring your attention. It will be nice to have a full-time medic again. John's been pulling double duty as our C.O. and our medic."

"Was Chief Rusk the team medic before?"

"No, John had medic training, but Cord was our official medic. John had never been an acting medic until Cord died. It did a number on his head. He wakes up with nightmares about that day. It was bad; he had to watch them all die. There was nothing he could do to save them."

Sophia bit her lip and stared at John. "Has he gotten any counselling for it? PTSD is serious."

Nick studied her for a moment. "Get some rest, Gonzalez. Tomorrow we start your training."

"More training? I've been training for two years straight. I'm ready to go on a real mission."

Nick chuckled softly. "Greens are all the same. You can't wait to jump into the fight and kick some ass, but despite what you think, you're not ready to go on a real mission yet. We have to train you how Echo moves and works together as a unit. John says you're really smart—your scores indicate genius. He has a lot of confidence in you. I'm sure you'll pick it up quickly."

The next morning, Sophia rose before dawn, quietly got into her locker, and got out her toothbrush. She walked to the bathroom where a few soldiers were at the outdoor sinks brushing their teeth. When she returned, John stood at the door of the tent with his arms folded over his chest blocking the entrance.

"Excuse me," she said politely as she side-stepped to circumvent him.

He side-stepped blocking her path. "You're not allowed in. The guys are changing clothes."

She gave him a questioning look but took a step back. A few minutes later, the rest of Echo exited the tent and headed to the bathroom.

"You can change clothes now. I'll stand outside the door to make sure no one walks in on you." John gestured for her to enter the tent.

She chuckled. "Thanks, but that's not necessary. At GITMO I had to change and shower with the men on base. At BUD/S it was the same. It won't bother me."

John cleared his throat and ran his hand over his burr. "It may not bother you, but it's a direct order. I don't want you changing or showering with the men on base. They are not used to having a female among them like this. This is a remote base. You are the only woman stationed here. This is a first for all of us. I don't want any trouble."

"I'm sure there won't be any trouble. We are all professional soldiers."

John glared at her. "Did I not make myself clear? You are not to parade around naked or in your skivvies in front of my men or any of the men on base. Likewise, we will not change in front of you to give you the same curtesy and to remove temptation on both sides of the fence. Are we clear, Petty Officer First Class Gonzalez?"

"Yes, Sir."

"When I give an order, I expect it to be followed. I will not tolerate any dissent from you. You've been in the field for one day. I've been here for twelve years. Don't think you know more than me or any of the senior officers on Echo. When we give you an order, you will follow it."

Sophia stood at attention and maintained eye contact with John while he glared at her.

Why the hell did I back talk him? I know better. He is my commanding officer. His word is law. Just because things were different in the Marines and at BUD/S doesn't negate his authority. I need to learn to keep my mouth shut and my ears open. He clearly gave me an order, and I clearly gave it my own interpretation. I won't make that mistake again.

"Are we going to have a problem, Gonzalez?"

"No, Sir! I will follow your orders to the letter from this moment on."

John nodded. She entered the tent, and he closed the flap and stood posted outside the door until she changed clothes. After Echo returned, she ate breakfast with them in the mess hall. She noticed that John had disappeared.

While the rest of Echo ate, John reported to Rowen's tent. He had to file the official report of the mission. He normally filed reports directly after missions, but Rowen had been tied up with more urgent matters the previous day. He'd been in the middle of collecting satellite data for two ongoing ops for two other SEAL teams.

"How did things go in China?" Rowen asked.

"We ran into some trouble, but we handled it."

Rowen nodded. "The target package?"

"It was handed off to our CIA contact at the border."

"Casualties?"

"None worth mentioning."

"I know you want time to train Gonzalez, but something has come up. I need Echo to deploy in an hour. We have a critical situation in Egypt. Echo will be backing up Charlie."

John went over the mission package with Rowen. Then he left to assemble Echo.

"We have a critical mission. Grab your gear. We chopper out at 0730."

The next forty-five minutes were spent packing equipment into packs, loading up MRE's, and getting on the chopper. John hadn't told them what the mission was. No one asked. A short while later, they were on a transport plane to Egypt. On the flight, John gathered them all together to go over strategies and target packages. When he finished briefing the team, he looked at Sophia.

"Gonzalez, you will shadow Sonny on this mission. We are not the primary team. We are here to provide back up." He looked at Sonny. "She has sniper training, but no field experience. I want her to learn the ropes from you, Sonny."

"No problemo, Bossman. I'll show her the ropes." Sonny winked at John.

John's stern expression didn't change. He looked back at Sophia. "You will follow Sonny's orders as if they were mine. He's in charge of you on this mission."

Sophia nodded. "Yes, Sir."

Her overwatch training started on the flight to Egypt. Sonny spent an hour going over Echo procedures with her. She listened intently to everything he said. When they reached their destination, she stuck close to Sonny. They took up a sniper position on the roof of a building located in the center of an open market.

SEAL team Charlie was scattered throughout the market dressed in appropriate attire to blend in with the crowd. Charlie had their own Overwatch positioned at the far end of the market. Their mission was to track and eliminate an arms dealer. The sell was supposed to go down in the market below.

"Keep yer eyes peeled," Sonny said quietly.

Sophia lay next to him on the roof with a pair of high-powered binoculars. She scanned the crowd for the faces in the target package. There were so many people moving among the market tents below; it was hard to determine within a few seconds if the person she was looking at was a target or an innocent civilian.

This is much harder than I imagined it would be. Everyone is moving so quickly, it's hard to recognize a specific face in the crowd.

"Got target D," Sonny said into his short-range coms. "He's moving from the fish market to the coffee house on the north end of the square."

Sophia focused her binoculars on the north end near the coffee house, but she could not identify anyone there as one of the five targets they were looking for.

"Got him," Bill from Charlie said as he stepped out from one of the tents below and followed.

Sophia quickly scanned ahead of Bill looking for target D, but she still couldn't identify which man Bill was following. There were so many. She suddenly realized how far in over her head she actually was. She'd believed that all her training in the Marine's, BUD/S, and sniper school had prepared her for field work. Now, John's words rang in her head.

You've been in the field for one day. I've been here for twelve years. Don't think you know more than me or any of the senior officers on Echo.

Sophia chewed at her bottom lip as she desperately tried to identify target D in the crowd.

"Target D has entered the coffee house," Bill said.

"Copy, I see him," Craig from Charlie said. "I'm in a booth in the back. He's headed this way. Target A just entered from the back alley. They are sitting at a table now."

"Spotted target B," Lance, Overwatch for Charlie, said into his coms. "He's getting out of his car. He's heavily armed and heading into the market now."

"I see him. In pursuit," Sean from Charlie said.

Sophia trained her binoculars on the crowd near the entrance. She spotted Sean heading toward the center of the market area, but she could not identify target B in the crowd.

"I see him," Sonny said. He's passing the rug dealer. He just nodded to Target E. E is walking along the western perimeter near the lamp vendor."

"Copy that," Murph from Charlie said. "Tailing him now."

Despite her best efforts, Sophia could not identify even one of the targets in the crowd. She felt frustrated and overwhelmed. Training had not prepared her for this. If she had been Overwatch today, she would have failed miserably. The mission continued. She heard them in her ear piece, but she didn't see what they saw. The only men she could identify were the SEALs from Charlie.

Charlie followed the targets, collected intel, and relayed it to the teams. Once the money changed hands via electronic transfer in the coffee house, targets B and E made the vehicle exchange in the parking lot on the north end of the market. After target E left with the merchandise, he drove the car to a remote area and switched vehicles.

Echo used the tracker they had placed on target E's vehicle to follow it to the switch. Then they hit target E, confiscated the merchandise, and destroyed any evidence of the skirmish. The stolen arms were transported to the rendezvous point where Echo turned the merchandise over to their CIA contact who had been tracking the electronic transfers.

On the flight back to Afghanistan, Sophia sat staring at the floor and berating herself for thinking she was ready to take on a whole world of villains by herself. The value of teamwork hit her full force. All the preaching in BUD/S about watching your teams back before your own made perfect sense now. She'd witnessed teamwork in action all day. It had taken thirty-two SEALs working together to successfully execute that mission.

Sonny sat down next to Sophia. "How'd it feel to get yer feet wet?"

"It was fine." She sighed and stared glumly at her combat boots.

Sonny frowned. "Not what you were expecting, was it?"

"No."

Sonny put a hand on her knee and leaned in close. "Don't worry. The first mission is always the hardest. It gets easier."

She sighed dejectedly. "I wasn't an asset to the team. I contributed nothing on this mission. I couldn't spot any of the targets in the crowd. How do you do it?"

Sonny gave her knee a gentle squeeze. "Like I said, it gets easier with practice. I've been doin' this fer a long time. My first few missions, I was like a lost puppy lookin' fer its tail. Kyle, my C.O., was pretty patient with me. He was a pro at all this stuff. He made it look easy. I felt like an incompetent, bumbling idiot compared to him, but he taught me the ropes. I got it eventually. Don't worry. I ain't gonna leave ya hangin' in the wind to dry. I got yer back, Little Sister. Stick with me, and you'll learn more than ya want to know."

"Thanks, Sonny."

He grinned and winked at her. Then he squeezed her knee a little harder before he got up and went back to his seat. John watched the exchange, and he didn't like it. He limped over to Sonny.

"What was that?" John demanded.

"What?" Sonny asked.

"I warned all of you not to put your hands on her. I just saw you flirting with her!"

Sonny chuckled. "I wasn't flirting. That ain't how I flirt, Bossman. I was just asking her how the mission went from her perspective. She was feelin' a little disappointed with herself. I was just trying to encourage her."

"Was her performance a problem on this mission?"

"No, she performed fine for someone who's never been in the field before. She'll get her sea-legs. It took me a minute before I got the hang of Overwatch."

"She has been in the field. She was a Marine at GITMO for four years before she joined us."

Sonny whistled. "She's a former Jarhead—like me! Well now—that gives me a whole new respect for her cute, little ass."

John's jaw tightened, and he glared at Sonny. "You better not be looking at her ass. Keep your eyes off her. I told you she's off limits!"

"Yeah, yeah, yeah. She's off limits, but a feller can window-shop, can't he?"

"No! No window-shopping, no flirting, no ogling!"

"Damn, John, you do take all the fun out of it."

John glanced around. Joe and Falco were eyeing Sophia like a piece of candy. Their lascivious grins and lustful eyes rubbed him the wrong way. He limped over to them.

"You boys have a problem? I saw the way both of you were looking at her. Keep it clean!"

"Yes, Sir," Joe and Falco said respectfully.

John turned his back on them and limped over to Sophia. "I need you to move to another seat."

"Okay." She unbuckled and followed him down the row of empty harness seats along the side of the cargo plane. He directed her to the last seat—as far away from the men as he could put her.

"Sit here."

She buckled up, and John took the seat next to her.

"Sir, did I do something wrong?" she asked confused.

"No." He closed his eyes and slouched down in the seat to get comfortable. "Get some sleep."

Her first day with the team and the guys are already drooling over her. This is going to be a problem. I'm going to have to keep an eye on these guys. For that matter, I'll have to keep an eye on her too. The men back on base won't be any different. I didn't anticipate this scenario when I chose her for the team. This is going to be a lot more work than I planned on.

Sophia looked around the cargo plane from her seat. She noticed a few of the men had gotten up from their seats and were curiously eyeing her and John from a distance. A couple of the men grinned at her and waved. She grinned and waved back.

Chief Rusk said I didn't do anything wrong, but this feels like some sort of punishment. Why is he separating me from the rest of the team?

After the curious onlookers returned to their seats, she turned her gaze on John. He seemed to be sleeping soundly. Her eyes traveled down to his left knee. She made a mental note to take a look at his knee when they returned to base. She didn't like that he was popping pain pills to deal with the injury. Pain pills were not a solution.

Suddenly, he jerked in his sleep and mumbled something incoherent. Then she noticed his right eye twitching.

Eye twitching is a sign of stress. I wonder if he's dreaming about the men he lost. I feel bad for him. That must have been hard. I can't imagine what that would be like. It's no wonder he has nightmares about it.

CHAPTER 40

June 7
2215
Afghanistan, mountains north of base

Echo was conducting a training op with the greens. John wanted to see how they would respond to a crisis without the ability to communicate with each other. He ordered them to HALO jump into separate zones and rendezvous fifty klicks north of base.

It was a dark, moonless night, and he and the senior officers on Echo had already taken positions in the field to ambush and eliminate the greens with paintball rifles.

The Op was going well. The greens had not been told that old Echo would be waiting in ambush. John wanted to ascertain how much of their previous lessons the greens had assimilated. It didn't take long for half of the greens to be taken out of the fight. Jerome and Andrew were the first to be eliminated. They were quickly followed by Joe and Mac. Hogan, Chris, and Matt were much harder to take by surprise. They made it much farther than John expected them to. The only greens left to eliminate were Falco and Sophia.

John met up with senior Echo, gave them each a sector to search, and the hunt was on.

Falco and Sophia reached the rendezvous, but the rest of the greens were not there.

"What do you think we should do?" Sophia asked.

Falco smirked. "If it was just one missing teammate, I'd suspect they were injured, but not seven. Knowing how sneaky John is, I suspect we are being set up for another poignant lesson."

"What do you suggest?"

Falco grinned at her. "See if we can turn the tables on the old dogs this time."

They split up and headed out on a hunt of their own. Falco managed to get the drop on Zach and Ezra, but he was taken out by Dorian a short while later.

Sophia crept quietly remembering Chris' story about John burying himself in the sand.

So, Chief Rusk likes to play games. We'll see if he likes the way I play.

Using every stealth technique she'd learned in the Marines and BUD/S, she cut away some scrub brush and half buried her pack. Then she camouflaged it with the branches.

If they are looking for a back pack, they won't find it.

She found a good spot near the rendezvous coordinates and dug a deep hole. Then she buried herself in it. The only thing visible was the very end of her paint gun barrel and the end of the scope. Everything else was completely covered by the loose sand of the Afghani desert and some branches of scrub brush attached to her helmet. She was as invisible as she could be. She mentally prepared herself for a very long wait.

John, Nick, Sonny, Ben, and Dorian searched the rest of the night for her. At dawn, John gathered all of Echo at the rendezvous site. Sophia watched from her hide.

"Do any of you know where Gonzalez is?" John asked.

Falco shook his head with a slight smirk.

"What do you know?" John demanded.

"She's hunting, Sir." Falco said respectfully.

"Hunting what?"

"You, Sir."

John let out a frustrated breath. "Where did you last see her?"

"Right here. We split up. I headed east. Last I saw her, she was headed west."

"Okay, Nick take half of the guys and go east. I'll take half and go west. We have to find her."

Sophia watched as the group split up in search of her. She wasn't sure if she should come clean and exit her hide or wait it out and see if they could find her. Her ego made the decision.

After three hours of fruitless searching, both groups returned to the rendezvous site.

Ben dragged a hand down his jaw. "What if she was captured by insurgents last night?"

John let out a frustrated breath. "Ben, take Mac and Joe with you in case there are insurgents in the area. Get back to base and have Rowen order a chopper sweep of the area. If they have her, they couldn't have gotten far on foot. The rest of us will keep looking here."

This plan backfired. I can't make Chief Rusk conduct a chopper search for me.

She took aim and pulled the trigger twice.

John felt the sting high on the inside of his right thigh and the thud on his flak jacket. He looked down to see orange paint. He jerked his eyes up scanning for the shooter. He saw nothing but sand. Then his ears were filled with the raucous laughter from the rest of Echo.

"Damn! She got you good, John. Where the hell is she?" Zach exclaimed.

Just then, Nick, followed quickly by Sonny, and Ezra felt the sting of paintballs hitting them. Everyone searched, but they couldn't figure out where she was.

"She's south of us!" John shouted. "Spread out and look for her!"

A wry grin spread over her mouth as she watched them through her rifle scope. Soon, they were all out of sight. They had passed her and were searching over the other side of the mountain peak for her. Soon enough, Echo returned to the rendezvous with the exception of John.

Where is Chief Rusk? Why didn't he come back with the rest of them?

She felt a hard tap against her helmet.

"Nice trick, Gonzalez."

John grabbed the end of her paint gun barrel and pulled it up from the sand. Sophia looked up to see him squatting next to her with a grin on his face. She grinned back. He offered her his hand and pulled her up out of the sand. Then he turned to the rest of Echo.

"Gonzalez just earned herself the first shower. Double time it back to base!"

By the time they reached base, it was dark. Like always, John stood guard in front of her shower to ensure no one disturbed her. His back was to her, but his eyes were vigilantly scanning for anyone heading their way. When she exited the shower, he blocked her path.

"Do me a favor, Gonzalez," he said sternly.

She looked up at him. "Sir?"

He lowered his voice and leaned in closer. "Next time you ambush me like that, can you aim a little farther away from my crotch?"

Her gaze dropped to the orange splatter of paint on his right thigh. "Did I hit—something?"

He cleared his throat noting her amusement. "No, but you came damn close—too damn close."

A wry grin spread over her mouth. "I apologize, Sir. It wasn't my intention to damage any equipment. I had my scope focused in on you. I aimed carefully to avoid your—package." She cleared her throat. "I could see my target was clear. I'm an excellent aim. I wouldn't have hit anything—sensitive. You were perfectly safe."

He took a step closer and lowered his voice even more. "You had your scope focused on—my package?" He cleared his throat. "Why would you—" His jaw worked as he stared down into her eyes. "Next time, don't aim there! Next time, keep your eyes off my—equipment."

She tried to suppress her grin and failed. "Yes, Sir. It won't happen again. Sorry, Sir."

He chewed at his bottom lip as he stared at her. He noted her smirky grin and took a step back. Her eyes dropped to the orange paint splatter on his thigh and slid over to his crotch.

"Are you sure I didn't damage anything. If I did—"

"Hey! Eyes up here, Gonzalez!" John suddenly felt overheated, and it had nothing to do with the Afghani desert climate.

She slid her eyes up to meet his and pressed her lips together to subvert her grin.

"You're not getting my pants off again to examine anything down there. Don't even think about suggesting it!"

A soft chuckle escaped her. "That wasn't what I was going to say."

"Oh—well—" He dragged a hand down his stubbled jaw. "You didn't—damage anything."

"But I did give you a scare."

"Affirmative. Just don't ever do that again. Dismissed, Gonzalez!"

She held his gaze for a moment. Then she saluted him with a playful wink and walked away.

He watched her walk away, and his lips turned up in a smirky grin.

At 2300, Sophia woke to the sound of John tossing and turning in his bunk. Then she heard him mumbling in his sleep. He kept repeating, 'No, no, no,' over and over. She got up to check on him. It was obvious he was having a nightmare. She gently laid her hand on his forearm.

"Sir, are you okay?" she asked quietly.

He jerked, grabbed her wrist, and sat up suddenly. "What are you doing up?" he growled.

"You were having a nightmare, Sir. Are you alright?"

"I'm fine! Go back to bed."

He let go of her wrist, and she sat down on her bunk staring at him in the dark tent. He threw off his covers, shoved his feet into his boots, and laced them up with her watching him.

"Go to sleep, Gonzalez!" He stood up and exited the tent.

When he didn't come back, she put on her boots and exited the tent. After a diligent search, she located John. He was sitting on a stack of crates staring at the ground.

"Sir, are you alright?"

A low growl emanated from his throat. "I told you to go back to sleep."

"I was worried about you, Sir. You've been gone for a while."

He stood up and glared at her. "Are you going to make a habit of disobeying my orders?"

"Your orders?"

"I told you to go back to sleep, yet here you are in the middle of the night wandering around. When I tell you to do something, I expect you to do it."

"I didn't realize telling me to go to sleep was an order, Sir. I apologize."

"Everything that comes out of my mouth is an order. I expect you to obey everything I tell you to do, even if it's to pass the salt in the mess hall. Are we clear yet?"

She nodded. "Yes, Sir."

"Go back to the tent, and go to bed, now!"

"Yes, Sir."

She turned and walked away. John waited until she was fifty yards away before he followed her. His eyes were alert as he scanned the area. There were a few soldiers on guard duty, but there was no one else roaming the base at the moment. He watched to ensure she was safe inside the tent. After a few minutes, he quietly looked inside the tent. Sophia was lying on her cot, and all the other members of Echo seemed to be sleeping. He dropped the tent flap and secured it. Then he took a jog around the perimeter of the base on the jogging path.

He needed to clear his head. He didn't want the nightmare of losing eight members of Echo to return. After running for two hours, he felt exhaustion weighing on him. He grabbed a towel and some fresh clothes and went to the showers. Standing under the cold water felt good after his hard work-out. He closed his eyes and let the water cascade down his body.

At 0215, Sophia headed to the bathroom. She passed the showers, and her eyes caught on John. He didn't see her, but she saw enough of him. The shower door may have covered the lower half of his body, but the top half that showed above the shower door was sexy as hell.

He is hot! I knew he had muscle definition, but—Wow! I bet his wife appreciates his hot body.

She stared as she hurried to the bathroom. When she came out, he was gone. She walked back to the tent to find him standing in front of the tent waiting for her.

"How many orders are you going to disobey in one day, Gonzalez?"

"I wasn't trying to disobey your order, Sir. I needed to use the bathroom."

He glared at her as she walked past him into the tent. He followed her in, and soon they were both lying in their bunks unable to sleep.

It took Sophia a while before she could drift back to sleep. Her encounters with John were weighing on her mind. It was obvious he was going through something traumatic. This wasn't the first night she'd woken to hear him moaning and restless. She kept thinking about what Nick had told her—John had to watch them all die.

John lay awake thinking. He had a lot to do to get Sophia ready for a real mission. Rowen was giving him a month to train her, but John wasn't sure it would take that long. Sophia was catching on much faster than the other greens had. After a while, he rolled over and stared at her in the dark. She was asleep now, and she looked peaceful. He stared at her for a while. Realizing he was staring, he rolled over and tried to go to sleep.

Damn! She even sleeps cute. She's curled up like a curvy, little kitten. I've got my work cut out for me. She's too pretty for her own good. It's not just the lonely men on base I have to be concerned about. Out in the field, any man who lays eyes on her is going to be attracted. She could be in danger from unscrupulous men on every mission. Then there's Sonny, Joe, and Falco to worry about. Sonny's a womanizer; he wouldn't hesitate to use her for his own pleasure. Joe and Falco are already showing an unhealthy interest in her. I've caught them both watching her.

At 0500, John went to the mess hall with the rest of Echo. He got a tray of food and walked to their usual table. What he saw confirmed his fears. Joe had taken a seat right next to Sophia and was grinning, joking, and doing his best to charm her. John watched him all through breakfast.

When Echo went out on training ops that morning, John deliberately paired Sophia and Joe so he could observe their interactions during the exercise. He didn't like what he observed. It was obvious that Joe was overtly flirting with Sophia.

It didn't take Falco long to notice that Joe was flirting with Sophia. He didn't care for it. He had his own designs for the beautiful SEAL. When John gave them thirty minutes to rest and eat an MRE, Falco walked over to Sophia. She looked up squinting against the sun. Falco stood in front of her with a grin on his face.

"Mind if I sit by you?" he asked.

He sat down with his MRE and stole another glance at her. She smiled, noting his attention. She had always had men stare at her with flirty grins. It wasn't unusual. Her eyes roamed over Falco for a moment. His dark, chocolate brown skin glistened with sweat from the extreme workout John had put them through. His bright, smile was friendly with a hint that more lurked beneath than mere friendly thoughts. He was five foot, ten inches, and 180 pounds of muscle.

He pulled his shirt up to wipe sweat from his face, and her eyes were drawn to the hard ridges of his eight pack. He was pure beauty. His body was perfect. His face was handsome enough to be on a magazine. She found him extremely attractive, but that didn't interest her. What drew her to him was his manner with her. He was extremely nice and full of helpful hints. He always went out of his way to give her advice on how to do things more efficiently. She appreciated being taken under his wing. It was nice to have someone work with you as opposed to against you.

She liked Falco. He'd made her feel welcome the moment she'd joined the team. She got along with him very well. Unlike GITMO or BUD/S, she was finding that most of the men on Echo seemed happy to have her on the team. There were two exceptions, John and Nick did not come across as friendly. Nick wasn't unfriendly; he merely treated her in an aloof manner. John was another story. She wasn't sure yet what to think of John. He'd picked her for the team and sent her for special training, but he wasn't anything like what she'd expected.

His manner with her was harsh, commanding, and judgmental. Nothing she did ever seemed to be right. If she strayed too far from the team, he came down on her. If she talked or joked around with other members of Echo, he came down on whoever she talked to.

Her thoughts strayed to their flight from Egypt. She still hadn't figured out what she'd done wrong on the plane. He'd made her sit as far away from the team as possible and had sat next to her to ensure she didn't move from her seat. It was obvious to her that everything she did must rub John the wrong way. He constantly went out of his way to punish her in subtle ways for infractions that she had yet to decipher.

John sat several feet away consuming his MRE. He watched the exchange between Falco and Sophia. He didn't like it. He noted Joe seemed unhappy that Falco was talking to Sophia.

This is going to be trouble. Both men want her, and they are developing an un healthy competition with each other over her. I'm going to have to talk to both of them about this.

John went back to observing Sophia and Falco. He couldn't determine if she was encouraging the unsanctioned attention. There was nothing overt in her manner, but she wasn't telling either man to take a hike. He couldn't help but wonder if she actually craved all the male attention she was getting. He decided to continue observing for now and gather more evidence before he acted.

After lunch, John switched up the pairs. He put Sophia with Falco for the afternoon exercises. He wanted to give Joe, Falco, and Sophia plenty of rope to hang themselves if that's where this was headed. By the end of the day, he ascertained that Joe and Falco were developing a much too intimate bond with Sophia. Sophia herself was still a mystery. She had done nothing to make him believe that she was instigating any of the flirting, but she wasn't putting a stop to it either.

At dinner, John noticed that Falco sat directly across from Sophia and Joe sat next to her. He could see the predatory way both men looked at her. It sent his radar into overdrive. He'd lectured the entire team for months prior to her arrival. He'd made it very clear that she was off limits. The fact that Joe and Falco were taking interest in her against his orders was infuriating.

CHAPTER 41

June 23
0600
Afghanistan base

Sophia picked up Echo's training methods like a sponge. John was so impressed with her that he decided to up her training from the basics to their overwatch procedures. He met with Echo.

"We are going on a three-day training op in Turkey. Gather up your supplies and pack your gear. We leave in two hours." John pulled Sonny off to the side. "I'm going to have Gonzalez shadow you on this op. I want her trained as a backup for Overwatch."

Sonny grinned. "I get the sexy senorita for three whole days all to myself? Yeehaw!"

John grimaced. "Keep the training professional and keep it in your pants! That's an order!"

Sonny studied him for a moment. "Cage the jealousy monster, John. I ain't gonna touch her."

"I'm not jealous! I just want your word that you won't try anything with her!"

"Yeah, yeah, Boss. She's off limits. I heard you the first time."

"Then act like you heard me! No more jokes! No more dirty insinuations!"

Sonny chuckled. "Fine, John. If you insist on taking all the fun out of it. I'll do a 180. Is that what you want to hear? I'll try to act more like Nick and less like me."

"That's exactly what I want to hear!"

"You virgins is somethin' else—I tell you— You and Nick is two peas in a pod. You both act like she don't exist, but I bet secretly—"

"Zip it, Sonny! You're the one with the dirty mind, not me, not Nick. Just cool it!"

"Fine! I'm coolin' it, but it don't change nothin'. You think she's hot the same as the rest of us. You just ignore it. I still haven't figured out how you two can ignore women the way you do. It ain't natural. I think you two has some screwed up hormones or whatnot. How can you watch her sweet, little ass sway past you and not get hard? She is so—"

John stepped up in Sonny's face and growled. "I told you to zip it! Go pack your gear!"

Sonny walked away chuckling and shaking his head.

At 0800, Echo climbed in the chopper. John noticed that Sonny and Joe took seats on either side of Sophia, and Falco took a seat across from her. He watched all three of them on the flight off base. He noticed Falco was grinning at her the entire flight, and Joe's thigh was pressed against hers like it was superglued there. He watched Sonny too, but Sonny wasn't doing anything objectionable—at the moment.

When they boarded a cargo plane for the flight to Turkey, John put his arm in front of Sophia to block her path onto the plane. He waited until all of Echo had taken seats. Then he chose the two seats farthest from the rest of the group, told her to have a seat, and he sat right next to her. Sophia buckled up, and her nerves started working on her. John had told her she'd be training for Overwatch for the next three days. She was excited, but fear roiled inside her too.

What if I screw up like last time? I felt like I was drowning in an endless ocean of faces.

She took a deep breath and let it out slowly.

John slouched down in his seat, closed his eyes, and settled in for a nap.

When the plane landed in Turkey, Echo disembarked and rode in the back of a transport truck to their temporary quarters. John surveyed the bunk room, and he didn't like the look of it. There was a door at either end of the cinder-block room. He walked to the center of the room and made bunk assignments. He made sure to put Sophia in the middle of the room right between himself and Nick. He assigned Sonny, Ben, and Ezra to the bunks directly across the aisle from her. He made sure to assign Falco and Joe at the far end of the room.

"Get some rest. The op starts at 2200," John said.

He laid down on his bunk and stared at the ceiling. When he heard the familiar cacophony of snoring, he rolled over and met Sophia's gaze. She was lying facing him, and she was as far from sleep as she could be. John stared back for a moment.

"Why aren't you asleep?" he asked quietly.

"I'm just thinking about the mission op."

"Stop thinking and start sleeping. You're going to be up for the next three days. You'll have plenty of time to think then."

He rolled onto his back and went back to staring at the ceiling.

"Aren't you going to sleep, Sir?"

"Close your eyes and go to sleep, Gonzalez!" he said tersely.

She closed her eyes and did her best to go to sleep, but there were too many thoughts, too many worries, and too much to fear. It took her a long time to go to sleep.

At 2100, Sophia woke to the feel of Sonny's hand on her shoulder.

"Soph, wake up. It's time," Sonny whispered.

She forced her eyes open with a yawn and sat up. Everyone else was asleep except for John.

"I thought the op starts at 2200," she said confused.

"It does," John said.

"Then why—"

"The Op starts at 2200, but you're in Overwatch training. Sonny will explain everything you need to know that pertains to this particular position."

She nodded, put her boots on, grabbed her bag full of gear, and followed Sonny past the rows of sleeping SEALs and out of the bunk house. John was waiting for them outside with a Jeep.

He gave Sonny a warning look as Sophia climbed into the back of the Jeep.

Sonny leaned in and lowered his voice. "Don't worry, Boss. I'll take good care of her."

Sonny climbed in the passenger's seat, and John slid in behind the wheel. Forty-five minutes later, John pulled to a stop in a narrow alley. Sonny and Sophia quietly scrambled out of the Jeep with their bags, and John pulled away.

"Now the real fun begins," Sonny said. "Follow me."

Sophia stayed close on his heels as he navigated the narrow alleys. She had no idea where they were headed. She wasn't sure what the mission was. All she knew was she'd been ordered to do whatever Sonny told her to do.

Two days later at 1650, Sonny and Sophia lay positioned on a rooftop in Turkey with their sniper rifles trained on the street below. There was a bustling crowd in the marketplace as patrons hurried to buy their wares before the shops closed for the day.

Echo had been running drills for two days straight. There had been no rest for anyone. Sophia was learning a lot from Sonny. Sniper school had taught her how to hit a target. Sonny was teaching her what it really meant to be a sniper. Long hours of concealment waiting on your target, how to identify a target in a crowd of people, and most importantly, how to stay focused on the task were all part of the Overwatch job.

"So, Senorita, I've been doing all the talking fer two days. It's your turn."

As she trained her scope on the target below, she felt Sonny reach up and mute her comlink.

"Why did you mute me?"

"Do you really want all of Echo to know your personal business?"

"I thought there were no secrets within the team."

Sonny chuckled. "There ain't—unless you mute them out on an Op."

"So, why are we muting?"

"Cause, the whole team don't need to know this. It's just between you and me."

She stayed focused on her task as she listened to Sonny.

"I been meanin' to ask you something important, but you always have a watchdog on yer tail."

"A watchdog?"

"John."

"What do you mean?"

"You don't notice the way he watches you, and all the guys on the team, and all the guys back at basecamp? He's like yer personal body guard. I mean—hell—he plays watchdog when you take a shower, and pretty much every other second of the day."

"I guess I hadn't thought about it like that. I figured he was just trying to run interference to avoid possible conflicts."

Sonny smirked. "Oh, he's runnin' interference alright."

"Is there a question in there somewhere, Sonny?"

"Yeah. How's your love life? Do you belong to anyone?"

She rolled her eyes. "Really? That's your important question?"

"Is that a yes or a no?"

"No. I don't have a boyfriend. I'm a SEAL. We don't have time for personal attachments."

"Yeah. I hear ya. So, how do you feel about personal unattachments?"

"Personal unattachments?"

"Would you be open to a no strings attached—just havin' fun—relationship?"

"I'm guessing you mean that in a sexual way?"

"Hell yeah, I mean it in a sexual way. Is there any other kind?"

She smirked. "No. I'm Catholic. I don't believe in sex before marriage."

Sonny grinned. "So, you haven't ever—"

"No."

"Damn! I think I just fell in love."

Sophia chuckled. "You must fall in love easy."

"Nope. I'm a wild stallion, Girl, but I'm willin' to put on a saddle and come inside your cozy little stable. You can ride me all night."

"Wow! I've heard pick-up lines from a lot of men, but I've never heard that one before."

He grinned. "Good. I aim to be original. So? What do you say? Want to rope a cowboy?"

"No, Sonny." She chuckled. "I see why you wanted this conversation muted."

"Don't mention this to John. If you do, he'll kill my ass and drag my carcass into the Afghani desert for the buzzards to pick clean."

"We can't have that. Echo needs its top sniper. Are we done with the muted conversation?"

"Nah. I'm still gatherin' intel."

"What sort of intel?"

"I don't know. Why don't you tell me what it would take for you to give me a chance? Then I'll do my best to be that guy. See, I know your type—a beautiful woman who gets hit on constantly by men. It's only natural that you would develop a defense mechanism."

"A defense mechanism?"

"Yeah, your first instinct is to shoot all men down at the first sign of interest, but in my case that would be the wrong move. See—I'm not like all those other guys."

She smirked. "You're not?"

"Nope. I'm a diamond in the rough. My outside layer might need a little work, but inside is where the good stuff is. You just have to dig a little to find my gem."

"Another line?"

"Nope. That's the truth."

"It sounds like a ploy to get in my panties."

Sonny grinned. "Does it? See—you're lookin' at it from the wrong angle. Maybe, I ain't trying to get in your panties. What if I'm trying to get in your heart?"

She fell silent. The conversation had taken an awkward turn.

"Did I step over the line, Soph?"

"No. I've just heard this all before from too many men to count."

"GITMO?"

"GITMO, BUD/S, and now Afghanistan."

"Am I the first man on base to ask you?"

"No, actually, several guys from other teams have asked me. I politely turned them down like I turn every man down."

"Well see, I ain't just any man. I'm Sonny Eldridge. You won't be able to resist my charms forever. Granted, yer first knee-jerk reaction was to shoot me down cold, but I don't give up easy. I'll wear you down; you won't remember why you ever said no in the first place."

"We can be friends, but I don't plan to have a relationship with anyone while I'm serving."

He grinned. "I'll change your mind eventually. You'll fall for me. It's inevitable."

"Inevitable?"

He leaned in closer until his lips barely brushed her ear. She could feel his warm breath against her skin. "It will just hit you one day. Out of nowhere, you'll realize that you're irrevocably in love with me. On that day, the only word in your vocabulary will be—Yes, Sonny, yes, yes, yes."

She smirked. "You have it all figured out then."

"I do."

"Then there's nothing more to say. Should we unmute and get back to work?"

"I've been workin'. See that guy in the pale blue robe?"

"Yeah."

"That's our next target."

"I know. I never stopped working."

"Neither did I. I'm good at multi-tasking. It goes with the job."

She felt his fingertips lightly grazing over the back of her short burr.

"Don't let yourself get distracted, Girlie." He grinned as he softly caressed his fingers down the back of her neck. "No matter what happens, make sure you paint that target. If a bug crawls in your ear, a snake slithers up yer leg and bites you, or a building falls and crushes your legs in the rubble, don't let your target out of your sight."

She focused harder on the target and completely ignored the way Sonny's fingers were travelling down her t-shirt covered spine. She ignored the way his hand slid over her ass and down the back of her thigh. She kept the target painted.

"Echo 1 to Echo 16." John said quietly into his coms.

Sonny reached up and unmuted her comlink.

"Echo 16, go for Echo 1." She kept her ultraviolet laser pointed on the man's pale blue robe.

She could feel Sonny's fingers slowly working their way up the inside of her thigh. She blocked it out and kept her head in the game.

"Target acquired. Echo 7 in pursuit. Keep the target painted."

"Copy that."

Sonny muted her comlink, scooted right up against her, and curled his leg over her ass. She could feel his breath on her ear again.

"Stay focused. Don't let your growing lust for my body come between you and your target."

A grin spread over her mouth. "Is that what's going on? I just thought you were suffering from hypothermia and needed some extra body heat."

"You know the best way to cure hypothermia is bare naked flesh to bare naked flesh. If you really want to save me, you'll take off our clothes and press your warm, little body against mine."

"Is this the best you've got? I'm not distracted in the least."

"Nah. This ain't my best. This is just a small tease of what's to come. By the time I'm through with you, you'll be beggin' ol' Sonny for it."

"Begging for what?"

"Don't play innocent."

"But I am innocent."

"Yeah, don't remind me right now. You'll make me lose focus. I'm havin' to quell the fantasy of breakin' you in like a spirited little filly."

"I see our next target."

Sonny slid his leg off of her and peered through his own scope. "Copy that. Better let Echo 1 know." He unmuted her com."

"Echo 16 to Echo 1."

"Echo 1 go for Echo 16."

"Next target acquired. He just entered the edge of the market square. He's heading straight for Echo 5."

"Echo 5 here. I see him."

"Good work, Echo 16." John said into his com.

Once the practice drills were run, Sonny and Sophia quickly packed up their gear and quietly made their way to the next test site.

"You're doin' real good." Sonny said as they hurried down the dark deserted alley behind the market square.

"Thanks, but I still have a lot to learn."

"You'll get it. You only missed two targets in the last forty-eight hours. That's better than my training record with Kyle. You're pretty good at ignoring distractions too."

She smirked. "You're pretty good at dishing out distractions."

"You're welcome."

She chuckled quietly as they darted into a building to set up their gear for the next round of tests. There was still another full day of target practice, but she was starting to feel more confident in her ability to recognize targets in a crowd. She was grateful for Sonny's helpful advice and practical suggestions. She only wished he'd been her instructor at sniper school.

They set up their gear and waited for a target to appear.

"So, are you interested in any man on base?"

She smirked. "Are you back on that again?"

"Well, what do you want to talk about? We got a speck of time to kill before Echo shows up."

"You've practically dragged my whole life story out of me. Tell me about yourself."

Sonny chuckled. "What do you want to know, Soph?"

"Everything."

"That could take a while."

"Like you said, we have time to kill."

"Alright. I'll start at the beginning then." He grinned at her. "I was born in Texas—"

Once the training Op was over, Echo caught a flight back to Afghanistan. John sat across from Sophia and Sonny on the crowded chopper. He couldn't help but notice the dynamic between them had changed. Sophia seemed more friendly—joking easily with Sonny—their thighs were pressed firmly together. He found it irritating.

I shouldn't have let Sonny train her. I should have done it myself. He's acting too familiar with her. He swore nothing happened on the Op, but he's Sonny. Can he really be trusted with a female? No! I'm an idiot! He probably already screwed her. He had ample opportunity.

John glared a hole through Sonny. Sonny acted oblivious to it. When they reached base, John ordered the team to take their showers first. When they were done and safely snoring the afternoon away on their bunks, he followed Sophia to the showers. There were four men from another team using the showers. John quickly steered Sophia away from the showers and around one of the tents.

"Is there a problem, Sir?"

"No, we'll just have to wait until the showers are free."

She nodded and suppressed the smirk she felt.

"How did Overwatch training go?"

"It was great! I feel like I really learned a lot from Sonny. He's a good teacher."

"You don't have any complaints about him then?"

"No. Why?"

John's eyebrow rose as he studied her. "He didn't do anything inappropriate, did he?"

"No."

"You're sure? We are talking about Sonny. He's the epitome of impropriety. You don't have to cover for him. If he did something that made you uncomfortable, I'll take care of it!"

"No. He was all business. I really got a good taste of what being Overwatch is like. It's not exactly how they describe it in sniper school."

"I'm sure it's not." John cleared his throat. "The shower is free. Clean up. I'll stand watch."

Sophia took a shower keeping a curious eye on John. He was doing a series of stretches while he stood watch. It was obvious to her that his knee was bothering him again. When she was done, he escorted her back to the tent and grabbed clean clothes to go take his own shower.

Sophia lay on her bunk staring at the ceiling. She was exhausted, and the snoring from the men around her only served to remind her that she hadn't slept in over three days. Still, she couldn't go to sleep. When John limped into the tent, her suspicions about his knee were confirmed. She waited until he reached his bunk before standing up to face him.

"Why aren't you asleep?"

"Is your knee bothering you?"

"I'll live. I've been through worse."

"Take your pants off. I want to examine it."

"Not necessary."

She gave him a stern look. "If you don't let me examine it, I'll have to report the injury to Rowen and have you sent to medical for a full work up."

John glared at her. "For a green you sure are obstinate!"

"I'm the team medic. It's my responsibility to look after the health of each team member."

"I can look after myself. I don't need you to babysit me. Go to sleep. That's an order."

"I will as soon as I confirm you haven't seriously damaged your knee."

John's jaw tightened, and he growled under his breath. "Turn around!"

She turned her back to him with a smirky grin.

After a minute, he growled, "Let's get this over with!"

She turned to find him sitting on the bed with his blanket covering him. She knelt down to examine his knee. The bruising was gone, but when she pulled his leg out straight, he winced.

"How bad did that hurt on a scale of one to ten?"

"Three."

She gently rubbed her fingers over the front of his knee and then the back. "Your muscles are very tight. I think you've overworked them."

"Nothing a little rest won't cure."

"I disagree. You need heat. That should help loosen them up a little."

Before John could protest, she got out a heat pack and instructed him to lie down. He lay back on the bed with an irritated growl. She put the pack behind his knee and wrapped it with a towel.

"I'll leave that on for a while, and then I'll see how you're doing."

"I'll be fine. You can go to sleep. I know you're tired. We all are."

"I can handle sleep deprivation just fine. It's part of being a SEAL. What I can't handle is you making this injury worse on my watch. What kind of medic would I be if I didn't treat you?"

He groaned and closed his eyes. "Fine. Do whatever. I'm too tired to argue."

"You can go to sleep, Sir."

"No, I can't. I still have to get dressed."

"Let the heat wrap do its work. I'll wake you up to get dressed in a little while."

He didn't mean to go to sleep, but after he closed his eyes his body betrayed him. He hadn't had any sleep since they left Afghanistan. Sophia set her watch alarm and went to sleep too. When her watch beeped a short while later, she got up to check his knee. He was still asleep. Not wanting to disturb him, she carefully removed the heat pack and gently felt of his muscles. They were still tight. She gently began kneading the muscles behind his knee.

He opened his eyes and stared at her for a moment. "You don't have to do that."

"It's my job, Sir." She finished the massage. "How does your knee feel now?"

He let out a frustrated sigh. "Better."

She smiled. "I'll turn around so you can get dressed."

She could hear him grunt with the effort to get vertical. His knee was bothering him much worse than he was admitting. She heard the swish of fabric and the zipper on his camo fatigues.

"Okay. I'm done."

She turned around and watched him carefully lower himself onto his bunk.

"I'll put another heat pack on it, Sir. That should help some."

He nodded and let her apply a new heat pack and wrap it with the towel over his pants.

She's a good medic. She really cares about the welfare of the team. Sonny said she's picking up Overwatch quickly. I made a good choice. I don't care what the jerks on this base say. She's dedicated, and she's willing to put in the work to get the job done. Plus, she's smart. She soaks up information like a sponge. I'm not sorry I picked her. She's going to make an excellent SEAL.

CHAPTER 42

July 7
0110
Transport plane over Russia

Echo lined up in the plane to make the jump. This would be Sophia's first official mission after over a month of training with Echo. She'd gotten to know most of the team pretty well. She knew Sonny better than anyone. They'd spent a lot of hours alone on training Ops. John wanted her to get up to speed on the Overwatch position, and Sonny was doing his best to accomplish that task.

As the first members of Echo made the jump, her stomach tightened. This would be her first real jump on her first real mission. Everything up until now had a certain air of safety about it. In a training Op the dangers were pretend. Once she stepped out of this plane the dangers would be absolutely real.

This mission wouldn't be like serving at GITMO. The base in Cuba was surrounded by a fence. It was patrolled constantly by Marines. Men stood on that wall and watched for the enemy with relentless diligence. She had been surrounded by a huge team of Jarheads who were ready for a fight every second of the day if it became necessary.

Now, she was on a small team of sixteen SEALs. They would be behind enemy lines, cut off, unprotected—alone. Stealth and awareness were the most important tools they possessed.

When it was her turn, she took a deep breath and jumped. All of her training echoed in her ears as she plummeted toward the Earth. At the appropriate mark she pulled the cord. Nothing happened. She pulled again and again. Then she panicked.

"My chute won't open!"

Sonny's drawl came over the comlink in her ear. "Don't panic, Girlie. I got you."

Some of her panic subsided at the sound of his voice. A few seconds later he reached her. He pulled her cord, but it still would not open.

She couldn't see the ground rushing up to meet them, but she knew it was close. They were already past the safe distance to open a chute. He hooked a clip to her and tethered them together.

"Grab on, Lil Sister!"

She held tightly to him as he pulled his cord, and they were suddenly jerked from their rapid decent. They floated down with her arms firmly wrapped around him. When their feet touched the ground, and they rolled to a stop, Sonny was lying on top of her with a big grin on his face.

"Did ya forget how to pack yer chute?"

Sophia couldn't speak for a moment. "I thought I packed it correctly."

Sonny got up off her and offered her a hand. He quickly checked her pack.

"Nah. It's packed correctly. You must have a faulty—yep—here it is. The pull string frayed and severed. That there's the problem."

He noticed she was shaking. He reached down and took her hands in his; they were trembling.

"You're okay, Girlie. You just got a little scare. Pull it together. No distractions—remember?"

She nodded. "Sorry. I just—How do I avoid this from happening again?"

He gently caressed her cheek with his fingertips.

"I'll teach ya, but not til we get back. Right now, we have to rendezvous with the rest of our team. We are off the target drop zone. Keep yer eyes peeled. I'll take point."

Sophia followed Sonny keeping a wary eye all around for any sign of the enemy. She managed to push the panic and fear down deep and refocus on the present moment—No distractions.

"Echo 3 to Echo 1." Sonny said quietly into his coms.

There was no answer. He tried several more times with no success.

"Must be some interference. Some of these mountains have magnetic rock. This ain't the first time our coms didn't work in Russia. Don't worry the guys will hit their mark; we'll find them."

Sonny is so nice. He never comes down on me for mistakes; he just gives me advice on avoiding future mistakes. I really like him. He's such a good friend.

John gathered Echo at the rendezvous. He noticed Sonny and Sophia were missing.

"Echo 1 to Echo 3. Echo 1 to Echo 16. Respond."

He was met with silence.

"Sir, I caught some static on my coms during the jump. I heard something about a chute not opening," Ben said.

John felt his guts twist. "Who's chute?"

"Hers. It was a female voice, but reception was cutting out."

"Did anyone hear anything from Sonny?"

No one ventured a comment.

John's pulse rate spiked. He checked his watch and waited half an hour before trying again. Then he tried every ten minutes for the next hour until he heard Sonny respond on the coms.

"We're on our way, Boss. We got a little sidetracked. We are five klicks from the rendezvous."

"Copy that, Echo 3. We'll see you soon."

CHAPTER 43

July 15
0700
Afghanistan base

John walked out of Rowen's tent after giving him a debrief of their latest mission in Pakistan. Everything had gone smoothly, and they'd accomplished their mission with resounding success. The only thing that bothered John was how well the team was taking to Sophia. Everyone liked her; that was the problem. Some of the men liked her too much. It wasn't setting well with him that his order to treat her like they would treat any other man was being ignored. His lectures about her being off limits seemed to have escaped nearly half the team. He'd seen too much flirting on the sly being done by too many. He had no intention of allowing it to continue. It seemed the threat of court martial was of no significance to these guys.

As he rounded the corner of a tent, he saw something that spiked his blood pressure. Joe was talking to Sophia outside the tent. Joe's body language was anything but professional. John froze in his tracks and watched the exchange.

He's flirting, but she looks like she's just tolerating it. She's not flirting back.

Sophia stood listening to Joe's story. It was obviously full of embellishments and not more than half of it could possibly be true, but she humored him. At GITMO, she'd found it was easier to get along with the men in her unit if she didn't smash their fragile egos to bits. Out of the corner of her eye she caught sight of John watching from a distance.

Sonny is right; he does watchdog me.

She focused her attention back on Joe and the story he was winding down, but she occasionally glanced John's way. He was still there. He was still watching. As soon as Joe headed toward the P.T. area, she noticed that John headed that way too. Curious, she followed them. Staying out of sight, she took up a post around the corner of a tent to eavesdrop.

"Karsa! Can I have a word with you?"

Joe turned back to see John right behind him. "Sure, Chief. What can I do for you?"

"For starters, you can follow orders."

"Sir?"

"I have repeatedly told you and the rest of Echo that Gonzalez is off limits! The UCMJ does not allow fraternization between enlisted within the same chain of command."

"Sir, I was not fraternizing. Sophia and I were just having a friendly chat."

"That's not what it looked like. Your body language spoke what your tongue might not have. It was obvious to anyone who happened upon you two that you were flirting with her."

"Sir, it wasn't intentional."

"Intentional or not, it has consequences that you won't like. You will learn to control every aspect of your mind, body, and tongue on this team. Just so you'll remember and think twice before you unintentionally flirt with her, run five klicks starting right now! Hustle, Karsa!"

"Yes Sir!" Joe took off at a dead run on the gravel track around the base perimeter.

Sophia quickly retraced her steps not wanting John to know she'd been listening.

He watches to keep these guys out of trouble. I don't think it's really directed at me personally.

After dinner that night, John quietly followed Sophia after she exited the mess hall. Sonny was with her, and they were laughing as they headed north across the base. He saw Sophia shove Sonny's arm as she cracked up laughing at something he said. Then he saw Sonny put his hand on her shoulder, lean in close, and whisper something in her ear. She laughed even harder. John's right eye twitched.

I don't like this. She's different with Sonny. All the other guys on base she ignores or tolerates, but when Sonny flirts, she doesn't deflect it in the least. She welcomes it! Can't she see he's a womanizer? Is she really that blind? Why do women have a blind spot when it comes to Sonny? Is he really that charming? Do women not mind being used if the user comes in a handsome, charming, blonde, cowboy package? I will never understand women!

July 27
1200
Chopper ride

The small rescue chopper was too small for the team to fit. Regardless, there was nothing for Echo to do but cram inside. The rescue chopper rose above the tree line, and the enemy opened fire. Echo returned fire as the chopper flew away. Once the chopper was clear of danger, John surveyed the team. Every bench seat was full, the floor was full, and three of the SEALs including John were standing bent over in the chopper hanging on to keep their balance.

Everyone looked exhausted. Many were scraped and bloody, and everyone was filthy from the arduous trek through the mountain terrain. His eyes fell to Sophia near the front of the chopper. She was sitting on Sonny's lap. John's jaw tightened in anger. Then he noticed that Joe and Mac were also sitting on someone's lap.

The small rescue chopper was over capacity. It looked as if the chopper crew had quickly extracted unnecessary weight before take-off. Any sign of first aid or rescue equipment was missing. It was obvious the crew had stripped it down to accommodate extra passengers. He noted that the customary chopper man who ran the cargo section was absent. In fact, there was only one pilot; the co-pilot seat was occupied by Falco.

They must have sent what they could in an emergency. At least, we all got out alive. That was a close one. If this chopper had been five minutes later, it could have been a different story.

His eyes drifted back to Sophia. Sonny had his mouth near her ear. John couldn't hear what Sonny was saying to her over the loud thrum of the chopper blades and the wind whipping past the open doorways. Still, he could plainly see that Sonny was flirting; his arms were wrapped snugly around her, and his hand was planted firmly on her ass. What irked John the most was that Sophia didn't seem bothered in the least by Sonny's overt advances—in fact—she was smiling and laughing at whatever he was saying in her ear.

John's jaw clenched tight.

He hasn't listened to a damn thing I've told him! He continually acts too familiar with her. I've seen his hands on her unnecessarily more times than I can count! He's a damn liar! He told me he's not after her. It's obvious that he is! His hand is on her ass right now—in front of the entire team! He's not fooling anyone! I'm going to have a talk with him when we get back to base! This is going to end! I didn't put her on this team so she could be corrupted by the likes of Sonny! He's crossed the line this time!

When the chopper touched down on base, the SEALs quickly exited and headed for the showers. John pulled Sophia aside for a chat while the men cleaned up.

"Are you okay?"

"Other than being tired, sore, and a little scraped up from the underbrush, I'm good."

"How about the chopper ride?"

She grinned. "I didn't know that many grown men could fit in a chopper that small."

"I noticed you didn't get a decent seat on the chopper."

She chuckled. "I think Falco had the only good seat on that ride."

John's jaw tightened. "How did you end up on Sonny's lap?"

"I gave up my seat so more men could squeeze in. I was going to stand, but the guys told those of us standing to sit on their laps so more men could squeeze into the floor space."

"And Sonny just so happened to be the one to offer?"

"No, I just quickly sat down on whoever's lap was closest to me, so did Mac and Joe."

"I noticed his hand was on your—ass. Was he—"

She smirked. "He had to hold onto me to keep me from sliding off onto the men sitting on the floor. The chopper ride wasn't exactly the smoothest."

"Yeah, I noticed that. I think all the extra weight was the problem."

"I noticed you had to stand the whole way. How is your knee doing?"

"My knee is fine."

"I saw you limping when we got off the chopper."

"It's just part of getting old. My joints don't work like they used to. I'll be fine."

Her eyebrow rose. "How old are you?"

"Thirty. Why?"

"Thirty is not that old, Sir."

"It is for a SEAL. Our bodies take more abuse than the average man. Stop worrying about my knee. I've had worse injuries. A little time, and it will be back to normal."

"I'll take a look at it after our showers."

"No! I don't want you to take a look at it."

"Why not?"

"Because it's not serious. I've had medic training too. I'm perfectly capable of diagnosing my own injury. I don't need you to tell me what I already know!"

"I'm just trying to help, Sir. I didn't mean to make you angry."

John let out a frustrated sigh. "I'm not mad at you. I'm just—"

"Just what?"

"Nothing. It's not important."

"I can tell something is bothering you, Sir. You've been more irritable lately."

He raked a hand over his burr and winced in pain.

"Is your arm hurt?"

"No."

"Something is. Your face registered some pretty intense pain just now."

"It's just my back. Bending over in the chopper didn't help it any. It's not an injury. It's just sore muscles. Stop worrying about me! I'm a grown man. I can take care of myself!"

"Sorry, Sir."

A long awkward silence ensued.

"The showers are probably free," Sophia said. "You should go clean up. I'll take mine last."

John shook his head. "No, you go first."

"I'm not the one in pain, Sir. I insist you go first."

His eyes narrowed on her. "Who gives the orders around here? Me or you?"

"Are you ordering me to take a shower first?"

His jaw tightened again. "Yeah. I am."

Sophia tried to suppress a grin, but she wasn't entirely successful.

She hurried through her shower and left John to take his. When he returned to the tent, he found her bandaging up several of the men who had gotten some scrapes and cuts on the hike through the dense underbrush. He swallowed a couple of his pain pills and sank down on his bunk. The welcome comfort of a soft bed was one of the few luxuries the base offered.

Sophia finished with her more than willing patients and turned to look at John.

I don't know how he can fall asleep with boots on. That can't possibly be comfortable.

She pulled a heat pack and a towel out of her med pack and walked over to his bunk. Then she proceeded to untie his boots, set them under his bed, and wrap his knee with the heat she knew he must certainly be needing. She'd seen him pop the pain pills. She knew it was bothering him. He only took them when he was in severe pain.

John watched her through slitted eyelids.

She just can't help herself! I told her not to worry about me, so she waited until she thought I was asleep to take care of me. She knew I'd tell her to take a hike if I was awake! What am I going to do about her? I never envisioned this sort of problem when I chose her for the team.

At chow that evening, John sat at the end of the table and warily watched the rest of his team. Sophia sat in the middle, and he noticed several men at the table intently watching her, smiling at her, and joking with her. He scanned their surroundings, and his frustration only grew. Quite a few men from other tables were eyeing Sophia like snakes poised to strike their prey. The lascivious stares he witnessed only served to add to his growing stress.

The longer she was on base, the more his protective nature grew. It seemed obvious—to him— that an enemy's bullet wasn't the only danger lurking in the shadows waiting to claim her. He'd been sleeping less and less lately, and what sleep he did get wasn't peaceful. Nightmares about that fateful day in China where they lost half of Echo plagued him, but they were accompanied by new nightmares. The last couple of weeks he'd been dreaming about Sophia being in danger. His dreams were never clear later, but he could always recall that her life was in peril and try as he might to save her—he continued to fail in every situation. He would wake in a panic only to discover he was safe in his bed, and she was safe right next to him.

His eyes darted back to Sophia. She was laughing and joking with several of the men at their table. She seemed perfectly at ease and perfectly unaware of the lascivious beasts all around her. He knew these men. He'd worked with them—trusted them with his life. The problem was—he couldn't find it in him to trust them with Sophia. He'd assessed the situation. He couldn't take the risk. He'd never forgive himself if something happened to her. Whether the danger was real or simply in his overactive imagination—he had to protect her from everything and everyone. Everyone included one of his best friends—when Sonny exited the mess hall, John followed.

"I need to talk to you, Sonny."

"Sure, what's up?"

"You swore to me that you were not going to try anything with Gonzalez."

"I haven't."

"That's not what it looks like."

Sonny stopped and stared at John. "What exactly does it look like, John?"

"I saw you today in that chopper."

"You saw what?"

"You had your hand on her ass, Sonny! Don't try to deny it."

"You're right. I did. I ain't denying nothing. We was crammed into that tiny chopper like a bunch of gators in a rabbit cage. I had to hold on to her to keep her from fallin' on top of Ezra."

"You didn't have to hold on to her ass! That was uncalled for!"

Sonny snickered. "Damn! If you ain't the most jealous man I ever seen."

"It's not jealousy! That was inappropriate behavior! It violated the UCMJ. It could be construed as sexual harassment, Sonny! This is serious. She can file charges if she wants to."

"Yeah, well, she won't. I already cleared it with Sophia. She didn't have a problem with where my hands were on that chopper ride. She knew just like the rest of us that it was more important to get on the bird and get the hell out of there than worry if someone's hand might be on a part of your body that it wasn't supposed to be on. Hell, I'm sure Joe and Mac don't have any complaints that they had to sit on Ben or Andrew's laps. That's just how that one rolled John. If she'd been sitting on Dorian's lap instead of mine, would you even be having this conversation? I think you are judging me unfairly here."

"If Dorian's hand had been on her ass then yes, I'd be talking to him right now. It wasn't his hand; it was yours. You could have found another place to put your hand, Sonny!"

Sonny shook his head and took a deep breath. "Maybe I could have, but to be honest, I wasn't really thinking about it. It wasn't a sexual move. I wasn't trying to flirt. All I was thinking about was if that chopper had enough fuel to get us home when it was obviously over its weight limit."

John glared at Sonny. "That wasn't all you were thinking about. I saw you whispering in her ear and making her laugh. What was that about?"

Sonny's eyebrow rose as he studied John. "Damn, Boy! You got it bad for her."

John crossed his arms over his chest and continued to glare at Sonny. "Don't try to deflect. This is about what you did on that chopper!"

Sonny's mouth turned up in the corner. "No, John, I already explained the chopper. This is really about what you wish you could do with her if the UCMJ wasn't in your way."

"You're delusional. I don't see her that way."

"The hell you don't. I seen the way you was watchin' her at dinner. I seen how you was glaring at any man you thought was scoping her out. If you ain't jealous, you ain't breathing."

"Don't make this about me. This is about your behavior with her all the time. You're too—"

"Too what?"

"Too you!"

"So, now I can't be myself?"

"No!"

"She and I are friends. We joke around. We talk about stuff. We have fun together, but I ain't got no designs to conquer her. She's made it pretty clear to every man on this base that she ain't here to find a man. She's just here to be a soldier."

"I am well aware of that! I know she's just here to serve like the rest of us. I'm trying to make sure she gets a fair chance to do just that without vultures like you circling the sky above her."

Sonny chuckled. "Now, I'm a vulture?"

"Aren't you?"

"Normally, I'd agree with that analogy, but in her case, I have to decline the compliment. When I first laid eyes on her I did see a hot piece of ass, but I've grown to respect her as a fellow SEAL. We are just friends, John, and I ain't going to change the way I am with her just to sooth your jealousy monster. Get over it. She ain't interested in you anyway. So, cage it."

"She's not interested in any man. She just wants to serve."

"True, but if she does develop interest in a man, you'd be at the very bottom of her list."

"What's that supposed to mean?"

Sonny smirked. "She and I are friends. We talk about personal stuff. She tells me things."

"She said something about me?"

"Oh, yeah."

"What did she say?"

"Friends don't rat on their friends."

John crossed his arms over his chest. "What did she say?"

"You couldn't torture it out of me."

John let out a frustrated breath. "Is she mad at me?"

Sonny studied him. "You would like to know, wouldn't you?"

"I won't say anything to her or anyone else. Just tell me what she said about me."

Sonny grinned. "First tell me why you care what she said."

"I don't—care—I'm just—curious."

Sonny smirked. "Curious—well that's one way of putting it."

John's jaw tightened. "Are you going to tell me or not?"

"Not."

"Then we are done! Just keep your hands off her going forward. You've been warned."

Sonny walked away with a smirk on his face.

John waited outside the mess hall just out of sight. When Sophia emerged with Falco and Zach, they headed toward the tents. He followed them at a distance until they entered the tent.

"Yeah, you got no designs on her." Sonny smirked from behind John.

John jerked in surprise and turned to face Sonny. "I was just making sure she got home safe."

"Right. And that don't smack of a man who's fallen for a pretty girl."

"I'm her C.O. I'm responsible for her safety the same as yours or any other man on Echo."

"Yet, I ain't never known you to follow any of us around on base to make sure we were safe."

John growled under his breath. "Don't push me!"

"I'm not pushin'. I'm just observin'."

"I'm going for a run."

John headed in the direction of the jogging path. Sonny followed him past the tents to the path.

"You really want to know what she said? She said not if you were the last man on Earth."

John stopped in his tracks, and his jaw clenched tight. He turned and looked back at Sonny. His entire body tensed, and his eye began twitching involuntarily. He let out a long breath, closed his eyes, and twisted his head cracking his neck. Then he looked back at Sonny.

Sonny could see the tortured pain in his friend's eyes.

"She actually said that? That's fine—" John's voice cracked a little. "That's good. She shouldn't have any interest in me. I'm her C.O. It's forbidden."

Without another word, John turned and headed down the well-worn jogging path.

Sonny watched him disappear around the bend in the track. "Not interested my ass!"

CHAPTER 44

August 1
2100
Afghanistan base

John stood watch at the showers while Sophia got cleaned up. When she exited, he stopped her before she could head back to the tent.

"I—um—are you mad at me about something?"

Sophia looked up at him with confusion on her face. "Mad? No. Why would you think that?"

"It's just—I heard from some of the guys on the team that you weren't too happy with me."

"Guys on the team—which guys?"

"I don't want to call anyone out. I just want to verify if it's true."

"I don't know why anyone would say that. I've never said anything bad about you to anyone."

"Have you thought it?"

"What?"

"Maybe you haven't said anything, but have you thought it? Do you have some kind of problem with me? If something is bothering you, you can tell me. Maybe I can do something to change it—make it better—improve the situation."

She shrugged. "I actually don't have any complaints about you. You are fair, honorable, and you always put the team ahead of yourself. You are an excellent leader. I truly respect you, Sir."

He nodded. "But on a personal level, is there something I do that bothers you?"

She shook her head. "No, Sir. To be honest, I can't really say that I know you on a personal level. You're pretty quiet when we are off duty. When we are on a mission, you're all business. I really don't know much about you. You never talk about yourself."

"Okay. I just wanted to make sure—I just—um—I guess that's all."

"No problem, Sir."

John followed her back to the tent. Then he took a walk on base. He needed to clear his head. Sonny's comments had been bothering him for days.

Sophia sat down on her bed with a heavy sigh.

"What's wrong?" Sonny asked from his bunk.

"Nothing."

He got up and moved over to sit on John's bunk. Most of Echo were too involved in a poker game at the far end of the tent to pay any attention to them.

"You can't lie to me, Girlie. I know that look."

She shrugged. "Chief Rusk just asked me if I have some kind of problem with him. He said some guys on the team were talking, and he got the impression I was mad at him."

Sonny hid the grin that threatened to give him away. "Where did he get an idea like that?"

"I don't know. I don't think I've ever said anything that could be construed as negative about him, but apparently some of the guys got that impression from me."

"I wouldn't worry about it. Did you set him straight?"

"I told him I have no problems with him and that I truly respect him as our C.O. That didn't really seem to affect him. He still looked—perturbed—no, that's not the right word. Maybe disappointed in my response would be more accurate. I'm not sure he believed me. What if he thinks I just lied to him to keep from getting in trouble? Maybe I should go talk to him."

"Nah. I'm sure he believed you. That's just how John is. He buries his true feelings down so deep they'll never see the light of day. He has trouble expressing himself to people. A lot of times, he comes across as hostile, but that's not who he really is. He's a really nice guy once you get past all them onion layers of defense he has. It takes time for John to open up to anyone.

He's socially awkward, but it ain't his fault. His parents didn't do him no favors the way they raised him. He didn't have a pleasant childhood. He grew up isolated and alone. Sometimes, he still seems isolated. It's hard for him to get past that defense shell he has and make real friends."

Sophia nodded. "I've noticed a little of that myself. He's very self-reliant. He doesn't like to ask for help even when he needs it."

"Yep, that's John. He's a hard nut to crack, but he's worth the effort."

She smiled. "I'm glad I talked to you. I was afraid he might be angry with me."

"Nah. He's about as far from angry with you as a man can get. He likes you. He respects you."

He's head-over-heels in love with you. A man don't protect a woman the way he protects you unless he's totally smitten.

"So, you don't think I need to go talk to him?"

Sonny shook his head. "You're good."

"Are you sure? The look on his face didn't really seem like we were good."

"Tell you what. How about I go talk to him and feel him out. I'll find out for sure."

"Thank you, Sonny. You are the best friend I've ever had. You always look out for me."

"Anytime."

Sonny gave her his most charming smile and a wink. Then he left the tent. He found John sitting on one of the supply crates staring at the ground with a dejected posture.

"You okay?" Sonny asked.

"Yeah, I'm fine."

"You look like the bull just bucked you and trampled you half to death. What's going on?"

"Nothing."

"We've known each other too long for me to believe that lie."

John let out a heavy sigh. "Too bad I don't have that superpower."

"What superpower?"

"The ability to detect your fabrications."

"What did I lie about?"

"Gonzalez."

"I didn't lie."

"You said she was mad at me. I talked to her. She said she's not."

"I never said she was mad at you."

"You insinuated it."

"When?"

"The other day."

Sonny pretended to think about it. "When? I'm not following you, John. What day? What were we talking about?"

"The chopper—your hand on her ass—ring any bells?"

"Oh, right. We was talkin' about how jealous you are of any man that glances her way."

"No, that's not what we were talking about!"

"That's what I was talkin' about."

John growled in frustration.

"Oh, wait! I remember. I did say that you'd be at the bottom of her list of eligible men."

John glared at Sonny.

Sonny grinned. "What's the matter John? Did you talk to her and confirm that it's the truth?"

John's jaw clenched tight.

"Ooh! Looks like I hit a nerve. Does it bother you so much? I mean—you did say you have no interest in her that way. You told me you just see her as a soldier. If that's true then it shouldn't concern you that she'd let the human race go extinct before she'd let you touch her."

"What do you need, Sonny? Why are you here?"

"I just came to see how you were doing after she rejected you so coldly. She told me about your conversation."

John sat up straight. "She told you about our conversation?"

"Yeah. I told you; she and I are real good friends. We don't keep secrets from each other. She tells me everything."

John's mouth turned down in a frown.

"She thinks you're bossy and ridiculously strict with her and the rest of the team. She thinks you're an ass. She doesn't realize you're such an ass because you're in love with her, you're bending over backwards to protect her, and you're jealous as hell."

John cleared his throat and stood up. "I'm not in love. I'm not jealous. You're way off."

"Am I?"

"Yeah!"

John started pacing back and forth. Sonny sat down on a crate and watched him. John dragged his hand over his burr, stopped, and stared at the ground.

"So, if you're not in love, and you're not jealous, why does it matter what she thinks of you?"

"It doesn't. I just—I—I'm trying to avoid any possible pitfalls. This is a unique situation. I don't want her presence here to give rise to a court martial or any other conflict that might arise. The rules of the UCMJ are clear. There is to be no relations between enlisted personnel in the same unit or under the same command. Most of the men on this base report to Rowen. That puts us all under the same command. Even if a man from another SEAL team were to—well, it would still be in violation of the code."

"What if she fell for one of the cooks or someone in the medical center? They don't report to Rowen."

John stopped in front of Sonny and glared at him. "I'm sure you've seen the way these guys look at her. They are here alone—away from female contact for most of the year. They are horny as hell, and they'd just be looking for a meaningless fling with her. They wouldn't care about her as a person or what an affair like that could do to her career. They'd just be using her."

"What if a meaningless fling is what she's looking for? Women have needs too, John. Maybe she's cool with sex with no strings attached."

John swallowed hard. "Did she say that?" He started pacing again.

Sonny watched him for a minute. John stopped in front of him and stared down at him. He noticed that John's fists were clenched tight.

"Did she?"

"Why would you care if she did?"

"Just answer the question!"

Sonny grinned. "No, she said the opposite. She told me she's Catholic, and she doesn't believe in sex before marriage. She's a virgin, John. She intends to stay a virgin until she gets married. She's one of the good girls."

John's hands relaxed, and he turned and walked a few feet away from Sonny. From his vantage point, Sonny didn't see the irrepressible grin on John's face.

"When did she tell you that?"

"On that Overwatch training Op in Turkey. I propositioned her, and she shot me down cold. She said we could be friends and nothing more."

John's grin widened. "She shot you down? The great Sonny Eldridge? I thought you always get what you want from women."

"Not all women. It's that religion hurdle. It's damn hard to overcome. Church girls seem to be immune to my particular charms."

John managed to wipe the grin off his face before he turned back to face Sonny.

"So, she's not interested in any of the men on this base then?"

"She is becoming pretty close to some of the guys on Echo. You never know what could develop over time."

"Nothing's going to develop. The UCMJ forbids it. She wouldn't be that stupid. She's worked too hard to get here to throw it away on a man."

"You might be right, John. No one can say for sure."

John stared up at the stars for a minute. Then he looked back at Sonny.

"Did she mention why she said that about me?" He cleared his throat and looked away.

Sonny smirked. "You mean why she wouldn't want you if you were the last man on Earth?"

John's eye twitched. "Yeah—that."

"It's really bothering you, isn't it?"

"No. I'm just curious if she gave you a reason."

"Hell, if I was you, I'd be curious too."

"Did she give you a reason?" he asked impatiently.

Sonny chuckled. "Damn! I'd love to torture you over this. Hell! I think I will. Nope. I'm not saying a word. If you want to know why, you'll have to ask her."

"You know damn well I won't ask her that. Why won't you just tell me? I'm just curious if it's the same reason other women reject me. I'm trying to figure out what's wrong with me."

"I can tell you what's wrong. You don't need Sophia for that. You're like a prickly pineapple. A woman can't see the sweet meat inside when the outside is full of sharp, pokey stickers."

"That's not helpful. I already know that. I was looking for something more specific."

"Like your ability to throw an offensive insult after only knowing them for less than an hour? Your mouth is your worst enemy, John That's nothing new. Unless you can figure out how to change that, you're pretty much doomed."

"Tell me something I don't know."

"So, this is not about Sophia? You're just agonizing over your bumbling ways with women?"

"Yeah."

"Maybe I should ask Sophia what she thinks. I could give her some examples of how you've screwed up on dates and see what she thinks from a woman's perspective."

"No! Don't do that!"

"Why not? She might have some helpful advice."

"No, I don't want her to know about any of that. I'm her C.O. I don't want her to lose respect for me based on personal issues that have nothing to do with the job. We have to work together. If she knew about all the stupid things I've done and said—just don't tell her about it."

"Okay. I won't."

"Good. I'm going for a jog."

"Make sure you get all the poisons out of your system before you turn in for the night. You don't want to have all those irrepressible urges bursting to get out while you lay staring at her in dark. You might be tempted to act them out."

"I told you, I'm not interested in her."

"Then why do you follow her around like a lost puppy and threaten any man who even looks at her? It sounds like you're interested to me."

John turned and left. He ran the base perimeter for a while.

Sonny is full of it. I'm not interested in her. She's just another Green. I just don't want anything to happen to her. Men don't have to worry about the same concerns she does. Her situation is special. I'm just trying to look out for her. That's all it is. I wish Sonny would drop this. Actually, I wish he'd come clean about why she ranked me at the bottom. I know I'm screwed up. I'd just like to know what she saw that was screwed up enough to put me in the not if he was the last man on Earth category. I really wish I could figure out exactly what is wrong with me. Maybe then—nah. It is definitely hopeless. My track record proves that. It's better if I just steer clear of all women from now on and face the fact that I'm always going to be alone.

An hour later, John stood under the cold water of a refreshing shower. He ducked his head under the water and stood there for a minute before lathering up and washing away all the sweat and sand. He ducked his head under again to rinse his hair. When he straightened back up, Sophia was walking away from the bathroom toward the row of tents. Her eyes were intently watching him until she realized he was watching her. She quickly averted her eyes, hurried past the shower stalls, and turned down a row of tents.

Was she just checking me out? No. She must have just been distracted and not paying attention. She wouldn't be looking at me. Why would she? I'm at the bottom of her list.

He stood in the shower drying off and pulling on his clothes with a grim expression.

Last man on Earth! Really? Am I that bad? Maybe I am. My parents never saw anything special in me. Special! That's a stretch. I'd settle for mediocre. At least a mediocre guy can settle for a mediocre girl. Guys like me—we have to settle for nothing. We have to settle for not if you were the last man on Earth. I guess I'm just utterly repulsive to women.

John walked into the tent and noticed that Sophia was already in bed with her back to him. He lay down on his bunk and stared at her back. After a while, she turned facing him, and their eyes met—held. He suddenly felt the awkwardness of the moment. Then she smiled at him, and he smiled back. Suddenly, the tension was broken.

I wonder if he noticed me staring at him while he was showering? I hope not. That would be so embarrassing if he thought—okay—I can't think about that, or I'll never get to sleep.

She closed her eyes and tried to go to sleep, but something was bothering her.

Sonny said John grew up isolated and alone, and he's still isolated. That doesn't make sense. Here he's surrounded by the team. Surely at home he's surrounded by his wife and kids. I'll have to ask Sonny what he meant by that.

She lay still for a while, but she couldn't go to sleep. Her thoughts would not be still long enough to allow it. She sat up and surveyed the tent. Everyone was asleep. She pulled on her boots and left the tent. As soon as she exited the tent, John got up and followed her. She didn't go to the bathroom like he expected.

Where is she going in the middle of the night? Does she really not understand how dangerous it is for her to roam around by herself on base in the dark? Anyone could—

He followed her to the P.T. area where she picked up a basketball and began shooting hoops. After a few minutes, he walked up next to her.

"Are you planning to shoot hoops all night?"

"Oh! You startled me."

"You should be more aware of your surroundings."

"You're right."

"It's not safe for you to wander around alone in the dark."

She retrieved the ball and walked back to him. "Not safe here—on base?"

"No. It's not."

Her eyebrow rose. "Sir? Are you married? You never talk about your wife or kids."

Her question took him by surprise.

"No. I'm not married. I joined the Navy straight out of high school."

"I joined the Marines straight out of high school too. My parents nearly had a heart attack."

"How do they feel now?"

"They don't like my career choice. My mom wants me to get out, get married, and have a dozen grandbabies for her."

"What do you want?"

"I'm doing exactly what I want. I've wanted to serve since I was in high school."

He nodded. "So, how long are you going to shoot hoops? Should I pull up a chair?"

She grinned. "You could shoot some with me."

"No thanks. Basketball isn't my game."

"What is your game?"

"I don't have one. I suck at sports."

She chuckled. "You suck? I can't imagine that. You're so athletic."

The image of his sculpted chest with the shower water running over him slammed into her brain. She couldn't help but picture him that way now despite his clothes.

She threw him the ball, and he easily caught it. "You'll have to prove it. I don't believe you."

He smirked, walked to the free-throw line, and shot the ball. It swished through the net.

"If you suck at sports, then that was one hell of a lucky shot." Her sarcasm was plain.

"My very first basket."

"Not believable."

He grinned at her. "I've always been a terrible liar. I have no poker face."

She grinned back. "Remind me never to play poker with you. I don't believe that either."

"What do you believe?"

"About you?"

He nodded.

"I think you are hiding."

"Hiding?"

"You have a wall up. Nobody really ever gets in do they? Not even Nick or Sonny."

He shook his head. "That's not true. Nick, Sonny, and Kyle have a key."

"What does it take to get a key, Chief Rusk?"

He stared at her as she walked toward him. She put her hands on the basketball in his hands and looked up at him. She stood there for a moment too long staring up into his eyes. He felt his pulse speed up. Then she grinned at him.

"My shot." She gently tugged the ball from his hands and turned to shoot it.

His eyes roamed down her back to her ass.

She has such a perfect ass. No! Stop looking at her ass! She's off limits!

She made the basket, retrieved the ball, and passed it to him. He took a shot from the half court line. Swish. Thud. It bounced on the dirt.

"I'm definitely not playing poker with you."

He grinned. "So, is basketball your game?"

She shook her head. "I never played sports in school."

"Why not?"

"Money. My parents had eleven kids to feed. There wasn't money for extracurricular sports."

"What did you do for fun?"

"We played with the neighborhood kids. What did you do for fun?"

He frowned. "Maybe you should turn in. It's getting late."

"Was that too personal? Is it inside your wall? I guess I don't have a key yet."

He cleared his throat. "My life wasn't what I'd call fun. I stayed in my room and did homework or read a book."

"All the time?"

"Pretty much."

"No brothers or sisters?"

"Only child."

"Yeah. I'm getting a mental picture now."

He frowned again.

"You were quiet, shy, no friends, stayed to yourself at school, reclusive, depressed. Your parents were abusive, weren't they?"

"No, they never laid a hand on me."

"There is more than one form of abuse."

He looked down at his boots, and his jaw tightened. Then he looked back up at her.

"It's time to turn in. I'm tired. I can't be out here babysitting you all night, Gonzalez."

That's a yes. I wonder what they did to him?

"I don't need a babysitter. I can take care of myself. I'm a trained killing machine."

"So is every man on this base."

"Are you really afraid one of these guys will try something?"

He chewed on his lip as he stared at the ground. "Yes—maybe—I don't know. I'd like to trust these guys, but—"

"But what?"

He dragged a hand over his burr, and let out a long sigh. "Have you looked in a mirror?"

She chuckled. "You're a little too paranoid."

"Am I? I'm just trying to protect you. Make my job easier and don't sneak out anymore."

She put the ball up in the heavy wire basket with the other balls, and he followed her back to the tent. John flopped down on his bunk and watched Sophia take her boots off and put them under her bed. She looked over and shook her head. Then she walked over, untied his boots, and tugged them off.

"Why do you always sleep with your boots on?"

He grinned at her. "Habit. Why does it bother you? I notice you're always taking them off when you think I'm asleep."

She grinned back. "I'm just trying to look after you."

He leaned up on his elbows and watched her lay down on her bunk. "Why do you care?"

"Why wouldn't I care? You're my C.O. We are teammates."

He chewed his bottom lip as he stared at her in the dark.

She doesn't act like she despises me. She obviously cares about my well-being as much as she cares about the rest of the men on Echo. Maybe it's just a lack of attraction—she feels no chemistry for me. That's why she told Sonny that she wouldn't want me if I was the last man on Earth. Still, that's pretty harsh. I must have done something to make her that disgusted with me.

"Are you okay, Sir?"

John snapped out of his daze. "Yeah, why?"

"You're thinking about something awfully hard."

"I'm fine. I just have a lot on my mind."

"Goodnight, Sir."

"Goodnight, Gonzalez."

She drifted off to sleep. He lay awake staring at the roof of the canvas tent unable to sleep.

August 12
0600
Mess hall on base

Sophia stood in line to get breakfast. She couldn't help that her eyes kept wandering in John's direction. After their moonlight basketball encounter, she had taken his advice and tried to become more aware of her surroundings at all times. She had noticed that she had a shadow everywhere she went on base. Her shadow's name was John Rusk—Sonny was right.

When she got her food, she deliberately took the seat at the end of the table directly across from John. He looked up at her for a brief moment and went back to shoveling in his food.

"Sir, did you ever have a pet growing up?"

He swallowed his bite. "No."

"Hobby?"

"No."

"Favorite color?"

He shoved in another bite, looked up at her, and chewed slowly. He stared at her with wary curiosity. Then he swallowed.

"Where is this going? I'm not in the mood for twenty questions."

"I'm just trying to get to know you better. I don't really know much about you, Sir."

"There's not much to know."

He shoved in another bite.

"Am I bothering you?"

"Yes. A lot." A half smirky grin played at his lips.

She took a bite and chewed while she watched him eat.

He looked back up at her, and his heart pounded a little harder.

"Do you need something, Gonzalez?"

"No."

"Why aren't you sitting with your friends this morning?"

He glanced down the table at the men she usually sat in the middle of at every meal on base. They were all casting curious glances his way.

"Am I not allowed to make a new friend?"

"Who? Me?"

She smiled at him.

"Why?"

"Why not?"

"Why would you bother?"

"Maybe I want a key too."

He shoved in his last bite, swallowed hard, and kept his eyes on his plate.

"I don't have any more keys."

He stood up and left the mess hall. She quickly polished off her breakfast and left. Most of Echo were still eating and joking with each other. It took her a while to find John. He was sitting on the sand behind the ammo supply building.

"Is this your getaway spot?"

She sat down next to him. The morning sun was just rising above the mountains to the east.

"What do you want?" he growled softly.

"To finish our conversation."

"I'd prefer not to."

"Why is that?"

"I'm your C.O."

"So, your favorite color is top secret?"

He smirked. "Black."

She grinned. "Big surprise. I should have guessed that one."

He gave her a questioning sideways glance.

"Mental picture is coming back. You were the loner in high school. You always wore black. You sat in the back row. You wanted everyone to ignore you, so you never answered any questions even though you knew the right answer to every single one. You slouched down in your seat to become as invisible at school as you were at home."

"You take psychology classes? I didn't see that in your file."

"So, I am right."

"Close."

"What did I get wrong? What is the real picture of young John Rusk?"

He smirked. "What difference does it make? Why would you care?"

"I'm just trying to get to know you better."

"Why?"

"Why don't you want to let me inside your wall?"

"Maybe I'm trying to protect you."

"From yourself?"

He didn't answer. He just stared at the sun slowly making its way above the mountain peaks in the distance.

"What are you afraid of?"

"Nothing."

"That's not true. Everyone is afraid of something."

"Nope. I've faced all my demons."

"Does that include your parents?"

His right eye twitched, and a frown marred his handsome face.

"What is your relationship like with them now?"

"We don't have one. I left for the Navy. We haven't spoken since."

"Your choice or theirs?"

"Mine. I have nothing to say to them."

Her eyebrow rose. "So, they were abusive. Is that why you hate them?"

"They weren't abusive. I don't hate them. I just don't care. They are living their life. I'm living mine. There's no reason for our paths to ever cross again."

"What if you get married and have kids? You don't want them to know their grandparents? Do you hate them that much? You have no desire to ever reconcile?"

His eye twitched three times.

No woman would ever agree to marry me.

"My destiny is not to reconcile with my parents. My destiny is to go home in a bag."

She swallowed hard. "That's a very negative attitude, Sir."

"It's a pragmatic attitude."

"It sounds like you've resigned yourself to that fate."

"Are we done with the interrogation yet?" he asked tersely.

"Are you angry with me? Did I cross an invisible line?"

"No." His jaw clenched tight as he glowered at the mountain vista outside the fence line.

Instinctively, she put her hand on his knee as a comforting gesture. He looked down at her hand and confusion showed on his face as he looked over at her. She quickly retracted her hand.

"Sorry, Sir. It's obvious that you want to be alone. Enjoy the sunrise."

She got up and walked away. He watched her leave.

Alone is the opposite of what I want, but what I want doesn't matter. I'll never get what I want.

He buried his head against his knees and groaned loudly. So much for watching the sunrise. He had to follow her and keep her out of trouble. He headed north in the direction she'd disappeared.

Sophia came around the southern corner of the ammo building in time to see him walking away. She followed him at a distance. When he covered the entire base searching for her, she decided to cut him some slack. She headed back to the P.T. area and joined a game of basketball with the men who were already playing. It wasn't long before she spotted John watching her from the corner of one of the tents. She pretended to be oblivious to his presence.

John's eyes followed the nine men playing basketball with Sophia. It was obvious to him that at least seven of those men were using the game as an excuse to get as close to her as possible.

CHAPTER 45

August 28
0230
Volga River, Russia

Echo made their way through the dense forest on the north bank of the Volga River. They were 100 klicks north of Astrakhan near the Caspian Sea where they would be extracted and return to base. It had been a recon mission to gain intel. They'd gotten in without detection, gotten the information they needed, and only had a twelve hour hike to the extraction point. Still, they were on enemy soil. They couldn't afford to become overconfident.

On the southern bank towns lay scattered between fields full of crops. The south bank was too dangerous to travel. The dense forest on the north bank offered better concealment though the way was more treacherous. The plan was to follow the river to the Caspian Sea.

Sophia was in line following Joe. The only one behind her was John. After an hour of trekking through the dense foliage over rocky terrain, John put his hand on her shoulder.

"Pick up the pace, Echo 16. You're lagging behind the group!"

"Yes, Sir!"

She did her best to keep up with Joe, but they had been hiking for three days straight, and her body was beginning to feel it. Her legs didn't want to go any faster no matter how hard she tried to push herself. After half an hour, she got a stitch in her side, but she pushed through it and kept going. Ten minutes later, the ground fell out beneath her, and she slid down the steep bank in a rain of rocks and small boulders. When she plunged beneath the water, the cold was a shock to her system. The water was barely above freezing. She struggled toward the surface against the pull of the current and broke free. She sucked in a breath just as a sharp pain shattered through her skull. Everything went black.

"Echo 16 is down. Going in after her. Do not follow me!" John shouted into his coms as he scrambled down the embankment after her. She was not in sight when he plunged into the cold water. Illuminated by the moonlight, the rest of Echo saw him surface searching for Sophia, but his last order still rang in their heads. He had ordered them not to follow. They watched until he was out of sight around a bend in the river.

"What should we do?" Andrew asked.

"We follow orders," Nick said into his coms. "Move out. We will try to catch up to them, but if we don't then we rendezvous with them at the rally point. We have a mission to complete."

John frantically searched the swiftly flowing rapids for Sophia. When he found her, he grabbed the metal bar at the top of her pack and tugged her toward the north bank. It was a struggle to pull her limp body up the muddy, steep incline, but he managed. Once on shore he stripped her out of the pack and checked her breathing. She wasn't!

He started CPR and chest compressions. He worked on her for several minutes before she coughed up water and lay unconscious but breathing. The August night was mild in temperature, but John was shivering from his swim in the frigid water of the Volga. He knew he had to get them both warm as soon as possible, but a fire was out of the question. There were too many towns and farms across the river. A fire might be noticed and reported by someone.

He got into his pack and pulled a dry blanket from its waterproof bag. Then he got into Sophia's pack. He pulled out her med kit and examined her thoroughly. She had a knot on her forehead, but otherwise seemed uninjured. He stripped her down to her bra and panties, wrapped her up in his blanket, and wrung as much water out of her clothes as he could. Then he hung them up on a nearby branch to dry. He stripped his own clothes off and wrung them out too, but he put his pants back on. Then he knelt down and rubbed his hands over her limbs to help restore circulation. She was too cold—so was he. The frigid water had dropped both their body temperatures. He pulled her up against his chest and wrapped the blanket around them both.

After an hour, their clothes had dried in the brisk wind. He redressed her, strapped her pack to the back of his pack, and hoisted her onto his shoulders. Then he headed south toward the mouth of the river. He checked his watch, checked his position against the stars above, and estimated how close he was to the rally point.

The trek was already treacherous, but carrying an extra 175 pounds did not make it any easier. John made sure to stay far away from the edge of the bank, but the farther from the river he trekked, the denser the foliage became. He decided not to go back to the river. It would cut several hours off his trek if he took a direct path. He checked his watch and checked the stars above. Then he followed his compass through the dense forest.

His knee started to bother him, but he pushed through the pain and kept going. When he reached the rally point, the rest of Echo were waiting for him. Nick called in the extraction, and they all headed to the rendezvous point on the shore of the Caspian Sea. Just before dawn they were picked up by boat.

August 30
0123
Military hospital, Naples, Italy

Sophia awoke in a hospital room. Everything seemed fuzzy.

"Where am I?" she mumbled.

John jolted awake at the sound of her voice. He stood up and limped over to her.

"Hey, how are you feeling?"

"Like my head was crushed under a boulder and some vampire sucked away all my energy."

He grinned. "Well, at least you still have your sense of humor."

"What happened? I remember being in the water, but everything is disjointed and fuzzy."

"The ground gave away beneath you, and you plunged into the river. You must have hit your head on a rock. You have a severe concussion."

"Where is the rest of the team?"

"Back on base."

"Where are we?"

"Naples."

"Why didn't you send me on alone? Rowen probably has another mission—"

"He probably does, but Nick can handle it. I don't leave a man behind, especially in a foreign hospital. Do you have any idea how dangerous these places are?" He grinned at her.

She smirked. "I seriously doubt that is the real reason. Why are you really here?"

John cleared his throat. "You were in bad shape, Sophia. I wanted to make sure you were going to pull through. I feel like it was partly my fault you got hurt. If I hadn't pushed you so hard to run faster, maybe you would have missed that rock slide."

"Don't blame yourself, Sir. It's not your fault. It was just bad luck. I shouldn't have been running so close to the edge."

"I'm sorry you got hurt."

"How did you guys get me out of that water?"

"I sent the team ahead to the rally point and dove in after you."

"You sent them ahead without us?" she asked confused. "I thought SEALs were all about teamwork and sticking together."

"We are, but the chances of rescuing you in that freezing water were minimal. It was a miracle that I actually found you. I didn't want to risk the whole team on a hopeless mission."

"So, you believed I had no chance to survive, but you dove in after me anyway."

"I really didn't think I would find you. The river was swift. The water was barely above freezing. We were swept miles downstream in a matter of minutes. By the time I found you and pulled you up on the bank, you were already dead."

"You brought me back." The truth of what he'd done hit her in an avalanche of disjointed facts. "You saved my life, Sir."

"That's what we do. We watch each other's back. I'm just glad you're recovering."

He limped closer to the bed. Even with blurry vision she could see him wince in pain.

"Your knee is bothering you again."

"It's nothing. I'm fine."

She swallowed hard. "You carried me—didn't you?"

"Yeah."

"By yourself—but—we were sixty miles away from the rendezvous."

He didn't say anything.

"I'm sorry, Sir. Your knee—that must have made it worse. It's my fault."

"No. It's not your fault. I'm fine. Stop worrying about me."

"It's my job. I'm the medic."

"Not today. Today, you're just a patient in recovery. Rest and get better. You can be the medic again when we return to base."

"How long will I be in here?"

"The doctor is not sure yet. You took a good knock to the skull. They want to make sure you didn't do permanent damage."

She smirked. "I don't think it's permanent. Besides, I've overcome worse injuries before."

"You're starting to sound like me."

She chuckled. "I guess I am. It must go with the territory."

He reached up and gently traced his fingertip down the delicate line of her jaw.

"Don't be such a hero, Gonzalez. Take the down time while you can."

Sonny was right. Under his hard shell, John really is a nice guy. He's actually kind of sweet.

November 16
0100
Poltava, Ukraine

Sophia was excited and nervous on the flight to the Ukraine. This would be her first solo mission as Overwatch. She'd trained with Sonny for months, and he'd told John she was ready.

John took six SEALs with him on a reconnaissance mission to retrieve data from a medical lab in Poltava, Ukraine. The CIA had received intel that the lab was not a cancer research lab, but a secret base of operations for unethical, unsanctioned experiments. Echo was there to retrieve any evidence that bio-chemical weapons of war were being developed there.

She took Overwatch position on a roof across the street from the med lab. John and Nick entered disguised as lab technicians, while Hogan, Matt, Mac, and Falco took assault positions.

John and Nick used the ID badges provided by their CIA contact to enter the facility and gain access to the lab. As soon as they entered the lab, they knew this was not what they'd been briefed on. There were no experiments and no lab equipment. The room was full of servers and one terminal. Nick quickly hacked into the system and downloaded the data. When they turned over the encrypted flash drive to their CIA contact, she seemed as surprised by their find as they were. John ordered Echo to meet at the rally point.

On the plane John sat next to Sophia. "Good job, Gonzalez. You handled that mission well."

"But I didn't actually do anything. I felt a little useless and separated from the action."

"Those are the best kinds of missions. Don't wish for trouble or it will find you."

Sophia smirked. "I didn't sign up to be a desk jockey, Sir."

John chuckled. "You never change. You're still as gung-ho as the first day I met you."

CHAPTER 46

December 1
1200
Los Angeles, California

When Sophia stepped foot inside her parents' home, Amparo grabbed her in a tight hug. Then she quickly let go and looked at Sophia questioningly.

"Who is your friend?" Amparo asked.

Sophia grinned. "This is Joe Karsa. He's a member of Echo. He doesn't have any family to come home to. So, I invited him to stay with us."

Amparo grinned as she studied Joe. He was five foot, ten inches tall, with light, sandy-brown hair, green eyes, and a friendly smile.

"Welcome to our home!" Amparo said enthusiastically. "Dinner is almost on the table. Come in and meet the family."

Sophia and Joe stepped inside, and she groaned inwardly. "Mama! Did you invite the entire Gonzalez clan?"

She looked around the room and saw not only her siblings and their families, but aunts, uncles, and cousins crowded in the small home as well.

"We haven't seen you in so long. Everyone wanted to be here to greet you," Juan said as he gave his daughter a hug.

"Papa! You're English is getting better."

"I heard what you said; I decided to go to class with your Mama. I'm trying to learn English better, and your brothers are teaching me the internet too."

"I can tell. I'm so glad."

Juan grinned at his daughter. Then he let go of her and held his hand out to Joe. "I am Juan, Sophia's dad. Are you her boyfriend?"

Sophia closed her eyes and groaned out loud.

Joe grinned at Juan. "We are team mates. We both serve on Echo, Sir."

"Papa! Just because I bring a man home with me doesn't mean we are dating! Joe and I are friends. That's all! Don't start with me!"

Juan chuckled and so did Joe.

While Sophia was in line to make herself a plate, Conseja pulled her away to the back hallway.

"So, who's the hottie? Is it Butch or Sam?"

"Neither. His name is Joe. He's on my team, and he's a friend. We are not dating."

"Yet!" Conseja could barely contain her excitement. "You brought him home to meet the family. You must like him."

"I brought him home because he doesn't have a family. I didn't want him to spend our entire leave alone. He's not going to stay here the whole time. He has plans of his own later this week."

"This is great! You've never brought any man home to meet your parents. Joe must be special."

Sophia could see she was making no headway with Conseja. "I'm going to go get some food before it all disappears."

Conseja chuckled. "No fear, Girl. There is enough food here to feed an army."

"We have enough relatives here to be an army." Sophia chuckled as she got in line for food.

Joe called to her from the doorway. "Soph! I already made you a plate."

Conseja playfully jabbed Sophia in the ribs. "That's so cute; he already has a pet name for you. He's good looking and sweet. Don't let him get away, Soph. Put a ring on that boy's finger."

Sophia playfully glared at Conseja. "Don't you start with me, Girl!"

Sophia walked into the crowded living room to find that Joe had saved her a seat on the fireplace hearth next to him. He had loaded down a plate full of food for her.

"Thanks, Joe. That was very nice of you to make me a plate."

"I saw your sister pull you out of line. I was afraid you wouldn't get any of the tamales or chili rellenos. You've been talking about how good your moms are for months. I can't wait to try them myself. There are a lot of people here. I didn't know your family was so big."

Sophia sat down next to him and dug into her plate. After several satisfying bites, she looked at Joe. He had already eaten half of his plate.

"I'm going back for seconds if there is any food left," Joe said around a mouthful.

"Conseja said they made plenty of food. I'm sure there will be a lot of leftovers. By the way, I don't have a sister. I have ten brothers. Conseja is one of my sister-in-laws."

Joe nodded. "I'm not sure your parents will have room for me with all these relatives here."

"Only two of my younger brothers are still living at home. All my relatives live close by. They won't be spending the night. There will be plenty of room for you."

He chuckled. "In that case, I may have to cancel my plans next week and stay here forever. I love your mom's cooking. Can you cook as good as she does?"

"Of course, I grew up cooking in my Mama's kitchen. She taught me everything she knows."

"Damn!" Joe leaned in and whispered. "If you can cook like this, I might have to marry you."

"Easy Joe!" She gave him a warning look.

He grinned and winked at her. "What? I'm not good looking enough for you?"

She rolled her eyes.

"Don't say that too loud. My family will think you're serious, and I'll never hear the end of it."

He pressed his lips to her ear and whispered, "I am serious."

Oh no! Not another Sam or Butch situation. I have to stop this before he gets any ideas.

She shoved in another bite to avoid commenting. Joe took the hint and finished his plate. He stood up to get seconds and turned back to her.

"Do you want me to make you another plate?"

Sophia shook her head. "No, I'm still working on this one. If I'm still hungry, I'll get more."

Joe nodded and headed toward the kitchen.

No sooner was he gone than Conseja took his spot on the hearth. "You have to give me the scoop. I saw the way he was looking at you. He likes you."

Sophia groaned. "Even if he does, it doesn't matter. We are in the same unit. We can't date. It's a violation of the UCMJ. Besides, I'm not looking for a boyfriend. I'm finally in a good place in my career. My C.O. actually trusted me with a solo Overwatch position for the first time. I'm getting some footing on the team. I came in later than they did. I'm still having to prove myself. I can't afford to get tangled up in a messy romance. That's why I broke up with Butch and Sam."

"You broke up with them? When did that happen?"

"Before I deployed. I needed to cut all strings. I have to stay focused. I have a very dangerous job. Mistakes mean lives."

"But I thought you really liked both of them."

"I did. That was the problem. I was getting too distracted. Sam wanted me to marry him before I deployed. He said he wanted to get me pregnant so I could get a special dispensation. He didn't want me to go overseas at all. That's when I realized that I loved Sam, but I wasn't in love with him. I wasn't willing to throw away all I'd worked for just to be his stay at home wife. I'm not ready to settle down, Conseja. I don't know if I will ever be ready. I can't imagine loving a man so much that I would give up everything just to be with him. It's just not for me."

Conseja laughed. Then she playfully shoved Sophia's shoulder. "Good for you. You are holding out for true love. When you meet the right man, you'll know. He will be the one you'll be willing to give up everything for. I know he's out there."

Sophia shook her head and sighed in frustration.

No one actually listens to what I say or understands what I mean. They all have to put their own spin on it. It is so frustrating to keep hitting my head against this same brick wall. Maybe I wasn't meant to be a wife or mother. Maybe I'm meant to just be a soldier. Why can't they see that? They all want me to conform to their idea of what I should be. I don't even believe in true love. I don't even want it. I saw how badly it devastated Sam when I turned him down. I don't need that kind of pain in my life. I don't! I am not going to fall in love! I refuse!

CHAPTER 47

December 1
1300
North Carolina

Kyle met Sonny and John at the airport. They exchanged hugs, grabbed their bags, and headed to Kyle's truck. On the drive home, Sonny entertained Kyle with semi-classified tall tales of his recent adventures while John sat staring out the window with a frown on his face. As Sonny drawled on, John's mind wandered. Kyle noticed John's sullen demeanor, but he didn't say anything. He listened to Sonny and laughed at his stories, but his mind was acutely focused on John. He wondered what was bothering his best friend.

When they arrived at the house, Megan greeted them all with a warm hug.

She grinned at Sonny. "Sonny, we haven't seen you in a long time. I'm so happy you decided to come for a visit. We've missed you."

"I figured I better come visit before you have so many babies you forget about ol Sonny."

Megan grinned and looked over at Kyle.

"Actually, Megan just found out that we are pregnant with baby number three."

John smiled. "Congratulations!"

Kyle shook John's outstretched hand. That's the first smile I've seen all day. Are you okay?"

John nodded. "Yeah. I'm fine. I just have a lot on my mind."

Sonny chuckled. "Yeah, she's five-foot-tall with a black burr."

John glared at Sonny. "Don't go there! We already had this discussion."

Kyle gave Sonny a questioning look. "Am I missing something. What's going on?"

"Nothing!" John snapped. He turned and stalked outside.

"Okay, something is going on." Megan stared out the window at John's retreating back as he headed down the path toward the horse stables.

"Oh, something is going on, alright," Sonny drawled. "John had to pick a new team after Lydell was discharged. He filled our number sixteen spot with a hot, little, Mexican girl that will make any man's mouth water. Then he lectured the team for six months about the rules of UCMJ, and how he better not catch any of us looking at her. He don't say nothin' in front of her, but if he even thinks one of us is lookin' at her with amorous eyes, he tears us a new one in private."

"Really!" Kyle said in surprise. He walked to the window to watch John until he disappeared from sight. "What do you think that's about?"

"The whole damn team thinks he's got the hots for her. He damn sure acts like a jealous lover. He frickin' stands guard outside the tent to make sure no one walks in on her when she's changing. He stands guard at the showers and won't let no one within fifty feet of a shower stall while she's showering. He guards her like a priceless treasure. He don't let her out of his sight. He even follows her around on base. He stays out of her line of sight, but he watches her like a hawk. That boys got a serious itch that needs to be scratched."

"You think that's really it?" Kyle asked. "Maybe he's just concerned for her safety. You are on a remote base full of nothing but men. He could just be taking precautions."

Sonny shook his head. "I've talked to him about it in private. He says the same thing you did; he's just trying to protect her and keep everyone from getting themselves into any trouble."

"But you don't believe him?" Megan asked.

"Nope! Maybe I might have half-believed him a week ago, but now—no chance in hell. As soon as Echo's leave was approved, everyone started making plans. This new kid, Joe, don't have no family. I think Sophia felt sorry fer the poor kid. She invited Joe to L.A. to stay with her and her family. She don't have no interest in him or any man that I can tell. She's pretty committed to the soldier life. She lives and breathes it."

Kyle and Megan waited impatiently for Sonny to continue. He grinned at them for a moment.

"See, John was perfectly fine until he found out that Joe was going to L.A. with Sophia. From that minute on, he's been sullen, moody, a real pain in the ass. I was goin' to go visit my mom in Texas, but I changed my mind when I seen how John was actin'. I figured I better tag along and babysit the poor boy. He might do something stupid and get himself into a spec of trouble without me to look out fer him."

Megan frowned. "Do you really think he would do something to Joe? John's pretty level-headed. I can't see him going off the deep end over a woman."

Kyle nodded. "I agree. He won't do anything stupid. It's not in his nature."

"He already done somethin' stupid, Kyle. He picked her fer the team. She told me she was passed over twice by the other teams. Them other team leaders know'd better than to stick a woman on a team full of testosterone and adrenaline. Women don't belong out in the field."

"So, you don't think she's doing a good job?" Megan asked.

"I didn't say that. She's a damn good soldier. Shoot! She's probably better than me. She speaks seven languages, and she's been learning new languages from the team. She's even a better shot than I am. The girl's got skills. I ain't going to lie. John already gave her a solo Overwatch op. The problem isn't that she can't hack it. She can hang with the best of us. The problem is simply that she's female."

"That's a pretty prejudiced statement," Megan said perturbed.

"I know. Call me a prejudiced son of a—" Sonny stopped himself realizing that little Mandy was watching him and hanging on his every word. "I know it ain't right, Megan. Women should be able to do any job they are capable of, but not a SEAL. There should be a line drawn somewhere. Whatever politician passed it to let women try out for the SEALs screwed us all."

"Why?" Megan asked.

Sonny sighed and looked at Kyle. "Kyle, you been there. Tell her why a woman don't belong."

Megan looked at her husband and smirked.

Kyle shook his head. "I'm not getting in the middle of that discussion. I'm happily married, and I intend to stay that way."

Sonny chuckled. "I knew you was whipped. The ol ball and chain got your tongue tied."

She crossed her arms over her chest and glared at Sonny. "Kyle was right. You are trouble!"

"Yes, Ma'am. That's me. Sonny Trouble Eldridge. I wear it proud."

Megan rolled her eyes.

Kyle looked at his wife. "Honey, just so you know, I don't agree with Sonny."

"About what? John being in love or women belonging in the SEALs?"

"Both. Women can do whatever they want. Have I ever tried to hold you back?"

She smirked. "No. Unless you count that time when you handcuffed me to Owen."

Kyle groaned. "Okay, that was stupid, but I only did it because I was worried about you."

She chuckled. "I know. I've forgiven you for being a stubborn, pigheaded fool."

He leaned in and claimed her lips.

Sonny groaned from his couch. "I didn't come here to see you two play kissy-face. You two are so sugar-sweet on each other it gives me a stomach ache."

Kyle pulled back from her lips grinning. Then he turned and looked at Sonny. "When are you going to settle down, Sonny?"

"Don't start with me, Kyle. I roam free. No woman is going to chain me down. I ain't the marrying kind. I'd make a rotten husband and a worse father."

"So, you don't want me to set you up on another blind date?" Megan chuckled.

"Hell no! Don't you even think about it. I'm sure Kyle's already told you that I don't date."

She nodded. "He has. What's your title again? The king of one-night-stands?"

Sonny grimaced and looked down at his cowboy boots. "Actually, I don't do that no more."

Kyle's eyebrow rose. "What brought about that change?"

Sonny rubbed his hand over his blonde burr and sighed. "This girl a while back. She made me realize that I'm kind of a scumbag when it comes to women. I decided to quit that scene."

"So, what do you do now?" Megan asked surprised.

"Nothing. I haven't been with a woman since her. She actually liked me with all my flaws and my horrible past, but I dumped her before I went back overseas. I know that was dirty, but she's better off without me. She deserves better than the likes of me."

"Are you in love with her, Sonny?" Kyle asked.

"Love! Hell! I don't know! Maybe I was starting to, but she's too sweet. I didn't deserve her."

Megan frowned. "What's her name?"

"Oh no, Little Miss! You ain't playin' matchmaker on me no more. I'm on to you."

Kyle stood up and headed to the front door. "I'm going to check on John."

"Good luck with that," Sonny called after him. "He's about as stubborn as you were. He don't want to admit that he's fallen hard fer our badass, little senorita."

Kyle walked into the stable to find John brushing a horse. "Want to take one out for a spin?"

John shook his head. "Nah. I'm just trying to blow off steam so I don't blow up on Sonny."

"Is he right about Sophia? Are you in love with her?"

"No."

Kyle leaned against the gate on the stall and studied John. "So, what's the story on her?"

"There is no story. She's a good soldier. She deserved a chance to prove herself on a team. No other team was going to take her. You know how it is out there. There's an invisible wall that women are not allowed through no matter how good they are. I'm just trying to be the bridge so she has the same chance as anyone else."

"So, you specifically chose her because she's a woman."

"No, I chose her because she speaks seven languages. She went to sniper school. She's smart as a whip, and she doesn't quit. She's a good soldier. The problem is, she's not just a woman; she's a beautiful woman. If she were dog-ugly, it would make everything a lot easier. I knew choosing her would cause a lot of waves and make my life harder. I figured she was worth the extra work. I don't like to see people held back because of petty prejudices."

Kyle nodded. "So, you have no interest in her whatsoever?"

"No. She's just another soldier, but Echo doesn't see it that way. That's my biggest problem. I've already had to reprimand more than one of my guys for taking an interest in her. I told them it's a direct violation of the UCMJ, and it's not allowed under any circumstances. I think they misinterpret everything I say and do when it comes to Gonzalez."

"What about this new guy, Joe?"

John growled, and his whole body tensed. "He's a problem."

"Why?"

"I see the way he looks at her when he thinks no one is watching. He definitely has a thing for her. I've warned him more than once, but he went to L.A. with her anyway."

"So, is Joe the reason you're angry?"

"I'm not angry. I'm frustrated. I knew discipline would be an issue once she deployed with our team, but I didn't expect my direct order to be blatantly disobeyed."

"You ordered him not to take leave with her?"

"Hell yeah, I ordered him not to. Obviously, he ignored me. I'll deal with him when we get back to Afghanistan."

"What if it's mutual? What if she likes him too?"

"It's not, and she doesn't."

"What if she takes a liking to him on leave?"

"She won't. She's all business all the time. She shows no interest in any man as far as I can tell. She told me she's just here to serve. She's probably the most dedicated soldier next to you that I've ever seen. She's serious. She stays focused. She follows orders to the letter. She gives 200 percent. Even if she was interested in Joe, she wouldn't be stupid enough to jeopardize her entire career over him. She's worked too hard to get where she's at to throw it away on some tryst with a teammate. That's just not who she is."

"I believe you, but I don't think Sonny does. He's worried about you."

John scoffed. "Sonny! He's worse than Joe. You know what a womanizer he is. He claims they are just friends, but I've seen the way he looks at her, the way he acts with her. It's anything but platonic."

"You really think Sonny has an interest in her?"

"He's Sonny! What do you think? The only criteria Sonny has for banging a woman is she has to be breathing. He's a worthless scumbag where women are concerned."

"Are you afraid she'll take an interest in Sonny?"

"I'd be stupid not to worry about that. He's God's gift to the female species. They can't resist him. You've heard his stories."

"Yeah, too many times."

John's jaw tensed. "I've had to warn Sonny more than once to keep his hands off her, but he can't seem to help himself. He's always touching her inappropriately. He claims he's not flirting, but he had his hand on her ass during one of our missions. I'm not buying his innocent act."

"So, you think Sonny likes her?"

"I know he does. He watches her all the time."

"Maybe he's just concerned for her safety—like you."

"No, he's got designs on her.

"He claims you do, and he's tagging along with you on leave to keep you out of trouble."

John's jaw tightened. He didn't say anything. He just continued to brush the horse in silence.

"So, you don't like Sophia. You have no interest in her whatsoever?"

"No."

"Good, because Megan has a couple of friends she wants you to meet while you're here."

"I'm not interested."

"She said they are pretty, smart, and very sweet."

"Don't care. I didn't come here to get set up on blind dates."

"You know she won't leave you alone until you say yes."

John's jaw tightened. "I said no!" he growled. "I don't feel like being harassed about this by anyone, including your wife!"

"Don't get angry."

"I'm not angry!"

"You sound angry."

"You know what! Coming here was a bad idea. I'll just call a taxi and go stay at a motel somewhere. I really don't need this, Kyle!"

"You're not going anywhere. I'll tell her to back off. I'll talk to Sonny too. Why don't you take one of the horses out for a ride? It might relieve some of your stress."

"I think I will go for a ride. Thinking about all this is giving me a headache."

Kyle walked out of the stable with a smirky grin on his face.

John aimlessly rode the trails on the property for hours. He had a lot on his mind, and he lost track of time. Dusk fell on a pitch black, moonless night. His horse wandered onto the beach, and he dismounted. The temperature was dropping, but he ignored the chill in the air. He tied the horse to the hitching post at the edge of the forest, walked down to the water, sat on the sand, and stared at the dark ocean before him.

Sonny is wrong. I'm not in love with Sophia. I don't love her any more or any less than the other guys on Echo. I respect her as a soldier. That's all there is to it.

"There you are," Owen called from behind John.

John didn't respond. He just stared blankly at the water. Owen walked over and sat down.

"Meg's got the posse out looking for you. When you didn't show for dinner, she got worried."

"That figures," John muttered.

"Something wrong?"

John shrugged. "Nothing and everything."

"That's vague and all encompassing."

"I'm just tired of people trying to force me into some romance. It's annoying."

Owen nodded. "Meg's matchmaking schemes are infuriating, but I have no room to complain. I wouldn't be married to Anna if Meg hadn't meddled in my life. She's good about that."

"I wasn't talking about Megan. I was referring to Sonny."

"Sonny's playing matchmaker now? Who's he trying to set you up with?"

"He's not trying to set me up. He thinks I'm in love with the new girl on our team. I'm not!"

"Are you sure?" Owen asked with a half grin.

"I'm sure! Even if I was interested, it's not allowed. The UCMJ is clear about relationships between soldiers on the same team or in the same chain of command. I'm her C.O. It's not allowed, but Sonny won't leave me alone. He's getting on my last nerve."

Owen cleared his throat. "I understand it's not allowed, but if the UCMJ wasn't an issue, would you be interested in her?"

John glared at the ocean for a long while in silence.

"No."

"So, you are in love with her," Owen said quietly. "I have a little experience with forbidden love. It's a tough road to navigate. All I can tell you is if you find yourself in a situation where you can tell her how you really feel, take it. Don't hesitate. Don't put it off and think you'll get a second chance. That's where I screwed up with Meg."

John cleared his throat. "I'm not in love with her, so that's not an issue."

Owen grinned. "You can tell yourself that lie, but it's obvious to anyone looking that you are."

John groaned and lay back on the sand with his eyes closed.

"Is that what it looks like? That's how rumors spread whether they are true or not. I won't let her career be ruined."

"What about your career? Won't yours be ruined too?"

"I don't care about my career, but I won't let this negatively impact her. That's not fair to her."

Owen grinned. "Man! You have it bad for her. How long have you known you love her?"

"I never said I love her."

John stood up to leave and saw Kyle standing a few feet behind them. He glared at Kyle.

"Don't look at me with that smirky grin! I'm not in love with her!"

CHAPTER 48

December 10

0900

West Virginia, VA rehab waiting room

Lydell sat in his wheelchair waiting for his turn with the VA rehab nurse. He'd undergone multiple surgeries, and he now had a steel rod where his right femur used to be. Now it was just a matter of learning to walk on it. It was an uphill battle every day, but it wasn't in him to quit.

At 1130, the nurse called loudly. "Chief Lydell Fry!"

Lydell rolled himself over to the nurse and followed her down the corridor to the rehab room.

"Don't look so chipper, Fry," Nurse Knight said as she held the door open for him.

He rolled in and stared at the familiar equipment. The cold steel stared back at him with no emotion. It had no interest in whether he succeeded or failed.

"Can you stand up on your own?" Knight asked.

"Not yet."

She leaned down and wrapped her arms around his torso and pulled him to a standing position. "Are you doing your exercises at home?"

"Yeah."

"It takes time. Don't get discouraged. You'll get there."

She helped him up on a table where she went through a series of stretching exercises. Then she put him on a weight machine. He was able to do the same amount he'd done the previous day on his right leg—none. After completing all the preliminary exercises, she wheeled him over to the parallel bars to see how far he could walk today.

She pulled him to a standing position again. He balanced on his good leg while she placed his hands on the cold, metal bars in front of him.

"I'm going to walk behind you like always. I won't let you fall."

"I know." His voice held no enthusiasm, no spark.

He took one step with his left leg and tried as hard as he could to move the right leg.

He let out a frustrated breath. "I still can't move it."

"We don't use that word in this room, Fry."

"What word would you like me to use?" he muttered.

"Don't get smart with me, young man. I'm here to help you. Try harder."

"I'm trying as hard as I can. I don't know how to make it move. I can't feel much in that leg."

"Don't you start quoting your file. I know all about the muscle damage. You can't let it atrophy, or you'll be in that chair the rest of your life. Now, try harder."

He did his best to focus all his energy on forcing the muscles to work. Nothing happened. After half an hour of failed attempts, she helped him back into his chair.

"Come back tomorrow, and we'll try again."

He nodded absently. Nurse Knight wheeled him back to the waiting room.

He called Grammy. "I'm done for the day."

"I'll be by to pick you up soon. I'm just dropping Ellery off at the house. How did it go?"

"The same as yesterday."

He hung up and wheeled himself out to the front sidewalk to wait. He stared absently at the trees planted in neat rows around the perimeter of the parking lot. His grandmother arrived, and with a lot of struggle and some help from her, he managed to maneuver himself into the front passenger's seat. Grammy put his wheelchair in the back and climbed behind the wheel.

"I should be the one taking care of you, not the other way around," he grumbled.

"We do what we have to, Sweetie. Life is a struggle of one sort or another from the day we are born to the day we die. The struggle is what makes us strong. Challenges make us grow."

A tear slid down his cheek, and he swiped it away.

"Tough day?"

"They're all tough."

She put her hand on his stubbled jaw. "Don't lose your hope, Lydell. It will get better."

"Can we just go home? I'm tired."

She drove home, and Donovan came out of the barn to help Lydell into the farmhouse. Lydell didn't like admitting he was wrong, but he had been wrong about Donovan. He'd decided that Donovan was the sweet innocent kid he appeared to be.

Two days later, Lydell wheeled himself out to the sidewalk after his therapy session and called Grammy.

"I'm done, Grammy."

"That's great. I was hoping you'd finish a little early today. I won't be coming to pick you up this time. Your ride should be there already."

"My ride? Who's picking me up? Gramps? I thought he went to pick up feed today."

"He did."

"So, who is—" Lydell trailed off as he saw John, Nick, Sonny, and Kyle headed toward him across the parking lot. "I'll call you later, Grammy."

"Have fun, Sweetie."

"Did we miss it?" Sonny asked, as he stepped up on the sidewalk. "Your grandma said you usually don't get out for another hour."

Lydell smiled at them. "What are you guys doing here?"

"We're on leave. We're just dropping by for a visit before we have to fly back," Nick said.

"How are you doing?" John asked.

"I'm doing fine."

John frowned. He didn't buy into the lie for a second.

"Are you hungry? We can go grab some dinner," Kyle suggested.

"Actually, I am hungry," Lydell said.

"Good. You're pickin' the place, cause we don't know where nothin' is around here. We got lost three times tryin' to find this here VA center," Sonny drawled.

Lydell chuckled. "I know that's a damn lie. Four SEALs don't get lost. You jokers know how to read a map and find coordinates."

All five men laughed.

Soon they were sitting at a table at a local steakhouse. The men caught up on old times, and the conversation eventually came around to John leading Echo.

"Yeah, ol John done screwed up. He picked a woman to join the team," Sonny teased.

"You did?" Lydell asked incredulously. "Why?"

"She made a good fit for the team," John said.

Sonny chuckled. Then he looked across the table at Lydell. "He's hopin' it will fit. She's a hot, little, Mexican senorita."

John growled as he glared at Sonny. "Sonny! That's enough! I will not tolerate any more insinuations from you. Crap like that can start rumors—rumors that could ruin her career! If you do it again, I'll file charges against you for harassment!"

Sonny chuckled. "I wasn't saying nothing in front of nobody who would get her in trouble. Nick knows you're in love with her. He ain't said nothin. Kyle and Lydell ain't going to tell nobody. Relax. We're just havin' a discussion among friends about how you got it bad for her."

John pushed back from the table and stalked out to the parking lot.

Kyle smirked. "I guess that means you're paying for his meal, Sonny."

"Hell. I was goin' to pay for everyone's meal anyways," Sonny drawled.

"Is he really in love with her?" Lydell asked.

Kyle nodded. "He's in love alright, but he refuses to admit it. Any time anyone mentions it he gets angry and walks away to cool off."

Lydell frowned. "How is he going to handle being her C.O.?"

Nick sighed. "He's actually handling it very professionally. He doesn't play favorites. He assigns us roles based on our skills and abilities. That extends to Sophia. The only special treatment he gives her is in regards to making sure she has privacy to shower and change clothes. I haven't seen him say or do anything to indicate that there's anything between them."

"Then why do you all believe he's in love with her?" Lydell asked.

"He is," Kyle said. "He might not admit it, but he already values her well-being over his own. He's trying to protect her reputation. He's jealous that she spent her leave with another member of the team. He's stressed out and worried that someone might think there is a romantic relationship between them. He doesn't want her to get in trouble. He's more concerned about the damage it would do to her career and reputation than to his own."

"That sounds like love," Lydell agreed.

"Speaking of love, have you heard from Bretta?" Sonny asked.

Lydell cleared his throat and stared at his plate for a moment. "No. Why would I?"

"Why wouldn't you?" Sonny countered. "If it wasn't for her intervention, we'd all be dead. She didn't steal a top secret, protype chopper from the Russians and cross enemy lines to save Echo; she did it to save your ass."

His lips turned down in a frown. "I haven't heard from her, and I'm not expecting to. I'm stateside now. It's not like she can just pop by for a visit."

Sonny grinned. "Well, seeing how she's a British spy, you're probably right. She's most likely saving the world as we speak."

Lydell nodded. "I'm sure you're right, Sonny. I don't think I'll ever see her again."

"I'm still trying to figure out how she knew where Echo was. That was a black op, mission."

Lydell cleared his throat. "She put a tracker in me."

Nick's eyebrow rose. "And you let her?"

"I didn't know about it until after she rescued us. She told me in the hospital."

"How did she put a tracker in you without your knowledge?" Kyle asked.

Lydell ran a hand through his loose, copper curls. "I still haven't figured that out."

"You took it out though, didn't you?" Sonny asked.

Lydell shook his head. "I figured out where it is, but I haven't removed it."

"Where is it?" they all asked in unison.

He grinned at them. "In my left ass cheek."

Sonny smirked. "So, you're just leavin' it there? You hopin' if she comes lookin' fer you again that you'll be easier to find with it in ya?"

Lydell shook his head. "No, Bretta has skills. I don't think she actually needs a tracker to know exactly where I am at all times. She probably knows I'm sitting here eating lunch with the four of you right now. She said she watches me all the time."

Lydell pointed up.

"You think she watches you via satellites?" Nick asked.

"I think she has a variety of ways to watch me. Traffic cams, satellite, trackers, the GPS on my phone—do I really need to go on?"

"Damn! That's like weird, high-tech, creepy stalker," Kyle said. "Doesn't it bother you?"

Lydell shook his head. "No, I don't know exactly what her agenda is, but I know she's a good person. She didn't have to save Negassi and his boys. She did that off the books on her own."

"You'll see her again," Sonny said. "She wouldn't have bothered to save your ass if she wasn't planning to screw you again."

Kyle's eyebrow rose. "How serious are you and Bretta?"

Lydell chewed at his lower lip. Then he shrugged. "As serious as she wants to be. I don't think she can have attachments in her line of work. It's just when it works out in her crazy schedule."

"Well, we've all avoided the elephant until now," Kyle said. "How is your rehab going?"

Lydell shrugged. "I'm doing all the exercises, but I still can't feel my right leg. I can't move it. I've hit a brick wall in therapy."

"What do the doctors say?" Nick asked.

"My leg has healed from the surgery. I should be able to use it. My doctor told me the reason I'm not walking yet is because I don't want to. She thinks it's some kind of mental block."

"Is it?" Nick asked.

Lydell shook his head. "I want to walk. I'm sick of being in this chair. I'm sick of my grandparents, my sister, and my sixteen-year-old neighbor having to help me. It's humiliating. My grandparents are too frail to be trying to help me. I hate this."

Kyle let out a long breath. "I don't know if you're interested, but I have an idea."

Lydell looked up at Kyle.

"Why don't you come stay with me and Megan for a while? We have plenty of extra rooms. You could do VA rehab in North Carolina. I could help you with your physical therapy."

"I don't want to burden you like that, Kyle."

"We're friends. It's not a burden, Lydell. I want to help you."

Lydell shook his head. "I won't do that to you and Megan. You have two little ones to look after. You don't need me there getting in the way."

Kyle pulled his phone from his pocket and dialed Megan.

"Hey, Sweetheart. Do you have a problem with me bringing Lydell back with me to stay with us for a while? He's having trouble with his physical therapy, and I offered to help him."

"No, I don't."

"Good, can you talk to him. He's afraid he'll be too big of a burden on us."

Kyle handed the phone to Lydell.

Lydell tried to argue with her, but it didn't take Megan long to convince him.

When Lydell explained it to his family a short while later they were sorry to see him leave, but also a little relieved to have the burden lifted for a while. He promised to come back to visit them once a month. He didn't want to monopolize every weekend and burden them more.

Kyle drove them all to the airport and Nick, Sonny, and John caught a flight. Kyle and Lydell waited an extra hour for their flight to leave. Lydell wasn't sure what to expect, but he trusted Kyle with his life, so trusting him with physical therapy was a no-brainer.

When they arrived, Megan was there to give Lydell a big hug and welcome him home. She had already made up a room for him on the first floor, and she had dinner in the oven.

"I invited Owen and Anna for dinner. I figured Lydell could meet all of us at once that way," she said, before planting a kiss on Kyle's lips.

Lydell was soon introduced to little Mandy and Buck. A short while later, he met the entire Wiley clan. By the time dinner was over and the Wileys had returned home, Lydell felt completely exhausted. He fell asleep that night feeling hopeful for the first time in a long time.

CHAPTER 49

December 14
2400
Afghanistan

Rowen sent Echo out on a local mission. SEAL team Whiskey had intel on a hostile Afghani terrorist group. Their orders were to capture or kill if necessary. The teams were choppered in and dropped off twenty-five klicks to the south of the reported terrorist location.

Seven klicks into the hike, a member of Whiskey triggered a landmine. The explosion went off a hundred yards ahead of Echo's position. John and Sophia raced ahead of Echo to lend a hand. Whiskey's medic was already working furiously to stop the bleeding of the man who'd triggered the mine. His left leg below the knee was gone, and he was gushing blood.

"Echo 16, check for any other injuries," John ordered her.

She started looking at the other men near the blast site. Two had taken shrapnel from the mine. She started working on the most serious of the two.

John assessed the man Whiskey's medic was working on and noted that Whiskey's medic was working with only one eye. Shrapnel protruded from his other eye.

"I'll take over," John said. "Go see our medic, now!"

John cinched the tourniquet tight and looked into the man's panic-filled eyes.

"You're going to make it. The bleeding is stopped. Do you have any other injuries?"

"My stomach hurts," he grunted in pain.

John removed the man's flak jacket and saw shrapnel protruding from his abdomen. "Don't move. A chopper is on the way to medivac you to a hospital. I'm giving you something for the pain."

John pulled out a needle filled with morphine and injected him with it.

Whiskey's communication officer was on the radio. "Chopper ETA is fifteen minutes."

Nick took charge of Echo while John was occupied with medic duties. "Form a perimeter. If enemy forces are in the area, they will have heard that mine. Watch your step. We don't need any more injuries this morning."

Whiskey's C.O. was doing the same with his men. When the chopper arrived, the injured men were loaded on board, and the chopper disappeared into the darkness.

"Circle up." Whiskey's Master Chief, Gabriel Hawkins, ordered the men who were left.

Gabriel quickly gave new orders. Figuring their position had been compromised, he ordered Whiskey to the left flank and Echo to the right. They would circle around to the north of their target and take them by surprise from an unexpected direction.

John nodded. "Agreed. You lost your medic. Is anyone else on your team trained for that?"

"Yes, but he was one of the casualties. We currently have no one with medical training."

"Echo 16 will accompany your team than," John said. "She is an excellent medic."

Gabriel nodded. "Agreed. We'll rendezvous to the north in three hours."

Whiskey and Echo moved out in the darkness. Sophia followed behind Whiskey. They moved stealthily as a unit watching out for any more landmines. When they reached the rendezvous point, Echo was not there. They waited, but Echo didn't show. Sophia felt panic fill her.

What if they triggered another mine? What if they need me, and I'm not there to save anyone?

Her gut felt like it had been twisted into a hard knot, but she had no time to contemplate Echo's fate further. Gabriel was giving the order to advance on the camp and assault.

As they neared the camp, they could hear a gunfight to the south of the camp. Whiskey's sniper took out the few militants in the camp, and the team advanced toward the sound of gunfire in the distance. The mountainous region was interfering with their shortrange coms. As they drew near the gunfight, they could hear garbled commands on their coms and a lot of static. Whiskey had no way of knowing the status of Echo's condition. All they could do was come in from behind and give the enemy two fronts to battle.

"Watch your targets. We don't want casualties from friendly fire," Gabriel ordered.

"Sir, I have sniper training," Sophia offered, "I can assist Overwatch."

Gabriel nodded. "Do it."

Sophia and Overwatch took up sniper positions as the rest of Whiskey advanced down the mountain toward the battle. Once Whiskey joined the fight, it didn't take long to eliminate the threat. Between Sophia, Sonny, and Whiskey's Overwatch half the combatants were eliminated. The remaining combatants were taken out by the rest of Whiskey and Echo.

A few hours later, they were choppered back to base. Echo and Whiskey hit the showers. Sophia waited until everyone was finished with their shower before she headed over. As usual John stood guard at the showers to make sure no one came too close to her. Sophia soaped up and stood under the cold water rinsing away the dust and grim. She looked over at John who stood with his back to her. A grin spread over her lips.

John is so paranoid. There is really no need for him to stand guard. He thinks he's protecting me, but I can take care of myself. If any of these guys tried something, they'd walk away in pain. That's assuming they could walk at all.

She finished her shower, dressed, and walked over to John. "I'm done."

"I need to speak with you before you return to the tent," he said sternly. "Let's take a walk."

She matched his pace as he headed toward the front of the compound away from the tents.

"How was your leave?" he asked.

"It was nice. I got to spend a lot of time with my family. How was your leave, Sir?"

"It was fine."

When he didn't say anything else, she fell silent. He stopped near the supply crates and gestured for her to have a seat. She sat down on a crate and looked up at him.

"I've lectured the men about the UCMJ since they joined our team, but I haven't really talked to you about it before now. Frankly, you never gave me a reason before now."

"The UCMJ?" she asked confused.

"Karsa took leave with you in L.A."

She nodded. "Yes, he stayed with my family for a few days before going to Yosemite."

John dragged a hand over his burr. "When he stayed with you, did he share your bed?"

Her mouth fell open. "Is that what this is about? You think we violated the UCMJ?"

"Did you?"

"No, Sir!"

"I'm your C.O. I'm going to give you some advice. You're the first woman to join a team like this. All eyes are on you. Command is watching you. Your peers are watching you. Any appearance of impropriety will be noticed and taken into consideration when you are up for promotion. If you get a reputation whether it's earned or not, things won't go well for you down the road. Taking a fellow teammate home on leave to meet your parents is unwise."

"I only invited him because he has no family. I was just trying to be a good friend."

"You can't afford to be friendly like that. Even if you didn't have relations with Karsa, there are a percentage of people on base who will assume you did."

"I didn't!"

John nodded and paced back and forth. "I know it's a double standard. If Karsa had taken leave with one of the other men on the team it wouldn't be an issue. Despite how innocent your intentions were, it won't be perceived that way. Going forward, I suggest you go on leave alone."

"Understood, Sir! Are you going to have this conversation with Karsa too?"

"I already had this conversation with him before he left. He ignored me and went with you anyway. Apparently, he doesn't care if your reputation gets tarnished."

"Why didn't you have this conversation with me before we went on leave?"

John leaned against a tall stack of crates. He closed his eyes and let out a weary sigh. "I should have." He looked back up at her. "You're much more rational and level-headed than Karsa. I believe you would have listened. Honestly, I didn't expect Karsa to disobey a direct order."

"You ordered him not to take leave with me?"

John nodded.

"I'm confused. Why didn't you give me the same order?"

"I should have. That was my mistake. I should have been a better commanding officer."

"It's okay, Sir. I should have known better. I guess I still keep expecting everyone to treat me like any other soldier."

John shook his head. "I'm sorry to say, they won't. You'll always be different in their eyes. Did Whiskey give you any trouble?"

"No, Master Chief Hawkins actually let me assist Overwatch."

"Good. I'm just glad no one else needed your medical training on that mission. It's going to be tough for Whiskey. They're going to have to find a new medic for the team."

Sophia nodded. "At least they are all going to live."

John nodded. "You did good work out there today."

"Thank you, Sir."

"You're dismissed. Go get some sleep."

She was almost to the end of the crates when she turned and looked at John. He was still leaning against the crates staring at the sand.

"Sir, you don't have to worry about me. I won't ever take anyone on leave again. I won't give anyone a reason to suspect the worst of me. I'm here to serve. I'm not here to find romance. I'm not looking for a husband. I doubt I'll ever get married. I chose the life of a soldier, and it's the only life I want to live. That makes me a huge disappointment to my mother. Her one goal in life is to find me a husband. My one goal in life is to serve my country."

John walked over to her and stared down into her chocolate brown eyes. His eyes involuntarily dropped to her plump, luscious lips. Then he forced his gaze back up to her eyes.

"You are not a disappointment to me. You have served admirably. You always give me everything you have. You never complain. You always follow orders. Most importantly, everything you say and do only affirms that you have a good heart, good morals, and you are an honorable soldier. I respect you. I just want you to know that I am in your corner even if no one else is. I know you have what it takes. You prove it to me every day. Thank you for your exemplary service, Gonzalez."

She swallowed hard. No one had ever given her such a compliment in all her years of service. A tear streaked down her cheek as she fought to suppress the emotion that was trying desperately to break free.

John reached up, cupped her jaw in his palm, and gently wiped away her tear with his thumb. "I didn't mean to make you cry."

She stared up into his dark brown eyes, and her heart skipped a beat. He dropped his hand to his side realizing he shouldn't have touched her.

"I should be stronger, Sir. I shouldn't be so emotional. It's just—no one has ever paid me a compliment like that before. Thank you. That means more to me than you can possibly know. I respect you too, Sir. You've always been fair with me. I asked you to treat me like any other male on the team, and you do. I appreciate that you don't treat me like a fragile china doll. You push me to my limits and challenge me to do better. I want you to continue to push me."

He nodded. "Don't worry. I will."

"Will there be anything else, Sir?"

"No. Get some sleep, Gonzalez."

CHAPTER 50

January 8
1400
Afghanistan base

Echo returned from an exhausting mission, and the entire team was sleeping soundly with the exception of John. He lay on his bunk tossing and turning. His dreams were plagued with the horrors he'd witnessed on previous missions.

Sophia woke to the sound of moaning. She sat up on her bed and surveyed the tent full of sleeping men. Her eyes fell on John. He was restless, and she heard him moan again. She got up and knelt on the wood floor between their bunks. She gently held his wrist in her hand and took his pulse. His blood pressure was a little high. She got into her med pack, pulled out a thermometer, and swiped it across his forehead; he was running a fever. He started mumbling in his sleep, but she couldn't make out his words. She leaned down closer to hear him.

"Don't go," he mumbled softly. "Sophia, wait. I just want to protect you."

He's dreaming about protecting me?

A grin spread over her lips. She gently trailed her fingers down the dark brown stubble that covered his angular jaw. He didn't stir, but his breathing grew more labored.

"Sir, you're running a temperature. You need to wake up and take some medicine."

When he didn't respond, she reached up and gently ran her hand over his dark brown burr. He moaned softly, and a dopey grin spread over his lips.

"What are you doin'?" Sonny asked quietly behind her.

She jumped in surprise. "Sonny! I didn't hear you get up."

Sonny leaned in close and whispered in her ear, "You shouldn't be touchin' him like that. If anyone was to see you, they'd think somethin' was going on between you two."

"I was just waking him up to take some medicine for his fever."

Sonny smirked. "No, you wasn't. I seen what you did. That ain't the way to wake a man up unless yer wakin' him up to seduce him."

Her eyes grew wide. "I-I wasn't—"

"Be more careful how you put your hands on a man around here, especially John. The whole damn base is already watchin' you two. Don't get him in no trouble."

She stood up facing Sonny. "What do you mean the whole base is watching us?"

Sonny pulled her in close and kept his voice low so only she could hear him.

"Everyone on base thinks he chose you for personal reasons. If they see evidence that you two are in a relationship, John could end up on the wrong side of a court martial and get sent to Leavenworth—so could you. Be more careful in the future."

Her mouth dropped open. "There is nothing going on between Chief Rusk and I. He's my C.O. I would never violate the UCMJ, and neither would he."

Sonny let out a sigh and shook his head. "If you only knew—

"Knew what?"

He leaned down until his lips almost touched her ear. "John ain't never been with a woman. If you go and start touching him, caressing him, and runnin' your fingers through his hair like you was doin', you're going to drive him crazy. A man has needs, and John's been denying his for a long damn time. Don't torture him with what he can't have. That's just cruel, Sophia. He's already sacrificed his career for you. Don't get him sent to prison too."

She gasped. "I wasn't trying to—"

"Weren't you?"

"No."

"What do you call it then?"

"I didn't mean it like that. I'll be more careful going forward."

Sonny nodded.

"What did you mean by he sacrificed his career for me?"

"Choosing you for his team painted a target on his back. Do you think he'll ever get promoted any farther than chief?" Sonny shook his head. "Everyone up the chain of command is going to look at his decision to put you on the team as a weakness. They'll automatically assume he wanted you on the team for unethical reasons. They'll suspect the two of you even if it isn't true. He sank his career the moment he chose you. He knew it. We know it. You're the only one who doesn't seem to get it. You're wearing blinders to the way the world works."

"Oh! That's terrible! Why would they punish him for choosing me? That's not fair!"

"Look, I know you. I know you wouldn't do nothin' intentionally to hurt any of us. This is just a unique situation. John's a good man. He's one of the kindest, most giving people I've ever known, but he is only human. You just can't flirt with him like that. If you do—he might not be able to resist your obvious charms."

"I wasn't flirting."

"Yeah—well—from the outside that's what it looked like."

She nodded. "I understand. I promise I'll be more conscientious with everyone from now on."

John moaned in his sleep, and they both looked over at him.

"He looks pale. I'm worried about him," she said quietly.

"He'll be fine. He survived Malaria a few years ago. A little virus won't kick his ass."

Sonny stepped around Sophia and gently shook John's shoulder. "Hey, Buddy. Wake up. You need to take some medicine."

"I'm not sick," John mumbled.

"That there thermometer begs to differ, Chief. Sit up and take yer meds, and don't give the doc no trouble about it. She's worried about you."

January 10
0130
Novosibirsk, Russia

Echo was inside the Russian border approaching Novosibirsk. CIA intel had discovered a connection between the data collected on their previous mission in Poltava, Ukraine to a medical facility on the outskirts of Novosibirsk. Echo's mission would be to investigate the facility and return with any intel they could acquire.

John ordered Nick, Ben, Dorian, and Ezra to infiltrate the facility. Sonny would act as Overwatch. Zach, Hogan, Chris, and Joe would cover the left flank of the building. Matt, Mac, Jerome and Andrew would cover the right flank. Falco and Sophia would roam and serve as sentries. John remained out of sight in an alley across the street to coordinate the op.

John leaned against the old stone wall of the building and tried to stay focused on the mission. His head hurt, and he was running another fever. His whole body felt chilled. The worst part was he couldn't quit coughing. It's why he'd sent Nick in to gather the data rather than going himself.

Nick downloaded data from the server while Ben gathered evidence of anything in the lab that looked suspicious. Dorian and Ezra stood guard inside the building. The rest of Echo were positioned outside ready to come to their aid if needed.

John listened intently to the feedback from his team. The op was going smoothly; the building seemed to be deserted much like the streets. The freezing temperatures discouraged the citizens of Novosibirsk from going out in the middle of the night.

Once his part of the op was complete, Nick spoke into his com link. "Echo 2 to Echo 1."

Silence was the only answer.

"I repeat. Echo 2 to Echo 1. Do you copy?"

There was no reply.

"Echo 2 to Echo 16."

"Echo 16, go for Echo 2," Sophia answered.

"Check on Echo 1 and report back."

"Copy." She immediately changed direction and headed back to the alley. She found John slumped against the wall unconscious.

"Echo 16 to Echo 2."

"Echo 2, go for Echo 16."

"Echo 1 is unconscious."

Nick grimaced. Then he took over command of the op. He ordered Falco to rendezvous with Sophia and carry John out of town. The rest of Echo met at the rally point outside of town.

Falco deposited John on the ground, and Echo took up defensive positions while Nick and Sophia knelt to examine him.

"He's burning up."

She got into her med pack and pulled out a pack of dissolvable acetaminophen. She carefully opened his mouth and pressed the medicine under his tongue.

"He pushed himself too hard," Nick said. "I told him to stay on base, but he wouldn't listen."

Nick looked around surveying their position. "This is not a safe place to hang out long. We need to move out immediately."

Dorian fastened John's pack to his own, and Sonny hoisted John onto his shoulders. Nick gave the order to move out. They were deep in enemy territory and needed to find cover before dawn.

After three hours of brisk hiking they found a farm fifty klicks southwest of Novosibirsk. There was a large barn on the south side of the farmhouse.

Nick took John from Sonny. "Echo 3, take Overwatch position. Echo 4, Echo 7 take sentry positions outside. The rest of you camouflage and take up watch positions on the property. We need to ensure we aren't being followed. Echo 16 and I will check him over and determine if it's safe to move him any farther."

Nick entered the barn and climbed up to the large loft above the livestock. It was lined with bales of hay. As soon as he laid John down in the back corner of the loft, Sophia examined him.

"His fever broke, but he's still unresponsive."

Nick nodded. "What can you do for him?"

"We need to keep him warm for now and hope for the best."

Nick watched as she spread out a blanket from his pack. He helped her lift John onto the blanket, and she tucked the blanket around him.

"Will he be warm enough with just the blanket?" Nick asked.

"He'll have to be."

"What does that mean?"

"It would be better if he had someone to share body heat with, but that's not really an option. We are in enemy territory. We all need to be ready to fight if it comes to that."

Nick shook his head. "We have fourteen lookouts. We'll have plenty of time to scramble for battle if it comes to that. If he needs body heat, give it to him. I'll stand guard in here."

"Is that really wise?" Sophia asked. "Shouldn't it be you to share body heat with him?"

Nick looked at her perplexed. "That makes no sense. With John out, I'm in command. You're the medic. Everyone else is on lookout duty. It's you or no one."

She nodded and got into her pack to take out her blanket. She unzipped their snowsuits, removed their flak jackets, and laid down next to him. Then she tucked the extra blanket around them and pulled John close to her to give him as much body heat as she could.

"You can get some rest while we wait. I'm not going to sleep, so you'll be safe. If anything comes up, I'll let you know," Nick said.

Sophia nodded and closed her eyes. She wasn't sure she could actually go to sleep. Her adrenaline was high, and after what Sonny had told her, she was worried about one of the other men coming up to the loft and getting the wrong idea about her and John.

Nick walked to the far end of the loft by the ladder and took up a lookout position. For a while, Sophia listened to the rest of Echo reporting to Nick.

The farmer came out just after dawn to feed the animals in the barn. After forty-five minutes, he returned to the house. It began snowing a short while later. Sophia stirred awake when she felt Nick tucking the blanket from his own pack around them.

"It's snowing now. The temperature is dropping. Make sure he stays warm enough," Nick said.

He returned to his post at the end of the loft. Sophia heard him checking in with the rest of Echo. Then the coms went silent. She went back to sleep. It was several hours later when she woke up. John's arms were curled snugly around her inside her open snowsuit; she couldn't move.

She tried to roll him off of her, but she couldn't budge him. She had no leverage.

She felt of his face; the prick of his heavy stubble pressed against her palm, but he wasn't feverish. She knew she should pull her hand away, but she didn't. Instead, she slid her hand up and ran her fingers through his burr. He moaned softly, and his left leg curled over her. She was trapped under him. Then she felt his lips pressing against her neck. She sucked in a surprised breath. Her eyes darted over to Nick at the far end of the loft. Nick's back was to them. He was intently watching the lower level of the barn.

She muted both their coms. "Sir! Are you awake?"

His head jerked back suddenly, and he stared down into her eyes. It took him a moment to process the situation.

"Get off me!"

"I'm sorry," he mumbled groggily as he tried to get off her.

He half fell, half rolled off her onto the blanket. He struggled to sit up, but she put a hand on his chest and gently shoved him back down.

"Just lie down," she said quietly. "You shouldn't try to get up and walk in your condition."

John lay back on the soft hay pallet and tried to focus on his surroundings. "Where are we?"

"A farm fifty klicks southwest of Novosibirsk."

"What happened with the op?"

"We got out without any incident."

He nodded and let out a sigh of relief. Then he reached down and pulled at the crotch of his fatigues. They were far too tight. He noticed the smirk on Sophia's face.

"Sorry about that. I didn't mean to—"

"Don't worry. You were asleep. It's not like you were aware of what you were doing."

He cleared his throat and looked away at the wooden wall to his left.

She chuckled softly. "Relax, Sir. I didn't take offense to anything you did."

He looked back at her and groaned. "What did I do?"

She glanced in Nick's direction. He hadn't heard them.

She put a finger to John's lips to quiet him. Then she leaned in closer and grinned down at him. "Nick is only a few feet away, Sir. Watch what you say."

John's eyes widened. He jerked his hand up to his ear.

"I already muted both our coms."

He let out a long breath. Then he leaned up on his elbows so he was closer to her. He could see Nick at the far end of the loft. He looked back into Sophia's eyes.

"What did I do?" he whispered.

She grinned at him and leaned in closer. Her cheek pressed against his stubbled jaw, and her lips lightly grazed his ear. "Nothing to be ashamed of, Sir. You were mostly a gentleman."

John's heart pounded in his chest like a jackhammer. "Mostly? What did I do, Gonzalez?" he whispered in her ear.

"You were dreaming. You tried to kiss my neck."

"Damnit!" he whispered. "I'm so sorry, Gonzalez. I would never have done that consciously."

"I know, Sir. I'm not holding it against you."

She slid her right hand up his chest and gently pushed him back to lie on the blanket. He closed his eyes and groaned softly. She pressed her palm against his forehead.

"You're not running a fever anymore. How are you feeling?"

He took a deep breath and let it out slowly. Then he opened his eyes and met hers. "Not great. I'm dizzy and a little disoriented. Everything is slightly blurry."

She nodded. Then she moved her hands down to his throat and checked his lymph glands.

"Swollen."

She got into her pack and pulled out an otoscope and a stethoscope. She put the stethoscope against the front of his shirt just over his left pec.

"Take a deep breath and let it out slowly."

He followed her instructions. She moved her stethoscope to his right pec and repeated her instructions.

"Your lungs don't sound great. You could have Pneumonia."

She used her otoscope to check his throat and his ears. "Sir, you have an ear infection in both ears, and your throat is very red. It could be Strep Throat."

"That's great," he muttered.

"I don't think you were in any condition to come on this mission. When we get back, you are going directly to see the doctor on base."

John couldn't help but grin at her. "Yes, Ma'am."

She grinned back.

Nick walked over and knelt down beside them. "How is he doing?"

"Not good," she sighed. "Two ear infections, possible Strep, and possible Pneumonia."

Nick frowned. "John, I told you; you should have stayed on base. I knew you were sicker than you were letting on. What good did it do you to come on a mission and pass out in the middle of an op? Sonny had to carry you for miles."

"You're right, Nick. I should have listened. Sometimes I'm too stubborn for my own good."

"We are a team. You can ask for help when you need it. You don't always have to be the lone hero," Nick said.

John nodded. "I know. I just feel guilty leaning on the team for anything. I am stubborn. I always think I can take care of everything myself. I'm sorry. I let the team down."

"You didn't let us down, but you are slowing us down. We are caught in a snow storm now. We'll have to wait it out and hope no one is following us."

John nodded. "I'll do my best to heal up during the storm. I'll walk out of here when it stops."

Nick shook his head. "No, you won't. One of the guys will carry you. If you're in that bad of condition, you shouldn't be overexerting yourself."

"I will walk out of here," John said. "I'm still giving the orders."

Nick rolled his eyes. "Stubborn ass! That's what you are, John. You never listen to reason."

John grinned. "I'm a typical SEAL just like you. We are all stubborn."

Nick held up a finger and unmuted his com. "Echo 2 here. Go for Echo 3."

"We have a bogy inbound in a black SUV," Sonny said.

Nick sprang into action and bolted toward the ladder. Sophia quickly put her flak jacket on and helped John refasten his flak jacket and zip his snowsuit. While John struggled to his feet. She grabbed the blankets and crammed them into the top of his pack. She put her medical equipment back in her pack and slid it back onto her shoulders. John fastened his pack and reached for his rifle.

When they reached the lower level of the barn, Nick signaled them to hold their position. Nick watched from the barn, and Sonny watched from his position five hundred yards away high up in a tree. The SUV crunched through the near blinding snow storm and stopped in front of the farmhouse.

Sonny clicked the safety off his sniper's rifle and trained his scope in on the SUV. Nick did the same inside the barn. A man exited the SUV on the driver's side and opened the back door. At the same time, a woman exited on the passenger's side and opened the passengers back door. After a minute, both the man and woman cradled their two small children against them as they made their way to the front door.

Nick breathed a sigh of relief. He spoke into his coms to the rest of the team. "This is Echo 2. False alarm. It looks like the kids and grandkids came to wait out the storm on the farm. We have a mother, father, and two kids. There doesn't seem to be any danger here."

Sonny clicked the safety back on and resumed his overwatch duties. "Copy that."

By 1330, the storm had subsided. It was still snowing, but only lightly. John gave the order to move out. Once past the farm, Echo used the forest for cover as they made their way south to the border of Kazakhstan.

Sophia followed close behind John. He'd insisted on walking, but Dorian had insisted that he would carry John's pack. Sophia was worried about him. He couldn't stop coughing, and he was walking slower and slower the farther they hiked. A few times, she saw him stop for a moment and brace himself against a tree. It was obvious he was still having problems with dizziness.

When they were ten klicks from the border, John fell to his knees in the deep snow. He braced his hands on the ground in front of him and struggled to maintain consciousness. He felt horrible. He wasn't sure he'd been this sick in his entire life.

Sophia was kneeling beside him a moment later.

"Sir, are you okay?"

"I'm fine. I just need a minute."

"Echo 16 to Echo 2."

Nike halted in his tracks and put his hand over his ear to hear better. "Echo 2, go for Echo 16."

The rest of Echo halted behind Nick.

"Echo 1 is struggling. He needs to rest for a few minutes."

"Copy that." Nick turned to look at the men behind him. "Take look out positions."

Echo spread out in the woods as Nick trekked back 500 yards to John and Sophia's position.

Nick dropped to his knee. "I'll have one of the men carry you, Sir."

"I can make it. I just need a minute."

Nick looked at Sophia. She shook her head, and he grimaced.

"Why don't I get two men to walk beside you. You can use them for support."

"I'm fine. I just need to catch my breath."

Nick frowned. "Don't be so stubborn. We can help you."

"We are in enemy territory. We all need to be alert. I can walk. I'm not helpless!"

Nick groaned. He knew it was pointless to argue with John. John was too stubborn.

When they crossed the border into Kazakhstan, Nick ordered Echo to take a break. He fell back to check on John who was dragging up the rear of the group with Sophia on his heels.

Sophia shook her head. "He's not doing well. His breathing is labored. His pace has slowed, and he's having difficulty walking a straight line."

She got into her pack and gave John medicine. He swallowed it with a pained look on his face.

"We need to keep moving. We're almost there." Another coughing fit overtook John.

"We've crossed the Russian border, Sir," Nick said. "Everyone could use a breather."

John nodded. Then he sank down on the snow and buried his head against his knees. "I just need a minute. I'll be fine." He started coughing again and couldn't stop for several minutes.

After half an hour, Nick ordered Echo to continue to the rendezvous point with Ben in the lead. He gave his pack to Mac, hoisted John onto his shoulders, and carried him the last forty klicks to the rendezvous point. John was in no condition to argue. He was having trouble breathing, and he couldn't stop coughing.

CHAPTER 51

January 25
0800
Afghanistan base

John stepped off the chopper after his stint in the Naples hospital. He reported to Rowen immediately. Rowen informed him that the team was on a mission and weren't due back until the following morning. He asked how John was feeling and took his report on the Novosibirsk mission. Nick had already turned in the official report, but John gave him his version of what he knew. Rowen dismissed him, and John went to the tent to lie down for a while. He was feeling much better, but he wasn't quite back to his old self yet.

When he woke up that afternoon, he called Kyle to check in.

"Hey, John. It's good to hear from you."

"Hey, Kyle. How is everyone doing?"

"Everyone is great. We got an ultra sound of the baby. Everything is good; the baby looks healthy, but Megan has been more exhausted with this pregnancy. I'm making her take it easy. How are you doing?"

"I just got out of the hospital. I caught some bug, and it kicked my tail for a while. I just got back to base. The team is out in the field, but they should be back soon."

"Bored out of your skull?"

John chuckled. "No, I actually slept most of the day. I just wanted to check in with you."

"I've got some really great news. Lydell's therapy is going better. He's starting to get a little feeling back in his leg. He was actually able to do a few leg lifts with the weights this week, and he took one step yesterday. He still has a long way to go, but he's making improvements."

"That's great! I'm glad to hear he's doing better. He was really down last time I saw him."

"He still is, but it's getting a little better. Taking that step yesterday lifted his spirits."

"Just curious, is Anna pregnant again?"

Kyle laughed. "Not that we know. Though her and Megan do seem to be on the same baby track. It wouldn't surprise me if she turns up pregnant soon."

John laughed. "You'd think that nine kids would be enough for Anna and Owen."

"I don't know how many they plan to have, but Owen told me they want a big family."

"How many do you plan to have?"

Kyle dragged his fingers through his silky, black hair and grinned. "We haven't decided on a number, but Megan wants to have a big family too. She and Owen were both only children. I think they both missed growing up with siblings. I had three siblings, but we weren't that close in age. Nissa is four years older, and Ireta is seven years older. There's an even bigger gap between me and Eli. I'm ten years older than him. By the time Eli was born, Ireta was almost out of high school."

"Are you guys close?"

Kyle sighed. "We try to be, but our lives were pulled in different directions once we moved out. Ireta is retired from the Marine's now, but she doesn't live close by. Her kids are in high school and middle school now. She's stays pretty busy. Nissa is a JAG lawyer. Her kids are still in elementary, but she is always busy with a case. Eli is another story altogether. He and I weren't exactly what you'd call close growing up. We played together, but it felt more like I was babysitting him than really playing with him—you know. When I joined the Navy, he was only eight years old."

"Yeah, I can see how that would put a wall between you two."

"I wouldn't call it a wall. We just haven't spent much time together as brothers. By the time I got out, he'd already joined a SEAL team. So, Eli stays busy all the time."

"Is that why you and Megan are having your kids so close together?"

"Partly. I would like our kids to be closer to each other than I was to my sisters and Eli. I want them to grow up playing together and having fun just being kids for a while."

"Sounds nice."

"How about you, John? Any plans to settle down yet? How is your situation with Sophia?"

John sighed. "I don't have a situation. I can't pursue it even if I wanted to. She's worked too hard to get here. I'm not going to be the guy to take that away from her. Besides, even if there weren't any obstacles between us, she has zero interest in me."

"There are other women in the world. Megan's tried to set you up with a lot of nice girls."

John shook his head. "I know you're right, but it's pointless, Kyle. Even if I wanted to pursue a girl who is free to be pursued, I suck at it. Every girl I've ever gone on a date with ends up hating my guts. You know how it is. I don't even know what I'm doing wrong until it's too late."

"You've had some bad luck, but that doesn't mean you won't succeed. You can't quit trying."

"I just can't face any more failures. It's a huge ego kicker!"

"Don't take it personally. A girl can't get to know you during one date. It takes time."

John scoffed. "Time? That's exactly the problem. None of them would give me time. After one date, none of them wanted to speak to me again. I'm a screw up. That's not going to change."

Kyle chuckled. "Maybe, you should consider an arranged marriage."

John rolled his eyes. "That's probably the only way I'll ever be able to get married. The problem is, if I screw up after the ceremony, we'll already be married. Then I'll be stuck with a wife that hates my guts, and it would end in divorce anyway."

Both men started laughing.

"Look, John, the right woman is out there for you. I have no idea what kind of woman it's going to take to get past your outer, offensive shell, but she's out there. Don't give up."

"I know you believe that, but I don't anymore. I'm giving up on women altogether."

Kyle frowned. "I don't like that kind of talk, John. You can't give up."

"I'm just tired of trying. I don't have it in me anymore, Kyle."

"I'm not trying to change the subject, but have you thought anymore about making amends with your parents? We've talked about it before, but you've never given me a straight answer."

John let out a heavy sigh. "I'm pretty sure they're happy I'm out of their lives."

"You don't know that unless you call them and talk to them. Maybe they miss you. Maybe they've had time to realize what a huge mistake they made with you growing up."

John rubbed his hand over his burr and closed his eyes. "I don't know. I'll think about it. They barely even talked to me when I lived there. When I told them I was joining the military right after high school, they had nothing to say about it. I think they truly regretted having a kid."

"I know. You've told me what it was like growing up in your family. I can't even imagine having parents that don't speak to each other or their kid. I'm sorry you had to grow up like that."

John sighed. "I try not to think about unhappy memories. I just try to focus on the present."

Kyle got up and grabbed little Buck before he made it over the baby gate. Then he deposited him on the floor next to Mandy, who was playing with her little plastic tea set.

"I don't want you to end this call on an unhappy subject. So, I'm going to put Mandy on."

"Hi, Unka John." Mandy's sweet voice cooed over the phone.

John grinned. "Hi, Mandy. What are you doing?"

"I play with my tea set."

"You are? Are you sharing with your brother?"

"No. Buck no like tea. He chew on my plates!"

John chuckled. "Well, maybe when he gets bigger he'll like tea."

"Buck try to eat Fluffy!" she pouted.

"He did!" John feigned surprise.

"He slobber on Fluffy! Daddy had to wash him."

"Is Fluffy clean now?"

"Yeah. He smell good. I love you, Unka John."

"I love you too, Mandy."

"She's done now," Kyle chuckled. "She's off chasing Buck. He took her teapot, and he's running as fast as his little legs will carry him."

John wrapped up his call with Kyle and sat on his bed staring at the empty bunks inside the tent. After a while, he stood up and opened Sophia's locker. He knew he shouldn't be snooping through her things, but he was bored—no—he was curious.

He pulled out her phone and opened up her picture gallery. Most of the photos were of her family. Some were of her and various men. It was obvious they were men she'd served with; everyone was in uniform. Some were Marines. Others were Navy. There were two selfies of her and two different men. One man had a blonde burr. The other had a black burr. They were both very handsome, and they were both staring at her like she was their priceless treasure. One selfie was labeled Sam. The other was labeled Butch. He scrolled through her text messages. There was a recent text from Sam. He knew he was being a complete ass by violating her privacy, but he was too curious to put the phone down. He opened the text.

January 14

Sam: Hey, Soph. It's been a while since we last talked. I know you said no, but I haven't given up. I still want to marry you. I know I screwed up. Please call me.

Sophia: Hi, Sam. You didn't screw up. We just want different things in life. You want a wife and kids. We aren't compatible. I'm not willing to give up the SEALs to stay at home. This is what I'm meant to do.

Sam: I'm not asking you to give up being a SEAL. I should never have suggested that. It was stupid on my part. I made a horrible mistake. It was my own fear that got in the way. I was wrong to ask you to get out of the Navy for my sake. I'll learn how to deal with the worry and stress of having a SEAL for a wife. I just don't want to lose you.

Sophia: I don't want to hurt you again. I hated watching you cry when I broke up with you, but nothing has changed. I'm not in love with you. I can't marry you. I won't cheat you like that. You're a good man. You deserve to have a woman who is all in. I'll never be that woman. I've dedicated my life to being a soldier.

I'm a single-minded weapon whose sole purpose is to defend our country. That's all I am. That's all I'll ever be. Stop hoping for something that's never going to happen.

John shut her phone off and put it back in her locker. He sat back down on his bed and let out a heavy sigh. Snooping through her things only confirmed what he already knew. Sophia was a soldier. That's all she wanted to be. She had no interest in men or relationships. Her only interest was to serve her country to her dying breath.

Stop thinking about her. She's off limits. If she wouldn't give her heart to Sam, she most definitely won't give it to me. Hell! Even my own parents couldn't love me. It's no wonder women find me repulsive. I don't know why I ever held out any hope that a woman would actually love me. I'm not lovable. I'm a worthless piece of—

He swiped away traitorous tears. The problem was, they wouldn't stop. He was usually good at tamping down his emotions, but today they were raw, and he couldn't tamp down the pain. He was grateful that he was alone in the tent. It wouldn't do to show weakness in front of his men.

February 14
0600
Afghanistan base, Mess Hall

Sophia finished breakfast and was on her way back to the tents when Sonny caught up to her.

"Hey, can we talk in private for a minute?" Sonny asked.

She smirked. "You're not afraid of what it would look like if we are seen walking off together? People might get the wrong idea, Sonny."

He chuckled. "I suppose you're right. How about we talk right here out in the open. No one can get the wrong idea that way."

She stopped and turned to face him. He stepped closer and lowered his voice so anyone walking past wouldn't hear him.

"I know we had that talk a ways back, and I've been watchin' you. I just wanted to say that I've seen vast improvements in your interactions.

Yer bein' a lot more careful about how you interact with all the men now. I'm officially apologizin' fer the way I come down on you. I see you don't have no interest in men at all. You're frickin' immune to us. So, I'm sorry."

"You don't need to apologize, Sonny. I know you were just trying to be a good friend and look out for me. I needed someone to be brutally honest with me. I did have blinders on. I thought if I was good enough it wouldn't matter if I was a woman. That was foolish on my part. People will always see the cover first."

He grinned at her. "So, are we okay?"

"We are great! You are the best friend I've ever had, and just between us—I'm not immune."

He winked at her. "I know. You got a soft spot in yer heart for me. I told ya I'd wear ya down eventually. So, anytime you feel lonely. You know where my bunk is."

She smirked, and he chuckled.

John cleared his throat from behind Sonny. "Can I talk to you, Sonny!"

"Sure, Boss."

Sonny followed John. Sophia's eyebrow rose, and curiosity sparked inside her. She followed them to the stacks of wooden crates near the front gate. She concealed herself between two tall stacks just out of their line of sight and listened intently to their conversation.

"Sonny, do I really need to go over this again?"

"Go over what?"

"I told all of you that Gonzalez is off limits! That especially applies to you! She is not interested in some tryst with any of you—especially with you! You have a well-earned, bad reputation! Stay away from her!"

"For your information, I wasn't tryin' to start nothin' with her, John! We was just talkin'. It was innocent conversation. Am I not allowed to have a platonic conversation with a teammate?"

"It didn't sound platonic to me! I heard you."

"What did you hear?"

"Anytime you feel lonely. You know where my bunk is. What was that?" John demanded.

"That there was a joke. She knew I was kiddin'."

"It didn't sound like a joke! It sounded like a proposition!"

"Don't start with me, John! It was just a joke. I wasn't trying to get in her panties."

John glared at Sonny. "Since when are you not trying to get into a pretty girl's panties. That's what you do, Mr.-King-of-the-one-night-stand!"

"Well, I seen the light, okay! I done give up sleepin' around. I don't do that no more."

John crossed his arms over his chest and continued to glare at Sonny.

"You can stand there and give me the evil-eye all day. It don't change nothin'. There ain't nothin' going on between Sophia and me. There ain't nothin' going on between Sophia and any man on this base. There especially ain't nothin' going on between you and her, no matter how bad you wish there was. She don't see you like that. She don't see any man like that. She's pure soldier, John."

"You're out of line, Sonny!"

"Am I? You sound pretty jealous to me. You didn't hesitate to rip me a new one the second you thought I was tryin' to move in on your territory."

John shoved Sonny back a step. "I said, you're out of line!"

Sonny shook his head and started walking away.

"I didn't dismiss you!" John growled.

Sonny walked back to face him. "What else do you want to say to me?"

"Gonzalez is here to serve. She's not here to get involved with anyone. I don't know if I believe you or not, but I'm warning you to steer clear of her from now on."

"You saying you don't trust me with her?"

"I—I'm just saying don't give me a reason not to trust you."

Sonny walked over to John shaking his head. "John, we been friends for a long time. I don't stab friends in the back. I especially don't steal a woman when I know my best friend's in love with her. You ain't got nothin' to worry about. I know she belongs to you. I ain't trying to start nothin' with her. I wouldn't hurt you like that."

"I'm not in love with her."

"You keep tellin' yerself that long enough, and you might actually start to believe it."

"I'm not. Stop trying to force something that isn't there. She's a soldier. I'm her commanding officer. That is the extent of our relationship. Don't make it into something it's not!"

"That might be the extent of your relationship, but that ain't what you wish it was."

"Sonny, I'm tired of having this conversation with you. You want to know the truth?"

"Sure."

"The truth is I'm never getting married to anyone. I'm not going out on one more of Megan's stupid blind dates! I'm not looking for a girl anymore! I'm done with it. I'm not in love with anyone, and I don't want to be."

"Now, that's a damn lie."

"No, it isn't."

"You're lying to yourself. You do want to be in love. The trouble is, you don't know how to talk to girls. That's why you have such rotten luck. You just need to take some lessons on how to flirt, how to charm a woman."

"No. I'm done with women for good!"

"You're just tired of being rejected. I get that. It don't feel good to have yer ego stamped into the dirt, but if you believe for one second that you don't want love—you're dumber than cotton candy in a rain storm. You want someone to love you so bad it hurts—don't it? I can see it all over you. It ain't enough that me, Nick, and Kyle love you like a brother. That ain't the kind of love you need right now. Your damn parents done messed your head up good. I don't think you even feel worthy of love. Am I wrong?"

John's jaw tightened, and a tear slid down his cheek. He turned his back on Sonny.

"Damn, John. I didn't mean to make you cry. I just don't want to see you make a mistake that you'll regret for the rest of your life. You need a woman's love. Don't give up looking for that."

Sophia swiped away the tears that had escaped down her cheeks.

"Just go away," John muttered.

Sonny shook his head, and walked away. Once Sonny was gone, Sophia peeked around the corner. She saw John sitting on the ground with his face buried against his knees and his arms covering his head. She couldn't hear him crying, but it was obvious that he was. His whole body was jerking with sobs. She watched him, and her own tears fell to the sand at her feet. She felt bad for him, but she knew better than to walk over to him at that moment. She knew it would hurt his pride if he knew she'd seen him crying. She wished there was something she could do, but she didn't know how to help him.

She returned to the tent to find most of Echo sitting on their bunks. A few men were playing card games. Two were writing letters. The rest were lying on their bunks staring at the roof.

Sonny wasn't there. She couldn't help but wonder where he'd gone.

It was a long while before John returned to the tent.

"Did you talk to Rowen?" Nick asked.

John nodded. "No news so far. Looks like we might actually get the whole day off."

Nick picked up the book he was reading and lay back on the bed. John sat down on his bunk and let out a long sigh.

Sophia sat up facing him. "Are you okay, Sir?"

"Yeah." His voice held no enthusiasm.

She frowned. "Are you feeling okay?"

"Yeah. I'm fine."

She stood up and placed her hand on his forehead. Then she sat back down and grinned at him. "I was just checking for fever. You don't like to admit when you're sick."

John grinned back at her. "I'm not sick. I'm fine."

"That's what you said last time."

He shook his head. "Not going to live that down, am I?"

She shook her head. "No, Sir. I won't take your word for it again. We nearly lost you. I won't let that happen again. I'm going to keep a close eye on you."

"We all are," Nick muttered from his bunk. "Next time you're sick stay home."

John smirked. "I'll think about it."

"No, you won't," Nick grumbled. Then he went back to reading his book.

Sophia glanced back at John, and he quickly looked away. He cleared his throat, stood up, and left the tent. She had the urge to get up and follow him, but she quelled it. It wasn't worth satisfying her curiosity to draw attention to John. Sonny's words kept playing in her head, and she knew it would look suspicious if she followed him outside.

CHAPTER 52

March 1
0300
Uzbekistan

Bretta watched from behind the one-way observation glass. The interrogation wasn't going well. The subject was stubborn and uncooperative. Despite being captured with highly incriminating evidence, he continued to proclaim his innocence. She pulled out her phone and called the man interrogating the subject.

"Give him the serum. We've wasted enough time. I need answers, and I need them now."

He looked at the man handcuffed to the chair and frowned. "That serum is not to be used lightly."

"We don't have time to get answers the old-fashioned way. Give him the serum. Then eliminate him and burn his body. We can't take any chances here. We are on precarious ground."

"As you wish."

March 3
1200
Civitavecchia, Italy

Bretta sat in front of her laptop in her hotel room. She glanced up when she heard a boat horn sound as it came into port. The Tyrrhenian Sea lay before her with it's beautiful blue water glistening in the noonday sun.

She saved and encrypted the file onto a flash drive. Then she slid the drive into her pocket and shut down her laptop. She checked her watch and hurried from the hotel to catch the next train to Rome. It would be a forty-five-minute ride, seventy klicks to her rendezvous.

She arrived at the Trevi Fountain in Rome twenty minutes ahead of schedule, surveyed the area, and did recon. Then she posed as a tourist taking photos of the famous fountain. She even threw in the customary three coins to wish for a safe return to find true love and marry.

Her watch beeped two minutes before the emissary was due to arrive. She spotted Vlad following her instructions to the letter. He threw three coins in the fountain and headed directly for the Spanish Steps. Following him, she weaved casually—inconspicuously—among the throng of tourists. When he was halfway up the Spanish Steps, Bretta closed the gap and pressed the encrypted flash drive into the emissary's palm as she passed him. Built in 1723, the 138-step work of art was the perfect place for a handoff. It was always swarming with tourists, and it was easy to get lost in the crowds.

Getting lost in a crowd was Bretta's specialty. As soon as she passed him, she stepped behind a group of tourists who were getting their picture taken by a friendly stranger. She quickly removed the ebony wig, the false nose and chin, and the white cardigan sweater and deposited them in her handbag. Then she stepped out from behind the group of tourists and walked directly in front of him. He looked right at her with her now blonde wig and showed no sign of recognition.

Vlad stood on the step searching the crowd for a moment, but his contact had vanished before his eyes. His boss would not be pleased. He'd been instructed to follow her and report everything. Now, he would come back empty-handed, save the flash drive he deposited into his pocket.

Bretta observed Vlad for a few minutes from a safe distance. She grinned knowing she had put that distraught expression on his face. He'd specifically requested a face to face meeting. Bretta didn't do face to face anything unless it was absolutely necessary. Too much personal contact led to messes that had to be cleaned up, like the mess in Congo, when she'd killed Jakeem Sayad. His handler had made quite a scene with her superiors when he'd accused her of making Sayad disappear. Luckily, Bretta was on a very long leash that required very little accountability. She was authorized to do pretty much anything as long as the bigger objective was achieved.

She left Vlad standing perplexed on the Spanish Steps and caught a train back to Civitavecchia to await further instructions. The stakes were high in this game of entropy. The slightest mistake could be catastrophic. An empire could be toppled, an economy crashed, or worse. If what she suspected were true, the major players were setting up the chess board for another world war. The pieces were in play. The only question was who would call checkmate in the end. She was determined to ensure that her side won at any cost.

The coup in Congo was only the beginning. The royal courts of the world were preparing to line their coffers with treasure in preparation for what was to come. Bretta was gifted with the unique advantage of position and knowledge. Knowledge was the only currency that mattered in the game she was playing. The more she knew, the better prepared she could be when the final plays were made.

She didn't have long to wait. The following morning, she received new orders. A big play was in the works. Pieces would have to be set in place. Certain sacrifices would have to be made.

CHAPTER 53

March 9
0500
Afghanistan base

John stood in Rowen's tent getting briefed on an urgent mission. Based on intel from the CIA, Echo would be transported to a U.S. Naval submarine currently located in the Arctic circle. They would infiltrate a military facility on one of the tiny islands of Zemlya Frantsa in the heart of the Arctic Ocean.

"Your CIA contact will be on the sub," Rowen said.

"Do we have a name?" John asked.

Rowen smirked. "Mark T. Wain."

"Not a very original cover name."

"I don't think it's meant to be."

Rowen dismissed John, and he immediately went to wake his team. To his surprise the tent was empty. He found Echo in the supply building filling their packs.

"Anytime Rowen gets you up this early for a mission it's critical," Nick said.

John nodded. "The chopper should be here in twenty minutes to pick us up." He glanced around at the men scurrying to pack their bags. "Where's Gonzalez?"

"She went to the bathroom to change. She didn't want to slow us down or defy your orders. She should be here any minute," Ben said.

"Has she packed yet?" John asked.

"I'm done. I brought her pack with me. I'll pack for her," Jerome said.

John began loading up his own pack. Sophia arrived three minutes later and took over preparing her pack.

"Thank you, Jerome."

"No, problem, Soph."

Echo was ready and waiting when the chopper arrived. A few hours later, they were on a transport plane from Turkey to Norway. That was followed by a flight over the Barents Sea to the Svalbard islands in the Arctic Ocean. A chopper ride from there brought them to their rendezvous with the Seawolf SSN-21, the most advanced submarine class in the U.S. Navy. They repelled down the rope to the sub and were escorted below deck. No sooner had the last member of Echo entered the sub than they sealed the hatch and descended back into the icy depths of the ocean.

Echo was shown to the empty mess hall where their CIA contact, Mark, was waiting.

"Have you been briefed on the mission?" Mark asked.

"Only on the destination," John said.

Mark went over the target package with specifics about what data he wanted them to gather. He also provided schematics of the facility and a satellite image of the entire island with up-close images of the military site.

"You can see there are exterior guards posted. This is a zero-footprint mission. Under no circumstances are you to alert the guards or anyone else to your presence. Get in and out undetected. If you are noticed by anyone at this facility, there will be catastrophic repercussions. This op is being run in conjunction with other ops. There is an interconnected web of conspiracy that we are trying to unravel. This is only one piece of the intricate puzzle. Whatever you do, don't screw this up," Mark said.

"Echo delivers results. We don't screw things up," John said.

Mark nodded. "I haven't worked with your team before, but I've heard good things about you. That's why I specifically requested you for this op. It's extremely sensitive and potentially volatile. You'll be on Russian soil, infiltrating a military guarded facility."

"That's kind of our thing," Sonny drawled. "Russia is our private playground; ain't it, Boys?"

Several men chuckled and grinned at Mark.

Mark grinned back. "Good. That's exactly what I want to hear."

For the next two hours, Mark went over schematics of the building and maps of the terrain surrounding the facility. Then John went to work strategizing entry points and assigning jobs to each member of Echo.

When it was time, Echo geared up and took a short swim in the Arctic water to the northern shore of the northernmost island in the Zemlya Frantsa chain. The Seawolf was submerged just off shore waiting for their return. Their window of opportunity for a zero-footprint infiltration was tight. There was no room for mistakes.

Sonny and Sophia took up Overwatch positions outside the fence line, and half of Echo took up assault positions nearby. Mac used rubber gloves to pull up a section of the electrified fence while the insertion team belly crawled under. The insertion team quietly made their way toward the facility. It was dark, but everything was covered in snow so visibility was good for any Russian soldier patrolling the grounds. With Sonny and Sophia's guidance, Echo managed to avoid contact with the patrolling guards, but the code Mark had given them did not open the door. Nick had to quickly hack the digital lock before another guard made a pass through the area. The last SEAL entered the facility only a few seconds before one of the guards passed by. They all breathed a sigh of relief.

Their next obstacle was avoiding the security cameras until they reached the interior guard post. They belly crawled past the window of the security office where an extremely bored guard sat sipping coffee and staring blankly at the live security footage of the facility.

When they reached the lab in sub-sector-2, Nick was once again forced to hack the digital lock; it seemed none of Mark's security codes worked. They entered the lab careful to avoid the security camera. In the corner, a robot methodically filled test tubes with a purple liquid.

John hand-signaled Ben, who was closest to the robot, to procure a sample of the purple liquid. Ben nodded and waited for the opportune moment to fill a vile and cap it off. Then he gave John the thumbs up.

A thorough scan of the lab revealed that robots were doing the tedious work of exact mixing, but there were two computer terminals on the south wall of the lab. John carefully adjusted the camera to point away from the terminals, and Nick went to work hacking into one.

The rest of Echo waited patiently while Nick downloaded the data to a flash drive. Once he finished, John slowly readjusted the camera to its original position.

There was one more task for them to complete before they could return to the Seawolf. They made their way down to sub-sector-5. Nick hacked the lock, and they entered the sub-zero level. John ordered Dorian and Andrew to stay on the landing by the door to guard it. The rest of Echo descended into the large sub-terranean room. Everything was covered in a thick layer of frost. They were careful not to slip on the narrow metal stairs that led down to the cryofreeze tanks.

Again, robots were doing the tedious work in this section of the building. There were no security cameras on this level, but that didn't make the task any easier. Their semi-damp wetsuits were beginning to stick to their skin in the frigid room.

There were five large cryo-tanks that were filled with frozen embryos. Mark wanted a sample embryo brought back in tact in a cryo-tube. Ben pulled the empty cryo-tube Mark had provided from the small pack on his back. Then he and John went to work procuring an embryo from one of the large cryo-tanks.

As instructed, Nick videoed everything in the large room. By the time Ben and John finished their task, Nick had thoroughly documented everything on that level. There were strange machines along the back wall that no one on Echo could identify. Their purpose seemed to be to knead a stringy, viscous substance that glowed orange. Ben procured a small sample of the orange substance in a vile, and they all exited sub-sector-5 together.

Getting out of the facility was as precarious as getting in. Avoiding the occasional drowsy guard in the hallways was the first obstacle. They belly crawled past the guard watching the security footage and made their way back to the exterior door.

Once outside, the biting wind reminded them exactly where they were—The Arctic! Sonny's drawl came over their comlinks.

"Ya'll took yer time in there. Our window is about to close. Hang out there for about another seventy-five seconds. Then make yer way back to the fence. The guard is almost to the end of the building."

They waited patiently until Sonny told them it was clear to proceed. Once outside the fence line, they hurried back to where they'd left their scuba gear. Ezra signaled the Seawolf that they were on their way back to the extraction point. Then Echo made the dive into the frigid Arctic Ocean once more.

Back on board they handed over all evidence to Mark and changed into dry uniforms. The Seawolf returned to the Norwegian coast near Svalbard where a helicopter rendezvoused to pick up the SEAL team and transport them back to land.

No sooner had Echo arrived on base than Rowen informed John that Echo would be shipping out first thing in the morning. The weary SEALs hit their bunks to get as much sleep as possible before their next mission.

CHAPTER 54

March 24
2400
Afghanistan base

Sophia sat on the chopper with the rest of Echo. She couldn't help that her eyes kept wandering to John. Since February, she'd been watching him. Hearing Sonny say that John was in love with her had piqued her curiosity. She needed to know if it was true. She wanted to know if she would have to kill his dreams. To her relief, she'd seen no evidence that John had any feelings for her. He virtually ignored her unless he was giving her an order. There were no outward signs that Sonny was right. She inwardly breathed a sigh of relief. She didn't relish having to crush a man's spirit the way she'd crushed Sam.

Once the chopper dropped them back on base, Echo cleaned up and hit their bunks. She went to bed and drifted into a light sleep but stirred when she heard John sit up on his bed. She opened her eyes and watched him put his boots on in the dark. Then he quietly walked out of the tent. Curiosity overcame her when he didn't come back. After half an hour, she quietly put her boots on and went to look for him. She found him sitting on the ground behind the ammo building. He looked dejected. She walked over to him.

"Sir, are you alright?"

He stood up and checked to make sure they were alone.

"I'm fine. You should be in bed. You never know when they are going to call us up on a mission. You need to get your rest while you can, Gonzalez."

"I could say the same for you. Why are you up? It's 0200."

"I can't sleep."

"What's keeping you up?"

"Nothing important."

She frowned. "If it wasn't important, you wouldn't be awake stressing about it."

"It's not something I can discuss with you."

"Sir, am I the subject of this problem? Is that why you can't share?"

John grimaced.

"I know there's something bothering you. I have a feeling that I'm somehow to blame for it."

"Why would you say that?"

"I've heard through the grapevine that your decision to put me on the team killed any chance you have at getting a promotion in the future."

"Who told you that?"

"Is it true?"

His jaw tightened, and he looked away.

"It is true, isn't it?"

"The truth is I have no idea what the future holds in regards to my career. To be honest, I don't really care. I didn't ask to be the leader of Echo. I never even wanted it. When the team was decimated, I was the most qualified to lead Echo. So, I stepped up. If choosing you for the team killed my career, then so be it. I'm not here to climb some career ladder in the Navy. I'm just here to be the best SEAL I can be. I saw that you were passed over by the other teams. When you were passed over twice—"

"You felt sorry for me."

He shook his head. "No. I've never felt sorry for you."

"Why did you choose me for the team?"

"I chose you because you were the best fit for Echo. Those other teams missed out on a great soldier. It's their loss."

"Why did you pick me to be the medic over the other men on the team?"

He grinned. "Six months of cramming your brain with medical knowledge is no easy task. I knew you could handle it the best. You're the smartest person on this team. Your intelligence scores are off the chart, Gonzalez. Your only rival is Nick, but I couldn't spare Nick for med training. I need him for too many other tasks."

"Thanks for satisfying my curiosity, Sir. I think I'll take a walk before I turn in."

She turned to leave, and John caught her by the wrist and pulled her back. She stumbled, bumped into his chest, and looked up into his eyes. There was something new in his serious expression—something pleading—sincere. Her heart skipped a beat.

"The men on Echo know I'd kick their ass if they even look at you wrong. The rest of the men on this base don't fall under that category. I don't like the way some of them look at you. I'm not doing this to be an ass or to treat you differently than the other men. I'm trying to protect you."

She looked at his hand curled firmly around her wrist. He immediately let go of her.

"Now, go back to bed. That's an order Gonzalez."

As soon as she walked away, he followed to ensure she made it safely back to the tent. He knew the men on base were all honorable soldiers, and his paranoia was probably unfounded, but he wasn't willing to risk it. He'd never forgive himself if something happened to her. Protecting her wasn't an option in his book.

CHAPTER 55

March 30
1100
Military base in Turkey

Echo landed in Turkey with a new set of orders. They would be splitting up for this particular mission. John didn't like it. He didn't agree with Rowen's decision, but he wasn't being given a choice. All he could do was follow orders and hope everything worked out the way it was supposed to. John split the team up and gave them instructions.

A small team of six consisting of John, Nick, Sonny, Mac, Falco, and Sophia would be infiltrating and documenting a facility in Siberia. Nine years ago, Echo had been sent on a mission to destroy this facility. Kyle had been the C.O. then. He'd disobeyed that order when he found the unexpected there. Now, Echo was being sent back a second time. This time they'd been ordered to leave zero-footprint. The CIA wanted viable intel, and it had to be kept top secret. If the Russian military were to discover any infiltration, things could go south like the previous mission.

Nine years ago, a super soldier project was being conducted at the remote Siberian facility. Kyle had returned with digital evidence of the experiment, but by the time the United Nations and the World Court took action to investigate the violation of Geneva Convention Protocols, the Russian military had wiped away any evidence of the project.

This time, the CIA wanted evidence to be collected in secret to prevent the military from being forewarned and destroying it before it could be acted upon. John had been ordered to take a small force into Siberia to collect evidence. The rest of Echo were being sent on a covert op to gather intel deep in the Saharan desert in southern Algeria.

John was less worried about the team he was leading into Siberia. He was taking two of the most qualified people with him. The second team would be comprised of four senior Echo members and six greens. Ben had never taken the lead position before, but John was less concerned about Ben and more concerned that the greens would try something reckless.

John watched over half his team board the transport plane without him. His gut tightened. He didn't like any part of this. The plane took off heading west with the second team led by Ben. On the flight to Algeria, their CIA contact Mark T. Wain went over the target package with the team.

At 2200, John's team did a HALO jump deep in Siberian territory. After what happened the last time, John was extra careful on the glacial ice. He led the way with the five members of Echo tethered behind him. They were on a deadline, but he intended to make up time after they traversed the precarious ice that lay between them and their target.

It had not escaped Sonny or Nick's attention that, even though Echo was split into two teams for this particular mission, John had assigned Sophia to his team. That put both snipers and both medics on one team, and left the other half of the team without those skill sets.

Sonny made his way across the ice tethered behind Sophia. He couldn't help staring at her ass; it was right there in front of him for hours and hours and hours.

Logically, she should have been assigned to Ben for this mission. They would have had a sniper and medic in one with her. There's only one way her being with us makes any sense. John's decision to bring her originated below the belt. He wants her close so he can protect her from every single thing he can control. I don't care what he says, he's in love with her.

March 31
2300
Sahara Desert, Algeria

Ben Obasi gave the signal to move in closer. Hogan, Ezra, and Zach crept down the sand dune toward the encampment below. The rest of Echo held defensive positions with their rifles trained on the grouping of tents in the valley. Ezra planted trackers on the trucks while Hogan and Zach kept watch for any movement in the camp. Once the trackers were placed, they rejoined Echo.

April 1
0200
Military facility, Siberia

John crept slowly toward the facility. The guards were more active than he had expected. Their patrols came in frequent intervals. He could see security cameras on the outside of the facility. It was going to be hard to get in undetected and get back out. He lay in the snow just outside the fence line scanning every detail of the building and its security with his night vision binoculars. He lay there for hours cataloguing everything. Two hours before dawn, he crept slowly back and rendezvoused with the rest of Echo in the forest to the southwest of the facility.

"I didn't see any weaknesses from my position. Did you?" Falco asked.

John shook his head. "They have it well guarded. Between the patrolling guards and the security cameras, it's not going to be easy."

Nick let out a heavy sigh. "I agree. Last time we were here we picked off the exterior guards and then took out the interior guards. We weren't worried about detection. We were here to destroy the building and everything in it."

"I don't like this. There is no good angle to approach the facility," John said.

"What about the trucks?" Sonny suggested.

"What about them?" Mac asked.

Sonny grinned. "We could hitch a ride on one of them trucks when they go out to do their vehicular patrol. They make a wide circle of the perimeter and then return to the motor pool on the north end of the building. They patrol every two hours like clockwork."

"There are soldiers in the back of those trucks," Nick countered. "You can't ride in the back."

"I was thinkin' of hitchin' a ride on the under carriage," Sonny drawled. "They stop outside the fence line to wait fer the guards to open the gate. Then they head straight to the garage."

John chewed on his bottom lip as he considered Sonny's suggestion. "That's risky. If that's your way in, it's also your way out. The fence is electrified."

"I think it would work," Nick said. "It would bypass the exterior security cameras, and it's the last thing they would expect."

John nodded. "We go two per truck. Nick and Mac take the first truck. Falco and I will take the second truck. Sonny and Sophia, you're Overwatch. Sonny you take the northwest spot. Sophia you take the southeast spot."

"When do you want to hit it?" Sonny asked.

"At 2100 just before the shift change. The guards will be tired and ready for their shift to be over. They'll be less likely to notice something out of the ordinary. We'll exit the same way at 0500 before the morning shift comes on. We'll have to be out of sight before dawn."

April 2
2100
Siberia

John, Nick, Mac, and Falco lay face down in the snow near the road. They could hear the sound of the approaching trucks. As soon as the trucks halted to wait for the gate to open, the SEALs rolled under the trucks and secured themselves to the chassis with rope and hooks.

"Echo 3 to Echo 16," Sonny spoke into his com.

"Echo 16, go for Echo 3."

"The mailman has picked up the packages."

"Copy."

Both had their rifle scopes trained on the building scanning for any sign of trouble.

Inside the garage, Echo waited for the soldiers to get out of the trucks. The weary soldiers trudged their way from the trucks to the interior door. They were gone within minutes. Echo unhooked from the chassis and scanned the garage. There was only one security camera pointed toward the trucks. Echo easily avoided its line of sight.

The next obstacle would be getting inside the door. "Fingerprint scanner," Nick whispered.

Mac handed the kit to Nick. Nick quickly defeated the lock with hairspray and a rubber thumb sleeve. They slipped inside and stayed out of the hallway camera's scope.

"This has changed since we were here," Nick whispered. "The first floor was mostly open. Now, it's full of small rooms."

They reached the main entrance to the labyrinth of laboratories. It was protected by a retinal scanner. They found a supply closet, and Nick and Mac infiltrated the labs via the ceiling ventilation system. John and Falco proceeded to the second floor to obtain any evidence there. They had to circumvent a retinal scanner in the same manner.

While Nick encountered chemical experiments and a server room to hack, John encountered something much different. He and Falco used the ventilation system to crawl over the immense lab on the second floor. Scientists in white coats were monitoring unconscious men in hospital beds on the south end of the floor. John recorded everything he passed. When he reached the north end of the room there were large tanks with a green, viscous liquid and live human subjects inside.

They are clones!

John scrolled back through the pictures he had taken and realized that every subject in the beds below had the same face. They were identical clones. He signaled Falco to head back. They rendezvoused with Nick and Mac on the first floor and carefully made their way back to the garage. There were a lot of cameras to avoid and the occasional scientist roaming the hallway.

Just before the shift change, they strapped themselves back to the under carriage of the trucks. They had to ride the entire patrol under the trucks and detach when the trucks returned to the gate. As soon as it was safe, they began the slow crawl to the woods. Sonny and Sophia joined them.

"Did ya get what we needed?" Sonny asked.

John nodded. "It's a cloning facility."

"That's not all," Nick said. "I found evidence in the labs downstairs of genetic manipulation. It looks like our little Russian pals are creating a genetically enhanced clone army."

Falco grimaced. "That's smart. They don't have to pay average citizens to do subpar work. They make their own soldiers bigger and better. An army with genetic enhancements that can be programed to do anything you want them to. Russia has gone too far."

"I don't think it's just Russia. I saw some formulaic calculations and periodic table combinations that were familiar," Nick said. "I've seen the same exact data in Novosibirsk and Poltava. It looks like we've stumbled onto something much bigger than one cloning facility."

"We didn't stumble onto anything," John muttered. "The CIA has been sending us on errands to gather evidence for months. So, if they know about it, why are they allowing it to continue?"

John ordered them to move out through the woods and put some distance between them and the facility. Soon, the temperature started to drop, and it began to snow.

"Should we stop and make camp to wait out the storm?" Mac asked.

"No, the fresh snow will cover our tracks. Keep moving. We are heading south," John said.

They trudged on the entire day in the immense forest. At dusk, they took a break to eat and sat leaning against tree trunks as they consumed the cold, tasteless MREs. It was then they heard the long, mournful howl of a wolf as the moon crested the horizon. That wolf was joined by more. Soon, there was a cacophony of wolf song filling the night sky.

"How many are you counting?" Falco asked.

All six SEALs got to their feet and trained their rifles toward the woods beyond.

"I lost count," Nick said. "That's a lot of wolves out there."

Mac braced his rifle against his shoulder. "They sound close.

The howling grew louder.

"I think we should take cover in the trees," Sonny suggested. "I don't like the sound of this. We might not have enough ammo to take down this bunch."

"Agreed." John signaled for them to climb.

No sooner than the last SEAL made it to safety in the branches above than the first wolf appeared in the small clearing below. Several more appeared within seconds. They sniffed the ground and the air. Then they spotted their prey in the branches above. Several wolves scrambled scratching against the tree trunks for purchase, but they could not reach the SEALs.

Soon the small clearing was crowded with the large, Siberian wolves. They clamored on each other's backs to get to their prey. The SEALs moved up higher in the trees to avoid the desperate wolves. A few wolves made it to the lowest branches and began scrabbling upwards. Their snarling jaws were hungry for a meal.

"Good call, Sonny," Falco called from his tree. "I'm counting at least seventy-five wolves in the clearing, and there are more coming from the forest."

"I thought wolves were supposed to run in small packs," Sophia said.

"They do, but I've read about these Siberian wolves," Nick said. "When food is scarce, they band together in larger packs and take down anything in their path. A few years back, a pack of 400 Siberian wolves were marauding the towns and villages. They were killing mass numbers of reindeer, horses, and cattle. The Siberian authorities actually lifted the restrictions on killing wolves and were paying wolf hunters a lot of money per pelt to decrease the wolf population."

Sonny chuckled. "Are they still payin' big bucks per pelt? I got me plenty of ammo. I could make a fortune right here. I'm countin' near abouts 200 of them critters down there."

"Conserve your ammo, Sonny," John said sternly. "We might need it later."

"How long are we going to wait them out in the trees?" Mac asked.

"As long as we have to," John said. "We've got MREs."

"Can we feed them MREs to the wolves?" Sonny joked.

After three hours, the wolves had not given up their quest for the SEALs. They were just as frantic as before.

"Fellers, I got me an idea."

Sonny pulled his silencer from his vest pocket and screwed it to the barrel of his rifle. Then he took aim and fired an entire mag into the roiling pack below. Once the wolves smelled the blood of their wounded, their frenzy turned on each other, and the pack tore the injured wolves to shreds in their quest for a meal. When the large majestic creatures moved on from the clearing, the only thing left behind were bones and blood on the fresh fallen snow.

Echo waited until dawn before climbing down from the trees. They wanted to have full visibility if the wolves returned. John gave the order, and Echo headed south through the dense forest.

April 4
1000
Sahara Desert, Algeria

The trucks Echo was tracking stopped at a village near the border of Libya. Echo watched the trucks from a distance. The militants were bartering with the locals. Andrew and Joe took up positions just outside of the village. They watched and reported back to Ben.

Echo wasn't the only one watching the small caravan. Bretta watched the satellite imagery on her laptop. She sent an encrypted e-mail reporting on the caravan's movement and the SEAL team's activities. Then she slid her laptop into her backpack and left the street side café in Paris.

April 4
1900
Siberia, Russia

Echo crossed into the Stanovoye Nagor'ye mountain range just east of Peleduy. That's where they encountered trouble. A Russian army platoon spotted them crossing the Lena river.

"Американский Спецназ!" (American Special Forces!) One of the Russian soldiers yelled.

Echo took cover in the trees, and the Russians opened fire on them. Shots were exchanged. Echo laid down cover fire while Sonny and Sophia got to higher ground. From their vantage point, they were able to take out most of the Russian soldiers but not before the Russian's called for backup. Echo left the scene as quickly as they could. They knew they'd be chased.

The SEALs made their way south along the mountain range. The heavy snow slowed their progress, but they were still making decent time. They used the trees for cover as much as possible, but by the time they reached Chuya on the southwest side of the Vitim River, the Russians engaged them again. Echo took out the small force and kept heading southwest. They kept to the western edge of the mountain range in a direct route toward Lake Baikal. John was hoping to lose the Russian army forces in the mountains on the northern border of the lake.

At 0430, a Russian force of thirty soldiers intercepted Echo near the northwest bank of the Reka Bol'shaya Chuya River. Echo took them out, but they were running low on ammo.

"Conserve your ammo," John ordered as they headed south through the wooded mountain range. "We don't know how many more we are going to encounter."

They crossed the Reka Bol'shay Chuya River on the sandbar to the northwest of the small mountain town of Gorno-Chuiskii. From there, they disappeared into the forest headed south.

April 5
1500
Sahara Desert, Libya

Ben gave the order for Zach to take Overwatch position. He ordered Ezra and Hogan to move in closer to gather evidence while the rest of Echo provided cover. They were just outside a small desert village near an oasis.

Ezra and Hogan crept up on the village and hopped the short, clay, brick wall. They proceeded to video the meeting that was proceeding inside a small adobe dwelling. A colorful tapestry swayed in the breeze through the open window, and the men inside spoke in Russian and Arabic. There was a translator between them. Neither Ezra nor Hogan spoke either language. They had no idea what the meeting was about. They only knew that Mark had insisted they gather evidence of whatever transpired.

After the Russian's left, Ezra and Hogan crept back to Echo's position. Echo waited for the cover of darkness before returning to their base camp twenty klicks away. Mark was waiting to review the data they'd collected. He immediately encrypted the video and sent it to his C.O.

April 7
0245
Kichera, Siberia

Thirty klicks north of Kichera, John consulted the GPS on his watch and compared it to his map. He changed their direction heading southwest to circumvent the town. They were almost to the northern shore of Lake Baikal. They had been pushing themselves for days with very little rest. Everyone was nearing the point of exhaustion.

"When we reach Baikal, we will find a secure location and get some rest," John said.

They powered through the mountainous trek and made the northern shore before dawn.

"Which way, Chief?" Mac asked.

"We'll travel along the western shore and cross the border into Mongolia."

John took the lead. Sophia brought up the rear. She was truly feeling the pain now. Her body had been pushed to its limits and beyond, but she wasn't about to fall behind the pack. John had given her his trust. The six SEALs on this team had been chosen for their skills and what they could bring to the mission. It was critical that they bring back the intel to their CIA contact. After what they discovered at the facility, it was obvious to everyone that a clone army would be a dangerous entity to unleash on the world. The Russians had to be stopped.

Falco scouted out a safe place for them to bed down for a few hours. It was high on the ledge of a ravine. There was plenty of cover from the rocky overhang to conceal them. John took the first watch. He insisted that everyone get some sleep. He knew his men were beyond exhausted. He posted himself at the top of the ravine in a tall tree. He could see in every direction from his perch. He continually scanned the horizon and the forest below with his binoculars.

At 1400, Nick exited the ravine to relieve John.

"Go get some rest, Sir. You should have woken one of us sooner. The day is half gone."

John climbed down from the tree. "We'll stay here until dusk. It's safer to travel after dark."

Nick climbed the tree and took over John's watch. John climbed down to the ravine ledge and curled up against the stone wall. He held his rifle against him in the event he needed to use it quickly. He was too keyed up to sleep. He could feel danger creeping up on them like a relentless predator. His mind was filled with too much fear and concern for his team. He closed his eyes, but sleep eluded him. Even the tiniest noise felt magnified in his ears. It was impossible to relax. When the rest of Echo woke a short while later, they made a quick meal of MREs and counted their ammo supplies.

"How are you on ammo?" Sonny whispered to Sophia.

"Four mags in my pack, half a mag in my rifle, four grenades, two fully loaded pistols, and my survival knife."

He nodded. The ledge wasn't tall enough to allow anyone to stand, so he crawled over to check everyone else's ammo count. When Sophia found out that everyone had less ammo than she did, she gave Sonny three mags and all her grenades to redistribute to whoever needed it the most. When Sonny climbed out of the ravine to check Nick's ammo, Mac and Falco decided to go back to sleep while they had the chance. When she heard them snoring, she crawled over to John and gently felt of his forehead.

A grin spread over his mouth. "Checking up on me?"

"Absolutely, Sir. How are you feeling?" she whispered.

"Tired."

"You should get some sleep."

"It's hard to sleep when you're being hunted."

"I'll stay awake, Sir. No one's getting in here on my watch. They'll have to get to you over my dead body. You're safe with me. Get some rest. I'll protect you and the rest of Echo."

John grinned. Then he shifted his arm to use it as a pillow and closed his eyes. The remainder of the daylight hours were uneventful. Echo rested up and prepared for what was to come.

April 9
0800
Lake Baikal, Siberia

Echo was nearing the sprawling town of Yelantsy near the western shore of Lake Baikal. They were sticking to the forested area, but there was a paved road that they would have to cross soon. They were careful to give the town a wide berth, but the road was well traveled. They waited until the road was clear before continuing. Three hours later, they encountered militants in the woods. A firefight ensued, but they were all low on ammo; every shot had to count. Echo took up positions and returned fire taking out several targets each. That's when disaster struck.

"Echo 1 to Echo 2," John grunted into his com link. "I took a bullet."

"Echo 2 to Echo 1. How bad is it?" Nick responded from his position a hundred yards north where he had taken up the rear position.

"Left thigh, it didn't hit an artery." John gritted his teeth against the pain.

"Echo 16, can you get to him?" Nick asked as he took out a target, and searched through his rifle scope for his next target.

"Negative!" John barked. "Echo 16 maintain position! I can take care of this myself!"

John pulled a tourniquet from his pack and tied it around his thigh. Then he applied pressure to the wound and pressed a wad of gauze against the bullet entry point. He wrapped duct tape around his thigh to hold the bandage in place and then removed the tourniquet. He rolled back onto his stomach taking up a sniper position. He took out several more targets before the crossfire ceased. Nick confirmed that all combatants were down, and John gave the order for Echo to continue south. The trees were to the west, and the lake was to the east.

After twenty minutes, John broke the silence. "Echo 1 to Echo 2."

"Echo 2, go for Echo 1," Nick responded.

"Echo 1 handing off the package to Echo 2, "John grunted into his coms.

Nick double timed his march to catch up to John's position.

"You okay?" Nick asked, as John handed him the waterproof bag with the digital data inside.

Nick shoved the bag into his cargo pocket on his right thigh.

"You okay?" Nick repeated.

"I'm fine." John gritted his teeth against the pain.

"I'll have Echo 16 take a look at your leg," Nick said.

"Negative. We don't have time for that. We need to get across the border."

Nick grimaced as he glanced down at John's leg. "You shouldn't be walking on that."

"This mission takes priority over a bullet wound that can be treated later." John gave new orders into his com link. "Echo 2 is taking lead position. Double time it. Complete the mission!"

As Nick took up the lead spot, John fell farther and farther behind the group. His order to double time it was costing him dearly. Every step he took was excruciatingly painful. Still, he was hanging in with the group. He could still see them ahead.

Sophia kept her eye on their leader. She agreed with Nick's assessment; John shouldn't be walking on that kind of injury. She slowed her pace and fell in step beside him.

"Echo 16, I told you to double time it!" John grunted, as he eyed the rest of the group pulling farther and farther ahead of him. "You can run faster than this! Double time is an order soldier!"

"Sorry, Sir! You can discipline me later when we get back."

"You're disobeying a direct order?" John growled as he tried to pick up his own pace.

"Sir, yes, Sir! I wasn't trained to leave a man behind, Sir!"

"This mission is more important than any one team member," he growled.

"Agreed, Sir! Echo 2 has it under control."

"The team needs their medic! Pick up your pace and rejoin the team!"

"Respectfully, Sir, I can't do that. The team needs their leader more than they need a medic!"

"Are you questioning my orders?" he barked at her.

"Sir, no, Sir! I'm just disobeying them."

He glared at her. Then he did his best to close the gap between the rest of the team. He noticed Sophia took up a position approximately three feet behind him no matter how slow or how fast he ran. The trek along the lake was not an easy one. The terrain wasn't always conducive to running. Still, they were making progress until John lost his footing and went tumbling down the hill. He slid across the ice on the frozen lake and came to a stop five meters from the shoreline. He lay on the ice trying to catch his breath. Then he struggled to get up on the slippery surface.

"Echo 16 to Echo 2," Sophia said into her coms as she hurried down the steep hill toward the ice-covered lake—toward John.

"Echo 2, go for Echo 16."

"Echo 1 is down. Making my way to him now."

Nick halted in his tracks and turned scanning for John and Sophia.

"Echo 16, what is your position? I'm coming for you," Nick said.

"Negative! Echo 2, I will catch up!" John grunted as he made it up on one knee. "Double time it to the rendezvous! Do not come back for me! Deliver the package! That's an order soldier!"

"Sir, yes, Sir!" Nick said.

Nick didn't resume his pace. Instead, he took up a position behind a tree and scanned looking for John and Sophia as the rest of the team caught up to him.

"Sir, Echo 1 ordered us to deliver the package," Mac said as he came to a halt in front of Nick.

"I'm aware of the order, Echo 11." Nick scanned the woods in search of John and Sophia.

"Are you disobeying a direct order?" Falco asked incredulously.

"Zip it!" Sonny growled. "Echo 2 outranks you. Show some respect!"

Falco shut his mouth and took up a defensive position searching the woods for possible enemy combatants. Nick hand signaled them to spread out. He made his way back in the direction they had just come. It was then he saw Sophia make it to the edge of the frozen lake. His eyes went to John five meters out struggling to get to his feet. Nick scanned the woods with his binoculars but saw no sign of the enemy. Still, he trained his rifle staying vigilant as he kept an eye on Sophia and John's progress.

Sophia carefully walked out on the ice to John. With great effort she helped him to his feet.

"Sir, you're bleeding again."

"Noted."

They started back toward shore with Sophia holding his arm to help him balance. That's when they all heard the echo of gunfire. A barrage of bullets sliced through the ice mere inches from their feet. Before either John or Sophia could process what was happening, the ice splintered beneath them, and they both plunged into the icy depths of Lake Baikal.

Nick immediately scanned the area and located the sniper. He quickly eliminated the threat, but when he looked back at the ice there was nothing there but a hole where John and Sophia had fallen in.

"Damnit!" Nick swore.

He didn't have time to contemplate his best friend's fate. A fresh barrage of bullets ripped through the trees, and Echo was busy taking down targets in the woods.

"Echo 2 to team," Nick said into his com link. "Move out! Double time it to the rendezvous!"

With that all four men fell in and picked up the pace as fast as they could. They were in hostile territory, and they were quickly running out of ammo.

CHAPTER 56

April 9
1156
Lake Baikal

Beneath the ice Sophia held on to John as tightly as she could. They were caught in an underwater current that was pulling them both down despite their best efforts to reach the surface. John knew their chances of survival were zero. Not only were they in frigid water, but at 600 feet deep, Lake Baikal was the deepest lake on the planet. They were being sucked down into its depths with a force too strong for either of them to overcome even if they weren't strapped down with heavy packs. John did the only thing he could think to do. To give Sophia any chance she might have of survival, he circled his arms around her, found her mouth in the dark, freezing water, and gave her his last breath.

Sophia's eyes grew wide as she realized what he had done. In the swift current, she felt his body jerk as his lungs filled with water. Then he went limp. She grabbed for him and managed to lock her fingers around the metal frame of his pack as they were both swept away in the swift current. She held her breath hoping for a miracle. Though like John, she doubted there was any chance of survival. Still, she refused to let go of John's pack. If they were going to die, it would be together. It was completely irrational. She knew he was already dead. He had expelled his last breath into her lungs. Logic wasn't driving her. It was something deeper.

John had been the only SEAL team leader to give her any consideration. When all the other SEAL teams passed her over, she had tasted despair. All her hard work, sacrifice, and dedication had meant nothing to those other teams. It wasn't just that she owed John, she respected him immensely. In all the missions they'd been on, she'd come to see that he was a mature, wise, dedicated, loyal leader. He was the man who always put his team's wellbeing ahead of his own—no matter what the situation. It came as no surprise to her that he had given her his dying breath in an attempt to save her. That's just the kind of man he was. She couldn't let go no matter how futile her efforts might be.

Just when she felt the pull on her lungs, the irrepressible need to suck in a breath, she surfaced. The current had pulled them to the exit point of the lake. They were being carried swiftly down the Angara River. She gasped for air as she struggled to stay above the surface in the swift tumultuous water. She kicked as hard as she could trying to reach the bank. When she finally found a hand hold on a group of rocks, she struggled to pull herself and then John up onto the southern bank.

She immediately shed her pack and unstrapped his pack. She rolled him onto his back, turned his head to the side, bent his legs up against his chest, and compressed as much water from his lungs as she could. Water gushed from his mouth. She pulled his legs out straight and began CPR on him immediately. He was unresponsive, but she wasn't going to give up.

Finally, after continued CPR he started breathing again, but he remained unconscious. She said a quick prayer over him and moved down to look at his leg. It was still bleeding, but not as bad as she expected. She redressed his wound applying pressure until the bleeding stopped. Then she duct-taped his leg and tried to wake him up.

"John." She lightly slapped his cheek.

There was no response.

I don't know if I can carry him. He probably weighs 200 pounds. That's twice my weight. Now I understand why the other teams passed me over for big, strong men. Why did John choose me?

Panic seized her for a moment. Then she remembered her BUD/S training.

If I can pull a toothpick that weighs 400 pounds, I can pull John. First, I need to get him out of these wet clothes before he goes into hypothermic shock.

No! First, I need to find us cover. We are being hunted. We are too exposed on the shoreline.

She scanned the narrow, sandy shoreline, but she saw no one in sight. The town was on the north bank of the Angara River. The south bank only had a very narrow strip of sand and a thick forest to the south. She managed to get him on her back with his arms over her shoulders. It was awkward to drag him the short distance into the woods, but she did it. Then she raced back to get their packs. Once in the cover of the trees, she quickly stripped him down naked and wrapped him in the blanket from his pack. Then she went to work making a makeshift travois from their two backpacks. She pulled him onto the travois, wrapped her blanket around him too, and lashed him to the packs with climbing rope from his pack.

She shivered against the frigid wind as it whipped through the forest, stirring up the powdered snow. Her white camo snowsuit was soaking wet, but there was no time to dry it out. She had to get as far away from the shoreline as possible. She knew from the mission maps that not too far down the Angara River was a major settlement. She had to keep them clear of that at all costs. She had to remain invisible.

Aside from avoiding the Russian soldiers in these woods, she had to find a way to get John warm before hypothermia killed him. She could feel the effects of it already beginning to affect her own mobility.

She used the shoulder straps from one end of the travois to loop over her shoulders. It was difficult to raise him up enough to get her arms through the straps. It was even more difficult to actually drag him behind her as she made her way farther south into the woods.

Her teeth chattered, and she could feel her body trembling as she struggled to pull him.

I'm not going to let him down. I'll find a way to save him. I'll find a way to get him out alive. I owe him my life. He just gave me his dying breath!

Sophia took her com link out of her ear and tapped it to drain the water. Then she put it back in. "Echo 16 to Echo 2."

Silence was the only answer. The water had killed her com link. She pulled the com link from John's ear and tried to contact Nick again. John's com was dead too. She stowed them in her pocket and focused on avoiding the enemy and finding shelter.

After two hours of running at top speed through the rough terrain of the forest, Nick reached the mouth of the Angara River. He halted at the edge of the forest to survey the terrain.

"Echo 3." Nick motioned for Sonny to join him.

Sonny came over and took up position next to Nick.

"What do you think?" Nick asked. "We can go down river and try to cross, but we'll be getting close to the settlement before we find a place tame enough to cross. Or we can take our chance on the lake and cross the ice to the other side."

"It's your call," Sonny said.

"I'm asking your opinion," Nick said quietly.

"They're both risky. On the ice there's no cover, but we could get there faster. Down river we are likely to run into more opposition, and we are all running low on ammo."

Nick nodded.

"If I was making the call, I'd say go across the ice. We'll get there faster. We've taken out a lot of the opposition. The chances that there are more soldiers nearby is minimal at the moment. A half hour from now, it could be another story. I say let's haul ass as fast as we can and get the hell home," Sonny drawled.

Nick nodded. "Okay, thanks."

The image of the black hole in the ice where John and Sophia disappeared slammed into Nick's brain. He studied the terrain for another minute. Then he gave the order.

"Echo 2 to team. We are going downstream to find a crossing. Keep your head on a swivel. Move out."

In the forest several miles to the south of Nick's position, Sophia was struggling against the weight of the packs and John. She kept her eyes peeled and her rifle ready as she stumbled over the uneven ground and fell to her knees in the deep snow. John stirred awake when he felt the jolt. He realized he couldn't move. Then the truth hit him full force.

I'm still alive. I remember drowning!

"Hey!" he croaked out. His throat felt raw.

She struggled out from under the travois and knelt beside him.

"Hey, how are you feeling?"

"Cold."

She nodded. "It's been snowing off and on. I'm trying to find shelter. I don't think it's safe to build a fire out in the open."

"Why am I tied up?"

"What? You don't like being tied up?" She grinned down at him and winked.

He smirked. "No."

She quickly untied him from the travois. That's when he realized he was completely naked.

"Where are my clothes?"

"I strapped them to the pack. They are stiff and frozen. I couldn't dry them out."

He reached up and felt of her snowsuit. It was coated in ice.

"We were in the water."

She nodded. "They shot the ice out from under us. The current must have taken us to the mouth of the Angara. We are in the forest to the south of it."

John nodded. "You must be freezing."

"Just a little."

"Give me my clothes."

"You'll be warmer in the blankets. At least they are dry."

"I need my clothes and boots to walk."

"You're not walking on that leg."

"The hell I'm not! I'm not letting you drag me. I'm not helpless."

"I can manage, Sir. I've dragged heavier than you before."

"Yeah, I know. I read your file. You dragged a toothpick. That's pretty impressive, but you're not dragging me another step. Give me my clothes."

She untied his clothes from the pack and beat as much ice from them as she could before handing them to him.

He looked up at her. "Turn around, so I can get dressed."

"Sir, I undressed you. I've already seen you naked."

"Just do it."

"You might need help, Sir."

"That's an order!"

She turned her back to him with a smirk on her pretty face. She could hear the rustle of fabric behind her. Then she heard him groan in pain.

"Please let me help you, Sir. We are a team. That's what teammates do."

John gritted his teeth against the pain, but he couldn't get his pants on no matter how hard he tried.

"Okay," he finally gasped.

She turned to see that he had the blanket over his thighs. She knelt down and carefully tugged his pants up to his knees. Then she put his boots on and laced them up.

"Can I see your wound. The bandages probably need to be changed."

He let out a frustrated sigh and pulled the blanket up just enough for her to redress the wound.

"You don't have to be embarrassed, Sir."

"I'm not."

"Are you sure?"

He cleared his throat and looked away.

"Has anyone ever told you that you're adorably cute when you get shy?"

His eyes darted back to meet her gaze. He swallowed hard as he stared into her eyes.

"No."

"Well, you are."

He could feel his heart pounding, his pulse racing. The look in her eyes was seductive. To his chagrin he felt himself get hard beneath the blanket.

Damnit! What is wrong with me?

His lips turned down in a frown. "You shouldn't say things like that."

"Why not?"

"It could be taken the wrong way."

"We are the only ones around for miles."

"I could take it the wrong way."

"What way are you taking it?"

"I—um—" he fell silent.

What way am I supposed to take that? She tells Sonny I'm at the bottom of the list. Then she tells me I'm cute. What is she trying to do? I know she's not looking for a man. She's told me so more than once. Hell, she's told practically half the men on base the same thing.

Sophia stared at him for a long moment.

Why does he have to look so sexy when he scowls? It's really not fair that he is so handsome.

"Let's get your pants on. We need to head out soon."

"I can get them on. I don't need help."

She stood up and watched him struggle to lift his hips and pull his pants up under the blanket.

"You really are stubborn."

"I could say the same about you."

She helped him to his feet. "I'll drag the packs. You follow behind. It will be easier for you to walk on the packed snow."

"No, I'll carry my pack. It will be easier for our tracks to be covered by the falling snow. It's better if we don't leave an unnecessary trail for the enemy to track us with."

Sophia took point, and John did his best not to stare at her ass.

After an hour of hiking through deep snow, they spotted a safe haven. It would be a difficult assent, but a cave up high on the cliff face would be more defensible if they encountered Russian soldiers in the woods.

Sophia gathered firewood and kindling, and John strapped it to his pack. He tethered himself to her, and they started scaling the steep cliff. Halfway up, she could feel the numbness in her fingers affecting her grip. She focused harder and dug down deep for the strength to hold on. Five meters from the cave entrance, she lost her grip, slipped, and slid down the cliff face.

John grabbed her wrist as she slid past him and easily pulled her 100-pound body back up beside him. He checked her climbing harness again before he dared let go of her.

"Are you okay?" he asked.

"Sorry, Sir. I lost my grip. I have no feeling in my fingers anymore."

He frowned. "We need to get you inside that cave and get you warm."

He helped her find hand holds on the cliff face, and she managed to regain her footing. They resumed the climb, and a few minutes later, they were pulling themselves into the cave entrance. It was a narrow opening. Sophia wormed her way inside followed by John. The narrow tunnel was barely wide enough for them to fit through dragging their packs behind them. After 100 yards, the tunnel opened up a little, and after another 100 yards, it turned to the left and went downhill for 300 yards. By the time it opened up into a cavern large enough for John to stand, they were deep inside the mountain.

The flashlights on their rifles only showed the craggy rock walls of the cave, but they could hear water. After a brief exploration, they found the entrance to a much larger cavern. There was a large crystal blue body of water in the cavern. The water was ice cold.

"It must be fed by Lake Baikal," John said.

He went to work building a fire. By the time he had the fire going, Sophia had stripped out of her frozen clothes and wrapped herself in a blanket. John rigged a clothesline with some of his climbing rope and hung her clothes up to dry. Then he stripped out of his clothes, wrapped up in the other blanket, and hung his things up to dry.

They both huddled near the fire trying to warm their frozen limbs. After a few minutes, John looked over at Sophia. She was shivering violently.

"Let me see your fingers," he said.

"I have frostbite."

"Let me see."

She held out her right hand to him. He grimaced. She definitely had the signs of frostbite.

"Let me see your feet."

"They aren't any better, Sir."

He reached out and felt of her cheek. Her skin was icy to the touch. He grimaced.

"We have to get you warm."

He doubled up his blanket and spread it out next to the fire. Her eyes slowly scanned his perfect, naked body. She averted her gaze just as he looked back at her.

"Come sit on this blanket."

She crawled over and sat down.

"I'm going to examine you."

He gently removed the blanket from her and took a good look at her body. She had frostbite on her fingers and toes, but otherwise seemed unscathed by their ordeal. He wrapped the blanket back around her. Then he limped down to the water and filled a canteen. He came back to the fire, poured the water into an aluminum pan from his pack, and put it on the fire to heat.

He looked down at Sophia who was shivering violently. "I'm not trying to get frisky, but you need some body heat."

She nodded. He sat down behind her on the blanket and pulled her onto his lap. She wrapped her blanket around them both and snuggled against his chest. Her body was much colder than his. He wrapped his arms around her and tucked her cold face against his warm neck.

"Thank you, Sir."

"I'll get you warm. Just snuggle up."

She fell asleep cuddled against him. She didn't wake up until he shifted her off his lap to take the water off the fire. He tested it. It was lukewarm. He gently placed her feet and hands into the tepid water. Then he sat down behind her, curled his body around her, and wrapped them both in her blanket. After treating her frostbite, they curled up on the blanket by the fire and shared body heat to stay warm.

John did his best not to think about how good her naked skin felt against his. He tried not to picture her perfect naked body. He tried to breath normal and allow his racing pulse to calm down. He failed on all counts. His thoughts raced out of control down paths that were forbidden—impossible. Sleep would have eased his pain, but sleep was an elusive ghost that danced just out of reach. As usual, he would have to endure his self-inflicted torture with no reprieve and no mercy. Holding her curvy, naked body against his was pure torture; it was the hardest thing he'd ever done in his life, but he was a SEAL, and SEALs pushed through the pain. No matter what the personal cost was, a SEAL always did the right thing. That's what he told himself over and over for the next several hours.

A few hours later, he checked their clothes, but they were not dry. It would be several more hours before either of them could get dressed. Then he checked the bandage on his leg while she slept. The bleeding hadn't entirely stopped. He didn't have a choice. He had to take care of it before he slowly bled to death. He injected himself with an antibiotic from her med pack. Then he took some pain pills. He scooted closer to the fire so he could see and carefully dug the bullet out of his thigh. The pain was excruciating, but he grunted his way through it. Then he opened a bullet and dumped the gunpowder into the open wound.

He gritted his teeth as he lit the powder to cauterize the wound. For a moment, he thought he would pass out from the pain. Once he regained control, he crawled over to Sophia and curled his body around hers. He lay awake worrying. He was worried about Sophia. He was worried about Nick, Sonny, Mac, and Falco. He was worried about the rest of Echo on a mission of their own in the Sahara. He couldn't sleep. It was pointless to try.

When the fire began to die down, and there was no more wood to feed it, he carefully tugged on his clothes, climbed out of the cave, climbed down the cliff, and gathered more firewood. He returned with a bundle large enough to keep the fire going for several days if necessary.

He'd decided that Sophia wasn't leaving the cave. Frostbite and hypothermia were serious health concerns. He wasn't going to risk her life in the frigid, Siberian weather until he was sure she was up to it. When her clothes were dry and toasty, he redressed her. She barely stirred.

"I can dress myself," she mumbled half asleep.

"I know you can. Just rest. You wore yourself out dragging me through the woods. It's one thing to drag a toothpick a hundred yards down a beach. It's much harder to drag a man twenty klicks in the mountains over rough terrain. Go back to sleep, Gonzalez."

She mumbled something incoherent and drifted back to sleep. He took their com links apart and set them near the fire to dry out. He hoped they weren't completely ruined. He hoped Nick had led the men successfully south of here by now, but just in case the rest of Echo was nearby, he intended to do everything in his power to make contact.

He lay next to her and watched her sleep. The firelight danced over her perfect features in the most enticing way. He had to quell the urge to lean in and plant a kiss on her perfect lips.

Stop looking at her. Stop thinking about kissing her! She is off limits! Stop torturing yourself!

April 9
2130
Angara River, Siberia

Nick signaled Echo to halt in the woods near the northern shore of the Angara River. They were still sixty klicks east of Irkutsk. The sprawling city spread out on either side of the river. There were four bridges that crossed the Angara; all four were located in the heart of Irkutsk. As they approached a small neighborhood on the northern shore, the cover of the forest was quickly disappearing. Sonny, Mac, and Falco huddled up around Nick.

"We need transportation. We can't walk through Irkutsk like this," Nick said. "Spread out. Look for a vehicle and report back."

Falco found a four-wheel drive that was unlocked on the gravel drive beside a house. He reported back to Nick and hotwired the SUV. They were able to traverse the city of Irkutsk undetected and made it through the neighboring city of Shelekhov. They made it past Poselok near the southern shore of Lake Baikal before they ran out of gas and had to abandon the vehicle. By then it was nearly daylight. They could no longer hide in plain sight. It was too risky. They pushed the car off the road into a ravine and headed back into the dense forest.

Nick tried to stay focused on the mission, but his mind kept wandering back to the sight of John and Sophia disappearing beneath the frozen lake. Guilt roiled in his gut.

I should have made sure John was with the group. I shouldn't have let him fall behind like that. Their deaths are on me. I can't let any more men die.

Nick felt sick inside. John was his best friend. Then a truly gut-wrenching thought hit him.

John gave me the package just before he— Was he bleeding to death trying to walk on that injury. Was he dying, and he knew it? Did he willingly sacrifice himself to ensure we completed the mission? I can't let him down. I won't let his sacrifice be in vain. I will deliver this package.

Suddenly, Nick stopped in his tracks, bent over, and puked up everything in his stomach.

Sonny ran over to him. "Are you okay?"

Nick staggered back a step. He felt light-headed. Sonny grabbed his arm to steady him.

Mac came to a halt next to them. "Are you getting sick, Sir?"

Nick shook his head. "I'm okay. I guess that MRE didn't set right."

Mac frowned. "MRE's never sit right."

Nick took a moment to let the dizziness clear before leading them deeper into the forest.

April 10
0700
Angara River region

As Sophia's groggy brain woke fully, she realized she was lying on top of John. She raised her head to see if he was asleep. He wasn't. The fire had died down to embers, but it was still putting off enough heat to sustain them.

He's so sweet. He must have been afraid I would get too cold.

She lay her head back on his chest and snuggled against him.

"Are you cold?" he asked concerned.

"No. You are very warm."

"I should put some more wood on the fire."

He carefully deposited her on the blanket and crawled over to the fire. Sophia watched him as he checked their boots. They were still damp inside. Then he got into their packs and produced MRE's. They sat on the blanket and ate them in silence.

"What's the plan now, Sir?"

"When you're ready to travel, we'll proceed to the rally point."

"I'm fine to travel, but I think you should rest your leg for a while. You took a bullet."

"I cut it out while you were asleep. I'm good to go, but we aren't leaving until our boots are completely dry and it's dark."

"You cut it out!" she gasped. "Let me see your leg, Sir!"

"It's fine."

"You shouldn't have done that."

"Triage. It had to be done. It wouldn't stop bleeding."

"How did you—"

"I sealed the wound with gun powder from a bullet."

"How did I sleep through that?"

"I was quiet."

"I want to look at it. I insist."

John smirked. "Another excuse to see me naked?"

She smirked back. "There's nothing to see."

His lips turned down in a frown. She suddenly realized what that sounded like.

"Oh! That's not what I meant. You have plenty—not that I was looking. I—uh—sorry, Sir."

He grinned. "I've never seen you get flustered before."

She cleared her throat and looked away. Then she shattered the awkwardness of the moment.

"Are you still angry with me?"

"Angry?"

"For disobeying your direct order?"

He grinned. "Well, seeing how you saved my life, I'm having trouble remembering what order you disobeyed." He winked at her.

Their eyes locked for a long, heated moment. On impulse, she framed his stubbled jaw in her hands, leaned in, and pressed her lips to his. John's heart beat out of control. He closed his eyes as he pulled back from her lips.

"We can't do that," he whispered.

She stared at his handsome face. His eyes were still closed, and his lips were turned down.

"Do you want to?" she asked softly."

He opened his eyes and stared into hers. "The UCMJ forbids it."

"That wasn't what I asked."

"It's not allowed."

"Do you want to kiss me?"

She leaned in, framed his jaw in her hands again, and pulled his bottom lip between hers in a soft, sucking kiss. He let her kiss him for a moment; then groaning, he pulled away from her lips.

"Sophia—don't."

He struggled to his feet and limped down toward the water. She got up and followed him.

"John, I've never felt this way about any man before. I like everything about you."

Life is cruel. The one woman I want more than anything in the world is the one woman I can't have under any circumstances.

Silent, he stood with his back to her staring at the blue water.

She laid her hand on his back. "Are you so afraid of an innocent kiss?"

Groaning loudly, he raked both hands over his burr, let out a heavy sigh, and turned to face her. He raised his hand and lightly trailed his finger down her jaw. Her heart sped up as their eyes locked. She felt like she was seeing the real John for the first time. His tortured eyes spoke what he would not.

"It wouldn't be an innocent kiss," he whispered.

Sonny was right! John is in love with me.

CHAPTER 57

April 10
0800
Lake Baikal

Nick, Sonny, Mac, and Falco perched high in the trees watching a troop of Russian soldiers march through the woods below. None of the SEALs dared to move. They did not have enough ammunition to take out a force that size. They had no cover. All they could hope was that the Russians passed by without noticing them.

Nick was glad it had been snowing all morning. Their tracks were covered and visibility was low. The Russians were more concerned with finding their footing on the rough terrain than they were with looking up and searching the trees above. The frigid temperature was only exacerbated by the biting wind. It had been a miserable morning in the woods surrounding Lake Baikal.

The only positive side was Echo was near the southern edge of the lake. Another thirty klicks and the lake would be behind them. Their rally point lay in Mongolia near the shore of Khovsgol Lake in Turt Typt where transportation awaited them.

Once he was certain there were no more Russians in the woods below, Nick gave the signal to climb down. On the ground they found an outcropping of rock to shelter against while they ate MREs. The wind speed had picked up, and the temperature had dropped.

"Anyone have frostbite?" Nick asked.

"My ass is completely frozen. Does that count?" Sonny joked.

Nick grinned. "We'll use the storm to cover our trail. We are close to the border."

He gave the order to head out, and they resumed their quest.

Struggling in the deep snow against an unforgiving wind was painful, but Nick pressed on. Echo followed. Nick was on a mission. He intended to deliver the package at any cost. He refused to let John and Sophia's deaths be for nothing. All he had to do was get across the border.

Every step he took cost him. Forcing his body through the waist deep snow was wearing him out. After an hour, Sonny took point to give Nick a break. After that, they all took turns acting as the snow plough. It was slow going, but every step brought them closer to the border—to safety.

April 10
1130
Sahara Desert, Libya

Ben lay on the edge of a dune crest. The unforgiving rays of the bright, Sahara sun beat down on his beautiful, chocolate brown skin creating beads of sweat that he kept having to wipe away to keep it from stinging his eyes. His binoculars were focused on the camp at the bottom of the dunes. There had been a lot of activity all morning. Men dressed in military fatigues had been running drills and target practicing since dawn. Zach lay beside Ben filming the activity below. The two men had noticed something peculiar. All of the men in training had the same face. They counted 200 men who all seemed to be identical mirror copies of each other.

They filmed the exercises for another hour before retreating down the backside of the dune. They rendezvoused with Mark and the rest of Echo back at camp. When they showed their footage to Mark, he didn't seem thrown by the odd anomaly.

"What are we looking at?" Zach asked. "Why do they all look alike? You need to tell us what's going on here. We're deep in enemy territory gathering evidence for you. We need to know what we're up against."

"It's classified. You don't have the clearance."

Zach's jaw tightened. "I'll classify you—You son of a—"

"Zach! Stand down," Ben barked. "Go cool off!"

Zach stalked away grumbling.

Ben leaned in toward Mark, and a low growl erupted from his throat. "Look! Clearance or not, I want to know what's going on here; otherwise, Echo is done doing your reconnaissance."

Mark smirked. "Done? You don't have the authority to cancel a mission. Either you do your job, or I make a call to Commander Rowen and tell him you are disobeying a direct order. You're not in charge here, Obassi! I'm in charge here. Just do what you're told!"

Ben stalked out of the tent with a snarl on his handsome face.

Zach walked up to him. "Sorry, Ben. I didn't mean to lose my cool. That guy just—"

"I understand, Zach. Don't worry about it. Whether Tom Sawyer in there likes it or not, we are going to get to the bottom of what's going on."

Zach chuckled. "Yeah, he is a Tom Sawyer now that you mention it. We've been white-washing his fence—doing all the grunt work—while he sits back and watches." Zach dragged his hand down his dark brown stubble. "So, what do you think is up with all the identicals?"

"Clones. They have to be clones. I can't come up with another explanation."

"Yeah, I agree, but the question is why?"

"That's what we are going to figure out, Zach."

April 10
1530
Angara River region

It had been a tense day in the cave. With nothing to distract him but attempting to restore the comlinks, John's nerves had been on edge. He was both shocked and flattered by Sophia's attempted kiss. He tried to refocus on the task at hand, but he couldn't get it out of his head.

Sophia sat watching John hunched over near the fire attempting to repair a comlink. Since her attempt to kiss him that morning, her mind had replayed his reaction at least a thousand times. She was used to being pursued by men. She was used to turning men down. She wasn't used to being on the other side of that fence. She tried to examine her feelings and motivations.

Did I kiss him because I feel grateful to him? Did I do it because I felt sorry for him? Was it just because he's sinfully hot? Do I have feelings for him? It's obvious from his reaction that he likes me, but he has the willpower to say no. Where's my willpower? Why did I really kiss him? What's wrong with me? He's my C.O.! He's off limits! I should definitely keep my distance. I should remove temptation from my path. Temptation! Am I tempted? Well—I kissed him! Obviously, I was tempted. Damnit! Why does he have to be so hot—so sweet—so perfect!

She walked over and sat down next to him. "Any luck?"

"No." He snapped the com link halves back together and shoved them into his pocket.

"I'm sorry about earlier. You are right; the UCMJ forbids fraternization. I was out of line. I don't know what got into me."

"You're a woman. Women are overly emotional. You can't help yourselves. Just don't let it happen again."

I'm a woman—I can't help myself! What the hell!

She looked at him with dagger eyes. John glanced her way and saw the look.

Yep, that did it. She's angry now. Good. Maybe it will help keep her in check. I'm the last man she should be pursuing. She could get herself in a lot of trouble, and she deserves a lot better than me. Besides, if she stays angry with me, it will remove temptation from both our paths.

He picked up a stick and stoked the fire. He didn't look back at her though he could feel her eyes burning into his back. From the look on her face he had infuriated her. Insulting her was the very last thing he wanted to do, but he wasn't sure how to keep her at a distance. It was the only plan he could think of so he went with it. When he returned to the blanket and sat down, she turned her back to him. He grimaced. It wasn't how he wanted things to go, but it was a necessary evil. She didn't speak to him, and he didn't speak to her.

At dusk he tugged on his boots and laced them. Sophia poured water on the fire, and they made the climb back to the cave entrance. A short while later, they were on the ground trudging through waist deep snow. It had been snowing all day, but it had let up for the moment. The wind had died down, and it was a beautiful night. Their visibility was good, and they were making decent time despite the deep snow.

Sophia insisted on taking the lead. She much preferred the sight of the pristine, Siberian forest covered in snow to the sight of John. She felt like there was a volcano inside her about to erupt. It was all she could do not to tell him exactly what she was thinking. Up until now, she'd always thought he was a fair-minded man who didn't allow petty prejudices to cloud his thinking. Now, she was sure he was just as small-minded as the other C.O.s she'd worked for in the past. His comment about her emotionalism had sent her over the edge.

John stared at her irresistible ass as she ploughed through the deep snow ahead of him. He kept a wary eye on the surrounding woods for the Russians too, but his eyes kept coming back to stare at her petite form. He couldn't help but picture her naked. He'd seen her naked. There was no mystery left. His problem now was staying focused on their surroundings when fantasies of making love to her kept invading his brain.

Only one thing helped keep his mind off the swarm of fantasies that wouldn't stop. The constant pain in his leg kept reminding him of the danger lurking in the woods all around them. Every step he took was painful. Painful didn't even describe it; excruciating agony came closer. His gut reaction was to scream with every step, but he stayed silent. Any noise could bring the enemy down on them.

John only had one goal; keeping Sophia safe, making sure she got across the border, and doing whatever it took to keep her alive. He didn't care about himself. His pain would be temporary. He was dying, and he knew it. The only thing he cared about was trudging through the snow ten feet in front of him. As long as he could ensure her safety, he was good with his fate.

He'd cheated death countless times before, but this time was different. He knew exactly where they were. He looked up and read the stars. He calculated the distance to the border, and the distance from the border to the rally point. He knew what kind of rough terrain lay between them and the goal. He knew he'd lost a lot of blood, but more importantly, he knew the wound was infected. He could feel it like an invasion. It was slowly taking over, taking him down. All he could do now was hang on for as long as possible in case they encountered an enemy force. Two guns were better than one in a firefight. As long as Sophia made it out alive, he was willing to trade his life for hers a second time.

He'd already accepted that he would never make it to the border. His body wouldn't hold out that long. He'd pushed himself to the limit many times before. He knew what his body could take, and it couldn't take a hike like that to the border. He was struggling to take each step. It was sheer willpower that kept him moving. He resolved to push himself until he dropped dead.

April 11
0500
Mongolian border

Nick held up his hand to signal his men to stop. They were ten klicks north of the Mongolian border. It would not be prudent to get cocky when they were so close to the finish line. He signaled Sonny to climb a tree and survey their surroundings.

At the top of the tree, Sonny had a good vantage point. It took him a few minutes to scan the area with his binoculars. Then he saw something that made him pause. There was a utility vehicle two klicks south of their position.

"Echo 3 to Echo 2," Sonny whispered.

"Echo 2, go for Echo 3," Nick whispered back.

"There's a Russian Humvee parked just down the way. Looks like they're settin' a trap fer us."

"Copy that."

Nick signaled Mac and Falco to keep an eye out.

"Is there a path through this or do we need to circle around?" Nick asked.

"I can't see none of them rascals, but if they came in that, there can't be more than eight guys."

"Copy. Keep a look out. We'll see if we can flush out these bogeys."

"Roger that."

Nick instructed Mac and Falco to spread out and see if they could locate their opposition. It took some searching in the dark to locate the Russian soldiers. There were five. Nick gave the signal, and Mac and Falco took out two targets each. Nick took out the last one. They waited for a few minutes to see if the shots would bring anyone else, but it was quiet.

"Echo 2 to team. Move out. Let's get to the rally point."

The last ten klicks to the border were the most nerve wracking. They kept expecting to meet further opposition. It was a relief once they crossed into Mongolia and put Siberia far behind them.

April 11
0800
Lake Baikal

John took the lead to give Sophia a break from making a path in the deep snow. She was still running on the adrenaline of her anger. She glared at the back of his snowsuit as he led the way.

I can't believe I thought he was a nice guy. He's a jerk! How dare he! Does he really think he's so hot that I can't control myself! What an ego! Okay, so maybe he is hot, but that doesn't give him the right to throw it in my face! I can't believe I wanted to kiss him! I'm an idiot! How could I fall for his charms? I'm better than this! I don't need a man! I don't want a man! I certainly don't want a petty, small-minded, prejudiced man like John!

She followed him for several hours before he halted.

"Do you want me to take the lead, Sir?" she asked as respectfully as she could manage.

"I need to take a break for a minute." He grunted as he sat down on a fallen tree trunk.

She took one look at his face and knew he was in serious pain. "I should take a look at your leg. You could have reopened the wound."

"It's not bleeding. It just hurts."

"I'm the medic. It's my job to assess the viability of a teammate to continue."

"I know what your job is. I'm telling you, it's fine. I just need to sit down for a minute."

Her jaw tightened and anger boiled up inside her. "If you're not going to let me do my job, then why did you make me train for it?"

John let out a low, frustrated growl. "Fine! Take a look at it but make it quick. We can't afford to stay in one place for too long."

She walked over and unzipped his snowsuit. When she reached for the zipper on his pants, he grabbed her wrist.

"I can do that."

She jerked her wrist free of his grip. "Fine! Then do it yourself!"

She's still angry. Good. Adrenaline will give her energy. It will keep her more alert.

He undid his pants and tried to pull them down. He winced in pain when he bent over. For a moment she felt sorry for him. Then she reminded herself of what a jerk he was. She couldn't help but smirk when she realized he was covering himself with his hands.

"I've already seen it, Sir."

She rolled her eyes and knelt down in front of him to examine his left thigh. She grimaced when she saw his patch job.

"You didn't stitch it up."

"I couldn't. I nearly passed out from cauterizing it."

"You've been through med training. You should know better. This should have been stitched up yesterday."

"It was all I could do not to scream. I didn't want to wake you up. You were exhausted; you needed your rest."

She swallowed hard and looked into his eyes.

There it is again! Am I going crazy? Does he like me or not? He looks at me like he's in love, but he acted like a complete jerk in the cave. Which is it? Does he love me or not? His mixed signals are infuriating! Okay—don't give into emotion. Don't prove him right!

"I'm going to stitch this up right now."

He nodded. "Okay."

She got out her med kit and went to work on his leg. He sat on the fallen log and did his best not to cry. He failed. It hurt worse than the previous day. Even her gentle touch was like a knife stabbing into every nerve ending. The needle piercing his flesh was much worse.

"I'm sorry, Sir. I'm trying to be gentle."

"I know," he groaned.

"I'm going to give you an antibiotic shot."

"I gave myself one yesterday."

"You need another. If this gets infected, you could lose your leg to gangrene."

He nodded and braced himself for the needle. When she was done, she gently pulled his pants up his thighs. "Sir, you'll have to move your hands, so I can pull them all the way up."

"No. Turn around. I can zip them myself."

She turned around with a wry smirk on her face. She could hear him grunting as he got to his feet. She heard his zipper. Then she turned around.

"I'll zip up your snowsuit, Sir."

He nodded. He was sure if he bent over, he would pass out. He steadied himself with his hand on the fallen tree.

"If you need me to, I can carry you."

He shook his head. "You're not carrying me. If I'd been awake, I'd never have let you drag me. You could have reinjured your back or given yourself a hernia. I weigh twice what you do."

"I'm tough. I can take it."

His expression softened, and he stared at her for a moment. "I know you're tough. You don't have to keep proving it to me. I only expect you to do your best. I'm not asking for a miracle, Sophia. I don't want you to hurt yourself trying to prove you can be just as tough and strong as a man twice your size. You don't always have to be the tough badass."

She swallowed hard as she stared back into his eyes.

He's doing it again. When he's like this I'm certain that he loves me. Then he turns around and acts like he disapproves of me. Why does he run hot and cold?

She nodded.

John got to his feet grimacing in pain.

"I'll take the lead," she said.

She tried to pick the easiest path she could find, but she could hear him breathing hard and occasionally grunting behind her.

By dusk, they had covered a surprising amount of ground, but it had taken a toll on John. He was beginning to lag behind, and she kept having to stop and wait for him to catch up. He'd developed a very pronounced limp by the time they stopped to rest.

"You don't have to play the tough guy."

She watched him carefully lower himself down on the ground.

"I'm not."

"I think you should have rested another day in the cave."

"It doesn't matter. We don't have a day to waste. We need to get to the rally point."

She walked over and removed her gloves. Then she knelt down and pressed her hand against his forehead.

"You're feverish. It could be a sign of infection."

"I'm sure it is."

The grim expression on his face made her guts twist. "I'm worried about you."

"Don't. I'm not worth wasting the effort on. If I fall behind, leave me. Get to the rally point and get home."

"You know I won't do that."

"Don't argue with me. I don't have the energy to argue. I'm ordering you to leave me behind."

That's an order I'll definitely disobey.

"We are going to make it out of here. Why would you even suggest that I leave you behind?"

"Because I'm not going to make it over these mountains. I'm struggling to even walk. The effort is wearing me out. The Russians are hunting us. The likelihood that I'll survive this mission is zero. If you leave me now, you'll be able to get across the border in a day. I'm slowing you down. The wound is infected. It hurts worse than any pain I've ever felt before. I'm feeling weak, dizzy, and I have a metallic taste in my mouth that won't go away. I think the wound is turning septic. I won't last much longer. There's no sense in both of us dying here. The Russian's will catch up to us sooner or later. It's best if all they have to show for their efforts is one dead American. Get across the border. Get home."

A tear streaked down her cheek. She knew John wasn't exaggerating. If he was feverish, the wound was definitely infected—and the Russians would catch up soon.

He's planning to fall on his sword to give me a chance to survive. I'm not leaving him. I don't care what he says. If we die, we die together. I won't let him sacrifice himself to save me.

She looked around and found a suitable tree with branches that would suit her needs. Then she used her survival knife to hack the branches free. When she turned back to look at John, his eyes were closed. She walked over to him, but he wasn't asleep. He was unconscious. She gave him some dissolvable acetaminophen though she doubted it would have much effect on him. She unzipped his snowsuit and pulled his pants down to check his wound. She confirmed it was infected. She quickly redressed him and went to work making a better travois from their packs and the branches. Then she tied John to it and headed south.

I have to save him. He doesn't deserve to die here like this. He must be in terrible pain to pass out like that, and he hasn't made one complaint all day. I'll get him home no matter what it takes.

April 12
1300
Afghanistan base

Nick waited outside Rowen's tent. When Maser Chief Wes Chilven from Delta exited the tent, Nick went in to give his report.

"Sir, we lost Gonzalez and Rusk. Their bodies were not recoverable. They fell through the ice on Lake Baikal and never resurfaced."

Rowen grimaced. "I'm sorry to hear that. Was the mission successful?"

Nick forced down the emotion that was roiling in his gut. "Yes, Sir. We recovered data and proof of a cloning project that seems to be connected to previous missions. I turned over the data to our CIA contact as ordered."

Rowen nodded. "Is there anything else to report?"

"No, Sir."

"Dismissed."

Nick left the tent and walked to the front of the compound. There were trucks leaving the compound and a helicopter was landing, but no one paid attention to Nick. He walked behind the ammo supply building and finally let go of all the pain that had been building inside him for days. He sank down on his knees, and the sobs wouldn't stop coming. Guilt and sorrow bombarded him, and he had no defense against it. He'd lost his best friend. He'd lost the team's medic and backup sniper. He'd failed to get everyone home safe.

I'm a failure. John turned the mission over to me because he knew he was going to die, and I didn't realize what he was doing until it was too late. I should have known. I should have seen how bad his injury was. I shouldn't have taken his word for it. It's my fault. I'm the one who lost him. I was responsible. I am to blame for this.

Nick didn't return to the tent for a long while. When he did, the look on Sonny and Mac's faces said it all. They both looked like they'd been kicked in the gut. Falco was asleep, but Nick was sure Falco blamed him too. He didn't know how he was going to face the team now. When the rest of Echo returned it would be a repeat of this horrible moment.

No one said anything. Nick walked to his bunk and sank down on it. He buried his head in his hands, and more tears started to fall. Sonny walked over and sat down next to Nick.

"It ain't goin' to be the same around here, but we'll survive. We don't have a choice." Sonny put his hand on Nick's shoulder.

Mac walked over and sat down on the opposite bunk. "No one blames you, Nick. You were following his orders. You couldn't have known that would happen. It was an accident that he ended up on that ice and bad luck that a sniper happened to be within range."

Nick wiped the tears away and stared at the floor. "I know, but it doesn't make it any easier. They're both dead. It's going to leave a hole in Echo that no one can fill."

April 12
1900
Lake Baikal

Sophia was on the verge of collapse. She had been pulling John all day through deep snow over precarious ground through a dense forest. The sound of gunfire broke through the silence of the forest. She dropped to the ground and trained her rifle in the dark forest. She saw nothing, but what she heard gave her some relief. There were howls erupting in the distance followed by more gunshots.

It's a wolf pack. Someone is shooting the wolves. They are not after us, but they are not that far away. I need to change my trajectory. I can't afford to cross paths with the Russians. I don't have enough ammo to take them on alone.

She rose to her feet and headed in a southwesterly route. It would take her out of her way and add time to her trip, but she wasn't going to take chances. John couldn't defend himself. He was still unconscious, and his fever was worse. No matter how much medicine she gave him, it seemed to have no effect. He needed a real doctor. As she pulled him through the snow, she prayed. She had done all she could; now it was in God's hands.

CHAPTER 58

April 13
0600
Sahara Desert, Libya

Echo was on another surveillance op. This was the third training camp they had investigated. The results were the same. Each camp had 200 look alike soldiers being trained for intensive combat. Mark would not enlighten them. All he wanted was for evidence to be gathered. They were not to intervene. Ben didn't like any of it, but he had orders to follow.

April 13
0630
Kiev, Ukraine

Bretta watched out a window from a third story apartment. She had been waiting for thirty-six hours, but her target hadn't shown yet. She glanced back at her laptop. The satellite images showed a distant view of a training camp in the Sahara. She could see Echo on the other side of the dune. She typed a quick email to update her boss. She encrypted it and hit send. Then her eyes went back to the street below. Traffic was picking up. There were a few pedestrians walking to work on the fresh fallen snow. The day was beginning to take form, but as of yet there was no sign of the woman she had been sent to assassinate.

She let out a sigh and clicked open a new window. A live satellite image came into focus. She zoomed in the image, and a smile flittered across her lips. She could see Lydell on horseback on the North Carolina beach. Kyle Masters was riding next to him.

"

She grimaced when they stopped, and Kyle had to help Lydell down off the horse. With Kyle's help he walked a few feet and sank down on the sandy beach. Kyle sat down beside him. They were having a conversation. She wished she could listen in. She wanted to know how Lydell was handling his recovery, but she was limited on how much surveillance she could spend her time on. She had a job to do, and spying on Lydell wasn't part of her duties anymore.

April 14
0940
Siberian Forest

Sophia stopped to drink some water and eat an MRE. She was fifty klicks north of the Mongolian border. Khovsgol Lake lay directly south. She'd been forced to take a major detour to avoid the Russians and the hungry wolf pack. She should have been in safe territory long before now, but she was close enough to taste it.

She checked on John. He was worse. She gave him another round of antibiotics and said another prayer. He had drifted in and out of consciousness over the last twenty-four hours, but his waking was consumed in delirium. As soon as she'd rested for a few minutes, she harnessed herself back to the travois and headed out. She was cautious for the rest of the day. John had taught her well that when the goal was in sight was the most precarious part of the journey.

At 0200, Sophia halted one klick south of the border in Mongolian territory. The silence of the forest had been shattered by the sound of a helicopter. She pulled John under the cover of the trees and readied her rifle. She was surprised when the helo hovered directly over her position and two SEALs from Tango repelled down.

"Gonzalez, we're here to take you home. What is Chief Rusk's condition?" James, the medic from Tango asked.

"He's unconscious. He might be septic. He has a gunshot wound in his left thigh."

Shock reverberated through her as she watched the two men take charge and harness John to the medic. The second man, Henry, cut their packs free of the travois, shouldered them, and harnessed her to himself. Two minutes later, she was sitting in the chopper headed to safety.

"How did you know where we were?" Sophia asked.

"CIA intel reported your position," Henry said. "Are you injured?"

"John is the one who needs medical attention. He's in bad shape."

James examined John and grimaced. "Chief Rusk needs immediate medical attention. He's circling the drain. I don't know if he's going to make it."

Sophia buried her head in her hands, and sobs wracked her body.

Henry took a seat next to her. "We'll do everything we can to save him."

April 20
1800
Naples, Italy

John forced his heavy eyelids open. It was too bright. He squeezed them shut and then squinted against the bright light.

"Welcome back, Chief Rusk," the nurse said. "How are you feeling?"

"Where is Sophia?" he mumbled.

"I'm right here." Sophia crossed the hospital room and took his hand in hers.

He gently squeezed her hand. "Are you okay?"

"I'm fine. I was treated for exposure and some frostbite, but I'm fine now."

The nurse took his vitals and went to find the doctor on duty.

Sophia let go of his hand. "I should go get Nick. He's been pacing the hall for hours. Rowen gave him permission to come see you."

"Wait." John grabbed her wrist and pulled her closer. "What happened?"

"Your wound became infected, and you lost consciousness. I had to drag you the rest of the way. Tango was notified of our position, and when we crossed the border, they picked us up."

"You dragged me all the way to Mongolia?"

She grinned down at him. "Yeah. You don't weigh as much as a toothpick. It was a cakewalk."

He frowned. "I told you to leave me."

"I had no intention of obeying that order."

"Damn! You are so stubborn."

She grinned at him. He stared at her with a grimace on his face. Then he reached up with his other hand, hooked it behind her neck, and pulled her down until her lips were almost touching his. He stared into her eyes for a long, heated moment.

"Don't ever disobey me again," he whispered.

She closed the gap and pressed her lips to his. He anchored his palm against her shoulder and gently pushed her back.

"Don't," he whispered.

She pressed her forehead to his and sighed. "Why not?"

"You know why. Don't kiss me ever again."

"I promise; I won't tell anyone."

"You're torturing me, Sophia. Please, don't tempt me with what I can't have."

"What if you can have—"

"Don't say it. Just go—before you make me lose my resolve."

She took a step back and stared at him. The tortured look and the sadness that stared back at her through his chocolate brown eyes was too much. Tears escaped down her cheeks, and she swiped them away.

John looked away. He couldn't bear to watch her cry especially since he was the cause. His jaw tightened, and he closed his eyes. He felt her thread her fingers through his, and then he felt her lips press a soft kiss to the back of his hand. He couldn't look at her. He kept his eyes closed.

"Before I crossed the border, you were so sick. I thought I was going to lose you, John. I can't lose you. I won't lose you. I've fallen in love with you."

A tear streaked down his cheek. "Don't say that. It's not allowed, Sophia."

"I don't care if it's allowed or not. I can't change the way I feel. If I had lost you, it would have destroyed a piece of my soul. Just thinking about a future without you in it hurts."

He opened his eyes and met hers. "Sophia, you have to stop this. You've worked too hard to get where you are. I won't let you throw all of that away. I'm not worth it. You're just emotional right now. You've been through an ordeal. You're not thinking clearly. When you've had time to process—"

"Don't you dare accuse me of being an emotional female again. I will kick your ass!" She grinned at him. "It took me a while to realize you said that to push me away. You're good at pushing people away. You're good at falling on the sword, but I'm not going to let you do it this time. I'm on to you, John Rusk. I see right through you. I know you love me too. You can deny it, but I saw it in your eyes."

He frowned and pulled his hand away from her grasp. "You don't know what you're talking about. I'm not in love with you. You're not in love with me. Stressful situations can mess with your head temporarily. That's all this is. You need to get a handle on it before you make a mistake that can't be overlooked. Violating the UCMJ is a serious crime. They will punish you for it if you make a mis-step. Tread carefully, Sophia. You can't display affection to anyone in your chain of command. They won't forgive it."

She took a step back, winked at him, and gave him a big grin. "Always trying to protect me even from myself. Deny it if you want, but I know the truth now. I do see you, John. You can't hide it from me anymore."

She left the room, and a minute later Nick came in. He walked over and gave John a hug.

"I'm so sorry. We thought you were dead. I never should have left without you."

"Stop, Nick. Don't blame yourself. There's no way you could have known we were still alive. There was no way to contact you. Our coms were dead. I gave you the intel so you could complete the mission."

"We did, but—"

"Then you did your job. There's no need to second guess yourself."

"I feel terrible. I should have tried to find you. I should have searched."

"You couldn't have found us. Looking would have wasted time and probably gotten you and the rest of the team killed."

They fell silent for a moment.

"Ben's not back yet."

John nodded. "Have we gotten any word from him?"

"Rowen only said the rest of Echo are still on site in the Sahara. They are coordinating with their CIA contact. We don't know when they'll be back."

John sighed. "I don't like having the team split up like this."

Nick nodded. "It's frustrating, but we don't have any control over this."

John let out a heavy sigh. "I need you to do me a favor."

"Anything."

"Until I get back, I need you to keep an eye on Gonzalez. I think the stress of this mission has messed with her head. She's not thinking rationally. Make sure she doesn't say or do anything that will get her in trouble—and stand guard when she takes showers."

Nick's eyebrow rose over his right eye. "You want me to babysit her?"

John cleared his throat. "She feels guilty that I nearly died. She's feeling overly attached to me at the moment. I know she'll get her head back in the game. I just want you to make sure she doesn't make any stupid mistakes between now and then."

Nick frowned as he stared at John. "Overly attached? As in—she likes you?"

John looked away, and his jaw tightened. "I know I can trust you to do the right thing. It's just a temporary response to a high adrenaline situation. She'll get past it."

Nick grinned. "So, what you're saying is she has an adrenaline crush on you?"

John looked back at him and glared. "Don't start with me, Nick!"

Nick laughed. "I'm going to need more details. I can't go into this mission blind. I need intel—you know—in case I have to head off anything amorous."

A low growl erupted from John's throat. "Just keep her out of trouble!"

Nick smirked. "How do you propose I do that?"

"I don't know. Use your best judgement."

"Did something happen on this mission that shouldn't have?"

John groaned.

"Oh, damn! You slept with her!"

His eyes locked on Nick like daggers. "No, I didn't!"

Nick studied his best friend for a moment. "Something happened."

"Nothing happened."

"I'm not buying that. The look on your face says otherwise."

"It's not what you think. It was mostly innocent."

"Mostly?"

"She got emotional, and she tried to kiss me."

"You kissed her!"

"No! I said she tried. I wouldn't let her. She just got caught up in the stress of the situation and made a bad call. I just don't want her doing something stupid now that it's over."

Nick crossed his arms over his chest. "A bad call? That's how you're going to phrase that?"

"She lost her head for a moment. She'll get it back in line. She just needs to get back into the normal routine. She'll realize it was a mistake."

May 30
1400
Afghanistan base

After an extended stay in the Naples hospital, John exited the helicopter on base in Afghanistan. He walked across the compound with a pronounced limp heading directly to Rowen's tent to report for duty.

"How are you feeling?" Rowen asked.

"Ready to kick some butt, Sir."

Rowen smirked. "Typical."

John stood at attention waiting for orders.

"The rest of Echo is back from Africa. Their mission was a success. They gathered more evidence of a clone army. It appears the Russians are up to something nefarious."

"What are our orders, Sir?"

"At the moment, you don't have any. We are waiting for direction from the CIA on what course of action to take."

John nodded. "I'll make sure we are ready to roll as soon as we receive orders."

Rowen nodded. "Dismissed."

John limped down the long rows of tents until he came to Echo's tent. He paused outside and took a deep breath. He wasn't ready for this, but he couldn't put it off any longer. It had to be done. He opened the tent flap and limped inside. Over half the men were asleep on their bunks. Those who weren't stood up and saluted him. John saluted back and limped to the back of the tent. He spotted Nick and Sonny playing poker on Nick's bunk. His eyes darted to Sophia's bunk. It was empty.

"Where's Gonzalez?"

"She's doing PT." Sonny stood up and grabbed John in a bear hug. "It's good to see you. You gave us all quite a scare."

John hugged him back. "I'm tougher than I look."

Sonny grinned. "That's fer dang sure."

"How long has she been gone?"

Nick's eyebrow rose. "About an hour, why?"

"Go find her and tell her to report to the mess hall immediately."

Nick stood up and walked toward John. "Is something wrong?"

"No."

Nick walked out of the tent to look for Sophia. John got into his locker and pulled out paperwork. Then he limped out of the tent to the deserted mess hall. A few minutes later, Sophia entered the mess hall. She was covered in sandy dust and sweat. She stopped in front of the table John was sitting at. She saluted him and stood at attention.

"Sir, reporting for duty."

"At ease. Have a seat, Gonzalez."

She sat down across from him and studied his face. He wore a grim expression.

"I'm having a hard time deciding how to handle this," he said sternly. "I should write you up for disobeying a direct order."

She swallowed hard. "Sir, if that's what you feel you need to do."

"Is it?"

"Sir?"

"Do I need to write you up for that? It will go against your permanent record and could affect future promotion opportunities."

"Sir, you did give me a direct order. I had no intention of obeying that order. You made a bad call. You weren't thinking clearly. I used my best judgement in the field to find a solution to the problem. I couldn't leave you behind, Sir."

His lips turned down in a frown. "When I give you an order, I expect it to be obeyed!"

"Yes, Sir."

"Do you think it's okay for you to pick and choose which orders you want to follow?"

"No, Sir."

"Then why did you disobey this order? In the field, sometimes lives are lost. Sometimes men have to be sacrificed for the greater good. In that situation, I made a call to preserve my team. It's better for some of the team to be saved than for one man to bring death to the entire team. I chose to save you, to preserve what was still a viable functioning part of Echo. You blatantly disregarded my order and did whatever the hell you wanted. That's not acceptable, Gonzalez!"

She sat silent staring at him.

"Do you have anything to say to me?" he growled.

"Yes, Sir!"

"Spit it out then!"

"Sir, in that situation, your rational thinking was compromised. Your ability to make a proper command decision was compromised. I felt it necessary to disregard that order and take appropriate action."

His fists curled against the table, and his jaw tightened.

"You're not in command. You don't get to decide which of my orders are to be followed. How is this not clear to you? Whether you felt I was compromised or not isn't the point. The point is you've become lax in your discipline. You've allowed your personal feelings to enter into your decision-making process. I won't have that, Gonzalez!"

"Yes, Sir."

"When I give you an order, you will follow it!"

"If the order is to leave you to die, I will not follow it, Sir."

John shoved his chair back from the table and stood up glaring at her.

She stood up facing him. "If you feel you need to write me up, I will take that punishment. I will take any punishment you feel is necessary, but I will never leave you behind to die. If that means I've destroyed my career as a SEAL, then so be it. I will not have your death on my conscious, Sir! You are too valuable to this team to let you die. I will not do that. I will never follow that order, Sir!"

A low growl erupted from his throat. "Consider yourself written up." He pulled out a paper from his folder and slid it across the table with a pen. "Sign it."

A smirky grin turned up the corner of her mouth as she took the pen and signed her name to the paper. She slid it back to him.

"Will that be all, Sir?"

"No, sit down!"

She took a seat and watched him intently. He paced back and forth with a painful limp. Her smirky grin fell to a frown. She watched him drag his hand over his dark brown burr. Then he stopped in front of her.

"I tried to do the right thing. I tried to be the nice guy. I wanted to give you a chance to prove yourself in the field, but you are walking a very thin line here, Gonzalez. Your behavior on this mission was out of line. I can't have that on this team. The nice guy is gone. If you want to continue with Echo, you will conform to the rules. You will follow my orders, and you will obey the UCMJ. Am I making myself clear?"

"Crystal, Sir."

"If we were in a battle situation and Nick was riddled with bullet wounds, bleeding out with less than a minute to live, would you follow an order to leave him behind?"

"Yes, Sir."

"If it were me instead of Nick, would you follow that same order?"

She swallowed hard and forced down the image of John bleeding to death. "Yes, Sir."

"Why did you hesitate?"

"I didn't."

"The hell you didn't! You had to think about it before you answered. Why?"

"You know why, Sir."

"Get those thoughts out of your head, Gonzalez! You can't afford to hesitate in the field. It can cost lives."

"Understood, Sir."

"Do you understand? Do you really know what these ideas can cost you?"

"Yes, Sir."

"I don't want to see any evidence of these unauthorized thoughts or feelings from you, Gonzalez. Follow the rules or there will be consequences."

"What sort of consequences?"

His eyes narrowed as he studied her. "The worst kind."

She stood up and stared back into his eyes. "The worst would be if you were dead. I can live with any other consequences."

"Prison?"

"Prison would be nothing compared to living with the knowledge that I let you die out there. I can take whatever is dished out. What I can't take is knowingly allowing you to die. I will never do that. Don't ever ask it again. I'm not capable of following that order, John."

"Don't call me John! Call me Sir or Chief Rusk. That's all you're allowed to call me!"

He dragged his hand over his burr and let out a frustrated sigh. Then he started pacing again. "You have to suspend your emotions from this equation."

"Is that what you're doing, suspending your emotions from the equation?" She studied him as he paced back and forth. His limp concerned her.

"There are no emotions for me to suspend. I'm referring to you."

She said nothing for a moment. Then she cleared her throat, stood up, rounded the table, and stood in his path. He halted in front of her.

"You want to come down on me for not following your order, but you were making decisions based on your emotions."

"No, I wasn't."

"You didn't stitch up your leg because you were in too much pain. You could have asked me to do it for you, but you didn't. You didn't want to wake me. You were worried about me."

He swallowed hard as he stared down into her eyes.

"We could have stayed in the cave so you could rest, but you wanted to make sure I made it across the border before we were caught by the Russians."

His jaw tightened.

"You pushed yourself too hard. You pushed until you were on the brink of collapse before you gave me the order to leave you behind. You weren't thinking about the good of the team. We were the only ones there. You were only thinking about how best to keep me alive. You didn't care about keeping yourself alive. Why is that, Chief Rusk? You can't tell me your emotions didn't play into that. Those decisions were riddled with emotions."

"I'm your commanding officer. It's my duty to ensure the safety of my team to the best of my ability. Letting you rest was vital to your recovery from the ordeal of dragging me through the woods. Staying in that cave would have been suicide for both of us. The Russians would have overtaken that area of the woods eventually. We would have been cut off from our exit route. I pushed myself as far as I could go, but ultimately, I knew I wasn't going to make it home. I had accepted that fate the minute that bullet tore into my leg. We were deep in enemy territory. The chances of me surviving that injury were minimal at best. If I didn't bleed out, there was always the possibility of infection waiting to take me down. It almost did. I'm grateful to be alive, but I shouldn't be alive right now. You took too big of a risk trying to save me. You could have ended up—dead!" His face twisted in pain. Then he went on. "I won't ask the men under me to make that sacrifice on my behalf. They are not here to keep me alive. They are here to serve our country. If they lay down their life it should be in the line of duty carrying out a mission. It should never be to save my ass. I'm expendable. The mission comes first, then my men. I'm last in line in that equation. Are we clear now?"

"So, everyone and everything comes before you."

"Exactly."

"Does that extend to your personal life, or are you only referring to the team, Sir?"

"I don't have a personal life, Gonzalez. I gave up that privilege when I joined the Navy. My life doesn't belong to me. It belongs to the military. Every time I renew my contract, I renew my vow to serve my country without limits. Everything I have belongs to the cause. I keep nothing for myself."

"In BUD/S they taught us that to be a SEAL is to be a team. Teamwork is the basis of our existence. Without the team we are nothing. Why are you insisting on going this alone? You are a part of the team, Sir. You rely on us. We rely on you. It's a symbiotic relationship."

"It is a symbiotic relationship, but when you become the C.O. of that team, things change. I'm responsible for the success of our missions and the safety of my team. The team has to come before me. That's just the way it is."

"So, you truly are left with nothing. You've separated yourself from the team. You've separated yourself from any hope of a personal life. You've isolated yourself into a box of your own making."

The steel resolve in his eyes didn't waver. "I did what had to be done."

"It must be very lonely inside that box."

His jaw tightened.

"You're dismissed, Gonzalez."

She frowned. Then she nodded and left the mess hall.

I only thought I knew who John was. I see now, I haven't even scratched the surface. Sonny said he has onion layers of defense. How many layers do I have to peel back before I get to his heart? He also said it takes John time to open up to people. Maybe he just needs more time to admit his feelings. I'll just have to be patient.

After she left, John sank down in the chair and stared at the paper Sophia had signed. He tore it into small pieces and threw it away. Then he sat at the table staring at the wall for a long time. He didn't want to go back to the tent. Going back meant having to face her. He wasn't sure how to act around her anymore. She had ruined everything.

CHAPTER 59

June 2
1200
VA rehab center, North Carolina

Lydell grunted as he struggled to push the weight with his right leg. If he could push the weight all the way this time it would make twenty reps. Halfway to his goal the muscles in his leg began to quiver. He closed his eyes and focused. With great effort he extended his leg completely and heard the soft clang of metal. He let out a breath and slowly allowed his leg to lower back down.

"Good job, Lydell," Nurse Walzer praised. "That's two more than last time. Your leg is getting stronger."

Lydell nodded, but his frown remained.

"Let's get you on the bars and see what you can do," Walzer said.

He picked Lydell up from the weight machine and carried him a few feet over to the parallel bars. Lydell stood with his hands on the bars staring at the goal ahead of him, a line of red tape on the floor. He mentally prepared himself for the task. Then he forced his right leg to bend.

One step down—forty-nine more to go.

Physical therapy had been grueling. It had taken a toll on him in more ways than one. His progress was coming much slower than he had envisioned it. Discouraged didn't begin to encompass how he felt, but he put on a brave face to the world. Quitting was not in his mental vocabulary. He struggled through the exercise and managed to get ten steps today before his body gave out, and he had to stop.

Kyle picked him up from the VA center. Kyle didn't ask how the session had gone. He could see from Lydell's dejected demeanor that his friend was having a rough day.

"How would you feel about helping me and Owen out with the restoration business?" Kyle asked as he navigated the road home.

"I don't know anything about restoring cars."

"Neither did I when I first started, but I picked it up. Owen is a good teacher."

Lydell let out a weary sigh and stared out the window at the green blur of trees and grass.

"I thought we could start you off on something easy like the exhaust assembly. Once you learn some of the basics, you can add to it and learn the whole process."

"Thanks, but I don't think so."

"Why not?"

"In case you haven't noticed, I can't walk without assistance."

"You don't have to be able to walk to roll up under a car and use your hands to attach parts."

Lydell sighed and closed his eyes. He wasn't in the mood to be cheered up. He didn't appreciate Kyle offering him more charity. He already felt like a freeloader as it was. Now Kyle was offering to make him feel useful when he felt utterly useless. It felt like pity on top of pity.

Kyle let it drop for the moment, and the truck fell silent as he drove home.

Megan had dinner almost ready when they arrived.

"Hi, Honey. We're home," Kyle called from the doorway.

Lydell put on a smile for Megan's sake, but through dinner his mind was working the problem.

Megan is going to have a new baby in the home in a month. I need to get out of here. I'm just in the way. They've been very gracious to open their home to me, but I've been here too long. My leg is only a little stronger than it was. At this rate I won't be walking for a long time. I won't be the third wheel anymore. I'm going to find my own place and move out.

That night he took a bath and sat in the tub evaluating his most recent scar. The bright pink scar that traversed the length of his right thigh wasn't pretty. It wasn't a gruesome scar. The doctors had done everything possible to minimize the scarring, but it was a reminder that the steel rod in his leg was an alien inside his body.

He got ready for bed and lay staring at the ceiling. Just before midnight, his phone buzzed on the nightstand. There was a text from an unknown number. He opened it and an irrepressible smile spread over his lips.

B: Hi Sweetheart. It's Bretta. How you are doing. I miss you.

L: I'm good. I miss you too.

B: How is your rehab going?

L: Slow.

B: You'll get there. I have faith in you.

L: That makes one of us.

B: You're not okay. What's wrong?

L: You mean other than feeling like a useless waste of space?

B: That's not true.

L: I'm a burden on my friends and family. I don't contribute anything anymore.

B: You will. Give yourself time. It takes a while to get over an injury like that.

L: Yeah, well, in the meantime, I'm a drain on the people I love.

B: I seriously doubt Kyle and Megan consider you a drain. They wouldn't have offered to help you if they felt that way. They love you.

L: You don't know. You're not here. They have a new baby on the way. They shouldn't have to deal with me. I'll be moving out soon. I won't put them through my struggle anymore.

B: I want to see you.

L: I don't want you to see me like this. It's not pretty.

B: Too bad. I'm already here. Unlock your window.

Lydell groaned softly. Then he sat up, hoisted himself into his wheelchair, and rolled over to the window. Bretta was standing there with a smile. He unlocked it, and a minute later she was inside sliding the window shut.

"What are you doing here?" he asked quietly.

"I'm worried about you. I've been watching. You don't seem your usual self."

"I'm not my usual self."

She leaned down and pressed her lips against his. He kissed her back, but there was no passion behind it. His kiss was as dejected as his attitude.

Bretta pulled back with a frown. "After all these months, this is the best kiss I can get from you? I know you can kiss better than that."

A half grin spread up his mouth. "Sorry."

"Let's try this again, but why don't we utilize that very comfortable looking bed of yours."

She wheeled him over to the bed and helped him onto the mattress. He sat on the edge staring at her in the dark room. She turned on the lamp beside the bed, and then she slid her fingers into his loose copper curls.

He grinned at her. "You changed your hair. Last time I saw you it was blonde."

"I'm in disguise." She reached up, tugged the red wig off, and dropped it on the floor.

His eyes widened a little. "Is this your real color?"

"Not attracted to a brunette?"

He reached up, hooked his hand behind her neck, and pulled her down for a kiss. She leaned him back on the bed and crawled on top of him as their lips danced in a frantic kiss. Her hands slid up under his t-shirt caressing over his rock-hard abs. His hands went to the zipper on her jeans to free her of the garment as quickly as possible. They made love the rest of the night. When dawn peeked through the window, she left before he woke up.

At breakfast, Lydell told Megan and Kyle about his plan to move out. They talked him out of it. He'd never imagined having friends like Kyle and Megan, but he was glad they were in his life. They were keeping him on track and making him feel like he belonged. It was nice to feel wanted. He gave into it and decided to stay with them for a while longer. He even decided to give car restoration a try. He figured having a job to do would keep his mind off his problems.

CHAPTER 60

June 4
0700
Afghanistan base

John stood in front of Rowen listening intently to the mission at hand. He was grateful there was finally something to do. The last five days on base had been hell. There was nowhere to go to escape Sophia. There was nothing to distract him from rehashing her observations.

He had been sure his decisions were based on rational foundations until she'd pointed things out from her perspective. Now, he couldn't help but wonder if she might be right. Had he based his decisions on a need to keep her alive because he had feelings for her?

He left Rowen's tent and informed Echo that they had a new mission. Everyone began packing for the mission immediately. As John fastened his pack, he glanced up. Sophia was putting the last few items in her pack. His eyes roamed down to her perfect ass and lingered for a moment too long. He jerked his eyes away from her just in time to see Nick frowning at him. John looked away and turned to check on the progress of the rest of the team. Everyone was nearly packed.

As soon as the last man finished, Echo headed to the waiting chopper. Nick sat opposite of John on the chopper. John deliberately kept his eyes off of Sophia, but he could feel Nick's accusing gaze on him the entire ride. Every time John looked up Nick was staring at him with a disapproving expression.

The chopper rendezvoused with a cargo flight out of Turkey to Bucharest, Romania. Echo was transported by SUVs to a centrally located safehouse. There they were introduced to their CIA contact, Leo D. Vinci. He escorted them up a spiraling staircase to the third floor and showed them into a suite of rooms. Five tables arranged in a circle held laptops and a variety of equipment. CIA agents were stationed at each table monitoring multiple locations within the city.

Leo showed them to a back room where chairs had been placed in rows. SEAL teams Lima and Bravo arrived a short while later, and Leo immediately launched into a formal briefing of the current situation. Heads of State from fifty countries would be attending a social gala at an ancient Bucharest castle in three days time. The NSA had decoded chatter on the web regarding an assassination attempt. The SEAL's job would be to coordinate with the CIA onsite to thwart any such attempt.

There was a lot of ground to cover and not much time to get all the pieces in place. Leo divided the SEAL teams into three sectors. Lima would cover street surveillance. Bravo would be the eyes inside the castle. Echo would be Overwatch for the mission. Echo would set up teams of two in selected buildings surrounding the castle. Anything suspicious in their line of sight would be their mission.

Leo showed John where the designated apartments and businesses surrounding the upcoming gala were located. There were eight hides for the SEALs to watch from. They were almost equally spaced in a circle around the stone castle. All John had to do was divide his team into pairs to watch the perimeter night and day.

Echo split off into a smaller room to strategize. Lima and Bravo did the same. John studied the map for a few minutes before spreading it out on the table for everyone to see. He pulled out a ruler and a red sharpie. Then he divided the map into eight equal pie shares.

"We'll rotate guard duty in four-hour shifts. Except on the day of the gala. I want everyone on high alert that day with all eyes on the prize. The more eyes we have on the problem the less likely the assassin will be able to slip through our net."

Everyone nodded in agreement.

John took a green sharpie and wrote on each section of the map who he was assigning there.

"Nick and Sophia take sector one. Ben and Mac, sector two. Zach and Jerome, sector three. Dorian and Falco, sector four. Ezra and Andrew, sector five. Sonny and Matt, sector six. Hogan and Chris, sector seven. I'll take sector eight with Joe."

John passed out a map to each team, and they respectively drew identical sections on their maps with the designated assignments. Then they all checked their comlinks, packed up, and headed to their respective stakeouts.

On his way out, Nick paused and waited until John was alone.

"I see I'm back on babysitting duty."

"I trust you."

"You don't trust the rest of Echo? We are all on the same team."

"Do you have a problem working with her?"

"No. She's fine. I have no problem with her. You're the one I have a problem with. You're letting this situation with her affect you. I'm not the only one who notices."

"Who notices?"

"The entire team."

"Have they said something to you?"

"No. They don't have to say anything. I see the way they look at you—at her. They know something is going on between you two. You can't hide it."

"Nothing is going on. I already told you what happened. I told you how I dealt with it."

"It's not effective. I'm not the only one who notices how she watches you now. She didn't used to, but she's changed since Siberia. She can barely keep her eyes off you."

John let out a heavy sigh. "Yeah, I've noticed. I'm trying to fix the situation; I really am."

"Why don't you start with yourself? You watch her as much as she watches you."

"I said I'll fix it!"

"You better fix it fast before someone outside of Echo notices."

John nodded. Nick left.

Once Echo set up their equipment and checked in, John addressed the whole team on coms.

"For the next two days, when you are off watch duty, I want you to sleep. I want everyone well rested and fully focused on the day of the gala."

Sector one and eight faced the front entrance of the 200-year-old Bucharest castle. Sectors two through eight fanned out clockwise from sector one. In sector one, Nick took the first shift. His view of the castle entrance was nearly the same as John's. He watched a stream of deliveries crossing the cobblestone bridge to the main entrance. The deliverymen were soon out of sight as they made their way around the castle to rear entrances.

An event this prestigious would have only the finest in décor and cuisine for the gala. Hundreds of people would be involved in pulling off such an event. That did not make the job easy for the SEALs or the CIA agents who were monitoring traffic cams and security cams from the safehouse. There were undoubtedly CIA undercover operatives inside the castle watching things from a very close angle, but the SEALs were not privy to that level of information.

On June 5, at 0100, Sonny watched from his hide in sector six. There had been no movement for hours, but now someone was skulking about in the shadows. His night vision goggles illuminated a male scaling the back wall of the castle.

"Echo 3 to Echo 1."

"Echo 1, go for Echo 3."

"I've got movement. Male—approximately five-foot-ten—scaling the back wall. Please advise."

"Copy that."

John grabbed the comlink for the CIA. "Leo, please advise. We have a bogey—male—scaling the back wall."

Leo tapped his com to unmute it. "Copy that. Bogey is one of ours. Stand down. We are running a test."

"Copy that. Will advise my team to stand down."

By the time John relayed the information to Sonny, the CIA operative had cleared the wall.

"Echo 1, can we get a better turnaround time for information relay? That bogey was over the wall before I heard back from you," Sonny said into his com.

"Copy that. I'll speak with Leo and have him inform us prior to any more tests," John said.

On June 6, at 1600, the first dignitaries began arriving at the castle entrance. Everyone was on high alert. The assassin had not been identified yet. After two hours, every guest had been admitted through the security protocol gate. Echo kept a watchful eye, but there was no suspicious movement on the exterior of the castle. Lima reported nothing on their patrol. Bravo saw nothing out of place inside the castle.

At 1900, Bretta entered the main dining hall of the castle with a long line of servers. She was dressed in the same black uniform as the other kitchen staff. She placed her appetizers in front of the two guests she'd been assigned to serve. The plates were small. The delicate works of culinary art were dainty and colorful. She filled wine glasses and returned to the kitchen for the next course. Miniature bowls of steaming soup were being lined up for the second course. The creamy broth was topped with a colorful garnish and the aroma was enticing. There would be seven courses in all, and each was a work of culinary genius prepared by a masterful chef.

While the guests dined, the SEAL teams remained vigilant. Bravo and Lima both made another round with bomb sniffing dogs as they kept an eye out for anything out of the ordinary.

A hum of conversation filled the dining hall. 100 party guests sat at the ancient table and conversed about politics and the social news of the day. After two hours of dining and polite discussions, dessert was served. Bretta carried her two plates and gently set the delicate desserts in front of her guests. Then she lit a match in unison with the other servers and the desserts were set ablaze for a moment. Sighs of delight came from the guests. The flames burned out quickly as the alcohol was consumed. Fresh glasses of wine were placed in front of the guests to accompany the desserts, and the servers quietly exited the dining hall.

Bretta slipped away from the kitchen where the staff were cleaning up and headed into the main hall of the castle. She passed the nearly invisible Bravo posts in the darkened hallway as she headed to the stairs. One of Bravo stepped in front of the stairs to block her.

"Excuse me, Miss. No one is allowed upstairs."

"The monkey runs at midnight." Her clipped British accent echoed in the dark hallway.

"Sorry, ma'am. I didn't know you were one of us." He stepped aside to allow her access and faded back into the shadows of the darkened hallway.

At 2100, CIA agent, Mark T. Wain, stood against the wall of the music hall in the castle. He was dressed in a black tuxedo, and he was watching the guests dance and sway to the elegant ballroom music from a live orchestra.

"Leo to Mark."

"Mark here."

"Doing the scheduled check in. Any trouble there?"

"No. Not a single hitch. The party is nearly over. The guests will be retiring soon."

"Copy that."

Leo contacted the leaders of Bravo, Lima, and Echo to let them know their services would be required all night until the last guest departed the following day. With no assassination attempt the danger was still lurking in the unseen shadows. John let out a sigh before passing along the news to his team. Then he refocused his attention on the exterior of the castle.

At 2130, Bretta crouched on the inside of a parapet and pulled out her scrambled burner phone. She pulled up Echo's com link code, hacked into it, narrowed the signal down to Sonny's earpiece, and connected to it.

"Sonny, it's Bretta."

Sonny jerked his head a little when he heard her clipped British accent in his ear.

"Echo 3 to Echo 1, we have interference on the line."

"No one can hear you but me. I hacked your com link. I need you to listen carefully."

"Copy that."

"Send Matt on a useless errand for about five minutes. This is between you and me."

"Negatory."

"This op is compromised. There's a double-cross in play. I'm trying to save lives here, Sonny. You're the only one I trust. I know you won't betray me."

"Says who?" Sonny whispered into his com.

"You never betrayed Lydell when you caught us kissing outside the bunkhouse in Congo. I know you are a loyal, true friend. I'm here to help. I think there is a mole in the CIA organization. I'm undercover at the gala, but there is no assassin in the castle. Everything is quiet and peaceful. Does that sound right to you?"

"It does sound fishy. We've been posted for three days straight. If this is an assassination attempt, it's the strangest one I've ever staked out."

"Exactly. Please trust me, Sonny. I need out of the castle without the CIA being made aware of it. I need to check something out before it's too late."

Sonny bit his lip. "What do you need to check? One of us can do it for you."

"What if one of you are in on the plot?"

"Ain't no chance in hell that a SEAL is a part of anything dirty. I know these guys. They ain't the traitor type."

"Sonny, time is of the essence. At midnight the party is over, and the dignitaries retire to their assigned rooms in the castle. I don't have much time to check out my hunch. I need your help. In two minutes, I'm going to climb down the back, castle wall. I need you to distract Matt until I get out of sight."

"Well, damn! You don't ask fer much, do ya. Just that I lie to my team and betray their trust."

"Do you want one of these heads of state to be assassinated?"

"No."

"Then help me."

"What if I help you and you end up being the assassin?"

Bretta chuckled. "Sonny, you would make an excellent MI-6 agent. You have a very suspicious mind."

"Don't flatter me, Little Miss. It don't work on me. Where are you?"

"I'm in the parapet."

Sonny trained his rifle scope on the parapet. "I don't see you. Prove it."

She held up her hand in the window. Sonny trained his rifle scope on her hand.

He smirked. "That could be anyone's hand. Prove it's you."

She shot him the bird. He chuckled. "You are feisty."

"Are you going to help me or not?"

Sonny contemplated the situation and grimaced. "I swear if you double-cross me on this, I'll hunt you down and take you out myself for fun. You better be legit!"

"Thank you, Sonny."

"Go on my mark. I have to get rid of Matt for a minute."

Sonny walked over to Matt, tapped him on the shoulder, and used hand signals to tell him that Bretta had contacted him and asked him to look the other way while she climbed down the back wall. He let Matt know to continue watching the wall, let Bretta climb down, and that he was going to follow her to see what she was up to.

Matt nodded and hand signaled that he would contact John. Sonny shook his head and let Matt know their coms had been hacked. Matt gave him the thumbs up, and Sonny slipped away. He took up a position where he could see Bretta without being in her line of sight. Then he took a deep breath and crossed his fingers hoping he had made the right decision.

"Sonny to Bretta."

"This is Bretta."

"Okay, Girlie. All is clear."

Bretta checked the hide across from her location and noted there was no longer a set of eyes with a rifle scope in the window. She quickly repelled down the castle wall and took off into the trees surrounding the castle. Sonny tailed her off the castle grounds, down several side streets, through a few back alleys, and finally came to a halt at the CIA safehouse.

What in hell is she doin' here? Does she think one of them CIA fellers in the safehouse is a double-agent? This don't make no sense!

Sonny crept up behind her and watched her link into the security feeds in the basement. He trained his rifle at the back of her skull with his finger on the trigger.

"Don't you trust me, Sonny?"

His jaw tightened.

Bretta smirked. "Did you notify the whole team or just Matt?"

"Wouldn't you like to know."

"I'm guessing just Matt. You didn't have time to get to anyone else. You should work on your tailing. I noticed you right after I left the castle grounds."

He smirked. "What makes you think I was really trying to hide. I'm good at what I do. If I wanted full concealment, you'd never see me coming, Little Princess. Now, why are we here?"

Her eyebrow rose. "I told you. There's a double-cross in play. I'm trying to save lives here."

"Let's just say I believe you. Who's the mole?"

"Someone on the safehouse team."

"Why one of them? They ain't even on-site. How are they supposed to assassinate anyone?"

"There are more ways to kill someone than a bullet or a bomb."

"You would know all about that. Don't play no head games on me. I ain't in the mood. Tell me what you're doin' right now, or I will blow your head off!"

Bretta turned to face him, his finger tightened on the trigger. She grinned as she sauntered over to him. She stopped inches away from the barrel of his sniper's rifle.

Bretta laughed. "It's hard to make a shot when the firing pin is missing."

Sonny squeezed the trigger, and his weapon clicked. He squeezed it again, and it clicked again.

"You little bitch!"

He swung the butt of the rifle at her head, but she easily ducked and countered with her fist to the side of his jaw. A struggle ensued that ranged from Martial Arts, to knives, to every defensive move Sonny had in his arsenal. He was no match for Bretta. In the end, he found himself on the ground with his own knife to his throat.

"I don't have time to play, Sonny. I don't want to kill you. Don't make me. I'm trying to stop an assassination. You can either help me, or you can lie here dead in a puddle of your own blood. Which will it be?"

He growled as he stared up at her. "I really hate you!"

"I'm sure you do."

"I don't trust you."

"You shouldn't. I'm not here to protect you. I'm on assignment and right now, you are causing delays. In five seconds, I'll make the decision for you, and you won't be happy with it."

Sonny gritted his teeth.

"Five, four, three, two, one—"

At 2215, John stood in position with his rifle on the front gate and his eyes scanning for any movement. Joe stood in position at the other window doing the same.

"Are you and Sophia an item or not?" Joe asked.

John glanced at Joe who was still watching the gate. He muted his com. "Keep your eyes on your work and cut the chatter," John growled.

"Don't worry. I muted my com. This conversation is just between us."

John's jaw tightened as he trained his eyes back on the castle gate.

"So, does she belong to you now? Did you mark your territory in Siberia?"

"No. Anything unprofessional with Gonzalez is a violation of the UCMJ. That goes for all of Echo—including me."

Joe smirked. "No. Something happened between you two. She's different now, and so are you. The way you look at her, or rather try to avoid looking at her tells the tale. She's more standoffish with the rest of the team now. She used to joke around and put up with my sly flirting. Now, she ignores it entirely. I think that's your doing."

"You shouldn't be flirting with her at all."

"Yeah, well—I asked her to marry me when we were in L.A."

John's whole body tensed as he kept his eyes trained on the objective below.

"The trouble is—I really like her. I like her family. They like me. We could be the perfect match once we both get out, but I think her heart belongs to someone else now. When we were in L.A. she was different. She was fun. She was flirty. She was open. Now, it feels like she slammed the door in my face. She's not the same Sophia she was when she joined Echo. If I had to guess, I'd say she's fallen in love with you, Sir."

"She's a soldier. She's not allowed to fall in love with anyone on Echo. Those are the rules. She's not going to break them and neither are any of us. Get your head back in the game, Joe. Stop entertaining things that are not possible."

Joe dropped the interrogation, and they both fell silent. After a few minutes, John unmuted his com and checked in with his team. Everyone reported back that there was nothing out of the ordinary except Sonny.

"Echo 10 report on Echo 3's position. Is his com link operational?"

"Copy that," Matt said. "Echo 3 is taking a smoke break. He should be back in a few minutes."

John's jaw tightened. He hand-signaled to Joe to keep eyes on while he went to check on Sonny. Joe nodded.

John left sector one and ran to sector six. His heart was pounding in his chest. Sonny didn't smoke, and none of his men would abandon their post in the middle of a critical op. Something was wrong. The minute he entered the room, Matt signaled him to remain quiet. For the next two minutes they communicated via hand signals, and Matt told him everything he knew.

John raked a hand over his burr and gritted his teeth. This wasn't like Sonny. Sonny didn't go off half-cocked with no back up and leave the team in the dark. The worst part of it was he had no way of knowing where Sonny might have tailed her to.

If he lives through this, I'm going to kill him! What the hell is he thinking? Bretta is a spy. You can't trust a spy.

At 2350, in the basement of the CIA safehouse, Bretta stood watching the feeds from the surveillance footage. Nothing seemed out of the ordinary. That was the problem. All was quiet—everywhere. She disabled the surveillance feeds, stepped over Sonny's body, and hurried up the stairs. She took out the four guards on the stairs before kicking in the door to the safehouse.

The startled agents went for their guns, but she took them out with speed and efficiency. The only agent who remained calm and didn't go for a weapon was Leo. Bretta aimed her gun at him.

Leo tusked. "Are you really going to kill me? That will only make all of this worse for you."

"You are a dirty snake, Leo."

He grinned wickedly. "Isn't that the business we are in?"

"You're betraying your country!"

"Am I?"

Her eyes narrowed on him. "You're following orders? Whose?"

He chuckled. "It doesn't work like that. Little fish don't get to swim in the big pond."

"Was there really chatter about an assassination, or is all of this some ruse to ferret out something else?"

"Perhaps it is."

"Don't clam up now. Your life depends on you talking. I will pull the trigger."

"I know you will. That's what you were trained to do. Kill first and ask questions later. You Brits will never learn. It's better to get all the information first before you make the kill."

"Why are you so smug about this? Is your life of so little value to you?"

"Is yours? If you kill me now, you will hang for all of this. You're the perfect patsy, Bretta. You're going to take the fall for everything that's about to happen. Your face will be all over the news as the latest traitor to your country. There will be so much notoriety, you won't be safe in even the most remote village on the planet. There will be nowhere to hide from it."

"I'll take my chances!"

She pulled the trigger and Leo laughed.

"It's hard to kill someone when you're shooting blanks, isn't it, Patsy!"

She gasped.

The other agents in the room all sat up with grins on their faces.

"How did you switch my weapon?"

"The same way we do everything, diversion, and sleight of hand."

"Why set me up for a fall?"

Leo smirked. "Necessity—convenience—the usual."

"Who's the target?"

"Everyone."

Her eyes grew wide. "You really did set me up! You poisoned the food, didn't you? —And I served it!"

Leo chuckled and shrugged his shoulders. "You are smart, Bretta. You're just not smart enough."

With a gasp, she turned to leave, but the exit was blocked by the four guards from the stairwell. Their rifles were aimed at her head.

Leo smirked. "There's no reason to run, Bretta. There is no escape. You will take the fall for the 100 dignitaries that will die in their sleep tonight. You will take the fall for the SEAL you left dead in our basement. You will take the fall for everything. Your life is over. We own your ass."

The four men in the doorway each grunted as a bullet ripped through his spine and lodged in his brain. Quick as lightening, Bretta grabbed Leo's handgun from its holster under his left arm. She quickly dispatched every agent in the room for real this time. She left Leo for last.

Leo grimaced as she pointed the gun at his head. Sonny walked into the room with his sniper rifle in hand and a wicked grin on his face.

"You out of bullets? Should I do the honors?" Sonny asked.

"No, this needs to look like Leo murdered his entire team and turned the gun on himself."

"You won't get away with this!" Leo sneered.

"Won't I? This op you're running is off the books, isn't it? There's no documentation of it anywhere, is there? Who do you really report to?"

"Why would I tell you that? You're going to kill me no matter what."

"True, but you can die with a clear conscience."

"I killed my conscience when I joined the CIA."

"Have it your way."

She pulled the trigger at point blank range. Then she placed the pistol in his hand.

Sonny looked at her. "How did you know he switched your gun?"

Bretta winked at him. "It's my business to know. I would never trust someone else with my gun. It's like an appendage. I know when a gun isn't mine. Leo should have known better than to try that with me. For that matter so should Mark; he had to be the one who pulled the switch. He must have done it just before dinner. I'll take care of him next."

"What about Leo's boss? He didn't say who he reported to."

Bretta scoffed. "Sonny, you really are naïve. I never enter an op without knowing all the players. In this game you have to watch your back every second of every day. There is always someone trying to kill you. The guilty parties won't come out of this unscathed."

Sonny nodded. "So, what now?"

"I'll stage this site for the cover up. I have some video footage to erase. I'll arrange for the dignitaries and the kitchen staff to be treated at the hospital. Go back to your op. Let your team know that the assassin hasn't been eliminated yet, but will be soon. I'll take Mark out myself."

Sonny nodded. "I'll let John know. By now, he's discovered I'm missing, and Matt will have filled him in on what happened."

Bretta smirked. "SEAL loyalty never ceases to amaze me. You men always fight as a unit. You never turn on each other."

"That's our code, Bretta. What is your code?"

"To do whatever it takes to make things turn out right. There are no lines I won't cross to ensure the right outcome—no lines."

Sonny nodded. "Glad you're on our side. You are on our side—right? I mean you're MI6, aren't you? You're not one of them double agent—triple agents, are you? I'm getting' confused a bit here."

"You can trust me, Sonny. It doesn't matter who I work for. What matters is what I'm working toward. I'm trying to save everyone. Just let me do my job."

He grinned at her. "In your spy world—you ever had a hick, cowboy from Texas before? Cause I could definitely go for some pretty, female spy seduction. Hell, you don't even have to seduce me. Tie me up and force me—spank me a little with a leather whip. I'm game."

She winked at him. "I like you, Sonny. You're a good man. Don't ever change."

He chuckled. "No chance of that. So, is that a yes? Cause I like bein' tied up."

"Sorry, Sonny, but my heart belongs to Lydell."

He grinned and winked at her. "That was a test. Glad you passed. I got standards too. I don't sleep with my friend's woman. That just ain't right. Lydell's plum gone and fell in love with a Red Coat. I ain't trying to take that away from him."

Bretta chuckled. "A Red Coat, huh? You really are a hick, aren't you, Sonny?"

"Cowboy to the core and proud of it. Hicks are some of the best people you'll ever meet."

"I'm glad we're friends, Sonny."

"Is that what we are?"

"You know you can't tell anyone what really went on here tonight."

"I can't keep secrets from my team."

"This could have serious repercussions for the U.S. if it is discovered that the CIA had a traitor who attempted to assassinate Heads of State from 50 countries."

"A bunch of them countries being allies too."

She nodded. Sonny stared at her in silence. He dragged a hand down his jaw as he studied her.

"What's really goin' on here, Bretta?"

"Someone is trying to start another World War. I'm trying to stop it. I need your silence."

Sonny left, and Bretta made a call to the local hospital. Then she made arrangements for all 100 guests and the kitchen staff to be transported there immediately. The only thing left to do was wait for Mark to show his head and then to snap it off. It would be a cake walk.

CHAPTER 61

June 15
0130
Afghanistan base

John lay awake. He couldn't get Sophia out of his head. Things were not getting better between them. They were getting much worse. On the chopper ride back to base, John had caught Sophia staring at him. She'd looked away, but not before he saw the lust in her eyes.

He sat up and looked around. The rest of the tent was asleep. Sophia was asleep. He could hear her regular breathing in the bed next to his. He could smell her. She smelled sweet, female. Her scent stood out from the other fifteen men who occupied the tent. It was her scent that was driving him crazy at the moment. It was too tempting. He got up, left the tent, and called Kyle.

"Hi, John."

"Hey."

"What's wrong?"

"Everything."

Kyle frowned. "What happened?"

John bit his lip and dragged a hand over his burr. "She kissed me."

Kyle set Buck down on the floor and walked past Megan who was playing tea with Mandy. He opened the front door and went outside.

"Is that all that happened?"

"Yes. I didn't kiss her back. I told her nothing can happen. I told her I'm not interested."

"But you are interested."

"I'm not allowed to be interested."

"Your contract is up soon. You could get out."

John groaned. "I can't do that."

"Why not?"

"A lot of reasons."

"Name one."

"We are involved in something big. It's not over. The CIA has been using us to gather intel. I can't walk away from this right now. Echo needs me."

"You can get out after this crisis is over. Name another reason."

John limped back and forth along the fence line. "If I get out for her, and it doesn't work out—I'll have nothing. Being a SEAL is my life. I have nothing else but that."

"That's not true. You have me. We are friends for life. What's your next excuse?"

John sighed. "I don't know if her kiss was born from curiosity, impulse, or something deeper. I don't know what angle she's coming at this from. I thought it was just an adrenaline, near-death-experience kiss, but I was wrong. She keeps looking at me. She keeps touching me inappropriately when no one else is looking. You know—putting her hand on my arm, my back, or sometimes my leg. She won't let this go. I don't know what to do."

Kyle sank down on the porch swing. "You have to talk to her. You have to find out where she's at. If she is serious about you, are you willing to get out to pursue a relationship with her?"

John leaned against the fence and stared at the dirt in silence. Finally, he said, "I don't know."

"That's a start. It sounds like you're toying with the possibility."

"Has it crossed my mind? Yeah—a thousand times a day. Do I think it's a good idea? No."

"Why not?"

"My track record with women is horrible. I have a one hundred percent failure rate. If I get out and pursue this, and it doesn't work, I'll be out of the SEALs and have nothing to show for it."

Kyle's lips turned down. "Is she the only reason you'd be getting out?"

"Yeah. I have no plans to retire early."

"Then you definitely need to talk to her and find out how she feels."

"I know. I just don't want to have that conversation. It has the potential to blow up in my face. If I've misread her intentions—which wouldn't be a first for me—we'll still be serving together with this awkward thing between us. It will make this worse, not better. Maybe I should just keep ignoring her like I've been doing. It's just—ignoring her is getting harder and harder to do."

"I don't know what to tell you, John. You're the only one who can decide. You'll be the one living with the consequences no matter which way it falls."

"I know."

John hung up and slid the phone back into his pocket. He limped back to the tent and sat down on his bunk. He stared at Sophia. She was sleeping peacefully, and she looked beautiful. He tried but he couldn't tear his gaze away from her. Finally, he lay back on his bed and closed his eyes. It was a fruitless effort. The sweet scent of her shampoo wafted across his perimeter. He was being tortured in the most excruciating way. He buried his face in his pillow and tried to block out her scent, but the fantasy of making love to her invaded his brain without permission.

He groaned softly into his pillow. He knew he was his own worst enemy. He was torturing himself slowly with no mercy and no reprieve. There was no escape. There was nowhere to hide, no cover to be found. He was laid bare to his own base desires with no possibility of fulfillment.

July 2
1030
Afghanistan base

John came in from his latest mission and checked his phone. There was a text from Kyle.

K: Welcome to the world, Kacy John Masters, six pounds, ten ounces. Congratulations, Uncle John!

John sat on his bunk staring at the text when Sonny walked over. John showed him the text.

"He named his kid after you? I'm jealous! He better have another one and put my name on it."

A smile lifted John's lip. "I can't believe he named his son after me."

"Why wouldn't he? Kyle loves you like a brother."

John nodded. "Yeah, but I'm not worthy of this honor."

Sonny shook his head and walked away.

Sophia sat on her bunk watching John. He looked happy and sad at the same time.

"Are you okay, Sir?" she asked.

"I'm fine." Avoiding looking at her, he stood up and left the tent to call Kyle.

"Hey, John."

"Congratulations."

"Thanks. Everyone is doing great. How are you doing?"

"I'm good."

"You don't sound good. Have you talked to her yet?"

"No."

"Are you going to?"

"I haven't decided. If I do this, there's no going back."

"I think you should talk to her."

"I have some thinking to do. I'll talk to you later."

John hung up and nearly bumped into Sophia as he rounded the corner of the supply building.

"Hi, John—uh—I mean, Sir."

The glower on his face didn't surprise her; it had become a permanent expression lately.

"Do you need something, Gonzalez?"

She grinned at him. "No."

"I thought you were hanging out in the tent with the guys."

"I decided to take a walk around base."

His jaw tightened. He let out a heavy sigh and put his hands on his hips.

"Do me a favor. Stay in public areas—where it's safe."

"Why? Worried about me?" She grinned up at him and playfully pushed his bicep. He immediately took a step back disconnecting from any contact as he quickly glanced around to ensure they were alone. He looked back to see her eyes slowly roaming down his body and back up. When she met his eyes, he was glaring at her.

"Really!" he grated. "Someone could walk by at any moment? This has to stop Gonzalez!"

"What has to stop?"

"Your behavior! Don't touch me. Don't ask me personal questions! Don't flirt!" He leaned in and lowered his voice. "And don't undress me with your eyes like you just did! It's not allowed!"

"I-I-I wasn't—"

"Yes! You were! Your behavior is inappropriate, Gonzalez! Find a way to control yourself!"

His lips formed a hard line, and the muscle in his jaw worked as he glared at her.

She felt her gut twist when she saw the angry look on his face. She turned quickly and walked away. When she was out of his sight, she wiped away tears, pulled her phone from her pocket, and dialed her mother.

"Hello, Sophia. It is so nice to hear from you."

"Hi, Mama."

"What's wrong?" Amparo could hear the tremor in her daughter's voice.

"I made a terrible mistake." Sophia tried her best to keep the sob inside, but she failed.

"What happened? Are you okay? Are you hurt?"

"I'm fine." She sniffed and swiped away tears as she walked toward the back of the compound. She wanted to put as much distance between herself and John as possible. "I'm not injured."

"You're crying. Something is wrong."

"I fell in love with the wrong man."

Amparo grimaced. "Are you pregnant?"

"No! Nothing like that. We can't be together. Military code forbids it. He's not willing to pursue a relationship with me. Being a SEAL is his whole life. It's all he cares about. It's all he wants. He doesn't want me."

"I am sorry, Sophia. If this man doesn't love you, he is the fool, and he doesn't deserve you. There are other men in the world. You will find the right man for you. Just keep looking."

"I don't want to keep looking. I never wanted to fall in love, but I did. If I can't have him—I don't want anyone. It hurts to know he doesn't love me back. I can't take this pain."

"I am sorry. I know it hurts, but it will get better. That pain will eventually heal."

Sophia swiped away tears. "I'll be okay, Mama. I just needed to hear a friendly voice."

She hung up and turned to see Sonny standing a few feet away watching her.

"You okay?"

She swallowed hard. "Were you listening to my phone call?"

"Only the tail end of it, but enough to know why you needed a friendly voice."

She bit her lip and looked away. Fresh tears slid down her cheeks.

Sonny grimaced. Then he stepped up and pulled her into his arms in a tight hug. She hugged him back and buried her face against his chest.

He leaned down to her ear. "Hey, don't lose heart, Girl. He might have rejected you, but you don't know what's comin' around the bend. The final chapter hasn't been written."

She sobbed against his chest. He tightened his hug and held her against him for a while. When her sobbing subsided, he framed her jaw in his hands and kissed the top of her head.

Neither saw John back away with a tortured expression on his face.

John stalked back to the tent with fury in his eyes. He walked past all the rows of empty bunks, opened his locker, stared at the neatly organized contents, and slammed the door several times.

Nick bolted up from his bunk. "You okay, John?"

"No!"

"What's wrong?"

John growled and slammed his fist into his palm.

Nick crossed his arms over his chest and stared at John. "Why are you so angry?"

"I just saw Sonny and Gonzalez violating the UCMJ!"

Nick's eyebrow rose. "They were having sex?"

"No, but I saw him kiss her!"

"I'm sorry, John. I never thought Sonny would go after her. He knows you like her."

"Why would that stop Sonny? All he cares about is bragging rights. He'll go after any woman who shakes her ass in front of him. He's a pathetic scumbag!"

John limped back and forth in the tent growling and swearing under his breath.

Nick grimaced. "You should calm down before you confront him about this. I've never seen you this angry before."

John scoffed. "Confront him—No! I'm going to file formal charges against both of them!"

"That would get them both dishonorably discharged!"

John dragged a hand down his stubbled jaw and stopped in the middle of the empty tent. "I can't look the other way on this. I can't have soldiers under my command fraternizing."

"Have you spoken to either of them about this?"

"No."

"Why don't you take a few minutes to calm down. I'll go find them."

Nick left John pacing and swearing inside the tent. He checked the mess hall and found Sonny and Sophia in line together. He walked over.

"Can I talk to you both for a minute?"

Sonny's grin turned to a frown when he saw the stern expression on Nick's face. They walked far enough away so no prying ears would hear.

"John is planning to file charges against both of you for violating the UCMJ."

"What!" Sonny exclaimed. "Why?"

"He saw you two kissing, and he said he's not going to look the other way."

"That's bull-hocky!" Sonny growled. "We ain't done nothin'. We sure as hell weren't kissing."

"What were you doing?"

"When did he allegedly witness this?" Sophia asked.

"I don't know, but he came into the tent mad as hell a few minutes ago."

Sonny smirked. "He must have seen me givin' her a hug earlier. We wasn't kissin'. She was upset, and I was just tryin' to encourage her."

"Sonny is telling the truth. There's nothing going on between us."

Nick nodded. "Go get some grub. I'll talk to John and see if I can calm him down."

Sonny and Sophia got a plate and sat down next to each other to eat. Just as Nick exited the mess hall he bumped into John. Nick grabbed his arm.

"I talked to both of them. I think you misinterpreted the situation."

John scoffed and jerked his arm free. "It figures you'd take his side."

Nick fell in step beside John. "I'm not taking sides. There is no side to take. He said she was upset, and he was just giving her a hug to encourage her. She concurred."

"Of course, that's what they would say."

"John, you're blowing this up into something it's not."

"Am I?"

"Yes, you are."

"That's your opinion."

Nick halted and watched John limp into the mess hall. There was no reasoning with him. He was literally seething with anger.

John spotted Sonny and Sophia on the far side of the room, and his jaw clenched in anger. He limped over to the table and sat down across from them with a hateful glare on his face.

Sonny shook his head. "Nick told us what you think. There ain't nothing going on."

A low growl erupted from John's throat. "I don't want to hear it, Sonny! Both of you report back here at 1300!"

Sonny nodded. "We'll be here."

John got up and limped away. Once he was gone, Nick joined Sonny and Sophia.

"He's not going to listen to reason," Nick said.

Sonny nodded. "I know. I saw the look on his face."

"This is my fault," Sophia sighed. "I should go talk to him."

"We'll both talk to him at 1300," Sonny said. "I'm to blame. I kissed the top of your head."

Nick rolled his eyes. "That's the kiss he saw?"

"That's the only kiss I gave her."

"He acted like he caught you two making out—like you were all over each other."

"It wasn't anything like that. I was upset. Sonny was just being nice. That's all it was."

"Apparently, I'm not allowed to be nice anymore," Sonny sneered.

The three of them finished their meals. Then they headed back to the tent. John wasn't there. They sat down on their bunks to wait.

At 1300, all three went back to the mess hall to meet John.

John glared at Nick. "I didn't tell you to be here. You're dismissed, Nick."

Nick shook his head. "I'm here to make sure you don't do anything stupid."

"If you stay, you'll get written up along with them."

"It's okay, Nick. We can handle this," Sonny said.

Reluctantly, Nick left the mess hall. He didn't have a good feeling about any of it.

Sonny and Sophia stood at attention in front of John.

"Have a seat!" John snapped.

They both sat down facing him.

"You both know why you're here," John said tersely.

"Nick said you think we violated the UCMJ," Sonny said. "That ain't true."

"I'm not listening to anymore lies!" John grated. "I know what I saw."

"You seen me kissin' the top of her head. That's all you seen!"

"You're not allowed to kiss any part of her or embrace her! I've been very clear about this!"

Sonny nodded. "You have, but if you was ballin' yer eyes out, I'd give you a hug too. I don't discriminate based on gender."

John's fist slammed down against the table. "I told you she is strictly hands off! You're not allowed to touch her. You're not even allowed to look at her!"

Sonny let out a low, rumbling growl. "So, I'm just supposed to ignore her? She was in pain. I was just trying to help."

"He's telling the truth," Sophia said. "I was upset. If you need to punish someone, punish me. I should be a stronger soldier. Sonny shouldn't have had to comfort me. I should have sucked it up and buried it down deep. That's what SEALs do."

"You're both guilty! You both had your arms around each other. I saw it. It was far from an innocent hug! I'm going to punish you both!"

"Please don't, John!"

He glared at her and crossed his arms over his chest.

"I meant Sir. Sonny isn't to blame for this. Please don't punish him. Put all the blame and punishment on me. I deserve it. You can even kick me out of the Navy if it makes you feel better. Just don't punish Sonny. I'll gladly trade my career to protect his. He's done nothing wrong."

John's jaw worked as he stared at her. "But you have—haven't you?"

Sophia bit her lip, and a tear streaked down her cheek. "Sir, I'm sorry to report that I have behaved inappropriately. I've allowed my personal feelings to come before my duty. I have pursued an officer in my chain of command. He made it very clear to me that he had no interest, and I did not relent. For that, I apologize. I'm not as strong as I thought I was. Maybe those other SEAL teams were right to pass me over. Maybe I don't deserve to be here. If I allow my emotions to rule my decisions, I'm not worthy to be a part of this team. Just kick me out now and put me out of my misery. I'm not sure how much more of this pain I can take anyway."

"Nice speech, Gonzalez! It sounds well-rehearsed. It's not going to work. Sonny will take equal punishment in this. It takes two to fraternize!"

"Don't be a pig-headed fool!" Sonny growled.

"How long has this been going on?" John demanded.

"There ain't nothing goin' on."

"Like hell there isn't! I know you, Sonny. I know how you operate. I know she's just one of your many conquests, but this one is going to cost you."

"He didn't conquest anything!" Sophia huffed. "It was an innocent hug. That's all it was!"

John's eyes darted back and forth between them. "Did you screw her on the missions too? All those hours you two were alone together were just one big—"

"Don't finish that." Sonny growled. "She ain't done nothing wrong and neither have I. You're way off here, John. I know jealousy is making you blind with rage, but you ain't got no reason to be jealous. Nothing happened. Nothing is going to happen. You need to get control of that green monster before he tears you up inside."

Sophia stared at John as Sonny's words echoed in her head.

"Sir, is Sonny right? Are you jealous?"

John's eyes narrowed on her and grew cold. "Don't try to pull me into your sick little game! I see what you're doing! You swore to me that all you wanted was to be given the same chance as any other man. I gave you that chance. You repaid it by betraying your word. You said you weren't here to find a man. Yet, you kissed me twice. I let you off with a warning then, but now it seems you've moved on to greener pastures. Obviously, you've set your sights on Sonny!"

Sophia stood up and slapped John hard across the cheek. His head recoiled from the hit. He pushed back from the table, stood up, and leaned in nose to nose glaring at her.

"You just earned yourself a court martial!"

"Good! I don't want to work for you anymore anyway!" she growled. "I thought you were a man of honor! I see I was wrong. You're just a petty, little man who can't see past his own ego!"

Sonny stood up, wrapped his arms around her, and pulled her back from the table.

"She didn't mean that, John. You just got her riled up. Don't do something you'll regret."

John's eyes narrowed on Sonny's arms wrapped around her. Then he met her defiant glare.

"I already have done something I regret!" John said with fury in his eyes. "I regret choosing you for this team. You are nothing but trouble. You flirt with every man on the team—on this whole damn base! You lead men on—make them fall for you—make them dance like a puppet. How many men were there between me and Joe before you moved on to Sonny? I am sick of this charade of yours. Well—it's coming to an end!"

She gasped in shock. "Sir, I have never flirted with anyone on this team or on this base."

"Joe would disagree with you. He told me about L.A."

"Nothing happened in L.A.!"

"Well something damn sure happened in that cave, Sophia! Or have you forgotten?"

Her hands started to shake, and a sob burst from her. "How could I forget? It was the worst moment of my life!"

John's lip curled up in a sneer. "Mine too!"

"I'm sorry, Sir. I was weak. I should never have tried to kiss you. If I had known my heart would be shattered into a million pieces, I would never have offered it to you. I was a fool to think you could ever love me. You can't even love your own parents."

She broke into more sobs as she sank into the chair and buried her face in her arms.

John felt her words like a kick in the gut. He turned and limped toward the door.

Sonny glared at John's back. "You just going to walk away? Go ahead! Kick her while she's down; then walk away! That's your style! Break a woman's heart and grind it into dust! No wonder all women hate your guts! You're a worthless piece of—" He trailed off as John disappeared through the doorway.

CHAPTER 62

John limped away from the mess hall. He wanted to hit something—to pulverize it! Anger seethed inside him and mixed with jealousy, hurt, and the pain of rejection. Seeing Sonny and Sophia together had shredded the thin hold he had over his emotions. He felt raw, exposed, and worse, he felt betrayed.

What kind of woman is she? She kissed me. She's been touching me. Obviously, she was just toying with me for her own amusement until she could run into Sonny's outstretched, waiting arms. I bet she never even liked me. Why would she? She's probably liked Sonny this whole time, and now that he's given her an open door, she's through with me. She was probably just using me anyway. I was probably just a convenient set of lips to kiss at the moment. Now, all she wants are Sonny's lips, his arms, his— Damnit! I can't let myself start thinking about him screwing her. It will drive me crazy!

John desperately needed a way to tamp down his anger. He needed to bury it deep before he did something he would truly regret—like kill Sonny Eldridge with his bare hands.

Inside the mess hall, Sonny glared at the empty doorway for a moment until the door swung shut. Then he turned his attention to the sobbing woman in front of him. He hated to see a woman cry. It always made him feel helpless. He sat down next to her and slid his arm around her shoulders.

"Hey, Girlie. It's going to be okay. John's just angry right now. He'll calm down. He's just hurt and jealous. He'll get over it."

"No, he won't. He hates me." She sniffed as she swiped at her tears.

"He don't hate you. He's angry because he loves you. He thinks you betrayed him, and it hurts. We'll just have to set him straight."

Sophia shook her head, stood up, and started for the door.

"I don't want you to get caught in the middle of this. I'll talk to him. I'll confess to whatever he wants to hear—whatever it takes to keep you out of trouble. I'm sorry, Sonny. I never meant for this to jeopardize your career."

Sonny caught her halfway to the door and pulled her into his arms. More tears traitorously slid down her cheeks.

"I ain't going to let you fall on the sword for me, Sophia. You're a good woman. You ain't done nothin' wrong."

She sobbed against his shoulder. "I don't know why I can't stop crying. I never cry."

"Your hearts been broke, Girl. It's okay to cry."

"I never wanted to be in love. This hurts too much. I'd rather be shot in the head."

"Now, don't go sayin' that!"

"It's true, Sonny. I don't think I can live with this empty, sucking hole in my chest."

Sonny slid his callused hands tenderly to frame her jaw as he stared into her eyes. The pain on her face tore at his heart. He pressed a soft kiss to her forehead and looked down into her eyes.

"Look, Girl, if John don't come to his senses, he's the fool. Don't let it ruin your life. Any man would be lucky to have you. You're sweet, and you care about every man on the team. I know it wasn't your dream to be a medic. That ain't really your calling, but when he asked you to do it, you stepped up. You've taken on that role with equal passion, and you're doing a great job at it. You're the hottest, little badass I've ever met. Don't let this drag you down. If John doesn't want you, don't give up on the whole male species. You're the whole package, Sophia. You're worthy of all the love and adoration a man can give.

A grin spread over her mouth.

"See, there's my girl. There's a smile."

She leaned in and hugged him tight. "How do you always know just what I need to hear?"

He playfully rubbed his hand over her ebony burr and grinned. "It's one of the few gifts God gave me—being able to charm any female that crosses my path."

"Is that what you're doing—trying to charm me?"

He pulled back with a mischievous grin. "Is it working?"

She laughed. "Not even for a second. I've heard about your reputation. I'm not going to be a notch on your bedpost, Sonny."

He stared at her, and his smile disappeared. A serious expression overtook his face.

"It wouldn't be like that with you, Sophia. I would never use you like that. I respect you. If you and I was to hook up, it wouldn't be for a roll in the hay. It would be the forever kind. It would be I do til I die. I'd put a ring on your finger, and never let you go. I'd never give you any reason to doubt my love, Girl. I'll be honest with you. If it weren't for John, I'd—"

She put a finger to his lips to silence him. His eyes locked with hers, and they were both caught in a moment. He gently took her hand, turned it, and pressed a soft kiss to the inside of her wrist. His eyes bore into her with such longing need and devotion; she couldn't look away. He'd never looked at her like that before. Her heart skipped a beat. Suddenly, the image of Sonny kissing her lips invaded her brain. She gasped softly as she felt his right-hand slide behind her neck. He slowly pulled her closer until the tip of her nose touched his. Her heart beat out of control as she stared into his sincere, brown eyes.

This is a Sonny I've never met before. It would be easy to fall in love with this Sonny—he's so sweet—so sincere.

She felt his left-hand slide down her side to her hip and curve around to cup her ass. As he gently pulled her firmly against him, his thumb caressed her neck, and then he framed her jaw in his palm. She felt frozen in place—at his mercy. It was impossible to look away from his sincere, brown eyes. Her heart pounded furiously like a cornered rabbit. There was no escape, no refuge from his eyes—his lips—his gentle hands. She was trapped in his soft web of seduction.

Is he going to kiss me?

Sonny's breath caught as he stared into her eyes. He felt her pulse racing beneath his fingers.

She's so sweet and vulnerable under her tough, little badass exterior. I wish I could protect her from ever getting hurt like this again. I can't bear to see her so sad. I just want to hold her in my arms and make slow, sweet, passionate love to her—for the rest of my life. Oh, Hell! I'm in love with her! — I don't fall in love! How in the hell did I let this happen?

They both stared at each other for a small eternity. Then, Sonny tilted his head to kiss her—the kiss he'd been dreaming about giving her night after night. Just before his lips touched hers, the image of John's face full of fury, rage, and hurt slammed into Sonny's brain. He froze—staring into her eyes.

Damn! What am I doing? I can't do this to John. He might be a pig-headed fool, but he's one of my best friends. I can't kiss her. I shouldn't even be touching her like this no matter how much I wish she was mine. John's in love with her. He's a good man. He deserves her. I've been a pig for the last decade. Even if John wasn't in the picture, I wouldn't deserve a girl like Sophia.

Sonny let go of her and took a step back. She felt the loss of his touch like a sudden release, and she stumbled forward a step feeling dizzy. The spell broke, and the moment passed. Her brain scrambled to make sense of what had just happened.

"Sonny—"

He shook his head. "We can't do this. John's in love with you. I won't hurt him like that. I won't steal his girl."

She swallowed hard. "Were you trying to steal me?"

He let out a long breath. "That's a dangerous question. I'm going to skidaddle before I do something really stupid."

Sonny walked to the door, paused, and looked back at her. Sophia stared at him. She could hardly believe that Sonny had almost kissed her. A pained look crossed his face, and then he left.

What just happened? Sonny almost kissed me! This is crazy! I was powerless to resist him. For a moment the world didn't exist—only Sonny existed. If he had kissed me, would I have let him? Is this what the guys are always talking about? They all say he has a charm with women—that they can't resist him. What is wrong with me? I'm not in love with Sonny; I'm in love with John.

Sophia stood staring at the door in a half daze.

I never lose my faculties with men, unless you count that cave in Siberia, but I just lost them with Sonny. I can't—I don't—have feelings for Sonny. He's my best friend—that's all he is. He can't be anything more. I can't let him be anything more.

How have I strayed this far off the path? I had a plan; it didn't include men! I can ignore men. I've been doing it for years. So, I can ignore Sonny and John. I have to make John understand; I can't let him ruin Sonny's career. None of this is Sonny's fault. It's my fault for being weak. It's my fault for falling for a man who will never love me back. I have to fix this.

She left the mess hall in search of John. She found him alone at the bathroom sink washing his left hand. She could see blood dripping off his knuckles.

"What happened?" she gasped.

His jaw tightened. "It's nothing."

He pulled his hand up and unsuccessfully attempted to extract splinters from his knuckles.

"Let me see your hand."

"I got this. Don't worry about it," he said coldly.

"I'm the medic. It's my job to look after you. Let me look at it before you make it worse."

He stuck out his hand toward her. "Fine! Look at it, but just so you know, this won't be your job for much longer!"

She nodded. "I understand. You're angry with me, and you should be. I was out of line. I never should have tried to kiss you. That was a stupid impulse that I fully regret. I swear to you; it will never happen again. Nothing happened between me and Sonny. The only man I've ever kissed was you, and since you didn't kiss me back, I'm not sure it qualified as a real kiss."

She gently took his hand and examined it. His knuckles had several imbedded splinters, and they were scraped and bloody. John watched her with a stern frown on his face.

"You never kissed Sam?"

Her heart sped up.

I forgot. I did kiss Sam. How could I have forgotten that? How does he know about Sam?

She cleared her throat. "Actually, I did kiss Sam. I'd completely forgotten about that. In fact, I'd forgotten about him. I haven't thought about him in a long time. He was my first kiss. It's strange that I would forget that."

John chewed at his bottom lip and studied her. "How many guys have you kissed since Sam?"

"Only you, Sir."

"You sure about that? You sure you didn't kiss Joe, Sonny, countless other men on this base? Maybe you forgot about them too. Is that what you do—kiss them and forget them?" he sneered.

Pain flitted over her face, and her lip trembled. It took her a moment to regain control.

"I haven't forgotten. You and Sam are the only men I have ever kissed."

John felt acid eating him up from the inside. "Were you in love with him?"

"No. I loved him as a person, but I didn't love him enough to give up everything to be with him. He wanted me to get out, stay at home, and raise children. I didn't want that. I love being a soldier. I want to serve. That's why I broke up with him."

"Convenient for you! Make men fall for you and crush them. Do you take pleasure in it?"

John felt so much anger inside he couldn't help but lash out at her.

Sophia felt like he'd driven his fist into her chest and was squeezing her heart. The sudden pain in her chest was unbearable. She let go of his hand and took a step back.

Why is he doing this? Does he hate me that much? All I did was kiss him. Why is he being so cruel? He's not the man I thought he was. He's not a nice guy. He's—vindictive and vicious!

It took her a moment to recover from his blow. She took a deep breath and resolved not to show how much he'd just hurt her. Defiance rose up inside her to take the place of heartache.

"For your information, Sir, I do not make men fall for me. It's not my fault if their lustful natures get the better of them. I can't help the way I look. This is how I was born. I've had to ignore their inane flirting for half my life. I have more important things to do with my time than waste it on men who only want to use me to pleasure their own egos. I have more respect for myself than to cater to that. The truth is, I thought you were different than all these idiots. I thought you were better than that. I thought you really understood me—respected me as a real soldier. It's why I fell in love with you. It's why I kissed you. I see now; I was mistaken. You're not better. You're the worst one I've ever crossed paths with. At least these ego-maniacs are nice to me even if it is in some lame attempt to get in my panties. You don't even have the decency to be kind. You pulled the claws out and tried to shred me over one stupid lapse in judgement. I'm sorry I tried to kiss you. I'm sorry I allowed myself to fall for you. Don't worry! I'm over it now! I will never kiss you again! I can't believe you turned out to be such a jerk!"

As she defiantly stared up at him, his fury disintegrated and confusion took its place. He stared down at her unsure what to believe.

Does she really like me? Am I so used to being rejected that I can't perceive when a woman actually likes me?

"How do you even know about Sam?" she demanded.

He grimaced. "I heard about him through the grapevine."

"What grapevine? I've never mentioned Sam to anyone here on base. I met Sam in BUD/S. I broke up with him before I deployed to Afghanistan."

John pulled his hand down his clean-shaven jaw.

"I read his texts on your phone. He begged you to take him back, and you told him to move on with his life. I shouldn't have snooped through your phone. That was wrong. I apologize."

She studied his face. He wasn't looking at her. He was staring at the ground in front of him. The look of guilt and shame he wore chipped away at the wall she'd just erected.

Is Sonny right? Is John acting like a complete ass because he's thinks I cheated on him?

"Why did you read my texts?"

He cleared his throat. "I was out of line. I never should have gone through your things."

"You didn't answer my question. Why did you go through my stuff?"

He forced his eyes up to meet hers. She was glaring at him.

"I apologize."

"I don't want your apology. I want the truth!"

He bit his lip and stared at the ground in silence.

"Sonny's right. You are jealous!"

"I'm not jealous." He looked away and stared at nothing.

"I think you are jealous. You thought something was going on between me and Sonny so you threatened to destroy both our careers. Nothing happened with Sonny. We are friends. That's all. If you let your emotions make your decisions, you'll only be proving me right."

He looked back at her. "What is that supposed to mean?"

"I know your decisions in Siberia were not rational. You tried to protect me at the expense of your own life. You did it twice. Once when you gave me your last breath in that lake. Twice when you told me to leave you behind to die. I'm not stupid. I see what you're doing. You were willing to die for me in Siberia, and now you're willing to have me and Sonny thrown out of the Navy because you believe I cheated on you. All those decisions are based solely on your emotions, Sir! Why don't you take a good look in the mirror and examine your motivations! You are the one in the wrong here, not Sonny, not me!"

John let out a long breath and looked away from her defiant, brown eyes. He stood staring at the sand lost in thought.

She's right! I am letting my emotions rule my decisions where she's concerned. I've been completely unprofessional. Does she really only see Sonny as a friend? Women always fall for Sonny. What makes her so different? Does she really love me? Have I completely screwed up my chances with her? What is wrong with me? Why can't I ever keep my mouth shut?

She watched the confusion play out on his face. Then he sat down on the sand, locked his fingers behind his neck, and planted his elbows on his knees. He let out a loud, frustrated groan.

"Are you okay, Sir?"

"I'm fine. It's just a few scrapes," he mumbled.

"I wasn't talking about your hand."

He looked up and met her gaze. "Oh. I—uh—" He trailed off unsure what to say.

Why does he do this to me? He makes me furious, and then he makes me feel—sympathy. Confusion! Grrr—Love! This isn't fair! Why do I care so much what he thinks? He acted like a jerk—but maybe he did it because he has feelings for me, and what he saw hurt him.

"I am truly sorry you saw that hug and thought something else was going on. I'm not interested in Sonny. He and I are just friends. He is actually the only person on the team who has been a true friend. He's been genuinely nice to me without an ulterior motive. Earlier, when you harshly told me to back off, I was upset about the way you've been treating me. I was crying like a pathetic sap. Sonny just happened along at the wrong moment, and he felt bad for me. I really hope you don't punish him for that. He was just trying to be nice. He was just being a friend when I needed a shoulder to cry on. I'm sorry I was so weak, Sir. You've made it obvious that you don't want me. I won't pursue you anymore, and I promise I'll never let my emotions get the best of me again. I'll be completely professional from now on."

I believe her. She seems sincere, and Sonny has never lied to me before. I made a mistake.

"I'm sorry, Sophia. I misjudged you. I won't be filing any charges."

"I'm sorry I slapped you. I didn't mean it. I just got so angry. I hope I didn't hurt you."

A grin tugged at his mouth. "I deserved it. I over-reacted. I was out of line."

She smiled at him. "I'm just glad you're not angry anymore. When you thought I cheated—I just want you to know that I would never cheat. If you'll give me a second chance, I'll be the best SEAL I can be for Echo. I've learned my lesson. SEAL's aren't meant to be in love. We are only meant to serve. I thought I understood before, but now I see things much more clearly."

Her gaze went back to his injured hand. She could see blood dripping from his knuckles.

"I need my med kit. We need to take care of your hand. Some of those splinters are in deep."

They returned to the tent and found it deserted for the moment. He walked to his bunk and sat down. Sophia got out her med kit. She didn't say anything. She just went to work removing the splinters. Then she cleaned the scrapes with alcohol and wrapped his knuckles in gauze.

"What should I put in my medical report regarding this injury?"

John grimaced. "Just put I tripped and scraped my hand."

She leaned in close. "I'll put that down, but just between us, what really happened?"

He cleared his throat and looked down at his combat boots. "I—uh—punched one of the wooden supply crates. I was so mad at Sonny—at you—I had to leave before I lost my temper."

"That's what I thought."

"It was stupid."

"I agree."

He looked up at her. She was grinning. A slight grin turned up the corner of his mouth.

"Well, I don't think you broke anything."

"No, I didn't." Suddenly, that uncomfortable pain returned to his chest. He leaned forward and whispered. "That's not true. I think I broke your heart."

"It's okay. I'll get over it."

"I'm sorry. I didn't mean to. That's not how I wanted to handle this situation."

"Don't worry about it, Sir. Every girl gets her heart broken at some point. Now that mine is broken, I can move on and let it scar up. It'll be tougher going forward. I won't fall in love again. It's too painful. You have nothing to worry about. I'll be the good soldier from now on."

Say something! Don't let her think you don't care! Don't let her slip through your fingers!

John dropped his eyes to the floor. He didn't know what to do. He had no idea what to say.

"I think I'll do some PT," she said.

"Yeah, okay," he mumbled.

As soon as she left the tent, he began mentally kicking himself for not handling things the right way. He left the tent to find Sonny. When he spotted Sonny in the ammunitions supply building, he walked inside. Sonny was getting supplies to clean his sniper rifle.

"Can I talk to you for a minute?" John asked.

Sonny grabbed his supplies and followed John outside.

"I owe you an apology," John said.

"Yer damn right you do!"

"I should have trusted you. I just got so—"

"Jealous. I know. If I was in your boots, I'd have probably thought the same thing. It probably looked incriminating."

"I'm sorry, Sonny. I talked to Sophia. I'm not going to file any charges."

"You're damn right you're not! I can't even believe you considered it. I'm going to tell you something, and you damn well better listen. That girl is madly in love with you. You broke her heart when you rejected her the way you did. You should know better. How many times have you gone on a date with someone and gotten rejected? Hell! You wasn't even in love with none of them women, but it still hurt. Imagine how it would feel if you was in love, and you told a girl, and she told you to take a hike off a tall cliff? It would hurt a thousand times worse. That's what Sophia's feeling right now. She actually told me she'd rather take a bullet to the head than feel the pain she's in. That's what you did to her, John! So, before you go mistreatin' her anymore, stop and think about that! She's in love with you. Try cutting her a little slack!"

"You're right, Sonny. I did her wrong. I don't know how to fix this."

"Why don't you try admitting that you're in love with her too. That would be a start!"

Sonny stalked off. He was as mad as a rattler in a fishbowl. Half of him wanted to beat some sense into John. The other half toyed with the idea of letting John hang himself with the rope.

Hell! It would be so easy to just let him self-destruct like he always does. I'm actually surprised Sophia fell for him in the first place. It ain't like he's got an ounce of charm in his whole damn body. The boy's a walking disaster! She must have x-ray eyes to see through his prickly outer shell.

Sonny went to the empty mess hall to clean his rifle on one of the tables. Soon he sat with a disassembled rifle spread out in front of him. He started cleaning and oiling all the necessary parts. He could clean and repair his rifle blind folded so naturally his thoughts strayed.

I can't let John do this. He's heading down the rapids toward a killer waterfall if I don't intervene. He may not have the guts to admit it, but he's in love with her. He might be rough around the edges, but he has a good heart. He's a good man. He deserves to be happy. If only he can manage to keep his foot out of his mouth, maybe Sophia will forgive him, and they can work it out. She'd be good for him. I could see them being really happy together. Dang-blasted! When in tarnation did I become a match-maker? That darn Megan is rubbing off on me!

Sonny finished, reassembled his rifle, and went to have a serious talk with John. He only hoped he could talk some sense into the durn-fool-idiot before it was too late.

CHAPTER 63

November 3
1806
Karpathos, Greece

Bretta aimed her sniper rifle at her target's skull. She followed him through the crowded market to his destination, an open-air café. She waited patiently for the perfect moment to squeeze the trigger. When the path was clear, she made the shot. A moment later, she dismantled her rifle, packed it into the small case, tucked it under her tunic, and exited the market. She was gone within forty-five seconds of making the kill shot. Five minutes later she was boarding the sailboat and pulling away from the dock. The op had gone off without a hitch. On the boat, she set a heading for Crete. Then she relaxed. It wasn't often that she had any downtime between ops. This time, she could enjoy a nice leisurely sail to her next destination.

November 17
0600
Mut, Egypt

Echo sat in a safe house briefing room with SEAL team Foxtrot. They would be working together in a joint effort to track one of the clone groups that had ventured into the southwest corner of Egypt in the Libyan Desert.

Master Chief Lee Shanley of Foxtrot was conducting the briefing. He went over the clone army's movements over the last month. He pulled up satellite images of heavy artillery being delivered to the clones along with tanks and stinger missiles.

"They haven't moved the tanks into Egypt yet." Shanley pointed to the latest satellite image from the previous day. "However, their unauthorized incursion into Egyptian territory is cause for concern. They entered via the Libyan Desert and seem to be conducting more training exercises. As of now, they are only in the southwest corner, but that could change. The fact that they crossed the border at all is a clear violation. We have to find out what they are up to and if we need to intervene. The CIA wants this to be a low-profile op. We are not to engage the clones. They don't want us to tip off the Russians that we know about the clones.

"Do we know how many clones they've produced?" Nick asked.

Shanley shook his head. "So far, the SEAL teams have counted a thousand clone soldiers being trained in the north African deserts. We do not have a tally on how many more there might be in other parts of the world. The group of clones we will be observing number fifty."

The next two hours were spent reviewing data and coming up with a strategic approach to the op. After the briefing, the SEAL teams organized their equipment, had a hearty meal, and bedded down for a few hours before it was time to depart. Sophia spread her bedroll next to John's. She lay down facing him and gave him a half smile. His jaw tightened, and he rolled so that his back was to her. A frown marred her pretty face.

It had been like this for months. Ever since he'd suspected her and Sonny of fraternizing, his demeanor had changed. He didn't just ignore her. He seemed to go out of his way to ignore her. No matter what she said or did, he treated her with disdain and a hint of contempt. She didn't know what she was doing wrong, but every time he snubbed her, it felt like a dagger to her heart.

She hadn't tried to flirt or make any advances toward him. She had done her best not to look at him more than was necessary, but it was hard to keep her eyes off him. She found herself watching him everywhere he went. Whether on a mission or on base, he always captivated her attention.

At 2000, Sophia climbed into the chopper with the rest of the SEALs. She took a seat next to Sonny and stole a glance at John. He wore a stern expression, and he didn't glance her way. She strapped in, and a few minutes later the chopper lifted off.

On the flight she kept glancing his way, but he kept his focus on the floor, the ceiling, or the other men in the chopper. Basically, he stared at everything else but her. Halfway to their destination she stopped stealing glances and blatantly stared at him. She was testing him. Soon enough, her suspicions were confirmed.

He is avoiding eye contact. Is he mad at me again? I haven't done anything wrong. He has no reason to be mad at me, but he won't look at me. It's not my imagination. He is deliberately ignoring me again!

They were choppered in part of the way, but in order to keep the op undetected, they had to traverse the remaining distance on foot. Sonny hopped down from the chopper in front of her and turned to offer her a hand getting down. He couldn't help but notice John glaring at him from inside the chopper. Sonny glared back. Things had been tense between them since the near-court-martial-incident. It hadn't escaped him that John's icy glares extended not only to him, but to Sophia as well. It didn't set well with Sonny. He felt a need to go out of his way to shelter Sophia as much as possible from John's coldness.

John hopped down from the chopper. His mind was full of suspicion. Sophia claimed she and Sonny were just friends, but the evidence in front of his eyes said otherwise. They were too familiar—too casual—too friendly—with each other. He didn't like it.

"Sonny! Take the lead with Nick and keep your eyes peeled."

Sonny halted and looked over his shoulder at John. "Aye, aye, Boss."

"Gonzalez! Bring up the rear and cover our flank."

"Yes, Sir," she said respectfully.

The rest of Echo fell in step behind Foxtrot as the chopper lifted away and disappeared into the night sky.

By 0130, the SEALs were making good time with Foxtrot in the lead. Traversing the desert at night was the safest way to avoid detection by the enemy, but night brought out the desert predators.

John came to a sudden halt, and Sophia, who was bringing up the rear, bumped into him. He stood watching a Sahara Desert Horned Viper sidewinding across the sand in front of him. Sophia gasped when she realized why he'd stopped. The deadly viper could travel across the sand at eighteen miles an hour when it wanted to, but the serpent slithering across the sand in front of John wasn't moving fast. They watched it flick it tongue testing the air. Then it slowed to a halt right in front of John.

The snake's deadly venom wasn't always fatal to humans, but considering their remote location and the likelihood that a chopper couldn't get them to a hospital fast enough, neither wanted to take a chance of getting bitten.

They both held their breath wondering what it would do. John didn't want to use his gun to take the snake out. They were too close to their target site. If the clones were nearby, a shot would draw their attention to the SEAL's position.

The snake flicked its tongue again, and its head moved slightly. John and Sophia froze in place. John slowly pulled his field knife from its sheath and prepared to defend himself against the dangerous predator. After a few minutes of testing the air, the snake slowly slithered away. They both breathed a sigh of relief.

"That was a close one," Sophia said quietly.

"Yeah. That thing popped up out of the sand right in front of me. Everyone running past must have disturbed it. I didn't even see it until it started moving. Keep your eyes open."

She nodded. "Sir, have I done something to make you mad?"

"No."

John started up the sand dune. Sophia quickly caught up to him. When they reached the top, they realized that the rest of the SEALs were already down the dune and nearing the top of the next dune.

"Double-time it," John ordered.

"Wait, Sir."

He turned and looked at her.

"I know you've been avoiding me. You won't look at me. You don't talk to me. You avoid being near me whenever possible. Have I done something wrong?"

"No. Now, double-time it, Gonzalez. We have distance to make up."

Sophia picked up her pace and stayed on John's heels, but after they met up with the rest of the team, her mind began to wander.

He didn't actually answer my question earlier. He side-stepped it entirely.

At 0330, Foxtrot located the clone camp and camouflaged themselves for recon. Echo's job was to provide cover for Foxtrot and serve as lookout. The clones didn't seem to be setting up permanent camp. They seemed to be doing an inventory of their supplies. Shanley sent in his best covert op, Wil Shakur, to get better intel. Wil returned just before dawn with an insightful report.

"Sir," Wil said. "The clones are not speaking any language I recognize. They seem to have developed their own language."

Shanley's mouth turned down. "That will make things more difficult. Did it have roots in anything recognizable?"

"Not that I could detect. I recorded as much as I could."

Shanley nodded. "Fall back to our hide coordinates. We will analyze this in a safer zone."

Echo took the lead this time, and Foxtrot brought up the rear. By the time the sun rose, the SEALs were fifteen klicks from the clone camp. When they reached thirty klicks, Shanley gave the order to make temporary camp.

After a breakfast of MREs, the SEALs got to work on Wil's recordings. They all crowded around to listen. Since there was such a wide diversity of languages spoken among the SEALs, some of them began to recognize not words, but patterns of words. As they watched the video for the fifth time, it became clear what the clones were communicating. It took several hours for the group to collectively decipher and translate the new language.

"We need more recon," John said. "This is only a small piece of their language. We've deciphered a few commands, some equipment vocabulary, and some verbs, but we need more data to fully decipher their entire language."

"We'll go back in tonight. In the meantime, I'll set up a watch rotation, and the rest of you get some rest. I have a feeling this is going to be a long mission," Shanley said.

Foxtrot took the first set of watch rotations. While they took turns standing guard, they memorized as much of the clone language as they could. When it was Echo's turn to stand watch, they began memorizing the language as well.

November 20
0800
Libyan Desert, Egypt

After three nights of recon, the SEALs had gathered a lot of data, but the clones were breaking down camp. The SEALs retreated to a safe distance to wait. They would tail the clones and try to ascertain their purpose for being in Egypt.

Over the next five days the clone army traveled south through Sudan. In the Sahel region, the clones were joined by three more groups of fifty from Chad bringing their total number to two hundred. As a cohesive unit, the larger clone army continued their journey south into Central African Republic. The clones from Chad brought heavier artillery, and multiple tanks.

The SEALs managed to tail the group without being detected, but their concern for what this army was created for was growing exponentially. Their CIA contact in Mut, Egypt, hadn't shared information with them. He had simply given them a directive and turned them loose. Neither John nor Lee liked where this was headed. They were concerned about what a clone army in Africa could be used for. Puzzle pieces were being fit in place, but the question loomed; what would the big picture look like?

November 26
0800
Obo, Central African Republic

Echo and Foxtrot took up positions just outside the small town of Obo. The clones seemed to have no interest in the inhabitants of the town. They only seemed interested in accessing the dirt road that ran along the southern border. Congo lay directly to the south. The cleared path would make it easier for their tanks to traverse the rainforest of Congo.

"Echo 1 to Foxtrot 1."

"Foxtrot 1, go for Echo 1."

"I don't like this," John said quietly into his com link. "They seem to be headed to Congo."

"Yes, that seems to be their general direction."

"I don't think this is a coincidence. Echo was on deployment in Congo three years ago. Things aren't what they seem there. If that's where the clones are headed, I think we need to report in. Something is up."

"The fact that the clones have moved from the Sahara training camps proves that something is up. What are you thinking?"

John was quiet for a moment. "You remember that coup in Congo three years ago?"

"Yeah, vaguely. We were busy with other problems at the time."

"It wasn't a legit coup. It was a set up. Negassi wasn't behind it, nor was he killed in the battle like they reported. Echo was ordered to assassinate Negassi and his army in January. The coup didn't happen until March. Some other power was at work behind that coup. Something is going on between the new government in Congo and the mining industry. It's all connected."

"Tell me something I don't know," Lee smirked. "The mining industry in Congo has been the source of trouble for decades."

"I think someone wants control over Congo's resources, and they are setting the stage to get it. The question is, what do Russian clones have to do with it? I can't quite fit the puzzle pieces together, but I don't like any of this."

Lee adjusted his binoculars to focus in on the clone army movement. "I don't like it either. It appears we have a new player on the scene. Military Humvee, ten o'clock."

John focused his binoculars in on the coordinates and saw a clone getting out of the passenger's side of the Humvee. His charcoal gray uniform was more formal than the green camo fatigues the rest of the clones wore. He had unfamiliar symbols of designation on the collar of his neatly pressed jacket.

"Who is this guy?" John said quietly into his coms. "I wasn't expecting a clone officer. I figured the clones were just the pawns and nothing more than cannon fodder. It looks like we underestimated the Russians. They seem to have a much more organized structure than we gave them credit for."

After a brief conversation with his men, the clone officer returned to the Humvee and pulled away. The clone army left soon after headed east on the dirt road that followed the border with Congo.

Shanley ordered John to take Echo to higher ground where they could get a clear signal to call their CIA contact. While Echo made a call to the CIA agent in Mut, Foxtrot continued to tail the clones and gather intel.

The clone army quickly grew into a force to be reckoned with. For two weeks clones poured into Africa. Echo and Foxtrot kept their CIA contact apprised of the clone activity, but they had not been given a green light to take any action.

When the clones took control of the mines, the capital, and every major city in Congo, the CIA ordered the SEALs to report to the rally point for extraction. Echo and Foxtrot were more than confused by the order. The cavalry wasn't coming. The clones were officially in control of one of the world's richest natural resources, and no one was doing anything to stop them.

December 21
0600
Afghanistan base

John stood in front of Rowen's desk.

"Sir, Echo is reporting back for duty."

Rowen nodded. "Echo is being given a two week leave as of 0600 tomorrow."

John's jaw worked as he stared at Rowen. "A two-week leave? We haven't requested any leave! The situation in Congo—"

"Is not Echo's problem. The leave isn't negotiable. Enjoy your time stateside."

"Since when are SEALs sent on mandatory leave?"

"Since I was ordered by my chain of command to remove you and Foxtrot from Congo and send you stateside for leave. It seems you've stepped on the wrong toes."

John frowned. "Something isn't right here, Sir."

Rowen nodded. "I know, but it's above your paygrade and mine. Just follow orders."

"Yes, Sir."

John limped back to the tent to give the rest of Echo the news. They too were confused and outraged that the clones were being allowed to take over Congo without any resistance.

CHAPTER 64

December 24
1100
Los Angeles, California

The Gonzalez home was filled to the brim with relatives, food, and Christmas presents. Everyone was having a good time laughing and telling stories. Sophia tried to keep a smile on her face, but it was difficult. After lunch, while the kids were opening presents, Conseja pulled Sophia away from the group crowded into the living room. Sophia followed her out to the patio.

"What is wrong, Sophia?"

Sophia shrugged. "Nothing. I'm fine."

"Don't lie to me. I saw you wiping away tears in the hall earlier. Something has happened."

Fresh tears betrayed her. "I made a mistake. I let myself fall in love with my C.O. John."

"Falling in love is not a mistake."

"He doesn't love me back."

Conseja frowned. "Well, he's an idiot. You can do better than him. What about Joe?"

Sophia shook her head. "I'm not in love with Joe."

"You could let yourself fall in love with him. He's obviously in love with you."

"No. I've decided to let my heart heal and never put it in the line of fire again."

"Just because John can't see how wonderful you are doesn't mean that another man won't."

"I thought John was different. I thought he was the one, but I was wrong. Not only did he reject me, but he won't talk to me anymore. Unless he has to communicate for the job, he completely ignores me. I never should have tried to kiss him. I was a fool."

Conseja hugged Sophia. "I'm so sorry. Just don't give up on love. I know it hurts right now, but it will get better. There are plenty of good fish in the sea. You don't need John."

Sophia nodded; she didn't voice what she thought. It was clear Conseja was there to convince her of a brighter tomorrow. She wouldn't hear that Sophia had given up on love—forever.

December 31
1800
Los Angeles, California

Sophia stood at the bus stop. The bus would be by any minute, but its arrival would bring her no joy. When it arrived, she boarded and took a seat at the back of the bus. She sat staring out the window with a solemn expression on her face.

All week Conseja had been calling and texting Sophia. Conseja wasn't the only one who was worried about her. Amparo had been mothering her a little too much. The entire family seemed to be on a mission to convince her that life goes on after heartbreak.

Sophia was tired of their sympathy. She had grown weary of lectures, advice, and a failed attempt to set her up on a blind date. She needed out of the house. She needed some fresh air. She needed to be away from her family when that clock struck midnight, and there was no one there for her to kiss. She needed to escape under a rock until morning.

She'd had a minor argument with her mother before leaving. Amparo wanted her to stay home and bring in the new year with the family. She suspected another attempt to set her up with a man. Even if it was a false suspicion, Sophia wasn't in the mood for celebrating. She was in the mood to drown her sorrows and disappear.

She lied and told her mother she was going to a party with friends to ring in the new year. The truth was she wanted no part of a party scene. She didn't think she could tolerate being hit on or watch other people have a good time. She just wanted to be alone—so no one would see her cry. She had a plan. Though she'd never had an alcoholic drink in her life, she planned to get a buzz, take a walk, and forget what time it was until dawn. She didn't want to know when midnight rang in the new year. She didn't want to think about how she was alone with no one to love her. Most importantly, she didn't want to have one single thought of John enter her mind that night. She figured if she got drunk enough, she could slide through the new year without the pain and heartache she was currently feeling. She rode the bus for a while staring out the window. She didn't know where she was going. She just needed to get away.

At 1900, she entered a seedy looking bar. It was already crowded with people. She squeezed in at the bar counter and ordered a shot of tequila and a beer. She downed the shot with a shudder and started on the beer. Four shots and three beers later she was feeling quite a buzz. Everything around her started feeling a little fuzzy. One of the patrons asked her to dance, and she found herself on the floor in his arms. The room began to spin a little as the music drowned out the hum of conversation in the crowded bar. It vaguely occurred to her that she was drunk. She thought about walking off the dance floor to find a quiet spot to enjoy her buzz, but when she tried to pull away from her dance partner, she stumbled, and he caught her. He pulled her back against him, and she leaned against his chest to regain her balance.

Across the street from the Los Angeles bar, John sat in a rental SUV. He'd been watching Sophia for a week from a discrete distance. He pulled a small velvet box from his pocket and flipped the top open. He stared down at the glittering diamond ring and let out a long breath. For a week the ring had lived in his pocket. He'd been trying to work up the nerve, but any time he had the opportunity, fear had roiled inside and paralyzed him. He slid the box back into his pocket and stared at the bar across the street.

Why would she say yes? I've treated her horribly. I accused her of cheating with Sonny. I threatened to have her kicked out of the SEALs. I've rejected her advances at every turn. Why the hell would she want me? Why the hell did she want me in the first place? I'm no catch. It probably won't work out even if she says yes. I'll do something to screw it up. That's what I do. Why am I even here? Following her around like this is pathetic. What am I really hoping for?

Happily ever after? It doesn't exist! I should just go. She obviously has a night of partying planned. It's better to just walk away before this blows up in my face.

He sat staring at the door for another forty-five minutes. When he watched her exit the bar with someone, a sharp pain stabbed into his chest.

So, she is moving on. That's a good thing. She deserves better than me anyway. Though that guy doesn't qualify. He looks like a loser-scumbag! Why would she give him the time of day? He's not even good looking. This guy looks like he crawled out of the gutter. She's way out of his league! Why is she hanging on him like that? — Is she drunk! — Where is he taking her?

He watched them weave through the throng of people that were heading into the bar. He watched them make their way down the sidewalk. He couldn't help but notice that the guy was practically carrying her. Her toes were barely touching the ground. That's when his radar went off. He reached for the door handle just as the guy turned down the alley with her. He bolted out of the SUV and ran across the street dodging traffic. When he hit the crowded sidewalk, he weaved his way through the laughing crowd of bar hoppers. It took him a minute to squeeze his way through them to the alley.

He reached the entrance and raced down the alley. Sophia was slumped against the wall. Her shirt lay in shreds on the ground along with her bra, and the man was cutting away her jeans. It took all the willpower he had not to snap the man's neck. Instead, he choked the man out before calling the cops. He left the man lying unconscious and knelt down beside Sophia. He checked her pulse and looked for injuries. Then he pulled his t-shirt off and tugged it down over her. The police arrived a short while later and started the investigation. Sophia was loaded into an ambulance, and John followed it to the hospital.

At the overcrowded hospital, the doctors told him she had a minor concussion and would be fine. They said she'd been given a date rape drug, but it would wear off in a few hours. They released her to John with instructions on how to care for her. He drove her back to his hotel room and put her in bed. Then he lay down beside her and gently trailed his fingertips down her jaw.

I should have known she wouldn't leave a bar with a sleazeball like that. I should have acted immediately. If I had, she wouldn't have gotten hurt. What was she doing in a bar anyway?

When dawn came streaming through the window, Sophia snuggled deeper under the covers to block out the morning light. She wasn't ready to get up. She didn't want to face her mother, or anyone from her family.

John sat down on the bed next to her. "How are you feeling?"

She smiled under the blanket. The familiar sound of his voice was comforting even if it was only in her dreams. It wasn't until she felt his fingers caress over the top of her ebony burr that she realized it wasn't a dream. She sat up in bed, threw off the covers, and came face to face with John. She blinked against the light as she scanned the room.

"Where am I?"

"My hotel room."

She shook her head to clear it, but that action brought a wave of pain inside her skull.

"What? How did I get here?"

"The man you left the bar with assaulted you. I pulled him off you and called the cops. The doctor said you have a minor concussion. The drugs your assailant gave you should work their way out of your system over the next day or so. You'll be okay."

"The bar—wait! What man? I don't remember a man."

"Good. It's probably better you don't remember what he did."

Sophia felt her heart skip a beat. "What did he do?" Her voice trembled.

John stood up, walked a few feet away, and stared at the wall. "Do you really want to know?"

"Yes."

He cleared his throat. "He cut your clothes off. If I hadn't gotten to you when I did—"

A tear slid down her cheek as she stared at his back. "Did he?"

"No, he didn't have time to do anything. I pulled him off you when he was cutting away your jeans. It took everything I had not to kill his sorry ass. He's rotting in jail right now."

Sophia gasped. "Thank you, Sir."

He rolled his shoulders and turned to face her. "We're not on duty. You can call me John."

The stern expression on his face was the same one she'd seen for the last several months. He stared at her for a moment; then he walked over to a chair, sat down, and stared out the window.

Sophia watched him for a moment. Then she looked down at herself for the first time. She was wearing one of John's t-shirts—and nothing else but her panties.

"I—uh—I should get dressed," she mumbled.

"You don't have any clothes. The police confiscated your shredded clothes as evidence. I'll have to go get you some. I thought about going to the store first thing this morning, but I didn't want to leave you alone. You have a slight concussion. I wasn't sure if you'd wake up while I was gone. I'll go get some right away. When I get back, I'll help you take a bath."

"I can take a shower by myself. I don't need your help."

He shook his head. "I'm not letting you take a shower unsupervised. If you get dizzy from the drug in your system, you could fall and hurt yourself."

Sophia smirked. "What are you planning to do—get in the shower with me and soap me up?"

"I'll do whatever I need to do to ensure your safety." His stern expression didn't waver.

She smirked. "What about your rule—no one gets within fifty feet of me while I shower?"

"I'll make an exception this time. You need help."

"Don't do me any favors."

"I'll pick you up some clothes. Stay in bed until I get back. I don't want you to fall."

"Is that another one of your direct orders, Sir!" Her tone dripped with sarcasm.

"Are you going to stay in bed or not?"

"Why do you care? We're on leave. I am not currently your responsibility."

He grimaced. "If you don't promise to stay in bed, I'm not leaving!"

"Fine! I'll stay in bed!"

John left, and she pulled the covers back over her head and tried to go back to sleep. It didn't work. The shirt she was wearing smelled like John.

It was distracting. She breathed in his scent, and a sleepy smile curved her lips. Her groggy brain kept pulling up their conversation and something wasn't adding up. Her head was pounding, but she couldn't stop working on the problem. Then it hit her. She sat up in bed with her mouth hanging open.

"That dirty, little Rat!"

She got up and made it to the bathroom despite her dizziness. She took a shower, brushed her teeth, dressed in one of his clean t-shirts from his duffle bag, and sat back down on the bed.

When John returned a short while later, she was waiting for him. She snatched the bags from him and headed toward the bathroom. He limped after her. She shut the door in his face and clicked the lock.

"Open the door. I'll help you take a bath."

"I took a shower while you were gone."

He frowned. "I knew I couldn't trust you to stay in bed."

She dressed in the clothes he'd bought and emerged from the bathroom.

"What are you doing in L.A.?" she demanded.

"I'm on leave."

She crossed her arms over her chest, and her eyes accused him.

"How did you happen to be there last night to rescue me?"

He cleared his throat and dragged his hand down his heavily stubbled jaw. "Fate."

"I'm not buying that. You were following me last night, weren't you?"

"You're lucky I was following you. If I hadn't been there—"

"Stop evading the real question."

He glared at her.

Sophia let out a frustrated breath. It was clear he wasn't going to cooperate. "Why are you even in California? You told me it is improper for anyone on the team to take leave with me."

"I'm not on leave with you."

"Nick told me you always take your leave at Kyle's. Kyle lives in North Carolina."

"When did he tell you that?"

"In Budapest. We had three days to talk about all sorts of things. I learned a lot about you."

"What else did Nick tell you?"

"Among other things, he said you are estranged from your parents, and you don't like to talk about it. Nothing I didn't already know from comments you've made."

John walked across the room to the window and stared down at the traffic below. "I've been thinking about what you said." He cleared his throat again. "You said how could I love you when I don't even love my own parents."

She didn't say anything. She just watched him. His whole body was tense.

"I don't know if you're right. Maybe I don't love them anymore. I don't know. I try not to think about them. Thinking about them is like pouring salt in the wound."

"What did they do to you, John?"

His head ducked for a moment, and she saw him swipe away tears.

"They didn't do anything to me."

"Then why haven't you spoken to them all these years?"

He turned to face her. "Actually, I have. I went to see them for the first time as soon as this leave started. Kyle has been bugging me to make amends with them, and you basically accused me of having a heart of stone. I thought I'd talk to them and try to mend some fences."

Her eyebrow rose with curiosity. "What happened?"

"They didn't want to talk to me. They wouldn't let me in the house. They wouldn't even come out on the porch. My dad told me to leave, and he slammed the door in my face." He swiped more tears away. "Growing up I always felt like they didn't love me. Now, I know they don't. I don't know which is worse, wondering or knowing."

Sophia walked toward him. Halfway there she felt a sudden wave of dizziness. She stumbled. Suddenly, she felt his strong hands on her shoulders steadying her. She looked up into his eyes, and her breath caught. He was looking at her like he used to, but then the coldness returned.

"You shouldn't be trying to walk. You have a concussion."

"You said it was a slight concussion."

His hand came up to frame her jaw. "Stop arguing. Why do you have to be so stubborn?"

An awkward silence ensued.

The heat of his hand on her jaw was intoxicating. She stared up at him, and he stared down at her. The longer they stared at each other the more awkward the tension grew.

Finally, Sophia broke the silence. "You could use a shave."

He smirked. "You don't like stubble?"

She grinned. "Actually, I think you look very sexy with a little stubble, but this looks like you've been growing it since we started leave."

He stared at her for a moment, and his pulse started to race. His eyes roamed over her body without his permission. Then a slight grin turned up his mouth. "How short is sexy?"

"Get your clippers, and I'll show you."

He scooped her up and carried her to the bathroom. Then he gently set her down on the countertop, got out his clippers, and handed them to her.

She set the clippers to the appropriate length and proceeded to trim his scraggly stubble. When she was done, she smiled up at him and set the trimmers down. "Much better."

He looked in the mirror and then down at her, and something in his eyes changed. He planted his hands on the counter to either side of her and leaned in. His lips barely brushed her ear.

"You think I look sexy now?" he murmured.

"You always look sexy." Her lips grazed up the side of his throat, and she pressed a soft kiss to his stubbled jaw.

He pulled back and stared down into her eyes. His heart beat faster, and his breath grew short. His eyes dropped to the swell of cleavage peeking above her low-cut shirt. He leaned down until his forehead touched hers. Then he closed his eyes, and his jaw clenched tight.

"Why do you do this?" he whispered.

"Do what?"

"Why do you tempt me with what we can't have?"

"Do you want it?"

He felt her legs curl around the back of his thighs pulling him in close. Her left hand settled on his hip, and her right hand slid up under his t-shirt. The soft caress of her fingertips over his ripped ab muscles tore down what was left of his defense.

"What are you doing?" he whispered, as he leaned his body into her.

"What do you want me to do?"

His eyes opened and locked with hers. His hands slid up to frame her jaw, and he brought his lips down on hers in a soft, sucking kiss. She gave in immediately and surrendered to his lips. Her heart beat wildly in her chest as he slid his hands down her body and curled them over her ass. He lifted her and pulled her tightly against him. Her eyes grew wide. He was so hard!

He continued to kiss her and stare into her eyes as he limped to the bed with her. He fought to stay in control, but he quickly lost that battle. It wasn't until she was on the bed under him that he pulled back from her lips.

"What do you want from me?" he whispered against her lips.

"Whatever you're willing to give me."

He groaned softly and rolled off her. He lay next to her staring at the ceiling.

She rolled on her side facing him. "Why do you keep this wall between us?"

"There is no wall. I just kissed you."

"You kissed me, but you didn't really kiss me."

He leaned up on his elbow and stared at her. "What does that mean?"

"You're holding back."

"You're damn right I'm holding back!"

"Why?"

He growled in frustration. "If I don't—"

"Yeah?"

"You don't believe in sex before marriage. I'm trying to respect that."

"Is that the only reason?"

"The UCMJ. I don't want you to get in trouble. We could hide sex, but you can't hide a pregnancy. I won't do that to you. I won't get you thrown out of the SEALs. You've worked too hard to get where you're at now."

Silence fell between them for a long moment.

"Why do you like me?" he asked.

"I love you."

His jaw tightened, and he swallowed hard. The room fell silent again. Their breathing was the only sound in the room.

"Why do you love me?"

"Because you're a good man."

He scoffed. "Don't put me in that category. I don't deserve it."

"Why don't you think you deserve it?"

He stood up and limped to the window. He stood staring out at the blur of cars passing by below.

"I'm a decent soldier. That's all I am. I'm not the kind of guy you can bring home to meet your parents. I'm a worthless loser. You deserve better."

She got up and walked over to him. He turned his head away to avoid eye contact with her.

"You are not a worthless loser. You're a great leader. You're caring, fair, and loyal. Those are all great qualities. Why do you have such a low opinion of yourself?"

She watched the muscle in his jaw work beneath his dark brown stubble.

"I promised myself I wouldn't do this."

"Do what?" she asked.

"Pursue you. I don't want to ruin your life, Sophia. I know how much the SEALs mean to you. I don't want to take that away from you. I don't want to destroy your dreams. I know what it feels like when someone takes away the one thing that's most important in the world to you. It hurts like hell. It leaves a sucking hole in your chest that never goes away. It never stops hurting. I don't want to do that to you. I just want you to be happy. I know you won't be happy with me. Women don't like me. There's something wrong with me. I haven't pushed your buttons yet, but I will eventually. That's what I do. I always find the wrong thing to say or do. You'll end up hating me. It's inevitable."

"Who hurt you, John? Where does this pain come from?"

He didn't answer her.

"Was it your parents? Are they the ones who left the sucking hole in your chest that never stops hurting?"

His voice cracked. "I don't want to talk about it."

She slid her hand into his and stepped in front of him. "You don't have to talk about it. I'm sorry they hurt you."

He closed his eyes as tears escaped down his cheeks. She let go of his hand and slid her arms around his chest and hugged him. He let her for a moment. Then he gently pushed her back and took a step away from her shaking his head.

"Don't."

"Why not?"

"It's better if I don't know what I'm missing."

She frowned and took a step toward him. He took another step back.

"What are you afraid of?"

"You," he whispered.

"I'm not going to hurt you, John."

"Not on purpose."

"Are you afraid I'll reject you?"

"I know you will. Everyone rejects me sooner or later: my parents, every girl I've ever gone out with. Even Kyle left me. He's still my best friend, but it's not the same. He has a life now. All I have is my duty to my country. Without the SEALs my life has no meaning. I'm just an empty shell, Sophia. I'm not worth wasting your time on. There are much better men out there. You deserve better than me. I'm not worthy of your love."

She gasped. "Sonny was right. You really don't feel worthy of anyone's love."

He looked away.

"Do you like me even a little?" she asked.

He dragged both his hands over his dark brown burr and groaned loudly.

"Tell me how you really feel about me."

"If I tell you, things will change between us."

"I know. I want them to change."

He took a deep breath, limped back to the bed, and sat down. She walked over to him, framed his jaw in her hands, and waited for him to answer.

"This is hard for me."

"I can see that."

"I've never been in love before. I'm afraid to give in to this."

"Why?"

"If you reject me too—"

"I'm not going to reject you."

"All women do."

"If I was going to dump you, I would have already done it in Afghanistan when you broke my heart. You're the one who rejected me, John. I never rejected you. Even when it hurt so bad I could barely breath, I couldn't bring myself to hate you. I couldn't stop loving you. I've had that sucking hole in my chest just like you, but you're the one who put it there. It hurt to tell you how I felt and have it thrown cruelly back in my face."

"I'm sorry."

She nodded. "I went to that bar last night to get drunk. I couldn't bear to think about not having you in my life. I just wanted to forget that pain for one night."

He hooked his hand behind her neck and gently pulled her down. "I'm so sorry." His lips pressed against hers, and she kissed him back.

He pulled her legs around him so she was straddling his lap. She tugged his t-shirt up, tossed it on the floor, and her hands explored his bare chest as they kissed. He surrendered to her as she playfully shoved him down on the bed under her. Then she planted soft, sucking kisses down his neck, down his chest, and finally down his ripped abs. Only when she went for the zipper on his pants did he stop her.

"Don't tempt me, Sophia. I'm barely in control."

"I want you to lose control. Just let go."

He groaned loudly.

She went for the zipper again. He grabbed her wrist and sat up shaking his head. "We can't. I don't have any protection. You could get pregnant."

She crawled up on him and rubbed her hand over his burr. Then she leaned down, kissed up his neck to his ear, and whispered, "I want your baby growing inside me, John."

With a tortured groan, he pulled her down on the bed and rolled on top of her. His lips ravished hers as his hips thrust against her.

"Make love to me, John."

His hands slid up under her shirt as his brain started the meltdown. He'd never wanted anything so badly in his entire life, but he managed to hold on to a shred of control. He rolled off her and lay panting hard. When she tried to crawl on top of him, he pinned her down against the bed and stared down into her wanton eyes.

"We can't," he panted. "I can't get you pregnant right now. We both have time left on our contracts. I already hate putting you in the line of fire. If you're pregnant with my baby, I won't be able to do it. I'm not sure I'll be able to do it anyway."

She grinned up at him as her hand pressed against the front of his pants.

"I'm sure you'll be able to do it."

She unzipped his dungarees and slid her hands down inside; he groaned as he stared down into her wanton eyes. Then he reached down, grabbed her wrists and pulled them up. He forced her hands down against the bed and threaded his fingers through hers. She grinned mischievously at him. He grinned back.

"I wasn't referring to that. I know I can do that. I was talking about putting you in danger. I don't think I can put you in danger ever again."

"It's our job. You'll have to, but only for five more months. I decided I'm not going to reup. I'll be out at the end of May."

"You don't have to do that. I told Rowen before I left that I'm not going to reup. I'll be out in May. You can stay in. You've worked hard for it. I don't want you to sacrifice that for me."

She swallowed hard. "You already told Rowen you're getting out?"

He nodded.

"Why? I thought being a SEAL was the most important thing in your life."

"No. You are."

"You just said you can't bear to put me in danger ever again."

"I can't. I can't be your C.O. anymore. I'm not cut out to be the leader of Echo. I never wanted it. Since I met you, I realized that I've changed. I'm not the man I used to be. I've stopped seeing the world in black and white. All I see now is gray. Whenever it's possible, I always put you in the least dangerous position on a mission. I'm already treating you different from the rest of the men. My judgement has been compromised. I think it's time for me to get out."

She let out a long breath. "I never thought I would give up my career for a man. I never thought I would fall in love. All I've ever wanted to do was serve my country. Then I met you. At first, I resisted my feelings. I tried to dismiss them. I can't ignore them anymore, John. Ever since the cave, something inside me has changed. I can't help but love you. I love you so much more than you realize. I already decided that I can't work under you anymore. The pain of having to see you every day and know you didn't love me back was too much. I talked to Rowen last month and told him I'm not going to re-enlist. He's already started my exit paperwork. I'll be out in May."

John groaned and buried his head next to hers. "I'm sorry, Sophia. I didn't mean to hurt you like that. At first, I thought you just had a crush on me that would go away. I was trying to keep you out of trouble. When I realized it was more, I knew I had to get out for both our sakes. If you want to stay in the SEALs, Rowen can change the paperwork."

"I don't want to. I've already made my decision. I'm getting out, John. Now that I know you're getting out too, there's no way I'm staying in. I want to be with you."

He pulled back to look into her eyes. "So, we are both getting out in May, and Rowen knows it. This is going to be tricky."

"You think he'll suspect—"

John nodded. "He and the rest of the base already suspect there's something between us. We'll have to be careful. We can't act like there's anything going on. In fact, we'll have to act like we can't stand each other, or he could bring up charges."

She nodded. "So, what now?"

John zipped up and tugged his shirt back on. "Now, we go get some lunch. I'm starving."

She gave him a smirky grin. "Food? That's what you're thinking about? I thought we were—"

He gave her a sly grin. "We can't do that until we are married. We'll just have to wait."

CHAPTER 65

January 1
1100
Los Angeles

John could hardly believe the puzzle pieces were falling into place. They were both scheduled to get out in May. Sophia was in love with him. Everything seemed perfect. He drove them to a nearby restaurant, and they ate lunch. Then John headed north. They took the BART to San Francisco, rode a cable car, and got off near the park. He took her by the hand and led her to the perfect spot overlooking the Golden Gate Bridge.

"What are we doing here?" she asked.

He got down on one knee and pulled the engagement ring from his pocket. He winked at her, and she grinned down at him.

"Sophia Maria Louisa Armanda Gonzalez, I love you. I fall more in love with each passing moment. You make me a better man. You make me whole. I want to spend the rest of my life falling more in love with you every day. Will you marry me?"

"Yes!" She leaned down and kissed him as he slid the ring on her finger.

He stood up. His arms circled around her holding her tightly against him as he devoured her lips in a passionate kiss. When he finally pulled back, she grinned at him.

"Now you've kissed me. That was our first real kiss. You didn't hold anything back."

He winked at her. "I may have held back a little."

Her look of confusion made him chuckle.

"I wanted to rip your clothes off and make love to you right here. I held back a little."

She chuckled too.

"I am worried about something," he said softly.

"What?"

"What if your parents don't like me?"

She smiled. "They are going to love you. If they don't, I'll kick their asses."

"I'm serious. My own parents hate my guts. What if yours do to?"

"It doesn't matter what they think. The only thing that matters is I love you, and I'm not ever going to let you go."

"I still don't understand why you love me, but I'm glad you do."

He has no idea. This is why I love him so much. He's so great and he doesn't even realize it. He's humble, sweet, and so perfect. He's fair, loyal, and trustworthy. He is everything I could ask for and more. I just wish he believed in himself half as much as everyone around him believes in him. He has so much untapped potential.

She caressed her fingers down his stubbled jaw and pulled him down for another kiss. They stood kissing in the park for a while. Then she pulled back.

"I should call my mother." She dialed Amparo's number.

"Sophia! Are you okay? I've been calling your phone all day. When you didn't come home last night, I feared the worst."

"I'm fine, Mama. My ringer on my phone must have gotten turned off."

"Thank goodness! Where are you?"

"San Francisco."

"San Francisco! What are you doing there?"

"Getting engaged."

Squeals of delight erupted from the phone.

"Who is he? How did you meet? When do we get to meet him?"

A stream of more questions followed.

"Mama!" Sophia interrupted. "I'm bringing him to dinner. You can meet him tonight."

"*¡Ay dios mío!*" There is no time to prepare! I have to call everyone. I'll have to send your papa to the store to buy extra food!"

"Mama! Please stop! I don't want to overwhelm him with the entire family tonight. Can we just have dinner with you and papa? You don't have to cook. We can go out to a restaurant."

"No, no, no! I will not have it. He is getting a good home cooked meal. Your brothers are going to want to meet him. If he is marrying you, he is marrying into a big family. He should know what he's getting himself into."

Sophia laughed. "Mama! I'm not trying to scare him off. I want to keep him."

John grinned at her. "Let me talk to her."

Sophia handed him the phone, and he started speaking to her in Spanish as he walked a few feet away. Sophia watched him shaking her head and grinning. John said *adios* and walked back.

"It's all settled." He handed her back the phone.

"What's settled?"

"We are not having dinner with your parents tonight. We are having a huge family lunch tomorrow afternoon. I'm going to meet the whole family. Your mom is very happy. She can't wait for me to taste her cooking. She says she taught you everything she knows."

Sophia rolled her eyes. "You have no idea what you just got yourself into."

"You've been holding out on me. I didn't know you could cook."

She chuckled. "I'm allowed a few surprises."

"Oh! So, it's like that? Okay. Then I'll just wait to tell you everything until later."

"You have a surprise?"

He grinned at her and winked.

"What is it?"

"It's a surprise. If you're allowed a few surprises, I am too."

"So, if we are not meeting my parents tonight, what are we doing?"

"I'll think of something."

He pulled her into his arms and went in for a long, slow, possessive kiss.

"Oh, wow!" she exclaimed when he finally pulled back. "I was mistaken. Now you've kissed me! You are a phenomenal kisser. You were holding out on me earlier."

Back at the hotel, John put the keycard in the lock and pushed the door open.

"This is going to be hard," he said, backing Sophia into the room.

She dragged her hand over the crotch of his pants. "It's already hard."

He grinned at her as the door swung closed behind him. "I meant sleeping together in the same bed is going to make it more difficult when we go back to Afghanistan."

"Probably, but I'm not giving up a second of my time with you."

They stripped each other down completely naked and crawled into bed. Kissing her and caressing her while holding back making love to her was torture for him, but it was the kind of torture he'd willingly endure. Having her in his arms was worth the angst of being unfulfilled.

After several hours, they both drifted to sleep in each other's arms. When she woke the next morning, the heat of his naked body curled over her felt better than anything she'd experienced before. It was comforting to know that he loved her as much as she loved him. She couldn't wait to get back to Afghanistan, serve their last five months, and marry him. She couldn't wait for their new life to begin. She'd never felt so much joy and excitement in her entire life. Even graduating BUD/S had not felt this good. She was so full of love for John she felt like she might burst. The only other obstacle was the family lunch they would face at her parents in a few hours.

At 1100, John pulled up to the curb in front of the Gonzalez home. There was a group of kids playing ball in the front yard.

"These kids belong to you?" he asked.

"Nieces and nephews. There will be more inside but younger."

He grinned. "You ready for this?"

She shook her head. "No. We are going to get accosted the moment we walk in the door."

He got out of the SUV and walked around to open Sophia's door, but she was already out. He took her hand in his, and they headed to the front door. Just as she predicted, the moment they stepped into the crowded living room, they were swarmed by curious family members and the questions started flowing like a roaring river.

Sophia answered as many questions as she could while tugging John along behind her in search of her parents. She found them both in the kitchen. Amparo was busy putting the last touches on the food. Juan was busy sampling his favorite dishes.

"Mama, Papa, this is John."

They both looked up, and their eyes grew wide.

"*¡El es un chico blanco!*" (He is a white boy!) Juan exclaimed in surprise.

"Yes, he is Caucasian," Sophia said.

"Your mama told me he was Mexican."

"Why would you think he's Mexican?" Sophia directed her question to Amparo.

"He speaks perfect Spanish. I just assumed—" Amparo trailed off.

"I speak Russian. That doesn't make me Russian. I also speak—"

"Alright! We get the point!" Amparo snapped. Then she looked at John and smiled. "I apologize. We meant no offense."

"None taken." John smiled at them both and extended his hand.

Juan shook his hand. "It is very nice to meet you."

Amparo ignored his outstretched hand and pulled him into a firm hug. "Welcome to the family, John."

He hugged her back. "Your food smells delicious. I can't wait to try it."

"I can't wait for you to try it. Sophia knows how to make all of these dishes," Amparo said proudly as she smiled at Sophia.

"Have you met the family?" Juan asked.

"Some." John replied.

"Come. I'll introduce you to everyone. Amparo has a few things to discuss with Sophia about the wedding."

"The wedding! We haven't even set a date yet!" Sophia protested.

"That's the first thing we need to decide," Amparo said with an irrepressible smile.

John grinned at Sophia and winked. "I'll leave you ladies to that."

He followed Juan out of the kitchen.

Amparo grabbed Sophia in a hug. "I'm so happy for you. He is very handsome."

"He is also very sweet. He is a good man."

"I know you would not be marrying him if he wasn't."

For the next half hour, Juan introduced John to everyone and then took John to the back yard for a father to future son-in-law talk. Sophia and Amparo were busy with their own discussion about the upcoming wedding. Amparo wanted to know Sophia's basic preferences so she could start planning the ceremony right away. Amparo insisted that Sophia give her hair time to grow out before the wedding—and all the wedding photos. She and Sophia agreed that a late August wedding would be doable. All Sophia had to do was talk to John and set an official date.

Conseja came in to rescue Sophia from Amparo's barrage of questions. She pulled Sophia into a back bedroom. "Is he the same John you told me about?"

Sophia nodded.

"So, it looks like you two worked out your problems."

"We worked out our misunderstandings."

Conseja nodded. "Girl, he is hot!"

"I know."

"He seems very nice."

"He is a sweetheart."

"How is he in bed?" Conseja grinned slyly.

"We haven't done that. We are going to wait until we get married."

"If I was in your shoes, I wouldn't be able to keep my hands off of that boy. Damn, Girl! Don't tell my husband I said that. He'll get insanely jealous. Sorry, I wasn't implying that I want your man. I was just saying God dipped that boy in the good end of the gene pool."

Sophia laughed. "Don't worry. I knew what you meant. Your secret is safe with me. Speaking of secrets. John and I have to keep this a secret from the team until we get out in May. It is illegal for us to date much less get engaged. The next five months are going to be tough."

"So, you can't wear this fabulous rock?" Conseja gasped.

Sophia looked down at the four-carat diamond on her finger. "No. It will be waiting in a safety deposit box until we get out."

"This boy is serious about you. Do you have any idea how much this ring costs?"

Sophia shook her head. "No, I'm not really that into jewelry."

"Well, I am. I love jewelry. Even if we can't afford it, I still like to look. This is an expensive ring. The four-carat diamond alone is worth a fortune, but all these smaller diamonds around it are expensive too. He wants every man in your vicinity to know that you are taken."

"I don't think that was his intention. He probably just thought it looked pretty."

"Girl! This ring probably cost more than my house."

"What! No. You're wrong about that. John doesn't make that kind of money. He's a SEAL. Even at Chief level, he couldn't afford a ring like that."

"Maybe he won the lottery."

Sophia chuckled. "No. You're probably just mistaken about the value of these diamonds."

Conseja held out her hand. "Can I see that ring?"

Sophia took it off and placed it in Conseja's palm.

"The only way this ring is not worth a small fortune is if it's cubic zirconia. Let's find out."

"No! I am not testing that ring. John wouldn't give me a cubic zirconia and try to pass it off as a diamond. That's not the kind of man he is."

Conseja walked over to the dresser and dragged the ring across a small makeup mirror.

"Diamond."

Sophia playfully glared at her. "I told you it was."

Grinning, Conseja handed the ring back. "This ring marks you as his territory. It's a warning to other men to back off or be destroyed. I know how men think."

The rest of the afternoon went as Sophia expected. Her relatives had a million questions for them. When Sophia left his side to get desert, she got a little more insight into John. She walked back into the room just in time to overhear John and her brother, Julio, in a conversation.

"So, when did you know she was the one?" Julio asked.

John dragged a hand down his stubbled jaw. "When I got shot."

"What? Did she shoot you?" Julio joked.

"No. We were behind enemy lines. I took a bullet in the leg, and I ordered the team to get to the rally point with the package. Sophia fell back to my position. I was lagging behind. I knew I wasn't going to make it. I ordered her to catch back up to the team. I knew Nick would get the team to safety. He's a great SEAL. He's a much better leader than I am. The trouble was. Sophia wouldn't obey my order. She insisted on following a few feet behind me. It really aggravated me that she wouldn't obey my order. It aggravated me more that hanging back with me was putting her in more danger."

Julio nodded. "We Gonzalez are all very stubborn."

"When I lost my footing and slid down the hill onto a frozen lake, I couldn't get back up. Sophia climbed down to the ice to help me. That aggravated me more. I knew on the ice we were exposed to the enemy. There was no cover. I didn't want her out there. I didn't want her help. I wanted her to catch back up to Nick, but she wouldn't listen to reason. Just after she got me to my feet, and we started back to the bank, enemy bullets ripped through the ice, and we both plunged into the icy water below."

"Damn, Dude!" Julio exclaimed. "What happened?"

Julio was completely captivated by John's story and so was Sophia. She stared at John's back hanging on his every word.

"I knew we weren't going to survive. We were both weighted down with heavy packs, and the current was swiftly pulling us away from the ice opening above. Not that we would have survived if we could have swum back up. The enemy was waiting on the shore to blow our heads off if we resurfaced."

By this time, John's story had drawn a small crowd of curious relatives.

"I knew we were going to die. I was almost out of air. I knew she had to be almost out of air too. So, I found her mouth in the dark water and expelled my last breath into her lungs. I just wanted her to live. I didn't care about myself. I just wanted to give her the only chance I could to survive. That's when I knew I loved her. That's when I admitted it to myself."

The room had grown quiet. Every eye was on John. Every ear was listening intently.

"So, what happened then?" Julio asked.

"I drowned."

Several people gasped.

"But you're still alive, so—" Julio prompted.

"I don't know what happened after that. I was dead. When I woke up, I was naked, wrapped in a blanket, and strapped down to a travois that Sophia had made from our two packs. She was dragging me through the forest. It was snowing, and I was freezing my ass off, but she was in worse condition. Her snowsuit had frozen to her. She was covered in ice and suffering from hypothermia and frostbite."

Julio looked around John and grabbed Sophia by the wrist. He pulled her out into the open.

"So, Little Sister, you stripped your man down naked, eh?"

Her cheeks turned crimson. "I had to. Our clothes were wet, and I couldn't dry them out. We were being hunted by the enemy. I had to keep moving. Drying him off and keeping him warm in the blankets was the best I could do at the time."

Julio nodded. "Was he really dead?"

Sophia nodded. "He drowned. We were lucky that the current swept us out of the lake and into a river before it was too late. Another few seconds and I might have drowned too. I gave him CPR, brought him back, and kept him alive long enough for us to reach a safe zone."

"So, when did you know that you were in love with him?" Julio asked with a sly grin.

Sophia grinned back. "I think I started falling in love with him from the moment we first met. He was the only SEAL team leader who was willing to give me a chance. I respected him for that. Plus, it didn't hurt that he's hotter than Hades."

John looked at her, and his eyebrow rose.

"The truth is, I fell in love with him a little more every day. Everything he does is honorable. He is good down to his core, and it shows. I couldn't help but fall for him, but I don't think I fully realized how far I had fallen until he tried to sacrifice himself to save me."

"You mean when he gave you his last breath?" Luisa, one of her sister-in-laws asked.

"It started there, but it really hit me when he told me to leave him behind and get to the safe zone. I argued with him, but he was adamant. He said he was a dead man anyway, and he didn't want to slow me down."

"Those weren't my exact words," John interjected.

"But that's what you meant."

He nodded.

"He wanted me to have an extra set of eyes and an extra gun in case we ran into trouble. His gunshot wound had become infected, but he didn't tell me. He knew he was going to die, so he pushed himself until he couldn't go any farther. Right before he passed out, he told me to leave him there and get home."

Several family members sniffed and wiped away tears.

"Of course, being a stubborn Gonzalez, I ignored his order and dragged his ass all the way across the border."

"That's my Sophia!" Juan said proudly. "She never gives up."

Sophia smiled at her father. "That's when I knew I was irrevocably in love with him. I couldn't leave him there to die. He was making the ultimate sacrifice for my safety, but I didn't care about my safety anymore. All I cared about was saving him. All I cared about was not losing him. That's when I truly knew he was the one—the only man I'll ever love."

The entire house was captivated by their story. The Gonzalez house had never been so quiet.

When John and Sophia were saying their goodbyes late that night, her oldest brother, Pedro, pulled John out to the front porch.

"When I first saw you walk in the door today, I didn't like you on sight. I was suspicious, and my protective, older brother radar went off, but after I heard your stories earlier, I realized that you two were made for each other. I just want to say, I was wrong. I think you will be the perfect husband for my little sister. Take care of her," Pedro said with sincerity.

"I will, Pedro."

Pedro grinned. "If you don't—Navy SEAL or not—I will kick your ass."

"I will never give you a reason to."

They both nodded and shook hands.

A short while later, John and Sophia got in the SUV and drove back to his hotel.

CHAPTER 66

January 26
1900
Afghanistan base

Sonny caught up to John on the jogging track. "Can we talk for a minute?"

"What do you want to talk about?" John slowed to a walk.

"You and the Senorita. You two seem different since you came back from leave."

"In what way?"

"In a weird way. You act like she's not even here. You look right through her. Used to be you couldn't keep your eyes off her cute, little ass. She doesn't look at you anymore either. What's up with you two?"

"Nothing."

"Before we left, she acted like a wounded puppy. She was in love with you, but she don't act too fond of you now. Did you hookup with her on leave and do that thing you do with women—the foot in the mouth thing?"

"No."

"I know you didn't go to Kyle's. I talked to him. He didn't even know you were on leave."

"I went to see my parents."

"Oh! How did that go?"

"It didn't. They had no interest in talking to me."

Sonny frowned. "Sorry."

John shrugged. "I'm letting it go. I'm not going to allow it to cloud my future anymore."

They fell silent for a moment.

"Is Sophia going to have any part in that future?"

"No, why would she?"

Sonny scoffed. "When are you going to admit that you love her?"

"I'm not because I don't. She's just another soldier."

Sonny studied John for a moment. "Yeah, you have definitely changed. Six months ago, you wanted to rip my head off for giving her a hug. Now, there's no emotion in you at all."

"I overreacted before. I was under a lot of stress at the time. I'm back on track now."

Sonny shook his head. "That's what you call this? You're just going to throw away the love of a good woman and call it getting back on track?"

"I'm not throwing anything away. I'm not in love with her. I never was."

"You practically needed a muzzle to keep you from tearing out every man's throat on this base who even looked at her. What would you call that?"

"A lapse in judgement that I have since corrected. I'm a SEAL; that comes before anything else. I have no feelings for her—whatsoever. Are we done now? I've got work to do."

February 19
0530
Afghanistan base

John and Sophia walked to the mess hall with the rest of Echo. They didn't get in line together. They didn't sit near each other. They didn't look at each other. Sonny took a seat across from her and stared at her for a moment.

"Dag blame it, Girlie! Ever since we came back from leave, you've been—happy."

"You act like that's a bad thing."

"No—it's just a little out of the ordinary for you—lately—since—well—you know—"

She shrugged, ate her breakfast in silence, and left the mess hall. Sonny caught up to her.

"Hey, Soph, can I talk to you?" He grabbed her wrist and tugged her behind a stack of crates.

"About what?"

He lowered his voice. "I've noticed that you and John ain't talkin' no more. He still follows you around like a watchdog and guards your showers, but it's different. It seems more like an obligation now. He acts like you don't exist, and you act like he don't exist."

"So."

"So, it's weird."

"Okay."

"Did you and him have a fallin' out?"

"Of sorts."

Sonny glanced around to make sure they weren't being watched.

"Is it permanent?"

"What do you mean?"

"I mean, did you two break up fer good?"

"We were never together, Sonny."

"Bull-hockey! You tried to kiss him. That don't just go away like a cloud on the breeze."

"That was my mistake. The UCMJ—"

"To hell with the UCMJ! Don't start spouting rules and regulations to me. I'm askin' you a serious question. I need an honest answer. For six months, I watched you cry in your bunk after everyone was asleep, but since leave, I ain't seen you cry once. Are you really over him?"

"What difference does it make?"

"It makes a difference; just answer the question."

Sophia stared up into his brown eyes. "There is nothing between us. Whatever may have been there is dead now. I'm over him."

He bit his lip as he stared into her eyes. "You're sure about that? No doubts?"

"I'm sure. The way he handled things was reprehensible. I just want to put it all in the past and forget it ever happened. I'm done with him for good."

"Sophia, I'm sorry he hurt you, but he's not the only man on this planet. I haven't been entirely honest with you these past months. It's been torture watching you go through that kind of heartbreak. So many times,

I wanted to tell you, but I was trying to be the good guy and not ruin his chances of winning your heart."

Sophia swallowed hard. "Sonny—don't."

He backed her up against the crates and stared down into her eyes.

"I can't hold this in anymore. I have to be honest with you."

Her heart sped up as she stared up into his sincere, brown eyes.

"I have never been in love before, but I'm in love with you, Sophia. I would do anything for you. All you have to do is ask."

"Sonny—"

She was interrupted by his lips pressing against hers. His hands came up to frame her jaw as his lips took hers in a soft, caressing, tender kiss.

Before Sophia could react, Sonny was yanked back in a choke hold by John.

"What the hell are you doing, Sonny?" John growled in his ear.

He threw Sonny to the ground. Sonny scrambled to his feet to find John had stepped in front of Sophia blocking her from his view.

"Listen, John—"

"No! You listen! I warned you before not to put your hands on her. Now, I find you kissing her! You've crossed the line, Sonny!"

Sonny glared at John. "I asked you nigh on a month ago if you still had feelings for her. You made it pretty plain that you was over her. She just told me she's over you. So, I reckon that don't give you no say in whether or not we kiss."

John stepped up to Sonny and lowered his voice. "I do have a say. We're engaged. You're out of line, Sonny."

"Engaged! You two been lyin' to me?"

Sophia stepped out from behind John. "We didn't want to put you in a position where you might have to lie to Rowen."

Sonny scoffed. "Lie? You're worried about me havin' to lie? That's rich. Lying is the least of my worries. Hell, I blow people's heads off for a living. You think I'd have a problem with telling a few measly lies?"

"We were just trying to protect you," Sophia said.

Sonny let out a frustrated breath. "You know—I can handle the brass. Hell, I been rooting for you to get together from the beginning. You should have told me the truth."

"Maybe, but that's not the point right now!" John growled. "You kissed her!"

"If I had known, I would never have gone and done that. I swear, John. I wouldn't do that to you. We been friends for fourteen years. I would never knowingly betray you that way. I honestly thought you didn't want her, and she didn't want you."

John raked a hand over his burr as he stared at Sonny

"So—what? You thought I wasn't interested—so without hesitation you swooped in to claim yourself another prize to brag about?"

"I wouldn't have done that to her. It would have been different with her, but if I had known the truth, I never would have made a move on her. I swear."

John growled angrily as he glared at Sonny. Sonny hooked his thumbs into his belt loops and dropped his eyes.

"Well, now that I know the truth, I won't ever do nothin' like that again. I promise."

John crossed his arms over his chest. "That better be the truth!"

Sonny looked up and met John's accusing eyes. "It's the truth. I'm hands off from now on. I'm sorry, John."

John let out a heavy sigh and dragged a hand down his stubbled jaw. "It wasn't all your fault. I should have told you the truth."

"So—we good now?"

"Yeah."

"Does Nick know yet?" Sonny asked.

"No, but I'll have to tell him I'm getting out soon so he can prepare to take over as Echo 1."

Sonny's eyebrow rose. "When are you getting out?"

"We are both getting out at the end of May," Sophia said.

Sonny whistled. "You two are taking a mighty big chance getting out at the same time. Is Rowen suspicious?"

John sighed. "Probably, but we are trying to eliminate as much suspicion as possible."

Sonny grinned and winked. "Go on back to fake hating each other. I won't say nothin'."

Sophia threw her arms around Sonny and hugged him tightly. "Thank you."

He hugged her back. "I'm just glad to finally see the two of you happy together."

February 19
1500
Afghanistan base

Sophia caught up to Sonny on the jogging track on the west end of the base. She fell in step beside him. Sonny didn't look at her.

"Are you allowed to talk to me?"

"What does that mean?"

Sonny lowered his voice. "It means I don't want to get my tail kicked by your boyfriend."

Sophia rolled her eyes. "He knows I'm here. We need to talk about what you said this morning."

"No, we don't. Forget I said that. Just forget everything that went down this morning."

"I can't forget it. I didn't know you felt that way. I'm sorry. I didn't mean to hurt you."

Sonny came to a halt on the path, and Sophia stopped and walked back to him. He stared at her with his hands on his hips.

"You can't be serious."

"What do you mean?"

He stepped up close and lowered his voice as he leaned in. "Are you seriously telling me that you had no idea how I feel about you?"

She cleared her throat and dropped her eyes to the sand at their feet. "We are good friends. I thought that's all there was between us. I didn't—"

He put his hands on her shoulders and pulled her in closer as he leaned down to her ear.

"We damn near kissed in the mess hall six months ago. Did you forget that?"

"No, I haven't forgotten."

"I thought—or maybe I just hoped that you felt the same way. I see now—I never stood a chance. The only man on your radar is John. You don't see the rest of us at all."

Sophia pulled back to look him in the eyes. "That's not true, Sonny. I—"

He stared back waiting for her to explain, but she fell silent. His eyes searched hers. "Sophia, why are you here? You're with him. Why come track me down to torture me like this?"

"I'm not—I don't want to torture you. I just wanted to—"

"To what?"

She pulled her lip between her teeth.

"You don't have to worry about me. I'm happy for both of you. If I had known, I never would have told you the truth."

She nodded. "I know, but I'm glad you told me the truth. I don't want there to be secrets between us. I hated lying to you all this time. It felt wrong to lie to you."

Sonny grinned and winked at her. "I don't want secrets between us either. I'm glad you told me the truth."

"I feel bad. I never meant for you to—"

Sonny shook his head. "Stop worrying about me. I'm tough. I can take disappointment, especially when it comes with such a happy ending. I'm glad he came to his senses, even if it means I don't get a chance with you. He deserves to be happy. He's a good man. He's been through a lot of pain in his life. I don't want to take away the one woman who gets him and can make him happy. I am truly happy for both of you. Truly."

"You're a good man, Sonny. The right woman is out there for you."

"Nah. I don't think there's a female alive that would want me and all my baggage."

"There is. Don't give up looking. If it wasn't for John—"

His eyebrow rose as he stared at her. He cleared his throat. "Are you serious—or are you just saying that to spare my feelings?"

She grinned at him and winked. "I think you are a great guy—baggage and all. Don't give up on finding love, Sonny. You're not as damaged as you proclaim."

Sonny grinned as he watched her walk away. Then he shook his head and resumed his jog.

So innocent—so naïve. My favorite kind. I wish I'd found her first. Damn if love ain't a bitch!

CHAPTER 67

May 26
0230
Transport plane over Russia

Sophia sat across from John. He was pretending to ignore her as usual, but she couldn't ignore him. This would be their last mission. After this, they would both be processed out. They would go home, get married, and start the life they'd planned. She could hardly wait.

All that stood between her and happily ever after was one HALO jump, a trek through the woods, and confiscating a little intel on the sly. Nothing they hadn't done a hundred times before.

She looked over at Sonny. He was watching her intently. He'd been watching her more than usual lately. She smiled at him. He smiled back and gave her a friendly wink. Her heart sped up a little. After knowing how he felt about her, she couldn't help but wonder what he was thinking. Did that wink mean more than it should? She dropped her gaze to the floor and didn't look back in his direction for a long time. When she ventured another glance, Sonny was still watching her.

He signed: *Last one. You ready for this?*

She breathed a sigh of relief. Maybe his intent gaze was completely innocent after all. He knew this was her last mission. It was likely she would never see Sonny again once she and John were out of the SEALs. Maybe he was just watching because he was about to lose a friend.

When it was time to make the jump, John stood in line behind her. They would be the last two off the plane. Just as she stepped up to the edge, he leaned down to her ear.

"Last one and we are home free. I can't wait to spend the rest of my life with you."

She smiled. "Me too."

She stepped off the plane smiling all the way down. Her perfect life was about to begin.

**...Continue this tale of love, intrigue, and mystery in
Book 3 of the Deadly Treasures Series
Deadly Treasures: What are the Chances**

9 798893 304046